IMPRIMATUR
Monaldi & Sorti

Translated from the Italian by Peter Burnett

First published in Italy in 2002
First published in Great Britain in 2008 by Polygon,
an imprint of Birlinn Ltd

West Newington House
10 Newington Road
Edinburgh
EH9 1QS

9 8 7 6 5 4 3 2 1

www.birlinn.co.uk

ISBN: 978 1 84697 076 4

British Library Cataloguing-in-Publication Data
A catalogue record for this book is available on request from the British Library.

Typeset by SJC

Printed and bound by ScandBook AB, Falun, Sweden

Divinatory interpretations
of the Arcana of the Judgement

Resurrection of the past
Reparation of past wrongs
Wise judgement of posterity.

Nothing is lost; the past lives on
in what pertains to the future.

OSWALD WIRTH, *The Tarot*

Contents

To the Congregation for the Causes of Saints   ix

Day the First—11th September, 1683   1

Night the First—Between the 11th & 12th September, 1683   20

Day the Second—12th September, 1683   29

Night the Second—Between the 12th & 13th September, 1683   80

Day the Third—13th September, 1683   92

Night the Third—Between the 13th & 14th September, 1683   144

Day the Fourth—14th September, 1683   162

Night the Fourth—Between the 14th & 15th September, 1683   190

Day the Fifth—15th September, 1683   219

Night the Fifth—Between the 15th & 16th September, 1683   254

Day the Sixth—16th September, 1683   282

Night the Sixth—Between the 16th & 17th September, 1683   303

Day the Seventh—17th September, 1683   324

Night the Seventh—Between the 17th & 18th September, 1683   341

Day the Eighth—18th September, 1683   362

Night the Eighth—Between the 18th & 19th September, 1683   381

Day the Ninth—19th September, 1683   403

Night the Ninth—Between the 19th & 20th September, 1683   430

Events Between the 20th & 25th September, 1683   475

Events of the Year 1688   497

September 1699   503

Addendum   511

Notes   534

Documents: Innocent XI & William of Orange   547

List of Pieces of Music Performed in *Imprimatur*   567

Como, 14th February, 2040

To His Excellency Msgr
Alessio Tanari
Secretary of the Congregation for the Causes of Saints
Vatican City

In nomine Domini

Ego, Lorenzo Dell'Agio, Episcopus Comi, in processu canonizationis beati Innocentii Papae XI, iuro me fideliter diligenterque impleturum munus mihi commissum, atque secretum servaturum in iis ex quorum revelatione preiudicium causae vel infamiam beato afferre posset. Sic me Deus adiuvet.

Dearest Alessio,

Be so good as to pardon me if I open my letter to you with the ritual oath: to maintain secrecy concerning anything I may have learned that might defame the reputation of a blessed soul.

I know that you will excuse your former tutor at the seminary for adopting an epistolary style less orthodox than that to which you are accustomed.

You wrote to me three years ago, on the instruction of the Holy Father, inviting me to throw light on a presumed case of miraculous healing which took place in my diocese over forty years ago, through the action of the Blessed Pope Innocent XI: that Benedetto Odescalchi from Como of whom you, as a boy, first perhaps heard tell from none other than myself.

As you will surely remember, the case of *mira sanatio* concerned a child, a little orphan from the country near Como whose finger was bitten off by a dog. The poor bleeding digit, immediately recovered by the little one's grandmother, who held Pope Innocent in special devotion, was wrapped by her in the holy image of the Pontiff and

ix

handed over to the doctors in casualty. After an operation to graft it back, the child instantly recovered feeling in his finger and was able to use it perfectly; both the surgeon and his assistants were utterly amazed.

In accordance with your indications and with the desire expressed by His Holiness, I have instructed the cause *super mira sanatione*, which my predecessor did not in his time see fit to initiate. I shall not expatiate any further on the inquiry, which I have just concluded, despite the fact that most of the witnesses to the event have since died, the records of the clinic were destroyed after ten years and the child, now in his fifties, resides in the United States. The acts will be sent to you under separate cover. As required by the procedure, you will, I know, submit these to the Congregation for its judgement, following which you will draft a report for the Holy Father. I am indeed aware of how eager our beloved Pontiff is to reopen the inquiry into the cause of canonisation of Pope Innocent XI so that, almost a century after his beatification, he may at last be proclaimed a saint. And it is precisely because I too care greatly about His Holiness's intention that I must now come to the point.

You will have noticed the considerable bulk of the folder which I have attached to my own letter; it is the typescript of a book that has never been published.

It will be hard to explain to you in detail how this came about, since the two authors, after sending me a copy, vanished completely. I fully trust that Our Lord will inspire the Holy Father and yourself, after reading this work, as to the best solution of the dilemma: *secretum servire aut non?* To pass over the text in silence or to publish? Whatever the decision arrived at, it will, for me, remain sacrosanct.

I beg to excuse myself at once if my pen—now that my spirit is free after three years of wearisome research—runs sometimes too freely.

I made the acquaintance of the two authors of the typescript, a young engaged couple, some forty-three years ago. I had just been appointed as a parish priest in Rome, where I had recently arrived from my dear Como, to which Our Lord was to accord me the grace to return as Bishop. The two young people, Rita and Francesco, were both journalists. They lived quite close to my parish church and so it was to me that they turned for instruction in preparation for matrimony.

The dialogue with the young couple soon developed beyond a simple teaching relationship and, with time, grew closer and more confidential. As chance would have it, the priest who was to conduct the ceremony suffered a serious indisposition only two weeks before the wedding. So it was quite natural that Rita and Francesco should ask me to perform the rite.

I married them on a sunny afternoon in mid-June, in the pure, proud light of the Church of San Giorgio in Velabro, a short distance from the glorious ruins of the Roman Forum and the Capitoline Arch. It was an intense ceremony, brimming over with emotion. I prayed ardently to the Most High that the young couple should be granted a long and serene life.

After the wedding, we continued to frequent one another for a few years. I learned thus that, despite the scant free time remaining to them after work, Rita and Francesco had never completely abandoned their studies. Although both of them, after obtaining their degrees in Literature, opted for the dynamic and cynical world of the written press, they still had not lost touch with their former interests. On the contrary, in their free moments, they continued to read good books and to visit museums and libraries.

Once a month, they would invite me to dinner or for afternoon coffee. Often, they would at the very last moment clear a chair heaped high with photocopies, microfilms, reproductions of antique prints and books, so that I could sit down; and these piles of paper seemed to grow higher with my every visit. I became curious and inquired what they were studying so enthusiastically.

They then told me how, some time previously, they had traced in the private collection of an aristocratic Roman book-lover a collection of eight manuscript volumes, dating back to the beginning of the eighteenth century. Thanks to the fact that they had friends in common, the owner, Marchese *** ***, had given the couple permission to study these antique volumes.

The find was a veritable gem for students of history. The eight volumes were the collected letters of Abbot Atto Melani, a member of an ancient and noble Tuscan family of diplomats and musicians.

Yet the real discovery came later: bound in one of the eight volumes, a substantial set of manuscript memoirs had come to light. It was dated 1699 and written in minute letters, by a hand manifestly different from that of the remainder of the volume.

The anonymous author of the manuscript affirmed that he had been an apprentice in a Roman inn and told in the first person of

surprising events which had taken place between Paris, Rome and
Vienna in 1683. The memoirs were preceded by a brief letter of pres-
entation, undated and naming neither sender nor addressee, the content of which was somewhat obscure.

For the time being, it was not given to me to know more. The
young couple maintained the strictest reserve about their discovery. I understood only that, ever since they had found them, these
memoirs had become the object and the cause of their animated
research.

However, since both had left the academic world for good, and
were thus no longer in a position to lend scientific dignity to their
studies, the two young people had begun to hatch out the idea of
writing a novel.

At first, they spoke of this as though in jest: they were going to
remodel the apprentice's memoirs in the form and the prose of a
novel. Initially, I was rather disappointed by the idea, which—prid-
ing myself on my passion for scholarship—I found faint-hearted and
superficial.

Then, between one visit and another, I understood that the matter was becoming serious. A year had not passed since their marriage,
and now they were dedicating all their free time to it. Later, they
confessed to me that they had spent almost their entire honeymoon
in the archives and libraries of Vienna. I asked no more questions,
resolving that I would be only the silent and discreet confidant of
their labours.

At the time I did not, alas, follow attentively what the couple told
me about the progress of their work. Meanwhile—spurred on by the
birth of a beautiful little girl, and tired of building on the quicksands
of our poor country—at the beginning of the new century, the couple
suddenly decided to move to Vienna, a city to which they had grown
attached, perhaps also because it held fond memories for them of
their first days as man and wife.

They invited me for a brief leave-taking shortly before their departure from Rome. They promised to write to me and to call on me
whenever they visited Italy.

They did none of those things, nor did I ever hear from them
again. Until, one day, months later, I received a parcel from Vienna.
It contained the typescript which I am now sending you: it was the
long-awaited novel.

I was happy to know that they had at least succeeded in completing it and wanted to reply and thank them. But I was surprised to find that they had not sent me their address, nor was there any covering message. As a frontispiece, a meagre dedication: "To the defeated". And on the back of the folder, just a scribble with a felt-tipped pen: "Rita and Francesco".

So I read the novel. Or should I rather say: the memoirs? Are these really memoirs from the baroque period, reworked for today's readers? Or is it a modern novel set in the seventeenth century? Or both? These are questions that still beset me. There are indeed places where one seems to be reading pages that have come down to us intact from the seventeenth century: all the characters invariably use the vocabulary to be found in treatises of the period. But then, when discourse gives way to action, the linguistic register changes sharply, the same characters express themselves in modern prose and their doings seem even to take on the character of a detective novel— one of the Sherlock Holmes and Watson variety, to put it plainly. As though, in those passages, the authors had deliberately left traces of their intervention.

And what if they had lied to me? I was surprised to find myself wondering just that. What if the tale of the apprentice's manuscript which they had found was all an invention? Was it not too much like the device employed by both Manzoni and Dumas for the opening of their masterpieces, *The Betrothed* and *The Three Musketeers*? Both of which, coincidentally, are set in the seventeenth century...

Unfortunately, I have not been able to get to the bottom of the matter, which is probably destined to remain a mystery. I have indeed been quite unable to trace the eight volumes of Abbot Melani's letters, from which the whole story began. The library of the Marchese *** *** was split up by his heirs and sold some ten years ago. After I had bothered a few acquaintances, the auctioneers who made the sale discreetly passed me the names of the buyers.

I thought I had found the solution and that the Lord was with me, until I read the names of the new owners: they were Rita and Francesco. And, of course, they had left no address.

During the course of the past three years I have, with the few resources at my disposal, conducted a painstaking series of checks on the contents of the typescript. You will find the outcome of my research in the pages which I have annexed at the end of the text.

These, I beg you to read most attentively. You will discover for how long I relegated to oblivion the work of my two friends, and the sufferings which that has caused me. You will also find a detailed examination of the historical events narrated in the typescript, and an account of the exhaustive research I conducted in the archives and libraries of half Europe, in order to understand whether these might correspond to the truth.

As you can judge for yourself, the impact of the facts narrated was indeed such as to alter the course of history violently, and forever.

Very well, having completed my research, I can affirm with certainty that the events and persons contained in the story which you are about to read are authentic. And, even where it was not possible to find the proofs of what I had read, I was at least able to establish the verisimilitude of the events recounted.

The affair narrated by my two former parishioners, while not gravitating only around Pope Innocent XI (who is indeed barely even a protagonist of the novel) does, however, bring to light circumstances which cast new and grave imputations as to the limpidity of the Pontiff's soul and the honesty of his words. I say new, insofar as the inquiry into the beatification of Pope Odescalchi, opened on 3rd September, 1714 by Pope Clement XI, encountered objections *super virtutibus* during the first preparatory stages, raised within the Congregation by the Promoter of the Faith. Thirty years were to pass before Pope Benedict XIV Lambertini silenced by decree all doubts expressed by the promoters and consultors as to the heroic virtues of Innocent XI. But, shortly afterwards, the process again came to a halt, this time for almost two hundred years: indeed, only in 1943, under Pope Pius XII, was another rapporteur appointed. The process of beatification took a further thirteen years, until 7th October, 1956. Ever since that day, Pope Odescalchi has remained shrouded in silence. Never again, until now, was there talk of proclaiming him a saint.

It would have been possible for me, by virtue of the legislation approved by Pope John Paul II over fifty years ago, to request further inquiries. But in that case, I would not have been able *secretum servare in iis ex quorum revelatione preiudicium causae vel infamiam beato afferre posset.* In other words, I would then have had to reveal the contents of Rita and Francesco's typescript, if only to the promoter of justice or to the postulator (the saints' prosecution and defence lawyers, as the press so crudely describes them).

In so doing, I would have permitted grave and irreversible asper-
sions to be cast on the virtue of the Blessed: a decision which could
be taken only by the Supreme Pontiff, certainly not by myself.

If, however, the work had in the meantime been published, I
would have been freed from the obligation to secrecy. I therefore
hoped that my two parishioners' book had already found a publisher.
I confided the search to some of the youngest and least experienced
members of my staff. But in the catalogues of books on sale, I found
neither any writings of the kind nor my friends' names.

I tried to trace the two young people (by now surely no longer
young): the registers showed that they had indeed moved to Vienna,
at Auerspergstrasse 7. I wrote to that address but received a reply
from the head of a university hostel, who was unable to provide me
with any assistance. I asked the Commune of Vienna, but nothing
useful came of that.

I feared the worst. I wrote to the parish priest of the Minoriten-
kirche, the Italian church in Vienna. But Rita and Francesco were
unknown to everyone there, including, fortunately, the keeper of the
graveyard records.

In the end, I decided to go to Vienna myself, in the hope of tracing at least their daughter, even though, some forty years after the
event, I could no longer remember her Christian name. As was to be
expected, this last attempt also came to nothing.

For three years, I have sought them everywhere. Sometimes I find
myself looking at girls with red hair like Rita's, forgetting that hers
will now be as white as my own. Today, she will be seventy-four and
Francesco, seventy-six.

Now, I take my leave of you, and of His Holiness. May God inspire
you in the reading which you are about to undertake.

Msgr Lorenzo Dell'Agio
Bishop of the Diocese of Como

To the defeated

Sir,

In conveying to you these Memoirs
which I have at last recover'd,
I dare hope that Your Excellency
will recognise in my Efforts
to comply with Your Wishes
that Excess of Passion and of Love
which has ever been the cause of my Felicity,
whenever I have had Occasion
to bear Witness thereof
to Your Excellency.

Memorials

Containing many
admirable
Occurrences
which took place
at the Inn known as the
Donzello
All' Orso
between the 11th
and the 24th of
September
in the Year 1683;
with Allusions to
other Events,
before and after those
Days.

At Rome, AD 1699

Day the First

11TH SEPTEMBER, 1683

✠

The men of the Bargello arrived in the late afternoon, just as I was about to light the torch that illuminated our sign. In their fists, they grasped planks and hammers; and seals and chains and great nails. As they advanced along the Via del Orso, they called out and gestured imperiously to the passers-by and knots of curious bystanders that they must clear the street. Truly, they were most wrathful. When they came level with me, they began to wave their arms about: "All inside, all inside, we must shut up the house," cried the man who gave the orders.

Barely had I time to descend from the stool onto which I had climbed than hard hands shoved me roughly into the entrance, while some began to bar the door with threatening mien. I was stunned. I came abruptly to my senses, jostled by the gathering which, drawn by the officers' cries, had piled up in the doorway as though a bolt of lightning had fallen from an empty sky. These were the lodgers at our inn, known as the Locanda del Donzello.

They were but nine, and all were present: waiting for supper to be served, as was their wont every evening, they wandered about the ground floor among the day-beds in the entrance hall and the tables of the two adjoining dining chambers, each feigning some business; but, in reality, all turning around the young French guest, the musician Robert Devizé who, with great bravura, was practising the guitar.

"Let me out! Ah, how dare you? Remove your hands from me! I cannot remain here! I am perfectly healthy, understood? Perfectly healthy! Let me by, I tell you!"

He who thus cried out (and whom I could barely descry through the thicket of lances with which the men-at-arms held him at bay) was our guest Padre Robleda, the Spanish Jesuit, who, panic-stricken, began to groan and to pant, his neck all red and swollen. So piercing were his screams that they minded me of the squeals of swine, hanging head downwards before slaughter.

The noise resounded down the street and, it seemed to me, as far off as the little square, which had emptied in a trice. On the far side of the street, I caught sight of the fishmonger who, with two servants from the nearby Locanda dell'Orso, was observing the scene.

"They are shutting us in," I cried to them, trying to capture their attention, but the trio remained unmoved.

A vinegar-seller, a snow vendor and a group of little boys whose cries had, only moments earlier, enlivened the street, now hid fearfully round the corner.

Meanwhile, my master, Signor Pellegrino de Grandis, had placed a small bench on the threshold of the inn. One of the officers of the Bargello laid thereon the register of the lodgers at our inn, which he had just received, and began the roll-call.

"Padre Juan de Robleda, from Granada."

Since I had never been present at a closure for quarantine, and no one had ever spoken to me of such a thing, I thought at first that they meant to imprison us.

"A dreadful, dreadful business," whispered Brenozzi, the Venetian.

"Come out, Padre Robleda!" called the officer, growing impatient.

The Jesuit who, in his vain struggle against the men-at-arms, had fallen senseless to the ground, now rose to his feet and, once he had made sure that every escape was barred by lances, responded to the call with a sign of his hairy hand. He was at once pushed towards me. Padre Robleda had arrived from Spain a few days earlier, and ever since morning, because of the day's events, he had sorely tried our ears with his fearful screaming.

"Abbot Melani, from Pistoia!" called the official, reading from the register of guests.

Darting up from the shadows came the fashionable French lace ornamenting the wrist of our latest guest, who had arrived only at sunrise. He raised his hand diligently when his name was called, and his little triangular eyes shone like stilettos piercing the shade. The Jesuit did not move a muscle to make room when Melani, with tranquil gait and in silence, joined us. It was the abbot's cries that had raised the alarum that morning.

We had all heard them, they came from upstairs. Pellegrino, the host, my master, was the first to stir his long legs and run swiftly. But hardly had he reached the large chamber on the first floor, giving onto the Via dell'Orso, than he stopped. There, two guests had taken up lodgings: Signor di Mourai, an aged French gentleman, and his companion Pompeo Dulcibeni, who hailed from the Marches. Mourai, in an armchair, with his feet soaking in the basin for his customary bath, sprawled sideways, his arms hanging down, while the abbot held him upright and strove to revive him, shaking him by the collar. Mourai's attention seemed fixed upon his helper's shoulders and he appeared to be scrutinising Pellegrino with great astonished eyes, while an indistinct gurgle issued from his throat. It was then that Pellegrino realised that the abbot was not calling for help but, with great uproar and agitation, interrogating the old man. He was speaking to him in French, which my master could not understand; but imagined that he was enquiring of him what had happened. To Pellegrino (as he was later to recount to us all) it did, however, seem that Abbot Melani was shaking Mourai with excessive vigour in his attempts to revive him, and so he rushed to release the old man from that all-too-powerful grasp. It was at that instant that poor Signor di Mourai, with an immense effort, uttered his last words: "Alas, so it really is true," he gasped in Italian. Then he left off from panting. His eyes remained fixed upon his host and a greenish dribble ran from his mouth to his breast. And so he died.

❧

"The old man, *es el viejo*," gasped Padre Robleda mixing languages in a terrorised whisper, no sooner than we had heard two men-at-arms murmur the words "pestilence" and "shutting up".

"Cristofano, physician and chirurgeon, from Siena!" called the officer.

With slow and measured gestures, our Tuscan guest stepped forward, holding the little leather bag containing all his instruments from which he was never parted.

"It is I," he responded in a low voice, after opening his bag, shuffling through a mass of papers and, with frigid dignity, clearing his voice. Cristofano was rotund and short of stature, careful of his appearance and with a jovial expression that set one at ease. That evening, his face was pale and dripping with perspiration, nor did he take the trouble to wipe it; his pupils focussed on something invisible in front of him and, before he moved, he made a quick gesture, smoothing his pointed beard. His every movement betrayed the extreme apprehensiveness behind his would-be phlegmatic calm.

"I wish to make it clear that, following a preliminary but careful examination of Signor di Mourai's body, I am by no means certain that this is a case of infection," began Cristofano. "The medical examiner of the Magistrate for Health, who asserts this with such confidence, spent very little time with the corpse. I have here," and he showed the papers, "my written observations on the case. I believe they could help you to reconsider the situation a little longer and delay any over-hasty decision on your part."

The Bargello's men, however, had neither the power nor the desire to enter into such points of detail.

"The Magistrate has ordered the immediate closure of this inn," said the officer who seemed to be in charge, adding that, for the time being, a proper quarantine had not been declared: the closure was for twenty days only, and without evacuation of the street; so long, of course, as there were no further deaths or suspected cases of distemper.

"Seeing as I too am to be locked up, and in order that I may the better arrive at my diagnosis," insisted Signor Cristofano with some irritation, "may I not at least know something more about the last meals on which the late Signor di Mourai supped, he being accustomed always to eat alone and in his chamber? It may have been no more than a simple congestion."

The objection had the effect of creating hesitancy on the part of the men-at-arms, who besought the innkeeper with their eyes. The latter had, however, not even heard the physician's request: slumped on a chair, plunged in dejection, he groaned and uttered imprecations, as was his wont, against the innumerable torments which life inflicted upon him. The last of these had been when, scarcely a week earlier, a small crack had appeared in one of the walls of the inn, no rare occurrence in the old houses of Rome. The fissure entailed no danger whatever, so we were told; yet it was more than enough to engender in my master both melancholy and rage.

Meanwhile, the roll-call continued. Evening shadows were lengthening and the officers had decided to admit of no further delay with the closure.

"Domenico Stilone Priàso, from Naples! Angiolo Brenozzi, from Venice!"

The two young men, the former a poet, the latter a glass-blower, stepped forward, looking at one another, seemingly relieved to be called up together, almost as though that lessened the apprehension. Brenozzi, the glass-blower—with fearful expression, his shining brown curls and small turned-up nose like a hillock between blushing cheeks—resembled a little porcelain Christ Child. What a pity that, as was his habit, he relieved himself of nervous tension by pinching obscenely the celery stem that lay between his thighs, almost as though he were plucking a one-stringed instrument. A vice which caught my eye more than anyone else's.

"May the Most High assist us," sobbed Robleda at that moment; whether in disapproval of the glass-blower's misplaced gesture or beweeping our plight, I knew not; and he let himself collapse, purple in the face, onto a stool.

"And all the saints," added the poet, "for I have come from Naples to catch the infection."

"And you did not do well," responded the Jesuit, wiping the sweat from his brow with a handkerchief. "You had only to remain in your own city, where the opportunities for contagion are not lacking."

"Perhaps so. And here, now that there is a good Pope, we believed we enjoyed the favours of heaven. But first we must see what those think who are, as they say, behind the Porte," whispered Stilone Priàso.

Tight-lipped and sharp-tongued, the Neapolitan poet had struck where none wished so much as to touch.

For weeks now, the Turkish army of the Ottoman Sublime Porte had been pressing at the gates of Vienna, thirsty for blood. All the Infidel hosts were converging implacably (or so the bare accounts that reached our ears would have it) on the capital of the Holy Roman Empire, and threatened soon to burst through its bastions.

The warriors in the Christian camp, almost on the point of capitulating, resisted only thanks to the power of the Faith. Short of arms and victuals, reduced by famine and dysentery, they were moreover terrorised by the first signs of an outbreak of the plague.

All knew that if Vienna were to fall, the armies of Kara Mustapha would have free passage to the West. And they would spread everywhere with blind and terrible joy.

To ward off the threat, many illustrious kings, princes and captains had mobilised: the King of Poland, Duke Charles of Lorraine, Prince Maximilian of Bavaria, Margrave Ludwig-Wilhelm of Baden, and others too. Almost all had been convinced to fly to the assistance of the besieged by the one true Bulwark of Christendom, Pope Innocent XI.

The Pontiff had, indeed, struggled long and strenuously to league together, gather and strengthen the armies of Christendom. And this he had done, not only by political means but also through precious financial support. From Rome there departed continuously generous sums of money: over two million scudi to the Emperor, five hundred thousand florins to Poland, more than a hundred thousand scudi donated by the nephew of the Pontiff, other subscriptions by individual cardinals and, lastly, a generous extraordinary levy on the ecclesiastical tithes of Spain.

The Holy Mission which the Pontiff was desperately seeking to accomplish followed upon innumerable pious works wrought during the seven years of his Pontificate.

Now aged seventy-two, the successor of Saint Peter, born Benedetto Odescalchi, had above all set the example. Tall, very thin, broad of forehead, with an aquiline nose, severe of mien, his chin prominent yet noble, wearing goatee and mustachios, he had gained renown as an ascetic.

Shy and reserved in character, he was but rarely to be seen riding in a carriage through the city, and took care to avoid popular acclamations. It was noted that he had chosen for himself the smallest, barest and most inhospitable apartments that ever a Pontiff inhabited, and that he almost never descended into the gardens of the Quirinale or the Vatican. He was so frugal and parsimonious as only to wear the habits and vestments of his predecessors. From the time of his election, he always wore the same exceedingly threadbare white cassock, and changed it only when it was pointed out to him that too negligent a dress ill-befitted the Vicar of Christ on earth.

Likewise, he had acquired the highest merit in the administration of the Church's patrimony. He had restored order to the funds of the Apostolic Chamber which, since the bad times of Urban VIII and Innocent X, had suffered all manner of robbery and fraud. He had abolished nepotism: no sooner was he elected than he summoned his nephew Livio, warning him—so it was said—that he would not have him made a cardinal, nor would he be allowed near the affairs of state.

Moreover, he had at last recalled his subjects to more austere and temperate usages. The theatres, places of disorderly entertainment, were closed. The Carnival which, only ten years earlier, had attracted admirers from all over Europe, was all but dead. Musical festivities and divertissements were reduced to a minimum. Women were forbidden to wear dresses too open and *décolleté* after the French fashion. The Pontiff had even sent forth bands of police spies to inspect the laundry hanging from the windows and confiscate any over-audacious bodices or blouses.

It was thanks to such austerity, both financial and moral, that Innocent XI had been able laboriously to raise money to combat the Turks, and great had been the succour given to the cause of the Christian armies.

But now the war had reached the critical moment. And all Christendom knew what to expect from Vienna: salvation or disaster.

So the people were in dire distress, at every sunrise looking to the East and wondering whether the new day would bring with it swarms of bloodthirsty janissaries and chargers thirsting to drink from the fountains of Saint Peter's.

৵৽৻

This, then, was what the squabble between the Jesuit and the poet had touched upon: a terror that ran through the town like an underground river.

The repartee of Stilone Priàso had piled fear upon fear in the already sorely tried spirit of Padre Robleda. Grim and trembling, the Jesuit's round face was framed by the angry pressure of the cushion of fat that danced beneath his chin.

"Is someone here of the Turkish party?" he gasped maliciously.

All those present turned instinctively towards the poet, whom a suspicious eye might easily have taken for an emissary of the Porte: brown, pockmarked skin, small eyes like coals, and an owl-like frown. His dark silhouette reminded one of those robbers with thick, short hair who are, alas, all too often to be encountered on the road to the Kingdom of Naples.

Stilone Priàso had not the time to reply.

"Silence, once and for all!" hissed one of the gendarmes, continuing the roll call.

"Signor di Mourai, from France, with Signor Pompeo Dulcibeni from Fermo, and Roberto Devizé, French musician."

The first name called was, as my master Signor Pellegrino hastened to explain, that of the old Frenchman who had arrived in the

Locanda del Donzello at the end of July and who had now died, allegedly of the infection. He was certainly a great nobleman, added Pellegrino, in very delicate health, and he had come to the inn accompanied by Devizé and Dulcibeni. Signor di Mourai was in fact almost completely blind and needed to be accompanied. About the old gentleman, almost nothing was known: the moment he arrived, he announced that he was very tired and every day he had his meal brought to him in his chamber, issuing forth only rarely for a short walk in the environs of the hostelry. The men-at-arms took rapid note of my master's statements.

"It is simply not possible, gentlemen, that he should have died of the plague! He had excellent manners and was very well dressed; it must have been old age—that is all."

Master Pellegrino's tongue had loosened and he began to address the militia in that soft tone of his which, although he employed it but rarely, sometimes proved highly effective for achieving his ends. Despite his noble features and tall, slim figure—his gentle hands, the easy and slightly stooped carriage of his fifty years, his face framed by flowing white tresses caught up with a ribbon, his vague and languid chestnut eyes—my master was, alas, prey to a bilious and choleric temper and ornamented his discourse with a great wealth of oaths and profanities. Only imminent danger restrained him from giving free rein to his nature on this occasion.

But no one was listening to him any longer. The young Devizé and Pompeo Dulcibeni were called up once again, and stepped forward at once. Our lodgers' eyes shone as the French musician, whose guitar had enchanted them only moments earlier, advanced.

The men of the Bargello were now eager to be gone and, without even giving Devizé and Dulcibeni the time to reach the wall, pushed them to one side, while the officer called, "Signor Eduardus Bedfordi, Englishman, and the Lady... and Cloridia."

The hasty correction and the vague smile with which the latter name was proffered left no doubt as to the ancient profession exercised by the one and only feminine lodger at the Donzello. About her, I really knew very little, for my master had not housed her among the other guests, but in the little tower, where she enjoyed a separate entrance. In the brief month of her stay, I had only to bring her provisions and wine, and to deliver (in truth, with singular frequency) notes in sealed envelopes which almost never showed the writer's name. Cloridia was quite young; she must have been about my own age. I had sometimes seen her come down into the chambers on the ground floor, and converse—quite charmingly, I must say—with one or other of our lodgers. Judging by her interviews with Master Pellegrino, she seemed intent on taking our hostelry as her fixed dwelling.

Signor di Bedfordi could not pass unobserved: with fiery red hair and a mantle of little golden freckles over his nose and on his cheeks, and squinting sky-blue eyes such as I had never seen before, he came from the distant British Isles. From what I had heard, this was not his first sojourn at the Donzello: like the glass-blower Brenozzi and Priàso the poet, he had already stayed there in the days of the previous hostess, my master's late cousin.

Mine was the last name to be called.

"He is twenty years old and has not been long in my employ," explained Pellegrino. "At the moment, he is my only apprentice, for at this time of year we have few guests. I know nothing about him, I took him in because he was alone in the world," said my master hurriedly, giving the impression that he wished to distance himself from any responsibility for the infection.

"Just show him to us, we must close," interrupted the men-at-arms impatiently, unable to identify me.

Pellegrino caught me by the arm, almost lifting me off the ground.

"Young man, you're nothing but a sparrow!" sneered the guard, while his companions guffawed.

From the windows all around, meanwhile, a few heads poked out timidly. The people of the quarter had found out what had happened, but only the most curious tried to draw near. Most kept their distances, already fearing the effects of the contagion.

The men-at-arms had concluded their mission. The inn had four entrances. Two on the Via dell'Orso: the great main door and the broad entrance next to it—kept open on summer evenings—which gave onto the first of the two dining chambers.

Then there was the side door which led from the alley directly to the kitchen, and, finally, the little door which led from the entrance hall to the courtyard. All were thoroughly sealed with stout beech planks made fast with nails a half-span long. The same was done to the door that led from Cloridia's little tower to the roof. The windows on the ground floor and the first floor, and those vents that opened onto the pavement from the top of the cellars had already been fitted with grates, and any attempt to escape from the second floor or from under the eaves would have involved the risk of falling or being seen and captured.

The leader of the Bargello's men, a fat individual with a half-severed ear, gave us our instructions. We were to lower the corpse of poor Signor di Mourai from one of the windows of his chamber after sunrise, when the dead-cart from the *Societas Orationis et Mortis* would pass by to collect it, and they would see to the burial. We were to be under the surveillance of a Watchman by Day from six of the clock in the morning until ten at night, and a Watchman by Night for the remainder of the time. We would not be able to leave until the safety of the place was duly established and certified, and in any case not before twenty days had expired. During that time, we must periodically answer a roll-call from one of the windows giving on to the Via dell'Orso. We were left a few large goatskins of water, pressed snow, a few round loaves, cheeses, lard, olives, some herbs and a basket of yellow apples. We were to receive a sum with which to pay for our victuals, water and snow. The inn's horses would remain where they were, in the hostler's stables next door.

Anyone who left or who so much as attempted to flee would receive forty lashes with the knotted cord and be delivered to the Magistrate for punishment. At the entrance, they nailed the infamous placard with the inscription SANITÀ—Health. We were then admonished to comply with whatever instructions might be given us thereafter, including the provisions adopted in times of infection, or plague; and whoever did not obey would be severely punished. From inside the hostelry, we heard dumbstruck that we were condemned to sequestration.

"We are dead, all dead," quoth one of the guests in colourless tones.

We were gathered in the long, narrow hallway of the hostelry, which had become dismal and dark since the barring of the door. We looked about ourselves, bewildered. None could make the decision to move to the adjoining rooms, where supper lay, already cold. My master, slumped on the great bench in the entrance, inveighed, holding his head in his hands. He uttered abuse and curses unfit to be repeated and threatened harm to anyone so bold as to venture near him. Suddenly, he began to rain down tremendous blows against the poor bench with his bare hands, causing the register of guests to jump up into the air. After that, he lifted the table and hurled it against the wall. We had to intervene and hold him back, clutching his arms and chest. Pellegrino tried to break free but lost his balance, dragging a pair of the guests to the ground with him, and dashing them one against the other with a great din. I myself managed to dodge out of the way a moment before the human heap threatened to bury me. My master was nimbler than his would-be controllers and almost at once was back on his feet, shouting and again unleashing his wrath on the bench with his fists.

I decided to abandon that narrow and now dangerous space and slipped away up the stairs. Here, however, after rushing up the first steps, I found myself face to face with Abbot Melani. He was coming down unhurriedly, stepping prudently.

"So they have really locked us up, my boy," said he, with that strange French rolling of his 'r'.

"What are we to do now?" I asked.

"Nothing."

"But we shall die of the pestilence."

"We shall see," he said with an indefinable nuance in his tone that I had already come to recognise.

Then he changed direction and led me up to the first floor. We went right to the end of the corridor and entered the large chamber which the old man who had just died shared with his companion Pompeo Dulcibeni from the Marches. A curtain divided the room in two. We drew it aside and there, crouching on the floor and fumbling in his little bag, we found the chirurgeon Cristofano.

In front of him, sprawled across the armchair, was Signor di Mourai, still half-dressed as Cristofano and the medical examiner had left him that morning. The dead man was somewhat malodorous because of the September heat and the foot bath in which his flesh was already beginning to rot, the Bargello having ordered that nothing was to be moved until the end of the roll-call.

"Boy, I asked you this morning kindly to clean up that noisome water on the floor," ordered Cristofano, with a note of impatience in his voice.

I was about to reply that I had done so immediately after he had ordered me to; but glancing down, I saw that around the basin there were indeed still several small puddles. I did as I had been commanded without protesting, using cloth and mop and cursing myself for not having been more careful that morning. In fact, I had until then never seen a corpse in all my life and I must have been confused by the emotion.

Mourai seemed even more meagre and bloodless than when he had arrived at the Locanda del Donzello. His lips were slightly parted and from them still dripped a little of that greenish froth which Cristofano, wishing to open his mouth a little more, began to remove with a cloth. The chirurgeon took pains, however, to touch this only after wrapping his own hand in another piece of cloth. As he had already done that morning, he scrutinised the dead man's throat carefully and sniffed at the froth. Then he got Abbot Melani to help him arrange the body on the bed. Once removed from the basin, the feet were greyish and from them emanated a dreadful odour of death which took our breath away.

Cristofano donned a pair of gloves in brown material which he took from the little bag. He returned to his inspection of the oral cavity, then observed the thorax and the groin. First, however, he prodded delicately behind the ears; then turned his attention to the armpits, removing the clothing so as to be able to observe the soft flesh with its covering of sparse hairs. Lastly, he pressed repeatedly with his fingertips the soft skin halfway between the organs of generation and the beginning of the thighs. He removed his gloves carefully and placed them in a sort of little cage divided into two compartments by a horizontal grate. In the lower half, there was a small basin into which he poured a brownish liquid, then closed the door of the compartment in which he had placed the gloves.

"It is vinegar," he explained. "It purges the pestiferous humours. One never knows. That being said, I stand by my idea: this really does not seem to me to be the infection. For the time being, we may rest our minds."

"You told the Bargello's men that it might be a congestion," I reminded him.

"That was only an example, given to gain time. I already knew from Pellegrino that Mourai ate only broths and clear soups."

"That is true," I confirmed. "Even this morning at dawn, he asked for one."

"Ah yes? Tell us more," asked the physician, showing interest.

"There is not much to be said: he asked my master for a clear soup with milk when, as every morning, he went to wake up Signor di Mourai and the gentleman from the Marches with whom he shared his room. But Signor Pellegrino was busy and so he asked me to prepare it. I went down to the kitchen, made it and brought it to him."

"Were you alone?"

"Yes."

"Did anyone come into the kitchen?"

"No."

"Did you ever leave the milk unattended?"

"Not even one moment."

"Are you sure?"

"If you are thinking that something in the broth might have harmed Signor di Mourai, know that I administered it to him personally, for Signor Dulcibeni had already gone out; and I myself drank a beaker of it."

The chirurgeon asked no more questions. He looked at the corpse and added: "I cannot perform an autopsy here and now, nor do I believe that anyone will do so, given the suspicion of plague. However, I repeat, this does not look to me like the infection."

"But then," I asked, "why have we been placed in quarantine?"

"Through excess of zeal. You are still young, but I believe that in these parts they remember the last visitation all too well. If nothing new occurs, they will soon realise that there is no danger. This old gentleman who, in any case, already seems not to have been enjoying good health, was not infected. And what is more, I would say that neither you nor I are. However, we have no choice: we shall have to pass poor Signor di Mourai's body and clothing out through the window, as the Bargello ordered. Each one of us will, moreover, have to sleep in a separate chamber. There are enough apartments in this inn, if I am not mistaken," said he, questioning me with his eyes.

I nodded in agreement. On each floor, four chambers opened onto the two branches of the corridor: one rather spacious apartment just next to the stairs, followed by a very small one and then an L-shaped one, while at the end of the corridor was the largest room, the only one to give not only onto the alleyway but onto the Via dell'Orso. This would mean occupying all the apartments on the first and second floors, but I knew that my master would not complain too much about that, since no other guests could join us for the time being.

"Dulcibeni will sleep in my chamber," added Cristofano. "He certainly cannot remain here with the corpse. However," he concluded, "if there are no other cases, true or false, in the next few days, they will release us."

"In how much time exactly?" asked Atto Melani.

"Who can tell? If anyone in the neighbourhood should feel unwell, perhaps only because he has drunk bad wine or eaten fish that has gone off, they will at once think of us."

"Then we risk remaining here forever," said I, already feeling suffocated by the thick walls of the inn.

"Forever, no. But calm down now: have you not been here, night and day, for the past few weeks? I have rarely seen you leave the house; you are already used to being shut in."

That was true. My master had taken me into service out of pity, knowing that I was alone in the world. And I worked from morning till night.

It happened early last spring, when Pellegrino had come to Rome from Bologna, where he worked as a cook, to take over the activity of the Donzello after the misfortune which had befallen his cousin, the late innkeeper, Signora Luigia de Grandis Bonetti. She, poor woman, had given up the ghost following the physical consequences of an attack suffered in the street at the hands of two gypsy scoundrels, who were trying to rob her of her purse. The hostelry had for thirty years been run by Luigia, together with her husband Lorenzo and their son Francesco, and subsequently by Luigia alone, when she had been widowed and bereaved of her son. For a time, it was quite well known and received guests from all over the world. Such was Luigia's veneration for Duke Orsini, the owner of the little building in which the inn was situated, that she bequeathed to him all that she possessed. The Duke, however, made no objection when Pellegrino (who had to feed his wife, an unmarried daughter and a little girl) arrived from Bologna and begged His Grace to allow him to continue his cousin Luigia's flourishing activity.

This was a golden opportunity for my master, who had already squandered another such: after a difficult career in the kitchens of a wealthy cardinal, in which he had reached the enviable rank of deputy carver, he was dismissed because of his choleric character and his all-too-frequent intemperance.

Hardly had Pellegrino settled near the Donzello, waiting for the few passing guests to free the premises, than I was recommended to him by the parish priest of the nearby church of Santa Maria in Posterula. With the coming of the torrid Roman summer, his consort, who was indeed full of enthusiasm for the idea of becoming an inn-keeper's wife, left for the Apennine mountains, where her parents still lived. They were due to return at the end of the month, and, in the meantime, I was the only remaining helper.

Of course, I could not be expected to be the best of appren-tices: but I put my all into pleasing my master. Once I had fin-ished the day's work, I willingly sought every opportunity to make myself useful. And since I did not care to venture out alone and face the dangers of the streets (above all the cruel jokes of those of my own age) I was, as the chirurgeon Cristofano had observed, almost always at work in the Inn of the Donzello. Nevertheless, the thought of being sequestered for a whole quarantine in those chambers, however familiar and welcoming, suddenly seemed to me an unbearable sacrifice.

❧

In the meanwhile, the hubbub in the entrance had died down and we were soon rejoined by my master and all those who had engaged in that lengthy and useless waste of their strength. Cristofano's recent pronouncement was explained to them, which raised everyone's spir-its, except my master's.

"I'll kill them, I'll kill them all," said he, again losing his temper.

He added that this misfortune had ruined him, for no one would ever again come to the Donzello, nor of course would it be possible to sell the hostelry's business, which had already been devalued by that accursed crack in the wall, and he would have to use up all his credit to obtain another such; in short, he would soon be poor and ruined, ruined forever, but first he would tell all to the College of Innkeep-ers, ah yes, even if they all knew that it was quite useless, quoth he, contradicting himself over and over, and I understood that he had unfortunately been at the Greco wine again.

The doctor continued: "We shall have to gather all the old man's blankets and clothing and tip them into the street when the dead-cart comes to collect the corpse."

He then turned to Pompeo Dulcibeni: "Did you meet or hear of infected persons coming from Naples?"

"Absolutely not."

The gentleman from the Marches seemed to be experiencing difficulty in hiding how deeply perturbed he was by his friend's death, which had, moreover, occurred in his absence. A veil of perspiration covered his forehead and his cheeks. The physician questioned him concerning a number of details: whether the old man had eaten regularly, whether his bodily functions were regular, whether he had been of melancholy humour; all in all, whether he had shown any signs of suffering other than those normally present in one of advanced age. But Dulcibeni was aware of no such thing. The man was rather massive, always wearing a black great-coat; but above all made to look awkward and cumbersome by a very old gorget of Flemish lace (as I believe must have been the fashion many, many years ago) and by his bulging paunch. This, together with his florid complexion, made one suspect a propensity for food not inferior to my master's for the Greco wine. Thick hair, now almost all white, a tendency to take umbrage, a slightly fatigued tone of voice and a grave and pensive expression conferred on him the semblance of an honest and temperate man. Only with the passing of time and closer observation was I to see in his severe blue-green eyes and ever-frowning eyebrows the reflection of a concealed and ineradicable bitterness.

Dulcibeni said that he had met the late Signor di Mourai quite by chance, in the course of a voyage, and he did not know much about him. Together with Signor Devizé, he had accompanied him from Naples; for the old man, being almost completely blind, was in need of assistance. Signor Devizé, the musician and guitar player, had, affirmed Dulcibeni (with Devizé nodding agreement), come to Italy to acquire a new instrument from a Neapolitan lute-maker. Later, he had expressed the desire to stay in Rome in order to learn the most recent musical styles, before returning to Paris.

"What will happen if we go out before the end of the quarantine?" I asked.

"Attempting to flee is the least advisable solution," replied Cristofano, "since all the ways out are sealed, including the passage that leads from the tower where Monna Cloridia lives on to the roof. The windows are too high or have been covered with grating, and the watch is patrolling below. What is more, attempting to escape from quarantine incurs an exceedingly severe punishment, and one would be imprisoned under far worse conditions for years and years. The people of the quarter would help recapture any fugitive."

Evening shadows were falling, and I distributed lamps and oil.

"Let us endeavour to keep up our spirits," added the Tuscan chirurgeon, looking meaningfully at my master. "We must give the impression that all goes perfectly with us. If nothing changes, I shall not examine you—not unless you so request. Should there be other cases of ill health, I shall have to do so for the sake of us all. Warn me if ever you feel unwell, even if it seems to be a mere trifle. For the time being, however, it will do no good to worry, for this man," said he, pointing at the inert body of Signor di Mourai, "did not die of the plague."

"What, then, did he die of?" asked Abbot Melani.

"Not of plague, I repeat."

"And how do you know, Doctor?" responded the abbot, distrustfully.

"We are still in summer and it is quite hot. If this were plague, it would be of the summer variety, which is caused by the corruption of natural heat and provokes fevers and headaches. In such cases, the cadavers at once become black and hot, and present tokens that are also black and putrescent. But this man has not the shadow of a token, or an abscess, a botch, a swelling or whatever you might wish to call it; neither under the armpits, nor behind the ears, nor in the groin. There was no rise in temperature, nor burning. And, from what his companions have told me, he seemed quite well until within hours of his death. That, as far as I am concerned, is sufficient to rule out contagion with the plague."

"Then it is another illness," replied Melani.

"I repeat: in order to understand that, it would be necessary to have recourse to anatomy: to open up the body and examine it from the inside; in other words, as the chirurgeons do in Holland. On the face of it, I could diagnose an acute attack of putrid fevers, which shows no signs until it is too late for any remedy. Yet I can find no sign of putrefaction on the body or bad odours other than those of death or old age. I might perhaps suppose it to be the malady of *mazzuco*, or *modoro*, as the Spaniards call it: that causes an aposteme, which is to say, an abscess within the brain, and is thus invisible. And once that is present, death must ensue. If, on the other hand, the illness is at the stage of its initial symptoms, it can be easily remedied. Had I been informed of it even a few days ago, I might perhaps have been able to save him. It would have sufficed to bleed one of the two veins under the tongue, to administer in his beverage an infinitesimal quantity of oil of vitriol, and to anoint stomach and head with holy oil. But, as far as we can see, old Mourai showed no signs of being unwell. Besides…"

"Besides?" urged Melani.

"*Mazzuco* certainly does not cause a swelling of the tongue," concluded the chirurgeon with a telling grimace. Perhaps it is… something very like poison."

Poison. While the physician returned to his chamber, each of us contemplated the corpse in silence. For the first time, the Jesuit made the sign of the cross. Master Pellegrino renewed his imprecations, cursing the misfortune of having a dead man in his hostelry and, what is more, one who had perhaps been poisoned. And who would have the courage to hear what his wife would have to say, on her return?

Talk then spread among the guests about the most notorious cases of poisoning, real or presumed: prominent among these were sovereigns of former times: Charles the Bald, for example, or Lothar, the King of the Franks and his son Louis; or, approaching modern times, the *acqua tofana* laced with arsenic, or the Spanish fly, both employed by the Borgias for their abominable crimes, as well as by the Valois and the Guises in their conspiracies. A shameful trembling ran through the group, for poison and fear are born of the same parents. Someone recalled how Henry of Navarre, before he became King Henry IV of France, was wont himself to go down to the banks of the Seine to draw the water which he drank at his meals, fearing that he might fall victim to toxic potions. Did not John of Austria die from wearing poisoned boots? Stilone Priàso recalled how Catherine de' Medici had poisoned Jeanne d'Albret, the mother of Henry IV, using perfumed gloves and collars, and how she had attempted to repeat the exercise by offering her own son a marvellous book on hunting, the pages of which were a little gummed together, so that he, licking his fingers to turn them, would imbibe the fatal Italian poison with which they were impregnated.

Such murderous preparations had, asserted another guest, been the province of perfumers and astrologers. And someone dusted off the tale of how Saint-Barthélemy, the servant of the ill-famed Prior of Cluny, had killed the Cardinal of Lorraine by paying him in poisoned gold coin. Henry of Luxembourg died—O subtle blasphemy!—of poison concealed in the consecrated host with which he took Communion.

Now, Stilone Priàso began to parley closely with one guest after another, admitting that so many fantastic things had always been said about poets and those who practised the art of fine writing; but he was only a poet, and born for poetry, may God pardon his immodesty!

They then all turned to me and began again to belabour me with questions about the broth which I had served Signor di Mourai that morning. I had to repeat several times that absolutely no one but myself had been near the dish. Only with difficulty were they at last convinced, and they then ceased paying attention to me.

I noticed all of a sudden that the only one to have left the company was Abbot Melani. It was late now, and I resolved to go down to the kitchen in order to wash up.

In the corridor, I almost collided with the young Englishman, Signor di Bedfordi, who struck me as being rather agitated; perhaps because, having transferred his effects to a new chamber, he had not been present for the chirurgeon's diagnosis. This guest was dragging himself along slowly and seemed unusually afflicted. When I stopped in front of him, he gave a start.

"It is I, Signor Bedfordi," I reassured him.

He looked dumbly, lost in his daydreams, at the lamp I bore in my hand. For the first time, he had abandoned his usual phlegmatic pose, which gave away his affected and haughty nature, one that caused him to be repelled (and he often gave me proof thereof) by my servant's simplicity. Born of an Italian mother, Bedfordi had no difficulty expressing himself in our language. On the contrary, his eloquence, in the conversations that accompanied their meals, was much appreciated by the other guests.

His silence that evening therefore struck me all the more. I explained to him that, in the doctor's opinion, there was no cause for anxiety, since this was certainly not a case of plague. It was, however, suspected that Mourai might have ingested a poison.

He stared at me, with his mouth hanging half open, and answered not a word. He retreated several paces, then turned round and returned to his chamber, where I heard him lock himself in.

Night the First

BETWEEN *the* 11TH *&* 12TH SEPTEMBER, 1683

✠

"Forget it, my boy."

This time it was my turn to be startled. I found myself facing Abbot Melani, who had come down from the second floor.

"I am hungry. Kindly accompany me to the kitchen."

"If you please, Sir, first I should tell Master Pellegrino. He has forbidden me to draw on provisions outside regular luncheon and supper hours."

"Never fear, your Master Pellegrino is now hard at it with Madam Bottle."

"And Doctor Cristofano's orders?"

"Those were not orders, but prudent advice; which I regard as superfluous."

He preceded me downstairs, where the dining chamber and the kitchen were situated. In the latter, to satisfy his request, I found a little bread and cheese and a beaker of red wine. We sat down at the work table where I and my master usually ate.

"Tell me, where do you come from?" he asked me, as he began to partake of his refreshment.

Flattered by his curiosity, I recounted briefly the story of my miserable life. At a few months of age, I had been abandoned and left outside a convent near Perugia. The nuns had then entrusted me to a pious woman who lived in the neighbourhood. When I grew up, I was brought to Rome, where I was placed in the service of that woman's brother, the parish priest of Santa Maria in Posterula, the little church not far from the hostelry. After employing me on a number of minor tasks, the priest recommended me to Signor Pellegrino, before he himself was transferred outside Rome.

"So now you are an apprentice," said the abbot.

"Yes, but I hope not forever."

"You would, I imagine, like to have your own inn."

"No, Signor Abbot. I would like to become a gazetteer."

"Now, that is a fine one," said he with a mischievous smile.

I explained to him that the pious and kindly woman to whom I had been entrusted had arranged for me to be instructed by a former serving maid. That old woman, who had previously been in a nunnery, had initiated me into the arts of the *Trivium* and the *Quadrivium*, in the sciences *de vegetalibus*, *de animalibus* and *de mineralibus*, in *humanae litterae*, in Philosophy and in Theology. She had then made me read many historians and grammarians, as well as Italian, Spanish and French poets. Yet, more even than arithmetic, geometry, music, astronomy, grammar, logic and rhetoric, I grew passionately interested in the things of this world, and, most of all, my spirit was inflamed by the telling of the exploits and successes, both near and far, of princes and reigning monarchs and of wars and other admirable things which...

"Good, good," he interrupted me, "so you want to become a gazetteer, or scribe, if you prefer. Men of wit often end up engaged in that trade. How did the idea come to you?"

I was often sent on errands to Perugia, I replied. In town, if I was fortunate enough to be present on the right day, I could listen to the public reading of gazettes, and for two pence one could purchase (but this one could in Rome, too) broadsheets with many notable descriptions of the most recent occurrences in Europe...

"My goodness, young man, I have never come across one like you!"

"Thank you, Sir."

"Are you not rather too learned for a mere scullion? Those of your kind usually do not even know how to hold a pen," said he, grimacing.

That remark upset me.

"You are very intelligent," he added, softening his tone. "And I understand you: at your age, I too was fascinated by the scribbler's trade. But I had so many things to do. To write skilfully for newspapers is indeed a great art, and always better than working. "And then," he added between one mouthful and the next, "to be a gazetteer in Rome is most exalting. You will know all about the question of the franchises, the Gallican controversy, Quietism..."

"Yes, I believe that... is so," I murmured, trying in vain to conceal my ignorance.

"Some things, young man, one must needs know. Otherwise, about what will you write? But of course, you are too young. And then, whatever could one write about these days in this half-dead city? You should have seen the splendour of Rome formerly, indeed, only a few years ago. Music, theatres, academies, the introduction of ambassadors, processions, balls: all was refulgent with a wealth, an abundance that you can scarcely imagine."

"And why is it no longer so today?"

"The grandeur and felicity of Rome ended with the ascension of this Pope, and they will return only with his death. Theatrical performances are forbidden, the Carnival has been suppressed. Can you not see it with your own eyes? The churches are neglected, the palaces are crumbling, the streets are full of potholes and the aqueducts are close to collapse. The master builders, architects and workmen are all returning to their own countries. The writing and reading of those handbills and broadsheets, for which so you have such a passion, are prohibited, although that ban is not always complied with; punishments are even harsher than in former times. Even for Christina of Sweden, who came to Rome abjuring the religion of Luther for our own, no longer are there festivities at the Barberini Palace, or spectacles at the Teatro Tor di Nona. Since the accession of Pope Innocent XI, even Queen Christina has had to cloister herself in her palace."

"In the past, did you live here in Rome?"

"Yes, for a time," he replied, then suddenly corrected himself, "indeed, more than once. I arrived in Rome in 1644, when I was only eighteen and studied with the best masters. I had the honour to be a pupil of the divine Luigi Rossi, the greatest European composer of all time. Then, in the Palazzo alle Quattro Fontane, the Barberini had a theatre with three thousand places and the theatre of the Colonna family in the Palazzo al Borgo was the envy of all the reigning Houses. The artists who designed the scenes bore the most celebrated names, and included even Gian Lorenzo Bernini himself, and the stage astonished, kindled the emotions and entertained, with apparitions of rain, suns setting, bolts of lightning, real living animals, duels with real wounds and real blood, palaces more palatial than real ones and gardens with fountains from which gushed fresh, clear water."

I realised at that point that I had not asked the abbot whether he was a composer, an organist or a choirmaster. Fortunately, I withheld that question. His almost hairless face, unusually gentle and womanish movements, and above all his very clear voice, almost like that of a small boy who had unexpectedly attained maturity, revealed that I was in the presence of an emasculated singer.

The abbot doubtless remarked the flash of recognition which my look must have betrayed at the instant when I received this illumination. He continued, however, as though nothing had transpired.

"Then, there were not as many singers as today. For a good many, the way lay open and they could travel far and attain unhoped-for goals. As for myself, besides possessing the talent which heaven was pleased to bestow upon me, I had studied with some alacrity. Thus it was that my patron, the Grand Duke of Tuscany, sent me to Paris in the retinue of my master, Luigi Rossi."

So that was where that strange "r" came from, thought I to myself, in which he seemed to take such delight.

"Did you travel to Paris in order to continue your studies?"

"Do you imagine that one would still need to study who possessed letters of recommendation to Cardinal Mazarin and to the Queen in person?"

"But then, Signor Abbot, you have had occasion to sing for those Royal Highnesses?"

"Queen Anne enjoyed my singing, I might say, more than ordinarily. She loved melancholy airs in the Italian style, in which I was perfectly able to satisfy her. No two evenings passed without my going to serve her, and every time for at least four hours in her apartments, no thought could arise of anything but music."

He broke off and looked out of the window, as though oblivious.

"You have never visited the court of Paris. How could one explain this to you? All those nobles and cavaliers rendered me a thousand honours, and when I sang for the Queen, I seemed to be in paradise, surrounded by a thousand angelic faces. The Queen went so far as to beg the Grand Duke not to recall me to Italy, so that she might still enjoy my services. My patron, who was her first cousin on his mother's side, complied with that request. It was the Queen in person who, a few weeks later, showed me, while gracing me with the sweetest of smiles, the letter from my patron permitting me to remain in Paris yet awhile longer. When I had read it, I felt myself dying from jubilation and contentment."

The abbot had then returned more and more often to Paris, also in the retinue of his master, Luigi Rossi, whose name caused his eyes to shine with pent-up emotion each time that he pronounced it.

"Today, his name means nothing. But then, all accorded him the honours which were his due: for he was a great—indeed, a very great—man. He wished me to play the hero of the *Orfeo*, the most splendid opera ever to be performed at the French court. It was a memorable success. I was but one and twenty years old then. And, after two months of continuous performances, I had barely the time to return to Florence before Mazarin begged the Grand Duke to send me back to France, so much did the Queen miss my voice. Thus it was that, after returning with Seigneur Luigi, we found ourselves caught up in the turmoil of the Fronde and were forced to flee Paris, together with the Queen, the Cardinal and the little King."

"So you knew the Most Christian King as a child!"

"Very well, even. During those terrible months of exile at the Château de Saint-Germain, he never left his mother's side, and would listen to me sing in silence, rapt silence. Often, in empty moments, I would try to distract him, inventing games for him; thus His Majesty recovered his smile."

I was for a while both galvanised and stunned by my double discovery. Not only had this bizarre guest a glorious past as a musician; he had been an intimate of the royal highnesses of France! And, what was more, he was one of those singular prodigies of nature who united with a man's form vocal gifts and a quality of soul that were utterly feminine. I had almost at once noticed that unusual timbre in his voice. But I had not dwelt sufficiently on other details, thinking that here might be a simple sodomite.

I had, however, chanced upon a castrato. I knew, in truth, that in order to conquer their extraordinary vocal powers, emasculated singers had to undergo a painful and irreversible operation. I knew the sad tale of the pious Origen, who had voluntarily parted with his masculine attributes in order to achieve supreme spiritual virtue, and I had heard that Christian doctrine had from the very beginning condemned castration. But fortune would have it that right here in Rome the services of castrati were highly valued and sought after. Everyone knew that the Vatican Chapel was accustomed to employ castrati on a regular basis, and I had sometimes heard the older inhabitants of my quarter comment jestingly on a snatch of song from a washerwoman with the words: "You sing like Rosini," or, "You are better than Folignato." They were alluding to the castrati who, decades before, had entranced the ears of Pope Clement VIII. Even more often, one heard mention of Loreto Vittori, whose voice had, I knew, the power to bewitch all who heard it. So much so that Pope Urban VIII had appointed him a Knight of the Militia of Christ. Little did it matter that, on several occasions, the Holy See had threatened with excommunication those who practised emasculation. And even less did it matter that the feminine charms of the castrati should perturb spectators. From the chatter and jokes of my contemporaries, I had learned that one need walk only a few dozen paces from the hostelry to find the shop of a complaisant barber who was ever ready to perform the horrendous mutilation, so long as the reward was adequate and the secret well guarded.

"Why wonder?" said Melani, calling me back from my silent reflections. "One should not be surprised that a Queen should prefer my voice to that—may God forgive me—of a mere *canterina*. In Paris, I was often accompanied by an Italian singer, a certain Leonora Baroni, who did try so very hard. Today, no one remembers her. Mark my words, young man: if women are not today permitted to sing in public, as Saint Paul so rightly willed it, that is certainly not a matter of chance."

He raised his glass as though for a toast, and solemnly recited:

> *Toi qui sais mieux que aucun le succès que jadis*
> *les pièces de musique eurent dedans Paris,*
> *que dis-tu de l'ardeur dont la cour échauffée*
> *frondoit en ce temps-là les grands concerts d'Orphée,*
> *les passages d'Atto et de Léonora,*
> *et le déchaînement qu'on a pour l'Opéra?**

I remained silent, allowing myself no more than a questioning glance.

"Jean de la Fontaine," said he, emphatically. The greatest poet in France."

"And, if I heard well, he wrote about you!"

"Yes. And another poet, a Tuscan this time, said that the singing of Atto Melani could be used as a remedy against a viper's bite."

"Another poet?"

"Francesco Redi, the greatest man of letters and science in all

---

* You who know better than anyone the success that music once enjoyed in Paris, what say you of the ardour with which the court flocked then so excitedly to the great concerts of Orpheus, the appearances of Atto and Leonora, and the enthusiasm that there was for opera?

Tuscany. Such were the muses on whose lips my name travelled, my boy."

"Do you still appear before the French royal family?"

"Once youth has vanished, the voice is the first of the body's virtues to become unreliable. As a young man, however, I sang in the courts of all Europe, and thus had occasion to make the acquaintance of many princes. Nowadays, they are pleased to ask me for advice, when they must take important decisions."

"You are then... a counsellor abbot?"

"Yes, let us say that."

"You must often be at court, in Paris."

"The court is now at Versailles, my boy. As for myself, that is a long story."

And, frowning, he added: "Have you ever heard of Monsieur de Fouquet?"

The name was, I replied, utterly unknown to me.

He poured himself another glass of wine and fell silent. His silence caused me no embarrassment. We remained thus awhile, without proffering a word, lulled by a spark of reciprocal sympathy.

Atto Melani was still dressed as he had been that morning: with his abbot's periwig, hood and grey-mauve soutane. Age (and his did not show) had enveloped him with a fine layer of fat which softened a rather hooked nose and severe features. The white powder on his face, which changed to carmine on his prominent cheeks, spoke of a perennial conflict of instincts; his broad, wrinkled forehead and arched eyebrows suggested a cold and haughty nature. Yet that was only a pose: it was contradicted by the mocking fold in his fine, contracted lips and in his slightly receding, but fleshy, chin, in the midst of which sat an impertinent dimple.

Melani cleared his throat. He drank a last draught and kept the wine in his mouth, letting it smack between his tongue and his palate.

"We shall make a pact," said he all of a sudden. "You need to know everything. You have not travelled, you have experienced nothing, seen nothing. You are perspicacious; one remarks certain qualities immediately. But without a helping hand at the outset, you will never arrive anywhere. Well, in the twenty days of claustration that lie before us, I can give you all that you need. You, in exchange, will help me."

I was astounded. "In what way?"

"What the deuce, to find out who poisoned Monsieur de Mourai!" answered the abbot, as though it were the most obvious thing in the world, and he gazed at me the while with a little half-smile.

"Are you certain that this was poisoning?"

"Absolutely," exclaimed he, standing up and moving around in search of something to else to eat. "The poor old man must have swallowed something lethal. You heard the physician, did you not?"

"And what does it matter to you?"

"If we do not stop the assassin in time, he will soon strike down other victims here."

Fear dried my throat at once, and any remaining appetite abandoned my poor stomach.

"By the way," asked Atto Melani, "are you quite sure of what you told Cristofano about the broth which you prepared and served up to Mourai? Is there nothing else that I should know?"

I repeated to him that I had never taken my eyes off the pan, and I had personally administered the broth, sip by sip, to the gentleman. Any outside intervention must therefore be ruled out.

"Do you know if he took anything earlier?"

"I would say not. When I arrived, he had just risen and Dulcibeni had already gone out."

"And afterwards?"

"No, I think not. After serving him the broth, I prepared the basin for his foot bath. When I left him, he was dozing."

"That means only one thing," he concluded.

"Namely?"

"That you killed him."

He smiled at me. He was jesting.

"I shall serve you in all things," I found myself promising him, with my cheeks on fire, torn between emotion at the challenge which I faced and fear of the danger.

"Bravo. For a start, you could tell me all that you know about the other guests, and whether, in the last few days, you have noticed anything unusual. Have you heard any bizarre conversation? Has anyone been long absent? Have letters been delivered or dispatched?"

I responded that I knew very little, apart from the fact that Brenozzi, Bedfordi and Stilone Priàso had lodged at the Donzello at the time of the late Signora Luigia. I then mentioned, not without some hesitancy, that it seemed to me that Padre Robleda, the Jesuit,

had gone at night to Cloridia's apartments. The abbot simply guffawed.

"My boy, from now on, you will keep your eyes open. Above all, you
will watch the two travelling companions of old Mourai, the French
musician Robert Devizé, and Pompeo Dulcibeni, the Marchigiano."

He saw that I had lowered my eyes, and continued: "I know what
you are thinking: you want to be a gazetteer, not a spy. Know then
that the two trades are not so different from one another."

"But shall I need to know all that you mentioned a moment ago?
About the Quietists, the Gallican Articles, and..."

"That is the wrong question. Some gazetteers have gone far, yet
know little: only really important things."

"And what are those?"

"Things which they will never write. But we shall speak of that
tomorrow. Now let us go and sleep."

While we were climbing the stairs, I glanced in silence at the abbot's white face by the light of the lantern: here was my new master,
and I savoured all the excitement of the situation. True, all had come
to pass so very suddenly, yet I was vaguely aware that Melani was
imbued with a similar secret pleasure at having me for a disciple. At
least for as long as the quarantine lasted.

The abbot turned towards me before we took leave of each other,
and smiled. Then he disappeared down the second-floor corridor,
without a word.

෧෧

I spent a good part of the night sewing together some old clean leaves
of paper piled up on the table where my master kept his accounts,
and then writing down on these the recent events which I had witnessed. I had decided: I would not lose a single word of what Abbot
Melani had taught me. I would transcribe it all and conserve it jealously.

Without the help of those ancient notes today, sixteen years later,
I could not be here compiling these memoirs.

Day the Second
12TH SEPTEMBER, 1683

✠

The morning after, I awoke to a strange surprise. I found Signor Pellegrino asleep on his bed, in the chamber which we shared under the eaves. He had made no preparation whatever for our guests' repast; which, despite our exceptional circumstances, was nevertheless required of him. My master, dressed in the clothes he had worn the evening before, lay sprawled across the bedcovers, showing every sign of having fallen asleep under the influence of some cheap red wine. After rousing him with some difficulty, I went to the kitchen. As I was descending the stairs, I heard, drawing ever nearer, a distant cloud of sounds, confused at first, albeit pleasant. As I drew closer to the entrance of the dining chamber, next to the kitchen, the music grew clearer and more intelligible. It was Signor Devizé who, clumsily perched on a wooden stool, was practising his instrument.

A strange enchantment overcame all who heard Devizé's playing, in which the joy of listening was conjoined with the pleasure of the eyes. His doublet of Isabella-coloured bourette and his unadorned apparel, his eyes whose colour shifted from green to grey, his fine cinder-grey hair: everything in him seemed to give way to the vivid tones which, with extravagant chromatics, he drew from the six strings. Once the last note had vanished into thin air, the enchantment broke; and there before one sat a sulky little red-faced man, almost scorbutic, with minute features, a small nose reaching down towards a fleshy, pouting mouth, the short, bull-like physique of an ancient Teuton, a martial gait and brusque manners.

He did not pay much attention when I entered and, after a brief pause, resumed his playing. Suddenly, from his fingers, there sprang up no mere music, but an admirable architecture of sounds which to this day I could describe, were heaven to grant me the words, and not just the memory. It began with a simple, innocent air which danced, *arpeggiato*, from the tonal chord to that of the dominant (thus the virtuoso was later to explain it to me, as yet utterly ignorant of the art of sounds), then reprised that movement, and, after a surprising free cadenza passage, repeated it all. This was, however, only the first of a rich and surprising collection of gems which, as Signor Devizé later explained to me, was called a *rondeau* and which was composed of that same first air, repeated several times, but each time followed by a new precious jewel, utterly original and resplendent in its own light.

Like every other *rondeau*, this one, to which I was to listen on many subsequent occasions, was crowned by the extreme and con-clusive repetition of the first stanza, which seemed to endow the whole with meaning and completeness. But, although the innocence and simplicity of that first stanza was utterly delicious, it would have been nothing without the sublime concert of the others which, one after the other, refrain upon refrain, arose ever freer, bolder and more exquisite from that admirable structure; so much so that the last of these was for the intellect and the ears a most sweet and extreme challenge, like those which knights issue to one another over ques-tions of honour. The final arpeggio, after descending prudently, even timidly, towards the bass notes, made a sudden ascent towards the high notes, then jumped to the highest, transforming its tortuous and timorous advance into a clear river of beauty, into which it loos-ened its long tresses of harmony with an admirable progression to bass. And there it remained, absorbed in mysterious and ineffable harmonies, which to my ear sounded forbidden, even impossible (which is the main reason why words fail me here), and at last moved unwillingly towards peace, making way for the final repetition of the initial stanza.

I listened rapt, without proffering a word, until the French musi-cian had stilled the last echo from his instrument. He looked at me.

"You play the lute so well," I ventured timidly.

"In the first place, this is no lute," he answered, "it is a guitar. And besides, you are not interested in how well I play. You like this mu-sic. One can see from how you listen. And you are right: I am rather proud of this *rondeau*."

Here, he explained to me how a *rondeau* was made, and how that which I had just heard differed from others.

"That to which you have just listened is a *rondeau* in the style we call *brisé*, or broken. In other words, it imitates the lute: the chords are not all played together but strummed, *arpeggiato*."

"Ah, I see," I replied, confusedly.

From my expression, Devizé must have understood how unsatisfactory his explanation had been, and he went on to say that, while the refrain was written according to the good old rules of consonance, the alternate passages contained ever new harmonic assays, which all concluded in an unexpected fashion, almost as though they were alien to good musical doctrine. And after reaching its apogee, the *rondeau* brusquely entered its coda.

I asked him how it was that he spoke our language so fluently (although with a strong French accent; but that, I did not mention).

"I have travelled much, and I have come to know many Italians whom, by inclination and in practice, I regard as the best musicians in the world. In Rome, however, the Pope has already had the Teatro Tor di Nona, which was near this hostelry, closed for years; but in Bologna, in the cappella of San Petronio, and in Florence, one can hear many fine musicians and many magnificent new works. Indeed, our great maestro Jean-Baptiste Lully, who ornaments the King's glory at Versailles, is a Florentine. Best of all, I know Venice where, of all Italian cities, music flourishes the most. I adore the theatres of Venice: the San Cassiano, the San Salvatore, and the famous Teatro del Cocomero where, before I went to Naples, I attended a marvellous concert."

"Were you intending to stay long here in Rome?"

"It scarcely matters now what I may have intended. We do not even know whether we shall leave here alive," said he, resuming his playing with a passage which, he said, came from a chaconne by Maestro Lully himself.

❧

Hardly had I left the kitchen where, after my conversation with Devizé I had closed myself in to prepare luncheon, when I ran into Brenozzi, the Venetian glass-blower. I advised him that, if he wished for a warm meal, it was ready. But he, without uttering a word, grasped my arm and dragged me down the stairs that led to the cellar. When I tried to protest, he closed my mouth with his hand. We stopped half-way down the stairs and he started at once: "Calm down and listen to me. Do not be afraid, you must only tell me certain things."

He whispered in a strangled voice, without allowing me to open my mouth. He wanted to know the comments of the other guests on the death of Signor di Mourai, and whether it was thought that there was a danger of yet another death by poisoning or some other cause, and if anyone in particular feared such an eventuality, and if others, on the contrary, feared no such thing, and how long the quarantine might last, if it might be more than the twenty days ordered by the Magistrate, and whether I suspected that any of the guests might be in possession of poisons, or even so much as thought that use had really been made of such substances; and lastly, whether any one of those present was proving inexplicably tranquil despite the quarantine that had just been imposed on the inn.

"Signore, I really…"

"The Turks? Have they spoken of the Turks? And of the pestilence in Vienna?"

"But I know nothing, I…"

"Now listen once and for all, and answer me," he continued, impatiently squeezing his rod. "Marguerites: does that mean anything to you?"

"I beg your pardon, Sir?"

"Daisies, marguerites."

"If you wish, Sir, I do have dried ones in the cellar for preparing infusions. Do you feel unwell?"

He snorted and raised his eyes to heaven.

"Forget all that I have said to you. My one command is this: if anyone should ask you, you know nothing about me, understood?" and he squeezed both my hands until they hurt.

I stood there looking at him, speechless.

"Understood?" he repeated impatiently. "What is wrong, is that not enough for you?"

I did not comprehend the meaning of his last question and began to fear that he was out of his mind. I broke free of his grip and rushed up the stairs, while my tormentor tried to hold me back. I emerged into semi-darkness, while Devizé's guitar began again to play that splendid and disquieting melody which I had already heard. Rather than tarry, however, I rushed up to the first floor. My fists were still tight with the tension provoked by the glass-blower's assault, and that is why it was only then that I became aware of something in my hand. I opened it and saw three little pearls of admirable lustre.

I put these in my pocket and headed for the chamber in which Signor di Mourai had died. There, I found three of our guests engaged in the saddest of tasks. Cristofano was carrying the corpse of the deceased, wrapped in a white cloth which served as a shroud, and beneath which one could sense the deathly rigour of his members. The physician was assisted by Signor Pellegrino and, in the absence of younger volunteers, by Dulcibeni and Atto Melani. The abbot wore no periwig, neither was his face powdered. I was astonished to see him wearing secular apparel—taffeta breeches and a muslin cravat—which seemed excessively elegant for so sombre an occasion. The only remaining sign of his rank was a pair of fiery red stockings.

The poor body was placed on a large oblong basket, lined with rags and blankets. On top of it was placed the bundle containing his few effects, collected by Dulcibeni.

"Did he possess nothing else?" asked Abbot Melani, noticing that the gentleman from Fermo had packed only a few of the dead man's clothes.

Cristofano replied that it was only obligatory to hand over clothing. Other effects could remain in the hands of Dulcibeni, who could deliver them to any surviving relatives. Then the three lowered the corpse with a thick rope through the window down to the street, where the *Societas Orationis et Mortis* awaited their sad consignment.

"What will they do with the body, Signor Cristofano?" I asked the physician. "Is it true that they will burn it?"

"That is not our business. It is not possible to bury him," he added, drawing breath.

We heard a slight tinkling. Cristofano reached down to the ground. "Did you drop something?... but what have you in your hand?" he asked.

From my half-open hand one of the pearls, with which I had been nervously playing, had fallen to the floor. The doctor picked it up and studied it.

"Really splendid. Where did you get it?"

"Oh, these were deposited by a customer," I lied, showing him the other two.

My master, in the meantime, left the apartment. He seemed tired. Atto, too, departed in the direction of his own apartment.

"That is bad. One should never allow oneself to be parted from pearls, least of all in our predicament."

"Why?"

"Among their numerous and occult virtues, they preserve one from poison."

"How is that possible?" I asked, growing pale.

"Because they are *siccae* and *frigidae* to the second degree," replied Cristofano, "and, if well preserved in a vase and not perforated, *habent detergentem facultatem*, and can exercise a cleansing action in the presence of fevers and putrefaction. They purge and clarify the blood—indeed, they limit menstruation—and, according to Avicenna, they cure the *corpum crassatum*, palpitations and cardiac syncope."

While Cristofano was displaying his medical learning, I felt unable to comprehend: what obscure signal did Brenozzi's gift hide? I knew that I must absolutely speak of this with Abbot Melani, and I sought to take my leave of the chirurgeon.

"Interesting," added Cristofano, examining the pearls and turning them attentively with his fingertips. "The form of these pearls indicates that they were fished before the full moon and in evening waters."

"And what does that mean?"

"That they cure the false imaginings of the soul and cogitations. Dissolved in vinegar, they are a sure remedy for *omni imbecillitate et animi deliquio,* above all, for apparent death."

At last Cristofano returned the pearls to me and I was able to leave him. I ran straight up the stairs to Abbot Melani's apartment.

Atto's chamber was on the second floor, just above that which the old Mourai had shared with Dulcibeni. These were the largest and brightest apartments in the entire hostelry: each had three windows, two of which faced onto the Via dell'Orso and one onto the corner of the alleyway. In the days of Signora Luigia, important personages had lodged there with their retinue. There was also an identical room on the third and last floor, under the eaves, where Signora Luigia had lived. Here, despite Cristofano's prohibition, my master and I continued to cohabit, although temporarily: this being a privilege that I would surely lose on the return of Signor Pellegrino's wife, when I would again be relegated to sleeping in the kitchen.

I was struck by the variety of books and maps of all sorts which the abbot had brought with him. Atto Melani was a lover of the antiquities and beauties of Rome, judging, at least, by the titles of some of the volumes which I glimpsed, carefully arranged on a shelf, and with which I was later to acquaint myself in quite another manner:

The Splendour of ancient and modern Rome, in which are represented all the principal Temples, Theatres, Amphitheatres, Circuses, Naumachiae, Triumphal Arches, Obelisks, Palaces, Baths, Curiae and Basilicas, by Lauri; and Fabricius' *Chemnicensis Roma*; and *The Antiquities of Rome in a Compendium of Authors both Ancient and Modern,* together with a *Treatise concerning the Fires of the Ancients* by Andrea Palladio. Nine great maps stood out, with their rods the colour of Indian cane and gold pommels, together with a mass of manuscript letters which Melani was sorting on the table and which he quickly put down. He offered me a seat.

"I wanted to talk to you. Tell me: have you any acquaintances in this quarter? Friends, confidants?"

"I think... well, no. Almost no one, Signor Abbot Melani."

"You may call me Signor Atto. A pity. I would like to have known, at least through the window, what is being said about our plight; and you were my only hope," he said.

He went to the window and began to sing in an exceedingly suave voice, which he barely restrained:

> *Disperate speranze, addio, addio.*
> *Ahi, mentite speranze, andate a volo...*[*]

The abbot's extemporaneous assay of virtuosity left me stupefied and full of admiration. Despite his age, Melani still possessed a rather light soprano voice. I complimented him and asked him if he had composed the splendid cantata of which he had just sung a snatch.

"No, 'tis by Seigneur Luigi Rossi, my master," he replied distractedly. "But tell me rather, tell me: how did the morning go? Have you noticed anything bizarre?"

"A rather strange episode befell me, Signor Atto. I had only just had a conversation with Signor Devizé when..."

"Ah, Devizé, it was precisely about him that I wished to talk to you. Was he playing?"

"Yes, but..."

"He is good. The King appreciates him greatly. His Majesty adores the guitar almost as much as, once, when young, he adored opera and giving a good account of himself in the court ballets. Fine times... And what did Devizé say to you?"

I understood that, unless I first exhausted the matter of music, he would not allow me to proceed further with my account. I told him

---

[*] Desperate hopes, adieu, adieu! / Alas, deceitful hopes, away you fly...

of the *rondeau* which I had heard from the French musician's guitar, and how the latter had spoken to me of the music he had heard in many Italian theatres, above all in Venice, with its celebrated Teatro del Cocomero.*

"The Teatro del Cocomero? Are you sure that you remember that properly?"

"Well, yes... the Watermelon... It is such a strange name for a theatre. Devizé told me he had been there just before he travelled to Naples. Why?"

"Oh nothing. It is just that your guitarist is telling tall tales, but he has not taken the trouble to prepare them well."

I was dumbfounded. "How can you tell?"

"The Cocomero is a magnificent theatre, where many splendid virtuosi do indeed perform. To tell the truth, I have sung there myself. I remember that, once, the organiser wished me to play the part of Apelles in *Alessandro, Vincitore di Se Stesso*. I of course refused and they gave me the main role, ha ha! A truly fine theatre, the Cocomero. A pity that it is in Florence and not in Venice."

"But... Devizé said he had been there before going to Naples."

"Exactly. Not long ago, then, since from Naples he came straight to Rome. But 'tis a lie: a theatre with such a name remains imprinted in the memory, as it did for you. I tell you: Devizé has never set foot in the Cocomero. And perhaps not in Venice either."

I was dismayed by the revelation of that small but alarming untruth on the part of the French musician.

"But pray, continue," resumed the abbot. "You said that something strange had happened to you, if I am not mistaken."

I was at last able to tell Atto about the questions which Brenozzi the Venetian had put to me so insistently, his bizarre request for daisies and the mysterious gift of three pearls, which Cristofano had recognised as being of the type used to cure poisoning and apparent death. For which reason, I feared that these little jewels might have something to do with the death of Signor di Mourai, and perhaps Brenozzi knew something, but had been afraid to speak clearly; I showed the pearls to Melani. The abbot took one look at them and laughed heartily.

"My boy, I really do not believe that poor Monsieur de Mourai..." he began, shaking his head; but he was interrupted by a piercing scream.

It seemed to come from the floor above.

We rushed into the corridor, and then up the stairs. We stopped halfway up the second staircase where, sprawled across the steps, lay the inanimate body of Signor Pellegrino.

Behind us, the other guests also came running. From my master's head flowed a rivulet of blood which ran down a couple of steps. The scream had without a doubt issued from the mouth of Cloridia, the courtesan, who, trembling, with a handkerchief that covered almost all her face, was staring at the apparently lifeless body. Behind us, who all still stood as though frozen, the chirurgeon Cristofano made his way forward. With a kerchief, he removed the long white hair from my master's face. It was then that he seemed to regain consciousness and, giving a great heave, vomited forth a greenish and exceedingly foul-smelling mass. After that, Signor Pellegrino lay on the ground without giving any sign of life.

"Let us carry him up to his chamber," exhorted Cristofano, leaning over my master.

No one moved save myself, when I tried with scant success to raise his torso. Pushing me aside, Abbot Melani took my place.

"Hold his head," he ordered.

The physician took Pellegrino by the legs, and, making our way through the silent onlookers, we bore him to his chamber and laid him on the bed.

My master's rigid face was unnaturally pale and covered with a fine veil of perspiration. He seemed as though made of wax. His wide-open eyes stared at the ceiling, and under them were two livid bags of skin. A wound on his forehead had just been cleaned by the chirurgeon, revealing a long, deep gash, on either side of which the bone of the skull was visible, probably injured by a heavy blow. My master, however, was not dead. His breathing was stertorous, but subdued.

"He fell down the stairs and struck his head. But I fear that he was already unconscious when he fell."

"What do you mean?" asked Atto.

Cristofano hesitated before answering: "He suffered an attack of a malady which I have not yet identified with any certainty. It was, however, a fulminating seizure."

"And what does that mean?" repeated Atto, raising his tone somewhat. "Was he too perhaps poisoned?"

At those words, I was seized by shivering and remembered the abbot's words the night before: if we did not stop him in time, the assassin would soon find other victims. And perhaps now, far earlier than expected, he had already struck down my master.

The doctor, however, shook his head at Melani's question and freed Pellegrino's neck from the kerchief which he usually wore knotted over his shirt: two swollen bluish blotches appeared below his left ear.

"From his general rigidity, this would appear to be the same sickness as that of old Mourai. But these," he continued, pointing out the two swellings, "these here... And yet he did not seem..."

We understood that he was thinking of the plague. We all drew back instinctively. Someone invoked heaven.

"He was perspiring, he probably had a fever. When we lowered Monsieur de Mourai's body to the street, he was far too easily fatigued."

"If it is the plague, he will not last long."

"However, the possibility does exist that this may be another similar but less desperate infirmity. For example, the petechiae."

"The what?" interrupted Father Robleda and Stilone Priàso, the poet.

"In Spain, Father, 'tis known as *tabardillo*, while in the Kingdom of Naples, it is called *pastici* and in Milan, *segni*," explained Cristofano, turning first to the one, then to the other. "Some call it the spotted fever. It is a distemper caused by blood corrupted by an indisposition of the stomach. Pellegrino has, indeed, vomited. The onset of the plague is violent, while the petechiae begin with very mild symptoms, such as lassitude and giddiness (which I noted in him this morning). It worsens, however, and causes the most diverse symptoms until it covers the whole body with red, purple or black spots, like these two. Which, it is true, are too swollen to be petechiae, but also too small to be tokens, that is, the bubos of the plague."

"But," intervened Cloridia, "is not the fact that Pellegrino fainted so suddenly a sure sign of the plague?"

"We do not know for certain whether he lost consciousness because of the blow to the head or because of the disease," sighed the doctor. "However, these two spots will reveal the truth to us tomorrow. As I said, they are indeed very black and show that the disease is greater and involves more putrescence."

"To sum up," interrupted Father Robleda, "is it contagious or not?"

"The petechial disease is caused by excessive heat and dryness and therefore those with choleric temperaments, like Pellegrino, are readily subject to it. From this, you will understand the importance, for keeping contagion at arm's length, of avoiding agitation and raving." Here, he looked significantly at the Jesuit. "The malady gives rise to extreme dryness. In a brief space of time, it extinguishes the radical humidity of the body and can in the end kill. But if sustenance is given to the weakened body of the patient, that in itself reduces the virulence, and very few die: that is why it is less grave than the plague. However, almost every one of us has been close to him during the past few hours and we are all therefore at risk. It is advisable that you should all return to your apartments, where I shall later visit you one by one. Try to keep calm."

Cristofano then called me to help him.

"It is good that Signor Pellegrino vomited at once: that vomiting cleared from his stomach the matter which was liable to putrefy and grow corrupt as a result of the humours," he said, as soon as I had joined him. "From now on, the sick man must be fed with cold foods, which refresh his choleric tendency."

"Will you bleed him?" I asked, having heard that such a remedy was universally recommended for all maladies.

"Absolutely to be avoided: bleeding might cool the natural heat too much and the patient would soon die."

I shivered.

"Fortunately," continued Cristofano, "I have with me herbs, balsams, waters and powders and all else that I need to treat disease. Help me to undress your master completely, for I must anoint him with oil for the *morbilli*, as Galen calls petechiae. This penetrates the body and preserves it from corruption and putrefaction."

He went out and returned soon with a collection of small ampoules.

After carefully folding Signor Pellegrino's great grey apron and clothes in a corner, I asked: "Then, is di Mourai's death perhaps due to the plague or the petechiae?"

"I did not find the shadow of a spot on the old Frenchman," was his brusque answer. "However, 'tis now too late to know. We have given away the body."

And he closed himself into the chamber with my master.

ॐ

The moments that followed were, to say the least, turbulent. Almost all reacted to the host's misadventure with accents of desperation. The death of the old French lodger, attributed to poison by the physician, had certainly not thrown the company into such confusion. After cleaning the stairs of my master's fluids, the thought of his soul's welfare crossed my mind, as he might soon be meeting the Almighty. I recalled, in this connection, an edict which commanded that, in every chamber of hostelries, a picture or portrait was to be placed of Our Lord, or of the Blessed Virgin, or of the saints, together with a vase of holy water.

Dismayed and praying heaven with all my heart that it should not deprive me of my master's kindness, I went up to the three chambers under the eaves that had remained empty since the departure of Signor Pellegrino's wife, in order to look for holy water and some holy image to hang above the sick man's bed.

These were the apartments where the late Signora Luigia had lived. They had remained almost unchanged, as the new host's family sojourn there had been so brief.

After a rapid search, I discovered above a rather dusty table, next to two reliquaries and a sugarloaf Agnus Dei, a terracotta statue of John the Baptist under a crystal bell; in his hands, he held a glass phial filled with holy water.

Beautiful holy images hung from the walls. The sight of them affected me deeply, and as I reflected on the sad events of my young life, a lump rose in my throat. It was not right, I thought, that there should be only profane images in the dining chambers, however charming: a picture of fruit, two with wooded landscapes and figures, two more oblong paintings on sheepskin, with various birds, two villages, two Cupids breaking a bow over their knees, and lastly, the one and only concession to the Bible, a licentious depiction of Susannah bathing, watched by the Elders.

Absorbed in these reflections, I chose a little picture of the Madonna of Sorrows which was hanging there and returned to the apartment, where Cristofano was busying himself around my poor master.

After arranging the picture and the holy water near the sickbed, I felt my strength abandon me and, collapsing in a corner, I burst into tears.

"Courage, my boy, courage."

I found again in the physician's tone of voice that paternal, jovial Cristofano who had in the past few days so raised my mood. Like a father, he took my head in his hands and I could at last unburden myself. I explained to him that the man who had taken me in, thus saving me from extreme misery, was dying. Signor Pellegrino was a good man, albeit of bilious humour, and although I had been but six months in his service, it seemed to me that I had always been with him. What would become of me now? Once the quarantine was over, even if I were to survive, I would be left without any means of support and I did not even know the new parish priest of Santa Maria in Posterula.

"Now everyone will need you," said he, raising my dead weight from the ground. "I myself was coming to look for you, as we have to calculate our resources. The subsidy which we shall receive from the Congregation for Public Health will be very small indeed, and we shall have to ration our provisions carefully."

Still sniffling, I reassured him that the pantry was far from empty, but he wished nonetheless to be taken there. The pantry was in the cellars and only I and Pellegrino possessed a key to it. From now on, said Cristofano, I was to keep both copies in a place known only to myself and him, so that no one could help themselves to the provisions. By the faint light that filtered in through the grates, we entered the pantry, which was on two levels.

Fortunately, my master, being a great steward and cook, had never failed to see to it that we were furnished with all manner of odoriferous cheeses, salt meats and smoked fish, dried vegetables and tomatoes, as well as rows of wine and oil jars which, for an instant, delighted the eye of the physician and caused his features to soften. He commented only with a half-smile, and continued: "If there are any problems, you will advise me, and you will also tell me if anyone seems to be in ill health. Is that clear?"

"But will what has befallen Signor Pellegrino also happen to others?" I asked with tears again filling my eyes.

"Let us hope not. But we shall have to do everything possible to ensure that it does not happen," said he, without looking me in the eyes. "You, meanwhile, may continue to sleep in the chamber with him, as you already did last night despite my orders: it is good that your master should have someone to watch over him at night."

I marvelled greatly that the physician did not consider the possibility of my becoming infected, but dared not ask questions.

☙❧

I accompanied him back to his apartment on the first floor. Hardly had we turned right, towards Cristofano's chamber, than we both gave a start: there we found Atto leaning against the door.

"What are you doing here? I thought that I had given everyone clear instructions," protested the doctor.

"I am perfectly aware of what you said. But if anyone has nothing to lose from keeping company with one another, it is we three. Did we or did we not carry poor Pellegrino? The boy here has lived shoulder to shoulder with his master until this morning. If we were to be infected, we are already."

A fine veil of perspiration covered Abbot Melani's broad, wrinkled forehead as he spoke, and his voice, despite the sarcasm of his tone, betrayed a certain dryness in the throat.

"That is no good reason for being imprudent," retorted Cristofano, stiffening.

"I admit that," said Melani. "But before we enter this claustration, I should like to know what our chances are of leaving here alive. And I wager..."

"I care not what you wager. The others are already in their apartments."

"... I wager that no one knows exactly how we are to organise the days to come. What will happen if the dead should begin to pile up? Shall we get rid of them? But how, then, if only the weakest should survive? Are we certain that provisions will be supplied? And what is happening outside these walls? Has the infection spread or not?"

"That is not..."

"All of this *is* important, Cristofano. No one can go on alone, as you thought to do. We must speak of these things, if only to lighten the burden of our sad predicament."

From the physician's weak response, I understood that Atto's arguments were breaching his defences. To complete the abbot's work, at that moment we were joined by Stilone Priàso and Devizé who seemed also to have many anxious questions to put to the physician.

"Very well," said Cristofano, yielding with a sigh before the two could even open their mouths. "What do you want to know?"

"Nothing whatever," replied Atto superciliously. "We need first of all to reason together: when shall we fall ill?"

"Well, if and when the infection comes," replied the physician.

"Oh, come, come!" retorted Stilone. "In the worst case, supposing that this is indeed the pestilence, when will that happen? Are you or are you not the physician?"

"Yes, indeed, when?" I echoed, almost as though to give myself strength.

Cristofano was touched to the quick. He opened wide his round black, barn-owl eyes and, arching an eyebrow in an unmistakeable sign that he was disposed to talk with us, he gravely raised two fingers to the pointed beard on his chin.

Then, however, he thought better of it and put off his explanations until evening, it being his intention, he said, to call us together after supper, on which occasion he would furnish us with whatever elucidations we might desire.

Thereupon, Abbot Melani returned to his apartment. Cristofano, however, retained Stilone Priàso and Devizé.

"It seems I heard, when I was speaking to you a moment ago, that you are suffering from a certain intestinal flatulence. If you wish, I have with me a good remedy to rid you of that nuisance."

The two consented, not without some embarrassment. All four of us then resolved to descend to the ground floor, where Cristofano ordered me to prepare a small portion of good broth with which to administer the four grains per head of Oil of Sulphur. The physician would, in the meanwhile, anoint the back and loins of Stilone Priàso and Devizé with his special balsam.

While Cristofano went to collect the necessary, which he had left in his chamber, the Frenchman went into a corner at the far end of the room to tune his guitar. I hoped that he would again play that intriguing piece which had so enchanted me in the morning, but, soon after, he rose and returned to the kitchen, where he stopped behind the table at which the Neapolitan poet was seated, and never again touched the instrument. Stilone Priàso had taken out a notebook and was scribbling something in it.

"Fear not, my boy. We shall not die of the pestilence," said he, turning to me as I busied myself in the kitchen.

"Perhaps, Sir, you foresee the future?" asked Devizé ironically.

"Better than chirurgeons can!" joked Stilone Priàso.

"Your wit is inappropriate in this hostelry," warned the doctor, arriving with his sleeves rolled up and with the balsam in his hands.

The Neapolitan was the first to uncover his back, while Cristofano as usual listed the numerous virtues of his physick: "... and last but not least, 'tis also good for the penile caruncle. One needs but rub it vigorously into one's tail until it is absorbed, and relief is assured."

While I was busy with tidying and warming up the broth which I had been asked to prepare, I heard the trio communing ever more closely among themselves.

"... and yet I repeat, 'tis indeed he," I heard Devizé whisper, his Gallic accent making his voice easy to recognise, above all when he pronounced words like "carriage", "war" or "correct" which made his elocution quite inimitable.

"There can be no doubt about it, no doubt," echoed Stilone Prià-so's excited response.

"All three of us recognise him, and each in different ways," concluded Cristofano.

I stationed myself discreetly where I could overhear them, without crossing the threshold dividing the kitchen from the dining chamber. I soon understood that they were speaking of Abbot Melani, whose reputation was already known to all three.

"This much is certain: he is an extremely dangerous individual," affirmed Stilone Priàso peremptorily.

As always when he wished to imbue his words with authority, he focussed severely on an invisible point in front of him, while scratching the bridge of his nose with his little finger and nervously shaking his fingers as though to rid himself of who knows what fine powder.

"He must be kept under constant observation," he concluded.

The trio talked without paying any attention to me, as was, moreover, usual with almost all customers, to whom a serving boy was little more than a shadow. Thus it was that I learned a number of facts and circumstances which made me repent no little my having conferred for so long the night before with Abbot Melani and above all having promised him my services.

"Is he now in the pay of the King of France?" asked Stilone Priàso in a low voice.

"I maintain that he is. Even if no one can tell with certainty," replied Devizé.

"Certain persons' preference is to side with all and with none," added Cristofano, continuing his massage and kneading Stilone Prià-so's back even harder.

"He has served more princes than he himself can remember," hissed Stilone. "In Naples, I am sure that they would not even allow him to enter the city. More to the right, please," said he, turning to the physician.

Thus I learned, with unspeakable dismay, of the dark and turbulent past of Abbot Melani; a past of which he had not breathed a word to me the night before.

Since his earliest youth, Atto had been engaged by the Grand Duke of Tuscany as a castrato singer (and this, the abbot had indeed told me). But that was not the only task which Melani performed for his master; in reality, he served him as a spy and secret courier. Atto's singing was indeed admired and in demand in all the courts of Europe, which gave the castrato great credit among crowned heads, in addition to unusual freedom of movement.

"On the pretext of entertaining the sovereigns, he would introduce himself into the royal courts to spy, to stir and to corrupt," explained Devizé.

"And then repeat everything to his principals," echoed Stilone Priàso acidly.

In addition to the Medici, Cardinal Mazarin had soon used Atto's double services, thanks to the ancient relations of friendship between Florence and Paris. The Cardinal had, indeed, become his foremost protector, and took him with him even on the most delicate diplomatic missions. Atto was regarded almost as one of the family. He had become the bosom friend of Mazarin's niece, for whom the King had so lost his head that he wished to marry her. And when, later, the girl was obliged to leave France, Atto remained her confidant.

"But then Mazarin died," resumed Devizé, "and life became difficult for Atto. His Majesty had just attained his majority and mistrusted all the Cardinal's protégés," explained Devizé. "What is more, he was compromised in the scandal involving Fouquet, the Superintendent of Finances."

I gave a start. Was not Fouquet the name which the abbot had mentioned in passing the night before?

"That was a false move," continued the French musician, "for which the Most Christian King pardoned him only after the passing of much time."

"Only a false move, you call it? But were not he and that thief Fouquet friends?" objected Cristofano.

"No one has ever succeeded in clarifying how matters really stood.

When Fouquet was arrested, a note was found containing the order to lodge Atto secretly in his house. That note was shown to Fouquet's judges."

"And how did the Superintendent explain it?" asked Stilone Priàso.

"He said that, some time previously, Melani had requested a sure refuge. That meddler had made an enemy of the powerful Duc de la Meilleraye, the heir to Mazarin's fortune. The Duke, who was a most irascible character, had succeeded in persuading the King to have Melani removed from Paris and had already hired ruffians to give him a beating. Some friends therefore recommended him to Fouquet: in his home, he would be safe, since the two were not known to frequent one another."

"But then Atto and Fouquet were not acquainted!" said Stilone Priàso.

"'Tis not that simple," warned Devizé with a knowing smile. "Twenty years have passed since then and I was a child at the time. Later, however, I perused the records of Fouquet's trial which in those days were more widely read than the Bible. Well, to his judges, Fouquet said: 'There existed no known frequentation between Atto and myself.'"

"What a sly fox!" exclaimed Stilone. "A perfect answer: no one could witness to having ever seen the two together; which did not, however, mean that they may not have been secretly in contact... In my opinion, the two did know each other, and that right well. The note speaks for itself: Atto was one of Fouquet's private spies."

"That is possible," said Devizé, nodding his head in agreement. "What is, however, certain is that Fouquet's ambiguous reply saved Melani from prison. He slept in Fouquet's house and immediately afterwards left for Rome, escaping the beating. In Rome, however, other bad news reached him: the arrest of Fouquet, the scandal, his good name besmirched, the King's fury..."

"And how did he extricate himself from that predicament?" asked Stilone Priàso.

"He managed very well," interrupted Cristofano. "In Rome, he placed himself at the service of Cardinal Rospigliosi who, like him, hailed from Pistoia, and who then became Pope. So much so that to this day Melani boasts that he had him elected Pontiff. Believe me, those Pistoiesi are the world's greatest braggarts."

"Perhaps," replied Devizé prudently. "But to make a pope, one must needs manoeuvre well in conclave. Now, during that conclave, Rospigliosi was indeed assisted by Atto Melani. And it is well known that not only has Melani always been on familiar terms with those cardinals who are most in the public eye, but also with the most powerful French ministers."

"He is an intriguer, to be feared and never trusted," cut in Stilone Priàso, conclusively.

I was utterly stupefied. Was the individual of whom the three lodgers were speaking really the same man with whom I had conversed only last night, a few paces from where they now sat? He had introduced himself to me as a musician, and now he was revealed to me as a secret agent, involved in turbid palace manoeuvres, and even in scandals. It seemed almost as though I had known two different persons. Surely, if what the abbot himself had told me was true (namely that he still enjoyed the favours of many princes) he must have recovered his reputation. But after hearing the conversation between Stilone Priàso, Cristofano and Devizé, who would not be suspicious of his word?

"Wherever there is a political question of any importance, Abbot Melani is always to be found," resumed the French musician, laying stress on the word "Abbot". "Perhaps it will be discovered only after the event that he too was involved. He always manages to worm his way in everywhere. Melani was among Mazarin's assistants during the negotiations with the Spaniards at the Isle of Pheasants, when the Peace of the Pyrenees was concluded. They also sent him to Germany, to convince the Elector of Bavaria to stand as a candidate for the Imperial Throne. Now that his age no longer permits him to travel as he used to, he endeavours to make himself useful by sending the King reports and aide-memoires concerning the court of Rome, which he knows well and where he still has many friends. In more than one affair of state, it is said that voices have been heard in Paris anxiously requesting the suggestions of Abbot Melani."

"Does the Most Christian King grant him audiences?" inquired Stilone Priàso.

"That is another mystery. A personage of such dubious reputation should not even be admitted to court, yet he enjoys direct relations with several ministers of the Crown. And there are those who swear that they have seen him slipping out from the King's apartments at

the most unseemly hours. His Majesty is said to have summoned him
for interviews most urgently and in the utmost secrecy."

So it was true that Abbot Melani could obtain audiences with His
Majesty the King of France. At least on that point he had not lied to
me.

"And his brothers?" asked Cristofano, as I approached with a bowl
of hot soup.

"They always move in a pack, like wolves," commented Devizé
with a grimace of disapproval. "Hardly had Atto settled in Rome, after the election of Rospigliosi, than he was joined by his two brothers,
one of whom immediately became *maestro di cappella* at Santa Maria
Maggiore. In their own city of Pistoia, they have laid their hands on
benefices and the collection of excise duties and are justifiably held
in execration by many citizens."

☙◦❧

There could be no further doubt. I had met not with an abbot, but a
deceitful sodomite, skilled in gaining the confidence of trusting sovereigns, and this too thanks to the rascally connivance of his brothers.
My promise to assist him had been an unpardonable error.

"It is time for me to check on Master Pellegrino," announced
Cristofano, after administering the oil of sulphur to his two boon
companions.

Only then did we realise that Pompeo Dulcibeni had returned
downstairs, who knows how long since: he had remained in complete silence, seated in an alcove of the other room, pouring himself liquor from a flask of aqua vitae which my master was wont to
keep on one of his tables, surrounded by small drinking glasses. He
must, I thought, surely have overheard the conversation about Atto
Melani.

So I followed the trio. Dulcibeni, however, did not move. On
the first floor, we encountered Padre Robleda. The Jesuit had restrained himself, controlling his mad fear of the infection, and had
remained for a moment on the threshold of his chamber, wiping the
perspiration which glued his grizzling curls to his low forehead and
struggling to maintain his dignity. Now he had propelled himself just
outside the chamber, and there he stood rigidly close to the wall, yet
without touching it, erect and comical. He stayed there, looking at
us, in the vague and anxious hope of gleaning some good news from

the physician, with all his great body weighing down on his toes and his chest exaggeratedly thrust backwards, so that his black profile formed a great curve.

Not that he was really fat, apart from the rather rotund forms of his brown face and his neck. He was tall, and the moderate prominence of his belly did not spoil his appearance but endowed him with an air of mature wisdom. However, his bizarre pose compelled the Jesuit to cast his eyes downwards, with his eyelids slightly lowered, if he wished to face whoever he would speak to; and this, together with his long and widely spaced eyebrows and the dark rings around his eyes, conferred upon him an air of extreme nonchalance. Much good did it do him, for scarcely had Cristofano caught sight of him than he invited him peremptorily to accompany us, as Pellegrino might be urgently in need of a priest. Robleda would have liked to make some objection, but as none came to mind, he resigned himself to following behind us.

Having climbed to the upper floor to look at what we feared might already be my master's corpse, we realised that he was still alive. And he was still breathing, hoarsely but regularly. The two spots had neither diminished nor grown: the diagnosis remained in the balance between the plague and the petechial fever. Cristofano proceeded to clean him all over and to refresh him with damp towels, after wiping away his sweat.

I then reminded the Jesuit, who had remained prudently outside the doorway that, as matters stood, the sacrament of Extreme Unction should be administered to Pellegrino. The edict which laid down that holy images were to be present in hostelries also—I made it clear—required that if anyone were to fall ill in hostelries or taverns, they were to be administered the Oil for the Sick.

Father Robleda gave a start, but could not refuse his services.

He then ordered me to bring him olive oil, as indicated specifically by Saint James, so that he could bless it for the ceremony; and also a little rod. A few minutes later, the Jesuit was by Master Pellegrino's bedhead to administer Extreme Unction.

The thing was over unbelievably soon: he dipped the rod into the oil and, making sure that he remained as distant as possible from the sick man, he anointed one of his ears, rapidly gabbling only the brief formula *Indulgeat tibi Deus quidquid peccasti per sensus*, which was very different from the familiar long form.

"The University of Louvain," said he, turning to his perplexed audience in self-justification, "ruled in 1588 that, in the event of the plague, it should be licit for the priest to impart the Holy Chrism with a rod rather than with his thumb. And instead of anointing the mouth, nostrils, eyes, ears, hands and feet, each time pronouncing the canonical formula *Per istas sanctas unctiones, et suam piissimam misericordiam indulgeat tibi Deus quidquid per visum, auditum, odoratum, gustum, tactum deliquisti*, many theologians there held that the Sacrament was valid with a single unction effected rapidly on one of the sensory organs, pronouncing the brief universal formula which you have just heard."

Whereupon, the Jesuit withdrew in great haste.

So as not to attract attention to myself, I waited until the group had dispersed, then at once followed Padre Robleda. I caught up with him just as he was crossing the threshold of his own apartment.

Still half out of breath, I said to him that I was most apprehensive for my master's soul: had the oil cleansed Pellegrino's conscience of sins, so that he would run no risk of perishing in the Inferno? Or must he confess himself before dying? And what would happen if he did not regain consciousness before he died?

"Oh, if that is what is troubling you," replied Robleda hurriedly, "you need not worry: 'twill not be your master's fault if, before dying, he is unable to return to his senses for long enough to render a full confession of his little sins to the Lord."

"I know," I promptly retorted, "but if there should also be mortal sins, as well as venial ones..."

"Do you perhaps know of some grave sin committed by your master?" asked the Jesuit, growing alarmed.

"As far as I know, he has never gone beyond some intemperance and a few glasses too many."

"Still, even if he had killed," said Robleda, signing himself, "that would not mean much."

And he explained to me that the Jesuit fathers, having a special vocation for the sacrament of Confession, had always made a careful study of the doctrine of sin and pardon: "There are greater sins that lead to the death of the soul, and these are in the majority. But there are also sins which are partially permissible," said he, lowering his voice bashfully, "or even sins which are permitted. That depends upon the circumstances, and for the confessor, I can assure you, the decision is always difficult."

The study of case histories was limitless, and was to be considered with the greatest prudence. Should absolution be accorded to a son who, in legitimate self-defence, kills his father? Does he commit a sin who, in order to avoid an unjust condemnation, kills a witness? And what of a wife who kills her husband, knowing that he is about to render her the same service? May a nobleman, in order to defend his honour before his peers (which for him is of the uttermost importance) assassinate someone who has offended him? Does a soldier sin who, obeying a superior's order, kills an innocent? Or again: may a woman prostitute herself in order to save her own children from hunger?

"And is stealing always a sin, Padre?" I insisted, remembering that my master's over-indulgence in the contents of the cellar did not always draw upon what belonged to him.

"Anything but. Here, too, one must consider the inner and outer circumstances in which the act was accomplished. It is certainly not the same when a rich man robs a poor one as when a poor man robs a rich one, or a rich man another rich man, or a poor man another poor man, and so on, and so forth."

"But cannot one gain pardon in all cases when one returns what has been stolen?"

"You are too hasty! The obligation to return stolen goods is, of course, important, and the confessor is in duty bound to bring this to the attention of whoever confides the matter to him. But the obligation may also be subject to limitations, or even be cancelled out. It is not necessary to return what has been stolen if that means impoverishing oneself: a nobleman may not deprive himself of servants, and a distinguished citizen may certainly not demean himself by working."

"But if I am not under any obligation to restore what was wrongfully taken, as you put it, then what must I do to obtain pardon?"

"That depends. It may sometimes be best to visit the offended party at home and to beg his forgiveness."

"And taxes? What happens if one does not pay what is owed?"

"Well, well, that is a delicate matter. Taxes fall within the category of *res odiosae*, in the sense that no one pays them willingly. Let us say that it is surely a sin not to pay those which are just, while in the case of unjust taxes, the matter should be examined case by case."

Robleda then enlightened me on many other instances in which, not knowing Jesuit doctrine, I would doubtless have reached very different conclusions: a man who has been unjustly condemned may escape from prison and may get the guards drunk and help his fellow prisoners to escape; it is licit to rejoice at the death of a relative who leaves one a great inheritance, so long as that is done without personal enmity; one may read books which have been banned by the Church, but for no more than three days and six pages at a time; one may steal from one's parents without sinning, but no more than fifty gold pieces; and whoever swears on oath but only pretends to do so is not obliged to keep his word.

"In other words, one may perjure oneself!" I concluded in utter astonishment.

"Do not be so crude. It all depends on the intention. Sin is deliberate detachment from the Word of God," intoned Robleda solemnly. "If, however, one commits it only in appearance, but without real intent, then one will be saved."

I left Robleda's chamber, vacillating between disquiet and prostration. Thanks to the learning of the Jesuits, I thought, Pellegrino had good chances of saving his soul. But from this discourse it seemed almost as though white were black, truth the same as lies, and good and evil one and the same thing.

Perhaps Abbot Melani was not as upright as he would wish one to believe. But, I thought, Robleda was even less to be trusted.

৶৽৵

Luncheon was already late, and our guests, who had fasted since the evening before, descended rapidly to the kitchen. After hastily regaling themselves with my broth containing little dumplings and hop shoots, which no one cared for, it was Cristofano who called our attention to what was to be done next. The men-at-arms would soon be calling us to appear at the windows. The presence of another sick person would surely cause the Congregation for Public Health to decree there was a danger of pestilence and the quarantine would then be maintained and strengthened. Perhaps a pest-house might be improvised to which we would all sooner or later be transferred. Such a possibility was enough to make even brave men tremble.

"Then, our only hope is to try to escape," gasped the glass-blower Brenozzi.

"It would not be possible," observed Cristofano. "They will already have erected gates and closed off the road, and even if we were to succeed in getting past them, we would be hunted down throughout the Papal States. We could try to cross the territory in the direction of Loreto, fleeing through the woods, and to embark on the Adriatic and flee by sea. But I have no sure friends along that way, nor do I think that any of us is better off in that respect. We would be reduced to begging strangers to take us in, always running the risk of betrayal by whoever offers us hospitality. Otherwise, we could try to take refuge in the Kingdom of Naples, travelling by night and sleeping by day. I am certainly no longer of an age to support such heavy exertions; and there are others among you who have perhaps not been favoured by nature. Besides, we would, of course, need a guide, a shepherd or a villager, who would not be so easy to persuade, to lead us through the hills and vales, and who must above all not guess that we are hunted fugitives, or he would hand us over to his master without thinking twice. Lastly, we are too numerous to escape, and none of us bear certificates of health: so we would all be stopped at the first border post. Our chances of success would, in other words, be negligible. And all that without counting the fact that, even were we to succeed, we would be doomed never to return to Rome."

"And so what?" rejoined Bedfordi, snorting disdainfully and letting his hands dangle ridiculously from his wrists in a gesture of impatience.

"And so, Pellegrino will reply to the roll-call," replied Cristofano without the slightest loss of composure.

"But if he cannot even stand on his feet," I objected.

"He will," replied the physician. "He must."

᠔᠂᠔

When he had finished, he retained us yet longer and proposed, in order to strengthen us against any possible infection, that we should take physick to modify the humours. Some remedies were, he said, already prepared, others he would make ready with the herbs and essences which he carried with him, and drawing upon Pellegrino's well-stocked pantry.

"You will like neither the taste nor the smell. But they are prepared with great authority," and here he stared significantly in Bedfordi's direction. "They include the *elixir vitae*, the quinte essence, second water and prepared mother of balsam, *oleum philosophorum*, the great liquor, caustic, diaromatic, the angelic electuary, oil of vitriol, oil of sulphur, imperial musk tablets and a whole series of fumigants, pills and odoriferous balls to be worn on the chest. These purify the air and will not allow any infection to enter. But do not abuse them: together with distilled vinegar, they contain crystalline arsenic and Greek pitch. In addition, I shall every morning administer to you my original quinte essence, obtained from an excellent matured white wine grown in mountainous regions, which I have distilled in a bain-marie, then enclosed in a glass decanter with a stopper of bitter herbs and buried upside-down in good, warm horse manure for twenty days and twenty nights. Once the decanter has been extracted from the manure—an operation which, I insist, must always be carried out with the greatest dexterity so as not to contaminate the preparation—I separate the sky-blue distillate from the lees: that is the quinte essence. I store this in small, hermetically sealed vessels. It will preserve you from all manner of corruption and putrefaction and from every other kind of disease, and such indeed are its virtues that it can resuscitate the dead."

"What matters to us that it should not kill the living," sneered Bedfordi.

The physician was piqued: "Its principle has been approved by Raymond Lull, Philip Ulstad and many other philosophers, both ancient and modern. But I should like to conclude: I have for each of you the most excellent pills, of half a drachm each, to be carried in your pocket and taken at once, the moment you feel yourselves to be in the least touched by the infection. They are all made up of the most appropriate simples: four drachms of Armenian bole, *terra sigillata*, zedoary, camphor, tormentil, burning bush and hepatic aloes, with a scruple of saffron and cloves, and one of diagrydium, juice of savoy cabbage and cooked honey. They are designed especially to dissipate the pestilence caused by the corruption of natural heat. The Armenian bole and *terra sigillata* extinguish the great fire in the body and mortify the alterations. Zedoary has the virtue of desiccating and resolving. Camphor refreshes, and it, too, has the effect of drying. Burning bush is a counter-poison. Hepatic aloes preserve one from putrescence and free the body. Saffron and cloves preserve and cheer the heart. And diagrydium dissolves the superfluous humidity of the body."

The audience remained silent.

"You may be confident," insisted Cristofano. "I myself have perfected the formulae, drawing inspiration from the famous recipes tried and proven by the most excellent masters during visitations of the most fearsome pestilences. Such as the stomachic syrups of Master Giovanni of Volterra, which…"

At that moment a hubbub arose in the group of onlookers: quite unexpectedly, Cloridia had arrived.

Until that moment, she had remained in her chamber, careless as ever of mealtimes. Her entry was greeted variously. Brenozzi tormented his sapling, Stilone Priàso and Devizé tidied their hair, Cristofano drew in his paunch discreetly, Padre Robleda blushed, while Atto Melani sneezed. Only Bedfordi and Dulcibeni remained impassive.

It was precisely between those two that the courtesan took her place, without being invited.

Cloridia's appearance was indeed singular: beneath the extreme whiteness of her face powder, her complexion was, despite her efforts, distinctly dark, forming a strange contrast with the thick, curly and artificially lightened tresses which framed her spacious forehead and the regular oval of her face. A snub nose, though small and graceful, large velvety black eyes, perfect teeth with never a gap between them in a full mouth: these were only the accompaniment to what most struck the eye: a most ample *décolletage*, underlined by a polychrome bandeau of entwined kerchiefs which encircled her shoulders and terminated in a large bow between her breasts.

Bedfordi made room for her on the bench, while Dulcibeni remained immobile.

"I am sure that some of you would like to know how many days it will be before we leave here," said Cloridia in amiably tempting tones, as she laid a pack of Tarot cards on the table.

"*Libera nos a malo*," murmured Robleda, crossing himself and rising hurriedly, without even taking his leave.

No one responded to Cloridia's invitation, which all believed to be merely introductory to other deeper but financially more onerous inquiries.

"Perhaps this is not the best of moments, dear lady," said Atto Melani courteously, to save her from embarrassment. "So sad is our plight that it overshadows even your delightful company."

To everyone's surprise, Cloridia then grasped Bedfordi's hand and drew it gently to her: precisely in front of that luxuriant bosom, *décolleté* after the French fashion.

"Perhaps it would be better to have a nice palm reading," proposed Cloridia, "but gratis, of course, and only for your pleasure."

This once, Bedfordi remained speechless, and, before he could refuse, Cloridia had lovingly opened his fist.

"Here we are," said she, caressing the Englishman's palm with a fingertip. "You'll see, you will really enjoy this."

All present (including myself) had imperceptibly stretched forward, the better to see and to hear.

"Has anyone ever read your palm?" asked Cloridia, gently smoothing first his fingertips and then his wrist.

"Yes. I mean no... I mean, not like this."

"Calm down, and Cloridia will explain to you all the secrets of the hand and of good fortune. First of all, the fingers of the hand are unequal for decency's sake, and for greater ease in using them. The great finger is known as the thumb or Pollex, *quia pollet*, meaning that it is stronger than the others. The second is called the Index, because it is used to indicate; the third is called Infamous, because 'tis a sign of derision and contumely; the fourth is the Medical or Annular, meaning that it is the ring finger; and the fifth is the Auricular, because 'tis used to pick and to clean the ears."

While she conducted her review of the digital apparatus, Cloridia underlined her every phrase by wantonly tickling Bedfordi's fingers, while he strove to conceal his agitation with a weak smile, showing a sort of involuntary aversion before the fair sex which I have observed only in travellers coming from northern climes. Cloridia went on to illustrate other parts of the hand: "Here, you see, this line which ascends from the wrist towards the index finger, right here, is the Life Line, or Heart Line. This one which cuts across the hand more or less from left to right is the Natural Line or Head Line. Its sister line, close by, is known as the Convivial Line. This little swelling is known as the Girdle of Venus. Do you like that name?" inquired Cloridia insinuatingly.

"I do, very much so," interrupted Brenozzi.

"Get back, you idiot," retorted Stilone, repelling Brenozzi's attempt to conquer a position closer to Cloridia.

"I know, I know, it *is* a lovely name," said Cloridia, turning first to

Bedfordi, then to Brenozzi with a knowing little smile, "but these too are beautiful: the Finger of Venus, the Mount of Venus, the Finger of the Sun, the Mount of the Sun, the Finger of Mars, the Mount of Mars, the Mount of Jupiter, the Finger of Saturn, the Mount of Saturn and the Seat of Mercury."

While she thus illustrated fingers, knuckles, wrinkles, lines, joints, swellings and hollows, in skilful and sensual counterpoint, Cloridia shifted her index finger alternately from Bedfordi's palm to her own cheeks, to the Englishman's palm and then to her own lips, again to Bedfordi's wrist, then to the first gentle slopes of her generous bosom. Bedfordi swallowed.

"Then we have the Line of the Liver, the Line or Way of the Sun, the Line of Mars, the Line of Saturn, the Mount of the Moon, and it all concludes with the Milky Way…"

"Oh yes, the Milky Way," gulped Brenozzi, swooning away.

By now, almost all the group had gathered around Cloridia, as not even the ox and the ass did with Our Lord on the night when he came into the world.

"However, you do have a fine hand, and your soul must be even finer," said Cloridia obligingly, drawing Bedfordi's palm for a brief instant to the brown skin between her bosom and her neck.

"As to your body, however, I cannot tell," said she, laughing and playfully pushing Bedfordi's hand far from her, as though in self defence, then seizing Dulcibeni's.

All eyes were fixed on the older gentleman. He, however, broke free of the courtesan's grasp with a brusque, ill-humoured gesture and, rising from the table, made his way towards the stairs.

"But what a to-do," commented Cloridia ironically, trying to hide her pique by vexedly arranging a lock of her hair. "And what an ugly temper!"

At that very moment, the thought crossed my mind that in the past few days Cloridia had sat ever closer to Dulcibeni, who had, however, repulsed her with growing irritation. Unlike Robleda, who made an exaggerated show of being scandalised by the courtesan but had perhaps willingly visited her on several nights, Dulcibeni seemed to experience a real, deep disgust in the young woman's presence. No other guest at the inn dared treat Cloridia with such disdain. But, perhaps precisely because of that, or because of the money which (as seemed clear) Dulcibeni did not lack, the courtesan seemed to have set her heart on speaking to the gentleman from Fermo. Since she was unable to extract one word from him, Cloridia had several times asked me about Dulcibeni, being curious to learn any particulars concerning him.

The doctor took advantage of the abrupt break in the palm reading to resume his explanations about the remedies against the risk of infection. He distributed various pills, odoriferous balls and other things to us. We then all filed up behind him when he went to check on the state of Pellegrino's health.

❧❧

We entered my master's chamber, where he lay on his bed, seeming now a little less livid. The daylight from the window gave us comfort while the physician inspected his patient.

"Mmmh," groaned Pellegrino.

"He is not dead," affirmed Cristofano. "His eyes are half-open, he still has a fever, but his colours have improved. And he has wet himself."

We commented on the news with great relief. Soon, however, the Tuscan physician found that his patient was catatonic and able to respond only weakly to external stimuli.

"Pellegrino, tell me what you understand of my words," murmured Cristofano.

"Mmmh," repeated my master.

"He cannot," observed the physician, with conviction. "He is able to discern voices but not to answer. I have already encountered such a one: a peasant who was crushed by a tree trunk blown down by the wind. For months, he was unable to utter a word, although he was perfectly able to understand whatever his wife and children said to him."

"And then what happened?"

"Nothing. He died."

I was asked to say a few words gently to the patient, to try to revive him. But I met with no success; not even by murmuring to him that the inn was in flames and his stock of wine in danger could I get him to overcome the torpor that enveloped him.

Despite this, Cristofano was relieved. The two protuberances on my master's neck were becoming lighter in colour and receding; so they were not tokens. Whether petechiae or mere bruises, they were now regressing. We no longer seemed to be threatened by a visitation of the plague. We could at last relax a little. We did not, however, abandon the sick man to his fate. We at once checked that Pellegrino was able to swallow both solids and liquids, however slowly; and I offered to feed him regularly. The inn remained nevertheless deprived of the person who best knew it and was best equipped to serve us. I was just reflecting on these considerations when the others, satisfied with their visit to their host's bedside, gradually dispersed. I remained alone by the physician's side, while he continued his careful observation of Pellegrino's inert and supine body.

"I would venture that matters are improving; but one must always beware of being over-sure when dealing with distempers," he commented.

We were interrupted by the vigorous ringing of a bell in the Via dell'Orso, just under our windows. I leaned out; there stood three men sent to make our roll-call and ensure that none of us had escaped the watchman's attention. First, however, Cristofano must report to them on our state of health. I ran to the other chambers and gathered all the guests together. Some looked apprehensively at my poor master, who was totally incapable of standing on his own feet.

Fortunately, the sagacity of Cristofano and Abbot Melani soon saw that problem resolved. We assembled on the first floor, in Pompeo Dulcibeni's apartment. Cristofano was the first to show himself at the window, assuring the men that nothing special had happened, no one had shown the slightest sign of infirmity and all seemed in perfect health.

We then began to file before the window, one by one, in order to be inspected. But the doctor and Atto had so arranged matters as thoroughly to confuse the three inspectors. Cristofano led Stilone Priàso, then Robleda, and finally Bedfordi to the window, while the three were calling the names of other guests. Cristofano excused himself several times for involuntarily mixing up names, but in the meanwhile a considerable confusion had arisen. When Pellegrino's turn came, Bedfordi succeeded in creating yet more chaos: he began to scream and shout in English, asking (as Atto Melani explained) to be freed forthwith. The three inspectors responded with insults and mockery, but in the meantime Pellegrino passed by rapidly. He seemed to be in perfect form: his hair was well combed, his pale cheeks had been coloured with Cloridia's rouge. At the same time,

Devizé began to gesticulate and to protest at our reclusion, completely distracting the inspectors' attention from Pellegrino. Thus it was that they concluded their visit without becoming aware of my master's wretched state of health.

❧❦

While I was considering these expedients, Abbot Melani plucked my sleeve and drew me through the door. He wanted to know where Pellegrino was wont to deposit the valuables which travellers entrusted to him on their arrival. I drew back, manifestly shocked by the question: the place was obviously secret. Even when no treasures were stored there, that was where my master always hid the sums of money which customers left in his care. I recalled the dismal repute in which Cristofano, Stilone Priàso and Devizé held Atto.

"I imagine," added the abbot, "that your master always keeps the key on his person."

I was about to reply when I glanced at Pellegrino through the doorway while he was being brought back into his chamber. The bunch of keys on an iron ring which my master kept attached to his breeches night and day was not in its place.

I rushed down to the cellar, where I kept the spare keys hidden in a hole in the wall of which only I knew the existence. They were there. Taking care not to attract the attention of the guests (who, still in a state of excitement at the success of our stratagem, were making their way downstairs for their evening meal), I returned to the third floor.

Now, I should explain that between each floor there were two flights of stairs. At the top of each of these was a landing. Well, on the landing between the second and third floors was the little door that gave access to the closet where the valuables were kept.

I made sure that no one was in the vicinity, then entered. I drew out the stone, set into the wall, behind which lay the little coffer. I opened it. Nothing was missing: neither money nor the notes of deposits countersigned by customers. I grew calmer.

"Now, the question is: who has taken Master Pellegrino's keys?"

The voice was Abbot Melani's. He had followed me. He entered and closed the door behind him.

"It would appear that we have a thief among us," he commented, almost amusedly. Then he stopped, looking alarmed: "Silence. Someone is coming." And he nodded in the direction of the landing.

He signalled to me to look outside, which I did most unwillingly. I heard vague notes from Devizé's guitar rising from the ground floor. Nothing more.

I invited the abbot to quit the closet forthwith, desiring as I did to keep our contacts to a minimum. While he was slipping out through the narrow doorway, I saw him look at the little coffer with a rather worried expression.

"What is it now, Signor Abbot?" I asked, striving to hide my growing anxiety and to restrain the discourteous tone that was rising to my lips.

"I was thinking: it makes no sense that whoever stole the bunch of keys should have taken nothing from the strong-box of the inn. Are you really sure that you looked through it thoroughly?"

I went back to see: the money was there, the deposit notes too; what else should there be? Then, I remembered: the little pearls which Brenozzi had given me.

Gone was the Venetian's bizarre and fascinating gift, which I had jealously concealed among the other valuables. But why had the thief taken nothing else? After all, there were considerable sums of money there, far more visible and readily exchangeable than my little pearls.

"Calm down. We shall now go down to my apartment and there we shall examine the situation," said he.

Then, seeing that I was about to refuse, he added: "If you want to see your pearls again."

Reluctantly, I consented.

Once in his chamber, the abbot invited me to take a seat. He was aware of my agitation.

"We are faced with two possibilities," he began. "Either the thief has already done all that he intended to, in other words, to steal your pearls, or else he did not succeed in completing whatever it was that he planned. And I tend towards the second option."

"Why? I have already told you what Cristofano explained to me: those pearls have to do with poison and with seeming death. And perhaps Brenozzi knows something."

"For the time being, at least, let us drop the matter, my boy," said he, laughing. "Not that your little pearls are worthless, on the contrary; nor that they lack the powers which our physician ascribes to them.

But I opine that the thief had something else to do in that closet. It is halfway between the second and the third floor; and ever since Master Pellegrino's inert body was found, there has been so much coming and going in that vicinity, that he has been unable to operate at ease."

"So?"

"So, I think that the thief will have more to do in that cupboard, and that he will act under cover of night. No one yet knows that you have discovered the theft of the keys. If you do not warn the lodgers, the thief will think that he can operate in peace."

"Very well," said I, acquiescing at last, albeit diffidently. "I shall let the night pass before I put them on their guard. Pray heaven that no ill befalls them."

I looked obliquely at the abbot and decided to put to him the question which I had been holding in reserve for some time: "Do you think that the thief killed Signor di Mourai and perhaps tried to do the same to my master?"

"Everything is possible," replied Melani, inflating his cheeks curiously and pursing his lips. "Cardinal Mazarin was wont to say to me: thinking bad thoughts, one commits a sin; but one always guesses rightly."

The source of my diffidence about him must have been clear to the abbot, yet he asked no questions and continued imperturbably: "As regards Mourai, this morning I was about to propose to you that we undertake a little exploration, but then your master fell ill."

"What do you mean?"

"I think the time has come to search the rooms of the poor old man's two travelling companions. And you have copies of all the keys."

"You intend to enter Dulcibeni's and Devizé's apartments by stealth? And you want me to help you?" I asked in consternation.

"Come, do not look at me like that. Think about it: if anyone is to be suspected of having something to do with the death of the old Frenchman, it must indeed be Dulcibeni and Devizé. They arrived at the Donzello together with Mourai, coming from Naples, and have stayed here for over a month. Devizé, with his tale of the Cocomero, has shown that he probably has something to hide. Pompeo Dulcibeni even shared his chamber with the dead man. They may well be innocent, but they surely know more than anyone else about the dead man."

"And what do you hope to find in their apartments?"

"I shall not know until I have entered," he replied coldly.

Once again my ears resounded with the horrible things which Devizé had uttered about Melani.

"I cannot give you a copy of their keys," said I, upon reflection.

Melani understood that it would be useless to insist and remained silent.

"For the rest, however, I am at your service," I added in a gentler tone, thinking of my lost pearls. "I could, for instance, put some questions to Devizé and Dulcibeni, and try to make them talk…"

"Please, please… You would obtain nothing from them and you would put them on their guard. Let us move step by step: let us first endeavour to understand who it was that stole the keys and your pearls."

Atto then explained his idea to me: after dinner, we would watch over the stairs from our respective chambers, I on the third floor and he on the second. We would pass a string between my window and his (our chambers being one exactly above the other) and both would tie one end to a foot. When one of us noticed something, he would pull hard, several times, to make the other run and thus to prevent the thief's escape.

While he spoke, I weighed up the facts. The knowledge that Brenozzi's pearls might be worth a fortune had in the end disheartened me: no one had ever given me anything so precious. Perhaps I should bear with Abbot Melani a little. I ought, of course, to keep my eyes open: I must not forget the dire judgements which I had heard concerning him.

I assured him that I would follow his instructions, as moreover—I recalled in order to reassure him—I had already promised last night during our singular and lengthy colloquy. I mentioned vaguely that I had overheard three guests at the inn discussing Superintendent Fouquet, whose name the abbot had mentioned to me the evening before.

"And what did they say?"

"Nothing that I can recall with any precision, as I was busy tidying up the kitchen. They simply caused me to remember your promise to tell me something about him."

A gleam appeared in Abbot Melani's penetrating pupils: he had at last found the source of my sudden diffidence towards him.

"You are right," he said, "I am indebted to you."

His regard suddenly grew distant, lost in past memories. He sang *sotto voce*, in melancholy tones:

> *Ai sospiri, al dolore,*
> *Ai tormenti, al penare,*
> *Torna o mio cuore...*[*]

"There," he added, seeing my questioning expression, "thus would my master, Seigneur Luigi Rossi, have spoken to you of Fouquet. But since it is now my turn to do the telling, and we must wait until dinner time, make yourself at ease. You ask me who Nicolas Fouquet was. I tell you, he was before all else a man vanquished."

He fell silent, as though at a loss for words, while the dimple on his chin trembled.

"A man defeated by envy, by *raison d'état*, by politics, but above all one vanquished by history. Because, bear this well in mind, history is always made by the victors, be they good or bad. And Fouquet lost. And so, now and forever, in France and in the world, you may ask anyone who Nicolas Fouquet was, and they will reply that he was the most thieving, corrupt, factious, frivolous and prodigal minister of our times."

"And you, besides being a man vanquished, who do *you* say he was?"

"The Sun," he replied with a smile. "Thus was Fouquet called, when Le Brun painted him in that guise in the *Apotheosis of Hercules*, on the walls of the Château of Vaux-le-Vicomte. And truly, no heavenly body was better suited to describe a man of such magnificence and generosity."

"And so the Sun King took that name because he wished to copy Fouquet?"

Melani looked at me pensively. He resumed, explaining to me that the arts, like the delicate inflorescence of roses, need someone who will arrange them in the right vase, or who will till and enrich the soil and, day after day, lovingly sprinkle the water with which to quench their thirst; as to the gardener, added Abbot Melani, he must possess the best of implements with which to care for his charges; a gentle touch, lest he offend their tender leaves, an expert eye to recognise their infirmities and, lastly, knowledge of how to transmit his art.

---

[*] To sighs, to suffering, / to torments, to chagrin, / return o my heart...

"Nicolas Fouquet had all that was needful to that end," sighed Abbot Melani. "He was the most splendid patron of the arts, the most grandiose, the most tolerant and the most generous, the most gifted in the art of living and making politics. But he was ensnared in the web of avid, jealous, proud, intriguing and dissimulating enemies."

Fouquet came of a wealthy family from Nantes, which had already a century before made a well-merited fortune trading with the Antilles. He was entrusted to the Jesuit Fathers, who found in him a superior intelligence and exceptional charisma: the followers of the great Ignatius made of him a nobly political spirit, able to weigh up every opportunity, to turn all situations to his advantage and to persuade his every interlocutor. At the age of sixteen, he was already a counsellor at the Parlement of Metz, and at twenty, he became a member of the prestigious corps of the *maîtres des requêtes*, the public servants who administer justice, finance and the military.

In the meanwhile, Cardinal Richelieu had died and Cardinal Mazarin had ascended: Fouquet, being a protégé of the former, passed without difficulty into the service of the latter. This was also because when the Fronde, the famous revolt of the nobility against the Crown, had broken out, Fouquet had defended the young King Louis well and had organised his return to Paris, after the troubles had compelled the Sovereign and his family to leave the city. He had shown himself to be an excellent servant of His Eminence the Cardinal, most faithful to the King and a man of daring. Once the tumult was over, at the age of thirty-five, he purchased the charge of Procurator-General of the Parlement of Paris, and in 1653 he was finally appointed Superintendent of Finances.

"But these facts," ventured Abbot Melani, "are merely the gilded frame of all his noble, just and eternal deeds."

His house was open to men of letters and artists and to business men; both in Paris and in the country, all awaited the precious moments which he stole from the duties of state to gratify those who had talent in poetry, in music and in the other arts.

It was no accident that Fouquet was the first to have understood and loved the great La Fontaine. The poet's scintillating talent was more than worthy of the rich pension which the Superintendent bestowed on him from the very dawning of their acquaintance. And to ensure that his friend's delicate soul should suffer no oppression, he asked him to repay his debt by periodic instalments, but in verse. Molière himself was indebted to the Superintendent, but never would this be held against him, because the greater debt was moral. Even the good Corneille, now aged and no longer kissed by glory's ardent and capricious lips, was, at this the most difficult moment of his life, gratified materially, and thus saved from the coils of melancholy.

But the noble nuptials of the Superintendent with letters and with poesy were not exhausted in a mere sequence of presents and patronage, however long the catalogue of his munificence. The Superintendent did not stop short at material assistance. He read works still in gestation, he proffered advice and encouragement, he corrected, admonished, criticised where necessary, and praised where praise was opportune. And he gave inspiration: not only in words but through his noble presence. The good heart which shone forth from the Superintendent's countenance instilled courage, comfort and confidence: those great childlike cerulean eyes, the long nose, retroussé at the tip, the wide fleshy mouth and the dimples which creased his cheeks when he smiled his open smile.

Early in life, architecture, painting and sculpture had knocked at the door of Nicolas Fouquet's soul. Here, however, warned the abbot, a sorrowful chapter opens.

In the country, near Melun, there stands a château, a jewel of architecture, marvel among marvels, which Fouquet had built with incomparable taste and executed by artists whom he himself had discovered: the architect Le Vau, the gardener Le Nôtre, the painter Le Brun, recalled from Rome, the sculptor Puget, and so many others whom the King was soon to take into his own service, making them the foremost names in French art.

"Vaux, the castle of illusions," moaned Atto, "an immense affront in stone: the décor of a glory that lasted a single summer's night, that of the 17th of August, 1661. At six of the clock in the afternoon, Fouquet was the real King of France, at two the next morning, he was nothing."

On that 17th of August, the Superintendent, who had recently inaugurated his château, organised a day of festivities in honour of the King. He wished to please and delight him. He did this with his usual gaiety and munificence, but alas for him, without having understood the Sovereign's warped character. He had delivered to

Vaux, for the still incomplete salons, day-beds decked in brocade with gold braided trimmings, tapestries, rare furniture, silverware, crystal chandeliers. Through the streets of Melun came a procession of treasures from a hundred museums and a thousand antiquaries: carpets from Persia and from Turkey, Cordovan leather wall coverings, porcelains sent from Japan by the Jesuits, lacquers imported from China via Holland, thanks to the privileged route which the Superintendent had created for the importation of rare merchandise from the Orient; and then, the paintings which Poussin had discovered in Rome and sent to him through his brother, the Abbé Fouquet. All the artists and poets who were his friends were recruited, including Molière and La Fontaine.

"In every salon, from that of Madame de Sévigné to that of Madame de la Fayette, the Château of Vaux was the one subject of conversation," continued Melani, lost now in memories of those days. "The entrance to the château welcomed the visitor with the austere tracery of its wrought-iron grille and the eight busts of deities who seemed to hover on either side. Then came the immense outer courtyard, the *cour d'honneur*, linked to the dependencies by a series of bronze pilasters. And, in the three round arches of the imposing entrance portal, the climbing squirrel, Fouquet's emblem."

"A squirrel?"

"In Breton, the Superintendent's native dialect, the word *fouquet* means a squirrel. And my friend Nicolas resembled the little creature in complexion and temperament: industrious, moving suddenly and rapidly, nervous in body, with a playful, attractive gaze. Under his coat of arms, the motto: *'Quo non ascendam?'*—or 'How high shall I not climb?'—which referred to the squirrel's passion for reaching ever-greater heights. By this, I mean of course, heights of generosity: Fouquet loved power as a little boy might. His was the simplicity of one who never takes himself too seriously."

Around the château, continued the abbot, spread the splendid gardens of Le Nôtre: "Velvet lawns and flowers from Genoa, where the begonia borders had the regularity of hexameters. Yews so clipped as to form cones, box bushes fashioned to resemble braziers, and then the great cascade and the lake of Neptune, leading to the grottoes; and, behind these, the park, with those celebrated fountains which so astonished Mazarin. All was ready to receive the young Louis XIV."

The King and the Queen Mother had left the Palace of Fontainebleau in the afternoon. At six, they arrived at Vaux with their retinue. Only Queen Maria Teresa, who was carrying the first fruit of
her husband's love, was not among the guests. Manifesting indifference, the royal party passed between the ranks of guards and
musketeers with their swelling chests and then through the busy
swarms of pages and valets bearing gold chargers overburdened
with the most ornate victuals, adjusting triumphs of exotic flowers,
dragging cases of wine, arranging chairs around enormous damasked
tables on which the candlesticks, the services and the cutlery were
of gold and silver, the cornucopias full of fruit and vegetables, and
the drinking glasses of the finest crystal, also ornamented in gold:
all these things combined to make a splendid, stupefying, inimitable,
irritating display.

"It was then that the pendulum of fate began to swing back,"
commented Abbot Melani, "and the reversal was as sudden as it was
violent."

The young King Louis disliked the almost insolent ostentation
of the fête. The heat and the flies, which were as anxious as the
guests to take part in the celebrations, enervated both the Sovereign
and his retinue, who were constrained by the conventions to make
a punishing tour of the gardens of Vaux. Roasted by the sun, throats
hemmed in by tight lace collars and lawn cravats pulled through the
sixth buttonhole of their justaucorps, they were dying to be rid of
their breeches and periwigs. It was with infinite relief that they saluted the cool of evening and at last sat down to dine.

"And how was the dinner?" I asked, my appetite whetted, imagining that the cuisine must have been on the same level as the house
and the ceremony.

"The King did not like it," said the abbot gloomily.

Above all, the young King did not like the array of thirty-six dozen
solid gold dishes and the five hundred dozen silver ones on the tables.
He did not like the fact that so very many guests had been invited,
hundreds and hundreds of them, or that the file of carriages and pages
and little coaches waiting outside the château should be so long and so
gay, almost a second fête. He did not like the whispered comment of a
courtier, uttered as though it were some gossip which he was entitled
to share, to the effect that the festivities had cost more than twenty
thousand *livres*.

The King did not like the music which accompanied the banquet—cymbals and trumpets with the entrées, followed by violins—nor did he like the enormous sugar basin which was placed in front of him, and which hampered his movements.

He did not like being received by one who, although not a crowned head, was demonstrating that he was more generous, more rich in fantasy, more skilled in astounding his guests and at same time winning them over, uniting hospitality and magnificence; and thus more splendid. In a word: more royal.

After the miseries of the meal, Louis must needs endure those of the open-air spectacle which followed. While the banquet dragged on, Molière in his turn, pacing nervously back and forth in the shelter of the great tents, cursed the Superintendent: *Les Fâcheux*, the comedy which he had prepared for the occasion, should have begun two hours earlier. Now the daylight was fading. In the end it was under the dark blue and green shield of the setting sun's last rays that he came on stage, while in the east the first stars dotted the heavens. There now followed yet another marvel: on the proscenium, there appeared a great clam, whose valves opened; whence a dancer, the sweetest of naiads, arose; and it was then as though all Nature spoke, and the surrounding trees and statues, moved by the subtlest of divine forces, gathered around the nymph to intone with her the sweetest of hymns: the eulogy of the King with which the comedy opened:

> *Pour voir sur ces beaux lieux le plus grand roi du monde*
> *Mortels, je viens à vous de ma grotte profonde...* *

At the end of the sublime spectacle came the fireworks prepared by that Italian, Torelli, who, thanks to the magic of those explosions and colours which he alone knew how to stir with such consummate skill in the black, empty cauldron of heaven, was known in Paris as the Great Wizard.

At two o'clock in the morning, or perhaps even later, the King signalled with a nod that the time had come to take his leave. Fouquet was dumbfounded to see that his visage was dark with anger; perhaps he understood, and he grew pale. He approached and, on bended knee, with a sweeping gesture of the hand, publicly offered him Vaux as a gift.

* To behold in this fine place the greatest King in the world, / Mortals, I come to you from my deep cavern...

Young Louis did not respond. He climbed into his carriage and cast a last glance at the château outlined in the dark: it was perhaps then (some swear to this) that there passed before his eyes an image from the Fronde, a troubled afternoon from his childhood, an image of which he no longer knew whether it was his own memory or what others had told him; an uncertain reminiscence of that night when, with the Queen Mother Anne and Cardinal Mazarin, he had escaped from Paris by stealth, his ears deafened by detonations and the clamour of the crowd, and in his nostrils, the sickening scent of blood mingling with the stink of the plebeians, ashamed to be King and despairing of ever returning to the city, his city. Or perhaps the King (some swear this, too) beheld the proud, arrogant jets of the fountains of Vaux, whose plashing he could still hear even as his carriage drove away, and suddenly realised that there was not a drop of water at Versailles.

"And then what happened?" I asked with a small voice, moved and troubled by the abbot's narration.

A few weeks passed, and the noose swiftly tightened around the Superintendent's neck. The King feigned the need to visit Nantes in order to make Brittany feel the weight of his authority and to impose those tributes which the Bretons had been slow to pay into the coffers of the realm. The Superintendent followed him without excessive anxiety, since Nantes was his own native city and many of his friends dwelled there.

Before he left, however, some began to suggest that he should cast an eye over his shoulder; his most faithful friends warned discreetly that a plot was being hatched against him. The Superintendent requested an audience with the King and opened his heart to him: he begged his pardon if the Treasury was in difficulties, but he had until a few months earlier been at Mazarin's orders, as Louis well knew. The King was perfectly understanding and treated him with the utmost consideration, asking his advice on even the most insignificant matters and following his indications without batting an eyelid.

Fouquet sensed, however, that something was wrong and he fell ill: he again began to suffer from those intermittent fevers which had struck him down following prolonged exposure to damp and cold when supervising the works at Vaux. More and more frequently he lost restoring sleep. He was seen once, weeping silently behind a door.

At last he left in Louis' retinue and, at the end of August, arrived in Nantes. At once, however, fever forced him again to take to his bed. The King, who had taken up lodgings in a castle at the far end of town, even showed signs of concern and sent visitors to inquire after his health. Fouquet recovered, although with difficulty. At last, on 5th September, the Sovereign's birthday, he was summoned at seven o'clock in the morning. He worked with the King until eleven, after which the Sovereign unexpectedly kept him back to discuss certain matters. When at length Fouquet left the castle, his carriage was stopped by a company of musketeers. A second lieutenant of musketeers, a certain d'Artagnan, read him the arrest warrant. Fouquet was incredulous. "Sir, are you certain that it is I whom you are to arrest?" Without according him one moment more, d'Artagnan confiscated all the papers which he had with him, even those which he carried on his person. All these were sealed and he was placed in a convoy of royal carriages which took him to the Château of Angers. There he remained for three months.

"And then?"

"That was but the first step on his *via dolorosa*. A trial was prepared, which lasted three years."

"Why so long?"

The Superintendent defended himself with incomparable skill. But in the end he was doomed to succumb. The King had him imprisoned for life in the fortress of Pinerol, beyond the Alps.

"And did he die there?"

"From that place, no one leaves save at the King's pleasure."

"But then it was the King's envy that destroyed Fouquet, because he could not tolerate his magnificence; and the fêtes…"

"I cannot permit you to speak like this," he interrupted. "The young King was, at that time, beginning to cast his eyes over the various aspects of the state, and those eyes were not indifferent: they were those of a master. Only then did he understand that *he* was King and that he had been born to reign. But it was already too late for him to call to account Mazarin, the now deceased master and godfather of his youthful years, who had refused him everything. There remained, however, Fouquet, the other Sun, whose fate was thus sealed."

"So the King took his revenge. And what is more, he had not appreciated the solid gold dinner service…"

"No one can speak of the King taking vengeance, for he is the most powerful of all the princes of Europe; and *a fortiori* no one can say that His Most Christian Majesty was envious of the Superintendent of the Royal Finances, when those finances belonged to the Sovereign and to no one else."

He again fell silent, but he himself understood that his reply was not sufficient to satisfy my curiosity.

"It is true," he added at last, staring at the last rays of daylight as they entered the chamber, "you would not know the truth unless I told you of the Serpent who caught the Squirrel in his coils."

If the Superintendent was the Squirrel, in his footsteps there followed insidiously the Serpent. This slimy creature is known in Latin as *coluber*, and, strangely enough, that appellation pleased Monsieur de Colbert, who was convinced that the similarity with a reptile could (an idea as erroneous as it was revealing) best lend lustre and magnificence to his name.

"And he truly did know how to conduct himself like a thousand-coiled serpent," said the abbot. "For it was the Serpent, whom the Squirrel so trusted, that was to thrust him into the abyss."

In the beginning, Jean-Baptiste Colbert, the son of a rich textile merchant, was lord of absolutely nothing.

"Even if," sneered Atto, "he did lay claim to august forebears by having himself made a false tombstone which he claimed to be that of an ancestor from the thirteenth century, and before which he was even so mendacious as to kneel."

"Poorly educated, fortune smiled on him early in the guise of a cousin of his father, with whose help he acquired a post at the Ministry of War. There, his talent for toadying enabled him to make the acquaintance of Richelieu and to tie himself to his chariot; then, after the Cardinal's death, to become secretary to Michel le Tellier, the powerful Secretary for War. In the meanwhile, Richelieu's place had been taken by an Italian Cardinal, Jules Mazarin, who was very close to the Queen Mother.

"During that time, thanks to the money accruing to him through trade, he had succeeded in purchasing himself a minor title. And if he needed more money, the matter was resolved by his marriage to Marie Charron and above all by her dowry of one hundred thousand *livres*," added Abbot Melani with a further touch of spite. "But what made his true fortune," he resumed, "was the King's misfortune."

In 1650 the Fronde, which had begun some two years earlier, reached its climax, and the Sovereign, the Queen and Cardinal Mazarin had to flee Paris.

"The main problem for the state was certainly not the absence of the King, who was still a boy of twelve, nor that of the Queen Mother, who was above all the Cardinal's mistress, but that of the Cardinal himself."

To whom were the affairs and secrets of state, which the Cardinal handled so skilfully, now to be entrusted? Colbert drew on all his qualities as a zealous functionary: he was to be found in the office at five o'clock in the morning, he kept the most absolute order and never undertook anything of importance on his own initiative. All that, while Fouquet worked at home, forging ideas in the white heat of his furnace-like mind, amidst the uttermost chaos of papers and documents.

Thus the Cardinal, who in 1651 was beginning to feel threatened by Fouquet's enterprising ways, chose Colbert to look after his affairs. The more so, as the latter had shown himself to be highly proficient in the art of coded correspondence. Colbert served Mazarin not only until his triumphal re-entry to Paris with Louis and Anne of Austria at the end of the Fronde, but until the Cardinal's death.

"He entrusted to him even the administration of his own property," said the abbot with a sigh which expressed all the bitterness of one who has seen so much trust placed in the wrong hands. "He taught him all that art which the Serpent would never have been able to cultivate on his own. The Serpent, instead of manifesting gratitude, ensured that he was well paid. And he obtained favours for himself and for his family," said he, rubbing his thumb against his index as a vulgar indication that he was speaking of money. "He succeeded in obtaining audiences with the Queen Mother almost every day. To look at, he was almost the exact opposite of Nicolas: squat and stocky, with a wide, marked face, a livid, yellowish complexion, long, sparse crow-black hair under his skull-cap, an avid expression, hooded eyelids, moustaches as fine as whiplashes over thin, unsmiling lips. His glacial, prickly and recondite character would have made him a man to be dreaded, were it not for his ridiculous ignorance, ill-camouflaged by those misplaced Latin quotations which he was wont to parrot, after learning them from young assistants especially appointed for the purpose. He became a figure of fun but was even less liked for it, so much so that Madame de Sévigné nicknamed him 'the North', the iciest and most disagreeable of the cardinal points."

I did not ask Melani why there transpired from his tale such aversion for Colbert but not for Mazarin, to whom Colbert seemed so closely tied. I already knew the answer: had I not heard Devizé, Cristofano and Stilone Priàso say that the castrato Atto Melani had, from his earliest youth, been helped and protected by the Cardinal?

"Were Colbert and Superintendent Fouquet friends?" I hazarded instead.

He hesitated an instant before replying.

"They met at the time of the Fronde and at first they quite liked one another. During the troubles, Fouquet's behaviour was that of the best of subjects, and Colbert revered him, rendering him services when he became Procurator-General of Paris, an office which he combined with that of Superintendent of Finances. But this did not last: Colbert could not bear that Fouquet's star should shine so high and so bright. How could he forgive the Squirrel his celebrity, his fortune, his charm, his agility at work and his promptitude of mind, (while he, Colbert, must sweat so hard to bring forth good ideas), and finally, for his sumptuous library which he, being uneducated, would not even have known how to use? So the Serpent played Spider, and set his hand to the web."

The fruits of Colbert's cunning were not long in coming. First, he instilled the poison of mistrust in Mazarin, then in the King. The realm was then emerging from decades of war and poverty and it was not difficult to falsify papers so as to accuse the Superintendent of accumulating wealth at the Sovereign's expense.

"Was Fouquet very rich?"

"He was not rich at all, but for reasons of state he needed to appear so: only thus could he continue to obtain more and more credit and thus satisfy Mazarin's pressing demands for money. He, the Cardinal, was exceedingly wealthy. Yet, when the King read his will a short time before he died, he found nothing to comment on therein."

This was, however, not the real question for Colbert. When the Cardinal died, a decision had to be made as to who was to take his place. Fouquet had adorned the realm, had endowed it with glory, had given of himself day and night to satisfy the demands for more revenue: he rightly thought that the honour should be his.

"But when the young King was asked who was to succeed Mazarin, he replied: *"C'est moi."* There was no room for another prime actor alongside the Sovereign, and Fouquet was of too refined a material to play the subordinate. Colbert, on the other hand, was perfect in the part of bootlicker: he was consumed by the thirst for power, and even resembled the King too much in his manner of taking himself seriously; and that is precisely why he made not a single false move. Louis XIV fell headlong into the trap."

"So it was Colbert's envy that led to the persecution of Fouquet."

"That is quite clear. During the trial, the Serpent covered himself in infamy: he suborned the judges, he falsified documents, he threatened and extorted. To Fouquet there remained only La Fontaine's heroic defence, the peroration of Corneille, the courageous letters which his friends wrote to the King, the wholehearted support and friendship of noble ladies and, among the people, a hero's fame. Only Molière kept cowardly silence."

"And you?"

"Well, I was not in Paris and there was little that I could do. Now, however, it would be better if you left me. I can hear the other guests making their way downstairs for dinner and I do not wish to catch our thief's attention: he must think that no one is on guard."

❧

In the kitchen, seeing the late hour and the fact that the other guests had already been waiting for a long time, the best I could do was to serve up the remains of luncheon, with the addition of a few eggs and white endives. Truly, I was a mere prentice with no experience at the cooking stove: I could not compete with my master, and the guests were beginning to become aware of the fact.

During the meal, I noticed nothing unusual. Brenozzi, with his rosy cherub's face, continued to pluck at the parsnip between his thighs, gravely observed by the physician, who with one hand tugged at the black goatee on his chin. Stilone Priàso, with his bristling black owl-like frown, was more than ever given over to nervous fidgeting: rubbing the bridge of his nose, cleaning his fingertips, shaking an arm as though he wanted to bring his sleeve down, pulling his shirt away from his collar and smoothing his temples with the palms of his hands. Devizé meanwhile ate as he was wont to: so noisily as almost to drown out the unstoppable loquacity which Bedfordi directed in vain at Dulcibeni, who grew ever more impenetrable, and at Padre Robleda, who nodded vacantly in the Englishman's direction. Abbot Melani consumed his meal in almost complete silence, only rarely looking up. He rose twice, seized by a great fit of sneezing, and brought a lace handkerchief to his nose.

When the meal was almost over and everyone was on the point of returning to their apartments, Stilone Priàso reminded the physician of his promise to enlighten us as to what hope we might entertain of escaping from the quarantine with our lives.

Cristofano needed no asking: "You must, before all else, know that the prime cause of the pestilence's coming into the world is the divine will, and there exists no better remedy for it than prayer. For the rest, no one knows with any certainty how the distemper is propagated. I can affirm that many visitations certainly began with a sick man bringing the disease from an infected zone," he answered. "Here in Rome, for instance, during the last visitation, the infection was said to have arrived from Naples, borne by an unsuspecting fishmonger. But my father, who was Proveditor for Public Health in the great Plague of Prato in 1630 and who cared for many struck down by the pestilence, confided in me many years later that the nature of the disease is mysterious, nor had any of the ancient authors been able to penetrate its secret."

"And he was right."

The harsh voice of Pompeo Dulcibeni, the aged traveller who had accompanied Mourai, took us all by surprise.

He began to hold forth in subdued tones: "A most learned man of the Church and of science has shown the way to proceed. But unfortunately, he was not listened to."

"A man of the Church and of science. Let me guess: Father Athanasius Kircher, perhaps," hazarded the doctor.

Dulcibeni did not reply, thus giving us to understand that the physician had guessed rightly. Then he recited: "*Aerem, acquam, terram innumerabilibus insectis scatere, adeo certum est.*"

"He is saying that the earth, the air and water pullulate with minuscule beings invisible to the naked eye."

"Now," resumed Dulcibeni, "these minuscule beings come from organisms in a state of putrefaction, but it has only been possible to observe them since the invention of the microscope, and so..."

"He is known to many, this German Jesuit," interrupted Cristo-fano with a hint of scorn, "whom Signor Dulcibeni is, it seems, quot-ing from memory."

To me, Kircher's name meant nothing. But he must have been very well known: on hearing the name of Father Athanasius Kircher, the whole audience nodded its assent.

"Kircher's ideas, however," continued Cristofano, "have not yet supplanted those of the great authors, who, on the other hand..."

"Perhaps Kircher's ideas may to some extent be founded, but only sensation can provide a solid, trustworthy basis for our knowledge."

This time, the interjection came from Signor Bedfordi, the young Englishman, who seemed freed from last night's terror and was again his usual bumptious self.

"The same cause," he continued, "may in different cases produce opposite effects. After all, does not the same hot water harden eggs and make meat tender?"

"I know perfectly well," hissed Cristofano harshly, "who it is that circulates these sophisms: Master Locke, and his colleague Sidenamio, who know all there is to be known about the senses and the intellect; but in London they claim to cure the sick without being physicians."

"And so what? Their interest is in obtaining a cure," rebutted Bedfordi, "and not in attracting patients with their quacking, like certain physicians. Twenty years ago, when the pestilence in Naples was killing twenty thousand people in a day, Neapolitan chirurgeons and specialists came to London to sell their secret prophylaxis against the plague. Fine rubbish it was too: papers to hang around one's neck with the Jesuits' mark I.H.S. in a cross; or the famous parchment to be hung from the neck with the inscription:

ABRACADABRA
ABRACADABR
ABRACADAB
ABRACADA
ABRACAD
ABRACA
ABRAC
ABRA
ABR
AB
A

At this point, the young Englishman, after arranging his red mane with some vanity and fixing his audience (except for me, to whom he paid no attention at all) with his glaucous, squinting eyes, stood up and leaned upon the wall, so that he could address us with greater ease.

The door posts of houses and the corners of streets were plastered over with doctors' bills inviting the people to buy "the INFALLIBLE preventive pills", "MATCHLESS potions", "ROYAL-ANTIDOTES" and "the UNIVERSAL anti-Plague-Water".

"And when they were not gulling the poor people with such-like quackeries," continued Bedfordi, "they sold potions based on mercury, which poisoned the blood and killed more surely than the plague itself."

This last phrase of the Englishman worked on Cristofano like a fuse, leading to a violent renewal of the dispute between them.

At that moment, Father Robleda joined the discussion. At first, he had muttered unintelligible comments under his breath, but now Robleda sallied forth in defence of his fellow Jesuit. The reactions were not long in coming and an indecorous altercation broke out, in which each struggled to impose his views by the force of his vocal cords rather than by that of reason.

It was the first time in my poor apprentice's life that I had witnessed so learned a contest, and I was both somewhat shocked and disappointed by the quarrelsomeness of the participants.

It was, however, thus that I obtained my first information about the theories of the mysterious Kircher, which could but arouse one's curiosity. In the course of a half-century of tireless study, the learned Jesuit had poured forth his multiform doctrine in over thirty magnificent works on the most varied topics, including a treatise on the plague, *Scrutinium physico-medicum contagiosae luis quae pestis dicitur*, published some twenty-five years previously. The Jesuit scientist claimed that he had with his microscope made great discoveries, which would leave the reader incredulous (as indeed they did) and which proved the existence of tiny invisible beings which were, in his opinion, the cause of the pestiferous infection.

In Robleda's view, Father Kircher's science was the product of faculties worthy of a seer, and in any case inspired by the Most High. And (I found myself thinking) what if that strange Father Kircher really had discovered how to cure the plague? However, the atmosphere was so torrid that I dared not ask questions.

Throughout all this, Abbot Melani was as attentive as myself, indeed more so, to the information concerning Father Kircher. He kept rubbing his nose, in a vain attempt to suppress several resounding sneezes, and while he did not intervene again, his sharp little eyes darted from one to the other of those mouths full of the German Jesuit's name.

I, for my part, was at once terrorised by the looming danger of the plague and fascinated by these learned theories concerning the infection, of which I was hearing for the first time.

That was why my suspicions were not aroused (as indeed they should have been) by the fact that Dulcibeni was so conversant with Kircher's old and forgotten theory about the plague. Nor had I noticed how Atto pricked up his ears when he heard the name of Kircher.

After hours of argument, most of the guests—overcome at last by boredom—had gradually slipped away to their beds, leaving only the antagonists. And a little later we all retired to sleep, without any peace being in sight.

Night the Second
BETWEEN *the* 12TH *&* 13TH SEPTEMBER, 1683

✠

No sooner had I returned to my chamber than I leaned out of the window and, using a cane, lowered to Atto's window one end of the string which we were to pull to give the alarm. I then laid me down on my bed, keeping my eyes half-open and my ears pricked up. Fearing though I did that I might not be able to resist sleep for long, I prepared nevertheless to keep watch; also because in the bed before me lay my poor master, and Cristofano had asked me to keep an eye on him. I placed some old rags over his loins in order to absorb any urine, and began my wake.

What Abbot Melani had told me had, I reflected, gone some way to making me more tranquil. He had without the least awkwardness admitted to his friendship with Fouquet. And he had explained why the Superintendent had fallen into disgrace: even more than the Most Christian King's disappointment, the determining factor had been Colbert's envy. Everyone knows the malignant force of envy: might not Devizé's, Stilone Priàso's and Cristofano's gossip about Atto also be attributable to precisely that? Perhaps too much jealousy had been stirred up by the ascent of a mere bell-ringer's son who, from his beginnings as a poor castrato, had so risen as to dispense counsel to the Sun King. Certainly, the three had shown that they recognised him, nor could their talk be the fruit of mere fantasy. Nevertheless, Cristofano's hostility might be explained by envy of a fellow-countryman: "*nemo propheta in patria*", says the gospel. What was one then to think of Devizé's strange lie? He had spoken of visiting the Teatro del Cocomero in Venice, when it was in Florence. Was I to mistrust him, too?

Atto's tale was not only credible but grandiose and moving. I felt bitter repentance arise in my breast for having thought him a scoundrel, a dissimulator ready to betray and to lie. In truth it was I who had betrayed the sentiment of friendship that had grown out of our

first conversation in the kitchen, and which I had taken to be genuine and sincere.

I glanced at my master, who for many hours had been sleeping a heavy and unnatural sleep. We seemed beset by too many mysteries: what had reduced him to that state? And, before him, to what had Signor di Mourai fallen victim? And, last of all, what had induced Brenozzi to present me with those precious pearls, and why had they now been stolen?

My mind was still occupied with these painful thoughts when I woke up: without realising it, I had fallen asleep. A sound of creaking awoke me: I jumped up and rolled out of bed, but immediately a mysterious force cast me to the ground, and only with the greatest of difficulty did I avoid a heavy fall. I cursed: I had forgotten the cord linking my right ankle with that of Abbot Melani. Rising, I had tripped over it; and when I fell, the noise awoke my master, who moaned softly. We were in the dark; perhaps for lack of oil, my lamp had gone out.

I listened carefully; in the corridor, there was not a sound. Hardly had I risen, however, fumbling for the edge of the bed, when I again heard creaking, followed by a heavy thud, then metallic sounds, then yet another creak. My heart was beating hard; this was certainly the thief. I freed myself of the string that had tripped me and groped in search of the lantern which was on the table in the middle of the chamber, but with no success. With great trepidation, I decided then to leave the room and intercept the thief, or at least to discover his identity.

I plunged into the dark corridor, without having the least idea of what to do. Laboriously, I made my way down the stairs to the closet. If I found myself face to face with the mysterious individual, was I to attack him or to call for help? Without knowing why, I ducked and tried to approach the door of the closet, holding my hands out in front of me both to defend my face and to explore the unknown.

The blow was cruel and unexpected. Someone, or something, had struck my cheek, leaving me confused and in pain. Terrified, I tried to avoid a second blow by backing against the wall and screaming. My anguish became insuperable when I realised that no sound was issuing from my mouth; for such was my panic that it crushed my lungs and blocked my vocal cords. I was about to roll desperately on the ground to escape from my unknown adversary, when a hand grasped my arm firmly and at the same time I heard: "What are you up to, you little fool?"

It was beyond any doubt Atto's voice, and it was he who had rushed up when I rose in alarm at the creaking and pulled on the string. I explained to him what had happened, complaining of the blow I had received to the face.

"That was no blow, it was I who was running to help you—but you came tumbling down the stairs like a half-wit and collided with me," he whispered, holding back his anger. "Where is the thief?"

"I have seen no one but you," I murmured, still trembling.

"I heard him. While I was climbing the stairs, I heard his keys jangling. He must have entered the closet," said he, lighting a lantern which he had had the foresight to bring with him. From above, we glimpsed a slit of light issuing from under the door of Stilone Priàso, on the right-hand side of the second floor corridor. The abbot asked me to lower my voice and indicated the entrance to the little passage into which he supposed that the thief had gone. The door was ajar. Within, all was dark.

We looked at each other and held our breath. Our man must be within, aware now that he was trapped. The abbot hesitated for a moment and then opened the door boldly. Inside, there was no one.

"It is not possible," said Melani, visibly disappointed. "If he had escaped downstairs, he would have run into me. If he had run upstairs, even if he had succeeded in getting past you, there is nowhere left to hide. The doorway from Cloridia's tower to the roof has been sealed from the outside. And if he had opened the door of one of the other rooms, we should surely have heard him."

We were utterly disconcerted; but just when we were on the point of beating the retreat, Atto gestured that I was to stay put, and went rapidly down the stairs. I followed his lantern with my gaze and saw him stop at the second-floor window onto the inner courtyard. He put the lantern on the floor and I saw him leaning over the window sill. Thus, he remained awhile. Growing curious, I too approached the grate of the little window which gave light to the closet during the day. But it was too high for me and I could see nothing but the pale moonlit night. Returning to the closet, the abbot knelt down and measured the length of the floor with his palms, until he reached under the sideboard loaded with household utensils which stood against the far wall. There he stopped for a moment, then repeated the operation, taking account this time of the thickness of the wall. He then measured the distance between the window and the end wall. When at last he raised his hands from the dust, he grasped me without uttering a word and lifted me onto a stool; then, putting the lantern on my head, so that I had to hold it in place with my hands, he set me before the grate. "Do not move," he commanded, tapping my nose with his finger.

I heard him grope his way down to the second-floor window. When at long last he returned, I was impatient to know what he was thinking.

"Follow this carefully. The closet is a little over eight hands long; about ten hands, if we include the wall. As one can see quite clearly from the courtyard, the little wing to which this closet belongs was built later than the main body of the inn. Indeed, from the outside, it looks like a great pillar rising up to here from the ground, attached to the posterior corner of the building's west wall. Only, there's something here that does not add up: the pillar is at least twice as wide as the closet. This little window is, as you can see, very close to the shelf, not more than a couple of palms from the end of the room. Therefore it should, when seen from the outside, be close to the outer corner of the wing. But, when I leaned out from the window on the second floor, I saw that the little window, lit up by the lantern which you were holding, was not even halfway along the wall."

The abbot stopped, perhaps waiting for me to reach my conclusions. But I, with my head cluttered to suffocation by all those geometric figures piled one on top of the other and adduced by Atto's rigorous reasoning, had understood nothing. So he continued: "Why so much wasted space? Why was not more room given to this closet, which is so small that the two of us cannot stand up in it without touching one another?"

I too went to look from the second-floor window, happy above all to breathe the fresh night air.

I screwed up my eyes. It was true. The light from the oil lamp which I could descry through the grate of the closet was curiously distant from the far corner, outlined by the pale moonlight. I had never paid attention to this, being too busy by day and tired by night to tarry by that window sill.

"And do you know what the explanation is, my boy?" asked Abbot Melani the moment I rejoined him.

Without awaiting my reply, he reached out with his arm to the sideboard and began busily to explore the wall behind the utensils. Panting, he asked me to help him shift the piece of furniture.

The operation was not too difficult. The abbot seemed not at all surprised by the revelation which met our eyes; half-hidden by the dirt which time's disrespectful hand had spread over the wall, there emerged the outline of a door.

"Here you are," he exclaimed, satisfied.

And without flinching, he gave a push on the door; the old hinges squealed.

ॐॐ

The first thing that I noticed was a damp, cold draught blowing in my face. Before our eyes, an obscure cavity opened up.

"He went into there," I concluded, stating the obvious.

"That does indeed appear to be the case," replied the abbot, peering apprehensively over the brink. "This wretched little closet had a double wall. Would you care to enter first?"

My silence spoke for itself.

"Very well," conceded Atto, reaching forward with his lantern to show the way. "It is always up to me to resolve everything."

Hardly had he spoken than I saw him clutch desperately at the old door which he had just opened, pulled down by an irresistible force.

"Help me, quickly," he called.

It was a well, and Melani was about to fall into it, with consequences which would surely have been fatal. He had just managed to hold onto the doorpost with his legs dangling in the voracious darkness opening beneath us. When he had climbed back, thanks to my feeble support, we found ourselves in the dark. The abbot had let go of the lantern, which had been swallowed up by the black hole. So I went to fetch another one from my chamber, which I took care to lock. Pellegrino was sleeping peacefully, happily unaware—thought I—of what was going on in his hostelry.

When I returned, Atto was lowering himself into the hole. He showed himself to be unusually agile for his age. As I often had cause to note thereafter, he possessed a kind of controlled but fluid vigour of the nerves, which constantly sustained him.

It was not really a well, as he showed me, waving the lantern, for in the wall was set a series of iron supports rather like steps, which

permitted a cautious descent. We climbed down gingerly into the vertical aperture, not without some trepidation. The descent did not last long: soon we were standing on a rough brick platform. We looked around us, pointing the lantern, and found that the way down was not cut off but continued on one of the short sides of the landing with a stone stairway around a square shaft. We leaned over, trying in vain to descry the bottom of this stairwell.

"We are under the closet, my boy."

I responded with a feeble moan in lieu of comment, seeing that this was of little consolation to me.

We went on in silence. This time, the descent seemed to be without end, also because of a fine slimy film which covered everything and rendered our progress quite perilous. At a certain point, the stairway changed completely in appearance; excavated from the tufa, it became exceedingly narrow and correspondingly uneven. The air had become dense, a sure sign that we were underground.

We continued our descent until we found ourselves in a dark and sinister gallery dug out of the damp earth: our only company, the dense air and the silence. I was afraid.

"This is where our thief went," whispered Abbot Melani.

"Why do you speak so quietly?"

"He could be nearby. I want to be the one to surprise him, not the contrary."

However, the thief was not a few paces off, nor was he beyond that. We proceeded along the gallery, in which Abbot Melani had to walk bending down because of the ceiling—if that it could be called—which was low and rather irregular. He watched me move easily in front of him: "For once I envy you, my boy."

We advanced very slowly along a pathway occasionally made compact by stones and bricks scattered haphazardly here and there. We continued a few dozen paces further, during which the abbot responded to my mute but foreseeable curiosity.

"This passage must have been built to enable one to emerge unseen at some remote point in the city."

"In times of pestilence, perhaps?"

"I think a long, long time before that. It will never have failed to be useful in a city like this. Perhaps it has been used by some Roman prince to unleash his men upon a rival. Roman families have always hated and fought one another with all their might. When the German mercenaries sacked Rome, some households helped them to plunder the city, so long as they struck only at their rivals. It is possible that our inn may originally have served as the headquarters of groups of assassins and cutthroats. Perhaps at the service of the Orsini, who own many houses in the neighbourhood."

"But who built the tunnel?"

"Look at the walls," said the abbot, bringing his lantern close to the side of the gallery. "The stone appears to be rather ancient."

"As ancient as the catacombs?"

"Perhaps. I know that in the past decades, a learned priest explored the cavities to be found in several places in Rome, and discovered and made drawings of innumerable tombs and remains of saints and martyrs. In any case, it is certain that beneath the houses and piazzas of several quarters there are passages and galleries, sometimes built by the ancient Romans, sometimes excavated in periods closer to our own.

"I have heard tell of an underground labyrinth built in Sicily by the great Emperor Frederick, the corridors of which conceal rods which, if trodden upon, release metal grates which fall from above and imprison visitors, or sharp blades which, propelled from invisible slits, are capable of wounding and killing passers-by. Other mechanisms suddenly open up deep wells into which those unwary of such dangers are unfailingly cast. Quite accurate plans have been drawn of some catacombs. It is said that under the ground in Naples, there also exist a surprising number of subterranean passages, but I have no experience there, whereas I have made a few visits to those in Paris, which are certainly quite extensive. I know too that in Piedmont in the last century, near to a place called Rovasenda, hundreds of peasants were ambushed by French soldiers who chased them into some caverns which were to be found near a river. It is said that none left those grottoes alive, neither the assailants nor the assailed."

"Signor Pellegrino never spoke to me of the existence of this passage," I whispered.

"I can believe that. It is not something to be revealed unless it is essential. And probably he himself does not know all its secrets, seeing that he has not been in charge of this inn for very long."

"Then, how did the person who stole the keys find this passage?"

"Perhaps your good master gave in to an offer of money. Or of Muscat wine," sneered the abbot.

While we advanced, I gradually felt myself overcome by a sensation of oppression in my breast and in my head. The obscure wandering on which we had ventured led in an unknown direction: in all likelihood, one that portended many dangers. The darkness, broken only by the oil lantern which Abbot Melani carried before him, was frightful and ominous. The walls of the gallery, because of the tortuous course they followed, made it impossible to look straight in front of us and caused us to foresee some disagreeable surprise with every step we took. And what if the thief had seen the light of our lantern from afar, and was waiting behind some projection to ambush us? I thought, shivering, of the perils populating the galleries of which Abbot Melani knew. No one would ever recover our bodies. The guests at the inn would have a hard time convincing the men-at-arms that I and the abbot had fled from the place, perhaps jumping from some window at night.

Even today, I could not say how long our exploration lasted. At the end, we noticed that the underground passage which had initially led us ever deeper, was gradually beginning to ascend.

"There," said Abbot Melani. "Perhaps we are about to emerge somewhere."

My feet hurt and the damp was beginning to sink its clutches into me. For a while we had not spoken, wanting only to see the end of that dreadful cavern. I was seized by terror when I saw the abbot stumble with a groan on something, almost falling, almost losing his grip on the lantern; to have lost our only source of light would have made our stay down there a nightmare. I rushed forward to support him. With an expression of mixed fury and relief, the abbot cast light on the obstacle. A flight of steps led upwards, as steep as they were narrow. We climbed them almost crawling, so as not to risk falling backwards. During the ascent, a series of curves forced Atto to squeeze through painfully. I, for once, was doing better. Atto looked at me: "I really envy you, my boy," he repeated amusedly, not caring that I showed how little I appreciated his joke.

We were muddied, our brow and our bodies befouled by disgusting sweat. Suddenly, the abbot screamed. A shapeless, rapid and furtive being fell upon my back, sliding clumsily down my right leg before plunging back into the darkness. I twisted my body, raising my arms in terror to protect my head, simultaneously ready to beg for mercy and blindly to defend myself.

Atto understood that the danger, if danger there had been, had lasted the space of a lightning flash. "Strange that we should not have met with any before," he commented as soon as he had regained his composure. "One can see that we really are off the beaten track."

An enormous river rat, disturbed by our arrival, had chosen to climb over us rather than be driven backwards. In its mad leap, it had clung to Abbot Melani's arm while he leaned against the wall, and had then fallen with all its weight onto my back, paralysing me with terror. We stopped, silent and fearful, until our breathing recovered its normal rhythm. We then resumed our ascent, until the steps began at intervals to be replaced by horizontal brick platforms, each one longer than the one before. Fortunately, we had a good supply of oil: contravening the repeated prohibitions issued by the College of Cardinals, I had decided also to use good edible oil.

We felt that we had reached the final stretch. By now we were walking up a gently ascending slope which made us forget the fatigue and the fears which we had only just traversed. We debouched suddenly in a quadrangular space which was no longer excavated but built in masonry. It looked very much like a storeroom or the cellar of a palace.

"We have returned among men," said the abbot, greeting our new surroundings.

From here, a last stairway led upwards, very steep but equipped with a rope handrail, secured to the right-hand wall by a series of iron rings. We climbed up to the top.

"Curses," hissed the abbot.

I understood at once what he meant. At the top of the stairs there was, as might be expected, a doorway. The door was quite solid, and it was closed.

Here was a good opportunity to take a rest, even in so inhospitable a place, and to reflect upon our situation. The little door was bolted with a rusty iron bar running into the wall. From the draught we felt coming through it, there was no difficulty in guessing that it gave onto the open air.

"Now I shall say nothing. You, explain all this," invited the abbot.

"The door is closed from the inside. Yet..." I struggled to make my deduction, "the thief did not leave the gallery. But since we did not meet him nor did we find any junction with another gallery, the conclusion must be that he did not take the same route as ourselves."

"Very well. Then, where did he go?"

"Perhaps he did not even descend into the well behind the closet," I suggested, without for one moment believing that.

"Mmmh," grumbled Atto. "So where did he hide then?"

He went back down the stairs and turned rapidly round the store-room. In a corner, an old half-rotten boat confirmed the suspicion which I had nourished from the moment of our arrival there: we were close to the banks of the Tiber. I opened the door, not without difficulty working the bolt. Illuminated by faint moonbeams, the beginning of a pathway was visible. Lower down, the river ran past, and I instinctively drew back from the chasm. The fresh, damp wind blew into the store-room, causing us to breathe deeply. Just outside the door, another uncertain path seemed to fork off to the right, where it vanished into the muddy riverbanks.

The abbot anticipated my thoughts: "If we flee now, they will capture us without fail."

"In other words," I moaned disconsolately, "we have come all this way for nothing."

"Quite the contrary," retorted Atto impassively. "Now we know this way out, should we ever need it. We have found no trace of the thief who, however, did not take this route. We have missed some other possibility, either through an oversight or through our incapacity. Let us now turn back, before someone becomes aware of our absence."

ॐ∽ॐ

The return to the inn was as painful and twice as tiring as the outward journey. Deprived of the hunter's instinct that had then driven us (or so it was, at least, for Abbot Melani), we dragged ourselves forward, suffering even more from the anfractuosities of the way, although my travelling companion was unwilling to admit it.

Once we had climbed back up the first well, with great relief leaving behind us the infernal underground passage, we regained the little closet. The abbot, visibly frustrated by this fruitless expedition, dismissed me with a few hurried instructions for the following day.

"Tomorrow, if you wish, you may advise the other guests that someone has stolen the second copy of the keys, or at least that they have been mislaid. Of course, we shall say nothing of our discovery or of our attempt to identify the thief. As soon as we have an opportunity, we shall consult together separately from the others, in the kitchen or in some other secure place, and we shall keep each other informed of any news."

I nodded lazily, because of my fatigue, but above all because of the doubts I still secretly harboured concerning Abbot Melani. During our return through the gallery, I had again changed my mind about him: I said to myself that, even if the gossip about him was excessive and malevolent, there did nevertheless remain obscure areas in his past; and so, now that the hunt for the thief had failed, I no longer intended to act as his servant and informer and thus to embroil myself in murky, and perhaps even perilous, affairs. And, even if it were true that Superintendent Fouquet, whose companion Melani had been, had been no more than too splendid a Maecenas, victim of the regal jealousy of Louis XIV and the envy of Colbert, it could still not be denied, I repeated to myself as we forged our tiresome way through the darkness, that here I was, in cahoots with one accustomed to the cunning, the sophistries and the thousand guiles of the court of Paris.

I knew how serious the quarrel was between our good Pope, Innocent XI, and the court of France. At the time, I was unable to tell why there should be such bitterness between Rome and Paris. But from the people's discourse and from those who were better informed about political affairs, I had clearly understood that whoever would faithfully serve our pontiff could not, and must not, be a friend of the French court.

And then, was not all that ardour in pursuing the supposed thief of the keys in itself suspect? Why take up that pursuit, so full of unknown consequences and dangers, rather than simply letting events take their course and telling the other guests at once of the keys' disappearance? And what if the abbot knew far more than he had confided in me? Perhaps he already had a precise idea of where the keys were hidden. And what if he himself had been the thief and had simply tried to distract my attention in order to be able to act more at ease, perhaps that very night? Even my beloved master had concealed from me the existence of the gallery, so why should a stranger like Abbot Melani have confided his real intentions to me?

I therefore gave the abbot my broad promise that I would follow his instructions, but did what I could to disengage myself from him as quickly as possible, taking back my lantern and closing myself at once into my chamber, where I intended to resume filling my little diary with the many occurrences of the day.

Signor Pellegrino was sleeping placidly, his breathing almost completely calmed. More than two hours had passed since we entered the horrid subterranean gallery, perhaps no more remained before it would be time to rise, and I was at the limit of my strength. It was by pure chance that, an instant before putting out the light, I glanced at my master's breeches and noticed the lost keys in plain view on his belt.

Day the Third

13TH SEPTEMBER, 1683

✠

Through the window streamed the sun's friendly rays, flooding the chamber with whiteness and spreading a pure, blessed light even over the sweaty, suffering face of poor Signor Pellegrino, abandoned in his bed. The door opened and the smiling face of Abbot Melani peered around it.

"It is time to go, my boy."

"Where are the other guests?"

"They are all in the kitchen, listening to Devizé play the trumpet."

How strange: I had not known that the guitarist was also a virtuoso on that resounding instrument; and why, then, was the silvery and penetrating sound of the brass not audible on the upper floors?

"Where are we going?"

"We must return down below, we did not search properly last time."

We again entered the closet, where the little door opened up behind the sideboard. I felt the damp on my face. I leaned over unwillingly, illuminating the mouth of the well with my lantern.

"Why not wait until nightfall? The others may discover us," I protested feebly.

The abbot did not reply. From his pocket he drew forth a ring, which he placed in the palm of my hand, closing my fingers around the jewel, as though to stress the importance of what he was giving me. I nodded my consent and began the downward journey.

We had only just reached the brick platform when I gave a start. In the darkness, a hand had clasped my right shoulder. Terror prevented me from either screaming or turning around. Obscurely, I understood that the abbot was telling me to remain calm. Overcoming with great difficulty the paralysis which gripped me, I turned to discover the face of the third explorer.

"Remember to honour the dead."

It was Signor Pellegrino, who with suffering mien was so solemnly warning me. I could find no words to express my discomfiture: who then was it that I had left sleeping in his bed? How had Pellegrino been able to transport himself instantly from our sunny chamber to this dark, damp tunnel? While these thoughts were forming in my mind, Pellegrino spoke again.

"I want more light."

I felt myself suddenly sliding backwards: the surface of the bricks was slimy and irresistibly slippery; I had lost my balance, perhaps when turning towards Pellegrino. I fell slowly, but with all my weight, towards the stairwell, with my back to the ground and my belly turned skywards (although down there, no sky seemed ever to have existed). I slid miraculously down the steps without meeting any resistance, although I felt as though I weighed more than a marble statue. The last thing that I saw was Atto Melani and Pellegrino watching my disappearance with phlegmatic indifference, almost as though life and death were the same to them. I fell, overcome by stupor and by desperation, as a lost soul falling into the Abyss becomes aware at last of his damnation.

What saved me was a scream that seemed to come from some unknowable fold in the Creation and awoke me, tearing me from my nightmare.

I had dreamed and, dreaming, I had screamed. I was in my bed and I turned towards that of my master who had clearly remained all the time just where I left him. Through the window came no fine white sunbeams, but that brightness tinged with red and blue which heralds sunrise. The sharp air of the early morning had chilled me and I covered myself, although I knew that I would not regain sleep easily. From the stairs came a distant sound of footsteps, and I listened intently, in case someone was approaching the door of the closet. I understood clearly that it was a group of guests, making their way down to the kitchen or to the first floor. In the distance, I could make out the voices of Stilone Priàso and Padre Robleda, who were asking Cristofano for news of Signor Pellegrino's health. I rose, fore-seeing that the doctor would soon be arriving to visit my master. The first person to knock at my door was, however, Bedfordi.

On opening, I found myself looking into a pale face with great dark half-moons under the eyes. On his shoulders Bedfordi wore a warm cape. He was fully dressed, and yet he shivered, his whole back and his head convulsed by great trembling fits, which he strove fruitlessly to suppress. He at once begged me to let him in, almost certainly so as not to be seen by the other guests. I offered him a little water and the pills which Cristofano had given us. The Englishman declined the offer, being concerned (so he said) that there existed pills capable of driving a patient to his death. That reply took me by surprise; nevertheless, I felt bound to insist.

"Yet I tell you," said he in a voice suddenly grown feverish, "that opium and purgatives for the various humours can even cause death, and never forget that negroes keep hidden beneath their fingernails a poison that kills with a single scratch; and then there are rattlesnakes, yes, and I have read of a spider which squirts into the eye of its persecutor a poison so potent that for a long time it deprives him of his sight..."

He seemed delirious.

"But Doctor Cristofano will do nothing of the sort," I protested.

"... and these substances," he continued, almost as though he had not heard me, "act by occult virtues, but those occult virtues are none other than the mirror of our ignorance."

I noticed that his legs were trembling, and to retain his footing, he had to lean against the doorpost. His very words were a sign of delirium. Bedfordi sat on the bed and smiled sadly at me.

"Excrement desiccates the cornea," he recited, raising his index finger severely, like a master admonishing his pupils. "Worn around the neck, the groundsel herb is good for curing tertian fevers. But for hysteria, one must needs apply salt poultices several times to the feet. And to learn the art of medicine, tell this to Signor Cristofano when you call him, instead of Galen and Paracelsus, he should read *Don Quixote*."

Then he lay down, closed his eyes, crossed his arms over his chest to cover himself and began to tremble slightly. I rushed down the stairs to call for help.

❧

The great bubo under his groin, together with another smaller one under the right armpit left few doubts in Cristofano's mind. This time, we were clearly faced with the pestilential distemper; and that inevitably cast dark shadows once more, both over the death of Signor

di Mourai and the singular torpor which had overcome my master. I felt myself utterly at a loss: was there a skilled and obscure assassin at large in the hostelry or, more likely, the all-too notorious pestilence?

The news of Bedfordi's illness threw the whole company into the deepest disarray. Only one day remained to us before the return of the Bargello's men for the next roll-call. I noticed that many were avoiding me, since I was the first to have come into contact with Bedfordi when the distemper assailed him. Cristofano, however, pointed out that every one of us had spoken, eaten and even played cards with the Englishman the day before. None, therefore, could feel safe. Owing perhaps to a good dose of juvenile temerity, I was the only one not to give way at once to fear. However, I saw the most fearful of all, namely Padre Robleda and Stilone Priàso, run and gather a few victuals which I had left out in the kitchen, returning thus laden to their apartments. I stopped them, having remembered then that Extreme Unction should be administered to Bedfordi. This time, however, Padre Robleda would not hear reason: "He is English and I know that he is of the reformed religion; he is excommunicated, unbaptised," he replied excitedly, adding that the oil for the sick was reserved for baptised adults and was not to be administered to infants, madmen, those denounced as excommunicated, impenitent public sinners, those condemned to life imprisonment, or to mothers in childbirth; nor might it be offered to soldiers deployed in battle against the enemy or to sailors in danger of shipwreck.

Stilone Priàso, too, inveighed against me: "Did you not know that holy oil accelerates death, causes the hair to fall out, makes childbirth more painful and gives infants jaundice, kills bees flying around the sick man's house, and that all those who have received it will die if they dance during the remaining months of the year; that it is a sin to spin in the sickroom because the patient will die if one leaves off spinning or if the yarn breaks, nor can one wash one's feet until long after receiving Extreme Unction, and one must always keep a lamp or a candle burning in the sickroom for as long as the distemper lasts, otherwise the poor man may die?"

And leaving me standing there, both ran to lock themselves into their apartments.

Thus, about half an hour later, I returned to the small chamber on the first floor where Bedfordi lay, to see in what state he was. I thought that Cristofano, too, had returned there, for the unfortunate

Englishman was talking and appeared to be in company. I at once perceived, however, that I and the sick man were alone together and that he was in fact delirious. I found him terribly pale, a lock of hair glued to his perspiring forehead and his lips abnormally cracked, suggesting a burning, painful throat.

"In the tower... it is in the tower," he babbled hoarsely, turning his tired gaze towards me. He was talking nonsense.

Without any apparent reason, he listed a series of names unknown to me and these I was able to commit to memory only because he repeated them so many times, larded with incomprehensible expressions in his native language. He was constantly sighing the name of one William, a native of the city of Orange, whom I imagined to be a friend or acquaintance of his.

I was about to call Cristofano, fearing that the distemper might abruptly worsen and come to a fatal conclusion, when the physician arrived, drawn by the sick man's moans. He was accompanied by Brenozzi and Devizé, who maintained a respectful distance.

Poor Bedfordi continued his mad monologue, mentioning the name of one Charles, whom Brenozzi later explained to be King Charles II of England; the Venetian, who thus showed himself to have an appreciable knowledge of the English language, explained that he thought Bedfordi had very recently traversed the United Dutch Provinces.

"And why did he go to Holland?" I asked.

"That I do not know," replied Brenozzi, silencing me while he again listened to the sick man's maunderings.

"You really do know the English language well," observed the physician.

"A distant cousin of mine, who was born in London, often writes to me about family matters. I myself am quick to learn and to memorise and I have travelled much on several kinds of business. Look, he seems to feel better."

The sick man's delirium seemed to have abated and Cristofano invited us with a nod of the head to remove to the corridor. There, we found most of the other lodgers waiting, anxious for news.

Cristofano spoke without mincing his words. The progress of the distemper was, he said, such as to make him doubt his own art. First, the far from clear circumstances of Monsieur de Mourai's death, then the accident which had befallen Signor Pellegrino, who was still

reduced to a most piteous state, and now the obvious case of infection
which had struck down Bedfordi: all this had discomfited the Tuscan
doctor, who, faced with such a conjunction of ill-fortune, admitted that
he did not know how to confront the situation. For several interminable moments, we looked at one another, pale and frightened.

ॐॐ

Some gave way to desperate lamentations; others took refuge in their
apartments. Some laid siege to the physician, hoping thus to assuage
their own fears; some fell to the ground with their face in their hands.
Cristofano himself hastened back to his own chamber, where he
locked himself in, begging to be left awhile alone, in order to consult
some books and to review our circumstances. His withdrawal did,
however, seem more like an attempt to take shelter than to organise
retaliatory action. Our enforced imprisonment had cast off the mask
of comedy and donned that of tragedy.

Pale as death, Abbot Melani had assisted at the scene of collective
desperation. But, more than anyone else, I was now a prey to authentic despair. Signor Pellegrino, I thought between sobs, had made the
hostelry into his tomb and my own, as well as that of our guests. And
already I imagined the scenes of distress that would ensue with his
wife's arrival, when she discovered with her own eyes the cruel work
of death in the apartments of the Donzello. The abbot found me
slumped on the floor in the corridor outside Cristofano's chamber,
where I had fallen to sobbing, hiding my tear-soaked face. Stroking
my head, he murmured a plaintive song:

> *Piango, prego e sospiro,*
> *E nulla alfin mi giova…*[*]

He waited for me to calm down, seeking gently to console me;
but then, seeing the uselessness of those first attempts, he lifted me
bodily to my feet and set me down energetically with my shoulders
to the wall.

"I do not want to listen to you," I protested.

I repeated the doctor's words, to which I added that within a
matter of days, perhaps only hours, we would all surely collapse in
atrocious agony, like Bedfordi. Abbot Melani grasped me forcefully,
dragging me up the stairs and into his apartment. Nothing, however,

---

[*] I weep, I pray and sigh / and in the end, nothing cheers me.

could calm me, so that the abbot had in the end to hit me hard with the back of his hand, which had the effect of arresting my sobs. For a few moments, I was peaceful.

Atto put a brotherly arm around my shoulders and tried with patient words to persuade me not to give in to despair. What mattered above all was that we should repeat the cleverly staged scene whereby we had hidden Pellegrino's illness from the men of the Bargello. To reveal the presence of one infected with the pestilence—and this time a real case—would certainly lead to closer and more frequent inspections; we would perhaps be deported to an improvised pest-house in a less populous quarter, perhaps the San Borromeo island where the hospital for the sick had been set up during the great visitation some thirty years before. We two could always attempt the escape route under the ground which we had discovered only the night before. To evade one's pursuers would always be difficult—that he did not conceal—but it would remain a practicable solution, if our plight should worsen. When I had almost recovered my calm, the abbot went over the situation, point by point: if Mourai had been poisoned, and if Pellegrino's presumed buboes were only the spotted fever or, even better, two simple bruises, the one and only certain case of the plague was Bedfordi.

Someone knocked at Atto's door: Cristofano was calling everyone to a meeting in the chambers on the ground floor. He said that he had an urgent announcement to make to us. In the hall, we found all the guests gathered at the foot of the stairs; although, after the latest events, they maintained a prudent distance from one another. Devizé, in an alcove, sweetened the grave moment with the notes of his splendid and disquieting *rondeau*.

"Perhaps the young Englishman has expired?" ventured Brenozzi, without leaving off from plucking at his celery.

The physician shook his head and invited us to take our seats. Cristofano's frown stifled the last note under the musician's fingers.

I went into the kitchen, where I began to busy myself around the pots and pans and the stove, in order to prepare the next meal.

When all were seated, the doctor opened his bag and took out a handkerchief, with which he carefully wiped the perspiration from his brow (as was his wont before making a speech) and, finally, cleared his throat.

"Most honourable gentlemen, I beg your pardon for having deserted your company a while ago. It was, however, necessary for me to reflect upon our present plight, and I have concluded," he declared, while all fell silent, "… and I have concluded…" repeated Cristofano, with one hand making a ball of his handkerchief, "that if we do not wish to die, we must bury ourselves alive."

The time had come, he explained, for us to cease once and for all wandering around the Donzello as though all was well. No longer would we be able to converse amiably with one another, in despite of the recommendations which he had been imparting to us for several days now. Hitherto, destiny had been all too kind to us, and the misadventures which had befallen Monsieur de Mourai and Pellegrino had proven to have no connection with any infection; but now, matters had taken a turn for the worse, and the plague, which had previously been evoked misleadingly, had truly struck at the Donzello. There was no point in counting how many minutes this or that guest had spent in the company of poor Bedfordi: that would serve only to nourish suspicion. Our one remaining hope of salvation was voluntary segregation, each in his own apartment, so as to avoid inhaling others' humours or coming into contact with the clothing of other guests, etc. etc. We were all to anoint and massage our bodies regularly with purifying oils and balsams which the physician would prepare, and we were to meet only on the occasion of the men-at-arms' roll-calls, the next of which was due on the morrow.

"Lord Jesus," baulked Padre Robleda, "are we to await death crouching on a corner of the floor, next to our own *dejecta*? If I may be permitted," he continued, softening his tone, "I have heard tell that my honourable brother Don Guzmán de Zamora carried out a remarkable work of preservation for himself and his fellow Jesuit missionaries during the Plague of Perpignan in the Kingdom of Catalonia with a *remedium* that was quite pleasant to the palate: excellent white wine to be consumed freely, in which had been dissolved one drachm of couperose and half a drachm of *Dictamnus albus*. He had everyone anointed with Oil of Scorpions and made them all eat well. And none fell ill. Would it not be advisable to try that, before immuring ourselves alive?"

Abbot Melani, whose inquiries would be severely hampered by such seclusion, nodded vigorously in support of Robleda's words: "I too know that white wine of the best quality is regarded as an excellent ingredient against the plague and putrid fevers," said he, forcefully, "and even better are spirits and Malmsey wine. In Pistoia, we have the renowned water which Master Anselmo Ricci adopted with great success to preserve the Pistoiesi from the infection. My father told me and my brothers that all the bishops who had succeeded one another in the pastoral administration consumed this liberally, and not only as a cure. The recipe consisted of five pounds of spirits aromatised with medicinal herbs, to be laid down in the cathedral for twenty-four hours in a hermetically sealed jar. After that, six pounds of the best Malmsey were added. This gave an excellent liquor of which Monsignor the Bishop of Pistoia drank two ounces every morning, with one ounce of honey."

The Jesuit clicked his tongue meaningfully, while Cristofano shook his head sceptically and endeavoured in vain to resume speaking.

"It seems to me undeniable that such remedies gladden the spirits," warned Dulcibeni, "but I doubt whether they can produce other, more important effects. I, too, know of a delicious electuary formulated by Ludovico Giglio of Cremona during the pestilence in Lombardy. It consisted of an excellent condiment of which four drachms were to be spread on toasted bread every morning before breaking one's fast: honey with rose water and a little vinegary syrup made into a paste with agarics, scammony, turbiths and saffron. But everyone died and Giglio avoided being killed only because the survivors were too few and too weak." Thus concluded the aged gentleman from the Marches, leaving it to be understood that, in his opinion, our chances of salvation were indeed few.

"Ah, yes," resumed Cristofano, "like the much-acclaimed cordial and stomach medicine of Tiberio Giarotto of Faenza. A master confectioner's folly: rose-water sugar, aromatised spirits, cinnamon, saffron, sandalwood and red coral, mixed with four ounces of citron juice and left to marinate for fourteen hours. The whole was then mixed with boiling skimmed honey. And to that he added as much musk as was needed to perfume it. He, however, was torn to pieces by the populace. Have trust in me, our only hope is to do as I have said; indeed…"

But Devizé would not allow him to complete his sentence. "Monsieur Pompeo and our chirurgeon are right: Jean Gutierrez, physician to Charles II of France, likewise held that what pleases the palate cannot purify the humours. Nevertheless, Gutierrez did prepare an electuary which it might well be worth trying. Bear in mind that the King was so seized with the virtues of this preparation that he gave

Gutierrez a very great living in the Duchy of Lorraine. Now, in his electuary, that physician incorporated sweetmeats such as cooked and skimmed honey, twenty walnuts and fifteen figs, also a great quantity of rue, wormwood, *terra sigillata* and gemmated salt. He prescribed this to be taken morning and evening, two ounces at a time, to be followed soon after by an ounce of very strong white vinegar, to augment the disgust."

There followed a most heated discussion between those, led by Robleda, who favoured remedies pleasing to the palate and those who saw disgust as providing the best therapy. I followed the discussion in a state approaching amusement (despite the gravity of the moment) at the fact that every single one of our guests seemed always to have been carrying in his pocket a remedy against the infection.

Only Cristofano continued to shake his head: "If you so desire, try all these remedies, but do not come looking for my help when next the distemper strikes!"

"Could we not opt for partial segregation?" proposed Brenozzi shyly. "It is well known that there was an analogous case in Venice during the Plague of 1556: one was allowed to circulate freely in the city's alleyways only if one held in one's hand certain odoriferous balls prepared by the philosopher and poet Girolamo Ruscelli. Unlike the stomach, the nose enjoys perfumes, but may be contaminated by stinks: musk from the Levant, calami, carnations, cloves, nutmeg, spikenard and oil of liquid *amber orientalis*, kneaded into paste. The philosopher made balls the size of walnuts from this and these balls were to be held in both hands at all times, day and night, for as many months as the infection lasted. They were infallible, but only for whoever did not let go of them one single moment, and I do not know how many those were."

Here, Cristofano grew impatient and, rising to his feet, proclaimed with the gravest and most vibrant accents that he cared little whether or not we desired to be secluded in our apartments: this was, however, the last possible remedy and, if we did not consent to it, then he personally would lock himself into his own chamber, begging me to bring him food, nor would he leave it until he knew that all the others were dead—and that would not take long.

There followed a sepulchral silence. Cristofano then continued, announcing that—if we were finally willing to follow his prescriptions— he alone, as our physician, would move freely through the hostelry to assist the sick and regularly to visit the other guests; at the same time, he would need an assistant, whose duty would be to take care of the guests' food and hygiene, as well as to anoint all and to ensure the correct penetration of the balms with which to preserve us from the distemper. Now, he dared not ask any one of us to incur such risks. We could, however, count ourselves fortunate in our misfortune, in that we had in our midst one who—and here, he glanced at me as I moved about the kitchen—according to his long medical experience, was certainly of a fibre well able to resist diseases. All looks turned towards me: the physician had appointed me to assist him.

"The particular condition of this little prentice," continued the chirurgeon from Siena, "renders him, and all those like him, almost immune to the infection."

And, while the listeners' faces all showed signs of astonishment, Cristofano began to enumerate the cases of absolute immunity in times of pestilence recorded by the greatest authors. The *mirabilia* succeeded one another in ascending order, and proved that one like myself could even drink the pus from buboes (as, it seemed, had actually happened during the Black Death three centuries earlier) without suffering anything worse than a little heartburn.

"Fortunius Licetus compares their astounding properties to those of the monopods, the baboons, the Satyrs, the Cyclops, the Tritons and the Sirens. According to the classifications of Father Caspar Schott, the better proportioned their members, the greater is their immunity to infection with the pestilence," concluded Cristofano. "Very well, we can all see that this lad is, as his type goes, rather well formed: solid shoulders, straight legs, a regular visage and healthy teeth. He is fortunate enough to be one of the *mediocres* of his race, and not one of the more unfortunate *minores* or, God forbid, one of the wretched *minimi*. So we may rest in all tranquillity. According to Nierembergius, those like him are born with the teeth, hair and organs of generation of an adult. By the age of seven, they already have a beard, at ten, they have the strength of giants and can generate children. Johannes Eusebius tells of having seen one who at four years of age already had the most elegant locks and a beard. Not to mention the legendary Popobawa who assails and, with his enormous attributes, sodomises in their sleep the robust men of an island in Africa; while they, in their vain struggles, also suffer bruises and fractures."

The first to side with the physician, who sat trembling and again covered in perspiration, was Padre Robleda. The absence of other solutions, together with the fear of being abandoned by Cristofano led the others meekly to resign themselves to claustration. Abbot Melani uttered not a word.

While all were rising to make their way to the upper storeys, the physician said that they could make a halt in the kitchen, where I would distribute a hot meal and toasted bread. He warned me to serve wine only after watering it well down, so that it should pass the more easily through the stomach.

I was all too well aware of the relief which our unhappy guests would have obtained from the culinary assistance of Signor Pellegrino. Instead, the entire administration of the inn now lay upon my shoulders and, despite the fact that I gave my all, I found myself reduced to serving up meals prepared from marinated seeds and whatever else I could find in the old wooden sideboard, while taking practically nothing from the well-stocked pantry in the cellar. I usually added to this some fruit or green vegetables and some of the bread which had been left to us, together with the goatskins of water. Thus, I consoled myself, I was at least saving my master's provisions, already exposed to Cristofano's continual plundering for his electuaries, balsams, oils, lozenges, elixirs and curative balls.

That evening, however, in order to comfort the guests in their misfortune, I made a special effort and prepared a little broth with eggs poached in *bain-marie*, together with vetchlings; to which I added an accompaniment of croquettes of soft bread and a few salt pilchards minced together with herbs and raisins; and, to complete the meal, chicory roots, boiled with cooked must and vinegar. The whole I sprinkled with a pinch of cinnamon; the precious spice of the wealthy would surprise the palates and refresh the spirits.

"It is very hot," I announced with forced good humour to Dulcibeni and Padre Robleda who sat down with lugubrious mien to examine the chicory roots. But I obtained no comments, nor did I remark any sign of cheer in the guests' dark, frowning faces.

৵৵৵

The prospect that my special condition might, in the doctor's opinion, become an arm against the assaults of the disease gave my life its first taste of Pride's inebriating vapours. Although a number of details had left me in some perplexity (at the age of seven I had, of course, been beardless, nor was I born with a set of teeth or with gigantic attributes), I suddenly felt myself a step above the others. And what, said I to myself, thinking over Cristofano's decision, what if I really did have these powers? They, the guests, depended on me. So that was why the physician had so lightly allowed me to sleep in the same chamber as my master, when he was still unconscious! Thus I recovered my good humour, while respectfully containing it.

> *A chi vive ogn'or contento*
> *ogni mese è primavera...* *

sang a lilting voice beside me. It was Abbot Melani.

"What a happy little face," he joked. "Keep it that way until tomorrow, for we shall be needing it."

The reminder of the imminent roll-call brought my feet back down to earth.

"Would you like to accompany me to my sad cloister?" he asked with a little smile after finishing his meal.

"You will return to your apartments alone," exclaimed Cristofano impatiently. "I need the boy's services; and I need them now."

After thus rudely dismissing Atto Melani, the physician ordered me to wash the guests' dishes and the pots and pans. From that moment on, he said, I was to do this at least once a day. He sent me to look for two large basins, clean cloths, walnut shells, pure water and white wine, and brought me with him to visit Bedfordi. He then went into his own chamber to fetch his chirurgeon's equipment and a few bags.

When he returned, I helped him to undress the young Englishman, who was as hot as a cauldron in the fireplace and from time to time launched again into his bouts of logorrhoea.

"The tokens are too hot," observed Cristofano anxiously. "They may require interment."

"I beg your pardon?"

"This is a great and miraculous secret left on his deathbed by the Cavalier Marco Leonardo Fioravanti, the illustrious physician from Bologna, to obtain a rapid cure from the plague: he who already has the tokens is to have himself completely buried in a trench, except

---

* For whoso lives content every hour / Every month will be Spring.

for the neck and the head and is to remain thus for twelve or fourteen hours, and then to be dug out. This is a secret which may be applied anywhere in the world, without incurring interest or expense."

"And how does it work?"

"The earth is mother and purifies all things: it removes all stains from cloths, it softens tough meat upon burial for four or six hours; nor should we forget that in Padua there are mud baths which heal many infirmities. Another remedy of great authority would be to lie from three to twelve hours in the briny waters of the sea. But we, unfortunately, are sequestered and so can do none of those things. The only remedy that remains to us is therefore to practise blood-letting on poor Bedfordi so as to chill his tokens. First, however, we must appease the spoiled humours."

He pulled out a wooden bowl.

"These are my imperial musk tablets, most attractive for the stomach."

"What does that mean?"

"They attract all that there is in the stomach and draw it out, exhausting in the patient that bad resistance which he might put up to the physician's operations."

And between two fingers he took a lozenge, one of those dried preparations of various forms which apothecaries prepare. Not without effort, we succeeded in making Bedfordi swallow this, following which he fell silent and soon seemed on the point of suffocating: he was shaken by trembling and by coughing, and began to foam at the mouth, until he threw up a quantity of malodorous stuff into the basin which I placed just in time under his nose .

Cristofano scrutinised and sniffed at the liquid with an air of satisfaction.

"Prodigious, these musk tablets of mine, do you not find them so? Yet, nothing could be simpler: one ounce of violet candied sugar, five of iris and as many of powdered eggshell, a drachm of musk, one of ambergris, and gum tragacanth and rose water, all dried in the sun," recited Cristofano with an air of satisfaction while he busied himself with collecting the patient's vomit.

"In the healthy, however, they combat loss of appetite, although they are less powerful than *aromaticum*," he added. "Indeed, remind me to give you some to take with you when you distribute meals, in case any should refuse to eat."

Cleaned and rearranged, the poor Englishman now remained silent, with half-closed eyes, while the physician began to prick him with his instruments.

"As Master Eusebio Scaglione from Castello a Mare in the Kingdom of Naples so well teaches, blood is to be extracted from the veins which have their origin in the places where buboes (or tokens, as we call them) have appeared. The vein of the head corresponds to the tokens on the neck and the common vein to those on the back, but not in this instance. Here, we shall bleed the vein of the wrist which starts from the token under his armpit. And then the vein of the foot, which corresponds to the great token in the groin. Pass me the clean basin."

He commanded me to search among his bags for the little jars labelled Burning Bush and Tormentil; he made me take two pinches of each and mix them with three fingers of white wine and then ordered me to administer them to Bedfordi. He then made me pound in the mortar a herb called crowsfoot, with which I was to fill two half walnut shells which the doctor used, once he had completed his blood-letting, to seal the holes in the wrist and the ankle of his unfortunate patient.

"Bandage the walnuts tight. We shall change them twice a day, until blisters appear, which we shall then break in order to squeeze out the poisoned water."

Bedfordi began to tremble.

"May we not have bled him too much?"

"Of course not. It is the pestilence which chills the blood in the veins. I foresaw this: I have prepared a mixture of stinging nettles, mallow, agrimony, centaury, oregano, penny-royal, gentian, laurel, liquid amber, benzoin and aromatico for a most health-giving steam bath."

And from a black felt coverlet, he drew forth a glass vessel. We descended again to the kitchen, where he made me boil the contents of the glass jar with much water in the hostelry's largest cauldron. He in the meanwhile attended to boiling a porridge of fenugreek flour, linseeds and marsh mallow roots, into which I saw him mix pig's lard taken from Signor Pellegrino's stores.

After returning to the sick room, we wrapped Bedfordi in five blankets and placed him above the steaming cauldron which we had carried there at great effort and the risk of severe scalding.

"He must sweat as much as he can: perspiration refines the humours, opens the pores and warms chilled blood, thus preventing the corruption of the skin from causing sudden death."

The unfortunate Englishman did not, however, seem to be of the same opinion. He began to groan more and more, sighing and coughing, reaching out with his hands and splaying his toes in spasms of suffering. Suddenly, he became calm. He seemed to have fainted. Still over the cauldron, Cristofano began to lance the buboes with a three- or four-pointed lancet, after which he applied a poultice of pig's lard. Upon completing the operation, we put the patient back to bed. He did not make a single movement, but he was breathing. What a quirk of destiny, I thought, that precisely his bitterest detractor should be the subject of Cristofano's medical treatment.

"Now, let us leave him to rest, and trust in God," said the doctor gravely.

He led me to his apartment, where he handed me a bag with a number of unguents, syrups and fumigants already prepared for the other guests. He showed me their therapeutic use and purpose, and also furnished a number of notes. Some *remedia* were more effective with certain complexions than with others. Padre Robleda, for example, being ever anxious, risked the most mortal pestilence in the heart or the brain. It would, however, be less grave if he were affected in the liver, which could be relieved by the tokens. I was, urged Cristofano, to begin as soon as possible.

—•—

I could bear it no more. I climbed the stairs, carrying those little jars which I already detested, heading for my bed under the eaves. When I reached the second floor, I was, however, hailed in a loud whisper by Abbot Melani. He was waiting for me, glancing circumspectly out from the half-open door of his chamber. I approached. Without giving me time so much as to open my mouth, he whispered in my ear that the bizarre behaviour of several guests during the past few hours had given him occasion to reflect no little upon our plight.

"Do you perhaps fear for the life of another of us?" I at once murmured in alarm.

"Perhaps, my boy, perhaps," replied Melani hastily, pulling me by the arm into his chamber.

Once he had locked the door, he explained to me that Bedfordi's delirium, which the abbot himself had overheard from behind the door of the sick man's chamber, revealed without the shadow of a doubt that the Englishman was a fugitive.

"A fugitive? Fleeing what?"

"An exile, awaiting better days to return to his country," the abbot pronounced with an impertinent air, tapping the dimple on his chin with his index finger.

It was thus that Atto recounted to me a series of events and circumstances which were to assume great importance in the days that followed. The mysterious William whose name Bedfordi had mentioned was the Prince of Orange, a claimant to the throne of England.

Our interview showed signs of being long-drawn-out: I felt my apprehensions, so strong only moments before, dissipate.

The problem, explained Atto, was that the present king had no legitimate children. He had therefore chosen his brother to succeed him; but the latter was a Catholic and would thus restore the True Religion to the throne of England.

"So, what then is the problem?" I interrupted, overcome by a yawn.

"It is that the English nobility, who follow the reformed religion, do not wish to have a Catholic king and are therefore plotting in favour of William, who is an ardent Protestant. Do lie down on my bed, boy," added the abbot with a voice grown gentler, as he pointed to his couch.

"But then England might remain heretical forever!" I exclaimed, putting down Cristofano's bag and lying down without further ado, while Atto moved to the mirror.

"Right. So in England there are now two factions: one Protestant and Orangist and the other Catholic. Even if he will never admit it, our Bedfordi must belong to the former," he explained, while the acute arching of one eyebrow, which I descried reflected in the mirror, betrayed the scant satisfaction which the abbot was obtaining from the examination of his own reflection.

"And how do you deduce that?" I asked, growing curious.

"From what I could gather, Bedfordi stayed awhile in Holland, a land of Calvinists."

"In Holland there are also Catholics: I know this from our guests who have sojourned long there, and they are surely faithful to the Church of Rome..."

"Of course. But the United Provinces are also William's country. Some ten years ago, the Prince of Orange defeated the invading army of Louis XIV. And now Holland is the stronghold of the Orangist conspirators," retorted Atto as, with a snort of impatience, he pulled out a little brush and a small box and rouged his rather prominent cheeks.

"In other words, you think that Bedfordi went to Holland in order to conspire in favour of the Prince of Orange," I commented, trying not to stare too hard at him.

"No, no, let us not exaggerate," he replied, turning to me after taking one last satisfied look in the mirror. "I believe that Bedfordi is simply one of those who would like to see William on the throne, also because—do not forget this—in England the heretics are very numerous. He will be one of many messengers moving back and forth across the English Channel, at the risk of being arrested sooner or later and imprisoned in the Tower of London…"

He paused, drew up a chair and sat down by the bedside.

"You see then that we are not far from the truth."

"It is incredible," I commented, while all sleepiness receded.

I was both intimidated and agitated by these marvellous and suggestive accounts. Remote and powerful conflicts between the reigning powers of Europe were materialising before my eyes, in this hostelry where I was but a poor apprentice.

"But who is this Prince William of Orange, Signor Atto?" I asked.

"Oh, a great soldier, overwhelmed with debts. That is all," replied the abbot drily. "For the rest, his life is absolutely flat and colourless, as are his person and his spirit."

"A penniless prince?" I asked incredulously.

"Indeed. And if he were not always short of money, who knows what he might not have achieved?"

I remained pensive and silent.

"Of course, never, but never would I ever have suspected that Bedfordi might be a fugitive," I resumed after a moment.

"We have another fugitive too. One who hails from a distant maritime city," added Melani with a little smile, while his face, which had drawn gradually nearer and nearer, looked down on me.

"Brenozzi the Venetian?!" I exclaimed, raising my head from the bed with a start and involuntarily striking the snub nose of the abbot, who let out a groan.

"Precisely him, of course," he confirmed, rising to his feet and massaging his nose.

"But how can you be so sure of that?"

"If you had listened to Brenozzi's words with greater perspicacity and, above all, if your awareness of worldly matters had been more extensive, you would certainly have noticed something unconvincing," he replied in a vaguely vexed tone of voice.

"Well, he did say that a cousin..."

"A distant cousin born in London, from whom he learned English simply by corresponding: now, do you not find that explanation a trifle curious?"

And he reminded me of how the glass-blower had dragged me downstairs by force and almost shocked me out of my senses and then subjected me to a flood of questions concerning the Turkish siege and the infection which was perhaps overcoming the resistance of Vienna, after which he had babbled of marguerites.

Only, continued Atto, he was not speaking of daisies, but of one of the most precious treasures of the Most Serene Venetian Republic, which it was prepared to defend by all means and which was doubtless the cause of our Brenozzi's present troubles. The islands which lie at the heart of the Venetian lagoon guard a secret source of wealth which the Doges, who for centuries have been at the head of that Most Serene Republic, watch over jealously. In those isles are manufactures of glass and of decorated pearls, known in Latin as *margaritae* (or "daisies"), and the art of manufacturing these depends upon secrets handed down for many generations, of which the Venetians are both proud and inordinately jealous.

"But then the daisies—the marguerites—which he mentioned and the little pearls which he put into my hand are one and the same thing," I exclaimed confusedly. "But how much could they be worth?"

"You cannot even imagine it. If you had travelled a tenth as much as I have, you would know that there clings to the trinkets of Murano the copious blood of the Venetians; and for these, it will perhaps flow until who knows when," said Melani, seating himself at his desk.

Many master glass-blowers and their apprentices had, indeed, attempted to flee to Paris, London, Vienna and Amsterdam, but also to Rome or Genoa, where they sometimes found more generous masters and commerce with fewer competitors.

Such fugues were not however to the taste of the magistrates of the Council of the Ten of Venice, who had no intention of losing control of that art, which had brought so much money into the coffers of the Doges; and they had therefore placed the matter in the hands of the State Inquisitors, the special council responsible for ensuring that no secret should be propagated which might be prejudicial to the interests of the Most Serene Republic.

The Inquisitors were most skilful: violence was followed by promises and blandishments, damage to new workshops and threats to relatives remaining in Venice; everything possible to persuade the glass-blowers to return.

"And did the glass-blowers return?"

"You should rather be asking 'do they return?', for the drama continues to this day and I think that it is being played out even in this hostelry. For those unwilling to return, there is the skilful and secretive work of the assassin. To steel, which announces violent death, they often prefer poison. That is why our Brenozzi is so worried," concluded Abbot Melani. "The maker of *margaritae*, glass or mirrors who flees Venice finds himself in hell. He sees assassins and betrayal everywhere, he sleeps with one eye open, he keeps looking over his shoulder. And Brenozzi, too, has surely known the violence and the threats of the inquisitors."

"And I, who ingenuously allowed myself to become so scared when Cristofano spoke to me of the powers of my little pearls," I exclaimed, not without some shame. "Only now do I understand why Brenozzi asked me, with such a nasty expression, whether those three pearls were enough. With those three little pearls, he wanted to buy my silence about our conversation."

"Bravo, you have grasped the point."

"Yet, do you not find it strange that there should be two fugitives present in this inn?" I asked, alluding to the presence of both Bedfordi and Brenozzi.

"Not so strange. In recent years, not a few have fled London, and no fewer, Venice. Your master is probably not the kind of person who tends to spy on his guests and nor, no doubt, was Signora Luigia Bonetti who kept the inn before him. Perhaps the Donzello is considered to be a 'discreet' hostelry where those fleeing from serious trouble can find refuge. The names of such places are often passed on by word of mouth from one exile to another. Remember: the world is full of people who want to flee their own past."

I had in the meanwhile risen from where I was lying and, taking the necessary from my bag, I poured into a bowl a syrup which the physician had indicated to me for the abbot. I explained to him briefly what it was and Atto drank it without complaint. Then he rose to his feet and, singing to himself, began organising some papers on the table:

In questo duro esilio… *

It was curious how Atto Melani could draw from his own repertory the perfect little aria for each occasion. He must, I thought, hold a truly lively and tender affection for the memory of his Roman master, Le Seigneur Luigi, as he called him.

"So poor Brenozzi is in a state of great anxiety," resumed Abbot Melani. "And he may, sooner or later, ask you again for help. By the way, my boy, you have a drop of oil on your head." He wiped the little spot from my forehead with a fingertip and carelessly brought it to his lips, sucking it.

"Do you believe that the poison which killed Mourai could have anything to do with Brenozzi?" I asked him.

"I would exclude that," he answered with a smile. "I think that our poor glass-blower is the only one to entertain such a fear."

"Why did he ask me, too, about the siege of Vienna?"

"And you, tell me: where is the Most Serene Republic?"

"Near to the Empire, just to the south, and…"

"That is quite enough: if Vienna capitulates, in a few days the Turks will spread out, above all to the south, entering Venice. Our Brenozzi must have spent quite a long time in England, where he was able to learn English discreetly in person, and not by correspondence. No, he would probably like to return to Venice, but he realises that the time is not propitious."

"In other words, he risks falling straight into the hands of the Turks."

"Precisely. He must have come as far as Rome, hoping perhaps to be able to set up shop and thus to find shelter. But he understood that here too the fear is great: if the Turks succeed in Vienna, after Venice, they will come to the Duchy of Ferrara. They will cross the Romagna and the Duchies of Urbino and Spoleto, and moving beyond the gentle hills of Umbria, they will leave Viterbo on their right and head…"

* In this hard exile…

"For us," I shivered, realising clearly for the first time the danger that hung over us.

"It is not necessary for me to explain to you what would happen in that eventuality," said Atto. The Sack of Rome a century and a half ago would be a mere trifle by comparison. The Turks will lay waste to the Papal States, taking their natural ferocity to its most extreme consequences. Basilicas and churches, beginning with Saint Peter's, will be razed to the ground. Priests, bishops and cardinals will be dragged from their houses and their throats cut, crucifixes and other symbols of the Faith will be torn down and burned; the people will be robbed, the women horribly violated, the cities and countryside will be ruined forever. And if that first collapse takes place, all Christendom may well end up a prey to the Turkish horde."

The Infidel army, bursting out from the woods of Latium, would next cross the Grand Duchy of Tuscany, then the Duchy of Parma, and, passing through the Most Serene Republic of Genoa and the Duchy of Savoy, it would overflow into French territory (and here perhaps I saw on Abbot Melani's face a trace of genuine horror) in the direction of Marseilles and Lyons. And at that point, at least in theory, it could head for Versailles.

It was then that, giving way again to discomfiture and taking my leave of Atto on a vague pretext, I picked up my bag and ran upstairs, stopping only when I reached the short stairway leading to the little tower.

❧

At this point, I gave free rein to all my anxieties, abandoning myself to a doleful soliloquy. Here was I, a prisoner in a cramped hostelry which was suspected, with good reason now, of harbouring the plague. Hardly had I succeeded in shaking off that terror, thanks to the words of the physician, who foretold my resistance to infection, when Melani came telling that I ran the risk of leaving the Locanda del Donzello only to find Rome invaded by the sanguinary followers of Mahomet. I had always known that I could count only on the kindness of a very few persons, among them Pellegrino, who had generously saved me from the hardships and dangers of life; this time, however, I could count only on the (surely not disinterested) company of a castrato abbot and spy, whose precepts were for me almost exclusively a source of fear and anguish. And the inn's other lodgers? A bilious-tempered Jesuit, a shady and inconstant gentleman from the Marches, a brusque-mannered French guitarist, a Tuscan physician whose ideas were confused and perhaps even dangerous, together with my master and Bedfordi, who lay supine in their beds. Never before had I experienced so deeply the sentiment of solitude, when my murmurings were suddenly interrupted by an invisible force which knocked me backwards, leaving me lying spread-eagled on the floor; and there, looking down on me, stood the guest whom I had omitted from my silent inventory.

"You frightened me, silly!"

Cloridia, feeling a strange presence behind her door (on which I had in fact been leaning) had opened it suddenly, causing me to roll into her chamber. I rose to my feet without even trying to excuse myself and hastily wiped my face.

"And anyway," she went on "there are disasters worse than the plague or the Turks."

"Did you hear my thoughts?" I responded, astonished.

"In the first place, you were not thinking, because whoever truly thinks has no time for snivelling. And besides, we are in quarantine on suspicion of infection, and in Rome these days no one can sleep a single night without dreaming of the Turks entering through the Porta del Popolo. Whatever should *you* have to whine about?"

And she handed me a dish with, on it, a glass half full of spirits and an aniseed ring-cake. I was about to seat myself timidly on the edge of her high bed.

"No, not there."

I stood up instinctively, spilling half the liquor on the carpet and somehow catching the cake but covering the bed with crumbs. Cloridia said nothing. I fumbled for an excuse and tried to make amends for the little disaster, wondering why she had not harshly scolded me, like Signor Pellegrino and indeed all the guests of the *locanda* (except, it is true, Abbot Melani whose conduct in regard to me was more liberal).

The young woman who stood before me was the one person of whom I knew so little, yet what I knew was certain. My contacts with her were limited to the meals which my master ordered me to prepare and bring to her, to the sealed notes which she would sometimes ask me to deliver to this or that person, to the maids whom she often changed and whom from time to time I would instruct in the use of the water and the pantry in the hostelry. That was all. For the rest, I knew nothing of how she lived in the little tower where she received guests who entered through the passage that gave on to the roof; nor did I need to know anything.

She was not a common prostitute, she was a courtesan: too rich to be a harlot, too avaricious not to be one. Yet all that is not sufficient to understand properly what a courtesan might be, and of what refined arts she might be mistress.

Everybody knew what took place in the "stufe", those hot vapour baths imported into Rome by a German and recommended for eliminating putrid humours through perspiration. Those baths were for the most part kept by women of easy virtue (indeed, there was one within a stone's throw of the Donzello which was generally regarded as the most famous and ancient in Rome and was known as the *Stufa delle Donne*, the Women's Baths. Everybody knew, except me, what commerce one could have with certain women near Sant'Andrea delle Fratte, or in the vicinity of Via Giulia, or at Santa Maria in Via; and it was common knowledge that at Santa Maria in Monterone an identical business took place even in the parish apartments; and in former centuries the pontiffs had found it necessary to forbid the clergy to live in the same neighbourhood as such women, yet these prohibitions had as often as not been ignored or circumvented. In any case, it was perfectly clear who hid behind such noble Latin names as Lucrezia, Cornelia, Medea, Pentesilea, Flora, Diana, Vittoria, Polissena, Prudenzia or Adriana; or what was the true identity of the Duchessa or the Reverendissima, who had been so bold as to filch their titles from illustrious protectors; or, again, what lusts Selvaggia and Smeralda enjoyed unleashing, or what was the true nature of Fior di Crema, or why Gravida—the Fragrant One—was called by that name, or indeed what trade Lucrezia-the-Slut carried on.

What point was there in investigating all this? That had already been done a century and more ago and, furthermore, a classification had even been made of all the categories: *meretrici, puttane, curiali* (those of the Curia), whores of the lamp, of the candle, of the Venetian blinds, of the silhouettes, and "women in trouble, or of lesser fortune", while some burlesque ballads sang, too, of the Sunday girls, the church mice, the Guelf girls, the Ghibellines and a thousand others. How many were they? Enough to give Pope Leo X the idea, when repairs had to be made to the road leading to the Piazza del Popolo, of levying a tax on the harlots, of whom many lived in that quarter. Under Pope Clement VII, some swore that every tenth Roman was engaged in prostitution (not even counting bawds and pimps), and perhaps Saint Augustine was right when he said that if prostitutes were to disappear, unbridled licence would flourish everywhere.

The courtesans, however, were of quite another kind. For, with them, mere amorous beguilements were transformed into a sublime exercise: one that gave the measure not of the appetites of merchants or the soldiery, but of the genius of ambassadors, princes and cardinals. Genius, because the courtesan jousted against men victoriously in verse, like Gaspara Stampa who dedicated an entire ardent *canzoniere* to Collatino di Collalto, or Veronica Franco who challenged the potentates of the Venier family both in bed and in poetry; or like Imperia, the queen of Roman courtesans, who would gracefully compose madrigals and sonnets, and was loved by men of such illustrious and opulent talents as Tommaso Inghirami, Camillo Porzio, Bernardino Capella, Angelo Colocci and the unbelievably wealthy Agostino Chigi, and who posed for Raphael and may have rivalled the Fornarina herself. (Imperia died by her own hand, yet on her deathbed, Pope Julius II granted her full absolution for her sins, while Chigi had a monument erected to her). The celebrated Madremianonvuole,* thus nicknamed following some imprudent juvenile refusal, knew all of Petrarch and Boccaccio by heart, as well as Virgil and Horace, and a hundred other authors.

So the woman before me belonged, in Pietro Aretino's words, to that shameless race whose pomp leaves Rome drained, while through the streets the wives go veiled and muttering paternosters.

"Have you, too, come to ask what the future holds in store for you?" asked Cloridia. "Are you in search of good news? Take care, for fortune—and so I tell all those who come here—does not always ordain matters as one might desire."

Taken by surprise, I was rendered speechless.

"I know nothing of magic. And if you wish to know the arcana of the stars, you must go to someone else. But if no one has ever read your hand, then Cloridia's is indeed the door to come to. Or perhaps you have dreamed a dream and wish to know its hidden meaning.

* My-mother-doesn't-want-me-to

Do not tell me that you came here without any desire, for I will not believe you. No one ever comes to Cloridia without wanting something."

I was at once curious and so excited that I found it hard to keep my composure. I remembered that I was supposed to administer Cristofano's remedies to her, too, but that I put off. Instead, I seized my opportunity and told her of the nightmare in which I had seen myself fall into the obscure cavity below the Donzello.

"No, no, it is not clear," commented Cloridia at the end, shaking her head. "Was the ring of gold or of base metal?"

"I could not say."

"Then the interpretation is unclear; because a ring signifies a reward or a punishment. A gold ring signifies great profit. I find the trumpet interesting, for it betokens secrets, hidden or revealed. Perhaps Devizé is the holder of some secret, which he may or may not be aware of. Does that mean anything to you?"

"No, I really know only that he is the most splendid guitar player," said I, remembering the marvellous music which I had heard issuing from the strings of his instrument.

"Of course, you can know no more, otherwise Devizé's secret would not be one!" laughed Cloridia. "But in your dream Pellegrino too is present. You saw him dead and then resuscitated, and the dead who rise again signify travail and damage. So, let us see: a ring, a secret, a dead man resuscitated. The meaning, I repeat, is not clear because of the ring. The only clear things are the secret and the dead man."

"Then the dream presages misadventures."

"Not necessarily: because in reality your master is only sick, and in a bad way, but not dead. And illness means simply idleness and little employment. Perhaps, since Pellegrino has not been well, you are afraid that you have been neglecting your duties. But do not be afraid of me," said Cloridia, lazily extracting another ring-cake from a basket. "I shall certainly be the last person to tell Pellegrino if you are a little disinclined to work. Tell me, rather, what are they saying downstairs? Apart from the unfortunate Bedfordi, it seems to me that the others are all still in good health, is that not so?" and, with a vague gesture, she added, "Pompeo Dulcibeni, for instance? I ask you, seeing that he is one of the oldest..."

Again Cloridia was asking me about Dulcibeni. I hung back, feeling dejected. She understood at once: "And don't be afraid of coming close to me," said she, drawing me to her and ruffling my hair. "I, for the time being, do not have the plague."

I then recalled my duties concerning health and mentioned that Cristofano had already delivered me the preventive remedies to be administered to all those in good health. Blushing, I added that I was to begin with the violet unguent of Master Giacomo Bortolotto from Parma, which I was supposed to spread on her back and her hips.

She fell silent. I smiled weakly: "If you prefer, I also have here the fumigants of Orsolin Pignuolo from Pontremoli. We could begin with those, seeing that you have a fireplace in your chamber."

"Very well," she answered. "So long as it does not take too much time."

She sat down at her dressing table. I saw her uncover her shoulders and gather her locks up into a white muslin bonnet tied with crossed ribbons. Meanwhile, I attended to making a fire and gathering the burning coals from the fireplace in a pot, trembling briefly when I thought of the nudity which those coals must have seen during those still warm mid-September nights.

I turned again towards her. On her head she had placed a piece of linen, folded double: she resembled a holy apparition.

"Carob, myrrh, incense, liquid amber, benzoin, gum ammoniac, antimony, made into a paste with the finest rose water," I recited, having studied Cristofano's notes well, while placing the bowl of coals lightly on the little table and breaking a bag into it. "I must insist, breathe in with wide open mouth."

And I pulled down the fine linen cloth until it covered her face. The room filled swiftly with a pungent odour.

"The Turks make far better health-bringing fumigants than these," she muttered after a while from under the cloth.

"But we are not Turks yet," I replied clumsily.

"And would you believe it if I told you that I am one?" I heard her ask.

"No, of course not, Donna Cloridia."

"And why ever not?

"Because you were born in Holland, in…"

"In Amsterdam, correct. And how come that you knew?"

I was at a loss for a reply, since I had learned that detail only a few days earlier, when I stopped at Cloridia's door before knocking to deliver a basket of fruit and overheard a conversation between her and an unknown visitor.

One of my girls will have told you, I suppose. Yes, I was born in a land of heretics almost nineteen years ago, but Calvin and Luther have never counted me among their own. I never knew my mother, while my father was an Italian merchant, who travelled a great deal."

"Oh, how fortunate you are!" I sighed from the depths of my mere foundling's estate.

She said nothing, and from the movement of her bust I guessed that she was inhaling deeply. She coughed.

"If one day you should ever have to do with Italian merchants, just remember: they leave only debts to others and keep the profits for themselves."

Cloridia explained that in Amsterdam she herself had known intimately the fame of the Tensini, the Verrazzanos, the Balbi, the Quingetti, and then the Burlamacchi and the Calandrini, who were also present in Antwerp: Genoese, Tuscans, Venetians, all merchants, insurers, shipowners, bankers and bill brokers, a few agents of Italian principalities and republics, and for freedom from scruples there were none who could outdo them.

"What does 'bill broker' mean?" I asked, leaning with my elbows on the little table, the better to hear and be heard.

"It is one who acts as go-between between a lender of money and someone who borrows it."

I brought my face close to hers: after all, she could not see me. And that made me feel very sure of myself.

"Is that a good profession?"

"If you wish to know whether those who exercise it are good people, well, that depends. If the question is whether this is work that makes one rich, why, that is for certain. Indeed, it makes those who practise it exceedingly wealthy. The Bartolotti, whose house on the Heerengracht is the finest in the whole city, started out as simple brewers and are now the most powerful people in Amsterdam, shareholders and financiers of the East India Company."

Then Cloridia gasped: "May I get up?"

"No, Monna Cloridia, not while there is still smoke!" I stopped her, although I myself felt the exhalations going to my head. I did not want to bring our conversation to so early a conclusion. Almost without realising it, I had begun to stroke a corner of the piece of linen which covered her head: she could not be aware of that.

"Are the shipowners and insurers as wealthy?" I asked.

She sighed. At this point, my ingenuous questions, together with my limited knowledge of the world (and of circumstances which I could not at present be blamed for not knowing) all had the effect of loosing Cloridia's tongue. Suddenly, she inveighed against merchants and their money, but above all against bankers, whose wealth was at the root of all manner of iniquity (only, here in truth, Cloridia used far harsher language and spoke with very different accents), especially when money was lent by usurers and brokers, and most of all, when those to whom it was destined were kings and popes.

Cloridia had risen from the hot coals and torn off the covering from her head, causing me to step sharply back, red with shame. She then cast off her bonnet and her long curly mane fanned out across her shoulders.

She appeared to me then for the first time in a new and indescribable light, capable of cancelling out all that I had hitherto seen of her—and above all, what I had not yet seen, but which seemed to me even more indelible—and I saw with my pupils and even more with my soul all that lovely lucent brown velvet complexion which contrasted with her luxuriant Venetian blond curls. Little did I then care that I knew them to be the creation of white wine lees and olive oil, if they framed those long black eyes and the serrated pearls of her mouth, that rounded yet proud little nose, those lips smiling with a touch of rouge just sufficient to remove their vague pallor, and that small but fine and harmonious face and the fine snow of her bosom, intact and kissed by two suns, on shoulders worthy of a bust by Bernini or so at least it seemed to me *et satis erat*, and her voice which, although distorted and almost booming with rage, or perhaps precisely because of that, filled me with lascivious little desires and little languid sighs, with rustic frenzies, with flower-strewn dreams, with a lusciously odorous vegetable delirium, until it seemed that I could become almost invisible to others' eyes, through the mist of desire that enveloped me and made Cloridia appear to me more sublime than a Raphael Madonna, more inspired than a motto of Teresa of Ávila, more marvellous than a verse of the *cavaliere* Marino, more melodious than a madrigal of Monteverdi, more lascivious than a couplet by Ovid and more edifying than an entire tome of Fracastoro. And I said to myself that, no, the poetics of an Imperia, of a Veronica, of a Madremianonvuole would never have such power (although my soul was weighed down with knowing that a few paces from the locanda, in the Stufa delle Donne, there lay in wait low females, ready and willing for anything, even for me, so long as I had but two scudi) and while I listened to her, in a lightning flash as rapid as Cardinal Chigi's horses, I was transfixed by the mystery of how I, who time and time again had brought to her door the tub, with pails of boiling hot water, for her bath, could possibly have remained indifferent to her presence behind those few wooden planks, with her servant-girl gently rubbing the nape of her neck with talcum and lavender water, so much did she now fire my mind and my senses and my whole spirit.

And thus absorbed I lost sight (and only later was I to realise this) of how bizarre was all that inveighing against merchants by a merchant's daughter, and above all how unexpected those protestations of horror for lucre in the mouth of a courtesan.

And in addition to being blind to such strange behaviour, I was almost deaf, too, to the rhythmic drumming of Cristofano's knuckles on Cloridia's door. She, however, responded promptly to his courteous request to enter and invited the physician in. He had sought me everywhere. He needed my help in preparing a decoction: Brenozzi was complaining of a great pain in the jaw and had requested a remedy. Thus was I unwillingly snatched away from my first colloquy with the only feminine guest of the Donzello.

We at once took leave of one another. With the eyes of hope I strove to discover in her countenance some trace of sadness at our separation, and that despite my descrying—as I was closing the door—the most horrible scar on her wrist, which disfigured her almost as far as the back of her hand.

∫⁕∫

Cristofano brought me down to the kitchen, where he instructed me to find a number of seeds, herbs and a new candle. He then made me heat a cooking pot with a little water while he reduced the ingredients to powder and sieved them, and when the water was hot enough, we put in the fine mixture which immediately gave off a most agreeable aroma. While I was preparing the fire for the decoction,

I asked him whether it was true, as I had heard say, that I could use white wine also for cleaning and whitening my teeth.

"Of course, and you would attain a good, indeed, a perfect result, if you only were to use it as a mouth-wash. If, however, you should mix it with white clay, you would see a very fine effect which will greatly please the young ladies. You must rub it into the teeth and gums, ideally with a piece of scarlet such as that over Cloridia's bed, on which you were sitting."

I feigned not to have noticed the double allusion and hastened to change the subject, asking Cristofano if he had ever heard tell of his Tuscan compatriots, such as the Calandrini, the Burlamacchi, the Tensini, and others (although in reality there were a couple of names which I could not recall without distorting them). And, while he ordered me to put the mixture of herbs and wax into the cooking pot, Cristofano replied that, yes, some of those names were quite well known in Tuscany. They were, however, all so bound up with trade with Holland, where they had bought lands, villas and palaces, that in Tuscany they were known as the *infiamengati*—the new Flemings. Some had made their fortune, had married into and had become kinsmen of noble families of that country; others were crushed under the weight of their debts and of them no more news had been heard. Others had died in ships that had sunk among the Arctic ice floes of Archangel or in the waters of Malabar. Others had eventually grown rich, and at an advanced age had preferred to return to their own land, where they were accorded well-merited honours: like Francesco Feroni, a poor dyer from Empoli, who had begun by trading with Guinea old sheets, bright buntings from Delft, cotton canvas, Venetian beads, quantities of spirits, Spanish wines and strong beer. With his trade, he had grown so rich that in the Grand Duchy of Tuscany he was famous even before his return home, also for having served as an excellent ambassador of the Grand Duke Cosimo III de' Medici, in the United Provinces. When at length he did decide to return to Tuscany, the Grand Duke himself had him appointed his Depositary-General, thus arousing the envy of all Florence. Feroni had brought back conspicuous wealth to Tuscany, and had purchased a splendid villa in the country of Bellavista, and despite all the evil that the Florentines could say of him, he could count himself fortunate to have returned to his home country and have escaped all dangers.

"Such as going down with one's ship?"

"Not only that, my boy! Certain trades involve enormous risks."

I should have liked to ask him what he meant, but the decoction was ready and Cristofano told me to bring it to Brenozzi in his little chamber on the second floor. Following the doctor's instructions, I recommended the Venetian to inhale the steam while it was still hot, with his mouth wide open: after such a treatment, his jaw would hurt far less or not at all. Afterwards, Brenozzi was to leave the cooking pot outside his door for collection. Thanks to his toothache, I was spared his garrulousness. Thus I could return at once to the kitchen to resume my conversation with the physician before he regained his apartment. It was, however, Abbot Melani whom I found there.

I struggled to hide my consternation. The brief time I had spent with Cloridia, concluding with the disquieting vision of her martyred wrist, together with her singular diatribe against merchants, made me feel a desperate need to interrogate Cristofano further. The doctor, however, following his own prescription, had prudently regained his chamber without waiting for me. And now Atto Melani, whom I found rummaging carelessly in the pantry, had come to oppress my thoughts yet further. I pointed out to him that his disobedience of the physician's instructions endangered all of us and it would be my duty to advise Cristofano; it was, moreover, not yet time for supper and I would in any case soon be busy preparing the wherewithal to satisfy the appetite of our honourable guests, if only (and here I cast a meaningful eye on the slice of bread which Melani held in his hand)... if only I could dispose freely of the larder.

Abbot Melani tried to conceal his own embarrassment, and replied that he had been looking for me to tell me certain things which were on his mind, but I cut him off and told him that I was tired of having to listen to him when we were all obviously in dire danger, nor did I yet know what he really wanted or was looking for, and I did not wish to be party to goings-on of which I did not understand the purpose and that the time had now come for him to explain himself and to dispel all possible doubts, for I had heard gossip concerning him which did not do him honour, and before placing myself at his service, I demanded adequate explanations.

The meeting with Cloridia must have endowed me with new and fresh talents, for my audacious discourse seemed to catch Abbot Melani utterly unprepared. He said he was surprised that someone in the hostelry should think that he could dare dishonour him without paying the price and demanded, without great conviction, that I reveal the name of that insolent fellow.

He then swore that he in no way intended to abuse of my services and affected utter astonishment: had I perhaps forgotten that he and I together were seeking to discover the unknown thief of Pellegrino's keys and of my little pearls? And indeed, before all that, was it not urgently necessary that we should understand if there was any connection between those events and the assassination of Monsieur de Mourai, and how all that related—if indeed there were any relation—to the misadventures which had befallen my master and the young Bedfordi? Did I no longer fear, he reproved me, for the lives of us all?

Despite the unstoppable flow of his words, it was clear to me that the abbot was becoming muddled.

Encouraged by the success of my sudden sally, I interrupted him impatiently and, with a corner of my heart still turning towards Cloridia, I demanded that Melani explain to me instantly what had brought him to Rome and what his intentions were.

While I felt my pulse pounding hard in my temples and mentally wiped the sweat from my brow at the audacity of my claims, I was utterly taken aback by the reaction of Abbot Melani. Instead of rejecting the arrogant pretensions of a mere apprentice, his expression changed suddenly and with all simplicity and courtesy he invited me to sit down in a corner of the kitchen so that he could satisfy my just demands. Once we had taken our places, the abbot began to describe to me a series of circumstances which, although they seemed fantastic, I must, in the light of what later transpired, take to be true or at least to possess the appearance of truth, and these I shall therefore report as faithfully as possible.

࠺࠾

Abbot Melani began by saying that in the last days of August, Colbert had fallen gravely ill, and was soon so close to death that it was feared this might follow within days. As happens on such occasions, in other words when a statesman who is the repository of many secrets is approaching the end of his life on earth, Colbert's house in the Richelieu quarter suddenly became the object of the most varied visits, some disinterested, others less so. Among the latter was that of Atto himself, who, thanks to the excellent references which he enjoyed from no less than his Most Christian Majesty in person, had been able without great difficulty to gain access to the four walls of the minister's home. There, the great coming and going of persons of the court calling to pay their last tribute to the dying man (or simply to show their faces) had enabled the abbot to slip quietly out of an antechamber and, circumventing the already lax surveillance, to enter the private apartments of the master of the house. Here he had in truth twice come close to being discovered by the servants as he hid behind an arras or under a table.

Somehow escaping discovery, he had in the end entered Colbert's study where, at last feeling himself to be safe, he had begun to rummage hastily among the letters and documents which were most readily and rapidly accessible. Twice, he had been compelled to break off his inspection, alarmed by the passage of strangers in the nearby corridor. The documents over which he had been able to cast a swift glance seemed practically devoid of interest: correspondence with the Ministry for War, affairs of the navy, letters concerning the Manufactures of France, appointments, accounts, minutes; nothing out of the ordinary. Then, once again he had heard through the door the approach of other visitors. He could not risk the bruiting abroad of the news that Abbot Melani had been surprised taking advantage of Colbert's illness to go clandestinely through the minister's papers. He had therefore confusedly grabbed and slipped into his breeches a few bunches of correspondence and notes piled in the drawers of the desk and the cabinets, to which he had without great difficulty found the keys.

"But had you permission to do this?"

"To ensure the King's security, every act is permitted," the abbot retorted drily.

He was already scrutinising the shady corridor before leaving the study (for his visit, the abbot had chosen the late afternoon, so as to be able to count on the declining light) when, through the corner of his eye, intuition caused him to catch sight of a small chest in an obscure recess half-hidden by the draperies of a heavy curtain and the massive flank of an ebony cupboard.

It lay under a considerable pile of white sheets of paper, on top of which balanced an imposing lectern with a richly carved foot; and on that lectern, a folder tied with a brand-new cord.

"It seemed as yet untouched," explained Atto.

Indeed, Colbert's illness, a violent renal colic, had peaked only a few weeks earlier. For several days, it was said that he had no longer attended to any business; this meant that the folder might still be waiting to be read. The decision was made in a flash: he put down all that he had taken and took the folder with him. Hardly had he picked it up, however, than his eyes again alighted on the pile of blank sheets of paper, deformed by the weight of the lectern

"'A fine place to leave writing paper,' I muttered to myself, attributing such a *bêtise* to the usual careless servant."

Taking the lectern under his left arm, the abbot tried to look through the still virgin sheets of paper, in case some interesting document should be hidden there. Nothing. It was paper of excellent quality, smooth and heavy. He did, however, find that some leaves had been cut in a way that was as accurate as it was singular: they all had the same form, like a star with irregular points.

"I thought at first that this might be some senile mania of the *Coluber*. Then I noticed that some of these papers bore marks of rubbing and, on the edge of one of the points, slight striations of what appeared to be black grease. I was still puzzling this over," continued Atto, "when I noticed that the great weight of the lectern was making my arm stiff. I decided to put it down on the writing desk when I remarked with horror that a corner of the delicate lace of my cuffs had been caught in a crudely fashioned joint of the lectern."

When the abbot succeeded in freeing the lace, it bore traces of black grease.

"Ah, you presumptuous little snake-in-the-grass, did you think you could deceive me?" thought Melani with a flash of sudden insight.

And swiftly he picked up one of the still new paper stars. Studying it carefully, he placed it on top of one of the used ones, turning it quickly until he could see which was the right point. Then he inserted it in the joint of the lectern. Nothing happened. Nervously, he tried again: still nothing. By then, the star was already crumpled and he had to take another one. This time, he inserted it in the joint with the greatest of care, holding his ear close to the operation, like a master clockmaker listening for the first tick of the mechanism he has returned to new life. And it was precisely a slight click that the abbot heard as soon as the tip of the paper reached the extremity of the slot: one end of the foot of the lectern had sprung open like a drawer, revealing a small cavity. In it lay an envelope bearing the effigy of a serpent.

"Such a presumptuous snake-in-the-grass," Abbot Melani muttered to himself before the emblem of the *Coluber* which so unexpectedly confronted him.

At that moment, Atto heard in the corridor the bustle of rapidly approaching footsteps. He took the envelope, adjusted his jacket in order to conceal as well as possible the bulge created by the parcel and held his breath, hidden behind an arras, while he heard a man arrive before the study door. Someone opened that door and said, turning to the others, "He will already have gone in."

Colbert's servants, not having heard Abbot Melani enter the dying man's sickroom, had begun to search for him. The door closed again, the servant returned whence he had come. Abbot Melani left in complete silence and moved without haste towards the main entrance. Here he greeted a valet with an easy smile: "He will soon be better," said he, looking him straight in the eye as he went through the door.

In the days that followed, no word reached him of the disappearance of any folder, and the abbot was able to peruse it at his ease.

"Pardon me, Signor Atto," I interrupted him, "but how did you understand which was the right point of the paper to insert into the joint?"

"Simple: all the paper stars that had already been used had traces of grease at exactly the same place. It had been a gross error on the Serpent's part to leave it there. Clearly, his senses had begun to grow dull of late."

"And why did the secret drawer not open at once?"

"Stupidly, I had thought it was a crude mechanism," sighed Atto, "which would be activated as soon as one touched the end of the aperture with the right key: in other words, with the point of the paper inserted at the right angle. But I had underestimated the French cabinet-makers' skill in inventing ever more remarkable devices. In reality (and here was why it was so important to use superior materials like those leaves of exquisitely fashioned paper) the mechanism was complex and involved many highly sensitive metal parts not situated directly behind the opening but at one remove from there, and only a slow stroking of both sides could activate all the parts in perfect succession."

I remained silent, lost in admiration.

"I should have understood at once," concluded Atto with a grimace. "The used stars were blackened not precisely at the tip but along both sides."

His instinct had not deceived him: into his hands had fallen one of the most extraordinary finds. Inside the envelope stamped with the face of the Serpent (and he emphasised the word) was a letter in Latin sent from Rome by someone unknown to Melani but whom he understood by his style and from other details to be certainly a cleric. The paper had grown yellow and seemed to date from many years previously. The missives referred to confidential information which the same informer had sent previously to the addressee. The latter, as was to be understood from the envelope, was the Superintendent General of Finances, Nicolas Fouquet.

"And why was this in Colbert's possession?"

"I have already told you, as you will recall, that at the time of his arrest and in the days that followed, all Fouquet's papers and correspondence, both private and relating to matters of state, were confiscated."

The language of the mysterious prelate was so cryptic that Melani was unable even to understand what might be the nature of the secret to which it alluded. He noted, amongst other things, that one of the epistles began curiously with the words *mumiarum domino*, but was unable to find any explanation for this.

But the most interesting part of Abbot Melani's tale was still to come, and here the material took on the contours of the incredible. The folder which Atto had found on top of the lectern contained very recent correspondence with which, because of his illness, Colbert had not yet been able to deal. Apart from a few matters of no importance, there were two letters sent from Rome in July and almost certainly (as appeared from the obsequious turns of phrase employed) destined for Colbert in person. The sender must have been a trusted servant of the minister, and he reported the presence in the city of the squirrel on the *arbor caritatis*.

"Meaning..."

"Elementary. The squirrel is the animal on Fouquet's coat of arms; the *arbor caritatis*, the tree of charity, can only be the city of loving kindness, that is, Rome. And indeed, according to the informer, the former Superintendent Fouquet had been seen and followed no fewer than three times: near a piazza called Fiammetta, in the vicinity of the church of Sant'Apollinare and in the Piazza Navona. Three places, if I am not mistaken, in the Holy City."

"But that is not possible," I objected. "Did not Fouquet die in prison, at..."

"At Pinerol, of course, a good three years ago, and in the arms of his son who at that extreme hour was generously granted access to him. Yet the letter from Colbert's informer, although written in cipher, spoke to me clearly: he was here in Rome little more than a month ago."

The abbot decided to leave at once for Rome in order to solve the mystery. There were two possibilities: either the news of Fouquet's presence in Rome was true (and that would have been beyond anything that could have been imagined, since it was common knowledge that the Superintendent had died following a long illness after almost twenty years' imprisonment in a fortress); or it was false, and then it would be necessary to discover whether someone, perhaps an unfaithful agent, was distributing false rumours with a view to disturbing the King and the court and comforting the enemies of France.

Once again I noticed how, when telling of such secrets and surprising events, Abbot Melani's eyes lit up with a twinkle of malicious joy, of private satisfaction and unspoken pleasure in recounting these things to someone like myself, a poor apprentice utterly ignorant of intrigues, plots and secret affairs of state.

"Did Colbert die?"

"No doubt, seeing the condition he was in; even if not before my departure."

In fact, as I learned far later, Colbert died on the 6th of September, exactly a week before Abbot Melani told me of his intrusion.

"In the eyes of the world, he will have died a victor," added Atto after a pause, "immensely wealthy and powerful. For his family, he bought the finest noble titles and high offices: his brother Charles became Marquis de Croissy and Secretary of State for Foreign Affairs; another brother, Edouard-François, was created Marquis de Maulévrier and became Lieutenant-General of the King's armies; his son Jean-Baptiste became Marquis de Seignelay, and Secretary of State for the Navy. Without counting all the other brothers and sons who made brilliant military and ecclesiastical careers, or the rich marriages contracted by his three daughters, all of whom became duchesses."

"But did Colbert not cry scandal, accusing Fouquet of being too rich and of having placed his men everywhere?"

"Yes, and then he himself engaged in the most blatant nepotism. He spun a network of his own spies such as there had never been, hunting down and ruining all the most loyal friends of the Superintendent."

I knew that Melani was also referring to his own exile from Paris.

"Not only that: Colbert had accumulated an estate of over ten million *livres* net, concerning the origins of which no one has ever expressed the slightest suspicions. My poor friend Nicolas, on the other hand, had contracted personal debts in order to provide funds for Mazarin and for the war against Spain."

"An astute man, your Signor di Colbert."

"And unscrupulous," added Melani. "All his life, he was praised to heaven for his vast reforms of the state which will, alas, guarantee him a place in history. Yet, all of us at court know perfectly well that every single reform was stolen from Fouquet: those to do with revenue and estates, the easing of the *taille*, tax relief, the great manufactures, and the naval and colonial policies. It is no accident that he had all the Superintendent's papers burned very early on."

Fouquet, explained the abbot to me, was the first shipbuilder and coloniser of France, the first to take up Richelieu's old dream of making the Atlantic coast and the Gulf of Morbihan the centre of the economic and maritime renewal of the kingdom. It was he, already the organiser of the victorious war against Spain, who first discovered and organised the weavers of the village of Maincy, whom Colbert later transformed into the manufactory of the Gobelins.

"Besides, it was soon common knowledge that these reforms were not flour from his own sack. For a good twenty-two years Colbert was Comptroller-General, a more modest title with which he, to please the King, had renamed the office of Superintendent, which was officially abolished. Fouquet, however, remained in government for eight years only. And here lay the problem: for as long as he was able to, the Serpent followed in the footsteps of his predecessor, and fortune smiled on him. But then he had to pursue on his own the reform plans which were confiscated from Fouquet at the time of his arrest. And from that point on, Colbert made one long series of false moves:

in industrial and mercantile policy, where neither the nobility nor the bourgeoisie gave him credit, and in maritime policy, in which none of his much-vaunted companies were long-lived, and no one ever succeeded in gaining supremacy over the English and the Dutch."

"And was the Most Christian King aware of nothing?"

"The King keeps his changes of judgement jealously to himself; but it seems that, no sooner had the physicians given Colbert up for lost than he began a round of consultations to choose a successor, taking a selection of names of ministers whose character and training were very different from that of Colbert. When this was pointed out to him, it is said that His Majesty replied: "That is precisely why I chose them.""

"Did Colbert then die in disgrace?"

"Let us not exaggerate. I should say, rather, that the whole of his career as minister was afflicted by the King's continuous rages. Colbert and Louvois, the Minister for War, the two most feared intendants in France, were overcome with trembling and covered in cold sweat whenever the King summoned them in council. They enjoyed the Sovereign's confidence, but they were his two first slaves. Colbert must have realised very early on how difficult it was to take Fouquet's place and, like him, to meet every day the King's demands for money for battles and ballets."

"How did he manage?"

"In the most practical way. The *Coluber* began to channel into the hands of one man, the Sovereign, all the wealth which had hitherto been that of the few. He abolished countless offices and pensions, he despoiled Paris and the kingdom of every luxury and all ended up in the coffers of the Crown. As for the people, those who previously had gone hungry now died of hunger."

"Did Colbert ever become more powerful than Fouquet had been?"

"My boy, he was far, far more powerful. Never did my friend Nicolas enjoy the liberties from which his successor benefited. Colbert laid his hands on everything, everywhere, interfering in areas that had remained completely beyond the reach of Fouquet, who faced the added difficulty of almost always acting in wartime. And yet the debts which the Serpent left behind him were far greater than those for which Fouquet was arraigned for ruining the state, he who ruined himself for the state."

"Did no one ever bring accusations to bear against Colbert?"

"There were several scandals: such as the one and only case of the forgery of money in France during the past several hundred years, and all of those involved were the *Coluber*'s men, including his nephew. Or the stripping and illicit trafficking of Burgundy's timber; or the criminal exploitation of the forests of Normandy; and these both involved the same henchman of Colbert, Berryer, who had materially falsified documents in the Fouquet trial. All devices to amass wealth for his family."

"A fortunate life, then."

"That, I would not say. He spent his existence pretending to be of the most exemplary integrity, accumulating a fortune which he was never able to enjoy. He suffered from envy that was boundless and could never be allayed. He had always to sweat blood and tears in order to come up with some paltry idea which was not to be thrown away. A victim of his own mania for power, he arrogated to himself control over every area of the country, spending a lifetime chained to his desk. He never enjoyed himself for one single hour, and despite that he was detested by the people. Every single day he suffered the terrible wrath of the Sovereign. He was mocked and despised for his ignorance. And it was a combination of these last two factors that eventually killed him."

"What do you mean?"

The abbot laughed heartily: "Do you know what brought Colbert to his deathbed?"

"A renal colic, you said."

"Precisely. And do you know why? The King, furious at his latest blunder, summoned him and showered him with insults and contumely."

"Was this some administrative error?"

"Far more. To emulate Fouquet's expertise, Colbert stuck his nose into the building of a new wing for the Château of Versailles, imposing his own opinions on the builders, who were unable to make him understand the risks incurred by his villainous intervention."

"But how so? Fouquet had died in prison three years before, and Colbert was still obsessed with him?"

"For as long as the Superintendent remained alive, although entombed at Pinerol, Colbert lived in a state of constant terror that the King might one day return him to his post. Even when Fouquet was no more, the memory of his all-too-brilliant, genial, cultivated, well-loved and admired predecessor remained etched into the *Coluber*'s soul. Colbert had many sons who were healthy and robust, and he enriched them all; he had immense power, while his adversary's family was dispersed far from the capital and condemned perpetually to struggle against creditors. Yet the *Coluber*'s thoughts could never be free of that one original defeat inflicted upon him by Mother Nature, who had so despised him as to refuse her own gifts and shower them prodigally upon his rival Fouquet."

"How did the building work go at Versailles?"

"The new wing collapsed, and all the court laughed. The King flew into a rage with Colbert who, overcome by humiliation, suffered a most violent attack of the colic. After days of screaming in pain, the sickness brought him to his death throes."

I was at a loss for words before the power of divine vengeance.

"You were truly a good friend of Superintendent Fouquet," was the only phrase I was able to utter.

"I would have wished to be a better friend."

We heard a door open and then close again on the first floor; then footfalls moved towards the stairs.

"Better leave the way open for science," said Atto, alluding to the approach of Cristofano. "But remember that we shall have work to do later."

And he ran to take shelter on the stairway leading to the cellars, while the doctor passed, after which he moved swiftly upstairs.

☙◦❧

Cristofano had come to ask me to prepare dinner, because the other guests were complaining.

"I thought I heard footsteps when I was coming downstairs. Has someone perhaps been here?"

"Absolutely not, you will have heard me: I was just getting ready to prepare the stove," said I, pretending to busy myself with the pots and pans.

I would have liked to retain the doctor but he, reassured by my reply, returned directly to his apartment, begging me to serve dinner as soon as possible. Thank heavens, thought I, that he had decided to serve only two meals a day.

I set myself to preparing a soup of semolina with beans, garlic and cinnamon, with sugar on it, to which I added cheese, sweet-smelling herbs, a few little pancakes and half a pint of the watered-down wine.

While I was attending to my cooking, a thousand turbid thoughts rushed through my poor prentice's mind. In the first place came what Abbot Melani had just told me. I was shaken: here, I thought, are all the present and past troubles of the abbot: a man capable of deceit and dissimulation (and to some extent, who is not?) but not inclined to deny the past. His former familiarity with Superintendent Fouquet was the one mark that not even his juvenile flight to Rome and the humiliations that had followed could cancel out, and which even now made him uncertain of the King's favour. Yet he continued to defend his benefactor's memory. Perhaps he spoke so freely only with me, as I would certainly never be able to report his words to the French court.

I went over again in my memory what he had discovered among Colbert's papers. In all tranquillity, he had confided in me how he had purloined a number of confidential documents from the *Coluber*'s study, forcing the devices which were designed to protect them. But this was no surprise, given the character of the man, as I had already learned both from others and from him in person. What had struck me was the mission which he had taken upon himself: to find in Rome his old friend and protector, Superintendent Fouquet. That could be no light matter for Abbot Melani, not only because the Superintendent had hitherto been believed dead, but also because it was precisely he who had, however involuntarily, involved Atto Melani in the scandal: and I seemed, according to the abbot, to be the one person privy to his secret mission, which only the sudden closure of the inn when we were placed in quarantine had, I thought, momentarily interrupted. Thus, when I had entered the gallery under the hostelry, I was in the company of a special agent of the King of France! I felt honoured that he should go to so much trouble to resolve the strange affairs which had taken place at the Donzello, including the theft of my little pearls. And indeed it was he who had insistently requested my help. By now, I would not have hesitated one moment to give the abbot copies of the keys to Dulcibeni and Devizé's chambers, which only a day before I had refused. However, it was too late: because of Cristofano's instructions, the two would, like the other guests, remain closed in their apartments all the time, making any search of those apartments impossible. And the abbot had already explained how inopportune it would be to ask questions of them, which might raise their suspicions.

I was proud to share so many secrets, but all that was as nothing when compared with the tangle of sentiments provoked by my colloquy with Cloridia.

༺༻

After bringing dinner to every guest in their chambers, I went first to see Bedfordi, then Pellegrino, where both Cristofano and I took care of feeding the patients. The Englishman was jabbering incomprehensible things. The doctor seemed worried. So much so that he went to Devizé's chamber next door, explaining Bedfordi's condition to him and begging him to lay aside his guitar at least for the time being: the musician was, in fact, practising sonorously, rehearsing on his instrument a fine chaconne which was among his favourite pieces.

"I shall do better," replied Devizé laconically.

And, instead of leaving off from playing, he launched into the notes of his *rondeau*. Cristofano was about to protest, but the mysterious enchantment of that music enveloped him, lighting up his face, and, nodding benevolently, the physician went out of the door without making a sound.

A little later, whilst I was descending from Pellegrino's chamber, up under the eaves, I was called in a stage whisper from the second floor. It was Padre Robleda, whose room was near the stairs. Leaning out from his door, he asked me for news of the two patients.

"And the Englishman is no better?"

"I would say not," I replied.

"And has the doctor nothing new to tell us?"

"Not really."

Meanwhile, the last echo of Devizé's *rondeau* reached us. Robleda, hearing those notes, permitted himself a languid sigh.

"Music is the voice of God," said he, explaining himself.

Seeing that I was carrying the unguents with me, I took the opportunity to ask him whether he had a little time for the administration of the remedies against the infection.

With a gesture, he invited me to enter his little chamber.

I was about to put my things down on a chair which was situated just past the door.

"No, no, no, wait, I need this!"

He hurriedly laid on the seat a little glass box with a black pear-wood frame, with inside it a Christ child and fruit and flowers, standing on little feet shaped like onions.

"I bought it here in Rome. It is precious, and it will be safer on the chair."

Robleda's weak excuse was a sign that his desire for conversation, after long hours passed in solitude, was now equal to his fear of contact with someone who must, he knew, touch Bedfordi every day. I then reminded him that I was to apply the remedy with my own hands, but that there was no cause for mistrust, as Cristofano himself had reassured everyone of my resistance to the infection.

"Of course, of course," was all he answered, marking his cautious confidence.

I asked him to uncover his chest, since I would have to anoint him and to place a poultice in the region of his heart and especially around the left pap.

"And why is that?" asked the Jesuit, perturbed.

I explained that this was what Cristofano had recommended, as his anxious character might risk weakening his heart.

He became calmer and, while I was opening the bag and looking for the right jars, lay supine on the bed. Above this there hung a portrait of Our Lord Innocent XI.

Robleda began almost at once to complain of Cristofano's indecision, and the fact that he had not yet found a clear explanation for the death of Mourai or for the distemper which had laid Pellegrino low; indeed, there were even uncertainties concerning the plague to which Bedfordi had fallen victim, and all this was sufficient to affirm without the shadow of a doubt that the Tuscan physician was not up to the task. He then went on to complain about the other guests and about Signor Pellegrino, whom he blamed for the present situation. He began with my master, who was, according to him, insufficiently vigilant about the cleanliness of the hostelry. He came next to Brenozzi and Bedfordi, who, after their long voyage, could certainly have brought some obscure infection to the inn. For the same reason, he suspected Stilone Priàso (who came from Naples, a city where the air was notoriously unhealthy) and Devizé (who had also journeyed from Naples), Atto Melani (whose presence at the inn and whose dreadful reputation surely called for recourse to prayer), the woman in the little tower (of whose habitual presence at the inn he swore that he had never heard, otherwise he would never have set foot at the Donzello); and lastly he inveighed against Dulcibeni, whose mean Jansenist expression, said Robleda, had never pleased him.

"Jansenist?" I asked, curious about that word which I was hearing for the first time.

I then learned in brief from Robleda that the Jansenists were a most dangerous and pernicious sect. They took their name from Jansenius, the founder of this doctrine (if indeed it could be called one), and among his followers there was a madman called Pasqual or Pascale, who wore stockings soaked with cognac to keep his feet warm and who had written certain letters containing matter gravely offensive to the Church, to our Lord Jesus Christ and to all honest persons of good sense with faith in God.

But here the Jesuit broke off to blow his nose: "What an immodest stink there is in this oil of yours. Are you sure it is not poisonous?"

I reassured him as to the authority of this remedy, prepared by Antonio Fiorentino to protect people from the pestilence at the time of the republic of Florence. The ingredients, as Cristofano had taught me, were none other than theriac of the Levant boiled with the juice of lemons, carline thistle, *imperatoria*, gentian, saffron, *Dictamnus albus* and sandarac. Gently accompanied by the massage I had begun to give his chest, Robleda seemed to be lulled by the sound of the names of these ingredients, almost as though that cancelled out their disagreeable odour. As I had already observed with Cloridia, the pungent vapours and the various techniques of touch with which I applied Cristofano's *remedia* pacified the guests to the depths of their souls and loosened their tongues.

"When all is said and done, are they not almost heretics, those Jansenists?" I resumed.

"More than almost," replied Robleda with satisfaction.

Indeed, Jansenius had written a book the propositions of which had been harshly condemned many years ago by Pope Innocent X. "But why are you of the opinion that Signor Dulcibeni belongs to the sect of the Jansenists?"

Robleda explained to me that on the afternoon before the quarantine, he had seen Dulcibeni return to the Donzello with a number of books under his arm which he had probably acquired from some bookshop, perhaps in the nearby Piazza Navona where many books are sold. Among these texts, Robleda had noticed the title of a forbidden book which precisely inclined towards that heretical doctrine. And that, in the Jesuit's opinion, was an unequivocal sign that Dulcibeni belonged to the Jansenist sect.

"Is it not strange, however, that such a book may be purchased here in Rome," I objected, "seeing that Pope Innocent XI will doubtless have condemned the Jansenists in his turn."

Padre Robleda's expression changed. He insisted that, contrary to what I might think, many acts of gracious attention towards the Jansenists had come from Pope Odescalchi, so much so that in France, where the Jansenists were held in the greatest suspicion by the Most Christian King, the Pope had for some time been accused of harbouring culpable sympathies for the followers of that doctrine.

"But how could Our Lord Pope Innocent XI possibly harbour sympathies for heretics?" I asked in astonishment.

Padre Robleda, stretched out with his arm under his head, looked obliquely at me, his little eyes twinkling.

"You may perhaps be aware that between Louis XIV and Our Lord Pope Innocent XI there has for some time been great discord."

"Do you mean to say that the Pontiff is supporting the Jansenists solely in order to damage the King of France?"

"Do not forget," he replied slyly, "that a pontiff is also a prince with temporal estates, which it is his duty to defend and promote by all available means."

"But everybody speaks so well of Pope Odescalchi," I protested. "He has abolished nepotism, cleaned up the accounts of the Apostolic Chamber and done all that can be done to help the war against the Turks..."

"All that you say is not false. Indeed, he did avoid the granting of any offices to his nephew, Livio Odescalchi, and did not even have him made a cardinal. All those offices he in fact kept for himself."

This seemed to me a malicious answer, even though it was so phrased as not to deny my assertions.

"Like all persons familiar with trade, he knows well the value of money. It is indeed acknowledged that he managed very well the enterprise which he inherited from his uncle in Genoa. Worth about five hundred thousand scudi, it is said. Without counting the residue of various other inheritances which he took care to dispute with his relatives," said he hurriedly, lowering his voice.

And before I could get over my surprise and ask him if the Pontiff had really inherited such a monstrous sum of money, Robleda continued.

"He is no lion-heart, our good Pontiff. It is said, but take care," he lowered his voice, "this is but gossip, that as a young man he left Como out of cowardice, in order to avoid arbitrating in a quarrel between friends."

He fell briefly silent, and then returned to the attack: "But he has the holy gift of constancy, and of perseverance! He writes daily to his brother and to his other relatives to have news of the family estates. It seems that he cannot remain two days in succession without controlling, advising, recommending... Moreover the assets of the family are considerable. They increased suddenly after the pestilence of 1630, so much so that in their part of the world, in Como, it was said that the Odescalchi had profited from the deaths, and that they had used suborned notaries to obtain the inheritances of those who had died without heirs. But those are all calumnies, by our Lord's charity," said Robleda, crossing himself and rounding off his speech: "Nevertheless, their wealth is such that in my opinion they have lost count of it: lands, premises leased to religious orders, venal offices, franchises for the collection of the salt taxes. And then, so many letters of credit, I would say, almost all in loans, to many persons, even to some cardinals," said the Jesuit nonchalantly, as though showing interest in a crack in the ceiling.

"The Pontiff's family gains riches from credit?" I exclaimed, surprised. "But did not Pope Innocent forbid the Jews to act as moneylenders?"

"Exactly," replied the Jesuit enigmatically.

Then he dismissed me suddenly, on the pretext that it was time for his evening orations. He made as if to rise from his bed.

"But I have not yet finished: I must apply a poultice now," I objected.

He lay down again without a protest. He seemed to be lost in contemplation.

Following Cristofano's notes, I took a piece of crystalline arsenic and wrapped it in a piece of sendal. I approached the Jesuit and placed the poultice above his breast. I had to wait for it to dry, after which I twice again wet it with vinegar.

"Please do not, however, listen to all the malevolent gossip which has been spread about Pope Innocent, ever since the time of the Lady Olimpia," he continued, while I attended to the operation.

"What gossip?"

"Oh, nothing, nothing: it is all just poison. And more powerful than that which killed our poor Mourai."

He fell silent then, with a mysterious and, to me, suspect air.

I became alarmed. Why had the Jesuit remembered the poison which had perhaps killed the old Frenchman? Was it only a casual comparison, as it seemed? Or did the mysterious allusion conceal something else, or had it, perhaps, to do with the Donzello's no less mysterious underground passages? I said to myself that I was being silly, yet that word—poison—kept turning around in my head.

"Pardon me, Padre, what did you mean?"

"It would be better for you to remain in your ignorance," said he, cutting me short distractedly.

"Who is Lady Olimpia?" I insisted.

"Do not tell me that you have never heard speak of the Papess," he murmured, turning to look at me in astonishment.

"The Papess?"

It was thus that Robleda, lying on his side supported by an elbow and with an air of granting me an immense favour, began to recount to me in an almost inaudible voice that Pope Innocent XI had been made a cardinal by Pope Innocent X Pamphili, almost forty years earlier. The latter had reigned with great pomp and magnificence, thus consigning to oblivion a number of disagreeable deeds which had taken place under the previous pontificate, that of Urban VIII Barberini. Someone, however—and here the Jesuit's tone descended by another octave—someone had observed that Pope Innocent X, of the Pamphili family, and his brother's wife, Olimpia Maidalchini were linked by bonds of mutual sympathy. It was murmured (all calumnies, of course) that the closeness between the two was excessive and suspect, even between two close relatives for whom affection and warmth and so many other things (quoth he, looking into my eyes for the space of a lightning flash) would be completely natural. The intimacy which Pope Pamphili granted to his sister-in-law was, however, such that she frequented his chambers at all hours of the day and night, put her nose into his affairs and interfered even in matters of state: she arranged audiences, granted privileges, assumed responsibility for taking decisions in the Pope's name. It was surely not beauty that gave Donna Olimpia her dominance. Her appearance was, indeed, particularly repugnant, although combined with the incredible force of an almost virile temperament. The ambassadors of foreign powers were continually sending her presents, aware of the power which she exercised in the Holy See. The Pontiff himself was, however, weak, submissive, of melancholy humour. Gossip in Rome ran rife, and some made a joke of the Pope, sending him anonymously a medal with his sister-in-law dressed as Pope, tiara and all; and, on the other side, Innocent X in women's clothing, with a needle and thread in his hand.

The cardinals rebelled against this indecorous situation, succeeding for a while in having the woman removed, but after that she managed to regain the saddle and to accompany the Pope even to the tomb; and that, after her own fashion: she concealed the Pontiff's death from the people for a good two days, so that she would have time to remove everything of value from the papal apartments. Meanwhile, the poor lifeless body was left alone in a room, a prey to the rats, while no one came forward to see to the burial. The funeral eventually took place amidst the indifference of the cardinals and the mockery and jibes of the common people.

Now, Donna Olimpia loved to play at cards, and it is said that one evening, in a gay assembly of ladies and cavaliers at her table, she found herself in the company of a young cleric who, when all other competitors had withdrawn from the game, accepted Donna Olimpia's challenge to play against her. And it is also said that there gathered around them a great crowd of people, to watch so unusual a contest. And for more than an hour, the two confronted one another, with no thought for time or money, occasioning great gaiety among those present; and, at the end of the evening, Donna Olimpia returned home with a sum of money of which the exact total has never been known, but which was by all accounts enormous. Likewise, rumour had it that the unknown young man, who in truth almost always held better cards than his adversary, was gracious enough so to arrange matters as to reveal those cards distractedly to a servant of Donna Olimpia, so that he lost all the decisive hands, without however (as chivalry requires) allowing anyone to see that, not even the winner; thus confronting his grave defeat with magnificent indifference. Anyway, soon after that, Pope Pamphili made

a cardinal of that cleric, who went by the name of Benedetto Odescalchi, and attained the purple in the flower of youth, at the age of
thirty-four years.

I had in the meanwhile completed my massage with the ointment.

"But remember," Robleda warned me hastily in a voice that had
returned to normal, while he cleaned the poultice off his chest, "this
is all gossip. There exist no material proofs of that episode."

Hardly had I left Padre Robleda's chamber than I experienced
a sense of unease, which not even I could explain to myself, as I
thought back over my conversation with that flabby, purple-faced
priest. No supernatural talent was needed to understand that the
Jesuit regarded Our Lord Pope Innocent XI, not as an upright, honest and saintly pontiff, but no less than a friend and accomplice of
the Jansenists; all for the purpose of thwarting the designs of the
King of France, with whom he had clashed. Furthermore, he saw him
as consumed by unhealthy material appetites, avidity and avarice;
and even as having corrupted Donna Olimpia to obtain his Cardinal's
hat. But, I reasoned, if such a portrait were truthful, how could Our
Lord Pope Innocent XI be the same person who had restored austerity, decorum and frugality to the heart of Holy Mother Church? How
could he be the same person who for decades had extended charity
to the poor, wherever he found them? How could he be the same man
who had enjoined the princes of Europe to unite their forces against
the Turks? It was a fact that previous pontiffs had showered their
nephews and families with presents, while he had broken off that unseemly tradition; it was a fact that he had restored a healthy balance
to the Apostolic Chamber; and finally, it was a fact that Vienna itself
was resisting the advance of the Ottoman tide thanks to the efforts
of Pope Innocent.

No, what that gossiping poltroon of a Jesuit had told me was
simply not possible. Had I not, moreover, immediately suspected
his manner of saying and not saying, and that capricious doctrine
of the Jesuits which legitimised sin? And I too was guilty of having
allowed myself to listen to him, even at a certain point encouraging
him to continue, led astray by Robleda's casual and misleading mention of the poisoning of Signor di Mourai. This was all, I thought
remorsefully, the fault of Atto Melani's attitude to investigation
and the craft of spying, and of my desire to emulate him: a perverse

passion which had made me fall into the snares of the Evil One and had disposed my ears to hearken to his whispers of calumny.

I returned to the kitchen where I found on the sideboard an anonymous note, clearly addressed to me:

THREE KNOCKS ON THE DOOR——BE READY

Night the Third
BETWEEN *the* 13ᵀᴴ *&* 14ᵀᴴ SEPTEMBER, 1683

✠

A little over an hour later, after Cristofano had taken a last look at my master, Abbot Melani knocked three times at my door. I was intent upon my little diary: I hid it carefully under the mattress before admitting him.

"A drop of oil," said the abbot enigmatically, immediately after entering.

I suddenly remembered how, when we last met, he had noticed a drop of oil on my forehead, which he had taken on a fingertip and brought to his tongue.

"Tell me, what oil do you use for the lamps?"

"The College of Cardinals has commanded that oil mixed with wine lees is always to be…"

"I did not ask you what you are supposed to use but what you do use, when your master," and he pointed to him, "is resting in his bed."

Embarrassed, I confessed to him that I also used good oil, because we had it in abundance, while the impure oil mixed with dregs was in short supply.

Abbot Melani could not hide a sly grin. "Now don't lie: how many lanterns have you?"

"To begin with, we had three, but we broke one when we were climbing down into the gallery. There are two left, but one needs a little mending."

"Good, take the better one and follow me. And take that too."

He pointed at a rod, leaning vertically in a corner of the chamber, with which in his rare free moments Signor Pellegrino was wont to go fishing on the banks of the Tiber, just behind the little church of Santa Maria in Posterula.

A few instants later, we were already in the closet, and had entered the well that gave access to the stairs leading down to the underground galleries. We lowered ourselves with the help of the iron rungs set into the wall until we felt the brick platform under our feet, and then we took the square stairwell. At the point where the stairway was excavated directly from the tufa, we encountered again the coating of slime on the steps, while the air became heavy.

At last, we reached the gallery, deep and dark as the night in which I had discovered it.

As I followed him, Abbot Melani must have felt my curiosity as though I were breathing down his neck.

"Now at last you will know what that strange Abbot Melani has in his head."

He stopped.

"Give me the rod."

He laid half the cane across his knee and with a sharp movement snapped it in two. I was about to protest, but Atto stopped me.

"Do not worry. If you ever have to report this to your master, he will understand that this was a matter of emergency. Now, do as I tell you."

He made me walk in front of him, holding the broken cane vertically behind me and dragging the end of it along the vault of the gallery, like a pen sliding on paper. Thus we advanced for a few dozen cane's lengths. Meanwhile the abbot asked me some bizarre questions.

"Does oil mixed with wine dregs have a special taste?"

"I would not know how to describe it," I replied, although in reality I knew the taste perfectly well, having more than once furtively sprinkled some onto a slice of bread purloined from the pantry, when Signor Pellegrino was sleeping and the meal had been too frugal.

"Would you call it rancid, bitter and acid?"

"Perhaps... Yes, I'd say so," I admitted.

"Good," replied the abbot.

We advanced a few paces further, and suddenly the abbot ordered me to stop.

"We are there!"

I looked at him in some perplexity.

"Have you still not understood?" he said to me, his grin queerly deformed by the lamplight. "Then let us see if this will help you."

He took the cane from my hands and pressed it hard against the vault of the gallery. I heard something like the groaning of hinges, then a tremendous reverberation, and finally, the skittering of a little shower of dirt and stones.

Then terror struck: a huge black serpent lunged at me and almost seized me, after which it remained grotesquely suspended from the ceiling like a hanged man.

I withdrew instinctively with a shiver, while the abbot burst out laughing.

"Come here and bring the lantern closer," he said triumphantly.

In the vault, a hole appeared, almost as wide as the entire cavity; and from it hung a thick rope. This was what, tumbling down when the trap opened, had brushed against me and terrified me.

"You let yourself be frightened by nothing, and for that you deserve a little punishment. You will go up first. Then you will have to help me up after you."

Fortunately I succeeded in climbing up without too much difficulty. Clinging to the rope, I swarmed up it until I reached the upper cavity. I helped Abbot Melani to join me there and he marshalled all his strength, twice coming close to dropping our one and only lantern.

We found ourselves in the middle of another gallery, aligned obliquely to the first one.

"Now, it is up to you to decide: right or left?"

I protested (weakly, fearful as I was): was this not perhaps the moment for Abbot Melani to explain to me how he had worked all this out?

"You are right, but then I shall choose: let us proceed to the left."

As I myself had explained to the abbot, oil mixed with dregs generally has a far less agreeable taste than that which is used for frying or for good cooking. The drop which he had found on my forehead the day after the first exploration of the gallery (and which, miraculously, had not come into contact with the blankets when I lay down) could not, according to its taste, come from the lanterns of the inn, which I myself had filled with good oil. Nor did it come from Cristofano's medicinal ointments, which were all different in colour. Therefore, it came from an unknown lantern which—who knows how—must have been situated above my head. From this, the abbot had concluded with his usual alacrity that there must be an opening in the vault of the gallery: an opening which also provided the thief's only possible way out, when he had so inexplicably vanished into nothingness.

"The oil that fell on your forehead must have dripped from the thief's lantern through a crack next to the hinges of the trapdoor."

"And the cane?" I asked.

"I was sure that the trapdoor, if it existed, must be very well hidden. But a cane like that of your master's fishing rod is very sensitive to vibrations, and we were sure to feel a shock when it moved from the stone of the gallery to the wood of the trapdoor. Which is what indeed happened."

I was secretly grateful to the abbot for having in some way attributed to both of us the credit for having discovered the trapdoor.

"The mechanism is somewhat rudimentary," he continued, "but it works. The rope, which so affrighted you when it came down from the ceiling, is simply stowed on the top of the trapdoor and closed together with it. When the trap is opened from the gallery below, pushing upwards, the rope falls down. It is important to put it back in the same way when one returns if one wants it to be available again."

"Then you think that the thief always moves back and forth along this gallery."

"I do not know; I suppose so. And I suppose too, if you wish to know, that this gallery leads somewhere else."

"Did you also suppose that solely with the aid of the cane we should find the trapdoor?"

"Nature makes merit, but fortune sets it to work," pronounced the abbot.

And by the faint light of the lantern the exploration began.

කතන්

In that gallery, too, as in the one we had left beneath us, a person of normal stature was obliged to stoop slightly because the vault was so low. And, as we at once observed, the material of which it was built, a pattern of diamond-shaped bricks, seemed identical to that of the previous gallery. The first stretch went in a long straight line which seemed gradually to slope downhill. "If our thief has followed this track, he must be strong and fit," observed Abbot Melani. "Not everyone could climb that rope and the terrain is rather slippery."

Suddenly we both suffered the most atrocious fright.

A stranger's footfalls, light but utterly clear, were approaching from a point which could not be identified. Atto stopped me, squeezing my shoulder hard, to signal the need for extreme caution. It was then that a reverberation caused us to tremble, similar to that when we had opened the trapdoor through which we passed not long before.

Hardly had we recovered our breath than we looked at one another, our eyes still wide with anxiety.

"Do you think it came from above or below?" muttered Abbot Melani.

"More above than below."

"I'd say so, too. So it cannot be the same trapdoor—it must be another one."

"And how many do you think there are?"

"Who knows? We were mistaken not to explore this ceiling too with the cane. Perhaps we might have found another opening. Someone must have heard us coming and have hurried to bar the passage between ourselves and him. The reverberation was too loud, I could not say whether it came from behind our shoulders or from the stretch which we have still to cover."

"Could it be the thief of the keys?"

"You keep asking me questions which cannot be answered. Perhaps he had the idea of taking a stroll this evening, perhaps not. Did you by any chance keep an eye on the entrance to the closet this evening?"

I admitted that I had not given much thought to that.

"Bravo," commented the abbot with a sneer. "So we have come down here without knowing whether we are following in someone's footsteps or he in ours, and, what is more... Look!"

We were at the top of a staircase. Lowering the lantern to our feet, we saw that the steps were in stone and skilfully carved. After an instant's reflection, the abbot sighed: "I have no idea what may await us down below. The steps are steep: if there is someone there, he knows that we are coming. *Is that not true?*" he concluded, calling down the stairs and creating a horrible echo which made me jump. Then, armed only with the feeble lamp, we began our descent.

When the steps came to an end, we found ourselves at last walking along a pavement. Judging by the echo of our footsteps, we appeared to be in a great hollow, perhaps a cavern. Abbot Melani thrust the lantern upwards. Great brick arches appeared in profile, cut into a wall so high that we could not distinguish its top, and through the arches led a passage towards which we had all the while been moving unawares.

Scarcely had we halted than all fell silent again. For a moment, the lantern flame weakened, until it almost went out. It was then that I noticed a furtive rustling to our left.

"Did you hear?" murmured the abbot, alarmed.

We again heard rustling, this time a little further off. Atto gestured to me not to move: and instead of following the passage that lay before us, he ran on tiptoe under the arch to our right, beyond which the light from the lantern no longer reached him. I stood waiting, with the lantern in my hand, petrified. Again there was silence.

A new rustling, this time nearer, came from behind my shoulders. I turned around sharply. A shadow slipped to my left. I rushed towards Abbot Melani, more to protect myself than to put him on guard.

"No-o-o," he whispered as soon as I could see him by the light of the lamp: he had silently shifted a few paces to the left and was squatting on the ground. Again, a grey silhouette emerged from who knows where and passed swiftly between us, trying to move away from the arches.

"Catch him!" screamed Abbot Melani, approaching in his turn, and he was right, because that someone or something seemed to trip up and almost fall. I rushed out blindly, praying God that Atto would reach him before I did.

But just at that moment, there fell upon me, and everywhere around me, a loud and horrible rain of cadavers, skulls and human bones, and mandibles and jawbones and ribs and shoulder-blades and disgusting filth, struck down by which, I fell to the ground and remained there. Only then did I fully distinguish that revolting stuff from close quarters, as I lay half-buried and almost dead. I tried to free myself from the monstrous crunching mortiferous mush, whose horrid gurgling mingled with a duet of infernal bellowing of which I could guess neither the origin nor the nature. What I could now recognise as a vertebra obstructed my vision and what had once been the skull of a living person looked at me threateningly, almost suspended in the void. I tried to scream, but my mouth uttered no sound. I felt my strength failing me, and while my last thoughts gathered painfully into a prayer for my soul's salvation, as in a dream, I heard the abbot's voice resounding through the vaults.

"That's enough, I can see you. Halt or I fire."

☙❧

It seemed to me that a long time passed (but now I know it was only a few minutes) before I was called back from the formless nightmare into which I had fallen by the echoing sound of a strange voice.

I noted with alarm that a strange hand was holding my head up, while someone (a third being?) freed my limbs from the frightful mass under which I was all but buried. Instinctively, I drew back from these strange attentions but, slipping clumsily, I found myself with my nose up against a nauseous-smelling member (impossible to tell which one). Suddenly overcome by the exertions of my stomach, in a few seconds I threw up all my dinner. I heard the stranger curse in a language that seemed similar to my own.

While I was still trying to recover my breath, I felt the kindly hand of Abbot Melani grasp me under the armpit.

"Courage, boy."

I rose painfully to my feet, and by the dim light of the lamp I caught sight of an individual, wrapped in a sort of gown, muttering as he bent down to the ground in a febrile attempt to isolate from my gastric secretions the no less vomit-inducing heap of human remains.

"To each his own treasures," sneered Atto.

I saw that Abbot Melani was holding a little device in his hand; from what I could make out, it ended with a piece of shining wood inset with gleaming metal. He was pointing it threateningly at a second individual, dressed like his companion and seated on a carved stone.

In the moment when the lantern lit up this figure, I was thunderstruck by the sight of his face, that is, if one could call it a face. For it was nothing but a symphony of wrinkles, a concerto of folds, a madrigal of ribbons of skin which seemed to hold together only because they were too old and tired to rebel against their enforced companionship. The grey and diffident pupils were crowned by the intense red of the eye, which made of the whole one of the most fearsome sights I had ever beheld. The picture was completed by sharp brown teeth, worthy of an infernal vision by Melozzo da Forlì.

"*Corpisantari*," murmured the abbot to himself, disgustedly, shaking his head.

"You could at least have shown a little more care," he added sardonically. "You scared these two gentlemen."

And he lowered the little device with which he had been keeping the first mysterious individual covered, returning it to his pocket in token of peace.

While I was cleaning myself up as well as I could under the circumstances, and struggling to overcome the nausea that still afflicted me, I was able to see the face of the second individual when he stood up for a moment. Or rather, to catch a glimpse of him, because he wore a filthy greatcoat with sleeves that were too long and a cowl that almost completely covered his face, leaving a slit through which, when the light permitted it, one could distinguish his features. And that was just as well, for after many patient attempts to observe him I discovered the existence of a whitish half-closed eye and of another swollen eyeball, enormous and protruding, as though it were almost about to fall to the ground; a nose like a deformed and cankered cucumber, and a yellowish, greasy skin; while, as to the mouth, I could never have sworn that he had one, were it not for the formless sounds that occasionally emerged from that vicinity. From the sleeves, two hands would furtively emerge from time to time, hooked and clawed, and as decrepit as they were swift and predatory.

The abbot turned and met my fearful and questioning gaze. With a nod, he pointed to the first of the two, impatient to recover his freedom so that he could rejoin his companion in his disgusting sorting of bones from the contents of my stomach.

"How curious," said Atto, dusting his sleeves and shoulders carefully. "In the hostelry I am forever sneezing, yet all the dust these two wretches have on them has not caused me to sneeze even once."

And he explained that the two strange beings whom we had encountered were members of the miserable (yet adequately fed) band of those who spent their nights exploring the innumerable cavities under the city of Rome in search of treasures. Not jewels or Roman statues, but the most holy relics of the saints and martyrs which abounded in the catacombs and tombs of the martyrs of the Holy Roman Church, disseminated throughout the length and breadth of the city.

"I do not understand," I broke in. "Are they really allowed to take these holy relics from the tombs?"

"Not only is it permitted: I daresay that it is even necessary," replied Abbot Melani with a hint of irony. "The places frequented by the first Christians are to be regarded as fertile ground for spiritual questing, and sometimes even hunting, *ut ita dicam*, by elevated souls."

Saint Philip Neri and Saint Carlo Borromeo had indeed been in the habit of praying in the catacombs, so the abbot reminded me. And at the end of the last century, a courageous Jesuit, a certain Antonio Bosio, had descended into the most recondite and obscure crevices and had explored all the cavities under Rome, making many marvellous discoveries and publishing a book entitled *Roma Subterranea*, which had met with great and general plaudits. The good Pope Gregory XV had, around 1620, laid down that the remains of saints were to be removed from the catacombs so that these precious relics could be distributed to churches throughout all Christendom, and he had instructed Cardinal Crescenzi to see to the implementation of this holy programme.

I turned towards the two bizarre manikins who were fussing around these human remains, emitting obscene grunts.

"I know it seems curious to you that a mission of such high spirituality should be entrusted to two such beings," continued Atto. "But you must bear in mind that descending into the catacombs and artificial grottoes, of which Rome has so many, is not to everyone's taste. One must enter dangerous places, cross watercourses, face the risk of rock-falls and collapsing galleries. And it takes a strong stomach to go rummaging among the corpses..."

"But they are just old bones."

"That is all too easily said, yet how did you react a few moments ago? Our two friends had just completed their round, as they explained to me while you lay half dead on the ground. In this cavity, they keep their collection. The catacombs are a long way off and there is no danger of encountering one of their competitors around here. So they were not expecting to meet with a living soul; and when we surprised them, they panicked and started to run in all directions. In the confusion, you came too near to their pile of bones and disturbed it, and it collapsed on top of you. And then you fainted."

I looked down and saw that the two strange little men had by now separated their bones from the vomit and had given them a quick cleaning. The little mountain under which I had been buried must have been far higher than myself; and now it all lay spread out on the ground. In reality, the human remains (a skull, a few long bones, and three vertebrae) were few when compared with all the remaining matter: earth, potsherds, stones, wood splinters, moss and roots, rags, all manner of rubbish. What, fuelled by fear, I had experienced as a deluge of death was but the contents of a sack filled by a peasant who had scraped too much from the soil of his little field.

"To exercise a dirty trade like this," the abbot continued, "you need a couple of characters like those whom you see before you. These tomb robbers are called *corpisantari*, after the sacred relics of saints for which they are always searching. If fortune does not smile upon them, they sell some rubbish to the next simpleton they meet. Have you not seen them, in front of your inn, selling Saint John's shoulder-blade or the jaw of Saint Catherine, feathers from angels' wings, splinters from the one True Cross borne by Our Lord? Well, the suppliers are our two friends, or their companions in the trade. When they are in luck, they find the tomb of some presumed martyr. Of course, those who reap the honours of translating the relics of Saint Etcetera to some church in Spain are the cardinals, or that old windbag Father Fabretti, whom Innocent X appointed, if I am not mistaken, *custos reliquiarum ac coemeteriorum*, the Custodian of Relics and Cemeteries."

"Where are we, Signor Abbot?" I asked, confused by our hostile and shadowy surroundings.

"I have mentally retraced the way we have covered and asked these two one or two questions. They call it the Archives, because this is where they heap up their ordure. I would say that we are more or less inside the ruins of the old stadium of Domitian, where during the Roman Empire they held sea battles, with ships. To make matters easier for you, I can tell you that we are under the Piazza Navona, at the end nearest the Tiber. If we had covered the distance from the inn to the same point on the surface, at a good walking pace, it would have taken no more than three minutes."

"So these ruins are from Roman times."

"But of course these are Roman ruins. Do you see those arches? They must be the old structures of the stadium where they held games and naval battles, above which were built the palazzi which now surround the Piazza Navona, following the old oblong design."

"As in the Circo Massimo?"

"Exactly: except that there, everything has remained visible; whereas here it was all buried under the weight of centuries. But you will see, sooner or later, they will excavate here too. There are things that cannot remain buried."

While he told me of matters that were utterly new to me, I was astonished to see for the first time shining in Abbot Melani's eyes the spark of fascination with art and antiquity, despite the fact that he was at that moment deeply involved in what would appear to be very different affairs. I had no way of knowing it at the time, but this inclination was to have not unimportant consequences in this and later adventures.

"Well, well, we should so like to be able to mention, one day, the names of our two nocturnal acquaintances."

"I am Ugonio," said the less runted of the twain.

Atto Melani looked questioningly at the other one.

"Gfrrrlubh," came the sound issuing from under his hood.

"And he is Ciacconio," said Ugonio, hastening to translate Ciacconio's gurglings.

"Can he not speak?" insisted Abbot Melani.

"Gfrrrlubh," replied Ciacconio.

"I understand," said Atto, reining in his impatience. "We humbly beg your pardon for having disturbed your perambulations. But, now that I come to think of it, may I avail myself of this opportunity to inquire whether you have, by any chance, seen someone pass this way, a little while before our arrival?"

"Gfrrrlubh!" broke in Ciacconio.

"He has invisioned a presence," announced Ugonio.

"Tell him that we want to know everything," said I, butting in.

"Gfrrrlubh," repeated Ciacconio.

We looked questioningly at Ugonio.

"Ciacconio entrified the galleria whence your worships emergencied, and was espied there by one who held a lamp-light; whereupon Ciacconio regressed upon his feetsteps. But the lamp-lifter must have entrified a trap-portal, for he disapparitioned like smoke, and Ciacconio sought sanctity here, most alarmified."

"Could he not have told us himself?" asked Abbot Melani, somewhat taken aback.

"But he has now descripted and confessated it," replied Ugonio.

"Gfrrrlubh," confirmed Ciacconio, vaguely piqued.

Atto Melani and I looked at one another in some perplexity.

"Gfrrrlubh," continued Ciacconio, becoming animated, and seeming by his grunts proudly to claim that even he, a poor creature of darkness, could render himself more than useful.

As his companion was most opportunely to interpret for us, Ciacconio had, after the meeting with the stranger, carried out a second minute investigation of the gallery, because his curiosity was stronger than his fear.

"He is a great miner of other people's busyness," explained Ugonio, in the tones of one reiterating an old and worn reproof, "which leads him only into troubleness and misfortunity."

"Gfrrrlubh," broke in Ciacconio, fumbling through his coat in search of something.

Ugonio seemed to hesitate.

"What did he say?" I asked.

"Naught , or only that..."

Triumphantly, Ciacconio produced a screwed-up piece of paper. Ugonio grabbed his forearm and with lightning speed tore it from his hand.

"Hand it over to me or I shall blow your head off," said Abbot Melani calmly, reaching into his right-hand pocket in which he had placed the device with which he had already threatened the two *corpisantari*.

Ugonio slowly reached out and surrendered to my companion the paper which he had scrunched up into a ball. Then without warning he set to kicking and belabouring Ciacconio, calling him, "You soursaggy old scumskinned, batskinned, sow-skinned, scrunchbacked, sodomitic skinaflinter, you puking mewlbrat, you muddy-snouted, slavering, sarcophagous shitebeetle, you bumsquibcracking sicomoron, you slimy old scabmutcheon-shysteroo, you shittard, sguittard, crackard, filthard, lily-livered, lycanthropic, eunichon-bastradion-bumfodder-billicullion-ballockatso, you gorbellied doddipol, calflolly jobbernol, you grapple-snouted netherwarp, you clarty-frumpled, hummthrumming, tuzzle-wenching, placket-racket, dregbilly lepidopter, you gnat-snapping, weedgrubbing, blither-blather, bilge-bottled, ockham-cockam pederaster," and other epithets which I had never heard before, yet which sounded somewhat grave and offensive to my ears.

Abbot Melani did not deign so much as to glance at these painful theatrics and spread out the sheet of paper on the ground, trying to restore it to its original appearance. I craned my neck and read with him. The left side and the right were, alas, badly torn and almost all of the title had been lost. Fortunately, the remainder of the page was perfectly readable:

nda.

MALACHI

ut Primum.

VARICATUS eſt autem Moab in
el, poſtquam mortuus eſt Achab. Ce-
itqueOchozias per cancellos cœnaculi
, quod habebat in Samaria , & ægro-
it : miſitque nuncios , dicens ad eos :
, conſulite Beelzebub deum Accaron
:rum vivere queam de infirmitate mea
:m Domini locutus eſt ad Eliam Thesbi-
: & aſcende in occurſum nunciorum Re-
:es ad eos : nunquid non eſt Deus in Iſraë
.ulendum Beelzebub deumAccaron ? Quæ
dicit Dominus : De lectulo ſuper quem aſc
.eſcendes , ſed morte morieris . Et abiit El
: ſunt nuncii ad Ochoziam.Qui dixit eis : Qt
:s? At illi reſponderunt ei : Vir occurrit nob:
.os : Ite & revertimini ad Regem , qui miſit
.is ei : Hæc dicit Dominus : Nunquid,quia nor
. in Iſrael , mittis ut conſulatur Beelzebub deus ,
? Idcirco de lectulo ſuper quem aſcendiſti, non ʠ
, ſed morte morieris. Qui dixit eis : Cujus figur
.us eſt vir ille , qui occurrit vobis & locutus
.ec ? At illi dixerunt ; Vir piloſus & zona pellic
ctus renibus . Qui ait : Elias Thesbites eſt.Miſitqu·
·quinquagenarium principem , & quinquaginta
ſub eo . Qui aſcendit ad cum: ſedentique in v
tis : ait : Homo Dei , rex præcepit ut deſcenʠ
denſane Fl.·   ·· ··ꞏꞏ·magenario: Si ʰ

"It is a page from the Bible," said I with complete assurance.

"I think so too," the abbot agreed, turning the paper in his hand. "I should say that it is…"

"Malachi," I guessed without hesitation, thanks to the fragment of a name in the upper margin which had almost completely survived recent events.

On the back there was no printing whatsoever but an unmistakable bloodstain (which I had already seen through the page). More blood covered what must be part of a title or heading.

"I think that I understand," said Abbot Melani, turning to Ugonio who was inflicting his last, listless kicks upon Ciacconio.

"What have you understood?"

"Our two little monsters thought they had made a good find."

He proceeded to explain to me that, for the *corpisantari*, the most precious booty came, not from the mere sepulchres of early Christians, but from the glorious tombs of saints and martyrs. It was, however, not easy to recognise these. The criterion for identifying such tombs had caused a never-ending dispute, which had dragged no few learned churchmen into endless controversies. According to Bosio, the bold Jesuit explorer of subterranean Rome, martyrs could be distinguished by symbols such as palms, crowns and vases containing grain or flames of fire, carved upon their tombs. But absolute proofs were glass or terracotta ampoules—found in tombs or sealed with mortar into their outer walls—containing a reddish liquid which was generally regarded as the holy blood of the martyrs. This burning question was long-debated and a special commission eventually cleared the air of all uncertainties, ruling that *palmam et cas illorum sanguine tinctum pro signis certissimis habendas esse.*

"In other words," concluded Atto Melani, "images of palms, but above all the presence of a small ampoule full of red liquid, were a sure sign that one was in the presence of the remains of a hero of the Faith."

"So these phials must be very valuable," I suggested.

"Of course, and not all of them are handed over to the ecclesiastical authorities. After all, any Roman can dedicate himself to the search for antiquities: all he needs is an authorisation from the Pope (Prince Scipione Borghese, for instance, did it, perhaps because the Pope was his uncle) and he can dig, and all he then needs is to find some obliging Doctor of the Church to authenticate any remains that are brought to light. After that, if he is not consumed by devotion, he will sell it. But there is no test to distinguish the true from the false. Whoever finds some fragment of a body can always claim that it is a relic of a martyr. If this were only a problem of money, one could pass over the matter. The fact is that these fragments are blessed and become objects of adoration, the object of pilgrimages, and so on."

"And has no one ever tried to clarify matters?" I asked incredulously.

The Society of Jesus has always enjoyed special facilities for excavating the catacombs, and has arranged the transport of various bodies and relics to Spain, where the holy remains are received in great pomp, and end up all over the world, even as far away as the Indies. In the end, however, the followers of Saint Ignatius themselves came to the conclusion, and confessed as much to the Pontiff, that there was no guarantee that such relics really did belong to saints and martyrs. There were cases, such as the corpses of children, in which proof was difficult. Thus the Jesuits were compelled to ask that the principle of *adoremus quod scimus* be introduced: only relics which can scientifically or reasonably be proved to have belonged to a saint or a martyr should be objects of veneration."

That was why, explained Atto Melani, it was eventually decided that only ampoules of blood could provide conclusive proof.

"And thus," concluded the abbot, "even ampoules are destined to enrich the *corpisantari* and to end up in some chamber of marvels or in the apartments of some very rich and very naive merchant."

"Why naive?"

"Because no one can swear that what the phials contain is the blood of martyrs, or even blood at all. I have examined one, purchased at great cost from a disgusting individual similar to... What is he called? Ciacconio."

"And what did you conclude?"

"That the reddish mud in the ampoule, watered down a little, consisted mostly of brownish earth and flies."

The problem was, explained Abbot Melani, returning to the present, that Ciacconio, after bumping into our thief, had found this page from the Bible stained with what showed every appearance of being blood.

"And finding, or better, selling the beginning of a chapter from the Bible stained with the blood of Saint Calixtus, to name but a name, can bring in plenty of money. That is why his friend is gently reproving him for having revealed to us the existence of the sheet of paper."

"But how is it possible," I protested, "that the thousand-year-old blood of a martyr could be found on a modern printed book?"

"I shall answer you with a story, which I heard last year in Versailles. A fellow in the market was trying to sell a skull which was, he guaranteed, that of the famous Cromwell. One of the would-be buyers pointed out to him that the skull was too small to be that of the great leader, who notoriously had a rather large head."

"And what did the vendor reply?"

"He replied: 'Of course, this was the skull of Cromwell as a child!' That skull, I am assured, was sold—and at a price. Think of it, Ugonio and Ciacconio should have no trouble selling their scrap of Bible stained with the blood of Saint Calixtus."

"Shall we return the page to them, Signor Atto?"

"Not for the time being," said he, raising his voice and turning to the *corpisantari*. "We shall hold onto it and we shall return it to them only when they have done us a couple of favours."

And he explained what we needed.

"Gfrrrlubh," assented Ciacconio, in the end.

అ•అ

Once he had imparted their instructions to the *corpisantari*, who vanished into the darkness, Atto Melani decided that it was time to return to the Donzello.

At that juncture, I asked him whether he did not find it somewhat strange to discover in these galleries a bloodstained page of the Bible.

"That page, in my view, was lost by the thief of your little pearls," was his only reply.

"And how can you be so sure of that?"

"I did not say that I was sure. But think for one moment: the paper seems to be new. The bloodstain (if it is blood, and I think so) does not seem old. It is too vivid. Ciacconio found it, if he was telling—sorry, if he was gurgling—the truth, immediately after his meeting with a stranger in the gallery into which the thief disappeared. Does that not suffice for you? And if we speak of the Bible, who does that bring to mind for you?"

"Padre Robleda."

"Precisely: a Bible smacks of priests."

"Still, the meaning of some details escapes me," I objected.

"What are you getting at?"

"'-*ut primum*' is all that remains of '*Caput primum*', while '*Malachi*' is clearly what remains of '*Malachiae*'. This made me think that under the bloodstain there must have been the word '*profetia*'. So here we have the chapter of the Bible concerning the prophet Malachi," I observed, remembering the lessons received during my almost monastic childhood. "However, I cannot understand the '*nda*' in the first line at the top. Have you any idea, Signor Atto? I have none whatever."

Abbot Melani shrugged his shoulders: "I certainly cannot claim to be an expert on the matter."

I found such a profession of ignorance concerning the Bible singular, coming from an abbot. And, when I came to think of it, his affirmation that "a Bible smacks of priests" sounded strangely crude. What kind of an abbot was he?

Meanwhile, we were returning into the conduit, and Melani had resumed his considerations. "Anyone can possess a Bible, indeed the inn has at least one, is that not so?"

"Certainly, two, to be precise; but I know both of them well and the page which you are holding could not have come from either."

"Of course. But you will agree with me that the page could have come from the Bible of any one of the guests at the Donzello, who might easily have brought a copy of the Scriptures with him on his travels. It is a pity that the tear has removed the ornate initial capital that opens the chapter, which surely comes from the beginning of a chapter in the Book of Malachi, and which would have helped us to trace the origin of our find."

I did not agree with him: there were other strange things about that paper, and I pointed them out to him: "Have you ever seen a page from the Bible printed on one side only, like this one?"

"It must be the end of a chapter."

"But the chapter has hardly begun!"

"Perhaps the prophecy of Malachi is unusually brief. We cannot know, the last lines have been torn off, too. Or perhaps it is common printing practice, or an error, who knows? Be that as it may, Ugonio and Ciacconio, too, will give us a hand: they are too afraid that they will never see their filthy scrap of paper again."

"Speaking of fear, I did not know that you had a pistol," said I, remembering the firearm with which he had threatened the two *corpisantari.*

"Nor did I know that I had one," he replied, looking at me obliquely with a wry grin, and he drew from his pocket the shining wooden metal-tipped barrel, of which the stock seemed to have disappeared inexplicably in Melani's hand when he brandished the instrument.

"A pipe!" I exclaimed. But how is it possible that Ugonio and Ciacconio did not see that?"

"The light was poor, and my face was threatening enough. And perhaps the two *corpisantari* did not wish to find out how much harm I could do them."

I was stupefied by the simplicity of the stratagem, by the nonchalance with which the abbot had carried it off and by its unexpected success.

"And what if one's adversaries should suspect that it is not a pistol?"

"Do as I did, when I faced two bandits one night in Paris. Yell with all your might '*Ceci n'est pas une pipe!*'" replied Abbot Melani, laughing.

Day the Fourth
14TH SEPTEMBER, 1683

✠

Next morning I found myself under the blankets with aching bones and my head in no small state of confusion, evidently as a result of insufficient and fitful sleep and all the adventures of the day before. The long descent into the gallery, the efforts of climbing through trapdoors and up stairways, as well as the horrifying struggle with the *corpisantari*, all had left me worn out in body and in spirit. One thing, however, both surprised and delighted me: the few hours of sleep left to me were not disturbed by nightmares, despite the dreadful death-filled visions which the encounter with Ugonio and Ciacconio had reserved for me. After all, not even the unpleasant (but necessary) search for the thief of the only object of value that I had ever possessed was worth disturbing my night's sleep.

Once I opened my eyes, I was—on the contrary—pleasantly assailed by the sweetest of dreamlike reminiscences: everything seemed to be whispering to me of Cloridia and her smooth and luscious countenance. I was unable to compose into a picture that blessed concert of illusory yet almost real sensory impressions: the lovely face of my Cloridia (thus I called her, already!), her melting, celestial voice, her soft and sensual hands, her vague, light conversation...

I was fortunately dragged away from these melancholy imaginings before languor could irremediably overcome me, giving rise to solitary pursuits which might have robbed me of the little strength that remained to me.

It was the sound of moaning to my right that caught my attention. I turned and saw Signor Pellegrino, sitting up in bed with his back resting against the wall, holding his head in his hands. Exceedingly surprised and delighted to see him in better condition (since the onset of his illness, he had indeed never raised his head from the pillow) I rushed to him and bombarded him with questions.

His only response was to drag himself with difficulty to the edge of the bed and to glance at me absently, without uttering a sound.

Disappointed, and also worried by his inexplicable silence, I rushed to fetch Cristofano.

The doctor came running at once and, trembling with surprise, began hurriedly to examine Pellegrino. But, just when the Tuscan was observing his eyes at close quarters, Pellegrino emitted a thundering *flatus ventris*. This was followed swiftly by a light eructation and then more flatulence. Cristofano needed only a few minutes to understand.

"He is somnolent, I would say aboulic; perhaps he has yet to wake up properly. His colours are still unhealthy. True, he is not speaking, but I do not despair that he may soon recover completely. The haematoma on his head seems to have gone down, and I am no longer so worried about that."

For the time being, Pellegrino seemed utterly stunned and his fever had gone; yet, according to Cristofano, one could not be completely reassured about his condition.

"And why can one not be reassured?" I asked, understanding that the physician was reluctant to entrust me with bad news.

"Your master is suffering from an evident excess of air in the belly. His temperament is bilious and it is rather hot today: that would suggest a need for caution. It will be as well to intervene with an enema, as indeed I already feared that I might have to."

He added that, from that moment onwards, in view of the kind of cures and purgative treatments that he would need, Pellegrino would have to remain alone in his room. We therefore resolved to carry my bedding into the little chamber next door, one of the three that had remained almost completely undisturbed since the death of the former innkeeper, Signora Luigia.

While I was seeing to this quick removal, Cristofano took out from a leather bag a pump with bellows as long as my forearm. At the end of the pump, he inserted a tube, and to that tube, he joined another long, fine one, which ended with a little aperture. He tried out the mechanism a couple of times in order to make sure that the bellows, correctly used, blew air into the conduit and expelled it through the little hole at the end.

Pellegrino assisted at these preparations with an empty stare. I observed him with a mixture of contentment, seeing that he had at last opened his eyes, and apprehension about his bizarre state of health.

"Here we are," said Cristofano at the end of his testing, ordering me to fetch water, oil and a little honey.

Hardly had I returned with the ingredients, when I was surprised to find the doctor busying himself with Pellegrino's half-naked body.

"He is not cooperating. Help me to keep him still."

So I had to help the doctor to denude my master's posterior rotundities, despite his unwillingness to accept the initiative. In the moments that followed, we came close to a struggle (more due to Pellegrino's lack of co-operation than to any real resistance on his part), and I was able to ask Cristofano the purpose of our efforts.

"It is simple," he replied. "I want to make him expel a good deal of useless wind."

And he explained to me that, thanks to the way in which the tubes were arranged at right angles, this particular apparatus enabled one to perform the inflation on one's own, thus saving one's modesty. Pellegrino, however, did not seem to be in any position to look after himself, and so we had to perform the action for him.

"But will it make him feel better?"

Cristofano, almost surprised by the question, said that a clyster (which is the name given by some to this remedy) is always profitable and never harmful: as Redi says, it evacuates the humours in the mildest manner possible, without debilitating the *viscera*, and without causing them to age, as is the case with medicines taken orally.

While he was pouring the preparation into the bellows, Cristofano praised purgative enemas, but also altering, anodyne, lithotriptic, carminative, sarcotic, epulotic, abstergent and astringent ones. The beneficial ingredients were infinite: one could use infusions of flowers, leaves, fruit or seeds of herbs, but also the hooves or head of a castrated lamb, animals' intestines or a broth prepared from worn-out old cocks whose necks had been duly wrung.

"How very interesting," said I, trying to please Cristofano and conceal my own disgust.

"By the way," the physician added, following these useful disquisitions, "in the next few days, the convalescent will have to follow a diet of broths and boiled liquids and waters, in order to recover from so great an extenuation. Today, you will therefore give him half a cup of chocolate, a chicken soup and biscuits dipped in wine. Tomorrow, a cup of coffee, a borage soup and six pairs of cockerel's testicles."

After dealing Pellegrino a series of vigorous piston strokes, Cristofano left him half-naked and charged me with watching over him until the bodily effects of the enema were crowned with success. This happened almost at once, and with such violence, that I could well understand why the doctor had made me remove my things to the little chamber next door.

༚⚬ᜰ

I went down to prepare luncheon, which the physician had recommended must be light but nutritious. I therefore prepared spelt, boiled in ambrosian almond milk with sugar and cinnamon, followed by a soup of gooseberries in dried fish consommé, with butter, fine herbs and scrambled eggs, which I served with bread sliced and diced, and cinnamon. I dished this up to the guests and asked Dulcibeni, Brenozzi, Devizé and Stilone Priàso when it would be convenient to apply the remedies which Cristofano had prescribed against the infection. But all four, taking the meal with signs of irritation, having sniffed it, sighed that for the time being they wanted to be left in peace. I had a suspicion that such unwillingness and irritability had something to do with my inexpert cooking. I therefore promised myself that I would increase the size of the helpings in the future.

After luncheon, Cristofano advised me that Robleda had asked for me, since he needed a little water to drink. I furnished myself with a full carafe and knocked at the Jesuit's door.

"Come in, my son," said he, welcoming me with unexpected urbanity.

And after copiously slaking his thirst, he invited me to sit down. Curious at this behaviour, I asked him if he had had a good night's sleep.

"Ah, tiring, my boy, so tiring," he replied laconically, putting me even more on guard.

"I understand," said I, diffidently.

Robleda's complexion was unwontedly pale, with heavy eyelids and dark bags under his eyes. It looked almost as though he had passed a sleepless night.

"Yesterday, you and I conversed," broached the Jesuit, "but I beg you not to accord too much weight to certain discussions which we may too freely have conducted. Often our pastoral mission encourages us, in order to excite new and more fecund achievements in young minds, to adopt unsuitable figures of speech and rhetorical devices, distilling concepts excessively and indulging in syntactical disorder. The young, on the other hand, are not always ready to receive such fruitful stimulation of the intellect and the heart. The difficult circumstances in which we all find ourselves in this hostelry may also incite us sometimes to interpret others' thoughts erroneously and to formulate our own infelicitously. Therefore, I beg you simply to forget all that we said to each other, especially concerning His Beatitude our most beloved Pope Innocent XI. And, above all, I am deeply concerned that you should not repeat such transitory and ephemeral disquisitions to the guests of the inn. Our reciprocal physical separation might give rise to misunderstandings; I am sure you understand me…"

"Do not worry," I lied, "for I retained little of our conversation."

"Oh, really?" exclaimed Robleda, momentarily vexed. "Well, so much the better. After reconsidering all that was said between us, I felt almost oppressed by the weight of such grave discourse: as when one enters the catacombs and, suddenly, being underground, one feels out of breath."

As he moved towards the door to dismiss me, I was astounded by that sentence, which I saw as being highly revealing. Robleda had betrayed himself. I strove swiftly to devise some argument that might prompt him further to expose himself.

"While standing by my promise not to speak again of these matters, I did in truth have one question on my mind concerning His Beatitude Pope Innocent XI, and indeed all popes in general," said I, the moment before he opened the door.

"Speak on."

"Well, that is…" I stammered, trying to improvise, "I wondered whether there exists a way of determining who, among past pontiffs, were good, who were very good and which ones were saints."

"It is curious that you should ask me this. It was just what I was meditating on last night," he replied, almost as though speaking to himself.

"Then I am sure that you will have an answer for me too," I added, hopeful that this might prolong the conversation.

So the Jesuit asked me again to be seated, explaining to me that there had, over the centuries, been an innumerable succession of statements and prophecies concerning the pontiffs, present, past and future.

"This is because," he explained, "especially in this city, everyone knows or thinks that they know the qualities of the reigning pope. At the same time, they lament past popes and hope that the next one will be better, or even that he will be the Angelic Pope."

"The Angelic Pope?"

"He who, according to the prophecy *Apocalipsis Nova* of the Blessed Amedeo, will restore the Church to its original holiness."

"I do not understand," I interrupted with feigned ingenuousness. "Is the Church, then, no longer holy?"

"I beg of you, my son... Such questions are not to be asked. Rome has always been the target of the propaganda of the papacy's heretical enemies: ever since, a long time ago, the *Super Hieremiam* and the *Oraculum Cyrilli* foresaw the fall of the city and Thomas of Pavia announced visions which foretold the collapse of the Lateran Palace, and both Robert d'Uzès and Jean de Rupescissa warned that the same city in which Peter had laid the first stone was now the City of the Two Columns, the seat of the Antichrist. Such prophecies have one aim: to instil the idea that the Church is to be completely demolished and that the pope is not worthy to remain in his post."

"Which pope?"

"Well, unfortunately, such blasphemous attacks have been directed against all the pontiffs."

"Even against His Beatitude, our own Pope Innocent XI?"

Robleda grew solemn, and in his eyes I noted a shadow of suspicion.

"They include all popes, including indeed His Beatitude Pope Innocent XI."

"And what do they foretell?"

I noticed that Robleda was returning to the subject with a bizarre mixture of reluctance and self-indulgence. He resumed in slightly graver tones, and explained to me that, among many others, there existed a prophecy which claimed to know the whole sequence of popes from about the year 1100 until the end of time. And as though for many years he had had nothing else on his mind, he recited from memory an enigmatic series of Latin mottoes: "*Ex castro Tiberis, Inimicus expulsus, Ex magnitudine montis, Abbas suburranus, De rure albo, Ex tetro carcere, Via transtiberina, De Pannonia Tusciae, Ex ansere custode, Lux in ostio, Sus in cribro, Ensis Laurentii, Ex schola exiet, De rure bovensi, Comes signatus, Canonicus ex latere, Avis ostiensis, Leo sabinus, Comes laurentius,*

Jerusalem Campaniae, Draco depressus, Anguineus vir, Concionator gallus, Bonus comes..."

"But these are not the names of popes," said I, interrupting him.

"On the contrary, they are. A prophet read them in the future, before they came into the world, but he identified them by the symbolic mottoes which I have just been reciting for you. The first was *Ex castro Tiberis*, meaning 'from a castle on the Tiber'. Well, the Pope designated by that motto was Celestine II who was indeed born at Città di Castello on the banks of the Tiber."

"So the prediction was accurate."

"Indeed, it was. But so was the next one, *Inimicus expulsus*, which surely indicated Lucius II of the Cacciaenemici family, a precise translation of the Latin which speaks of expelling enemies. The third pope is *Ex magnitudine montis*: this is Eugene III, born in the city of Grammont, which in French is an exact translation of the motto. Number four..."

"These must be very ancient popes," I interrupted. "I have never heard of them."

"They are of great antiquity, it is true. But even the modern ones were foretold with the greatest of exactitude. *Jucunditas crucis*, number 82 in the prophecy, was Innocent X. And he became pope on the 14th of September, the Feast of the Holy Rood. *Montium custos*, the guardian of the mountains, number 83, was Alexander VII, who founded the *Montes Pietatis*.* *Sydus olorum*, or the star of the swans, number 84, is Clement IX. He in fact lived in the Chamber of the Swans in the Vatican. The motto of Clement X, number 85, was *De flumine magno* or 'from the great river', and he was in fact born in a house by the Tiber, just where the river overflowed its banks."

"So, the prophecy has always come true."

"Let us say that some, indeed many, maintain that," said Robleda indulgently.

At that juncture, he fell silent, as though awaiting a question. In the list of popes foretold by the prophecy, he had stopped at Pope Clement X, number 85. He knew that I would not be able to resist the temptation to ask about the next one: this was His Beatitude Pope Innocent XI, our Pope.

"And what is the motto of number 86?" I asked excitedly.

* Monti di Pietà: a system of pawn offices, now run by the Italian State. (Translator's note.)

"Very well, since you ask me..." said the Jesuit with a sigh, "his motto is, shall we say, rather curious."

"And what is it?"

"*Belua insatiabilis*," said Robleda with a colourless voice, "'insatiable beast'."

I struggled to hide my surprise and dismay. While all the mottoes of the other popes were innocuous enigmas, that of our beloved pontiff was atrocious and menacing.

"But perhaps Our Lord's motto does not refer to his moral qualities!" I objected indignantly, as though seeking reassurance.

"That is unquestionably possible," agreed Robleda tranquilly. "Now that I come to think of it, the arms of the Pope's family include a lion *passant gardant* and an eagle: in other words, two insatiable beasts. That could be, indeed it must be, the explanation," concluded the Jesuit with a calmness more conniving than any smile.

"In any case, you need lose no sleep over this," he added, "for according to the prophecy, there will be 111 popes all in all, and today we are only at number 86."

"But who will be the last pope?" I insisted.

Robleda frowned and seemed thoughtful.

"From Celestine II, the series includes 111 popes. Towards the end, will come the *Pastor angelicus* or the Angelic Pope of whom I spoke to you earlier, but he will not be the last. Five popes will indeed follow, and, at the end, says the prophecy, *in extrema persecutione Sacrae Romanae Ecclesiae sedebit Petrus romanus, qui pascet oves in multis tribulationibus; quibus transactis, civitas septicollis diruetur, et judex tremendus judicabit populum.*"

"In other words, Saint Peter will return, Rome will be destroyed and the Last Judgement will come."

"Bravo, that's it exactly."

"And when will that happen?"

"I told you: according to the prophecy, there is still much time to run. But now it would be in order if you were to leave me: I would not wish you to neglect the other guests listening to these unimportant fables."

Disappointed by the sudden ending of the colloquy, and without having succeeded in obtaining any other useful clue from the mouth of Robleda, I was already on the threshold when I realised that I wanted to satisfy one last, this time genuine, curiosity.

"By the way, who is the author of the prophecy of the popes?"

"Oh, a holy monk who lived in Ireland," said Robleda hurriedly, while closing the door. "He was, I seem to remember, called Malachy."

తోగ

Excited by the unexpected and alarming news, I ran straight to Atto Melani's chamber at the other end of the same floor, to inform him of it. Hardly had I opened the door than I found the room submerged in a sea of papers, books, old prints and packets of letters, all spread in disorder over the bed and the floor.

"I was studying," said he, welcoming me.

"It is he," said I breathlessly.

And I told him of the colloquy with Robleda in which the latter had without any apparent reason referred to the catacombs. The Jesuit had then (but only because I had encouraged him to talk) begun a lengthy discourse in which he spoke of vaticinations concerning the coming of the Angelic Pope, and then, a prophecy concerning the end of the world after a series of 111 pontiffs, which speaks of an "insatiable beast," who is said to be Our Lord Pope Innocent XI, and in the end he had admitted that the prediction had been made by the Irish prophet Malachy...

"Calm down, calm down," broke in Atto. "I fear that you are becoming somewhat confused. I know that Saint Malachy was an Irish monk who lived a thousand years after Christ, quite different from the Prophet Malachi in the Bible."

I assured him that I knew that perfectly well too, nor was I confusing anything, and I repeated the facts, this time setting them out more calmly.

"Interesting," commented Atto at the end. "Two different prophets called Malachi cross our path in the space of a few hours: too much to be pure coincidence. Padre Robleda mentioned to you that he was meditating on Saint Malachy's prophecy just last night, while we found the chapter from the Book of Malachi in the underground galleries. He claims not to remember the Saint's name with any certainty, yet it is known universally. And then he comes out with the catacombs. That the thief of the keys should be a Jesuit would come as no great surprise to me: they have done far worse than that. I would, however, like to know what he might have been looking for under the ground. Now, that would be really interesting."

"To be quite sure that it was Robleda, we should check on his Bible," I observed, "and see if the torn page comes from it."

"Correct. And, to do that, we have but one opportunity. Cristofano has warned us that there will soon be another roll-call for the quarantine: you will have to take advantage of Robleda's absence from his chamber to sneak in and look for his Bible. I think you know where to find the Book of Malachi in the Old Testament."

"After the Book of Kings, among the twelve minor prophets," I promptly replied.

"Bravo. I can do nothing, since Cristofano will be keeping an eye on me. He must have got wind of something: he asked me whether by chance I left my chamber last night."

It was just then that I heard the physician's voice calling my name. I quickly joined him in the kitchen where he informed me that he had heard the Bargello's men announcing from the street that they were ready to make their second roll-call. The hope which all of us had secretly been nourishing, namely that the inspectors might have been distracted by the wait for the outcome of the battle of Vienna, had vanished.

Cristofano was in a state of great anxiety. If Bedfordi did not pass the test, we would almost certainly be transferred to a pest-house.

Following Cristofano's instructions, the whole group assembled in trepidation on the first floor, before the chamber of Pompeo Dulcibeni. I felt a tender twinge when I saw sweet Cloridia smiling at me, sadly too (or at least so I fondly imagined) at the thought that no verbal or other intimacy would be possible at that time. I saw the doctor arrive last, with Devizé and Atto Melani. Contrary to what I had hoped, they were not carrying Bedfordi's almost inert body with them: the Englishman (and this was plain from the consternation on Cristofano's face) was absolutely in no condition to stand on his feet, let alone to reply to the roll-call. While they approached, I saw Atto and the guitarist terminate an intense conversation with nods of agreement.

Cristofano made way for us in the chamber and leaned first out of the window below which the Bargello's ruffians were already craning their necks to observe us. The physician introduced himself and showed at his side the youthful and obviously healthy face of Devizé. Abbot Melani, Pompeo Dulcibeni and Padre Robleda were then called and briefly observed. There was a short pause, during which the inspectors conferred among themselves. I saw that Cristofano and Padre Robleda were almost beside themselves with fear. Dulcibeni, however, stood by impassively. I noticed that, of all the group, only Devizé had left the room.

The inspectors (who even to a layman like myself did not seem very expert in the art of medicine) put a few more generic questions to Cristofano who had in the meanwhile hastened to lead me too to the window, so that I could be duly observed. Then came Cloridia's turn, and she immediately met with some coarse banter on the part of the inspectors, together with allusions to unspecified diseases of which the courtesan might be a carrier.

Our fears were at their height when Signor Pellegrino's turn came at last. Cristofano led him firmly to the window, but without any humiliating tugging or jerking. We all knew that Cristofano was trembling: the very fact of leading my master into the presence of the authorities without expressing any prior reservations meant that he was the first to attest his good health.

Pellegrino smiled weakly at the three strangers. Two of them exchanged questioning glances. A few rods' distance now separated Cristofano and my master from their inquisitors. Pellegrino tottered.

"I warned you!" exclaimed Cristofano angrily, extracting an empty bottle from my master's breeches. Pellegrino belched.

"He has been talking too much with the Greek," jested one of the three from the Bargello, alluding to my master's now notorious weakness for wine. Cristofano had succeeded in passing Pellegrino for drunk rather than ill.

It was then (and I shall never forget the scene) that I saw Bedfordi appear miraculously among us.

He strode towards the window, affectionately greeted by Cristofano, and offered himself to the view of the fearsome triumvirate. I was, like everyone, terrified and confused, almost as though I had witnessed a resurrection. I could have believed that I was seeing his spirit, so utterly did he seem free from the sufferings of the flesh. The trio from the Bargello were not so surprised, being ignorant of the illness that had struck him down in the preceding hours.

Bedfordi uttered something in his own language, which the three ruffians showed with some vexation that they did not understand.

"He is again saying that he wants to be free to leave," explained Cristofano.

The trio, remembering Bedfordi's protests on the occasion of the previous roll-call, and being certain that they would not be understood, mocked him with great and vulgar amusement.

Bedfordi—or rather, his miraculous simulacrum—responded to the jokes of the officious trio with a symmetrical volley of insults and was immediately led away by Cristofano. All of our group then returned, some glancing incredulously at one another, astounded by the Englishman's inexplicable recovery.

Hardly had I entered the corridor than I sought out Atto Melani, in the hope of receiving some explanation. I caught up with him just as he was about to climb the stairs to the second floor. He looked at me with an air of amusement, guessing at once what I yearned to know, and mocked me, singing:

> *Fan battaglia i miei pensieri,*
> *e al cor dan fiero assalto.*
> *Così al core, empi guerrieri,*
> *fan battaglia, dan guerra i miei pensieri...* *

"Did you see how our Bedfordi has recovered?" he asked ironically.

"But it is not possible," I said, protesting incredulously.

Atto stopped halfway up the staircase.

"Did you really believe that a special agent of the King of France would allow himself to be manipulated like a small boy?" he whispered derisively. "Bedfordi is young, small of stature and fair haired; and you just saw a small, fair young man. The Englishman has blue eyes and our Bedfordi this evening likewise had bright glaucous orbs. At the last roll-call, Bedfordi protested because he wanted to leave, and this time he did so yet again. Bedfordi speaks a language which the three from the Bargello do not understand, and indeed they understood nothing of what he said this time either. So, where is the mystery?"

"But it could not be he who..."

"Of course it was not Bedfordi. He is still half-dead in his bed, and we pray that he may one day rise from it again. But if you had a good

* My thoughts do battle, / And proudly storm my heart. / Thus, to my heart, pitiless warriors / Give battle, my thoughts make war...

memory (and to become a gazetteer, you must have a good memory) you would recall that there was some confusion during the last roll-call: when I was called, Cristofano brought Stilone Priàso to the window; when it was Dulcibeni's turn, Cristofano presented Robleda, and so on, all the time pretending that he was making mistakes. In your opinion, after that pantomime, could the Bargello's three men be sure of recognising all the guests at the inn? Bear in mind that the Bargello does not have our effigies, for none of us is the Pope or the King of France."

My silence answered for me.

"Of course, they could recognise no one," the abbot reaffirmed, "apart from the young gentleman with fair hair who protested in a foreign language."

"And so Bedfordi…"

I broke off and had a sudden illumination as I watched Devizé disappear through the door of his chamber.

"… plays the guitar, speaks French, and sometimes pretends that he knows English," said Atto with a conspiratorial smile.

"But then Signor Devizé went to the window a second time in the place of Bedfordi and I did not realise it!"

"You did not realise it because it was absurd, and absurd things, even when true, are the most difficult to see."

"But the Bargello's men called us one by one," I objected, "when the inn was closed down on suspicion of infection."

"Yes, but that first inspection was too confused and chaotic, because the officials had to see to the blocking of the road and the boarding up of the inn as well. And several days have passed since then. The visual obstacle, namely the grille over the first-floor window, did the rest. I myself, from behind that grille, would not be able to identify any of our jailers with any certainty in a day or two's time. And, speaking of eyes, pray, remind me again: what colour are Bedfordi's?"

I reflected for a moment, and a smile came to my lips: "They are… crossed."

"Exactly. If you think carefully on the matter, his squint is his most distinctive trait. When the three inspectors saw two converging blue eyes looking at them (and here, our Devizé played his part well) they had no doubt: it was the Englishman."

I remained lost in silent amazement, turning the matter over and over in my mind.

"And now, go to Cristofano," said Atto, dismissing me. "He will certainly want you to be with him. Do not discuss with him the little tricks which he has helped me to put into effect: he is ashamed of them because he fears he may betray the principles of his art. He is mistaken, but we had better leave him to think as he will."

☙❧

No sooner had I rejoined him than Cristofano gave me comforting news: he had conferred with the Bargello's men, whom he had assured that the condition of the entire group was good. He had then offered them his personal guarantee that any news of importance would be communicated to an emissary, who would call on the hostelry every morning in order to check on the situation with Cristofano himself. This would free us of the need to appear together for a roll-call, as we had indeed done (and miraculously) hitherto.

"At other times, such frivolity would not have been possible," opined the doctor.

"What do you mean?"

"I know what measures were taken in Rome during the Pestilence of 1656. Scarcely had news been received of suspected cases of infection in Naples, than all roads were closed between the two cities, and all movements of persons and goods with other bordering territories were prohibited. Commissioners were sent to the four parts of the Pontifical State to see to the implementation of public health measures. The coast guards were reinforced, so as to limit or prevent landings by ships, while in Rome a number of the city's gates were immediately barred, and those which remained open were subject to rigorous filtering in order to limit the passage of persons to what was strictly necessary."

"And all this was not sufficient to prevent the infection?"

It was already too late, explained the doctor sadly. A Neapolitan fishmonger, one Antonio Ciothi, had already come to Rome from Naples in the preceding month of March, to escape from an accusation of homicide. He had taken up lodgings in a hostelry at Trastevere, in the Montefiore quarter, when he was suddenly taken ill. The wife of the host (Cristofano had learned these details from conversations with a number of persons who had witnessed these events) had immediately arranged for the fishmonger to be transported to Saint John's Hospital, where the young man died a few hours later. The post-mortem found no cause for alarm. A few days later, however, the wife of the host died, then her mother and her sister. In these cases, too, no tokens were found of infection with the plague, but it was nevertheless decided, in view of the all too clear coincidence, to send the host and all his servants and apprentices to the pest-house. Trastevere was cordoned off from the remainder of the city and the special Congregation for Public Health was convened to deal with the emergency. Commissions were set up for every ward, consisting of prelates, gentlemen, chirurgeons and notaries, who carried out a census of the city's inhabitants, noting their trade, their material conditions and the state of their health, precisely so as to enable the Congregation for Public Health to have a clear view of the situation and to visit and succour such houses as might need assistance, on alternate days.

"But now all the city can think only of the battle for Vienna," observed Cristofano, "and our three inspectors told me that the Pope was seen recently prostrated before the crucifix, weeping in dismay and apprehension for the fate of all Christendom; and when the Pope weeps, so the Romans reason, we must all tremble."

The physician added that the responsibility which he had taken upon himself was extraordinarily grave, and that it fell also upon my shoulders. Henceforth, we must scrutinise with the closest attention every slight variation in our lodgers' health. Moreover, any shortcomings on the part of either of us (and he would certainly report any breaches I might commit) would entail grave penalties for us. In particular, we must at all costs ensure that no one should leave the inn before the end of the quarantine. However, to ensure the necessary control, the two rounds of the watch would continue to make sure that no one would attempt to undo the boards or lower themselves from the windows.

"I shall serve you in all things," I said to Cristofano in order to appease him; yet, I awaited nightfall impatiently.

The otherwise welcome suspension of the roll-call had the unfortunate effect of compromising the plan, hatched out with Atto Melani, of looking into Padre Robleda's Bible. I informed the abbot discreetly of this, slipping a note under his door and returning at once to the kitchen, for I feared that Cristofano (who was moving from one chamber to the next in order to visit his patients) might surprise me in conversation with him.

It was Cristofano himself, however, who called me to the chamber of Pompeo Dulcibeni on the first floor. The gentleman from Fermo had suffered an attack of sciatica. I found him in bed, lying on one side, while he begged the doctor to set him back on his feet as soon as possible.

Cristofano manipulated Dulcibeni's legs pensively. He would raise the one and order me at the same time to bend the other one: with each such movement, the physician would stop and await the patient's reaction. Every now and then, he would cry out, and Cristofano would nod solemnly.

"I see. Here we need a magisterial cataplasm with cantharides. My boy, while I prepare this, anoint all his left side with this balm," said he, handing me a small jar.

He then informed Dulcibeni that he would have to wear a magisterial cataplasm for eight days.

"Eight days! Do you mean that I must remain immobilised for that long?"

"Of course not: the pain will be attenuated a long time before that," retorted the doctor. "Obviously, you will not be able to run. But what does that matter to you? As long as the quarantine lasts, you will not be able to do more than while away the time."

Dulcibeni grumbled somewhat ill-temperedly.

"Take comfort," added Cristofano. "There is one here younger than yourself, yet full of infirmities: Padre Robleda does not show it, but for several days now he has been suffering from rheumatism. His must be a delicate constitution, for the inn does not seem damp to me and the weather these days is fine and dry."

I gave a start on hearing these words. My suspicions in regard to Robleda became yet more acute. I saw, meanwhile, that the doctor had taken from his bag a jar full of dead coleoptera. He drew out two of a golden-greenish colour.

"Cantharides, or the Spanish fly," said he, putting the beetles under my nose, "dead and desiccated. They are miraculous as vesicants—and as aphrodisiacs, too."

Saying this, he began to pulverise them carefully over a piece of saturated gauze.

"Ah, the Jesuit has rheumatism," exclaimed Dulcibeni after a while. "So much the better; that way he will leave off sticking his nose into everyone else's business."

"What do you mean?" asked Cristofano, busying himself on his beetles with a little knife.

"Did you not know that the Society of Jesus is a nest of spies?"

My heart leapt into my mouth. I must know more. But Cristofano did not seem to be drawn to the subject and Dulcibeni's assertion was thus on the point of dying unanswered.

"Surely you do not mean that seriously?" I asked forcefully.

"Very much so!" replied Dulcibeni with conviction.

In his opinion, not only were the Jesuits masters of the art of espionage, but they claimed it as a privilege of their order, and whosoever practised that art without their express permission was to be severely punished. Before the Jesuits came into the world, other religious orders had also played a part in the intrigues surrounding the Apostolic See. But since the followers of Saint Ignatius had applied themselves to the exercise of espionage, they had outrun them all. This was because the pontiffs had always had an absolute need to penetrate the most recondite affairs of princes. Knowing that no one had ever succeeded in the business of spying as well as the Jesuits, they made heroes of them. They sent them to all major cities and favoured them with privileges and papal bulls, elevating them above all other orders.

"Excuse me," objected Cristofano, "but how could the Jesuits spy so well? They cannot frequent women, who always gossip too much; they cannot be seen in the company of criminals or persons of low station, and moreover..."

The explanation was simple, replied Dulcibeni: the pontiffs had assigned the sacrament of Confession to the Jesuits, not only in Rome but in all the cities of Europe. Through Confession, the Jesuits could insinuate their way into the minds of all, rich and poor, princes and peasants. But above all, they thereby scrutinised the inclinations and disposition of every counsellor and minister of state: with practised rhetoric, they mined the depths of men's hearts for all the resolutions and reflections which their victims were secretly nurturing.

In order to dedicate themselves entirely to Confession, and to gain ever greater profit from that source, they had obtained from the Holy See the right to exemption from other holy offices. Meanwhile, the victims took the bait. The kings of Spain, for instance, had always used Jesuit confessors and wished their ministers to do likewise in all the lands under Spain's rule. Other princes, who had hitherto lived in good faith and were unaware of the malice of the Jesuits, began to believe that these fathers possessed some special virtue as confessors.

Gradually, they came to follow the example of the kings of Spain and also chose Jesuits as their confessors.

"But someone must surely have exposed them," argued the physician, while he continued to make the carcasses of the cantharides crackle under his little scalpel.

"Of course. But once their game was discovered, they placed themselves at the service of this or that prince, as the opportunity presented itself, always ready to betray them."

That was why everyone loved them and everyone hated them, said Dulcibeni: they were hated because they served everyone as spies, they were loved because no better spies could be found to fulfil the sovereigns' purposes. They were loved, because they offered their services voluntarily as spies; they were hated because they thereby gained the greatest profit for their order and inflicted the greatest damage upon the whole world.

Cristofano applied the magisterial cataplasm to Dulcibeni, sprinkled with little fragments of beetle, and we both took our leave of him. I was absorbed in a jumble of thoughts: first, the physician's reference to Robleda's curious rheumatisms, then the revelation that the Spanish Jesuit had, at the seminary, been trained more to spy than to pray: all confirmed me more in my suspicions about Robleda.

I was about to retire at last (I really needed rest after the exertions of the previous night) when I noticed that the Jesuit had left his chamber, accompanied by Cristofano, in order to go to the pit near the kitchen where it was possible to deposit organic dejections. Faced with so propitious an opportunity, thought and action were one: I moved silently to the second floor and carefully pushed the door of the Jesuit's chamber, slipping inside. But it was too late: I thought I heard Padre Robleda's footsteps climbing back up the stairs.

I rushed out and turned hurriedly towards my own chamber, disappointed by this failure.

౸‐౸

On my way, I stopped to call on my master, whom I found sitting up in bed. I had to help him loosen his bowels. He put some confused and listless questions to me concerning his own state of health because, he stammered, the Sienese physician had treated him like a child, hiding the truth from me. I endeavoured in my turn to calm him down, after which I helped him to drink, arranged his bedding as best I could and stroked his head for a long time, until he fell asleep.

Thus I could shut myself into my own room. I took out my little notebook and, in a state of extreme fatigue, I wrote down—in truth, somewhat hurriedly—the latest events.

Once I had retreated to the bed, my need for rest struggled with all the thoughts which came crowding in, striving in vain to arrange themselves into a reasonable and orderly whole. Perhaps the page of the Bible found by Ugonio and Ciacconio had belonged to Robleda, and he had lost it in the underground galleries near the Piazza Navona: it was probably he who had stolen the keys, and in any case, he had access to the tunnels. The assistance which I had given to Abbot Melani had exposed me to unspeakable terrors, as well as the struggle with the loathsome *corpisantari*. Yet the abbot himself had resolved the situation with the aid of a mere pipe disguised as a pistol: a success which he had then repeated, planning and carrying out the deception of the three emissaries of the Bargello, and thus circumventing the danger of a state of pestilence being declared, with all the frenzied controls to which that would have given rise. My lingering mistrust for Abbot Melani was subtly tempered by thankfulness and admiration, so much so that I awaited with a certain impatience the moment when the search for the thief would resume, almost certainly that very night. I wondered whether the fact that the abbot was suspected of espionage and involvement in political intrigues might not be something of a disadvantage for us all; but then, I thought, it was if anything the contrary: thanks to his cunning, the whole group of guests of the hostelry had been saved from the dreadful prospect of internment in a pest-house. He had, moreover, informed me of his mission, and thus given a token of his trust in me. He had purloined letters from Colbert's house; but such doings were, he affirmed, the direct and ineluctable consequence of his devotion to the French sovereign; nor did proofs exist to the contrary. I rejected with a shiver the sudden appearance, among my lucubrations, of the disgusting mass of human remains which Ciacconio's heap had disgorged onto me, and suddenly felt an overwhelming flood of gratitude for Abbot Melani. Sooner or later, I reflected, finally giving way to the promptings of Morpheus, I would be unable to prevent myself from revealing to the other guests the presence of mind he had shown in dealing with the two *corpisantari* and holding them at bay with promises and threats in equal measure.

Such, I imagined, must be the actions of a special agent of the King of France, and I only regretted that I had neither the knowledge nor the experience necessary adequately to convey such admirable undertakings: a network of secret passages under the city; an agent of the King of France selflessly and and at great peril hunting down rogues and ruffians; an entire group of gentlemen sequestered as a result of a mysterious death and suspected of infection with the plague; and finally, Superintendent Fouquet, believed dead, yet sighted in Rome by informers of Colbert. Now almost overcome by tiredness, I prayed heaven that I might one day, as a gazetteer, be able to write of similar marvellous events.

The door (which I ought in truth to have closed more carefully) opened on squeaking hinges. I turned towards it just in time to see a shadow hide swiftly behind the wall.

I arose and, leaping from my bed to surprise the intruder, rushed out into the corridor. I saw a figure a few paces from the door. It was Devizé, who held his guitar in his hand.

"I was sleeping," I protested, "and Cristofano has forbidden us to leave our chambers."

"Look," said he, pointing towards the object of his visit on the ground.

Suddenly, I realised that I was walking on a carpet of small stones, whose crunching had accompanied me from the moment I had left my bed. I felt the ground with the palm of my hand.

"It looks like salt," I said to Devizé.

I brought one of the little stones to my tongue.

"It is indeed salt," I confirmed in alarm, "but who can have spread it on the ground?"

"In my opinion, it was..." said Devizé, but as he pronounced the name, he handed me his guitar and his last words were lost in the silence of the night.

"What did you say?"

"This is for you," said he with an ironic little laugh, as he handed me the instrument, "seeing that you like the sound of it so much."

I felt myself vaguely touched. I was not certain that I could not produce from those gut strings some agreeable sound, or perhaps even a pleasing melody. Indeed, why not attempt that ineffable

melody which I had heard performed by the French musician? I decided to try at once, in his presence, despite knowing that I was exposing myself to his scorn. I was already exploring the fingerboard
with my left hand, while the other felt the gentle resistance of the
strings near to the sound hole in the instrument beloved by the Most
Christian King, when I was surprised by a touch as familiar as it was
unexpected.

"It has come to see you," remarked Devizé.

A fine tabby cat with green eyes, imploring a little food, was
laying siege to me, rubbing its tail with polite insistence against
my calf. I was more alarmed than ever by this surprise visit. If a cat
had found its way into the inn, I thought, perhaps there existed
another way of communicating with the outside world which Abbot Melani had not yet discovered. I raised my eyes to share my
thoughts with Devizé. He had disappeared. A hand gently shook
my shoulder.

"Should you not have closed yourself in?"

☙❧

I opened my eyes. I was in my bed, and Cristofano had roused me
from my dream, asking me to prepare and serve dinner. Reluctantly
and confusedly, I abandoned my visions.

After quickly restoring some order to the kitchen, I prepared a
soup of artichoke stalks with dried fish stock and good oil, onions,
peas and *involtini*, little rolls made up of tunny-fish slices with a lettuce filling. This I served up with a generous piece of cheese and a
quarter of a pint of watered-down red wine. Over everything, I sprinkled cinnamon, as I had again promised myself that I would. Cristofano himself assisted me with serving, personally feeding Bedfordi
while I was thus freed to bring food to all the others and, above all,
to feed my master.

Once I had fed Pellegrino, I felt a compelling need for a little
pure air in my lungs. The long days of seclusion, most of them spent
in the kitchen with the door and window sealed and barred, amidst
the smells of cooking continuously wafting from the fireplace, had
weighed down on my chest. I therefore resolved to tarry a while in
my little chamber. I opened the window, which gave onto the alleyway, and looked down: not a soul was to be seen on that sunny late
summer afternoon. Only the watchman dozed placidly, huddled in

the corner of the building on the Via dell'Orso. I leaned on the sill with my elbows and breathed in deeply.

"But sooner or later, the Turks will clash with the most powerful princes in Europe."

"Ah yes? And with whom exactly?"

"Well, for example, with the Most Christian King."

"Well then that will be the ideal occasion for them to shake hands without hiding."

The voices, excited yet prudently muted, were unmistakeably those of Brenozzi and Stilone Priàso. They came from the second floor, where the windows of their adjoining chambers were set quite close together. I leaned out discreetly to take a look: like some new Pyramus and Thisbe, the two had devised a rather simple mode of communication beyond Cristofano's strict surveillance. Both being restless and curious by temperament, they could thus give free rein to their irrepressible anxiety.

I wondered whether I ought to profit by that unhoped-for opportunity: unseen, I could perhaps glean some additional information from these two singular personages, one of whom had proven to be a fugitive. And perhaps I might learn something useful for the complicated investigations in which I was assisting Abbot Melani.

"And Louis XIV is the real enemy of Christendom: he, not the Turks," proclaimed Brenozzi in bitter, impatient tones. "You will be well aware that in Vienna the Christian princes are fighting to save Europe from the Infidel. Yet the King of France was unwilling to lend his assistance to the enterprise. That was no accident, truly no accident!"

As I have already told, and as I had crudely learned in those months from the chattering of the populace and from the new visitors to the hostelry, Our Lord Pope Innocent XI had worked strenuously to form a Holy League against the Turks.

"It is shameful," assented Stilone Priàso. "And yet he is the most powerful sovereign in all Europe."

"I tell you, better Mahomet than those arrogant Frenchmen! They bombarded Genoa with a thousand cannon-shots for no better reason than that their fleet had received no salute when passing before the port."

Brenozzi stopped, perhaps gloating over the disconsolate expression which I could imagine painted on the Neapolitan's countenance.

Stilone, for his part, soon resumed with other pressing observations, so that the conversation became more animated.

I leaned out cautiously from my unsuspected position, looking down on their heads from above: in the heat of their conversation, the pair recovered the vitality lost in the darkness of solitude, and political passion almost dispelled fear of the pestilence. Did not the same thing occur with the other guests, whenever my visits or those of the physician—sometimes accompanied by inhalations of pungent vapours, spicy oils and gentle pressures—loosened their tongues and caused them to release a flood of their most intimate reflections?

"In all Europe," resumed Stilone Priàso, "only Prince William of Orange, despite the fact that he is always hunting for loans, has succeeded in stopping the French, who have gold to spare, and in imposing the Peace of Nijmegen."

Once again, the Dutchman William of Orange made an appearance in our lodgers' talk, he whose name had first arisen in Bedfordi's delirium and then been sketched by Abbot Melani. I was curious about this noble and impoverished David whose military prowess was equalled by the fame of his debts.

"For as long as the Most Christian King's mania for conquest remains unassuaged," insisted Brenozzi, "there will be no peace in Europe. And do you know when that will come to pass? When the Imperial Crown shines on the head of the King of France."

"You are, I imagine, referring to the Holy Roman Empire."

"But of course! To become Emperor, that is what he wants! That is why France is so much at ease with the Turkish invasion: if they press on Vienna, the eastern flank of the Empire is broken while France expands into its western flank."

"True! A pincer manoeuvre."

"Precisely that."

That was why, Brenozzi continued, when Innocent XI called upon the European powers to rally their forces against the Turks, the Most Christian King and first-born son of the Church refused to send troops, although he was begged to do so by all Christian leaders. Louis XIV had even tried to impose upon the Emperor in Vienna an odious agreement: making his neutrality conditional upon recognition of the conquests such as Alsace and Lorraine gained by his banditry on the western borders of the Habsburg Empire.

"He even had the gall to describe his claims as 'moderate'. Yet, the Emperor, although up to his neck in trouble, did not acquiesce. Now the Most Christian King is abstaining from hostilities: and do you think that is out of scruple? No! It is a tactical decision. He is waiting until Vienna is exhausted. Then he will be able to resume his invasions with all ease. Already, at the end of August, it was being said that the French troops were on a war footing."

If only Brenozzi could have read on my face the grave thoughts which these words inspired! Perched above the pair and eavesdropping on their conversation, I was biting on a bitter pill: to what manner of monstrous sovereign had Atto Melani sworn his services? I could not deny that I had grown inexorably attached to the abbot; and despite all the ups and downs between us, I had not yet ceased to regard him as my master and guide.

Thus, yet again the victim of my own mania for investigation and the discovery of knowledge, I found myself condemned to learn *nolens volens* things of which I would have preferred never to hear a word breathed.

"Ah, but that is nothing," added Brenozzi with a viperous hiss. "Have you heard the latest news? Now the Turks are protecting the French merchant fleet from pirates. So now trade with the Orient is in the hands of the French."

"And what will the Turks gain in exchange?" asked Stilone.

"Oh, nothing," sneered Brenozzi ironically, "perhaps only... victory in Vienna."

Hardly had the inhabitants barricaded themselves within the city, explained Brenozzi, than the Turks excavated a network of trenches and tunnels which went under the walls and placed very powerful mines, several times breaching the fortifications. Now, this was the very technique of which the French engineers and sappers were past masters.

"You are saying, in other words, that the French are in league with the Turks," concluded Priàso.

"It is not I who am affirming that; this was the opinion of the military experts in the Christian camp in Vienna. The armies of the Most Christian King had learned the art of using trenches and tunnels from two soldiers in the service of Venice, during the defence of Candia. The secret then reached Vauban, a military engineer in the service of the Most Christian King. Vauban perfected it: vertical trenches, with which to bring mines forward, and horizontal trenches to move troops from one point to another in the camp. This is a deadly stratagem: hardly has the right breach been made than the troops enter the besieged city. Now, suddenly, the Turks have become masters of this technique, in Vienna. Do you think that is a coincidence?"

"Speak more softly," warned Stilone Priàso. "Do not forget that Abbot Melani is just next door to us."

"Ah yes, that French spy who's no more an abbot than Count Dönhoff. You are right. Let us leave off here," said Brenozzi, and after exchanging salutations, the two withdrew.

Now other long shadows were being cast over Atto. What was the meaning of that observation which aimed a shot at some unknown personage? While closing the window, I turned over in my mind the matter of Melani's ignorance of the Bible. Curious, I thought, for an abbot.

∂∞↔

"Guitar, salt and cat," laughed Cloridia, much amused. "Now we have something better."

I had tidied up the kitchen with only one thought in my mind: to return to her. Brenozzi's grave statements surely called for a later confrontation with Abbot Melani: but the night was there for such matters, when he himself would come to my door to lead me back into the underground galleries. I had hurriedly brought their victuals to the other prisoners, using various pretexts to leave those who, like Robleda and Devizé, tried to retain me. It was, however, far more urgent that I should once again be able to enter into colloquy with the fair Cloridia, and this I did with the excuse that I wanted to interpret the second curious dream I had had since the doors of the inn had been sealed by the hand of the Bargello's men.

"Let us begin with the scattered salt," said Cloridia, "and I warn you that it is not a good sign. It means assassination, or opposition to our designs."

She read the disappointment on my face.

"But each case must be carefully weighed up on its own merits," she added, "because it is not said that this meaning refers to the dreamer. In your dream, for instance, it could refer to Devizé."

"And the guitar?"

"It means: great melancholy, or work without recognition: like that of a peasant who labours all the year round without ever gaining any satisfaction. Or an excellent painter, or architect, or musician, whose work no one knows and who is always neglected. You see that it is almost synonymous with melancholy."

I was deeply upset. Two rather bad symbols in the same dream, to which, Cloridia announced, a third was to be added.

"The cat is a very clear sign: adultery and lust," she declared.

"But I have no wife."

"For the exercise of lust, matrimony is not necessary," retorted Cloridia, maliciously twisting a tress of her hair on her cheek, "and as for adultery, remember: every sign must be carefully valued and weighed up."

"But how? If I am not married, I am a bachelor and that is that."

"But then you really know absolutely nothing," Cloridia gently reproved me. "Dreams can also be interpreted in a manner completely opposed to their appearance. Thus, they are infallible, because one can just as easily conjecture the pro and the contra."

"But if that is so, a dream can mean everything and its contrary..." I objected.

"You think so?" she replied, arranging the tress behind her neck and, with a wide circular movement of her arms, raising the round and firm cupolas of her breasts.

She sat upon a stool, leaving me standing.

"Please," said she, untying a velvet ribbon ornamented with a cameo, which she kept tied around her neck, "be so kind as to adjust this properly, for I cannot manage with the mirror. Place it a little lower, but not too much. Do it gently, my skin is so delicate."

As though it was necessary to facilitate my task, she spread her arms wide behind her head, thus exposing immoderately the bosom which spilled from her *décolletage*, a hundred times more flowery than the meadows of the Quirinale and a thousand times more perfect than the dome of Saint Peter's.

Seeing me colour at the sudden spectacle, Cloridia took the opportunity to evade my objection. She continued imperturbably, while I busied myself around her neck.

"Some hold that dreams which precede sunrise relate to the future; those which come while the sun is rising refer to the present, and those which follow the sun's appearance concern the past. Dreams are surer in summer and in winter than in autumn and spring, and at sunrise, rather than at any other hour of day. Others claim that dreams made at Advent or the feast of the Annunciation augur solid and lasting things; while those which occur on moveable feasts (such as Easter) designate variable things, on which one may not count. Yet others... Ouch! no, that will not do, it is too tight. How come your hands are trembling?" she asked with a cunning little smile.

"Really, I have almost done it, I did not mean..."

"Calm down, calm down, we have all the time that we want," she winked, seeing that I had failed to tie the knot for the fifth time. "Yet others," resumed Cloridia, uncovering her neck unduly and raising her breasts even closer to my hands, "say that in Bactriana there is a stone called Eumetris which, if placed under the head during sleep, will convert dreams into solid and certain predictions. Some utilise only chemical preparations: perfume of mandrake and myrtle, water of verbena and powdered laurel leaves applied behind the head. But there are also those who recommend cats' brains with bats' dejections, seasoned in red leather, or who stuff a fig with pigeon's droppings and coral dust. Believe me, for nocturnal visions, all these remedies are very, very stimulating..."

Suddenly, she took my hands between hers and looked at me in amusement: I still had not succeeded in tying the knot. My fingers, clumsily entangled with the ribbon, were icy; hers were boiling. The little ribbon fell into her corsage and disappeared. Someone would have to retrieve it.

"In sum," she resumed, squeezing my hands and fixing me in her gaze, "it is important to have clear, certain, lasting, true dreams, and where there's a will there's a way. If you dream that you are not married, that may perhaps mean the exact opposite, in other words, that you soon will be. Or perhaps it means you are not, and that is that. Have you understood?"

"But in my case, is it not possible to understand whether the appearance of the dream is true, or the contrary?" I asked in a very small voice and with my cheeks burning.

"Of course it is possible."

"And why will you not tell me, then?" I implored, involuntarily lowering my gaze to the perfumed cleft which had swallowed up the ribbon.

"Simple, my dear: because you have not paid."

She ceased smiling, pushed my hands brusquely away from her bosom, retrieved the little ribbon and tied it around her neck in a flash, as though she had never needed help.

I went down the stairs with as sad a soul as a human soul can be, cursing the whole world, which was so incapable of bending to meet my desires, and wishing myself in hell for having been so inept an interpreter of that world. I being miserably impoverished, the dreams which I had confided to Cloridia had fallen naked and defenceless into the lap of a courtesan: how could I have so lost touch with reality? How could I have imagined, dolt that I was, that I could win her favours without paying royally for them? And how could I hope, simpleton that I was, that she might, *liberaliter*, open her mind, and what is more, to me rather than to others a thousand times more talented and more deserving and admirable? And should I not also have been suspicious of her request, on the occasion of both her consultations concerning dreams, that I should lie down on her bed, while she sat on a chair by the bedhead, close to my shoulders? Such an incomprehensible and dubious request should have reminded me of the sadly mercenary nature of our brief encounters.

Because of my sad thoughts, it was a pleasant accident to encounter Abbot Atto Melani before my door at the foot of the stairs, already impatient at having been kept briefly waiting. The latter risked betraying our appointment to Cristofano when, on my arrival, he was unable to hold back a resounding sneeze.

Night the Fourth

Between *the* 14ᵗᴴ & 15ᵗᴴ September, 1683

✠

This time we traversed the series of galleries under the Donzello more swiftly and more safely. I had brought with me Pellegrino's broken fishing rod, but Abbot Melani was opposed to inspecting the ceiling of the tunnels, as we had done when we had discovered the trapdoor to the upper cavity. We were, he reminded me, due at an important meeting; and in view of the circumstances of that encounter, there could be no question of delay. He then noticed my surly face and remembered that he had seen me descending from Cloridia's little tower. An amused smile played on his lips and he intoned:

> *Speranza, al tuo pallore*
> *so che non speri più.*
> *E pur non lasci tu*
> *di lusingarmi il core...* *

I had no desire to be entertained and decided to silence Atto by putting to him the question which had been on my mind ever since I had overheard Brenozzi. The abbot stopped abruptly.

"Am I an abbot? But what kind of question is that?"

I begged his pardon and said that never would I have wished to put such inappropriate queries to him, but Signor Angiolo Brenozzi had spoken at great length with Stilone Priàso from his window and in the course of that conversation, many things had been recounted and many considerations touched upon, amongst which, the conduct of the Most Christian King in his dealings with the Sublime Porte and the Holy See; and among the many words exchanged, the Venetian had expressed the opinion that Melani was no more an abbot than Count Dönhoff.

---

* Hope, from your pallor / I know you hope no more. / And yet you do not cease / From flattering my heart...

"Count Dönhoff... How clever of him!" hissed Atto Melani sardonically, hastening at once to explain. "Obviously, you have no idea who Dönhoff is. It should suffice for your purposes to know that he is the Diplomatic Resident of Poland in Rome, and that during these months of war with the Turks, he has been very, very busy. To give you an idea, the money which Innocent XI is sending to Poland for the war against the Turks also passes through his hands."

"And what would that have to do with you?"

"It is no more than a low and offensive insinuation. Count Jan Kazimierz Dönhoff is indeed not an abbot: he is a Commander of the Order of the Holy Spirit, Bishop of Cesena and Cardinal with the title of San Giovanni a Porta Latina. I, on the other hand, am Abbot of Beaubec with letters patent from His Majesty Louis XIV, confirmed by the Royal Council. What Brenozzi means is that I am an abbot only by the will of the King of France, and not the Pope. And how did they come to this question of abbots?" he asked, as we moved on once more.

I gave him a brief account of the conversation between the pair: how Brenozzi had represented the growing power of the King of France and how the Sovereign intended to ally himself with the Sublime Porte in order to put the Emperor in difficulties and to have a free hand to pursue and consolidate his conquests, and how such designs had made him an enemy of the Pontiff.

"Interesting," commented Melani. "Our glass-blower detests the French Crown and, judging by his hostile remarks, his feelings for yours truly can scarcely be sympathetic. I shall do well to bear that in mind."

Then he looked at me with narrowed eyes, showing clear signs of annoyance. He knew that he owed me an explanation concerning his abbot's title.

"Do you know what the Right of Regalia is?"

"No, Signor Atto."

"It is the right to appoint bishops and abbots and to have title to their property."

"Therefore it is one of the Pope's rights."

"No, no... One moment!" broke in Atto. "Listen carefully, for this is one of those things which will serve you well in the future, when you are a gazetteer. The question is a sensitive one: who owns church property, when it is on French soil? The Pope or the King? Remember: this concerns not only the right to appoint bishops and to grant ecclesiastical benefices and prebends, but the material ownership of convents, abbeys and land."

"Indeed... it is hard to tell."

"I know. In point of fact the pontiffs and the kings of France have been squabbling over this for the past four hundred years or so because, obviously, no king will voluntarily cede a piece of his kingdom to a pope."

"And has the issue been resolved?"

"Yes, but the peace was broken with the arrival of this pope, Innocent XI. In the last century, the jurists finally came to the conclusion that the right of regalia belonged to the King of France. And, for a long time, no one queried that decision. Now, however, two French bishops (note the coincidence: both Jansenists) have reopened the matter with Innocent XI immediately extending his support to them. Thus, the dispute has resumed."

"In other words, were it not for Our Lord the Pope, there would be no discussion whatsoever concerning the question of regalia."

"Of course not. Only he could have hatched the idea of so clumsily disturbing relations between the Holy See and the Firstborn Son of the Church."

"If I understand correctly, you, Signor Atto, were appointed abbot by the King of France and not by the Pope," I concluded, scarcely concealing my surprise.

He replied with a mumbled assent, stepping up his pace.

I gained the distinct impression that Atto Melani did not desire to wish the matter any further. I, however, had at last rid myself of a doubt, which had taken hold when I was in the kitchen, listening to Cristofano, Stilone Priàso and Devizé recount Atto's obscure past to one another. That doubt had deepened when we examined the torn page from the Bible found by the *corpisantari*. His scant familiarity with the Holy Scriptures now coincided with his revelations concerning the right of regalia, which permitted the King of France to make an abbot of whomsoever he wished.

I was, then, not in the presence of a true churchman, but of a mere castrato singer who had received a title and a living from Louis XIV.

"Do not place overmuch trust in Venetians," resumed Atto, breaking in on my thoughts at that very moment. "To understand their nature, one need only observe how they behave with the Turks."

"What do you mean to say?"

"The truth is that the Venetians, with their galleys full of spices, fabrics and all manner of goods, have always maintained a rich commerce with the Turks. Now, their trade is falling off, with the arrival on the scene of superior competitors, among them the French. And I can well imagine what else Brenozzi will have told you: that the Most Christian King hopes Vienna will fall so that he can then invade the German Electorates and the Empire and share all the spoils with the Sublime Porte. That is why Brenozzi mentioned Dönhoff: he meant that perhaps I was in Rome to lend a hand to some French plot. It is indeed from this city that, by the will of Innocent XI, money is convoyed for the relief of besieged Vienna."

"While in fact that is not the case," I added, almost as though I were demanding some confirmation.

"I am not here to set traps for Christians, my boy. And the Most Christian King does not conspire with the Divan," was his grave reply.

He then added solemnly: "Remember: crows fly in flocks; the eagle flies alone."

"What does that mean?"

"It means: use your head. If everyone tells you to go to the right, you go to the left."

"But, in your opinion, is it or is it not legitimate to form an alliance with the Turks?"

There followed a long pause, until Melani, without once raising his eyes to meet mine, pronounced these words: "No scruple should prevent His Majesty from renewing today the alliances which so many Christian kings before him have formed with the Porte."

There had, he went on to explain, been dozens of cases in which Christian kings and princes had made pacts with the Ottoman Porte. Florence, to name only one example, had sought Mehmet II's assistance against Ferdinand I, King of Naples. Venice, in order to expel from the Levant the Portuguese who were disturbing its trade, had used the forces of the Sultan of Egypt. Emperor Ferdinand of Habsburg had not only allied himself with but become a vassal and tributary of Soliman, of whom he had, as a humble supplicant, begged to be granted the throne of Hungary. When Philip II set out to conquer Portugal, in order to obtain the good offices of the king of nearby Morocco, he had made a present to him of one of his possessions, thus placing Christian lands in the hands of the Infidels:

and this, for the sole purpose of despoiling a Catholic monarch. Even Popes Paul III, Alexander VI and Julius II had, when necessary, gone to the Turks for assistance.

Naturally enough, the question had been raised several times among the casuist fathers and in the Catholic schools as to whether those Christian princes had sinned in so doing. However, almost all the Italian, German and Spanish authors considered that this was not the case, and they had arrived at the conclusion that a Christian prince might succour an Infidel in war against another Christian prince.

"Their opinion," the abbot expounded, "is grounded in authority and in reason. The authority is drawn from the Bible. Abraham fought for the King of Sodom, and David against the children of Israel; not to mention the alliances formed by Solomon with King Hiram, or that of the Maccabees with Sparta and with Rome—in other words, with pagans."

How well Atto knows the Bible, I thought, when it deals with politics.

"Reason, however," continued the abbot with an expression of firm conviction, "is founded on the notion that God is the author of nature and of religion: therefore, it cannot be said that what is just in nature is not just in religion, unless some divine precept obliges us to consider it so. Now, in this instance, there are no divine precepts which condemn such alliances, especially where they are necessary, and the right of nature renders honest all reasonable instruments upon which our preservation depends."

Having thus concluded his diatribe, Abbot Melani scrutinised me again from under didactically raised eyebrows.

"Do you mean to say that the King of France may form an alliance with the Divan for purposes of legitimate self-defence?" I asked, still a trifle dubious.

"Of course: in order to defend his states and the Catholic religion from the Emperor Leopold I whose base scheming runs contrary to all laws, both human and divine. Leopold in fact formed an alliance with the heretical Dutch, and was thus the first to betray the True Faith. But in that event, no one uttered so much as a word of comment or condemnation. Everyone is, however, always ready to inveigh against France, which is guilty only of having rebelled against the constant threat of the Habsburgs and the other princes of Europe.

Louis XIV has, since the beginning of his reign, fought like a lion in order not to end up being crushed."

"Crushed by whom?"

"By the Habsburgs, in the first place, who surround France on the east and the west; on the one hand, the Empire of Vienna, on the other, Madrid, Flanders and the Spanish dominions in Italy. While, from the north, heretical England threatens, together with Holland, which commands the seas. And, as though all that were not enough, the Pope himself is France's enemy."

"But if so many states say that the Most Christian King endangers Europe's liberty, there must surely be some truth to the assertion. You too told me that he..."

"What I said to you about the King is completely irrelevant. Never, never make irrevocable judgements, and consider every single case as though it were the first you had ever encountered. Remember that, in relations between states, absolute evil does not exist. Above all, never assume that condemnation of one party implies the honesty of the other: in most cases, both are guilty. And the victims, once they have changed places with their tormentors, will commit the same atrocities. Remember all this, otherwise you will play into the hands of Mammon."

The abbot paused, as though to reflect, and heaved a melancholy sigh.

"Do not chase after the mirage of human justice," he continued, with a bitter smile, "for when you reach it, you will find only that from which you hoped to flee. God alone is just. Be wary especially of whoever loudly proclaims justice and charity, while accusing his adversaries of being creatures of the devil. That is no king, but a tyrant; no sovereign, but a despot; he is faithful not to the gospel of God but to that of hatred."

"It is so difficult to judge!" I exclaimed disconsolately.

"Less than you think. I told you, crows fly in flocks, the eagle flies alone."

"Will knowing all these things help me to become a gazetteer?"

"No. It will be a hindrance to you."

We proceeded for a while without another word being uttered. The abbot's maxims had left me speechless, and silently I turned them over in my mind. I was especially surprised by the ardour with which Melani had defended the Most Christian King, whom he had presented to me in a dark and arrogant guise when narrating the Fouquet affair. I admired Atto, even if my youth did not yet enable me fully to comprehend the precious teachings which he had just imparted to me.

"Know, in short," added Abbot Melani, "that the King of France has no need to plot against Vienna: if the Empire should fall, it will have been brought down by the cowardice of the Emperor Leopold himself: when the Turks drew too close to Vienna, he fled like a thief in the night, while the desperate and angry populace rained blows against his carriage. Our Brenozzi should know this perfectly well, since the Venetian ambassador to Vienna was also a witness to that wretched scene. Hearken to Brenozzi's words, if you will; but do not forget that when Pope Odescalchi enjoined Europe to resist the Ottomans, apart from France, only one power ignored the call: Venice."

I was thus doubly silenced. Not only had Atto Melani convincingly refuted Brenozzi's accusations against France, diverting them against Leopold I and Venice; he had also clearly understood the mistrust which the glass-blower had tried to engender against him. I was, however, allowed no time in which to reflect upon my companion's sagacity for we had already reached the dark lair in which, a day or so before, Ugonio and Ciacconio had tried to ambush us. A few minutes later, as promised, the pair of tomb robbers appeared.

As I had occasion to observe later, it was never possible to know with any certainty where these two obscure beings had emerged from. Their arrival was generally heralded by a pungent odour of goat, or of mildewed food, or of damp straw, or more simply by that fetid smell typical of the beggars who slouched through the streets of Rome. Then, in the dark, their curved profile would be gradually revealed. Anyone seeing this for the first time would take it for the epiphany of some creature out of the Underworld.

❧

"And do you call this thing a map?" raged Abbot Melani. "You are two beasts, that is what you are. Boy, take this and use it to wipe Pellegrino's fundament."

Scarcely had all four of us sat down around the lantern to conclude the business which had been settled the night before than abbot Melani gave vent to his fury. He passed me the piece of paper which Ciacconio had given him, on examining which I was unable to withhold a gesture of disappointment.

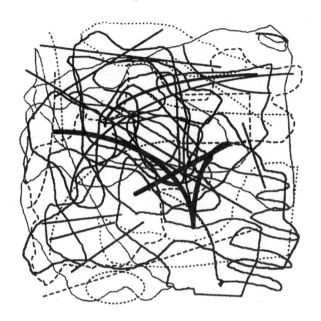

We had made a pact with the *corpisantari*: we would return to them the scrap of Bible, which they so coveted, only if they prepared for us an accurate plan of the passages which they knew stretched through the bowels of the city, from under the *locanda*. We were ready to honour our commitment (partly because Atto thought that the *corpisantari* might be useful to us on other occasions) and we had brought the blood-soaked paper with us. In exchange, however, we had received nothing but that dirty little scrap, which a long time previously must have been paper. On it was visible only a crazed tangle of hundreds of tremulous, indeciperable lines, of which one could often find the beginning but not the end, and which it was barely possible to distinguish from the natural folds of the paper. The latter, on closer examination, could not hold together for long before crumbling into a thousand pieces. Atto was beside himself and spoke to me as though the pair before us, swept aside by his scorn, did not even exist.

"We should have thought of this. Those who spend their lives rooting around under the earth like beasts cannot be capable of any-thing else. Now; if we are to be able to move around down here, we shall need their help."

"Gfrrrlubh," protested Ciacconio, clearly offended.

"Silence, animal! Now you are to listen to me: you will get back your page from the Bible only when I decide to give it. I know your names: I am a friend of Cardinal Cybo, the Pope's Secretary of State. I can so arrange matters that the relics which you find will not be authenticated, and that no one will buy any more of the rubbish which you gather down here. I shall therefore avail myself of your services, Malachi or no Malachi. And now show me how one gets out into the open air."

The *corpisantari* were shaken by a tremor of alarm. Then Ciacconio placed himself despondently at the head of our quartet and gestured to a vague point in the dark.

"I do not know how they manage," murmured Atto Melani, understanding my concern, "but they always find their way in darkness, like rats, without any lantern. Have no fear, let us follow them."

The way out to the Piazza Navona, which we took thanks to the guidance of the two *corpisantari*, emerged from under the ground more or less opposite the stairway which one must descend when coming from the Donzello. To get there we had, however, to pass through a hole so suffocatingly tight that even Ugonio and Ciacconio, whose horribly twisted and deformed backs rendered the task easier for them, had clumsily to crouch and scramble in order to get through. Atto cursed at the effort, and because he had just soiled his cuffs and his fine red stockings with the damp earth against which we had to squeeze.

The abbot was most curious to behold, he who spent his days cloistered in his chamber and his nights under the ground, clothed always in the most precious materials: Genoese satin, serge, ratteen from Spain, silk bourette, striped poplin, camlet from Flanders, drugget, Irish linen; and all stitched with the finest embroidery, with gold and silver thread and plaques, pleated, and garnished with fringes, lace, tassels, bows, ribbons and braiding. In truth, he had no ordinary apparel in his portmanteau, and thus these splendid creations were doomed to a wretched, premature end.

Beyond the narrow tunnel, we found ourselves in a gallery similar to those which came from the Donzello. Just as I was emerging (more easily than the others) from that tight passage, a question began to gnaw at me. Abbot Melani had, until that moment, shown himself to be most keen to surprise the thief of the keys and of the marguerites, who might perhaps have something to do with the death of Signor di Mourai. To me he had subsequently confided how he had come to Rome in order to resolve the mystery of Fouquet's alleged presence in the city. I suddenly found myself wondering whether the first justification was sufficient cause for his zeal in the pursuit of our nocturnal peregrinations. And thus I came very close to doubting the second pretext. Too flattered by the possibility of close acquaintance with that individual, who was as extraordinary as the circumstances under which I had come to know him, I decided that the time had not yet come to follow up such questionings. At that moment, we set off into the darkness, barely assisted by the weak light of our two lanterns.

A few dozen yards along the new gallery, we came to a bifurcation: to our left, a second passage of the same dimensions led away from the main one. A few steps further, and we found yet another fork: a sort of cavern opened up to our right, without revealing what it concealed in its depths.

"Gfrrrlubh," said Ciacconio, breaking the silence which had descended upon the group since we began our march.

"Explain!" Atto commanded harshly, turning to Ugonio.

"Ciacconio says that one may also exitate via this egression."

"Very well. Then why are we not doing so?"

"Ciacconio knows not whether you desiderate to exitate to the surface via that egression or, decreasing the scruples so as not to increase one's scruples,* you would rather be gratified to benefit from a less hazardous itinerary."

"You would like to know whether we would prefer to emerge from here or elsewhere. And how am I to know? Let us do it this way: let us take a look down here and try to work out what we should best attempt. It will not take us long to gain an idea of these accursed galleries."

"Gfrrrlubh?" inquired Ciacconio curiously, turning to his companion.

"Ciacconio dubitates whether he has correctly comprehensified," announced Ugonio, translating for Atto.

"I said: let us take a quick look at the galleries down here, as that should not be too complicated. Are we all agreed?"

---

* This means: "By decreasing the dosage of medicine rather than increase the doubts about the rightness of one's course of action." A scruple (or scruple) is, among other things, a small unit of weight. The point is to do as little harm as possible. (Translator's note.)

It was then that Ugonio and Ciacconio exploded into thick, bestial, almost demonic laughter, emphasised by obscene and joyous rolling in the filthy mud on which we were walking and by guttural grunting and explosive peptic exhalations. Grotesque and almost painful blubbering completed the picture of our two *corpisantari*, utterly incapable of any self-restraint.

Once the beast-like wallowing had come to an end and the two relic-hunters had calmed down somewhat, we obtained a few clarifications.

In his own highly coloured jargon, Ugonio explained that he and his companion had found the idea of exploring *breviter et commoditer* the passages in that area, or indeed throughout the city, most surprising, seeing that for many years the two *corpisantari* had, along with innumerable others, been endeavouring to understand whether the ways of the buried city had a beginning, a middle or an end; and whether the human mind could reduce them to a rational order or, more modestly, whether there so much as existed any certain way of reaching safety, if one were to become lost in its depths. That was why, continued Ugonio, the map of underground Rome which the two *corpisantari* had prepared for us would have been invaluable and we should have appreciated it. No one had hitherto attempted the audacious undertaking of representing the whole of subterranean Rome; and few, apart from Ugonio and Ciacconio, could boast so detailed a knowledge of the network of tunnels and caverns. Yet so precious a repository of subterranean intelligence (to which in all probability no one else was privy, as Ugonio was once more at pains to stress) had not met with our favour, and so...

Atto and I glanced at each other.

"Where is the map?" we asked in unison.

"Gfrrrlubh," said Ciacconio with a half-suffocated voice, opening his arms disconsolately.

"Ciacconio respectifies the cholerical rejection proffered by your most sublimated and cosmical decisionality," said Ugonio impassively, while his companion lowered his head and, with a horrid regurgitation, vomited into the palm of his hand a mush in which, alas, were recognisable a few fragments of the scrap on which the map had been drawn.

No one came forward to save what remained of the map.

"Being more padre than parricide, whensoever Ciacconio (or one of his acquaintances) finds a matter not to his approbriation, he avails himself of his mandibles."

We were confounded. The map (of which we had only now learned the importance) had been devoured by Ciacconio who, according to his colleague, was in the habit of swallowing whatever was disagreeable to himself or to his acquaintances. The precious drawing, now almost digested, was lost forever.

"But what else does he eat?" I asked, appalled.

"Gfrrrlubh," said Ciacconio, shrugging his shoulders, and indicating that he really did not care too much what crossed the threshold of his jaws.

Ciacconio informed us that the second bifurcation, the one which at first resembled a little grotto and turned off to the right, certainly led up to the surface, but the way was rather long. Atto decided that it would be worth exploring the first turning, which led to the left. We turned back and entered the gallery. We had walked only a few score yards when Ugonio caught Atto's attention by pulling hard at his sleeve.

"Ciacconio has scented a presence in the galleria."

"The two monsters think that there is someone in the vicinity," murmured Atto.

"Gfrrrlubh," confirmed Ciacconio, pointing to the tunnel from which we had emerged.

"Perhaps we are being followed. I and Ciacconio shall wait here, in the dark," decided Abbot Melani. "You two, however, will proceed slowly with both lanterns lit. Thus, we shall be able to intercept him when he follows your light."

I did not welcome the prospect of remaining alone with Ugonio, but we all obeyed without a murmur. Melani and Ciacconio stayed hidden in the dark. Suddenly, I felt my heart beating harder, while my breath became shorter.

Ugonio and I advanced for twenty or thirty paces, then we stopped and listened intently. Nothing.

"Ciacconio has scented a presence and a foliage," Ugonio muttered to me.

"Do you mean to say a leaf?"

Ugonio nodded in affirmation.

A figure could be vaguely discerned in the gallery. I tensed all my muscles for I knew not what: to attack, to face an attacker; more probably, to flee.

It was Atto. He gestured that we should join him.

"The stranger was not following us," he announced as soon as we had rejoined him. "He is proceeding alone, and he has taken the main gallery, that which goes straight, after the narrow hole. It is we who shall follow him. We must make haste, or we may lose him."

We caught up with Ciacconio, who was waiting for us, motionless as a statue, leaning forward into the darkness with the tip of his nose.

"Gfrrrlubh."

"Mascular, juvenilious, robustious, scarified," pronounced Ugonio.

"Male, youthful, in good health, frightened," translated Atto under his breath. "I cannot bear them, those two."

We turned to the left, again taking the main conduit and keeping a single lantern lit with as small a flame as possible. After advancing for a few minutes, we at last glimpsed before us a faint and distant glimmer. It was the lamp borne by our prey. Atto gestured to me to extinguish our own lantern. We walked on tiptoe, striving to move noiselessly.

For a good stretch, we followed the mysterious traveller, without, however, being able to catch sight of him, because the gallery curved slightly to the right. If we were to move too far forward he in turn might catch sight of us, in which case there was a risk that he might flee.

Suddenly, from under my foot there came a slight crackling. I had trodden on a dry leaf.

We halted with bated breath. The individual stopped, too. Absolute silence enveloped the gallery. We heard a rhythmic rustling grow steadily nearer. A shadow cast by the light of the man we were following stretched out towards us. We prepared for a clash. The two *corpisantari* remained motionless, impenetrable behind their cowls. In the penumbra, I descried a faint gleam in Atto's hand. Despite my fear, I managed a smile: it was surely his pipe. Then, where the gallery curved, came the revelation.

We had been following a monster. On the left-hand side of the cavity, the light of the stranger's lantern revealed the shadow of a horrible hooked arm. There followed a pointed, oblong cranium, from which sprouted disgustingly thick and robust fur. The body was formless and out of proportion. An infernal being, which we had imagined we could surprise, crawled forward menacingly as it approached our little group. We stood as though frozen. The silhouette of the monster took one, two, three paces forward. It was on the point of appearing round the corner of the gallery. It stopped.

"Go away!"

We all gave a start, and I felt my strength drain away from me. The shadow on the wall became enormous, deformed beyond any logical expectation. Then it shrank, regaining normal proportions, while the being itself appeared before our eyes in flesh and blood.

It was a rat the size of a little dog, with a clumsy, uncertain gait. Instead of springing away rapidly upon seeing us (like the sewer rat which I and Atto had run into during the course of our first incursion into the subterranean world), the big creature advanced laboriously, indifferent to our presence. The lantern had projected its silhouette onto the wall of the gallery, magnifying it enormously.

"Disgusting brute, you frightened me!" said the voice again. The light began to move away from us again. Before darkness descended upon us once more, I exchanged a glance with Atto. Like me, he had no difficulty in recognising the voice of Stilone Priàso.

കൈൗ

Having left the dying rat behind us, we patiently continued on our way. The surprising revelation had provoked in me a turmoil of suppositions and suspicions. I knew very little about Stilone Priàso, beyond what he had let slip. He called himself a poet, yet it was clear that he did not live by verse alone. His clothing, although not luxurious, revealed a degree of affluence far beyond that of a mere poetaster of circumstance. I had immediately suspected that the true source of his income must be very different. And now, his inexplicable presence in those underground passages rekindled my every doubt.

We followed him for another stretch, to a stairway which led upwards and which suddenly became narrow and suffocating. We were now in darkness. We moved in single file, led by Ciacconio, who had no difficulty in following in the tracks of Stilone Priàso. At the same time, he sensed the variations in the terrain and communicated them to me, who came second in the group, by means of rapid taps on my shoulder.

Suddenly, Ciacconio halted, then moved on again. The steps had come to an end. I felt a new air caressing my face. From the faint echo of our footfalls, I surmised that the space we had entered was quite vast. Ciacconio hesitated. Atto asked me to light the lantern.

Great was my confusion when, half-blinded by the light, we looked around us. We were in an enormous artificial cavity, the walls of which were entirely covered with frescoes. In the middle, there stood a great marble object, which I was unable as yet to distinguish clearly. Ugonio and Ciacconio too seemed out of their element in this unknown place.

"Gfrrrlubh," complained Ciacconio.

"The malodour conceals the presence," explained Ugonio.

He referred to the strong odour of stale urine which reigned in this room. Atto stared transfixed at the paintings which looked down on us. One could distinguish birds, the faces of women, athletes, rich floral decorations and everywhere a gay abundance of ornamentation.

"We have no time," said he, immediately breaking the spell. "He cannot just disappear like this."

We quickly found two exits. Ciacconio had regained his composure and showed us which, judging by his nose, was the right one to take. He guided us at a frenetic pace through a maze of other rooms, which we were unable to take in, because of our haste and the weak light of our lantern. The absence of windows, of fresh air and of any human presence proved that we were, however, still under the ground.

"These are Roman ruins," said Atto with a hint of excitement. "We may be under the Palace of the Chancellery."

"Have you ever been in there?"

"But of course. I knew the Vice-Chancellor, Cardinal Barberini, very well; he requested a number of favours of me, too. The palace is magnificent and the halls grandiose, even the travertine façades are not bad, although..."

He had to break off, because Ciacconio was making us climb a staircase which rose, perilously devoid of any handrail, through the dull emptiness of another great cavity. We all joined hands. The stairs seemed endless.

"Gfrrrlubh," exulted Ciacconio at the top, pushing open a door that led to the street. Thus, half-dead with fear and fatigue, we again found ourselves in the open.

Instinctively I filled my lungs, heartened, after five days of quarantine inside the Donzello, by the fine, refreshing night air.

For once, I could make myself useful. I immediately recognised at once where we were, having been there several times with Pellegrino who purchased provisions for the Donzello at this place. It was the

Arco degli Acetari, near to the Campo di Fiore and Piazza Farnese. Ciacconio, his nose in the air once more, immediately dragged us towards the broad open space of Campo di Fiore. A light drizzle silently swept over us. In the piazza we saw only two beggars curled up on the ground near to their poor possessions, and a boy who was pushing a hand cart towards an alleyway. We came to the opposite end of the piazza and suddenly Ciacconio pointed out a small building to us. We were in a familiar street, the name of which escaped me. No light came from the windows of the building. At ground level, however, a door was ajar. The street was empty, but in order to exercise the greatest possible caution, Ugonio and Ciacconio mounted guard on either side of us. We drew near: the muffled sound of a distant voice reached us. With extreme caution, I pushed the door open. A little staircase led down to where, behind another half-open door, light seemed to be issuing from a room. The voice came from there, joined now by that of the person addressed.

Atto preceded me until we reached the foot of the stairs. There, we realised that we were walking on a veritable carpet of scattered leaves. Atto was gathering some of these up, when suddenly the voices drew nearer, just behind the half-closed door.

"... and here are forty scudi," we heard one of the pair say.

We rushed up the stairs and went out of the street door, taking care, however, to leave it ajar, so as not to raise any suspicions. With Ugonio and Ciacconio we hid by the corner of the building.

Our aim had been true: Stilone Priàso emerged from the door. He glanced around him and walked rapidly towards the Arco degli Acetari.

"And what now?"

"Now let us open the cage," replied Atto. He murmured something to Ugonio and Ciacconio, who replied with a sordid and cruel smile. And off they trotted on the trail of Stilone.

"And what about us?" I asked, covered in confusion.

"We are going home, but calmly. Ugonio and Ciacconio will await us underground, after completing a certain little errand."

We returned by a more circuitous route, avoiding crossing the middle of the Campo di Fiore, so as not to be seen by anyone. We were, Atto mentioned in passing, not far from the French embassy and there was a risk of being surprised by the night guard. Thanks to his acquaintances, he could even have asked for asylum. But at

that hour, rather than arrest us, the embassy's Corsican guards might
perhaps have preferred to rob us and cut our throats.

"As you may know, in Rome there exists 'the freedom of the quarter': meaning that the Pontiff's men and the Bargello can arrest no
one in the quarter of the embassies. This arrangement is, however,
becoming all too convenient for fugitive assassins. That is why the
Corsican guards do not waste much time on subtleties. My brother
Alessandro, who is *maestro di cappella* to Cardinal Pamphili, has ab-
sented himself from Rome at the present time. Otherwise he could
have provided us with an escort."

We returned under the ground. Thanks be to heaven, our lanterns
were undamaged. We walked through the subterranean labyrinth in
search of the hall with the frescoes, and we were on the point of giving ourselves up for lost when, from some unknown passageway, the
corpisantari appeared at our side.

"Did you have a pleasant conversation?" asked Atto.

"Gfrrrlubh!" answered Ciacconio with a smug grin.

"What did you do to him?" I asked with concern.

"Gfrrrlubh."

His grunt calmed my fears. I had the bizarre impression that I was,
by some obscure means, beginning to understand the *corpisantaro*'s
monochord language.

"Ciacconio has but affrighted him," assured Ugonio.

"Suppose that you had never seen our two friends," explained
Atto, "then imagine them both jumping upon you screaming, in a
dark underground passage. Next, suppose that they asked you a
favour, in exchange for which they would leave you in peace, what
would you do?"

"I should certainly do whatever they asked!"

"There you are, they merely inquired of Stilone what he had just
been up to, and why."

Ugonio's account, briefly, ran as follows. Poor Stilone Priàso had
visited the shop of a certain Komarek, who from time to time worked
in the printing press of the Congregatio De Propaganda Fide, and at
night undertook a few clandestine jobs on his own to supplement
his earnings. Komarek printed gazettes, anonymous letters, perhaps
even books placed on the Index: all prohibited material, for which he
ensured that he was very well paid. Stilone Priàso had commissioned
him to print a few letters containing political predictions, on behalf

of a friend in Naples. In exchange, the two were to share the profits. That was why he was in Rome.

"And the Bible, then?" asked Atto.

No, said Ugonio, Stilone knew absolutely nothing about any Bibles. And he had taken nothing from Komarek's shop, not even a single page.

"So it was not he who lost the bloodstained page underground. Are you sure that he told the truth?"

"Gfrrrlubh," sniggered Ciacconio.

"The scarified presence did pissify upon himself," explained Ugonio gleefully.

To complete their good work, the pair had searched Stilone Priàso, finding on him a minuscule and much fingered booklet which he probably always kept under his clothing. Atto scrutinised it by the light of the lantern, as we were setting out on our return journey:

ASTROLOGICALL
TREATISE
CONCERNING THE INFLUENCES OF THE HEAVENLY BODIES
Pro, and Contra Matters Sublunary for the entire Year 1683
CALCULATED FOR THE LONGITUDE, AND LATITUDE
of the Most Serene City of Florence
BY BARTOLOMMEO ALBIZZINI OF FLORENCE
and by the Same Dedicated
to the most Illustr. Lord, and most Ven. Patron
Sig.
GIO: CLAUDIO BUONVISI
Ambassador of the Most Illustrious & Excellent Republic of Lucca
to His Most Serene Highness Cosimo III. Grand Duke of Tuscany

"Tut tut, an astrological gazette," exclaimed Atto with great amusement.

> *Son faci le Stelle*
> *che spirano ardore...**

He trilled melodiously, arousing in Ciacconio grunts of admiration.

"Ooohh, castricated cantor!" applauded Ugonio, with a servile expression.

"A gazetteer, that much I had understood," continued Atto without paying any attention to the *corpisantari*. "But that Stilone

---

* The Stars are torches / Which inspire ardour...

Priàso should be a judicial astrologer, no, that I could not have imagined."

"Why did you suspect that Stilone was a gazetteer?"

"Intuition. However, a poet he could surely not be. Poets are of melancholy humour, and, unless they have a prince or a cardinal to protect them, I can recognise them at once. They will read you their doggerel on the slightest pretext, they are poorly dressed, and they invariably try to get themselves invited to one's table. Stilone, however, had the apparel, the words and the eyes of one who 'has a well-lined belly', as they say in his part of the world. At the same time, however, his is a reserved character like, for example, that of Pompeo Dulcibeni, nor does he talk out of place, as Robleda is wont to do."

"What does judicial astrology mean?"

"You will of course know more or less what astrologers do?"

"Yes, more or less: they try to foretell the future by means of the stars."

"In general, that is so. But that is not all. You would do well to bear in mind what I am about to tell you, if you really intend to become a gazetteer. Astrologers are divided into two categories: astrologers pure and simple and judicial astrologers. Both are agreed that the stars and planets, besides producing light and heat, have mysterious qualities, whereby they exercise a number of effects upon inferior bodies."

We were now moving through the long curved gallery in which we had been terrorised by the rodent's shadow.

"But judicial astrologers go beyond that, engaging in a highly perilous game," said Abbot Melani.

Not content with asserting the influence of the stars and planets upon natural things, they maintained that this extended to mankind too. Thus, knowing only the place and date of birth of an individual, they endeavoured to determine what would be the celestial effects upon that person's life, including, for instance, his character, health, fortune and misfortune, time of death, and so on and so forth.

"What does that have to do with gazetteers?"

"It has very much to do with them. For some astrologers are also gazetteers, and on the basis of the influences of the stars, they devise their political prophesies. Just like Stilone Priàso, who goes about imprudently with an almanack of horoscopes in his pocket and by night has forecasts printed."

"And is this prohibited?"

"Absolutely prohibited. It is not at all unusual for judicial astrologers and their friends, including ecclesiastics, to be meted out severe punishments. A few years ago, the problem caught my attention and I read something on the matter. Pope Alexander III, for example, suspended for one year a priest who had had recourse to astrology, despite the fact that the priest's purpose had been to recover the spoils of a theft perpetrated in his church."

Anxiously I turned the little volume confiscated from Stilone over and over in my hands, raising it to the light of the lantern.

"Almanacks like this," said Atto "I have already seen by the dozen. Some bear titles like *Astrological Jests* or *Astrological Phantasies*, in order to allay the suspicion that they might deal with more serious matters, like judicial astrology, which is, however, capable of influencing political decisions. In themselves, admittedly, these are innocuous manuals containing advice and speculation about the current year, but certainly our Stilone can be no model of shrewdness," mocked the abbot, "if, with the dangerous trade he is plying, he haunts clandestine printing presses with such material upon his person!"

Frightened, I immediately returned the slender booklet to Atto.

"No, no, of course you can keep it," he reassured me.

Out of prudence, I nevertheless slipped it into my breeches, under my clothing.

"Do you yourself think that astrology can really be of use?" I asked.

"No, I do not. But I do know that many physicians take it seriously. I know that Galen wrote an entire book *De diebus criticis*, on the cures to be applied to the sick depending upon the positions of the planets. I am no astrologer, but I do know that some argue, for instance, that in order to cure bile, it is good that the moon should be in..."

"In Cancer."

We were both taken short by Ugonio's interjection.

"With the moon in Cancer, where it is domiciled, (or with Mercury) in trine," continued the *corpisantaro*'s viscous, inspissated muttering, "the bile may felicitously be purged; with the sun in sextile, or trine, the phlegm; where there is an aspect of Jupiter, melancholy; in the sign of Draco, in Capricorn and in Aries, ruminant signs, subversion will be provoked the closer one approaches the septentrional, or austral constitution (for the vitiated humours flow in pairs) and in those boreal, increased impression and compression will provoke flux and distillation, wherefore evacuation is not to be attempted in those who are beset by the fluxes; it will therefore be beneficial and necessary to observe the aspects signified, if one is not to be a rustic physician, and would obtain more benefice than malefice, and be more padre than parricide, appeasing one's conscience, for by fulfilling one's obligations the Christian's jubilations are increased, and by decreasing the scruples so as not to increase one's scruples, and applying the most appropriate, and indigent remedies: if, for example, one has recourse to magisterial julep."

We both remained speechless.

"Well, well, here we have a veritable expert on medical astrology," commented Abbot Melani an instant later. "And where did you learn all these precious notions?"

"Gfrrrlubh," interjected Ciacconio.

"We have multiplicated our knowingness by the lecture and memorisation of foliables."

"Foliables?" asked Atto.

Ciacconio indicated the little book in his hand.

"Ah, you mean books. Come along, boy, let us not tarry: I fear that Cristofano may take a look around the inn. It would be difficult to explain our absence."

"Stilone Priàso, too, was absent."

"No longer, I trust. After his encounter with our two little monsters he will surely have regained the hostelry as fast as his legs will carry him."

Stilone Priàso, Atto continued, had come to Rome in pursuit of his trade of judicial astrologer, in other words a nefarious business. He therefore needed a discreet way out of the Donzello at night. He must previously have discovered the underground route, since he said he had already stayed at the Donzello.

"Do you think that Stilone had something to do with the assassination of Signor di Mourai and the theft of my little pearls?"

"It is too early to tell. We must think a little about him. He will surely have visited the underground galleries any number of times. We have no such good fortune. Curses! If only we had the map prepared by Ugonio and Ciacconio, however messy and confused, that would give us an immense advantage. Fortunately, we had at least one other advantage: we knew that Stilone had been in the underground galleries, whereas he did not know about us.

"Meanwhile," added the abbot, "before you go to bed, go and take a look at him. I do not trust these two individuals," said he, turning to indicate the grinning faces of the *corpisantari* who followed us.

We returned all the way along the subterranean passage until we reached the mouth of the narrow hole which led to the ruins of Domitian's stadium, under the Piazza Navona. Atto dismissed the two *corpisantari*, making an appointment with them for an hour after nightfall the next evening, and promising a reward.

"Gfrrrlubh," protested Ciacconio.

The two *corpisantari* demanded the return of the page from the Bible. Atto, however, decided to keep it, since he had still not established its provenance, and indeed he handed it over to me to keep carefully. He did, nevertheless, offer the *corpisantari* monetary compensation.

"Fair is fair, after all, you did prepare the plan," said he cordially as he took out the money.

Suddenly, Abbot Melani's eyes narrowed. He bent down and picked up a lump of earth which he threw at Ciacconio's shoulder, while the latter remained petrified with surprise. Then he took the page from the Bible, opened it and pressed it against Ciacconio's rustic cloak, at the point where he had just soiled it.

"Beasts, animals, bastards," said he, looking at them disdainfully. Motionless, the pair meekly awaited punishment. On the sheet of paper, a sort of dense labyrinth remained imprinted, the shape of which was all too familiar.

"Remember: never again try that kind of thing on me. Never."

He then fell silent, returning to his pocket the money which he had prepared for Ugonio and Ciacconio.

"Do you understand?" he asked me later, after their departure. "They wanted to cheat us like two idiots. They pressed the sheet of paper onto that sort of goatskin they wear. They then added a couple of scribbles, and there is your precious plan of subterranean Rome. But I—oh no!—I am not so easily duped. The figure in the middle of the map was an exact mirror image of a piece of patching on Ciacconio's shoulder: that is how I found them out!"

Exhausted, we returned to the Donzello in silence, in the depths of night.

∞∞∞

I was climbing the stairs after leaving Atto when, on the second floor, I glimpsed a faint gleam coming from Stilone Priàso's chamber. I remembered Abbot Melani's recommendation that I should keep an eye on the young Neapolitan. I approached the door which was slightly ajar, trying to look in.

"Who is there?" I heard him ask in a trembling voice.

I announced myself and entered. He huddled in his bed, pale and dirt-stained. In the semi-darkness, I pretended not to notice this.

"What are you doing awake at this hour, my boy?"

"My master wanted to relieve himself," I lied. "And you?"

"I... I have had a terrible nightmare. Two monsters attacked me in the dark, and then they robbed me of my books and of all the money I had on me."

"Your money too?" I asked, remembering that Ugonio and Ciacconio had made no mention of that.

"Yes, and then they asked me... well, they tortured me and gave me no quarter."

"That is terrible. You should rest."

"Impossible, I can still see them before my eyes," said he, shivering, fixing an indefinite point in the dark.

"I too have had some strange dreams recently," said I, in order to distract him, "the meaning of which was incomprehensible."

"The meaning..." repeated Stilone Priàso in a daze. "You cannot understand the meaning of dreams. You would need an expert in oneiromancy; but a real one, not a charlatan or a harlot trying to extort money from you."

I blushed on hearing these words and tried to change the subject.

"If you are not tired, I could keep you company for a while. I, too, have no desire to return to sleep tonight," I suggested, in the hope of being able to converse with the Neapolitan and perhaps to obtain from him some information useful to Abbot Melani's inquiries.

"That would not displease me. Indeed, it would be a great help to me if you could brush my clothes while I wash."

He rose and, after undressing, went to the wash-bowl, where he began to rinse his muddy hands and head. On his bed, where he had left me his clothing and a brush, I discovered a notebook on which a number of strange signs were drawn. Nearby, a number of old books, of which I scanned the titles: *Myrotecium, Reverberant Chemicall Proto-Light* and, finally *Horoscopant Physickall Anti-Lampion*.

"Are you interested in alchemy and horoscopes?" I asked, struck by these obscure titles.

"No, no," exclaimed Stilone turning round with a start. "It is just that they are written in rhyme and I was consulting them for inspiration. You are aware that I am a poet?

"Ah yes," said I, pretending to believe him, while I laboured with the brush. "And besides, astrology, if I am not mistaken, is forbidden."

"That is not exactly the case," he retorted crossly. "Only judicial astrology is prohibited."

In order not to alarm him, I pretended to be completely ignorant of the matter and thus Stilone Priàso, while rubbing his head energetically, repeated to me in doctoral tones all that Atto had already told me.

"Finally, about half a century ago," he concluded "Pope Urban VIII, in the very middle of his pontificate, unleashed the full force of his fury against judicial astrologers who, for some thirty years, had enjoyed ever-increasing tolerance and renown, even among cardinals, princes and prelates desirous of obtaining forecasts of their fortunes. It was like an earthquake, so much so that even today whoever reads destinies in the stars runs the gravest of risks."

"A pity, as it would be very useful to us now to know what end we shall come to at the Donzello: whether we shall perish in a lazaretto or come out safe and sound," I provoked him.

Stilone Priàso did not respond.

"With the help of an astrologer, we could perhaps understand whether di Mourai died of the plague or whether he was poisoned, as Cristofano maintains," I assayed once more. "Thus we protect ourselves from any further threats from the assassin."

"Forget it. Poison, more than any other lethal weapon, is concealed from the vigilant eye of the stars. It is stronger than any attempt at divination or prediction: frankly, if I had to kill someone, I would choose poison."

I felt my blood draining away on hearing those words; and here, it seemed to me, was a clue with which to follow up my suspicions.

Astrologers and poison: suddenly I recalled the conversation about poisons which had exercised our guests around the body of poor Signor di Mourai on the very evening of our incarceration. Was it not asserted that astrologers and perfumers were notably expert in the preparation of mortal poisons? And Stilone Priàso, I thought with a shiver, was a gazetteer and an astrologer, as Abbot Melani had just discovered.

"Really?" I replied, feigning candid interest. "Perhaps you already know of cases of suspected poisoning which it was impossible to foresee in the stars."

"One above all: Abbot Morandi," said Stilone, anticipating me. "That was the most compelling case."

"Who was Abbot Morandi?" I asked, ill concealing my anxiety.

"A friar, and the greatest astrologer in Rome," came his curt reply.

"How is that possible? Friar and astrologer?" I retorted, feigning incredulity.

"I shall tell you: until the end of the last century, Bishop Luca Gaurico was official astrologer to the court of no fewer than four popes. A golden age!" he sighed, "alas, gone forever."

I saw that his tongue was loosening.

"After the affair of Father Morandi?" I prompted.

"Exactly. You must know that Father Orazio Morandi, abbot of the monastery of Santa Prassede, owned—some sixty years ago—the best astrological library in Rome: a real landmark for all the astrologers of the time. He corresponded with the most noted men of letters of Rome, Milan, Florence, Naples and other cities, even outside Italy. Many were the men of letters and of science who asked his opinion on the stars, and even the unfortunate Galileo Galilei, when he sojourned in Rome, had been his guest."

At the time when these events took place, Abbot Morandi, continued Stilone, was just over fifty years of age: he was eloquent, always gay, rather tall, with a fine chestnut-coloured beard, and was only just beginning to lose his hair. Astrology then enjoyed no little tolerance. Laws did exist against it, but in practice they were ignored.

Orazio Morandi's fame was at its height when (it was 1630) the abbot thought fit to state, on the basis of his astrological calculations, that Pope Urban VIII Barberini would die within the year. The abbot, before divulging this calculation, consulted with other renowned astrologers, who redid the calculations and obtained the same results.

The sole dissenter was Father Raffaello Visconti, who taught mathematics in Rome, and who thought that the Pope, so long as he did not expose himself to dangers, would not die for at least another thirteen years, in other words in 1643 or 1644. The professor was, however, not heeded by his colleagues, who all agreed on the imminent demise of Pope Barberini. The abbot of Santa Prassede's prophecy spread through Rome and the other capitals at lightning speed. Such was the abbot's renown as an astrologer that a number of Spanish cardinals made haste to leave for Rome in order to take part in the conclave, which was seen as imminent. The rumour also spread through France, so much so that Cardinal Richelieu had to beg the court of Rome to take urgent measures to put an end to this embarrassing situation.

Thus, the word reached the ears of the Pontiff himself, who was not pleased to learn, in this manner, that his last hour was approaching. On 13th July, Pope Urban VIII ordered that proceedings be opened against Abbot Morandi and his accomplices. Two days later, Morandi was gaoled in the prison of Tor di Nona, and his library and chambers sealed and searched. Soon afterwards, all twelve monks of Santa Prassede were arrested. The friars confessed and in the end Morandi himself, under pressure from the judge, revealed the names of his colleagues and friends, who in their turn gave away others' names.

"And thus the trial was concluded," said I.

"By no means," replied Stilone Priàso. "It was just at that point that matters started to become complicated."

In the concatenation of denunciations, there was a risk of embarrassing names coming to light, especially cardinals who, with their secretaries and entourages, having heard of the prediction of the coming death of Urban VIII, had requested further astrological consultations in order to know what their chances were of obtaining the Tiara. At his very first interrogation, Morandi had given his accusers a number of important names, including even that of the Pope's nephew, Cardinal Antonio Barberini.

The Pope understood at once what loomed on the horizon: a scandal which would besmirch the whole Consistory, and above all, his own family. Urban VIII therefore took preventive measures, requiring that the names of pontiffs, cardinals, prelates and even lay persons be omitted from the charges and marked in cipher in the margin, or simply left blank in the text. The decision as to whether such names should be entered would rest with him in person.

Wherever the interrogations went too far, the omissions desired by the Pope came into effect: "I know many who understand astrology. Vincenzo Bottelli was my master. He told me that many in the palace understood astrology, such as Cardinals ***, *** and ***, as well as ***, ***, *** and also *** and ***."

"In other words, cardinals galore," exclaimed Stilone. "The judge was shocked to hear so many distinguished names; he knew perfectly well that those astrological dealings were being carried out on behalf of the cardinals themselves; and that the latter ran the risk, if one single word too many were to be uttered by their servants, of being covered in dishonour. And farewell then to all hopes, for whoever might have nourished them, of ever being elected pope."

"And how did it all end?" I asked, impatient to hear what all this story had to do with poison.

"Oh, providence… saw to that," replied Stilone with a meaningful grimace. "On the 7th of November, 1630 Abbot Morandi was found dead in his cell, lying on his bed, in the modest robe and sandals which he had worn all his life."

"Killed!"

"Well, seven days later, the physician of the prison of Tor di Nona submitted his report: Morandi had died following twelve days of illness. He had caught a sextan fever which had become malignant and, in the end, fatal.

"'I neither have nor saw any evidence of poison,'" confirmed the physician, supported by two other colleagues. They all, however, passed over in silence the fact that only two days previously, another prisoner detained with Morandi had died in identical circumstances after eating a cake of unknown provenance."

Persistent rumours and suspicions of poisoning circulated for months, insistent and impossible to uproot. But what did all that matter now? Father Morandi was dead, and he alone had shouldered the tremendous burden of the vices of the entire pontifical court. To the great relief of all, the veil, which had been so incautiously lifted, was hastily lowered once more.

Urban VIII, in a brief hand-written note, ordered the judge to suspend the case, granting impunity to all copyists and to the astrologers and monks, and ordering that there should be no further judicial action concerning them.

Stilone Priàso fell silent and looked at me. He had dried himself and slipped into bed, awaiting my reaction to the story.

So, in the case of Abbot Morandi, as in that of Signor di Mourai—thus I reflected as I replaced the brushed apparel on the chair—poison was concealed under the guise of illness.

"But were not all the others equally guilty?" I objected, gripped by the sad tale.

"In truth, the copyists had copied, the monks had hidden the evidence, the astrologers had speculated on the death of the Pope; and, above all, the cardinals had been involved. It would not have been unjust to punish them, but to do so it would have been necessary to reach a verdict," observed Stilone Priàso, "which would have caused a scandal. And that was precisely what the Pope wished to avoid."

"So Urban VIII did not die in that year."

"No, indeed he did not. Morandi was completely mistaken in his prophecy."

"And when did he die?"

"In 1644."

"But was that not precisely the date calculated by Father Visconti, the mathematician?"

"It was," replied Stilone Priàso. "If only the abbot of Santa Prassede had heeded the word of his friend the professor, he would truly have predicted the death of Urban VIII. Instead, he foretold his own death."

"And what happened to the astrologers after the death of Morandi?" I asked, dejected by that lugubrious observation.

"That tale is soon told: Galileo recanted, Argoli went into exile, Centini went to the stake; all this in the space of a very few years. And astrology ended up crushed under the weight of papal bulls."

Here, Stilone fell silent, as though observing a moment of mourning.

"However," he resumed, "when Abbot Morandi's prophecy of his imminent death was circulating, the Pope became very afraid that it would come true."

"So, even Urban VIII, who did so much to combat astrology, believed in it!"

"But of course! I have already told you that everyone, but everyone, in every epoch, has paid tribute to Dame Astrology," laughed Stilone Priàso, bitterly.

"Pope Barberini, so it was said, was beset by the blackest terror when the prediction of his death began to do the rounds. While he publicly professed scorn for Abbot Morandi's prophecy, in secret, he summoned a Dominican friar, Tommaso Campanella and, fearful and trembling, begged him to dispel the threat. The Dominican did what he could, sprinkling aromas and perfumes against malefic effluvia, making the Pontiff wear white vestments in order to cancel out the effects of eclipses, lighting lamps which symbolised the seven planets, and so on and so forth. But now I had better break off. Thanks be to heaven, I am again feeling a little drowsy."

It was dawn. I greeted the ending of this discussion with silent relief. I again blamed myself for having initially encouraged it. Not only had I discovered nothing about the poisoning of Signor di Mourai, or the theft of my little pearls; but, at the end of such a long an interview, I was now more confused than ever.

Day the Fifth

15TH SEPTEMBER, 1683

✠

After leaving Stilone Priàso, I returned exhausted to my chamber. I do not know where I found the strength to complete my diary, but I did succeed in so doing. Then, I read swiftly through the pages which I had already written. Dejectedly, I went over the results of the tentative investigations which I had conducted concerning the guests at the Donzello: and what had I discovered? Practically nothing. Every apparent breakthrough had proved to be a false dawn. I had learned of facts and circumstances which had little to do with the sad end of Signor di Mourai, and which had thrown my ideas into even greater confusion.

But what, I wondered, did I know about Mourai? At my table, I lay my head on one arm, asking myself that question. Enveloped in the blanket of sleep, my thoughts receded into the distance, but did not disappear entirely.

Mourai was French, old and ill, and his eyesight had become very weak. He was between sixty and seventy years of age. He was accompanied by the young French musician Devizé and by Pompeo Dulcibeni. He seemed to be of elevated rank and more than merely prosperous, which contrasted with the very poor state of his health: it was as though he had in the past undergone long-drawn-out sufferings.

But then, why would a gentleman of his rank lodge at the Donzello?

I knew from Pellegrino that the Ponte quarter, where our hostelry was situated, had long since ceased to house the great inns, which were now to be found in the environs of the Piazza di Spagna. To sojourn at the Donzello was perhaps more fitting for a person of limited means; or perhaps for someone desiring to avoid the company of neighbours of high rank; but why?

Mourai, moreover, never left the inn, save at nightfall; and even then, only for the shortest of walks in the immediate environs; certainly not beyond the Piazza Navona or Piazza Fiammetta.

Piazza Navona, Piazza Fiammetta: suddenly, my temples began to throb painfully, and, rising with great difficulty from the chair, I let myself collapse onto my couch like a marionette.

I awoke in the same position the next morning, in broad daylight. Someone had knocked at the door. It was Cristofano, angry that I had still not fulfilled any of my duties.

I sat up in the bed with extreme indolence, having had only a few hours of sleep. In my breeches, I espied the gazette of horoscopes which the tomb robbers had purloined from Stilone Priàso. I was still affected by the extraordinary events of the previous night: the peregrination through the underground passages full of uncertainties and surprises, the stalking of Stilone and, lastly, the terrible affairs of Abbot Morandi and Campanella, which the Neapolitan had narrated to me in the last hours before dawn. That abundant harvest of sensory and spiritual impressions was still very much alive in me, despite the fatigue that assailed me, when I lazily opened the little book. Perhaps also because of a powerful headache, I did not resist the temptation to lie down once again; at least for a few minutes, thought I. And I began to peruse the book.

The first words that met my eyes were a lengthy and learned dedication to Ambassador Buonvisi, and then another no less polished prologue addressed to the reader.

There followed a table entitled "Calculation of the Introitus of the Sun", which I did not read. Finally, I found a "General Discourse on the Year 1683":

> It will begin, according to the Custom of the Holy Roman Catholicke Church, on the First of January and, according to the ancient Astronomical Style, when the Sunne has completed its Round of the Twelve Signs of the Zodiac, returning again to the Cusp of the Sign of Aries, because Fundamentum principale in revolutionibus annorum mundi et introitus Solis in primum punctum Arietis. Thus, it is by Means of the Tychonian System...

Irritated by all this show of astronomical wisdom, I gave up. Further on, I read that there would be four eclipses during the course of the year (none of which would, however, be observable in Italy); then came a table with a mass of figures, all of them completely incomprehensible to me, entitled "Direct Ascension of the Celestiall Figure in Winter". I felt discouraged. It all seemed to me to be unconscionably complicated. I was only trying to find some prediction for the current year and, what was more, I had little time. At long last, I found a promising heading: "Lunations and Combinations with other Planetary Aspects for all the Year 1683". I had finally discovered detailed predictions, set out according to the seasons and months and covering the entire year. I skimmed through the pages until I came to the four weeks of September:

Saturn, Ruler of the Eighth House, threatens the aged, endangering their lives.

I was perturbed. This prediction referred to the first week of the month, but it was clear that, only a few mornings earlier, old Mourai had died a mysterious death. I looked hurriedly for the second week, since Mourai had died on the 11th, and soon discovered:

As regards Maladies, Jupiter rules the Sixth House and will strive to bring Health to many who are sick; however, Mars, in a Fiery Sign and in Opposition to the Moon seems intent on subjecting many Individuals to malignant Fevers and venomous Distempers, for it is written that in this position Lunam opposito Martis morbos venenatos inducit, sicut in signis igneis, terminaturque cito, & raro ad vitam. Saturn rules the Eighth House, and greatly threatens senile Age.

Not only had the author clairvoyantly perceived that the aged were again threatened by Saturn, which fully corresponded with the demise of Signor di Mourai, but he had also foreseen the sufferings of my master and Bedfordi as a result of "malignant Fevers and venomous Distempers". Not to mention the fact that the reference to poison perhaps concerned the aged Frenchman most of all.

I went back a few lines and resumed my reading for the first week, with the firm intention not to leave off from it, even if Cristofano were to knock yet again.

The Emergencies which result from the Study of the heavenly Bodies during this Week are directed by Jupiter in his quality as Ruler of the governing House, which, being in the Fourth House with the Sunne and Mercury, seeks with fine Astuteness to reveal a hidden Treasure; *the same Mercury, dignified by Jupiter in a terrestrial Sign, signifies* Outbreaks of subterranean Fires, and Tremors with Terrors and Alarums for Mankind; *wherefore it is written: Eo item in terrae cardine, & in signo terreo fortunatis ab eodem cadentibus dum Mercurius investigat eumdem, terraemotus nunciat, ignes de terra producit, terrores, & turbationes exauget, minerias & terrae sulphura corrumpit. Saturn, Ruler of the Seventh House, in the Third House, promises* great Mortality as a

Consequence of Battles, and Assaults against the City, *and, being square with Mars, means* the Surrender of a considerable fortified Place, as foreseen by Ali and by Leopoldus Austriacus.

Despite some difficulties (as with the learned references to masters of astrological doctrine) I did in the end succeed in understanding. And again, I shuddered; for, in the prediction of the revelation of "a hidden Treasure and Outbreaks of subterranean Fires, and Tremors, with Terrors and Alarums for Mankind", I recognised clearly the most recent occurrences at the Donzello.

What was the "hidden Treasure" which was to be brought to light in the first days of the month if not the enigmatic letters hidden in Colbert's study and appropriated by Atto just before the minister's death? It all seemed so clear and terrible in its inevitability. Above all, the death of Colbert, who surely did not die young, coincided perfectly with the threats to the aged of which the gazette spoke.

Even the earthquakes and subterranean fires were familiar to me. I could only think of the rumbling which we had at the beginning of the month heard coming from the cellars. The tremendous reverberation had made us fear that an earthquake was coming; fortunately, it had left no more trace than a crack in the wall of the stairs leading to the first floor. But Signor Pellegrino almost had a seizure.

And what could one say about the "great Mortality as a Consequence of Battles, and Assaults against the City" as foreseen by Ali and by Leopoldus Austriacus? Who would not see in this the battle against the Turks and the siege of Vienna? The very names of the two great astrologers were disturbingly reminiscent of the Emperor Leopold of Austria and the followers of Mahomet. I grew afraid of reading on and went back to the preceding pages. I stopped at the passage concerning the month of July, in which, as I expected, the Ottoman advance and the beginning of the siege were predicted:

The Sun in the Tenth House signifies… the Subjection of Peoples, Republics and Neighbours by a stronger bordering Power, as foreseen by Ali…

At that precise moment, Cristofano knocked on my door.

I hid the astrological gazette under the mattress and rushed out. The doctor's call came almost as a relief: the accuracy with which events seemed to have been guessed at by the author of the gazette (especially, sad and violent events) had upset me deeply.

In the kitchen, while I was preparing luncheon and at the same time assisting Cristofano with the preparation of a number of remedies for Bedfordi, I kept turning matters over and over in my mind. I was spurred on by my anxiety to understand: I felt as though I were somehow a prisoner of the planets, and all our lives, in the Donzello as in Vienna, no more than a vain struggle in narrow fore-ordained straits, in some invisible torrent which might bear us where we would perhaps rather not go, while our sad but trusting prayers languished under a black and empty heaven.

"What rings you have around your eyes, my boy! You have not perchance been insomniac these last few nights?" Cristofano inquired of me. "Insufficient sleep is quite a serious matter: if the mind and the heart remain awake unceasingly, the pores no longer open and allow the evaporation of the humours corrupted by the cares of the day."

I admitted that I was indeed not sleeping enough. Cristofano then warned me that he could not do without my services, especially now that, with my help, he was at last managing to keep the lodgers in perfect health. And truly, he added in order to encourage me, all had praised the quality of my assistance.

It was plain that the physician was unaware that I had as yet given no treatment to Dulcibeni, to young Devizé or even to Stilone Priàso, in whose company I had, however, spent almost an entire night. And so, the health of at least these three guests was due to Mother Nature and not to his remedies.

Cristofano, however, planned to do more: he set to work on a preparation to make me sleep.

"All Europe has tried it thousands of times. It restores sleep and is good for most of the body's intrinsic infirmities, as well as healing all manner of wounds. If I were to tell you here and now all the wonders I have wrought with this, you would not believe me," the Tuscan assured me. "It is known as *magnolicore*, the great liquor; and it is prepared in Venice too, at the Apothecary of the Bear, on Campo Santa Maria Formosa. The process of preparation takes quite some time, but can be completed only in the month of September."

And, with a smile, he pulled out from his bags, the contents of which had already spilled onto the great kitchen table, a curious clay jar.

"It is necessary to begin preparation of the *magnolicore* in the springtime, boiling twelve pounds of common oil together with two of mature white wine..."

While Cristofano, with his usual extreme meticulousness, listed the composition and miraculous qualities of his preparation, my mind continued to wander.

"... and now that it is September, we shall add balsamic herbs and a good quantity of Master Pellegrino's finest aqua vitae."

I awoke abruptly from my thoughts upon hearing this news of the latest spoliation of my master's cellar for apothecary's purposes.

"My boy, what is it that so preoccupies your heart and your mind?"

I told him that I had awoken that morning with a sad thought: if, as some affirmed, our lives were governed by the planets and the stars, then all was in vain, including the medicines which Doctor Cristofano himself was preparing with such care. But I at once excused myself, explaining away my ravings as the fruit of fatigue.

He looked at me with perplexity and I detected a shadow of apprehension: "I do not understand how such questionings arose in your mind, but these were no ravings; far from it. I myself take astrology greatly into account. I know that many physicians deride this science, and to them I reply what Galen wrote, namely that *medici astrologiam ignorantes sunt peiores spiculatoribus et homicidis*: physicians ignorant of astrology are worse than speculators and murderers. Without counting what was said by Hippocrates, Scotus and other most learned writers, whose part I take in deriding my sceptical colleagues in their turn."

It was thus that Cristofano, while busying himself with preparing the *magnolicore* in accordance with the recipe, informed me that it was even thought that the Black Death had been brought about by a conjunction of Saturn, Jupiter and Mars which occurred on 24th March, 1345, while the French pox was thought to have been caused by the conjunction of Mars and Saturn.

"*Membrum ferro ne percutito, cum luna signum tenuerit, quod membro illi dominatur*," he declaimed. "That signifies: may every chirurgeon avoid amputating that member which corresponds to the sign of the zodiac in which the moon is situated that day, especially if the moon is in opposition to Saturn and Mars, which planets are malefic for health. For example, if the birth or, in other words, the horoscope of the patient predicts a negative issue to a certain malady of his, the physician my reasonably attempt to save him, applying cures on the days which the stars indicate as most opportune."

"So, to each constellation in the zodiac there corresponds a part of the body?"

"Certainly. When the moon is in Aries, and Mars and Saturn are in opposition, one must postpone any operations to be performed on the head, the face and the eyes; in Taurus, on the neck, the nape or the throat; in Gemini, on the shoulders, the arms and the hands; in Cancer, on the chest, the lungs and the stomach; in Leo, on the heart, the back and the liver; in Virgo, on the belly; in Libra, on the shins, the loins, the navel and the intestines; in Scorpio, on the bladder, the penis, the backbone, the genitals and the anus; in Sagittarius, on the thighs; in Capricorn, on the knees; in Aquarius, on the legs; in Pisces, if I am not mistaken, on the feet and the heels."

He added that the most suitable time for a good purgation was when the moon is in Scorpio or in Pisces. One should, however, avoid administering a medicine when the moon, in the ruminant signs, is in conjunction with a retrograde planet, because there is a risk that the patient might vomit it up and suffer from other harmful impairments.

"'With the moon in signs ruminant, in the sick, symptoms extravagant,' as was taught by the learned Hermes. And," he concluded, "that is especially valid this year, when in spring and in winter, there were four retrograde planets, three of them in ruminant signs."

"But then our lives are no more than a struggle between the planets."

"No, on the contrary, this simply shows that with the stars, as with all else in creation, man may shape his fortune or his ruin. It is up to him to make good use of the intuition, intelligence and wisdom which God has given him."

He explained to me that, in his experience as a physician, planetary influences indicated a tendency, a disposition, an inclination, never a predetermined path.

Cristofano's interpretation did not deny the influence of the stars, but reaffirmed the judgement of men and above all the supremacy of the divine will. Little by little, I felt relieved.

I had in the meanwhile completed my duties. For luncheon, I had cooked a bread-soup with rice flour, pieces of smoked sturgeon, lemon-juice and, lastly, an abundant sprinkling of cinnamon. But as a few hours remained before the mealtime, Cristofano let me go: not, however, before handing me a bottle of his *magnolicore* with the injunction to drink barely a drop thereof and to sprinkle some on my chest before going to bed, so as to inhale its health-giving vapours and enjoy a good sleep.

"Do not forget that it is also excellent for curing wounds and all pains; excepting, however, the lesions caused by the French pox which, if anointed with the *magnolicore*, will occasion the most acute spasms."

❧

I was climbing back up the stairs, when from the first floor, I heard the echo of Devizé's plucked notes: he was again performing the *rondeau* which so charmed me and which seemed so wonderfully to pacify the soul of every one of us.

Arriving on the second floor, I heard my name whispered. I turned to the corridor and glimpsed Abbot Melani's red stockings through his barely open doorway.

"I need your syrup. Last time, it did me much good," he called out with a clear voice, fearing that Cristofano might be in the offing, while with frenetic gestures he indicated that I was to enter his chamber where, rather than the administration of a syrup, important news awaited me.

Before closing the door behind me, the abbot inclined a delighted ear to capture the echo of the *rondeau*.

"Ah, the power of music," he sighed ecstatically.

He then moved with swift steps to his writing desk: "Let us get down to business, my boy. Do you see all this? In these few papers, there is more work than you could ever imagine."

Spread out on the table was the mass of manuscript notes which I had seen him put away with a certain apprehension on the occasion of my last visit.

He explained to me that he had for some time been writing a guide to Rome for French visitors, since he considered that those which were available in trade were neither suited to travellers' needs, nor did they do justice to the importance of the antiquities and works of art which were to be admired in the papal capital. He showed me the last pages which he had written in Paris, in a close, tiny hand. This was a chapter dedicated to the Church of Saint Athanasius of the Greeks.

"And so?" I asked in surprise, as I took a seat.

"I had hoped to make use of my free time during this sojourn in

Rome to complete my guide-book. This morning, I was just sitting down to work on it when I had a revelation."

And he told me how, four years previously, in this very Church of Saint Athanasius, he had had a bizarre and unexpected encounter. After examining the noble façade which was the work of Martino Longhi, he had gone inside and was admiring a fine canvas by Trabaldesi in a side chapel. Suddenly, with a shudder, he became aware of the presence of a stranger by his side.

In the penumbra, he saw an aged priest who, from his headdress could be identified as a Jesuit. He was rather bent and a prey to a slight but incessant trembling of the trunk and the arms. He leaned on a cane but was supported on either side by two young servant girls who helped him to walk. His white beard was carefully trimmed and the lines on his forehead and cheeks were mercifully fine and few. His eyes were blue and as piercing as two daggers, suggesting that, a few years earlier, he would have lacked neither sharp wits nor a ready tongue.

The Jesuit fixed Atto in his gaze and, with a weak smile, pronounced the following words: "Your eye... is indeed magnetic."

Abbot Melani, vaguely disquieted, glanced questioningly at the two girls accompanying the old priest. The pair, however, remained silent, as though they dared not speak out without the old man's permission.

"The magnetic art is most important, in this vast world," continued the Jesuit, "and if you also master gnomonic catoptricks or the new specular horologiography, you may be spared every coptic prodromous symptom."

The two servant girls remained silent, but were plainly dismayed, as though this embarrassing situation had arisen before.

"If, then, you have already undertaken the *iter extaticus coelestis*," the old man resumed with a hoarse voice, "you will need neither Maltese astronomical observatories nor physico-medical Scrutinies, for the great art of light and shade, dissolved in the diatribe of the prodigious cruces and in the poligraphia nova will give you all the arithmology, musurgy and phonurgy that you may need."

Abbot Melani had remained silent and motionless.

"But the magnetic art cannot be learned, because it is part of human nature," the aged prelate then argued. "Magnets are magnetic. Yes, that is indeed so. But the *vis magnetica* also emanates from visages. And from music. And this, you know."

"Do you recognise me, then?" Atto had asked, thinking that the old man might know that he was a singer.

"The magnetic power of music, you may see in the tarantulas," continued the stranger, as though Atto had not spoken. "It can cure tarantism, and can cure much else. Have you understood?"

And, without giving Atto time to respond, the old man succumbed to a bout of almost silent laughter which made him quake from within, in a crescendo of spasms. The trembling shook him vigorously from head to foot, so much so that his youthful escorts had to struggle to prevent him from losing his balance. This mad outburst of hilarity seemed at times to border on suffering and monstrously deformed his features, while tears ran copiously down his cheeks.

"But take care," the Jesuit raved on, struggling to speak. "The magnet also lies concealed in Eros, whence sin may arise, and you have the magnetic eye; but the Lord does not want sin, no, the Lord does not want that," and he raised his stick clumsily, trying to strike Abbot Melani.

At that point, the two servant girls restrained him and one of them calmed him, leading him to the door of the church. Several churchgoers, distracted from prayer, looked curiously at the scene. The abbot stopped one of the two girls: "Why did he come to me?"

The girl, overcoming the natural shyness of simple people, explained that the old man often accosted strangers and importuned them with his lucubrations.

"He is German. He has written many books, and now that he is no longer his own master, he keeps repeating their titles. His colleagues are ashamed of him, he keeps confusing the living and the dead, and they rarely let him out. But he is not always in that state: I and my sister, who usually accompany him on his walks, find that at other times he has all his wits about him. He even writes letters, which he gives us to send."

Abbot Melani, after initially being irritated by the old man's aggression, was in the end softened by this sorry tale.

"What is his name?"

"He is known to many in Rome. His name is Athanasius Kircher."

Such was my surprise that I trembled from head to foot.

"Kircher? But was that not the Jesuit man of science who you said had found the secret of the plague?" I exclaimed excitedly, recalling how the guests at our inn had discussed Kircher animatedly at the beginning of our imprisonment.

"Exactly," Atto confirmed. "But perhaps the time is ripe for you to know who Kircher really was. Otherwise, you would not understand the rest of the story."

And so it was that Atto Melani helped me to understand how resplendently Kircher's star and that of his infinite doctrine once shone in the firmament and how for many years every single word of his was treasured as the wisest of oracles.

Father Athanasius Kircher spoke twenty-four languages, many of them learned after lengthy sojourns in the Orient, and he had brought with him to Rome many copies of Arabic and Chaldean manuscripts, as well as a truly vast exposition of hieroglyphs. He also had a profound knowledge of theology, metaphysics, physics, medicine, mathematics, ethics, aesthetics, jurisprudence, politics, scriptural interpretation, moral theology, rhetoric and the combinatory art. Nothing, he was wont to say, is more beautiful than the knowledge of the totality, and he had indeed, in all humility and *ad maiorem Dei gloriam* revealed the gnomonic mysteries and those of polygraphy, magnetism, arithmology, musurgy and phonurgy and, thanks to the secrets of the symbol and of analogy, he had clarified the abstruse enigmas of the kabbala and of hermeticism, reducing them to the universal measure of primal sapience.

He then carried out extraordinary experiments with mechanisms and marvellous machines of his own invention, collected by him in the museum which he founded at the Roman *Collegio*, including: a clock activated by a vegetable root which followed the sun's peregrination; a machine which transformed the light of a candle into marvellous forms of men and animals; and innumerable catoptric machines, spagyric ovens, mechanical organs and sciatherical dials.

The learned Jesuit gloried justly in having invented a universal language whereby one could communicate with anyone throughout the whole world, and which was so clear and perfect that the Bishop of Vigevano had written to him enthusiastically, claiming that he had learned it in just over an hour.

The venerable professor of the Roman College had also revealed the true form of Noah's Ark, and succeeded in establishing the number of animals which it contained, in what manner were ordered within it cages, perches, mangers and water troughs and even where the doors and openings were situated. He had demonstrated *geometrice et mathematice* that if the Tower of Babel had been completed, its weight would have been such as to tilt the terrestrial globe.

But, above all, Kircher was a natural philosopher exceedingly well versed in antique and unknown languages. He had deciphered the hieroglyphs of the Alexandrine obelisk which now stood in the fountain erected in the Piazza Navona by the Cavalier Bernini. The tale of the obelisk was perhaps the most extraordinary to be told concerning him. When the enormous stone relic was found buried among the ruins of the Circo Massimo, the Jesuit was immediately called to the place where it had been discovered. Although only three of the four sides of the obelisk were visible, he had foreseen the symbols which would appear on the side that remained buried, and his prediction had proved correct even in its most abstruse details.

"But, when you met him, he was... how could one put it?..." I objected at that point in the narration.

"Say it outright. He was senile."

Indeed, that was so, at the end of his life, the great genius grew demented. His spirit, explained Atto, had evaporated, and his body was soon to know the same fate. Father Kircher in fact died one year later.

"Folly makes all men equal, kings and peasants," said Abbot Melani, who added that he had in the days that followed made a couple of visits to well-connected acquaintances, and had received confirmation of the painful situation, despite the Jesuits' endeavours to ensure that it was bruited abroad as little as possible.

"I now come to the point," said the abbot, cutting short the discussion. "If your memory serves you well, you will recall that in Colbert's study, the main thing that I found was correspondence sent from Rome and addressed to Superintendent Fouquet, written in prose which appeared to be that of an ecclesiastic, in which mention was made of unspecified secret information."

"I remember, of course."

"Well, the letters were from Kircher."

"And how can you be sure of that?"

"You are right to doubt: I must again explain to you the illumination which came over me today. I am still overcome by the emotion that it caused me—and emotion is the handmaid of chaos; while what we need is to put facts in order. As you will perhaps recall, when examining the letters, I noted that one of them curiously began with the words *mumiarum domino*, which I was at the time unable to understand."

"That is true."

"*Mumiarum domino* means 'to the master of the mummies' and certainly refers to Fouquet."

"What are mummies?"

"They are the corpses of ancient Egyptians contained in sarcophagi and preserved from decay using bandages and mysterious treatments."

"Still, I do not understand why Fouquet should be 'the master of the mummies'."

The abbot picked up a book and handed it to me. It was a collection of poems by Signor de la Fontaine, he who in his verses had lauded the singing of Atto Melani. I opened at a page where he had placed a bookmark and indicated a few lines.

> *Je prendrai votre heure et la mienne.*
> *Si je vois qu'on vous entretienne,*
> *J'attendrai fort paisiblement*
> *En ce superbe appartement*
> *Où l'on a fait d'étrange terre*
> *Depuis peu venir à grand-erre*
> *(Non sans travail et quelques frais)*
> *Des rois Céphrim et Kiopès*
> *Le cercueil, la tombe où la bière:*
> *Pour les rois, ils sont en poussière.*
> *...*
>
> *Je quittai donc la galerie,*
> *Fort content parmi mon chagrin,*
> *De Kiopès et de Céphrim,*
> *D'Orus et de tout son lignage*
> *Et de maint autre personnage.*

"It is a poem dedicated to Fouquet. Have you understood?"

"Not a lot," I replied, irritated by that prolix and incomprehensible poem.*

"Yet it is all quite simple. Cephrim and Kiopès are the two Egyptian mummies which Superintendent Fouquet had acquired.

---

* I shall take your time and my own. / If I see that you're conversing, / I shall wait most patiently / in this superb apartment / where, from a strange land, / recently, after great wanderings / (not without labour and at some expense) / of Kings Cephrim and Kiopès were brought / the coffin, tomb or bier: / for the kings themselves are dust. / ... / So I left the gallery / most content, despite my chagrin, / for Kiopès and Cephrim, / For Horus and all his lineage / and for many another personage.

La Fontaine, who was his great admirer, speaks of them in this witty little poem. Now, I ask you: who, here in Rome, was interested in ancient Egypt?"

"That I know: Kircher."

"Correct. Indeed, Kircher had personally studied Fouquet's mummies, travelling to Marseilles, where they had just been disembarked. He then reported on the results of his studies in the treatise entitled *Oedipus Aegiptiacus*."

"Then Kircher and Fouquet knew one another."

"Certainly. I even recall admiring in that treatise a fine drawing of the two sarcophagi which Kircher had had made by a Jesuit colleague. Therefore, the author of the letter and Kircher are one and the same person. Only today, however, did I put all this together and understand it."

"I too am beginning to understand. In one of the letters, Fouquet is addressed as *domino mumiarum* or 'master of the mummies', because he has purchased the two sarcophagi mentioned by Kircher."

"Bravo, you have grasped the essence of it."

The situation was indeed thoroughly complicated. Briefly, Abbot Melani had understood that Kircher had been in contact with Superintendent Fouquet in connection with the mummies which the latter had acquired at Marseilles and brought with him to Paris. Perhaps meeting him in person or by some other means, Kircher had confided a secret to him. Concerning this, however, the correspondence between the two which Atto Melani had taken from Colbert's house contained no explanation, but only allusions.

"So you came to Rome not only to inquire into the presence of Fouquet, but also to uncover the secret referred to in those letters."

I saw Abbot Melani grow pensive, as though a disagreeable thought had traversed his mind.

"And it was not at all by chance that you came to the Locanda del Donzello, is that not so?"

"Well done. How could you tell?"

"I have thought it over a little. And then I remembered that, according to the letters which you found, the Superintendent had been seen by Colbert's spies in Piazza Fiammetta, near the church of Sant'Apollinare, as well as in the Piazza Navona: in both cases, a few yards from here."

"Again, bravo! I knew at once that you had talent."

It was then that, encouraged by that compliment, I took a chance. When I put the question, my voice trembled a little.

"Signor di Mourai was Fouquet, is that not so?"

Atto Melani remained silent, but his face was answer enough. That mute admission was, naturally, followed by my explanations. How had I worked it out? Not even I could say. Perhaps it was simply the combination of a series of, apparently insignificant, facts that had put me on the scent. Fouquet was French, and Mourai too. Mourai was old and ill, and his eyesight had become very weak. After almost twenty years in prison, such would also be the Superintendent's condition. The age of both was the same: about sixty years, perhaps nearly seventy. Mourai had a young companion, Signor Devizé, who however did not know Italy as well as his own country and, what is more, understood only music. A fugitive would need a guide skilled in the ways of the world; and that could well be Pompeo Dulcibeni. The aged gentleman seemed indeed, from some of his observations (concerning the price of textiles in Rome, the grist-tax, the supplying of foodstuffs to the Roman market) to be exceedingly well informed about commerce and merchandise.

Nor was that all. If Fouquet were really hiding in or passing through Rome, it is probable that he would not have moved far from his lodgings. And if he had been a guest at our inn, wherever would he have gone for a stroll at nightfall, if not to the Piazza Navona or to Piazza Fiammetta, passing in front of Sant'Apollinare? Moreover, as I had already confusedly guessed that morning on my couch, to sojourn at the Donzello was a choice more appropriate for someone of limited means; for our quarter, which once had contained the best hostelries, was now in a state of inexorable decay. Yet the old Frenchman certainly did not give the impression of being short of money, on the contrary. It was therefore probable that he wished to avoid encountering his peers, perhaps Frenchmen who might, even after so long a time, recognise a countenance as well known as that of the Superintendent.

"But why did you not tell me the truth?" I asked with a wavering voice at the end of my discourse, striving to contain my emotions.

"Because it was not yet indispensable. If I always told you everything that I know it would only cause your head to ache," he replied shamelessly.

Soon, however, I saw his mood change and he was clearly touched.

"I have still much to teach you, apart from the art of making deductions," he said, clearly troubled.

For the first time, I was certain that Abbot Melani was not simulating but, on the contrary, showing his pain at his friend's sad fate. So it was that, sometimes fighting back his tears, he told me that he had not come to Rome simply to investigate whether the news of Fouquet's presence was true, and thus to establish whether false rumours had been spread with a view to perturbing the Most Christian King and all of France. He had undertaken the long voyage from France to Italy in the fond hope of seeing again his old friend, of whom he now retained only painful and distant memories. If (he had thought) Fouquet was really in Rome, he would surely be in danger: the same informer who had advised Colbert of the Superintendent's presence in the Holy City would sooner or later receive orders from Paris. He would perhaps be ordered to capture Fouquet or, failing that, to eliminate him.

That was why Melani, as he himself explained, had arrived in Rome torn by a confusion of conflicting emotions: the hope that he might again see the friend whom he had believed dead after years of harsh imprisonment, the desire to serve the King faithfully and, lastly, the fear that, if he were really to find Fouquet, he might be involved in what might follow.

"What do you mean?"

"In Paris, everyone knows that the King never hated anyone more than the Superintendent. And if he discovered that Fouquet had not died at Pinerol but was alive and free, his wrath would know no bounds."

Atto then explained to me that a trusty servant of his had, as on previous occasions, helped him to conceal his departure.

"He is a copyist of extraordinary talent, and knows perfectly how to imitate my handwriting. He is a good man, his name is Buvat. Every time that I leave Paris secretly, he looks after my correspondence. They write to me from all the courts of Europe to obtain the latest information, and princes must be answered at once," said he, boastfully.

"And how does your Buvat know what he is supposed to write?"

"A few utterly predictable items of political news, which I left for him before my departure. As for news of the court, that he could procure by paying a few servants, who are the best source of information in all France."

I was about to ask him how he had managed to conceal his departure from the King himself, but Atto did not let me interrupt him. Once in Rome, he said, he had at last traced Fouquet to our inn. But the very morning when he set foot at the Donzello, he whom we still called Signor di Mourai tragically died. Thus, the abbot came barely in time to see his former benefactor, whom he had retraced in so singular a fashion, die in his arms.

"And did he recognise you?"

"Alas, no. When I entered the apartment, he was already moribund, babbling meaningless words. I tried with all my strength to reanimate him, I shook him by the shoulders, I spoke to him, but it was already too late. In your hostelry, there died a great man."

Abbot Melani looked away, perhaps trying to hide a furtive tear. I heard him intone with trembling voice an agonisingly poignant melody:

> *Ma, quale pena infinita,*
> *sciolta hai ora la vita...* *

I was dumbfounded. I felt overcome by emotion, while Atto withdrew to a corner of the chamber, suddenly closed in upon himself. I called to mind old Mourai's features and gestures, as I had known him during those days at the Donzello. I tried to recollect words, expressions, accents which might link him with the great and unfortunate figure of the Superintendent, as I imagined him to be from all Abbot Melani had told me. I remembered his eyes, veiled and almost unseeing, his pale, old, trembling body, his cracked, gasping lips; but found nothing, nothing that might remind me of the Squirrel's proverbial vivacity. Or perhaps... yes: now that I thought of Mourai's minute and delicate form, of his cheeks, lined but not dried up by age; and his curved profile, and fine, nervous hands... yes, an old squirrel, that was what Signor di Mourai resembled. With not a gesture, not a word, not a gleam in his eyes: the Squirrel had settled into his eternal repose. One last effort, and he had made that sudden, final climb up the tree of freedom: that was enough. In the end, I concluded, while my tears flowed silently, what did it matter how Fouquet died? He died free.

* But, what infinite sadness, / your life has now dissolved...

The abbot turned towards me, his features contorted by emotion.

"Now my friend sits on the right hand of the Most High, among the just and the martyrs," he exclaimed emphatically. "You should know, Fouquet's mother looked with apprehension upon her son's ascent, which made him powerful over the things of this world, but weakened his soul. And every day, she prayed to God that he should alter the Superintendent's destiny, so as to guide him onto the path of redemption and sanctity. When his faithful servant La Forêt came with the news of his arrest, Fouquet's mother knelt, full of joy, and thanked the Lord, exclaiming: 'Now he will surely become a saint.'"

Atto broke off for a moment to control the anguish that tightened his throat and prevented him from speaking.

"That good woman's prediction," he resumed, "came true. According to his confessor, Fouquet, in the last period of his imprisonment, had admirably purged his soul. It seems that he even wrote a number of spiritual meditations. Certainly, he often repeated in his letters to his wife how grateful he was for that prayer of his mother, and how happy he was that it had been answered." The abbot sobbed: "Oh Nicolas! Heaven demanded the highest price of you, but accorded you a second grace: it spared you from that miserable destiny of worldly glory which leads inevitably to a vain cenotaph."

After allowing the abbot and myself a few more moments in which to soothe our souls, I tried to change the subject: "I know that you will not agree to this, but has the time perhaps not come to question Pompeo Dulcibeni or Devizé?"

"Not at all," he retorted sharply, promptly abandoning every trace of his previous despair. "If those two have anything to hide, any question will put them on their guard."

He rose to wipe his face. Then he rummaged among his documents and finally handed me a paper.

"There are other matters to think about, for the time being: we must unravel such clues as we have. You will recall that when we set foot in Komarek's clandestine printing press, the floor was littered with sheets of paper. Well, I found time to pick up a couple of these. Tell me if this reminds you of something."

Carattere Testo Paragone Corsivo.
_____

LIBER JOSVE.
Hebraice Jehoshua.
Caput Primum.

ET *factum est post mortem Moysi servi Domini, ut loqueretur Dominus ad Josue filium Nun, ministrum Moysi, & diceret ei; Moyses seruus meus mortuus est surge & transi Jordanem istum tu & omnis populus tecum, in terram, quam ego dabo filiis Israel. Omnem locum, quem calcaverit vestigium pedis vestri, vobis tradam, sicut locutus sum Moysi. A deserto & Libano usque ad fluvium magnum contra Solis occasum erit terminus vester. Nullus poterit vobis resistere cunctis diebus vitae tuae: sicut fui cum Moyse, ita ero tecum: non dimittam, nec derelinquam te. Confortare & esto robustus: tu enim sorte divides populo huic terram...*

"It seems to be another passage from the Bible."

"And so?"

I turned it over in my hands: "This, too, is printed on only one side!"

"Correct. The question then follows: is there some new fashion in Rome for printing Bibles on one side only? I do not think so: it would call for so much paper, the books would weigh twice as much and would perhaps cost double too."

"And what does that tell you?"

"That tells me these pages are not from a book."

"What are they then?"

"An assay of skill."

"Do you mean a printer's proof?"

"Not just that: it is a sample of what the printer is able to offer his clients. After all, what did Stilone Priàso tell the *corpisantari*? Komarek needs money, and in addition to his humble duties in the print-shop of the Congregation for the Propagation of the Faith, he takes on a few clandestine jobs. But, at the same time, he will need to find, so as to speak, 'ordinary' clients. Perhaps he has already requested an authorisation to print on his own account. He will have prepared a sample to show future customers the quality of his work. And, to show a sample of characters, one page will suffice."

"I do believe that you are right."

"I do believe so too. And I shall show you the proof of this: what does the first line of our new page say? 'Carattere Testo Paragone Corsivo.' I am no expert, but I maintain that 'Paragone' is the name of the typeface used in this text. On the other page, and in exactly the same place, I read 'nda'. Probably, the complete word was '*rotonda*', for some rounded typeface."

"Does all this mean that we must now go back to suspecting Stilone Priàso?" I asked in no small state of agitation.

"Perhaps so, perhaps not. But what is certain is that to find our thief we must search among Komarek's customers. And Stilone Priàso is one of them. Moreover, like our gazetteer, the thief of your little pearls cannot be weighed down by riches. And, lastly, he hails from Naples; the very city from which Fouquet left for the Donzello. Strange, is it not? However…"

"However?"

"That is all too obvious. Whoever poisoned my poor friend is cunning and skilful, and will have taken steps to ensure that he is above suspicion, and to pass unobserved. Can you imagine a perennially anxious character like Stilone Priàso in that role? Do you not think it would be absurd, if he were the assassin, that he should go about with an astrological gazette under his arm? To pass oneself off for an astrologer would certainly not be a good cover for an assassin. Even less, to indulge in petty thieving by filching your pearls."

Of course. Stilone really did seem to be an astrologer. I told Atto with what melancholy and pain the Neapolitan had narrated the tale of Abbot Morandi.

As I was leaving his chamber, I decided to put to Melani the question which I had been holding in reserve for some time.

"Signor Atto, do you or do you not believe that there is some connection between the mysterious thief and the death of Superintendent Fouquet?"

"I do not know."

❧❧

He was lying. I was sure of it. When, back in my bed after serving luncheon, I gathered my ideas together, I felt a cold, heavy curtain fall between me and Abbot Melani. He was certainly hiding something else from me, as he had hidden the presence of Fouquet at the inn under barefaced lies and, before that, the letters discovered in Colbert's study. And with what impudence he had narrated to me the story of the Superintendent! He had spoken of him as though he had not seen him for years, while he and Pellegrino had seen him die (and in my mind I weighed up that tremendous event) only a few hours before. He had then had the effrontery to suggest that Dulcibeni and Devizé were hiding something about Mourai, alias Fouquet. And who was he to talk? What high priest of deceit, what virtuoso of simulation could Abbot Melani be? I cursed myself for not heeding those things which I had learned concerning him when I overheard Cristofano, Devizé and Stilone Priàso conversing. And I cursed myself for having felt flattered when he praised my perspicacity.

I was exceedingly irritated, and so all the more desirous of squaring up to the abbot in order to put to the proof my ability to stay ahead of his moves, to unmask his omissions, to interpret his silences and to cut through his eloquence.

Indulging myself in the subtle and envious rancour which I felt for Melani, worn out by my sleepless night, I fell very gently asleep. On the point of giving myself up to Morpheus, I unwillingly banished the thought of Cloridia.

For the second time that day, I was awoken by Cristofano. I had slept for four hours without a break. I felt well, I know not whether because of my nap or the *magnolicore* which I had taken care to drink and to spread on my chest beforehand. On seeing that I had recovered, the doctor left, reassured. I remembered then that I must complete my round of visits to administer the remedies against infection. I dressed and took with me the bag containing the little jars. I intended first of all to administer a stomach theriac and a decoction of ivy with syrup to Brenozzi, and a fumigation to Stilone Priàso, then to descend to the first floor and visit Devizé and Dulcibeni. I passed through the kitchen in order to boil a little water in the kettle.

I ordered matters so as to deal quite swiftly with the Venetian. I could no longer tolerate his manner of interrogating me, putting questions and then answering them himself before I could so much as open my mouth. Nor could I refrain from observing his disgusting habit of grasping his nether parts in restless counterpoint, like those youngsters who have just lost their innocence but, being inexperienced in life, cannot stop pestering their little celery stalk with vain digital interrogations. I saw that he had not touched his food but avoided asking questions, fearing that this might unleash another flood of words.

I then knocked on the Neapolitan's door. He called me in but, while I was laying out my things, I saw that he too had left his meal untouched. I asked him if by any chance he felt unwell.

"Do you know where I come from?" he asked me in response.

"Yes Sir," I replied in some perplexity. "From the Kingdom of Naples."

"Have you ever been there?"

"Alas, no, I have never visited any other city in my whole life."

"Very well, know then that in no land has heaven been so prodigal of its beneficent influences in every season," he began grandiloquently, while I prepared his inhalation. "Naples, gentle and populous capital of the twelve provinces of the kingdom, is situated in a magnificent theatre overlooking the sea, framed by soft hills and rolling plains. Founded by a nymph named Partenope, it enjoys the myriad fruits, the purest fountains, the famed fennel and all manner of herbs offered by the nearby plain known as Poggio Reale, all of which may justifiably raise eyebrows into arches of wonderment. Then, on the fertile littoral of Chiaia, as on the hills of Posilippo, cauliflowers are harvested, and peas, cardoons and artichokes, radishes, roots and the most exquisite salads and fruit. Nor do I believe that there exists a place more fertile and delightful, o'erflowing with every amenity, than the proud shores of Mergellina, ruffled only by soft zephyrs, which deservedly received the ashes of the immortal Marone and of the incomparable Sanazzaro."

So it was not purely by chance that Stilone Priàso styled himself a poet. He, in the meanwhile, pursued his discourse from under the sheet with which I had covered his head, immersed in balsamic vapours: "Moving further, we come to the antique city of Pozzuoli, with its copious bounty of asparagus, artichokes, peas and pumpkins out of season; and in the month of March, early sour-grape juice, to the good people's astonishment. Luscious fruit on Procida; on Ischia, medlars both white and red, fine Greco wines and pheasants plentiful. At Capri, the finest of heifers and splendid quails. Pork at Sorrento, game at Vico, the sweetest of onions at Castell'a Mare, grey mullet at Torre del Greco, red mullet at Granatiello, Lachrimae on the Monte di Somma, once known as Vesuvius. And watermelons and saveloys at Orta, Vernotico wine at Nola, *torrone* at Aversa, melons at Cardito, apricots at Arienzo, Provola cheeses at Acerra, cardoons at Giugliano, lampreys at Capua, olives at Gaeta, legumes at Venafro; and trout, wine, oil and game at Sora..."

At last, I understood.

"Do you perhaps mean to suggest, Sir, that the food which I am serving you does not meet with your approval?"

He stood up and looked at me with a hint of embarrassment.

"Er... to tell the truth, we eat nothing but soups here. But, that is not the point..." said he, stumbling in his search for words. "Well, in short, your mania for putting cinnamon in all your broths, sauces and soups will end up accomplishing the extermination which we were expecting from the plague!" And unexpectedly, he laughed out loud.

I was confused and humiliated. I begged him to lower his voice lest we be overheard by the other guests; but I was too late. From the chamber next door, Brenozzi had already heard Stilone's protest and was laughing unrestrainedly. The echo spread to Padre Robleda's apartment, and in the end both of them leaned out of their windows. Stilone Priàso went on to open his door, caught up in the chorus of hilarity: I begged him to close it, but in vain. I was overwhelmed by a barrage of scornful jokes and mockery, and they laughed until they cried, all at the expense of my cooking. Only, it seemed, the charitable accompaniment of Devizé's music rendered it all a little less unbearable. Even Padre Robleda struggled to suppress a guffaw.

None of them had yet confessed the truth to me, explained the Neapolitan, for they had learned from Cristofano of Pellegrino's awakening and were counting upon my master's swift return, besides which, these were the least of their cares during those days. The recent increase in my doses of cinnamon had, however, rendered the situation untenable. Here, Priàso broke off, seeing from my countenance how humiliated and offended I was. The other two closed their doors again. The Neapolitan put a hand on my shoulder.

"Come on, my boy, do not take it to heart: quarantine is not conducive to good manners."

I begged his pardon for having thus tormented him with my cinnamon, collected my little jars and took my leave. I was furious and unhappy but I decided for the time being not to show it.

I descended to the first floor, intending to knock on Devizé's door. When, however, I got there, I hesitated.

From behind the door came the sound of still uncertain notes. He was tuning his instrument. Then he launched into a dance, perhaps a villanelle; and next, what I would today recognise without the slightest difficulty as a gavotte.

I resolved to knock at the next door, that of Pompeo Dulcibeni. Should the gentleman from Fermo be available for a massage, I would at the same time be able to enjoy the echoes of Devizé's guitar.

Dulcibeni accepted the offer. He received me as always with an austere and weary manner, his voice mournful yet firm, his eyes glaucous yet perspicacious.

"Come in, dear boy. Put your bag down here."

He often called me thus, as one speaks to a servant. He was the guest at the Donzello of whom I stood most in awe. His tone, which was tranquil when speaking to inferiors, yet utterly lacking in warmth, seemed always on the point of betraying some impatient or scornful gesture which, however, never materialised; and this caused those approaching him to show exaggerated self-control in his presence and, in the end, to take refuge in silence. That, I thought, was why he remained the most solitary of all the guests. Never once, when I served meals, had he kept me back to converse with him. He did not seem troubled by solitude; quite the contrary. Yet, on his low forehead and ruddy cheeks, I noted a deep and bitter crease, and sensed an underlying torment, such as appears only in one burdened by lonely suffering. The one light note was his weakness for my master's good cooking, which alone drew a rare but genuine smile from him or some witty comment.

Who knows how much he too has suffered from my cinnamon, I thought, at once dismissing the conjecture.

Now, for the first time, I was about to spend an hour, or perhaps more, alone in his company, and I felt greatly troubled at the prospect.

I had opened my bag and taken out the jars which I would be using. Dulcibeni asked me what they contained and how they were to be applied, and feigned polite interest in my explanations. I then asked him to uncover his back and sides and to sit astride a chair.

Having opened up the back of his black costume and removed his comical old-fashioned collar, I noticed that he had a long scar across his neck: so that, I thought, was why Dulcibeni never removed that antiquated item of apparel. He then sat as I had suggested and I began to spread the oils which Cristofano had shown me. The first few minutes passed in light banter. We both enjoyed the echo of Devizé's notes: an allemande, then, perhaps, a gigue, a chaconne and a minuet *en rondeau.* I went over in my mind what Robleda had said about the Jansenist doctrines which Dulcibeni seemed to follow.

Suddenly, he asked me if he could stand up. He seemed to be in pain.

"Do you feel ill? Is the smell of the oil perhaps troubling you?"

"No, no, dear boy. I just want to take a pinch of snuff."

He turned the key of the big chest and pulled out three rather well-bound little books in vermilion leather with golden arabesques. Then he brought forth the snuff-box, which was well made, in inlaid cherry-wood. He opened it, took a pinch of powder, raised it to his nostrils and inhaled forcefully, two or three times. He remained for an instant as though in a state of suspense, then took a deep breath. He looked at me and his expression became rather more cordial. He seemed pacified. He asked with genuine concern after the health of the other guests at the inn. Then the conversation began to falter. Every now and then, he would sigh, closing his eyes and briefly stroking his white hair, which must once have been fair.

Looking at him, I wondered how much he knew about the story of his late companion. I could not rid my mind of the revelations concerning Mourai-Fouquet which I had just learned from Atto. I was tempted to put some vague question to him about the old Frenchman whom he had accompanied from Naples (perhaps without knowing his identity). And who knows, perhaps the two had met some time previously; perhaps they had even enjoyed a lengthy acquaintance, despite what Dulcibeni had claimed when speaking to the physician and to the Bargello's men. If that were the case, few indeed were my chances of gaining any confirmation from the lips of the *Marchigiano.* Therefore, after taking counsel with myself, I concluded that my best course would be to converse on some neutral subject so as to start up a conversation and induce him to talk for as long as possible, in the hope of gaining some useful clue from him; exactly as I had already done—although with scant success—with the other guests.

I therefore endeavoured to elicit Dulcibeni's opinion concerning some important occurrence, as one does when one wishes to converse with old men of whom one stands in awe. I asked him, with elaborate deference, what he thought of the siege of Vienna, where the fate of all Christendom hung in the balance, and whether he thought that the Emperor might in the end defeat the Turks.

"Emperor Leopold of Austria can defeat no one: he has fled," he replied drily and then fell silent, leaving it to be understood that the conversation was now closed.

I hoped, nevertheless, that he might express some further opinions, while struggling desperately within myself for some rejoinder whereby to salvage the dialogue. But no inspiration came to me, and so deep silence again descended between us.

I swiftly completed my task and took my leave of him. Dulcibeni remained silent. I was about to leave when there arose in my mind the desire to put another question to him: I could not resist the pressing urge to know whether he too disapproved as much of my cooking.

"No, dear boy, far from it," he replied. "Indeed, I'd say that you have a flair for it."

I thanked him, feeling encouraged, and was about to close the door behind me when I heard him add, as though speaking to himself in a strange whisper rising from the belly: "Were it not for your excremental brews and all that damned cinnamon. *Pumilio*! Booby of a scullion that you are!"

That was enough for me. Never had I felt so humiliated. Yet, what Dulcibeni thought of me was, I reflected, quite true. I could strive with all my might and main but it would not raise me one single inch in the eyes of others, not even, alas, those of Cloridia. Anger and pride flared up in me. So I, who aspired to so much (one day to become a gazetteer) was not even capable of raising my station from that of scullion to cook.

While I was thus groaning inwardly outside Dulcibeni's doorway, I thought I heard a sound of mumbling. I brought my ear closer the better to listen, and what was my surprise when I heard Dulcibeni conversing with someone else.

"Do you feel unwell? Does the smell of oil perhaps inconvenience you?" the other voice asked solicitously.

I was troubled. Was that not the same question I had put to Dulcibeni only moments earlier? Whoever could have hidden in the chamber to listen? And why repeat my words now? But in those words, one detail shocked me: they were spoken by a woman's voice; and it was not Cloridia's.

There followed a few moments of silence.

"Emperor Leopold can defeat no one; he has fled!" Dulcibeni exclaimed suddenly.

That, he had also said to me! I continued to listen, suspended between astonishment and the fear of being discovered.

"You are unfair, you ought not..." replied the woman's voice timidly, in curiously weak, hoarse tones.

"Silence!" interrupted Dulcibeni. "If Europe is blown up, we shall have cause only for rejoicing."

"I hope that you are not serious."

"Listen, then," Dulcibeni resumed in a more conciliatory tone. "These lands of ours are, now, after a manner of speaking, like a great house: a house in which there dwells a single great family. But what will happen if the brothers become too numerous? And what will happen, too, if their wives are all sisters, and so their children all are cousins? They will be forever quarrelling, they will hate one another, each will malign the others. Sometimes, they will form alliances, but these will be too fragile. Their children will couple in an obscene orgy, and will in turn produce mad, weak, corrupted offspring. What is to be expected of so unfortunate a family?"

"I do not know. Perhaps someone... will succeed in pacifying them. And above all, the children will leave off marrying among themselves," the feminine voice responded uncertainly.

"Very well, if the Turk conquers Vienna," retorted Dulcibeni, "at least we shall at last have some new blood on the thrones of Europe. Obviously, after the old has flowed like rivers."

"Excuse me, but I do not understand," the woman ventured shyly.

"It is simple. By now, all the Christian kings are related to one another."

"What do you mean, all related?" asked the little voice.

"I understand. You need a few examples. Louis XIV, the Most Christian King of France, is twice cousin to his wife Maria Teresa, the Infanta of Spain. Both their parents were in fact siblings. This was because the mother of the Sun King, Anne of Austria, was the sister of Maria Teresa's father, Philip IV, King of Spain; while the Sun King's father, Louis XIII, was a brother of Maria Teresa's mother, Elisabeth of France, the first wife of Philip IV."

Dulcibeni paused for a few moments; I heard him taking his snuff box out from a nearby chest and mixing the contents carefully while he continued speaking.

"The respective parents-in-law of the King and Queen of France are, therefore, blood relations: their uncle and aunt. Now, I ask you, what effect will it have to be the nephew and niece of one's parents-in-law? Or, if you prefer, the son and daughter-in-law of one's uncle and aunt."

I could not restrain myself: I had to know who this woman was to whom Dulcibeni was speaking. How the deuce could she have entered the Donzello, despite the quarantine? And why was Dulcibeni addressing her with such passion?

I tried very gradually to open the door, which I had not completely closed when leaving. Now, there was a crack, and with bated breath, I put my eye to it. Dulcibeni was standing, leaning with his elbows on a large chest and fiddling with his snuff-box. Speaking, he directed his attention towards the wall on his right, where the mysterious guest must be. Unfortunately, my field of vision did not extend far enough for me to distinguish this feminine presence. And if I were to open the door wider, I risked being discovered.

After forcefully taking several pinches of snuff, Dulcibeni became agitated, then began to swell up his chest, as though he were about to hold his breath.

"The King of England is Charles II Stuart," he resumed. "His father married Henrietta of France, a sister of Louis XIV's father. Therefore, the King of England is likewise cousin twice over both to the King of France and to his Spanish wife; and they, as you have seen, are doubly cousins to one another. And what about Holland? Henrietta of France, the mother of King Charles II, besides being the Sun King's paternal aunt, was also the maternal aunt of the young Dutch prince William of Orange. In fact, Mary, a sister of King Charles and his brother James, went to Holland as bride of William II of Orange, and from that marriage was born Prince William III who surprised the world six years ago by marrying James's first-born daughter, his first cousin. In other words, four sovereigns have mixed the same blood eight times."

He shook his snuff-box and brought it to his nose, breathing in frenziedly, as though he had long been deprived of tobacco. Then he resumed his harangue, his face grown livid and his voice, hoarse: "Another sister of Charles II wed his cousin, the brother of Louis XIV. They, too, mixed the same blood."

He broke off, seized by a coughing fit. Leaning on the big chest, he brought a handkerchief to his mouth as though he were about to be sick.

"But let us go to Vienna," Dulcibeni resumed, with a trace of exertion in his voice. "The Bourbons of France and the Habsburgs of Spain are, respectively, four and six times cousins to the Habsburgs of Austria. The mother of the Emperor Leopold I of Austria is the sister of Louis XIV. But she is also the sister of the father of his wife Maria Teresa, King Philip IV of Spain, and daughter of the sister of her husband's father, the late Emperor Ferdinand III. The sister of Leopold I married her maternal uncle, again, Philip IV of Spain. And Leopold I married his niece Margaret Teresa. So, the King of Spain is the uncle, brother-in-law and father-in-law of the Emperor of Austria. Thus, three families of sovereigns have mixed the same blood a thousand times over!"

Dulcibeni's voice had grown higher and his expression ever stranger.

"What do you think of it?" he cried out suddenly. "Would you like to be aunt and sister-in-law to your son-in-law?"

In a furious rage, he swept away the few objects placed on the chest (a book and a candle) so that they struck the wall and the floor. The room fell silent.

"But has it always been like this?" the woman's voice stammered at last.

Dulcibeni resumed his usual stern pose and made a sarcastic grimace: "No, my dear," he went on pedantically. "In the distant past, the reigning families assured their posterity by marrying their offspring with the best of the feudal nobility. Every new king was the purest quintessence of the noblest blood of his own land: in France, the sovereign was the most French of Frenchmen. In England, he was the most English of Englishmen."

It was at that juncture that my excessive curiosity caused me to lose my balance, and I pushed against the door. Only by a miracle did I manage to hold onto the doorpost, thus avoiding falling any further forward. Consequently, the opening widened only a little. Dulcibeni had heard nothing. Sweating and trembling with fear, I glanced to the right of the gentleman from the Marches, where the woman should be.

It took me many minutes to overcome my surprise: instead of a human figure, on the wall there was but a mirror. Dulcibeni was talking to himself.

In the instants that followed, I found it even more difficult to follow that paroxysm of anger and scorn vented against kings, princes
and emperors. Was I listening to a madman? With whom was Dulcibeni pretending to speak?

Perhaps, I thought then, he was beset by the memory of a dear
one (a sister, a wife) who was now dead. And it must be a most painful memory to inspire that sad and disquieting scene. I felt at once
embarrassed and moved to pity by that fragment of intimate and solitary suffering which I had stolen like a burglar. I realised that, when I
had attempted to persuade him to talk about the same topics, he had
drawn back. Perhaps he had preferred the company of a dead person
to that of the living.

"And so?" resumed the *Marchigiano*, mimicking the little voice of a
young girl with an innocent, troubled tone.

"And so, and so..." intoned Dulcibeni. "So... all gave way to the
lust for power, which impelled them to intermarry with all the sovereigns of the earth. Take the house of Austria. Today their fetid blood
defiles the sepulchres of valiant ancestors: Albert the Wise, Rudolph
the Magnanimous, and then Leopold the Brave and his son Ernest I
the Iron-willed, all the way down to Albert the Patient and Albert the
Illustrious. Blood which, three centuries ago, began to putrefy, when
it generated the unfortunate Frederick Fat-Lips and his son Maximilian I, both of whom died of a wretched bellyful of melons. And it was
precisely from these two that there arose the insane desire to reunite
all the Habsburg lands, which Leopold the Brave had so wisely divided between himself and his brother. These were lands that could
not be brought together: it was as though a mad chirurgeon were
attempting to force upon the same body, three heads, four legs and
eight arms. In order to assuage his lust for lands, Maximilian I married
no fewer than three times: his wives brought him as their dowries the
Netherlands and Franche-Comté; but also the monstrous chin that
disfigures the countenance of their descendants. His son, Philip the
Fair, in the twenty-eight years of his life, annexed Spain by marrying
Joan the Mad, daughter and heir to Ferdinand of Aragon and Isabel of
Castile, and mother of Charles V and Ferdinand I. Charles V both
crowned and undid the plans of his grandfather Maximilian I: he abdi-
cated and divided his kingdom, on which the sun never set, between
his son Philip II and his brother Ferdinand I. He divided his kingdom,
but he could not divide his blood: among his descendants, madness was

by now unstoppable, brother lusted after sister and both desired to marry their own offspring. The son of Ferdinand I, Maximilian II, Emperor of Austria, married his father's sister and with his aunt-wife produced a daughter, Anne Marie of Austria, who married Philip II of Spain, her uncle and cousin, being the son of Charles V; from these inauspicious nuptials, Philip III of Spain was born, who married Margaret of Austria, daughter of his grandfather's brother, Maximilian II, and from her begot Philip IV and Maria Anna of Spain, who married Ferdinand III, Emperor of Austria, her first cousin, being the son of her mother's brother, and they in turn brought into this world the present Emperor Leopold I of Austria, and his sister Maria Anna..."

Suddenly, I was seized by disgust. That orgy of incest had given me vertigo. The revolting interweaving of marriages between uncles and aunts, nephews and nieces, brothers and sisters-in-law and cousins had something monstrous about it. After discovering that Dulcibeni was speaking to the mirror, I had listened distractedly. But in the end that lugubrious secret oration both intrigued and sickened me.

Dulcibeni, overexcited and purple in the face, remained standing there with his gaze lost in the void, as though the excess of ire had strangled his voice.

"Remember," he managed to groan at last, turning once more to his imaginary companion, "France, Spain, Austria, England and Holland: for centuries jealous of peoples of other races, are now all under the yoke of one single race with neither land nor loyalty. This blood is *autàdelphos*, twice brother to itself, like the children of Oedipus and Jocasta: blood alien to the history of any people, yet which dictates the history of all peoples. Blood without land and without honour. Traitorous blood."

ॐ•ॐ

Excremental brew: once in the kitchen, I remembered the terms with which Pompeo Dulcibeni had labelled my culinary efforts and their seasoning of precious cinnamon.

Once I had recovered from the disgust which the elevated and solitary considerations of the gentleman from the Marches had provoked in me, I turned my mind to the nausea which I myself had generated in the stomachs of the guests at the inn. I resolved to remedy this.

I went down into the cellar. I continued to the lower level, quite under the ground, and there spent, I think, about an hour, at the risk of catching some illness from the sharp cold that always reigned down there. I examined that space with its low ceiling from end to end, exploring by the light of my lantern the most hidden corners, where I had never yet ventured or stopped, and the shelves all the way to the top, and delving into the cases of snow until I almost reached the bottom. In a wide crevice, hidden behind rows of jars filled with wines and oil, there lay all sorts of dried legumes and seeds, candied fruit, green vegetables in gallipots and bags of macaroni, gnochetti, lasagne and zeppoli, resting under great jute covers and, in the cold amidst the snow, a great variety of salted, smoked, and dried meats and meat in jars. There, Signor Pellegrino, like a jealous lover, kept tongues in pottage and sucking-pigs, as well as pieces of various beasts: sweetbreads of deer and of sucking-kid; tripe of sucking-calf; hedgehog's paws, kidneys and brains; cows' and goats' teats; boars' and sheep's tongues; haunch of doe and of chamois; liver, paws, neck and throat of bear; flank, sirloin and fillet of venison.

And I found hare, black grouse, turkey, wild chicken, chicks, pigeons and wood pigeons, pheasants and blackcock, partridges and woodcock, peacocks, peahens and peachicks, ducks and coot, goslings, geese, quails, turtle-doves, redwings, hazel-hens, ortolans, swallows, sparrows and garden-warblers from Cyprus and Heraklion.

With beating heart I imagined how my master would have prepared them: stewed, roast, in soups, in consommés, spitted, fried, in simple or crusted pastry, in arms, in broths, in snacks, in cakes, with sauces, with vinegars, with fruit and in great centrepieces.

Drawn by the strong odour of smoked meat and of dried seaweed, I continued with my inspection; and under yet more pressed snow and jute sacking, as I expected, salted and packed in little casks, or hanging in small bunches from nets and hooks, I discovered: barbels, dories, razor fish, striped mullet, red mullet, sea-perch, sea-snails, tusk-shells, mushrooms, shrimps, trough-shells, crabs, shad, lampreys, sand-smelt, sole, snails, pike, hake, bass, black umber, limpets, fillets of swordfish and gurnard, turbot, plaice, angler-fish, frogs, pilchards, sea-scorpions, mackerel, sturgeon, turtles, clams and tench.

Of all that abundance, I had hitherto seen only such fresh produce as was from time to time delivered by the tradesmen for whom I had opened the back door. Most of the provisions, I had, however, glimpsed only briefly when (alas, all too rarely) my master ordered me to fetch victuals from the cellars, or when accompanying Cristofano.

I was seized by a doubt: when, and to whom, did Pellegrino plan to serve such food in such quantities? Did he perhaps hope to receive one of those sumptuous trains of Armenian bishops who, as neighbourhood gossip still told, had been the pride of the Donzello in the days of the late Signora Luigia? I suspected that my master might, before his dismissal from his post as carver, have skilfully bribed the keepers of the Cardinal's pantry.

I took a jar of cows' teats and returned to the kitchen. I shook the salt off them, tied the ends together and put them to boil. Then, I cut some into fine slices, which I rolled in flour, glazed and fried before covering them with sauce until I was satisfied with the result. Another portion I chopped up and stewed with aromatic herbs and spices, a little clear soup and eggs. Yet more I roasted in the oven with white wine, sour grape pips and lemon juice, some fresh fruit, raisins, pine kernels and slices of ham. I prepared some, too, diced and mixed with white wine, then closed into pies with soft pastry, together with spices, ham and other salted meats, and bone marrow, with *brodetto* and sugar. The rest, I prepared slightly interlarded with slices of bacon fat and cloves, all wrapped in a net and spitted.

In the end, I was exhausted. Cristofano arrived in the kitchen at the end of my long travail and found me crouching, weary and bathed in sweat, in a corner of the fireplace. He examined and sniffed at the dishes lined up in a row on the kitchen table. Then he turned to me with a satisfied, fatherly expression.

"I shall look after the matter of serving the food, my boy. You, go and take a rest."

Satiated by the repeated and generous tastings which I had allowed myself while cooking, I climbed the stairs to the top of the house, but I did not enter my chamber. Seated on the stairs, I enjoyed my well-deserved success in all discretion: while the guests partook of their evening meal, for a good half-hour, the corridors of the Donzello echoed with clinking, moans of pleasure and satisfied lip-smacking. A chorus of stomachs coughing noisily signalled at last that the time had come to collect the dishes. The victory which I had snatched from the jaws of defeat brought me close to tears.

෧‍⬦

I then prepared to make my round of the apartments: I did not wish to forego the compliments of the Donzello's guests. However, arriving before Abbot Melani's doorway, I recognised his deeply mournful singing. I was struck by the heart-rending tone of his voice, so much so that I stopped to listen:

> *Ahi, dunqu'è pur vero;*
> *dunque, dunqu'è pur vero...*

He was repeating the phrase so softly, and with ever-new and surprising melodic variations.

I was perturbed by those words, which I seemed to have heard already at a time and in a place unknown to me. Suddenly, a revelation came to me: had not my master Pellegrino perhaps mentioned to me that the old Signor di Mourai, alias Fouquet, had, before expiring, with a last supreme effort murmured a phrase in Italian? And now, I remembered: the dying man had pronounced the very words which Atto was now intoning: "*Ahi, dunqu'è pur vero*".

Why, I wondered, why ever had Fouquet pronounced his last words in Italian? I recalled, too, that Pellegrino had seen Atto, leaning close to the old man's face and speaking to him in French. Why, then, had Fouquet murmured those words in Italian?

Meanwhile, Melani continued his song:

> *Dunque, dunqu'è pur vero,*
> *anima del mio cor,*
> *che per novello Amor*
> *tu cangiasti, cangiasti pensiero...**

At the end, I heard him struggle to hold back his sobs. Torn between embarrassment and compassion, I dared neither move nor speak. I felt a stab of pity for that eunuch, no longer in the flower of youth: the mutilation imposed on the little boy's body by a father's greed had brought him fame, while condemning him to shameful solitude. Perhaps, I reflected, Fouquet had nothing to do with it. Those words pronounced by the Superintendent at the point of death might simply be an astonished exclamation in the face of death; I had heard that such things were not unusual among the dying.

The abbot had, in the meantime, begun another aria, the accents of which were even more anguished and lugubrious:

* So it is really true, / soul of my heart, / that for a new Love / you've changed, changed your mind...

Lascia speranza, ohimé,
ch'io mi lamenti,
lascia ch'io mi quereli.
Non ti chiedo mercé,
*no, no, non ti chiedo mercé…**

He emphasised the last phrase, and repeated it ad infinitum. What, I wondered, could so torment him, that in his discreet and subdued song he should exclaim broken-heartedly that he would ask no pity? At that moment, Cristofano arrived behind me. He was doing his rounds.

"Poor fellow," he whispered to me, referring to Atto. "He is suffering from a moment of discomfort. Like all of us, what is more, in this wretched reclusion."

"Yes, indeed," I replied, thinking of Dulcibeni's solitary discourse.

"Let us leave him to relieve his feelings; I shall come and visit him later and make him drink a calming infusion."

We went on our way, while Atto sang unceasingly:

Lascia ch'io mi disperi…†

---

* Ah Hope, let me lament, / let me complain. / I ask you no mercy, / no, no, I ask you no mercy…
† Let me despair…

Night the Fifth
Between *the* 15ᵗʰ & 16ᵗʰ September, 1683

✠

My mood was rather melancholy when the abbot called on me to descend yet again under the ground. The supper of cows' teats had given fresh heart to our lodgers; but not alas to me, weighed down as I was by the sequence of revelations and discoveries concerning Mourai and Fouquet, not to mention the gloomy judgements of Dulcibeni. Nor had the task of writing my diary improved matters.

The abbot must have sensed my state of mind, for while we went on our way, he made no effort to enliven the conversation. Nor was he in the best of moods, although visibly more tranquil by comparison with the desperate laments which I had heard him singing after dinner. He seemed to be suffering under the weight of some unspoken anxiety, which rendered him unusually taciturn. As might have been expected, Ugonio and Ciacconio did what they could to make the situation worse.

The two *corpisantari* had already been awaiting us for some time when we joined them under the Piazza Navona.

"Tonight, we must clarify our ideas a little concerning the underground city," announced Melani.

He produced a sheet of paper on which he had traced a series of lines schematically.

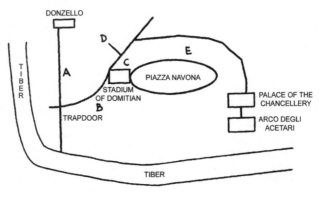

"Here is what I would have liked to obtain from these two wretches, instead of which we have to depend upon ourselves."

It was a rough map of the galleries which we had explored to date. On the first night, we had descended from the Donzello to the opening onto the Tiber, taking a gallery which Atto had marked with the letter A. In the roof of that gallery we had, later, discovered the trapdoor through which we had taken the passage which led to the ruins of Domitian's Stadium, under the Piazza Navona, corresponding to the letter B. From the Piazza Navona, through the narrow hole in which we had to bend double, we took passage C. From that point, there began a long curve (marked E) along which we had followed Stilone Priàso and which had led us to the space painted with frescoes, in all probability beneath the Palace of the Chancellery. Thence, we had emerged at the Arch of the Acetari. Finally, passage D branched out from the left-hand side of passage C.

"There are three galleries of which we know the beginning but not the end: B, C and D. It would be wise to explore them before undertaking any further pursuits. The first is the left-hand branch of the gallery which one takes upon emerging from the trapdoor. It goes in the general direction of the Tiber, but we know nothing else about it. The second gallery is that which turns off from the Piazza Navona and proceeds in a straight line. The third deviates from that gallery to the left. We shall begin with the third one, gallery D."

We advanced cautiously until we reached the point where Ugonio and Ciacconio had stationed themselves the night before when they assaulted Stilone Priàso. Atto made us stop there to check our position from the map.

"Gfrrrlubh," said Ciacconio, to catch our attention.

A few paces in front of us, an object lay on the ground. Abbot Melani ordered us all to halt and advanced first to examine our find. It was a small green glass phial from which there had spilled a (now dry) stream, then clear drops, of red blood.

෨෴෧

"What miracle have we here?" sighed Abbot Melani with a tired voice.

It took no little time to calm down the *corpisantari*, who were convinced that the phial was one of the relics for which they were forever searching. Ciacconio had begun to patter around it, gurgling frenetically. Ugonio had attempted to seize the phial, and Atto had been compelled to thrust him back, without sparing him a few blows. In the end, the *corpisantari* ceased their agitation and we were all able to gather our ideas together. It was clearly not the blood of a martyr: gallery D, in which we had found the blood was neither a catacomb, a columbarium, nor indeed any ancient holy place, Abbot Melani reminded us, exhorting the two treasure hunters to calm down. Above all, however, the blood which it contained was hardly dry, and had even spilled onto the ground: therefore it belonged to a living being, or to one not long dead—not to a martyr who had lived centuries ago. Atto wrapped the phial in a fine piece of cloth and put it in the pocket of his doublet, erasing with one foot the blackish traces of liquid remaining on the ground. We decided to continue our exploration: perhaps the solution to the mystery would be found further on.

Melani said nothing, but it was all too easy to guess his thoughts: yet another unexpected find, yet another object whose provenance was hard to determine; and yet again, blood.

As on the night before, the underground passage appeared to turn gradually to the left.

"That, too, is strange," commented Abbot Melani. "It is what I least expected."

Finally, the gallery seemed to be leading back towards the surface. Rather than a stairway, this time we encountered a rather gentle incline. Suddenly, however, a spiral staircase appeared before our eyes, with stone steps skilfully set into the ground. The *corpisantari* seemed unwilling to go any further. Ugonio and Ciacconio were ill-tempered: after having to give up the page from the Bible, the phial, too, had been snatched from before their eyes.

"Very well, then, you are to remain here until our return," Melani reluctantly conceded.

As we were beginning our ascent, I asked the abbot why he was so surprised that gallery D, which we had just traversed, should curve to the left.

"It is quite simple: if you have carefully studied the map which I gave you, you will understand that we have returned almost to our point of departure, in other words, to the vicinity of our hostelry."

We climbed the stairs slowly, until I heard a muffled noise, followed by Abbot Melani's lamenting. He had struck his head against a trapdoor. I had to help him push until the wooden lid opened.

Thus we gained access to an enclosed space in which the air was acrid with urine and damp with the reek of animals. We were in a stable.

Standing there was a small two-wheeled carriage, which we briefly examined. It had a leather hood, protected by waxed canvas stretched over a metal framework embellished with smooth iron knobs. Inside, a rosy sky was painted on the roof, while the seats were made comfortable by a pair of cushions. Next to it stood a more ordinary but larger carriage, with four wheels, and again a cowhide hood; and nearby, silent, but somewhat perturbed by our presence, stood two rather old and neglected horses.

Taking advantage of the faint light of the lamp, I looked inside the coach. Hanging behind the back seat, I discovered a large crucifix. From the wooden cross there hung a little iron cage which contained a glass sphere, within which was visible a small, indistinct brownish mass.

Atto too had approached, to illuminate the interior of the carriage.

"It must be a relic," said he, bringing his lantern closer. "But we must not waste time."

All around us lay buckets for washing the carriages, and combs, currycombs and horse-brushes (which almost caused us to trip up noisily).

Without tarrying any longer than necessary, we identified a doorway which, in all probability, led into a house. I tried the door carefully. It was closed.

In disappointment, I turned towards Abbot Melani. He too seemed to be hesitating. We could certainly not dream of forcing the lock, thus risking being surprised by the house's inhabitants and perhaps facing a double sentence, for escaping and for attempted housebreaking.

I was just thinking how fortunate we had been not to chance upon anyone in the stables, when suddenly I saw a monstrous hooked hand clutch at Abbot Melani's shoulder. I somehow managed to stifle a scream, while Melani stiffened, preparing to confront the stranger who was attacking him from behind. He told me to grab something, a stick, a bucket, anything and to strike the attacker. Too late. The individual was between us.

It was Ugonio. I saw Atto blanch with terror, so much so that he suffered a fit of dizziness and had to sit down for a few minutes.

"Idiot, you almost killed me with fright. I told you to remain down below."

"Ciacconio has scented a presence. He desiderates to be commandeered."

"Very well, let us return down the stairs and... but what have you in your hand?"

Ugonio held out both his forearms and looked questioningly at both his hands, as though he did not know what Atto was referring to. In his right hand, however, he grasped the crucifix with the relic which we had seen hanging inside the carriage.

"Put it straight back," ordered Abbot Melani. "No one must know that we have entered this place."

After grudgingly returning the crucifix to its place, Ugonio approached the closed door and brought his face close to the keyhole, examining the lock.

"What are you wasting time with, animal? Can you not see that it is closed and that there is no light on the other side?" Atto rebuked him.

"It may be that the portal can be unclavitated. To obtain, of course, more benefice than malefice," replied Ugonio, without losing his composure. And from his filthy overcoat he produced as though by enchantment an enormous iron ring to which were tied dozens, indeed hundreds of keys of the most varied styles and dimensions.

Atto and I were astounded. At once, Ugonio began with feline rapidity to sort through that clinking mass. In a few moments, his claws stopped at an old half-rusted key.

"Now Ugonio unclavitates and, if one is not to be a rustic physician, by fulfilling one's obligations the Christian's jubilations are increased," said he, cackling with laughter as he turned the key in the lock. The mechanism opened with a click.

⇛⇚

Later, the two *corpisantari* would explain this last surprise of theirs. To gain access to the underground city, they often needed to make their way through cellars, store-rooms or doors which were locked or padlocked. In order to resolve the problem (and, as Ugonio insisted, "by decreasing the scruples rather than increasing the scruples") the pair had dedicated themselves to the methodical corruption of dozens of servants, serving-maids and menservants. Well aware that the owners of the houses and villas who possessed the keys would never, but never, allow them to lay their hands on them, the two *corpisantari* had haggled with servants to obtain copies of those keys. In exchange, they passed some of their precious relics to the servants. They had, of course, made sure that in the course of such trafficking, they did not release the best items of their collection. At times, however, they had been constrained to make painful sacrifices; for the key to a garden through which one obtained access to catacombs near the Via Appia, they had, for instance, had to give up a fragment of Saint Peter's shoulder-blade. It was less than obvious how they succeeded in such bargaining, what with Ciacconio's garglings and Ugonio's circumlocutions, yet it was clear that they possessed the keys to the cellars and palace foundations of a goodly part of the city. And those doors for which they did not possess the keys could often be opened with one of the many other more or less similar ones in their possession.

Therefore, once the door from the stable had been opened with Ugonio's key, we could be sure that we were in an inhabited house. Muffled by distance, we could hear sounds and voices drifting down from the upper floors. Before extinguishing the only lantern that we still had lit, a few seconds remained in which to take in our surroundings. We had entered a great kitchen, full of dishes, with a huge cauldron, three smaller ones, iron pans, basins large and small, copper cooking pots, moulds with iron handles, various stoves, kettles, jugs and coffee pots. All the kitchen equipment was hanging on the wall or kept in a sideboard of silver poplar wood or in a small cupboard, and almost all were of the best quality, as I would have wished the few utensils at my disposal in the kitchen of the Donzello to be. We crossed the room, taking care not to make any noise by tripping over one of the cooking pots that lay on the floor.

At the opposite end of the kitchen, there was another door; and through this we entered the next room. We were forced to light the lantern for a moment, but I covered it prudently with my hand.

We found ourselves facing a four-poster bed with a striped yellow and red satin cover. On either side stood a pair of little wooden tables and, in a corner, a simple chair, covered in worn stamped leather. Judging by the old furnishings, and by a certain stale and stuffy odour, the chamber must have been in disuse.

We gestured to Ugonio to go back and wait for us in the stable: in the event of our having to beat a rapid retreat, two intruders might perhaps succeed in escaping, but with three, we should certainly be in worse trouble.

The chamber which we had just visited also had a second door. After again extinguishing the lantern, we listened carefully at that doorway. The residents' voices seemed distant enough for us to risk opening it, which we did most delicately, entering another, fourth, space. We were now in the entrance-hall of the house. The front door, as we could sense despite the almost complete darkness, was to our left. In front of us, at the end of a little corridor, began a spiral staircase, set into the wall and leading to the upper storey. From the top of the stairs, there filtered an uncertain glimmer which just enabled us to find our way.

With extreme caution, we approached the stairs. The noises and speech which we had first heard in the distance now seemed to have almost died out. Mad and foolhardy though the idea seemed to me, Atto began to climb the stairs, and I behind him.

Halfway up the stairs, between the ground and the first floor, we found a little room lit by a candelabrum, with various fine objects in it which we stopped briefly to examine. I was astounded by the wealth of the furnishings, the like of which I had never seen before: we must be in the house of a well-to-do gentleman. The abbot approached a little inlaid walnut table covered with a green cloth. He raised his eyes and discovered a number of fine paintings: an Annunciation, a Pietà, a Saint Francis with Angels in a gold-bordered walnut frame, another picture representing John the Baptist, a little picture on paper with a tortoiseshell and gilt frame and, lastly, a plaster octagon bas-relief representing Mary Magdalene. I saw a wash-stand which seemed to me to be in pear-wood, turned with great art and skill. Above it, there hung a small copper and gold crucifix with a cross fashioned from ebony. Completing the little parlour, there was a little table in light-coloured wood with its fine little drawers, and two chairs.

In a few more steps, we reached the first floor, which seemed at first to be deserted and enveloped in gloom. Atto Melani pointed out to me the next flight, leading even higher, and on which the light fell clearer and stronger. We craned our necks and saw that on the wall by the stairs was a sconce with four large candles, beyond which one came to the second floor, where, in all probability, the people of the house were at that moment.

We remained briefly immobile on the stairs, listening intently. There was not a sound; we continued to climb. Suddenly, however, a loud noise startled us. A door on the first floor had been opened and then roughly slammed, and in the interval we heard two men's voices, too confused to be intelligible. Gradually, we heard steps approaching the stairs from the chambers. Atto and I looked at one another in confusion; hurriedly, we rushed up the four or five remaining stairs. Beyond the sconce, we found a second little room halfway up, and there we halted, hoping that the footsteps would not continue up the stairs, in the direction of our temporary hiding place. We were lucky. We heard one door close, and then another, until we could hear neither footsteps nor the two men's voices.

Crouching awkwardly in the little room halfway up the stairs, Atto and I exchanged looks of relief. Here too, a candelabrum afforded us sufficient light. Once we had recovered our breath and allowed our panic to subside, we took a look around us. Around the walls of the second small room, we discovered tall and well-stocked bookshelves, with many volumes placed in good order. Abbot Melani took one in his hand and examined the frontispiece.

It was a *Life of the Blessed Margaret of Cortona*, by an unknown author. Atto closed the book and returned it to its place. There then passed through his hands: the first of an eight-volume *Theatrum Vitae Humanae*, a *Life of Saint Philip Neri*, a *Fundamentum Doctrinae motus gravium Vitali Iordani*, a *Tractatus de Ordine Iudiciorum*, a fine edition of the *Institutiones ac meditationes in Graecam linguam*, a French grammar, and lastly, a book which explained *The Art of Learning to Die a Good Death*.

After rapidly leafing through this last curious volume of moral reflections, Atto shook his head in irritation.

"What are you looking for?" I asked him in the lowest voice of which I was capable.

"Is it not obvious? The owner. These days, everyone marks their books, at least those of value, with their name."

So I assisted Atto and there soon passed through my hands the *De arte Gimnastica* of Gerolamo Mercuriale, a *Vocabularium Ecclesiasticum* and a *Pharetra divini Amoris*, while Atto set aside with a snort the *Works* of Plato and a *Theatre of Mankynde* by Gaspare de Villa Lobos, before greeting with surprise a copy of *Bacchus in Tuscany* by his be-loved Francesco Redi.

"I do not understand it," he whispered impatiently at the end of the search. "There is everything here: history, philosophy, Christian doctrine, languages ancient and modern, devotional works, various curiosities and even a little astrology. Here, take a look: *The Arcana of the Stars* by a certain Antonio Carnevale and the *Ephemerides Andreae Argoli*. Yet in no book is there the owner's name."

Seeing that fortune had thus far remained on our side, and that we had avoided only by a hair's-breadth being surprised by the mas-ter of the house, I was about to suggest to Atto that we should be on our way when, for the first time, I came across a book on medicine.

I had in fact been searching on another shelf, where I came across a volume by Vallesius, then the *Medicina Septentrionalis* and *Practical Anatomy* by Bonetus, a *Booke of Roman Antidotes*, a *Liber observationum medicarum Ioannes Chenchi*, a *De Mali Ipocondriaci* by Paolo Tacchia, a *Commentarium Ioannis Casimiri in Hippocratis Aphorismos*, an *Enciclopedia Chirurgica Rationalis* by Giovanni Doleo and many other precious texts on medicine, chirurgie and anatomy. I was, among other things, struck by four volumes of a seven-volume edition of the works of Galen, all rather finely bound, in vermilion leather with golden lettering; the three others were not in their place. I picked one up, enjoying the feel of the precious binding, and opened it. A small inscription, at the foot of the frontispiece and on the right-hand side read: *Ioannis Tiracordae*. The same thing, I rapidly established, was to be found in all the other books on medicine.

"I know!" I whispered excitedly. "I know where we are."

I was about to share my discovery when we were again surprised by the sound of a door opening on the first floor, and by an old man's voice:

"Paradisa! Come down, our friend is about to take his leave of us."

A woman's voice replied from the second floor that she would be coming at once.

So we were about to be caught between two fires: the woman de-scending from the second floor and the master of the house await-ing her on the first. There was no door to the little room and it was, moreover, too small for us to crouch in unseen. We should be discovered.

Hearing, understanding and acting came together in a single movement. Like lizards hunted by a hawk, we scuttled down the stairs in furtive desperation, hoping to reach the first floor before the two men. Otherwise, there would be no escape.

In less than a second came the moment of truth: we had just come down a few stairs when we heard the voice of the master of the house.

"And tomorrow, do not forget to bring me your little liqueur!" said he, under his breath but in a rather jovial tone of voice, obviously addressing his guest, while they approached the foot of the stairs. There was no more time: we were lost.

Whenever I think back on those moments of terror, I tell myself that only divine mercy saved us from many punishments, which we doubtless deserved. I also reflect that, if Abbot Melani had not had recourse to one of his ploys, matters would have gone very differently.

Atto had a flash of inspiration and energetically blew out the four candles which illuminated this flight of stairs. We again took refuge in the little room where, this time in unison, we puffed up our chests and blew out the candelabrum. When the master of the house looked up the stairs, he was confronted with pitch darkness and heard the woman's voice begging him to light the candles again. This had the double effect of not giving us away and making the two men return, bearing a single oil lamp, in order to fetch a candle. In that brief lapse of time, we groped our way swiftly down the stairs.

Hardly had we reached the ground floor than we rushed into the abandoned bedchamber, then into the kitchen and, thence, to the coach-house. There, in my haste, I tripped and fell headlong on the fine layer of hay, making one of the nags nervous. Atto rapidly closed the door behind us, and Ugonio had no difficulty in locking it in time.

We remained motionless in the dark, panting, with our ears glued to the door. We thought that we could hear two or more people descending into the courtyard. Footsteps moved over the cobbles in the direction of the doorway to the street. We heard the heavy door open, then slam shut. Other footsteps turned back until they were lost on the stairs. For two or three minutes, we remained in sepulchral silence. The peril seemed to have passed.

We then lit a lantern and went through the trapdoor. As soon as the heavy wooden lid had closed on us, I was at last able to inform Abbot Melani of my discovery. We had entered the house of Giovanni Tiracorda, the old court physician to the Pope.

"Are you certain of that?" asked Abbot Melani as we again descended into the subterranean city.

"Of course I am," I replied.

"Tiracorda, what a coincidence," commented Atto with a little laugh.

"Do you know him?"

"It is an extraordinary coincidence. Tiracorda was physician to the conclave in which my fellow-citizen Pope Clement IX Rospigliosi was elected. I was present, too."

I, however, had never addressed a word to the old *Archiater*. Tiracorda, having been chief physician to two popes, was honoured in the quarter, so much so that he was still addressed as *Archiater*, although in reality his office was now that of locum. He lived in a little palazzo belonging to Duke Salviati, situated in the Via dell'Orso, only a few houses beyond the Donzello, on the corner of the Via della Stufa delle Donne. The map of the underground galleries which Atto Melani had drawn had proven to be accurate: moving from one gallery to another and coming to Tiracorda's stable, we had almost arrived back at our point of departure. I knew little, indeed very little indeed, about Tiracorda: that he had a wife (perhaps the Paradisa whose name we had heard him call not long before), and that in their large and fine house there also lived two or three maidservants who helped with the work of the household, and that he practised his art at the Arcispedale di Santo Spirito, at Sassia.

He was more rotund than tall, with rounded shoulders and almost no neck, and a great prominent stomach on which he often rested his joined hands, as though he incarnated the virtues of patience and tolerance. All this suggested a phlegmatic and pusillanimous character. Sometimes I had seen him from a window walking down the Via dell'Orso, trotting along in a garment that reached almost to his feet; oft had I observed him, smoothing his mustachios and the goatee on his chin, in lively conversation with some shopkeeper. Caring little for periwigs despite his baldness, with his hat constantly in hand, his slightly bumpy pate, crowning a low, wrinkled forehead and pointed ears, shone in the sun. Crossing his path, I had once been struck by how rosy his cheeks were and how kindly his expression: with eyebrows that screened the deep-set eyes and the tired eyelids of a physician accustomed, yet never resigned, to looking upon the suffering of others.

When we had covered the most difficult portion of the return journey, Abbot Melani asked Ugonio if he could procure him a copy of the key which he had used to open the stable door.

"I assure your most worshipful decisionality that I shall not emit to execute your desïderation; and that, upon the earliest importunity. However, to be more padre than parricide, it would have been more perfectly ameliorating to have had it fabricated upon the past nocturn."

"Are you telling me that it would have been better to have the copy of the key made last night?"

Ugonio appeared to be surprised by the question.

"Indubiously, in the street of the chiavari, the key-facturers, where Komarek impresses."

Atto's forehead creased. He plunged a hand into his pocket and drew out the page from the Bible. Several times, he passed the palm of his hand over it, then held it up to the light of the lantern which he held in his hand. I saw him carefully examine the shadows which the folds cast in the lamplight.

"Confound it, how can I have allowed that to escape me?" cursed Abbot Melani.

And he pointed out with his finger a form which I only then seemed able to detect in the middle of the paper: "If you observe carefully, despite the precarious condition of this piece of paper," he began explaining to me, "you will be able to find more or less in the middle of the paper the outline of a large key with an oblong head, exactly like that of the closet. Look, just here, where the paper has remained smoother, while on either side it is crumpled."

"So this piece of paper is just the wrapping of a key?" I concluded, in surprise.

"Precisely. And it was indeed in the Via dei Chiavari, where all the locksmiths and makers of keys have their shops, that we found the clandestine workshop of Komarek, the printer used by Stilone Priàso."

"Ah, then I understand," I deduced. "Stilone Priàso stole the key and then went to have a copy made in the Via dei Chiavari, near Komarek's place."

"No, dear boy. Some of the guests—you yourself told me this, do you not remember?—said that they had stayed at the Locanda del Donzello previously."

"That is true: Stilone Priàso, Bedfordi and Angiolo Brenozzi," I recalled, "in the days of the late lamented Signora Luigia."

"Good. That means that Stilone most probably already had a copy of the key to the little room that leads from the inn to the underground galleries. Moreover, he already had sufficient reason to visit Komarek, in order to have some clandestine gazettes and almanacks printed. No, we need not look for one of Komarek's clients, but simply one of our own guests. The person who briefly removed Master Pellegrino's bunch of keys needed to have a copy made of the key to the closet."

"And then the thief is Padre Robleda! He mentioned Malachi to see how I would react: perhaps he realised that he had lost the sheet of paper with the prophecy of Malachi underground and thought up a trick worthy of the best spies to unmask me, just as Dulcibeni says," I exclaimed, after which I told Atto of Dulcibeni's harangue about the Jesuits' vocation for spying.

"Ah yes. Perhaps the thief is none other than Padre Robleda, also because…"

"Gfrrrlubh," interrupted Ciacconio politely.

"Errorific and fellatious argumentations," translated Ugonio.

"How, pray?" asked Abbot Melani incredulously.

"Ciacconio assures that the provenance of the foliables is not Malachi: this, with all due circumspect for your decisionality, and, of course, decreasing the scrupules rather than increasing one's scruples."

At the same time, from under his clothing Ciacconio produced a little Bible, worn and filthy, but still legible.

"Do you always keep it on you?" I asked.

"Gfrrrlubh."

"He is exceedingly religious: a bigot, almost a trigot," explained Ugonio.

We looked in the index for the Book of Malachi. It was the last of the twelve books of the minor prophets, and so was to be found among the last pages of the Old Testament. I turned the pages rapidly until I found the title and, with some difficulty because of the microscopic characters, began reading:

PROPHETHIA
MALACHIÆ

CAPVT I.

Onus verbi Domini ad Israel in manu Malachiae.

Dilexi vos, dicit Dominus, & dixistis: in quo dilexisti nos? Nonne frater erat Esau Iacob, dicit Dominus, & dilexi Iacob, Esau autem odio habui? & posui montes ejus in solitudinem, & hereditatem ejus in dracones deserti.

Quod si dixerit Idumaea: Destructi sumus, sed revertentes aedificabimus quae destructa sunt: Haec dicit Dominus exercituum: Isti aedificabunt, & ego destruam: & vocabuntur terminis impietatis, & populus cui iratus est Dominus usque in aeternum.

Et oculi vestri videbunt: & vos dicetis: Magnificetur Dominus super terminum Israel.

Filius honorat patrem, & servus dominum suum: si ergo Pater ergo sum, ubi est honor meus? & si Dominus ego sum, ubi est timor meus? dicit Dominus exercituum ad vos, & sacerdotes, qui despicitis nomen meum, & dixitis: In quo despeximus nomen tuum?...

I broke off: Abbot Melani had taken from his pocket the sheet of paper found by Ugonio and Ciacconio. We compared the two. Although mutilated, one could read in it the names Ochozias, Accaron and Beelzebub, all of which were absent. Not a single word corresponded.

"So... it is another text of Malachi," I observed hesitantly.

"Gfrrrlubh," retorted Ciacconio, shaking his head.

"To be more auspicious than haruspicious and more medicinal than mendacious, the foliable is, as Ciacconio suggested and ingested, with all deference to the sagacity of your decisionality, from the secondesimal Book of Kings."

And he explained that "Malachi", the truncated word which could be read on the scrap of Bible, was not "Malachia", the Latin name of the prophet, but what remained of the word "Malachim", which in Hebrew means "Kings". This is because, Ugonio explained patiently, in many Bibles, the title is written according to the version of the Hebrews, which does not always correspond to the Christian one. The Christians do not, for example, admit among the Holy Scriptures, the two books of the Maccabees. Consequently, the complete title, mutilated and masked by the bloodstains, originally read, according to the *corpisantari*:

Carattere Lettura Tonda.

LIBER REGUM.
Secundus Malachim.
Caput Primum.

"Liber Regum" meant "Book of Kings", while "Secundus Mala-chim" stood for the "Second Book of Kings" and not for "Malachi". We looked up the Second Book of Kings in the Bible of the *corp-isantari*. And indeed, the title and text corresponded perfectly both with the scrap of paper and with the explanation of Ugonio and Ciac-conio. Abbot Melani's face darkened.

"I have but one question: why did you not say so before?" he asked, and I could already imagine the reply which the *corpisantari* would utter in unison.

"We had not the honorarium to be bequested."

"Gfrrrlubh," confirmed Ciacconio.

So, Robleda had not stolen the keys and the little pearls, nor had he entered the underground galleries, he had not lost the loose page from the Bible, nor did he know anything of the Via dei Chiavari or Komarek. And even less of Signor di Mourai, that is Nicolas Fouquet. Or to put it more precisely, there was no reason to suspect him more than anyone else, and his long discourse concerning Saint Malachy had been purely coincidental. In other words, we were back to our starting point.

In compensation, we had discovered that gallery D led to a great and spacious dwelling, the owner of which was chief physician to the Pope. But another mystery had arisen that night. To the discovery of the Bible had been added our finding the phial of blood which some-one had inadvertently (or perhaps deliberately) mislaid in the gallery leading to the house of Tiracorda.

"Do you think that the phial was lost by the thief?" I asked Abbot Melani.

At that moment, the abbot tripped on a stone protruding from the ground and fell heavily. We helped him to his feet, although he re-fused all assistance; he dusted himself down hurriedly, most put out by what had happened, and uttered many imprecations against the builders of the gallery, the plague, physicians, the quarantine and, finally, against the blameless *corpisantari* who, overwhelmed by so many unmerited insults, exchanged glances full of humiliation.

I was thus able, thanks to that apparently insignificant incident, to measure clearly the unexpected change which had, for some time, come over Abbot Melani. While, on the first days, his eyes had sparkled, now they were often lost in thought. His proud bearing had taken on a more cautious aspect, his once confident gestures had grown hesitant. His acute and perspicacious reasoning sometimes gave way to doubts and reticence. True, we had successfully penetrated the house of Tiracorda, exposing ourselves to the gravest risks. True, we had boldly explored new passages almost blindly, guided more by Ciacconio's nose than by our lanterns. Yet Abbot Melani's hand seemed from time to time to tremble slightly, while his eyes would close in a mute prayer for salvation.

This new state of mind, which for the time being surfaced just occasionally like a half-submerged wreck from the past, had become manifest only recently, indeed very recently. It was difficult to tell exactly when it had begun. It had, indeed, arisen from no particular event, but from occurrences both old and new, which were now settling awkwardly into one single form: a form which, however, remained undefined. Its substance was, however, black and bloody, like the fear which, I was now certain, troubled Abbot Melani's thoughts.

࿇

From gallery D, we had returned to gallery C, which we would doubtless need now to explore thoroughly. This time, however, leaving to our right branch E, which led to the Palace of the Chancery, we went straight on.

I noted the absorbed expression of Abbot Melani and above all his silence. I guessed that he must be meditating upon our discoveries, and therefore decided to question him with the curiosity which he himself had instilled in me only a few hours before.

"You said that Louis XIV never hated anyone more than Superintendent Fouquet."

"Yes."

"And that, supposing he had discovered that Fouquet had not died at Pinerol but was here in Rome, alive and free, his wrath would certainly have been unleashed anew."

"Precisely."

"But why such implacable rage?"

"That is nothing compared to the Sovereign's brooding fury at the time of the arrest and during the trial."

"Was it not enough for the King that he had been dismissed?"

"You are not the only one to have asked such questions. And you must not be surprised, for no one has ever found an answer to that. Not even I. At least, not yet."

The mystery of Louis XIV's hatred for Fouquet, explained Abbot Melani, was a matter of endless discussion in Paris.

"There are things which, for lack of time, I have not yet been able to tell you."

I pretended to accept this excuse. But I now knew that, because of his new state of mind, Atto was prepared to confide in me many things which he had hitherto kept to himself. It was thus that he again evoked those terrible days in which the noose of the conspiracy tightened around the Superintendent's neck.

Colbert began to spin his web from the day when Cardinal Mazarin died. He knew that he must act under cover of the state's interests and the glory of the monarchy. He also knew that he did not have much time: he must act quickly while the King was still inexpert in financial matters. Louis was unaware of what had really been going on under the government of Mazarin, whose machinations escaped him. The only one with access to the Cardinal's papers was Colbert, the master of a thousand secrets. And, while he was already tampering with the documents and falsifying evidence, the Serpent lost no opportunity to instil in the Sovereign, like a subtle poison, mistrust for the Superintendent. In the meanwhile, he soothed the latter with pledges of loyalty. The plot was working perfectly: three months before the festivities at the Château de Vaux, the King was already meditating on how to bring down his Superintendent of Finances. There remained, however, a final obstacle: Fouquet, who still held the office of Procurator-General, enjoyed parliamentary immunity. The *Coluber*, adducing the pretext of the King's urgent need for money, persuaded the Squirrel to sell his office.

Poor Nicolas fell headlong into the trap: he earned one million four hundred thousand *livres* from the transaction and as soon as he received an advance of a million *livres*, donated it to the King.

"And when he received the money, the King said, 'He is putting his own hands in irons,' Atto remembered bitterly, brushing a little dirt from his sleeves and then examining his still soiled cuffs with disappointment.

"How horrible!" I could not restrain myself from exclaiming.

"Not as much as you think, my boy. The young King was tasting his power for the first time. He could do this only by imposing his royal prerogative, and therefore injustice. What proof of power would it have been to favour the best, those whose qualities already destined them for the highest honours? He is powerful who can elevate the mediocre and the cunning over the wise and the good, by his sole caprice subverting the natural course of events."

"But did Fouquet suspect nothing?"

"That is a mystery. He was warned from several sides that something was being plotted behind his back. But he felt that his conscience was clear. I recall that he would respond with a smile, quoting the words of a predecessor: 'Superintendents are made to be hated.' Hated by kings, with their ever increasing demands for money for battles and ballets; and hated by the people, who have to pay the taxes."

Fouquet, Atto continued, even realised that something important was to take place in Nantes, where he was soon to end up in irons, but he would not look reality in the face: he convinced himself that the King was about to arrest Colbert, not him. Once in Nantes, his friends persuaded him to take up lodgings in a house which had a secret underground passage. This was an ancient conduit leading to the beach, where a fully equipped boat was kept at the ready, to bear him to safety. In the days that followed, Fouquet saw that the streets surrounding the house were full of musketeers. He began to open his eyes, but told his family that he would never run away: "I must run the risk: I cannot believe that the King means to ruin me."

"That was a fatal error!" exclaimed Atto. "The Superintendent knew only the politics of confidence. He could not see that those had had their day and been displaced by the crude politics of suspicion. Mazarin was dead, all was changed."

"And how was France before the death of Mazarin?"

Abbot Melani sighed. "How was it?... Ah, it was the good old France of Louis XIII: a world—how could I put it?—both more open and more mobile, in which speech and thought were free, and gay originality, bold attitudes and moral equilibrium seemed set to reign forever. So it appeared: in the circles of the *Précieuses*, Madame

de Sévigné and her friend Madame de la Fayette, in the maxims of
the Sieur de la Rochefoucauld and in the verses of Jean de la Fontaine. None could foresee the glacial, absolute domination of the new
King."

Six months were all the Serpent needed to ruin the Squirrel.
After his arrest, Fouquet languished in gaol for three months before obtaining a trial. At last, in December 1661, the Chamber
of Justice which was to judge him was constituted. It consisted
of Chancellor Pierre Séguier, President Lamoignon and twenty-six
members appointed from the regional parlements and from among
the referendaries.

President Lamoignon opened the first session by describing
with tragic grandiloquence the wretched condition of the people of
France, crushed each year under the weight of fresh taxes and beset
by hunger, disease and desperation. To make matters worse, their
plight had of late been aggravated by several years of bad harvests. In
many provinces, people were literally dying of hunger; yet the rapacious hand of the tax collectors knew no pity and preyed upon the
poor villagers with ever greater avidity.

"What had the misery of the people to do with Fouquet?"

"It had much to do with him. It served to introduce and to illustrate a theorem: in the countryside, the peasants were dying of
hunger because he had enriched himself scandalously at the expense
of the state."

"And was that true?"

"Of course not. In the first place, Fouquet was not really wealthy.
And, secondly, after his imprisonment at Pinerol, the wretched condition of France's villages became considerably worse. But listen to
what followed."

At the opening of the trial, a notice was read out in all the churches
of the realm in which citizens were invited to denounce all collectors of the salt tax and tax farmers, collectors and financiers who had
committed financial abuses. In a second edict, those accused of such
misdeeds were forbidden to leave their cities. Any who did so would
at once be arraigned on charges of embezzlement, a crime punishable
by death.

This had an enormous effect. All financiers, tax farmers and collectors were immediately denounced to the people as criminals; the
immensely wealthy Superintendent of Finances, Nicolas Fouquet,

was thus depicted as the head of a band of brigands which terrorised the peasantry and had reduced it to famine.

"Nothing could have been more false: Fouquet had always pointed out to the Crown, but in vain, the danger of imposing excessively high taxes. When he was sent to the Dauphiné as Intendant for Finances, for the purpose of squeezing more taxes out of those refractory people, he had even succeeded in getting himself dismissed by Mazarin. After thorough inquiries, Fouquet had in fact concluded that the taxes levied in that region were intolerably high and he had even made so bold as to present in Paris an official request for exemption. The members of the Parlement of Dauphiné had all mobilised in his defence."

Those times seemed, however, to have been forgotten. At the beginning of the Superintendent's trial, no fewer than ninety-six charges were read out, which the rapporteur of the Bench sensibly reduced to about ten: above all, he was accused of having made the King bogus loans, on which he had unjustly charged interest; secondly, of illicitly confusing the King's money with his own, and using it for private purposes; thirdly, of receiving from subcontractors more than three hundred thousand *livres* in exchange for granting them favourable conditions; and of having personally encashed the revenue from this operation, using false names; fourthly, he was charged with having given the state expired bills of exchange in return for cash.

When the hearing opened, the people's hatred for Fouquet was most violent. In the days following the arrest, the guards took care to avoid certain villages in which the mob was ready to tear him to pieces.

Locked in his tiny cell, isolated from everything and from everyone, the Superintendent was unable fully to grasp into what an abyss he had been cast. His health declined and he asked to be sent a confessor; he sent memoranda to the King in his defence; four times, he begged him in vain for an audience; he had letters circulated in which he proudly pleaded his cause; he cherished the illusion that the incident could be concluded honourably. All his requests were rejected, and he began to realise that there was no breach in the wall of hostility raised against him by the King and Colbert.

In the meantime, Colbert was manoeuvring behind the scenes: he summoned the members of the Chamber of Justice in the King's presence and subjected them to innuendo, coercion and threats. He did worse with the witnesses, many of whom were investigated in their turn.

We were interrupted by Ugonio. He showed us a trapdoor through which he and Ciacconio had lowered themselves a few weeks earlier, thus discovering the gallery which we were now moving along.

"Where does the trapdoor lead?"

"To the hinder part of the Subpantheon."

"Bear this in mind, my boy," Atto said to me. "If I have understood correctly, this trapdoor leads to some underground chambers behind the Pantheon. Thence, one finds one's way into some private courtyard and, finally, we can use one of your keys to open the gate and go out into the street, is that not so?"

Ugonio nodded, with a coarse, self-satisfied smile, adding that there was no need for any key, as the gate was always left open. Having taken in that news, we all continued our march, and Abbot Melani, his narration.

At the trial, Fouquet defended himself alone, without any lawyers. His eloquence was prodigious, his reflexes ever prompt, his argumentation, subtle and insinuating, his memory, infallible. His papers had all been requisitioned and probably purged of anything that might be used in his defence; but the Superintendent defended himself as no one else could. For every challenge he had a ready answer. It was impossible to catch him out.

"As I have already mentioned, the counterfeiting of certain documentary proofs by one Berryer, Colbert's man, was discovered. And, in the end, all the documents in the case, a veritable mountain of paper, did not suffice to prove *a single one* of the charges against Fouquet! What did, however, tend to emerge was the responsibility and involvement of Mazarin, whose memory must, however, remain immaculate."

Colbert and the King, who had trusted in a swift, utterly servile and merciless judiciary, had not foreseen that many of the judges of the Chamber of Justice, who were old admirers of Fouquet, might refuse to treat the trial as a mere formality.

Time passed quickly: from one hearing to another, three long years had soon gone by. Fouquet's passionate harangues had become an attraction for all Paris. The people, who, at the time of his arrest, would have torn him apart, had come gradually to feel pity for him. Colbert had stopped at nothing to raise ever greater taxes, which were to serve for the pursuit of more wars and the completion of the Palace of Versailles. More than ever, the peasants had been tormented, abused, even summarily hanged. The Serpent had increased the pressure of taxation far beyond anything that Fouquet had ever dared impose. Moreover, the inventory of all the property owned by Fouquet at the time of his arrest proved that the Superintendent's accounts were in deficit. All the splendour with which he had surrounded himself had been no more than dust thrown in the eyes of creditors, with whom he had personally exposed himself, not knowing how otherwise to meet the costs of France's wars. He had thus contracted personal debts amounting to sixteen million *livres*, against a fortune in land, houses and offices valued at no more than fifteen million *livres*.

"Nothing when compared with the thirty-three million *livres* net which Mazarin left to his nephews in his will."

"Then Fouquet should have been able to obtain an acquittal," I observed.

"Yes and no," replied the abbot, while we stopped to replenish the oil in one of the lanterns. "In the first place, Colbert succeeded in preventing the judges from seeing the inventory of Fouquet's property. In vain, the Superintendent requested that it be placed among the documents before the court. And then, immediately after the arrest, came the discovery that was to bring about his downfall."

This was the last of the charges levelled against him, which had nothing to do with financial malpractice or any other question involving money. This was a document which was found hidden behind a mirror when Fouquet's house at Saint-Mandé was searched. It was a letter to friends and relatives, dated 1657, four years before his arrest. In it, he expressed his anxiety at the growing mistrust which he sensed on the part of Mazarin and the intrigues whereby his enemies sought to ruin him. Fouquet then gave instructions concerning the action to be taken in the event of Mazarin's ordering his incarceration. This was no plan for an insurrection but for subtle political agitation, destined to alarm the Cardinal and lead him to negotiate, in full awareness of Mazarin's inclination to back off when faced with an awkward situation.

Notwithstanding the fact that there was no word in the document of any uprising against the Crown, the procurer presented this as a plan for a coup d'état; in other words, something like the Fronde, which all the French remembered only too well. Again, according to the procurer, the rebels were to take refuge in the isolated fortress of Belle-Île, which belonged to Fouquet. Emissaries of the investigators were sent to Belle-Île, off the coast of Brittany, and these did their best to present as proofs of guilt the work on the fortifications, the cannons and the stocks of gunpowder and ammunition laid up there.

"But why had Fouquet fortified the island?"

"He was a genius of the sea and of marine strategy and he planned to use Belle-Île as a support base against England. He had even thought of building a city in that place with its excellent natural harbour and particularly favourable position, so as to divert from Amsterdam all the commercial traffic of the North, thus rendering a great service to the King of France."

Thus, Fouquet, who had been arrested for embezzlement, found himself tried for fomenting sedition. Nor was that all. At Saint-Mandé, a padlocked wooden box had been found containing the secret correspondence of the Superintendent. The King's representatives found therein the names of all the accused's most faithful friends, and many trembled at this. Most of the letters were sent to the King and in the end they were all entrusted to Colbert's care. He kept many of them, being well aware of their potential usefulness as a means of bringing pressure to bear upon those involved. Only a few letters, which Colbert was able to select in his own good time, were burned so as not to compromise some illustrious personage.

"Do you then think," I interrupted, "that the letters from Kircher which you discovered in Colbert's study were found in that box?"

"Perhaps."

"And how did the trial end?"

Fouquet had requested that several judges should be challenged on grounds of partiality: for instance, Pussort, Colbert's uncle, who persistently referred to the Serpent his nephew as "my party". Pussort attacked Fouquet so coarsely as even to prevent him from responding, thus upsetting all the other judges.

Chancellor Séguier also sat in the court, yet during the Fronde he had been among the insurgents against the Crown. Fouquet observed: how could Séguier judge a state crime? The next day, all Paris applauded the brilliant counter-attack of the accused, but the challenge was rejected.

The public began to murmur: not a day passed without some new accusation being levelled against Fouquet. His accusers had made the rope so thick that it was becoming too unwieldy to strangle him with.

So, the decisive moment drew nigh. Some judges were requested by the King in person no longer to take an interest in the trial. Talon himself, who in his speeches for the prosecution had showed great zeal without obtaining much success, had to make way for another Procurator-General, Chamillart. It was he who, on 14th November, 1664, set out his own conclusions before the Chamber of Justice. Chamillart called for Fouquet to be condemned to death, and for the restitution of all sums illicitly taken from the state. It then fell to the rapporteurs of the trial to make their concluding speeches. Judge Olivier d'Ormesson, vainly subjected to Colbert's attempts at intimidation, spoke passionately for five whole days, unleashing his fury against Berryer and his men. He concluded by calling for a sentence of exile: the best possible solution for Fouquet.

The second rapporteur, Sainte-Hélène, spoke in more languid and tranquil tones, but called for the death sentence. Then each judge had to utter his own verdict.

The ceremony was long-drawn-out, agonising and ruinous for some. Judge Massenau had himself carried into court, despite a grave indisposition, murmuring: "Better to die here." He voted for exile. Pontchartrain had resisted Colbert's allurements and his threats: he too voted for exile, thus ruining his own career and that of his son. As for Judge Roquesante, he ended his own career in exile, for not having voted in favour of a death sentence.

In the end, only nine out of the twenty-six commissaries opted for the death sentence. Fouquet's head was saved.

As soon as it became known, the verdict which saved Fouquet's life and gave him back his freedom—albeit outside France—met with great relief and was greeted by much rejoicing.

It was here that Louis XIV entered the scene. Overcome by wrath, he resolutely opposed exile. He annulled the sentence of the Chamber of Justice, thus rendering utterly pointless the three long years of the trial. In a decision unique in the annals of the Kingdom of France, the Most Christian King reversed the royal right to commute sentences, hitherto used only to pardon, and condemned Fouquet to life imprisonment, in solitary confinement, in the distant fortress of Pinerol.

"Paris was utterly shocked. None could comprehend the reasons behind that gesture. It was as though he nurtured a secret and implacable hatred for Fouquet," said Abbot Melani.

It was not enough that Louis XIV should dismiss him, humiliate him, despoil him of all his property and have him imprisoned on the faraway borders of France. The King himself sacked the Château de Vaux and his residence at Saint-Mandé, decorating his own palace with Fouquet's furniture, his collections, carpets, gold services and tapestries and incorporating into the Royal Library the thirteen thousand precious volumes lovingly chosen by the Superintendent in the course of years of study and research. The whole was valued at no less than forty thousand *livres*.

To Fouquet's creditors, who suddenly emerged on all sides, there remained: the crumbs. One of them, an ironmonger named Jolly, forced his way into Vaux and the other residences, furiously tearing off with his bare hands all the padding and wall-coverings of precious leather; he then dug up and carried off the exceedingly modern lead pipes and hydraulic conduits, thus almost reducing to nothing the value of the parks and gardens of Vaux. Stucco decorations, ornaments and lamps were hurriedly stripped away by a hundred angry hands. When the pillage came to an end, the glorious residences of Nicolas Fouquet resembled nothing so much as two empty shells: the proof of the wonders which they contained rests only in the inventories of his persecutors. Fouquet's possessions in the Antilles were meanwhile plundered by the Superintendent's overseas dependents.

"Was the Château de Vaux as fine as the Palace of Versailles?" I stupidly asked Atto Melani.

"Vaux anticipated Versailles by a good five years," said Atto with calculated bombast, "and in many ways it was the inspiration behind it. If only you knew how heart-rending it is for those who frequented Fouquet, when moving through the Palace of Versailles, to recognise the paintings, the statues and the other marvels that belonged to the Superintendent and which still have the savour of his refined and sure taste..."

I said nothing and even wondered whether he was about to give way to tears.

"A few years ago, Madame de Sévigné made a pilgrimage to the Château de Vaux," Atto resumed. "And there she was seen to weep for a long time at the ruin of all those treasures and their great patron."

The torment was compounded by the system of incarceration. The King gave orders that at Pinerol Nicolas Fouquet was to be forbidden to write or to speak with anyone, apart from his gaolers.

Whatever the prisoner had in his head or on his tongue was to remain his and his alone. The only one entitled to hear his voice, through the ears of his keepers, was the King. And if Fouquet did not desire to speak with his tormentor, he had but to keep silence.

Many in Paris began to guess at an explanation. If Louis XIV wished to silence his prisoner for all eternity, he had only to arrange for him to be served a soup with suitable condiments...

But time passed, and Fouquet was still living. Perhaps the question was more complicated. Perhaps the King wanted to know something which the prisoner, in the cold silence of his cell, was keeping to himself. One day, they imagined, the rigours of prison would convince him to talk.

Ugonio called for our attention. Distracted by our conversation, we had forgotten that, while we were in the house of Tiracorda, Ciacconio had smelled a foreign presence. Now the *corpisantaro*'s nose had again scented something.

"Gfrrrlubh."

"Presence, perspiraceous, antiquated, scarified," explained Ugonio.

"Can you perhaps tell us what he ate for luncheon?" asked Atto Melani derisively.

I feared that the *corpisantaro* might take this amiss, for his exceedingly fine sense of smell had been useful to us and would probably continue to be so.

"Gfrrrlubh," came Ciacconio's calm response, after he had again sampled the air with his deformed and carbuncle-encrusted nose.

"Ciacconio has scented cow's udderlings," translated his companion, "with a probability of hen-fruit, hamon and white vino, mayhap with broth and saccar."

Atto and I exchanged astonished glances. This was exactly the dish which I had taken such great pains to prepare for the guests at the Donzello. Ciacconio could know nothing about that; yet he was able to discern from the odorous traces left by the stranger not only the smell of cows' teats but even the aroma of a number of the ingredients which I had added to the dish. If the *corpisantaro*'s sense of smell was accurate, we concluded incredulously, we must be following a lodger at the Donzello.

The narration of Fouquet's trial had lasted quite a while and during that time we had explored a fairly lengthy portion of gallery C. It

was hard to say how far we had come from beneath the Piazza Navona
and where we now were; but, apart from some very slight bends, our
trajectory had involved no deviation whatever: we had therefore followed the only direction possible. Hardly had we made that observation, when all changed.

The ground became damp and slippery, the air denser and heav-
ier, and in the gloomy silence of the gallery a distant rustling sound
could be heard. We advanced cautiously, while Ciacconio's head
rocked from side to side, as though he were suffering. A nauseating
odour could be detected, which was, I knew, familiar, but could not
as yet identify.

"Sewers," said Atto Melani.

"Gfrrrlubh," confirmed Ciacconio.

Ugonio explained that the sewage was disturbing his colleague no
little, and making it impossible for him to identify other odours clearly.

A little further on we found ourselves walking through real puddles. The stink, which had at first been indistinct, grew intense. At
last we found the cause of all this. In the wall to the left, there was a
wide and deep opening, through which poured a flood of black, fetid
water. The rivulet followed the slope in the gallery, partly flowing
along the sides, partly ending up in the seemingly endless darkness
of the passageway. I touched the opposite wall: it was damp and left
a fine coating of slime on my fingertips. Our attention was attracted
by a detail. On its back in the water before us, and indifferent to our
presence, lay a large rat.

"Mortified," proclaimed Ugonio, nudging it with one foot.

Ciacconio took the rat by the tail with his two clawed fingers and
let it hang. From the rat's mouth into the greyish water there ran a
fine stream of blood. Ciacconio lowered his head, observing the unexpected phenomenon with an air of surprise.

"Gfrrrlubh," he commented thoughtfully.

"Mortified, bloodified, maldistempered," explained Ugonio.

"How does he know that it was ill?" I asked.

"Ciacconio loves these little animals very much, is that not so?"
intervened Abbot Melani.

Ciacconio nodded affirmatively, showing with an ingenuous and
bestial smile his horrible yellow teeth.

We continued on our way, moving beyond the stretch of gallery
soaked by the flood from the sewers. Everything suggested that the

leakage was recent and that normally we should have found there no trace of water. As for the rat, this was no lone discovery. We soon came across three more dead rodents, more or less of the same dimensions as the first one. Ciacconio inspected them: all bled abundantly from the mouth because, said the *corpisantari*, of some undefined illness. Here was yet another encounter with blood: first, the bloodstained page from the Bible, then the phial, now these rats.

Our exploration was interrupted by yet another surprise. This time we found no infiltration, however copious, but a veritable watercourse, which rushed rapidly through a gallery perpendicular to our own and appeared to be fairly deep. This was in all probability an underground river, whose waters were perhaps mixed with some of the waste materials normally borne by the sewers. There was, however, no bad smell like that which had so upset Ciacconio.

With no little disappointment, we had to admit defeat. We could go no further, and a long time had passed since we left the Donzello. It would not do to remain any longer outside the inn, given the risk that our absence might be discovered. Thus, tired and worn, we decided to turn back.

While we turned around, Ciacconio once more sniffed the air suspiciously.

Atto Melani sneezed.

Day the Sixth
16TH SEPTEMBER, 1683

✠

The return to the Donzello was long, sad and tiring. We came back to our bedchambers with our hands, faces and clothing mud-stained and wet. I threw myself onto my bed exhausted and almost at once fell into a deep sleep.

When I stirred in the morning, I found that I was still lying in the same uncomfortable posture as when I lay down the night before. It was as though my legs were tormented by a thousand swords. I stretched out an arm to raise myself into a sitting position and my hand met the rough, crumpled surface of an object with which I had obviously shared my bed. It was Stilone Priàso's astrological almanack, which I had so precipitously put aside some twenty-four hours before, when Cristofano called me to work.

The night which had just passed had fortunately helped me to forget the tremendous occurrences which the almanack had, by occult means, precisely foretold: the death of Colbert, that of Mourai (rather, of Fouquet) and the presence of a poison; the "malignant fevers" from which my master and Bedfordi would suffer; the "hidden treasure" which would come to light at the beginning of the month, or in other words, the letters hidden in Colbert's study and stolen by Atto; the "subterranean earthquakes and fires" which had resounded through our cellars; and, lastly, the prediction of the siege of Vienna: or, in the words of the gazette, " battles and assaults against the City", as foreseen by "Ali and Leopoldus Austriacus".

Did I wish to know what would happen in the days to come? No, I thought, with a tightening of my stomach, at least for the time being, I did not desire that. I looked instead at the preceding pages and my eyes alighted on the last week of July, from the 22nd until the last day of the month.

This Weeke, News of the World will be received from Jupiter, who governs the ruling House. That being the Third House, he sends many Dispatches, perhaps concerning the Illnesse of a Ruler, who will in the End tearfully quit a Kingdom.

So, at the end of July, the death of a sovereign was expected. I had heard of no such thing and so it was with satisfaction that I saluted the arrival of Cristofano: I would ask him.

But Cristofano knew nothing of this. Once again, he wondered, and inquired of me, how it was that I should be concerned with matters so distant from our present predicament: first, astrology, then, the fortunes of sovereigns. Thanks be to heaven, I had enjoyed sufficient presence of mind to conceal the astrological gazette in my couch in good time. I felt pleased to have discovered an inaccuracy, and one of some importance, in the almanack's hitherto all too precise predictions; this meant that they were not infallible. Secretly, I breathed a sigh of relief.

Cristofano, meanwhile, looked pensively at my eyes. He said that youth was a most happy season in human life, one that tended to unleash all the forces of body and mind. However, he added emphatically, one must not abuse this sudden and sometimes disorderly flowering, thus dissipating its new and almost uncontrollable energies. And while, with concern, he prodded the bags under my eyes, he reminded me that dissipation was above all sinful, as was commerce with women of easy virtue (and here he nodded in the direction of Cloridia's little tower), which could, moreover, lead to the French pox. He knew this well, having had personally to cure many with his authoritative remedies, such as the Great Ointment and Holy Wood. Yet, for health, such commerce was perhaps less inauspicious than solitary dissipation.

"Excuse me," said I, in an endeavour to deflect the discussion from that thorny subject, "I have another question: do you perhaps know what illnesses rats suffer from?"

Crisofano laughed. "That is all we need. I can see it all now... One of our guests must have asked you whether there are rats in the hostelry, is that not so?"

My smile was uncertain, neither affirming nor denying.

"Well, I ask you, are there rats in the hostelry?"

"Good heavens, no, I have always cleaned everywhere with the greatest of care."

"I know, I know. If that were not the case, in other words, if you had found any dead rats, I myself would have put you on your guard."

"And why is that?"

"Why my poor boy, rats are always the first to catch the pestilence: Hippocrates recommended that one should never touch them, and in this he was followed by Aristotle, Pliny and Avicenna. The geographer Strabo tells that in ancient Rome the dreadful meaning of rats appearing sick in the streets was well known; for it portends a visitation, and he reminds us that in Italy and Spain, prizes were awarded to whoever killed the greatest number of them. In the Old Testament, the Philistines, being afflicted with a frightful pestilence which affected their posterior parts, causing the putrefied intestines to issue forth from the anus, noticed that the fields and villages had been invaded by rats. They then questioned the seers and the priests who replied that the rats had devastated the earth and that, to placate the wrath of the God of Israel, they must offer Him an *ex voto* with a representation of the anus and of the rats. Apollo himself, a deity who caused the plague when wrathful and turned it away when placated, was known in Greece as Smintheus, or destroyer of mice and rats: and indeed, in the *Iliad*, it was Apollo Smintheus who destroyed with the pestilence the Achaeans besieging Troy. And Aesculapius, too, was represented during visitations of the plague, with a dead rat at his feet."

"Then rats cause the plague!" I exclaimed, thinking with horror of the dead rodents which I had seen under the ground the night before.

"Calm down, my boy. I did not say that. What I have just told you are only ancient beliefs. Today we are fortunate enough to be living in 1683 and modern medical science has made immense progress. Vile rats do not cause the plague, which results, as I have already had occasion to explain, from the corruption of the natural humours and principally from the wrath of the Lord. It is, however, true that rats fall sick with the plague and die from it, just like men. But it suffices not to touch them, as Hippocrates said."

"How does one recognise a rat with the plague?" I asked, fearing the reply.

"Personally, I have never seen one, but my father did: they suffer from convulsions, their eyes are red and swollen, they tremble and squeal in agony."

"And how does one know that it is not another malady?"

"It is simple; they soon lose all their natural fluids and die, pirouetting and spitting blood. And, when dead, they become bloated and their whiskers remain rigid."

I blanched. All the rats found in the galleries had a rivulet of blood flowing from their pointed muzzles. And Ciacconio had even taken one by the tail.

I was not afraid for myself, being immune to the distemper; but the discovery of those little carcasses meant perhaps that the plague was spreading through the city. Perhaps other houses and other inns had already been shut up and within them wretched unfortunates shared our anguish. Being in quarantine, we had no means of knowing. I therefore asked Cristofano whether, in his view, the pestilence had spread.

"Fear not. In the past few days I have several times requested information from the watchmen who mount the guard in front of the inn. They have told me that there are no other suspected cases in the city. And there is no reason not to believe that to be the case."

As we descended the stairs, the doctor ordered me to rest for a few hours in the afternoon, obviously after anointing my chest with the *magnolicore*.

Cristofano had come to my room to warn me that he himself would see to the preparation of something quite simple and nutritious for luncheon. Now, however, he needed my assistance: he was concerned about some of the guests who, the evening before, after the dinner based on cows' teats had been beset by fits of heavy eructations.

As soon as we reached the kitchen, I saw, placed upon a little stove, a heavy glass bell equipped with a spout shaped like an alembic, in which oil was beginning to distil. Underneath, something was burning in a little pot, giving off a great stink of sulphur. Next to it, there stood a flask in an earthenware container which the physician grasped and began to tap delicately with his fingertips, producing a delicate ringing sound.

"Do you hear how perfectly it sounds? I shall use it for reducing to ash the oil of vitriol which I shall apply to the tokens of poor Bedfordi. And let us hope that this time they will mature and at last burst. Vitriol is rather corrosive, most bitter, of black humour, and unctuous; it greatly chills all intrinsic heat. Roman vitriol—of which I was fortunate enough to purchase a stock before our quarantine—is the best, because it is congealed with iron, while the German product is congealed with copper."

I had understood very little, except that Bedfordi's condition had not improved. The physician continued: "In order to help our guests' digestion, you will help me to prepare my angelical electuary, which by its attractive and non-modifying virtues, resolves and evacuates all indispositions of the stomach, heals ulcerated wounds, is a salve for the body and calms all altered humours. It is also good for catarrh and for toothache."

He then handed me two brown felt bags. From one, he extracted a couple of flasks of wrought glass.

"They are very beautiful," said I.

"For electuaries to be maintained in good condition according to the art of the herbalist, they must be stored in the finest glass, and for this purpose other flasks are worthless," he explained proudly.

In one, Cristofano explained, was his quinte essence, mixed with electuary of fire of roses; in the other, red coral, saffron, cinnamon and the *lapis philosophorum Leonardi* reduced to powder.

"Mix," he ordered me, "and administer two drachms to everyone. Go to it at once, for they must not partake of luncheon for at least another four hours."

ȣȣȣ

After preparing the angelic electuary and pouring it into a bottle, I did the rounds of all the apartments. I left Devizé's for last, since he was the only one to whom I had not yet administered the remedies which preserve from the plague.

As I approached his door, with the bag full of Cristofano's little jars, I heard a most graceful interweaving of sounds, in which I had no difficulty in recognising that piece which I had so many times heard him play, and whose ineffable sweetness had invariably enchanted me. I knocked timidly and he quite willingly invited me to come in. I explained the purpose of my visit to him and he assented with a nod, while still playing. Without proffering a word, I sat down on the floor. Devizé then put down his guitar and fingered the strings of an instrument which was both far bigger and far longer, with a wide fingerboard and many bass notes to be played unfretted. He broke off and explained to me that this was a theorbo, for which instrument he himself had composed many suites of dances with the most vigorous succession of preludes, allemandes, gavottes, courantes, sarabandes, minuets, gigues, passacaglias and chaconnes.

"Did you also compose that piece which you play so often? If only you knew how that enchants everyone here at the inn."

"No, I did not compose that," he replied with a distracted air. "The Queen gave it to me to play for her."

"So you know the Queen of France in person?"

"I knew her: Her Majesty Queen Maria Teresa is dead."

"I am sorry, I..."

"I played for her often," he continued without pausing, "and even for the King, to whom I had occasion to teach some rudiments of the guitar. The King always loved..." His voice trailed off.

"Loved whom, the Queen?"

"No, the guitar," replied Devizé with a grimace.

"Ah yes, the King wanted to marry the niece of Mazarin," I recited, regretting at once that I should thus have given away the fact that I had overheard his conversations with Stilone Priàso and Cristofano.

"I see that you know something," said he, somewhat surprised. "I imagine that you will have gleaned this from Abbot Melani."

Although taken by surprise, I succeeded in neutralising Devizé's suspicions: "For heaven's sake, Sir... I have endeavoured to keep my distance from that strange individual, ever since..."—and here I pretended to be ashamed—"ever since, well..."

"I understand, I understand, you need say no more," Devizé interrupted me with a half-smile. "I do not care for pederasts either..."

"Have you too had cause for indignation towards Melani?" I asked, mentally begging pardon for the ignominious calumny with which I was staining the honour of the abbot.

Devizé laughed. "Fortunately, no! He has never... um... bothered me. Indeed we never addressed a word to one another in Paris. It is said that Melani was an exceptional soprano in the days of Luigi Rossi, and of Cavalli... He sang for the Queen Mother, who loved melancholy voices. Now he sings no more: he uses his tongue for lies, alas, and betrayal," said he acidly.

It could not have been clearer: Devizé did not like Atto and knew of his fame as an intriguer. However, with the help of some necessary calumny about Abbot Melani, and by pretending to be even more of a rustic than was in fact the case, I was creating a certain complicity with the guitarist. With the help of a good massage, I would loosen his tongue even further, as with the other guests, and perhaps I would thus gain from him some intelligence concerning old Fouquet. The main thing, I thought, was that he should treat me as an ingenuous prentice, with no brain and no memory.

From my bag, I drew the most perfumed essences: white sandalwood, cloves, aloes and gum benzoin. I mixed them according to the recipe of Master Nicolò dalla Grottaria Calabrese, with thyme, calamite styrax, laudanum, nutmeg, mastics, spikenard, liquid amber and fine distilled vinegar. From these I made an odorous ball wherewith to rub the shoulders and flanks of the young musician, until it dissolved, while exerting light pressures on the muscles.

After baring his back, Devizé sat astride his chair, facing the window: to look upon the light of day was, he said, his only comfort in these distressing days. At the start of the massage, I said nothing. I then began clumsily to hum the melody that so enchanted me: "Did you not say that Queen Maria Teresa gave this to you: perhaps she composed it?"

"No, no, what kind of idea is that? Her Majesty did not compose. Besides, that *rondeau* is no beginner's piece; it is by my master, Francesco Corbetta, who had learned it on one of his journeys and, before he died, donated it to Maria Teresa."

"Ah, your master was Italian," I remarked vaguely. "From what city did he come? I know that Signor di Mourai came from Naples, like another of our guests, Stilone..."

"Even a mere prentice like yourself," Devizé interrupted me, "has heard of the love between the Most Christian King and Mazarin's niece. That is shameful. Of the Queen, however, no one knows a thing, save that Louis was unfaithful to her. Yet, the greatest wrong that one can do to a woman, especially Maria Teresa, is to let oneself be gulled by appearances."

Those words, which the young musician seemed to have pronounced with sincere bitterness, affected me profoundly: when judging the female sex, never be contented with first impressions. Despite the fact that I still felt the wound which I had sustained during our last encounter burning too cruelly, my thoughts moved instinctively to Cloridia, when she shamelessly reproached me for not paying the offering which she expected. Perhaps, however, Devizé's observation might not apply to her. I felt a certain shame, then, at having compared the two women, the Queen and the courtesan. More than anything else, however, I felt myself suddenly overwhelmed by nostalgia, loneliness and awareness of the cruel distance that separated me from my Cloridia. Being unable at this time to cope with these feelings, I became most anxious to know more about the spouse of the Most Christian King, at whose sad and tormented fate Devizé had hinted. I hoped that in some way, obscurely, her tale might reconcile me with the object of my languor.

I held out the bait to him with a venial lie: "I have indeed heard speak of Her Majesty Queen Maria Teresa. But only from passing guests at the inn. Perhaps I have..."

"Perhaps nothing: you surely need to be better governed," he brusquely interrupted me. "And you would do well to forget courtiers' chatter if you truly wish to know who Maria Teresa was and what she meant to France, and indeed, all of Europe."

He had bitten the hook.

The nuptial entry of the young Maria Teresa, Infanta of Spain, into Paris in 1660 was, so I learned from Devizé while kneading the odorous ball into his shoulders, one of the most joyous events in all the history of France. The young Queen was seated in a triumphal coach finer even than that of Apollo; the silver of the ornaments in her hair was as luminous as the very rays of the sun and triumphed over her fine black gown embroidered with gold and silver and set with innumerable precious stones of inestimable worth. The French were enthusiastic and, transported by the joy and devoted love which only faithful subjects can know, prayed for a thousand blessings upon her. Louis XIV, King of France and of Navarre, was in his turn the poets' perfect representation of a mortal deified; his apparel was woven of gold and silver and surpassed in dignity only by its wearer. He rode a superb mount, followed by a great number of princes. The peace between France and Spain, which the King had just given France through so auspicious a marriage, renewed the zeal and fidelity in the hearts of the people, and all those who had the good fortune to behold him on that day felt happy to have him for their sovereign lord. The Queen Mother, Anne of Austria, watched the King and Queen pass from a balcony on the rue Sainte-Antoine: one had but to see her face to know the joy which she felt. The two young sovereigns were united in exalting the greatness of both their kingdoms, at last at peace.

This was also a triumph for Cardinal Mazarin: the Peace of the Pyrenees, which restored calm and prosperity to France, was the crowning glory of his subtle policies. There followed months of festivities, ballets, operas and music, and the court was never richer in gaiety, gallantry and opulence.

"And after that, what happened?" I asked, fascinated by the history.

"After that, after that..." chanted Devizé.

It was a matter of only a few months, he continued, before Maria Teresa was fully apprised of what was to be her destiny, and of what fidelity her consort was capable.

The first appetites of the young King were satisfied by Maria Teresa's maids of honour. And even if his wife had not completely understood the stuff of which Louis was made, she was helped in that by the King's other, not even very secret, erotic trysts with Madame de la Vallière, maid of honour to her sister-in-law Mary Stuart. Next, came the turn of Madame de Montespan, who gave Louis no fewer than seven children. All this intense adulterous activity took place in broad daylight, so much so that the people soon called Maria Teresa, Madame de la Vallière and la Montespan "the three Queens".

The King knew no limits: he had banished the poor husband of la Montespan from court and several times threatened to imprison him. Louis de Gondrin had dared to protest by wearing mourning and adorning his carriage with horns. Yet, Louis had built two splendid palaces for his mistress, with a profusion of gardens and fountains. In 1674, la Montespan remained almost without rivals, since Louise de la Vallière had retired to a convent. The new favourite travelled with a coach and six, always followed by a cart loaded with provisions, and with a retinue of dozens of servants in attendance. Racine, Boileau and La Fontaine sang her praises in their verses and all the court regarded it as a great honour to be received in her apartments, while no one paid tribute to the Queen, save for the minimum required by etiquette.

The fortune of la Montespan was, however, lost the moment that the King laid eyes upon Marie-Angélique de Fontanges, as lovely as an angel and as silly as a goose. Marie-Angélique, not content with supplanting her rivals, found it difficult to understand the limits which her position imposed upon her: she wanted to appear in public at the King's side and to salute no one, not even the Queen, notwithstanding the fact that she was part of her retinue.

In the end, the Sovereign allowed himself to be caught in the nets of Madame de Maintenon, to whom he confided without any distinction his legitimate children and his many bastards by other mistresses. For Maria Teresa, the affronts did not, however, end here. The Most Christian King despised the Dauphin, his first-born son by the Queen, and preferred his illegitimate children. To the Dauphin, he gave in marriage Maria Anna Victoria, the rather plain and ugly daughter of the Elector of Bavaria. All beautiful women were, of course, only for His Majesty's pleasure.

Here Devizé stopped.

"And Her Majesty?" I asked, incredulous after all that dizzying traffic in women, and anxious to know the reaction of Maria Teresa.

"She suffered all in silence," the musician replied sadly. "What really took place in her heart of hearts, no one will ever know."

The adulteries, the humiliations, the pitiless mockery of the court and the people: in time, Maria Teresa had learned to swallow it all with a smile on her lips. So the King deceived her? She became all the more charitable and frugal. The King displayed his conquests before the whole world? She multiplied her prayers and devotions. The King courted Mademoiselle de Théobon or Mademoiselle de la Mothe, his wife's maids of honour? Maria Teresa dispensed smiles, words of advice and the kindest of attentions to all around her.

In the days when the Queen Mother, Anne of Austria, was still living, Maria Teresa had once dared to sulk at Louis for a couple of days. How little that was compared to all the outrages which she had put up with. Despite that, weeks and weeks passed before Louis deigned so much as to look at her again, and that thanks only to the Queen Mother who had laboured night and day to restore the situation. Maria Teresa had then understood that she must accept all that the marriage brought her: all, especially the pain and trouble; and that, without expecting anything in return, only the little which her spouse granted her.

In love, too, Louis had conquered. And since he knew and venerated the art of conquest, he had in the end decided upon what was—for him—the best and most appropriate conduct. He treated his wife, the Queen of France, with all the honours due to her condition; he ate with her, he slept with her, he fulfilled all his family obligations, he conversed with her as though his mistresses had never existed.

Apart from her spiritual devotions, the distractions which Maria Teresa permitted herself were few and harmless. In her retinue, she kept a half-dozen jesters whom she called Little Boy, Little Heart and Little Son, and a mass of small dogs whom she treated with a besotted, excessive affection. On her promenades, she had a separate carriage assigned to all that absurd company. Often the dwarves and little dogs ate at Maria Teresa's table, and to have them always near her, she was prepared to spend huge sums of money.

"But did you not say that she was a frugal and charitable lady?" I asked, taken aback.

"Yes, but this was the price of loneliness."

From eight to ten o'clock in the evening, Maria Teresa would play at cards, waiting for the King to take her to dinner. When the Queen played, princesses and duchesses would sit around her in a semicircle, while behind her stood the lesser nobility, panting and perspiring. The Queen's favourite game was *hombre*, but she was too ingenuous and always lost. Sometimes the Princess d'Elbeuf would make a sacrifice and allow herself to lose against the Sovereign: a sad and embarrassing spectacle. Until the end, the Queen felt more alone every day, as she herself confided to her few intimate friends. And before she died, she engraved all her suffering in a single phrase: "The King feels for me only now that I am about to leave him."

This narration, which had made me feel such great pity, was now making me impatient: I had hoped to obtain very different information from mouth of the musician. While continuing to massage Devizé's back, I glanced at the table a few paces away from us. Distractedly, I had placed a few of my medicinal jars on some pages of music. I begged Devizé's pardon for this but he gave a violent start and jumped up to check on the pages, in case they had been stained. He found a little oil-stain on one of them and became rather angry.

"You are no prentice, you are a beast! You have ruined my master's *rondeau*."

I was horrified. I had soiled the marvellous *rondeau* which I so loved. I offered to spread a fine dry powder on the leaf wherewith to absorb the oil; meanwhile, Devizé cursed and heaped insults upon me. With trembling hand, I strove to restore to its pristine state that page of music on which were traced the sounds which had so delighted me. It was then that I noticed an inscription at the top: "à Mademoiselle".

"Is that a dedication of love?" I asked, stammering, showing how embarrassed I still was by what had occurred.

"But who would love Mademoiselle?... The only woman in the world more lonely and sad than the Queen herself."

"Who is Mademoiselle?"

"Oh, a poor woman, a cousin of His Majesty. She had sided with the rebels during the Fronde, and she paid dearly for that: just think of it, Mademoiselle had fired the cannons of the Bastille against the King's troops."

"And was she sent to the scaffold?"

"Worse: she was condemned to remain forever a spinster," laughed Devizé. "The King prevented her from marrying. Mazarin said: 'Those cannon killed her husband.'"

"The King has no pity even for his relatives," I commented.

"Indeed. When Maria Teresa died, last July, do you know what His Majesty said? 'This is the first displeasure she has given me.' And nothing else."

Devizé continued talking, but now I was no longer listening to him. One word was pulsing in my head: July.

"Did you say that the Queen died in July?" I asked, brusquely interrupting him.

"What did you say? Ah yes, on the 30th of July, after an illness."

I asked no more. I had finished cleaning the page, rapidly removing the powder from both sides of the sheet and returning it to its cover. I took my leave and left the chamber almost panting with agitation. Closing the door, I leaned on the wall to reflect.

A sovereign, the Queen of France, had died of an illness in the last week of July: exactly in accordance with the prediction of the astrological almanack.

It was as though I had received a warning through the mouth of Devizé: a piece of news (of which only I, a poor prentice, had remained unaware) had provided yet another confirmation of the infallibility of the astrological gazette and the ineluctability of fate's writing in the stars.

Cristofano had assured me that astrology was not necessarily contrary to the Faith, and was indeed of the greatest utility for medicine. Yet, in that moment there came to me the memory of the unfathomable reasoning of Stilone Priàso, the strange story of Campanella and the tragic destiny of Father Morandi. I prayed heaven to send me a sign that might free me from fear and show me the way.

It was then that I again heard the notes of the wonderful *rondeau* arising from the deep tones of the theorbo: Devizé had begun playing again. I joined my hands in prayer and remained motionless, with my eyes closed, torn between hope and fear, until the music came to an end.

I dragged myself back into my chamber and there collapsed onto the bed, my soul emptied of all willpower and all vigour, tormented by events in which I could discern neither meaning nor order. Giving way to torpor, I hummed the sweet melody which I had just heard, almost as though it could confer on me the favour of a secret key wherewith to decipher the labyrinth of my sufferings.

❧

I was awoken by some noise from the Via dell'Orso. I had drowsed for only a few minutes: now my first thought went again to the almanack, mixed, however, with a bitter-sweet concert of desire and privation, the first cause of which I had no difficulty in discerning. To find peace and relief, I knew that I had only to knock at a door.

For several days now, I had left Cloridia's meals before her door, only knocking to signal their serving. Since then, only Cristofano had had access to her apartment. Now, however, the conversation with Devizé had opened up the wound of my distance from her.

What did it matter now that she had offended me with her venial request? With the pestilence circulating among us, she could be dead within a day or two; so I thought to myself with a pang in my heart. Pride, in extreme circumstances, is the worst of counsellors. There would surely be no lack of pretexts for me to visit her again: I had much to tell her and no less to ask.

"But I know nothing about astrology, that I have already told you," said Cloridia defensively when I showed her the almanack and explained to her how precise its predictions had turned out to be. "I know how to read dreams, numbers and the lines of the hand. For the stars, you must go to someone else."

I returned to my bedchamber thoroughly confused. That, however, was not so serious. Only one thing mattered: the blind god with little wings had again pierced my breast with his darts. It did not matter that I might never entertain any hope with Cloridia. It did not matter that she was aware of my passion and might laugh at it. I was still fortunate: I could see her and converse with her as and when I wished to, at least for as long as the quarantine lasted. This was a unique opportunity for a poor prentice like me; priceless moments which I would certainly remember for the remainder of my grey days. Again, I promised myself that I would return to visit her as soon as possible.

In my chamber, I found a little refreshment which Cristofano had left for me. A prey to love's drunkenness, I sipped the glass of wine almost as though it were the purest nectar of Eros, and swallowed a piece of bread and cheese as though it were the finest manna, sprinkled upon my head by the tender Aphrodite.

Replete, and with the dissipation of the soft aura which the encounter with Cloridia had left in my soul, I resumed my meditations upon my colloquy with Devizé: I had succeeded in obtaining nothing from him about the death of Superintendent Fouquet. Abbot Melani was right: Devizé and Dulcibeni would not speak easily about that strange affair. I had however succeeded in not arousing the suspicions of the young musician. On the contrary: with my ingenuous questions, and the damage which I had clumsily done to his score, I had imprinted in his mind the indelible image of an uncouth and stupid servant.

I went to visit my master, whose condition I found to be slightly improved. Cristofano was present, having just fed him. Pellegrino began to speak with a certain fluency and seemed sufficiently to understand what was said to him. Of course, he was far from enjoying perfect health, and still slept through most of the day, but, concluded Cristofano, it was not unreasonable to expect that he would soon be able to walk normally.

After spending some time with Pellegrino and the doctor, I returned to my chamber and at last allowed myself to enjoy sleep worthy of the name. I slumbered for hours, and when I descended to the kitchen, it was already dinner time. I hastened to cook for the guests, preparing a few slices of lemon with sugar, to stimulate the appetite. I continued with a Milanese soup, whose recipe called for egg yolk, Muscatel in which some crushed pine kernels had been soaked, sugar, a discreet dose of cinnamon (which, however, I decided this time to omit) and a little butter: all of this pounded in the mortar, sieved and placed in a little boiling water until it thickened. To this I added a garnish of a few bergamots.

After I had completed my round, I returned to the kitchen and prepared half a small jug of hot roasted coffee. Then I climbed to the little tower on tiptoe, so as not to be caught out by Cristofano.

"Thank you!" exclaimed Cloridia radiantly, as soon as I had opened her door.

"I prepared this only for you," I had the courage to tell her, blushing violently.

"I adore coffee!" said she, closing her eyes and sniffing ecstatically at the fumes which spread across the room from the little jug.

"Do they drink much coffee where you come from, in Holland?"

"No, but I do like very much the way in which you have prepared it, diluted and abundant. It reminds me of my mother."

"I am pleased. I had the impression that you had never known her."

"That was practically the case," she replied hurriedly. "I mean: I hardly remember her face, only the aroma of coffee, which, as I was later to learn, she prepared wonderfully well."

"Was she, too, Italian, like your father?"

"No. But did you come here to pester me with questions?"

Cloridia had become gloomy; I had ruined everything. Yet, suddenly, I saw her seek my eyes with hers and bestow on me a beautiful smile.

She invited me kindly to take a seat, pointing to a chair.

From a chest of drawers she took two little goblets and a dry roll with aniseed, and poured me some coffee. Then she sat before me, on the edge of the bed, sipping greedily.

I could think of nothing to say with which to fill the silence. And I was too ashamed to ask more questions. Cloridia, however, seemed pleasantly occupied, dipping a piece of the cake into the hot beverage and biting it with both grace and voraciousness. I melted with tenderness looking upon her and felt my eyes grow moist as I pictured myself plunging my nose in her hair and brushing her forehead with my lips.

Cloridia looked up: "For days now, I have spoken only with you, and yet I know nothing of your life."

"There is so little in it to interest you, Monna Cloridia."

"That is not true: for instance, where do you come from, how old are you, and how did you come to be here?"

I told her succinctly of my past as a foundling, my studies, thanks to the instruction of an old nun, and the benevolence of Signor Pellegrino towards me.

"So you have received instruction. I imagined that from your questions. You have been most fortunate. I, however, lost my father at the age of twelve and I have had to make do with the little which he had time to teach me," said she, without losing her smile.

"You learned Italian only from your father. Yet you speak it admirably."

"No, I did not learn it only from him. We were living in Rome when I was left alone. Then other Italian merchants brought me to Holland with them again."

"It must have been so sad."

"That is why I am here now. I wept for years, in Amsterdam, re-calling how happy I had been in Rome. Meanwhile, I read and stud-ied alone, in the little time that remained to me between..."

She did not need to finish her sentence. She was surely referring to the sufferings which life inflicts upon orphans, and which had led Cloridia onto the road to an abominable life of prostitution.

"But thus I succeeded in obtaining my freedom," she continued, as though she had guessed my thoughts, "and I could at last follow the life which is hidden in my numbers..."

"Your numbers?"

"But of course, you know nothing of numerology," said she with ostentatious courtesy, making me feel slightly ill at ease. "Well," she continued, "you must know that the numbers of our date of birth, but also those of other important dates in our lives, contain in them-selves our whole existence. The Greek philosopher Pythagoras said that, through numbers, all could be explained."

"And the numbers of your date of birth brought you here to Rome?" I asked, slightly incredulous.

"Not only: I and Rome are one and the same thing. Our destinies depend the one upon the other."

"But, how is that possible?" I asked, fascinated.

"The numbers speak clearly. I was born on the 1st of April, 1664, while the birthday of Rome..."

"What? Can a city, too, celebrate its birthday?"

"But of course. Do you not know the tale of Romulus and Re-mus, the wolf and the flight of birds, and how the city came to be founded?"

"Certainly, I do."

"Well, Rome was founded on a specific day: on the 21st of April in the year 753 before Christ. And the two birth dates, mine and that of the city of Rome, give the same result. Always provided that one writes it correctly, as is done in numerology, that is, counting the months from March, the month of spring and the beginning of new life, onwards; as did the ancient Romans and as still is done in the astrological calendar, which begins, of course, with Aries."

I realised that she was entering slippery terrain, in which the borders with heresy and witchcraft were very narrow.

"April, then, is the second month of the year," continued Cloridia, taking up ink and paper, "and the two dates are written thus: 1/2/1664 and 21/2/753. If you add up the two groups of numbers, you obtain, first: $1+2+1+6+6+4 = 20$. And then: $2+1+2+7+5+3 = 20$. Do you understand? The same number."

I stared at these figures hurriedly scribbled onto the sheet of paper and remained silent. The coincidence was indeed surprising.

"Not only that," continued Cloridia, dipping into the inkwell and resuming her calculations. "If I add day, month and year, figure by figure, I obtain $21 + 2 + 753 = 776$. If I add the figures of that total, $7 + 7 + 6$, I again obtain 20. Yet, adding $1 + 2 + 1664$, I obtain 1667, the digits of which also add up to 20. And do you know what the figure 20 stands for? It is the Judgement, the major arcana of the tarot, bearing the number 20, and signifying the reparation of wrongs and the wise judgement of posterity."

How sharp-witted was my Cloridia. So much so, that I had understood very little of her divinatory calculations or why she applied herself to them with such fervour. Little by little, however, my scepticism was overcome by her great ingenuity. I was in ecstasy: the grace of Venus competed with the intellect of Minerva.

"So, you are in Rome to obtain reparation for a wrong which you have suffered?"

"Do not interrupt me," she retorted brusquely. "The science of numbers proclaims that the reparation of wrongs will one day lead posterity to correct its own judgement. But do not ask me exactly what that means, because even I do not yet know."

"Was it also written in your numbers that you would one day come to the Locanda del Donzello?" I asked, drawn to the idea that my meeting with Cloridia might have been predestined.

"No, not in the numbers. When I arrived in Rome, I chose this hostelry following the guidance of the *virga ardentis*, the burning, or trembling, or projecting rod (there are many names for it). Do you know what I am speaking of?" said she, standing up and holding out her arm at the height of her belly, as though imitating a long stick.

It looked very much like an obscene allusion. I held my tongue and felt discouraged.

"But we shall speak of that another time; if you wish to, of course," she concluded with a smile which seemed ambiguous to me.

I took my leave of her, promptly completing my round of the apartments to collect the dishes in which I had served dinner. Whatever had Cloridia meant by that strange gesture? Was it perhaps a lascivious invitation or, worse, a mercenary one? I was not that stupid: I knew that, given my humble condition, it was ridiculous to expect that she might ever think of me as anything other than a poor servant; but, had she not understood that I had not a penny to my name? Did she perhaps hope that, for her, I might take some money from my master? I dismissed the thought with horror. Cloridia had referred to a wrong which had been suffered, in connection with her return to Rome. No, she cannot have been alluding to meretricious traffic at so grave a moment. I must have misunderstood.

I was delighted to see the guests of the inn visibly satisfied with their meal. When I knocked at his door, Dulcibeni was still sipping his soup, which was cold by now, and greedily sucking it between tongue and palate.

"Do take a seat, dear boy. Pardon me, but today my appetite was slow to come."

I obeyed silently, waiting for him to finish his meal. My attention wandered to the objects scattered across the chest of drawers next to his armchair, and stopped at three small volumes with vermilion covers and gilt lettering. They were very beautiful, I thought: but where had I seen them before?

Dulcibeni looked at me curiously: he had finished his soup and was holding out the dish for me. I took it with the most ingenuous of smiles and went out with lowered eyes.

Hardly was I out of the apartment than, instead of descending to the kitchen, I rushed up to the second floor. When I knocked breathlessly on Atto Melani's door, my arms were still laden with crockery.

"Pompeo Dulcibeni?" exclaimed the abbot incredulously, as I terminated my report.

The day before, I had in fact visited Dulcibeni's chamber in order to give him a massage and, during the treatment he had wanted to take a little snuff. He had, then, opened the chest in search of his snuff-box of inlaid cherry-wood and, in order to tidy the drawer a little, he had taken from it a few little books with a rather fine vermilion binding and gilt lettering. Now, in Tiracorda's library, I had

noticed a number of identical books: an edition of the works of Galen in seven volumes from which, however, three were missing. And
precisely these three I had just seen in Dulcibeni's chamber. On the
spine of each was inscribed *Galeni Opera* and they belonged without
the shadow of a doubt to the same set of the complete works of Galen in seven volumes as the four books in the house of Tiracorda.

"Of course," the abbot reasoned, "it is always possible that Dulcibeni and Tiracorda last met before the quarantine began. And it was
perhaps then that Tiracorda lent those books to Dulcibeni."

Nevertheless, he objected, both he and I were witnesses to the
fact that the *Archiater* had received a guest in the middle of the night:
a most curious hour for a visit! Nor was that all: he and his visitor had
made an appointment for the following day at the same hour. Therefore, Tiracorda's mysterious guest was wont to wander around the
city at the same hours in which we were able to leave the Donzello
unseen. That guest must be Dulcibeni himself.

"How is it that Tiracorda and Dulcibeni know one another?"

"You are asking that question," Atto replied, "because you are
unaware of one factor: Tiracorda is a Marchigiano."

"Like Dulcibeni!"

"What is more, Dulcibeni is a native of the Marches of Fermo, and
I seem to remember that Tiracorda too comes from Fermo."

"So they are fellow citizens."

"Just so. Rome has always been home to many illustrious physicians coming from that ancient and noble city: Romolo Spezioli, for
instance, the personal physician to Queen Christina of Sweden, the
chief court physician Giovan Battista Benci and even Cesare Mac-
chiati, if my memory does not betray me, who like Tiracorda was
physician to the conclave. Almost all the citizens of Fermo live in this
quarter, around the church of San Salvatore in Lauro, where their
High Confraternity meets."

"Tiracorda, however, lives a few yards away from the Donzello,"
I objected, "and he surely knows that we are in quarantine. Does he
not fear to be infected by Dulcibeni?"

"Obviously not. Perhaps he has repeated Cristofano's original
view that this was not the pestilence, passing over Bedfordi's illness
and the strange accident that befell your master."

"Then it is Dulcibeni who stole my master's keys. He, who seems
so severe!"

"Never trust to appearances. He will probably have been instruct-ed by Pellegrino in the use of the subterranean passageways."

"While I knew nothing of them. It seems incredible…"

Noi siam tre donzellette
semplicette semplicette,
oh, oh, senza fallo… *

He teased me, striking up a comic pose and chanting with his little voice. "Wake up, my boy! Remember: secrets are made to be sold. Originally, Pellegrino must have opened up the secret passage for him in return for payment. However, at the beginning of the quar-antine, your master became comatose. Dulcibeni must then have had to borrow the bunch of keys in order to have a copy of the key to the closet made by an artisan in the Via dei Chiavari, the road where (as Ugonio puts it) Komarek impresses."

"And what has Komarek to do with it?"

"Nothing whatever. I have already explained that to you, do you not remember? A pure coincidence; one which misled us."

"Ah yes," I replied, worried by my incapacity to keep pace with the congeries of discoveries, refutations, intuitions and false trails of the past few days. "But why did Pellegrino not give Dulcibeni a copy of the key?"

"Perhaps your master, as I said, takes payment every time a client wishes to use the underground passages; meaning that no keys are provided."

"Why, then, does Stilone Priàso have his own copy?"

"Do not forget that the last time that he sojourned at the Donzel-lo was in the days of the late Signora Luigia: he will have asked her for one, or purloined it."

"That does not explain why Dulcibeni should have stolen my lit-tle pearls, since he seems to be anything but poor."

"And I have a question which is even more difficult to resolve: if he is indeed the mysterious thief whom we have taken such pains to follow, how is it that, on every single occasion, he has proven to be a hundred times faster than we, and has always given us the slip?"

"Perhaps he knows the galleries better than we do. However, now that I come to think of it, he cannot possibly move so fast: only two

* Three little maids are we / Simple, oh so simple / Oh, oh with not a fault.
In Italian, the last word "fallo" may be a *double-entendre*, since it also means "phallus". (Translator's note).

days ago, he suffered an attack of sciatica. And Cristofano told him that it would last for several days."

"All the more reason. Add to that the fact that Dulcibeni is no longer a youngster and is somewhat corpulent, and whenever he speaks for any length of time, he becomes breathless: how the deuce does he manage to crawl every night up the hole which leads to the trapdoor?" concluded Atto with a hint of sourness, he who perspired and panted every time that we climbed through that narrow place.

I then told Atto all that I had recently learned concerning Pompeo Dulcibeni. I mentioned to him that, according to Padre Robleda, the elderly Marchigiano belonged to the sect of the Jansenists. I also told him of the harsh judgement which Dulcibeni had pronounced against the activities of the Jesuits in the sphere of espionage and of his fiery soliloquy against the consanguineous marriages which had for centuries been taking place among the royal families of Europe. The gentleman from Fermo was, I insisted, so scandalised by that practice and had become so heated as to exclaim in a loud voice—in an imaginary conversation with a woman, held before a mirror—that he longed for a Turkish victory at Vienna; thus, he hoped, a little fresh and uncorrupted blood would come to the thrones of our continent.

"A discourse, or should I say, a soliloquy worthy of a true Jansenist. At least, in part," commented Abbot Melani frowning pensively. "And yet, why desire a Turkish invasion in Europe, only out of pique against the Bourbons and the Habsburgs? That does seem to me somewhat excessive even for the most fanatical follower of Jansenius."

Be that as it may, Atto concluded, my discovery compelled us to return to the house of Tiracorda. As we had heard last night, Dulcibeni would be returning there too.

Night the Sixth

BETWEEN *the* 16TH & 17TH SEPTEMBER, 1683

✠

As usual, we waited until all the guests, including Cristofano, seemed finally to have retired, before descending the well which led to the labyrinth beneath the hostelry.

We covered the distance to our meeting point with Ugonio and Ciacconio under the Piazza Navona without any unforeseen occurrences. When, however, we met the *corpisantari*, Atto Melani found himself faced with a number of demands and an animated argument.

The two strange beings complained that, because of the adventures in which we had involved them, they had been unable to dedicate themselves freely to their activities. They claimed, moreover, that I had damaged some of the precious bones which they had carefully stacked, and which had collapsed upon me when we first met. The claim was scarcely credible, but Ciacconio had begun to wave under the nose of Abbot Melani an enormous, nauseatingly evil-smelling bone, with still some flesh attached to it, which, the *corpisantaro* pretended, had been harmed during that incident. If only to be rid of that filthy, stinking fetish, Atto preferred to give in.

"Very well, so be it. But I insist that you will cease henceforth to bother me with your problems."

He drew forth from his pocket a handful of coins and offered them to Ciacconio. In a lightning movement, the *corpisantaro* grasped the money in his hooked fingers, almost clawing Abbot Melani's hands.

"I cannot bear them, those two," murmured Atto under his breath, massaging his palm disgustedly.

"Gfrrrlubh, gfrrrlubh, gfrrrlubh…" Ciacconio began to grunt quietly, passing the coins from one hand to the other.

"He is totalising the pecuniary valorisation," said Ugonio in my ear, with an ugly, knowing grin. "He is economiserly."

"Gfrrrlubh," commented Ciacconio at last, with satisfaction, letting the money slide into a grimy, greasy sack where it fell jingling onto what must be a sizeable heap of coin.

"Nevertheless, the two monsters are invaluable to us," said Abbot Melani to me later, while Ugonio and Ciacconio moved into the darkness. "That revolting thing which Ciacconio held under my nose was some butcher's refuse, anything but a relic. But at times it is better not to be too tight-fisted and to pay up; otherwise, we should risk making enemies of them. Remember, in Rome one must always win, but never crushingly so. This holy city reveres the powerful but takes pleasure in their ruin."

After obtaining their reward, the *corpisantari* had delivered to Atto what we needed: a copy of the key to Tiracorda's coach-house and kitchen. Once we had emerged from the trap into the physician's little stables, entering the house was a matter of no difficulty. The late hour made it reasonable to suppose that only the old court physician would still be up and about, awaiting his guest.

We crossed the kitchen and entered the chamber with the old four-poster bed, then the lobby. We moved in the dark, finding our way only by memory and with the help of the faint moonlight. Thus, we climbed the spiral staircase: here we found the welcoming light of the large candles higher up the stairs, which Atto had had to extinguish the evening before in order to safeguard our retreat. We passed the first parlour halfway up the stairs in which were displayed the fine objects which we had so admired on our previous inspection. We then came to the first floor which, as on the night before, was plunged in darkness. This time, however, the door giving access to the chambers was open. All lay silent. The abbot and I exchanged glances of complicity: we were about to cross that almost fateful threshold and I felt myself strong with a courage as unusual as it was misplaced. The night before, all had gone well, so I thought, and we could again succeed this time.

Suddenly, three loud knocks coming from the lobby sent our hearts to our mouths. Almost instantaneously, we took refuge on the stairs from the first to the second floor, outside the other little room which housed the library.

We heard a stirring above our heads and then, down below, the shuffling of distant footsteps. Once again, we were caught between two fires. Atto was on the point of again blowing out the candles (which this time would certainly have aroused the suspicions of the master and mistress of the house) when Tiracorda's voice came clearly to our ears.

"I shall go, Paradisa, I shall go."

We heard him descend the stairs, cross the hall and utter an exclamation of happy surprise. The visitor entered without a word.

"Enter dumb into here," said Tiracorda joyfully, closing the door. "Number to dine: three."

"Pardon me, Giovanni, I am in no mood for laughter this evening. I must have been followed, and so I preferred to take another passage."

"Come in, my friend, my dearest friend."

Atto and I held our breath, glued like two snails to the wall of the staircase. The brief dialogue had been sufficient for us to recognise the voice of Pompeo Dulcibeni.

❧

Tiracorda led his guest to the first floor. We heard the pair move away, and at length a door closed. As soon as we were alone, we descended from our hiding place and looked into the large vestibule on the first floor. I would have liked to ask Abbot Melani a thousand questions and to obtain his comments on as many matters, but silence was our only hope of salvation.

We entered a spacious chamber where, in the semi-darkness, we could descry two four-poster beds and a number of other pieces of furniture. By some miracle, I avoided tripping over a low coffer. When, however, my pupils grew accustomed to the darkness, I suddenly realised that two icy, frowning faces lay silently in ambush in the darkness.

Frozen with terror, I needed several seconds to realise that these were two busts, one of stone, the other of bronze, placed at my height upon two pedestals. Beside them I could now see a plaster Hercules and a gladiator.

Turning to the left, we passed into an ante-chamber along the walls of which stood a long row of chairs. Thence, we moved to a second more spacious ante-chamber, immersed in gloom. From a neighbouring room came the voices of Tiracorda and his fellow-townsman. With great circumspection, we approached the crack of the door, which was not completely closed. There, transfixed by the fine blade of light that issued from within, we overheard the strangest conversation.

"Enter dumb into here... Number to dine: three," intoned Tiracorda, as when he had welcomed his guest at the front door.

"Number to dine: three... three..." repeated Dulcibeni.

"And so, consider calmly now; did you not perhaps come for this?"

The physician stood up and off he trotted to the left, out of our field of vision. Dulcibeni remained seated with his back to us.

The chamber was lit by two large candles of gilded wax, standing on the table at which the two were seated. The pomp of the furnishings, such as I had never seen before, left me both surprised and filled with admiration. Next to the candles stood a silver basket overflowing with wax fruit; the place was also illuminated by two large candelabra, one standing upon a little sandalwood table, the other on an ebony writing desk decorated with black mouldings and gilded bronze coats of arms. The walls were covered with rich crimson satin; everywhere hung fine pictures with varied and delightful figures: looking around, I recognised paintings of landscapes, animals, flowers and figurines: a Madonna and Child, a Pietà, an Annunciation, a Saint Sebastian and perhaps an Ecce Homo.

But dominating the room, in the middle of the longest wall, immediately opposite us, hung an imposing portrait of Our Lord Innocent XI, with a great gilt frame, carved with arabesques adorned with cut-glass foliage and garlands. Under this, on a pedestal, I espied an octagonal reliquary in silvered and gilt bronze which I imagined to be full of holy relics. More to the left, I could see a bed and a commode covered in red brocade. This last particular seemed revealing to me: we were in all probability in Tiracorda's study, where he received his patients.

We heard the doctor returning to the middle of the room, after opening and closing a door.

"How silly of me, I put it on the other side."

He turned to the right and went to the wall on which, immense and imposing, hung the portrait of His Holiness. To our surprise, in the wall before us, there opened up another door: there were two invisible panels, covered in the same crimson satin as the walls. The secret doorway concealed a dark closet in which were stored the instruments of his art. I could distinguish pincers, forceps and lancets, vases of officinal herbs and a number of books and piles of paper; these were perhaps notes on medical consultations.

"Are they still in there?" asked Dulcibeni.

"They are here and they are well," said Tiracorda busying himself in the little room. "But I am just looking for a couple of pleasant little things which I had set aside for the two of us. Ah, here we are."

He came out from the cupboard triumphantly waving a half-crumpled piece of paper, closed the secret door and sat down, preparing to read.

"Now, listen to this: if a father has seven daughters..."

At that precise moment, Atto Melani shocked me by clamping his hand sharply over his mouth. His eyes closed and he stood on tiptoe, his chest suddenly swelling, then doubled up desperately, with his face tucked into his armpit. I was seized by panic: I could not understand whether this was a fit of pain, hilarity or anger.

His anguished and impotent look made me understand that Atto was on the point of sneezing.

I have already drawn attention to how, in those days, Abbot Melani suffered from brief but uncontrollable fits of sneezing. This was, fortunately, one of the rare occasions when he succeeded in containing one of these loud outbursts. For a moment, I feared that he might lose his balance and fall against the half-open door. He leaned against the wall and, miraculously, the danger passed.

Thus, however, although only for a few instants, we were distracted from listening to Tiracorda and Dulcibeni. The first scrap of conversation which I managed to follow, as soon as Atto had recovered his composure, was as incomprehensible as what had gone before.

"Fourteen?" Dulcibeni was asking in a bored voice.

"Eight. And do you know why? One brother is brother to all the girls. Ha, ha, ha, ha! Ha, ha, haaaaa!'

Tiracorda had abandoned himself to unbridled asthmatic laughter, in which he was not joined by his guest. Hardly had the doctor calmed down than Dulcibeni endeavoured to change the subject.

"So, how did you find him today?"

"Ah, he fares not so well. If he does not cease fretting, there will be no improvement, and he knows it. Perhaps we shall have to forget about the leeches and try some other mode of intervention," said Tiracorda, pulling on his nose and drying his tears of laughter with a handkerchief.

"Really? I thought…"

"I, too, would have continued by the usual means," replied the physician, pointing towards the secret door behind him, "but now I myself am no longer quite so sure…"

"Permit me to say, Giovanni," Dulcibeni interrupted, "although I do not belong to your art: to each remedy, due time must be allowed."

"I know, I know, we shall see how we proceed…" the other responded absently. "Unfortunately, Monsignor Santucci is in a poor state of health and can no longer care for his patient as in the good old days. It was proposed to me that I should replace him, but I am too old. Fortunately, there are several persons who can one day take our place; like young Lanucci, whom I have done all in my power to help."

"He too is from the Marches, if I am not mistaken?"

"No, he was born here in Rome. But I have adopted him, so to speak. First, he was a pupil of our colleague from the Marches, then I made him my assistant at the Archispedale of Santo Spirito in Sassia."

"So, you will change the treatment?"

"We shall see, we shall see. Perhaps a little country air will suffice to obtain an improvement. Talking of which," said he, reading again from the crumpled paper, "On a farm…"

"Giovanni, listen to me," interrupted Dolcibeni with some warmth. "You know how much I enjoy our meetings, but…"

"Have you dreamed again of your daughter?" asked the other. "It is not your fault, I have told you that a thousand times."

"No, no, it is not that. It is…"

"I understand: you are again concerned about the quarantine. I have already told you: it is a trifle, a mere trifle! If matters are as you have described them to me, there is no danger of infection, let alone of being interned in a pest-house. He is absolutely right, that… what is he called? that Cristogeno of yours."

"Cristofano, he is called Cristofano. But I am concerned about something else. It seems to me that I was followed when I was coming to your house through the galleries."

"Ah well, one thing is for sure, you have been trampled on by some water rat, ha, ha, haaa! By the way, the other day, I found one right here in the stable. It was as big as this," said Tiracorda, stretching his short, round arms full length.

Dulcibeni remained silent, and although we could not see his face, I had the impression that he was losing patience.

"I know, I know," said Tiracorda then. "You are still ruminating upon that business. I do not understand why you torment yourself thus after so, so many years. Is it perhaps your fault? No; and yet you believe it and you think: 'If only I had served another master! Ah, if I had been a painter, a steward, a poet, a blacksmith or a stable-boy! Anything, but not a merchant.'"

"Well, yes. At times, I do think that," confirmed Dulcibeni.

"And I, do you know what I say to you? If it had been so, you would not even have known your daughter Maria."

"It is true. Far less would have sufficed: simply that Francesco Feroni should never have crossed my path."

"There we are again. Are you so sure that it was he?"

"It was he who backed the sordid designs of that swine Huygens."

"You could at least have revealed the facts and demanded an investigation."

"An investigation. But I have already explained to you: whoever would have undertaken a search for the bastard daughter of a Turkish slave? No, no, in difficult cases no help can be obtained from the Bargello's men, only from rogues and scoundrels."

"And the scoundrels told you that there was nothing to be done."

"Exactly, nothing to be done: Feroni and Huygens had carried her off, up there where that wretch lived. I went to search for her, to no effect. Do you see this old black great coat which I am wearing? I have had it ever since then. I bought it in a shop in the port when I was at the end of my strength and of my hopes; I shall never take it off again, never... I searched again and again, I paid informers and spies halfway across the world. Two of the best told me that of Maria there was no longer any trace: sold or, as I fear, dead."

The two fell silent for a few moments. Atto and I looked at each other; and in his eyes I read the same surprise and the same questions.

"I have told you many times: in this affair, there is neither resolution nor hope," Dulcibeni continued softly. "A drop of the usual?" he then asked, drawing out a flask and placing it on the table.

"What a question!" said Tiracorda, as his face lit up.

He rose to his feet, again opened the secret door and entered the cupboard. Groaning, he stretched up on tiptoe and, reaching out to a shelf near the ceiling, with his stubby fingers grasped two large goblets of fine green glass.

"It is a miracle Paradisa has not yet discovered my new secret hiding place," he explained, while closing the closet. "If she found my wine glasses, she would make such a scene. You know, with all her mania about sins of gluttony, and Satan... But let us return to you: what happened to Maria's mother?" asked Tiracorda.

"I have already told you: she was sold a little while before Maria's abduction. And of her, too, no more was ever heard."

"Could you not oppose her sale?"

"She belonged to the Odescalchi, not to me; as did my daughter, alas."

"Ah yes, you should have married her."

"Of course. But, in my position... with a slave..." stammered Dulcibeni.

"Had you done so, you would have obtained paternal rights over your daughter."

"It is true, but you do understand..."

A sound of breaking glass made us start. Dulcibeni cursed under his breath.

"I am sorry, oh, I am so, so sorry," said Tiracorda. Let us hope that Paradisa has heard nothing. Oh dear, what a mess..."

Moving one of the wax candles which lit the table, Tiracorda had struck Dulcibeni's flask, causing it to fall to the floor and shatter into a thousand pieces.

"It does not matter. I should have some more at the inn," said Dulcibeni in conciliatory tones, and he began to gather up the largest fragments of glass from the floor.

"Take care, you will cut yourself. I am going to fetch a cloth," said Tiracorda. "Please do not go to so much trouble, as you did when you served the Odescalchi, ha, ha, haaa!"

And laughing, he moved towards the half-open door behind which we were hiding.

We had a few seconds in which to act, and no choice. While Tiracorda opened the door, we flattened ourselves against the wall on either side of the door. The doctor passed between us, as between two sentries standing rigid and erect with fear. He crossed the whole ante-chamber and went out through the door at the far end.

It was then that the genius of Abbot Melani came to our aid, that and, perhaps, his insane inclination for disguises and ambuscades. He gave me a nod, and we both ran to the opposite wall, as silently and swiftly as two mice. Here, we again glued ourselves against the wall on either side of the doorway, this time with the advantage of being able to hide behind the open double doors.

"Here we are," said Tiracorda, who had evidently found a cloth.

The *Archiater* returned to the ante-chamber, passing between myself and Atto. Had we remained at the opposite end, I then realised, he would have faced us and there would have been no escape.

Tiracorda returned to the chamber where his guest was waiting for him, and closed the door behind him. Just before the last sliver of light disappeared, I had time to catch sight of Dulcibeni, still seated, and turning his head toward the door. With a dubious frown, he stared into the darkness of the ante-chamber, looking, without knowing it, straight into my frightened eyes.

❧❧

We remained immobile for a few minutes, during which I did not dare so much as to wipe the sweat from my forehead. Dulcibeni announced that he felt unusually tired and decided to take his leave and return to the Donzello. It was as though the failure of their toast had suddenly robbed his visit of all meaning. We heard the pair rise to their feet. We found no better solution than to run back to the first room, that which gave onto the staircase, and to hide behind the plaster statues. Tiracorda and Dulcibeni passed near us, unaware of our presence. Dulcibeni left with a lantern in his hand, the same one which he would use to return to the inn, while the physician kept apologising for breaking the flask, thus spoiling their evening.

They descended the stairs to the lobby. We did not, however, hear the main door of the house open. Surely, Atto whispered to me, Dulcibeni was returning to the Donzello by the underground route, the only possible one because of the watchmen who kept guard over the inn, day and night.

A little while later, Tiracorda returned up the stairs and went to the second floor. We were in utter darkness. With a thousand precautions, we descended to the kitchen and thence into the stables. We prepared to follow Dulcibeni.

"There is no danger: like Stilone Priàso, he will not escape us," whispered Atto.

However, matters went otherwise. Very soon, in gallery D we caught sight of the light of Dulcibeni's lantern. The gentleman from the Marches, with his heavy and corpulent physique, was advancing at a moderate pace. The surprise came at the junction with gallery C: instead of turning to the right, in the direction of the Donzello, Dulcibeni proceeded to the left.

"But that is impossible," Abbot Melani gestured to me.

We advanced a fair distance, until we were close to the watercourse which crossed the gallery. Beyond that, darkness reigned: it was as though Dulcibeni had extinguished his oil lamp. No point of reference remained to us and we advanced blindly.

We slowed down, fearing an encounter with our prey, and pricked up our ears. Nothing was to be heard save the rushing of the underground stream. We decided to proceed further.

Abbot Melani tripped and fell, fortunately without any consequences.

"The Devil with it, give me that wretched lantern," he cursed.

He himself lit our lantern and we both remained utterly confounded. A few yards ahead of us, the gallery came to an end, cut off obliquely by the watercourse. Dulcibeni had disappeared.

꙳

"Where do we start from?" asked Abbot Melani, visibly piqued, as we returned to the inn. In a painful endeavour to discern some logical sequence in the latest events, I summarised all that we had learned.

Pompeo Dulcibeni had several times visited Giovanni Tiracorda, his fellow-citizen of Fermo and physician to the Pope, to discuss mysterious matters the essence of which we had not succeeded in understanding. Tiracorda had mentioned obscure questions concerning brothers and sisters, farms, "number to dine, three", and other incomprehensible expressions.

Tiracorda also had a patient who seemed to be causing him some concern, but whom he hoped soon to restore to good health.

We had received important news concerning Pompeo Dulcibeni: he had (or, in his own words, had had) a daughter called Maria. The mother was a slave of whom he had soon lost all trace. The woman had been sold.

Pompeo Dulcibeni's child had, according to him, been abducted by a certain Huygens, the right-hand man of a certain Feroni (a name which, in truth, did not sound new to me) who seemed to have had a hand in the affair. Dulcibeni had not been able to prevent the abduction and believed that the girl was now dead.

"In all probability, it was to his lost daughter," I observed, moved to pity, "that Dulcibeni imagined he was speaking during his soliloquy, poor man."

But the abbot was no longer listening to me.

"Francesco Feroni," he murmured. "I know the name: he enriched himself trafficking slaves to the Spanish colonies in the New World, and returned to Florence in the service of Grand Duke Cosimo."

"A slaver, then."

"Yes. He is said to be a man of few scruples: in Florence, much ill is told concerning him. And, now that I remember, it was about him and that Huygens that a rather ridiculous tale circulated," said Atto with a little laugh. "Feroni dreamed of an alliance with some Florentine nobleman, instead of which, his daughter and heiress quite literally lost her health for love of that Huygens. The problem was that Huygens was Feroni's trusted collaborator and managed all the most important and delicate affairs on his behalf."

"What happened? Did Feroni dismiss him?"

"On the contrary: the old merchant neither would nor could do without him. Thus Huygens remained in the family business, while Feroni endeavoured almost obsessively so to exercise his power as to fulfil his young assistant's every caprice. In order to keep him away from his daughter, he arranged for him to have all the women he wanted, even the costliest ones."

"And how did it all end?"

"I do not know, that is of no interest to us. But I think that Dulcibeni's little girl fell, poor creature, under the eyes of Huygens and Feroni," sighed Atto.

Dulcibeni, I resumed, and this was the most surprising discovery, had in the past been a merchant in the service of the Odescalchi: the Pope's family.

"And now, put your questions to me," said Melani, guessing that I had a long list of queries on the tip of my tongue.

"First of all," I said as with a little jump down, we came to gallery D, "what service will Dulcibeni have performed for the family of the Pope?"

"There are various possibilities," replied Atto. "Dulcibeni said 'merchant'. But the term is perhaps misleading: a merchant works on his own account, while he had a master. He may therefore have served the Odescalchi in the capacity of a secretary, an accountant, a treasurer or an agent buying for them. Perhaps he travelled for them. For decades, that family bought and sold grain and textiles throughout Europe."

"Padre Robleda told me that they lend money with interest."

"Did you speak of this too with Robleda? Bravo, my boy; well, yes. They subsequently withdrew from trading and dedicated themselves above all to moneylending. I know that in the end they invested almost everything, purchasing public offices and savings bonds."

"Signor Atto, who can the patient be of whom Tiracorda spoke?"

"That is the easiest question to answer. Think about it: this is a patient whose illness must remain secret, and Tiracorda is physician to the Pope."

"Good heavens, it must be..." I swallowed as I dared to draw the inference "Our Lord Innocent XI."

"I do believe so. Nevertheless, I was surprised. When the Pontiff falls ill, the news spreads like wildfire. Yet, Tiracorda wishes to keep it secret. Clearly, they fear in the Vatican that the time is too sensitive: it is still unclear who will win in Vienna. With a weakened Pope, there is in Rome a danger of discontent and disorder; abroad there is a risk of raising the morale of the Turks and sapping that of the Christian allies. The trouble is, as Tiracorda said, that the Pontiff is not recovering, so much so that it will soon be necessary to change his treatment. That is why the news must not be bruited abroad."

"Yet Tiracorda confided this to his friend," I observed.

"He evidently thinks that Dulcibeni knows how to keep his lips sealed. And Dulcibeni, like ourselves, is shut up in an inn under quarantine: he certainly has no opportunities to let out the secret. The most interesting thing, however, is not this."

"What is it, then?"

"Dulcibeni was travelling with Fouquet, now he is visiting the Pope's physician to talk of mysterious things: farms, brothers, 'enter dumb into here'... I would give an eye to understand what they were talking about."

While returning to the Donzello, we encountered the *corpisantari*, in their archives among the ruins under the Piazza Navona.

I noticed that the pair had reconstituted their filthy heap of bones, which now appeared to be considerably higher and more bulky. The *corpisantari* did not in any way salute our arrival: they were engaged in an intense discussion and appeared to be arguing over the ownership of an object. Ciacconio had the better of it, with a sudden ugly gesture grabbing something from Ugonio's hand and placing it, with an all-too servile smile, in the hands of Atto Melani. It was a few fragments of dry leaves.

"And what is this?" said Atto. "I cannot possibly pay for all the stupid things that you would like to sell me."

"It is an estranged foliage," said Ugonio. "To be more medicinal than mendacious, Ciacconio disgoverned it in the vicinity of the mortified, bloodified rodents."

"A strange plant near to dead rats... how curious," remarked Atto.

"Ciacconio says that it reeks in a stupefactual manner," continued Ugonio. "It is an excitifying, inquisitating, besotting plantation. In sum, to obtain more benefice than malefice, he is representing it to you, for by fulfilling one's obligations the Christian's jubilations are increased."

Atto took one of the leaves; while he was raising it to the light of the lamp in order to examine it, I had a sudden reminiscence.

"Now that I come to think of it, Signor Atto, I too seem to have seen dry leaves in the galleries."

"That is a fine one," he commented, clearly amused. "We are full of leaves down here. How is that possible? Trees do not grow under the ground."

I explained to him that, when we were following Stilone Priàso in the conduit, I had trodden on dry leaves, so much so that I feared I might be heard by Stilone.

"Silly lad, you should have told me. In situations like ours, nothing should be neglected."

Taking some of those friable vegetable fragments, I promised myself that I would make up for that inattention. Seeing that I was unable to help Atto to decipher the business of the farms, brothers and "enter dumb into here" discussed by Tiracorda and Dulcibeni in the course of their incomprehensible conversation, I would at least endeavour to discover from what plant those dry leaves came: thus we might discover who had disseminated them throughout the underground galleries.

෩෨

We left the *corpisantari* busy with their bones. During our return to the inn, I remembered that I had not yet reported to Abbot Melani my conversation with Devizé. In the whirl of our recent discoveries, I had forgotten it, all the more so in that I had learned nothing of importance from the musician. So I told Atto of this encounter (obviously omitting the fact that, in order to gain the guitarist's confidence, I had cast a slur on the abbot's honour).

"Nothing of importance, did you say?" he exclaimed, without allowing me to finish. "You are telling me that Queen Maria Teresa had contacts with the famous Francesco Corbetta, and with Devizé, and you call that nothing of importance?"

Atto Melani's reaction took me by surprise: the abbot seemed almost beside himself. While I was recounting these matters to him, we would proceed for a short distance, then suddenly he would stop, open his eyes wide and ask me to repeat what I had said; whereupon he would again move on in silence, and then halt yet again, lost in thought. In the end, he had me recapitulate the whole story from the beginning.

So I told him yet again how, on my way to Devizé's apartment to give him a massage, I had heard that *rondeau* which he so often played and which had so delighted all the other guests at the Donzello before the quarantine. I then asked him if he was the author of that piece and he replied that it was his master, one Corbetta, who had learned the melody of that *rondeau* during one of his frequent voyages. Corbetta had rearranged it and had made of it a tribute to the Queen; she had then handed the musical score to Devizé, who in his turn had reworked it in part. In other words, it was not clear whose the music was, but we did at least know through whose hands it had passed.

"But do you know who Corbetta was?" asked the abbot, with eyes that had narrowed down to two slits, and stressing every single syllable.

The Italian Francesco Corbetta, he explained to me, had been the greatest of all guitarists. It was Mazarin who had called him to France to teach music to the young Louis XIV, who adored the sound of the guitar. His fame had soon spread and King Charles II of England, another lover of the guitar, had taken him with him to London, had arranged a good marriage for him and had even elevated him to the peerage. However, in addition to being a wonderfully refined musician, Corbetta was also something else which almost no one knew: a most skilful master of ciphers and codes.

"Did he write letters in code?"

"Even better: he composed music containing ciphers, in which secret messages were encoded."

Corbetta was an exceptional individual: both fascinating and intriguing, and a hardened gambler. For much of his life, he had travelled between Mantua, Venice, Bologna, Brussels, Spain and Holland, even becoming implicated in a number of scandals. He had died scarcely two years ago, in his sixtieth year.

"Perhaps he too did not disdain the profession of... counsellor, alongside the art of music..."

"I would venture to say that he was very much involved in the political affairs of the states which I have mentioned," said Atto Melani, thus admitting that Corbetta must have had a hand in some affairs of espionage.

"And did he use the tablature of the guitar for that purpose?"

"Yes, but that was certainly not his invention. In England, the celebrated John Dowland, who played the lute at the court of Queen Elizabeth, wrote his music in such a manner that, through it, his patrons could transmit secret information."

Atto Melani took no little time to convince me that musical notation could include meanings completely foreign to the art of sound. Yet, this had always been so: both monarchs and the Church had for centuries had recourse to musical cryptography. The matter was, moreover, familiar to all men of doctrine. To give an example accessible to everyone, he said that in *De furtivis litterarum notis* Della Porta had listed all the systems whereby secret messages of every kind and length may be encrypted. By means of a suitable key, for example, every letter of the alphabet could be associated with a musical note. The succession of notes, annotated on the pentagram would thus provide whoever held the key to the code with complete words and phrases.

"Thus, however, there arises the question of the *saltus indecentes*, or in other words, of disagreeable dissonances and disharmonies, which might even arouse suspicion in one simply casting an eye over the music. Someone then thought up more refined systems."

"Who was that?"

"Our Kircher, to be precise: for example, in his *Musurgia Universalis*: instead of assigning a letter to each note, he distributed the alphabet among the four voices of a madrigal or an orchestra, the better to govern the musical material, thus rendering the composition less rough and disagreeable: after all, if the message was intercepted, such flaws would be enough to arouse suspicion in anyone. There are infinite possibilities for manipulating the sung text and the notes to be intoned. For example, if the musical note—'fa', 'la' or even 're'—coincides with the text, then only *those* syllables are to be taken into account. Or one can do the opposite, conserving only the remainder of the sung text which, at that point, will reveal its hidden meaning. It is, in any case, certain that Corbetta will have been aware of Kircher's innovation."

"Do you think that, apart from his art, Devizé will have learned from Corbetta this... art of communicating secretly?"

"That is just what is rumoured at the French court; especially as Devizé was not only Corbetta's favourite pupil but above all a good friend of his."

Dowland, Melani, Corbetta and now perhaps also his pupil Devizé: I was beginning to suspect that music was inevitably accompanied by espionage.

"What is more," continued Abbot Melani, "Corbetta knew Fouquet well, seeing that he was guitarist to Mazarin's court until 1660: only then did he emigrate to London, even though he in fact continued to make frequent visits to Paris, where he finally returned ten years later."

"But then," I concluded, without even wishing to believe my own words, "even that *rondeau* might conceal a secret message."

"Calm down, calm down, first let us consider the other things we know: you told me that the *rondeau* was given by Corbetta to Queen Maria Teresa who in turn gave it to Devizé. Well, this provides me with another piece of precious information: I had no idea that the Queen was in touch with the two guitarists. The thing is so extraordinary that I find it almost hard to believe."

"I understand," I interrupted. "Maria Teresa led an almost reclusive existence..."

I then told him of the lengthy monologue in which Devizé described the humiliations which the Most Christian King had heaped upon his poor consort.

"Reclusive?" said Atto at the end. "I would not use that term."

And he explained to me that Devizé had painted me perhaps too immaculate a portrait of the late Queen of France. At Versailles, even now, one might still encounter a young mulatto girl who bore a curious resemblance to the Dauphin. The explanation of that wonder was to be found twenty years previously, when the ambassadors of an African state had sojourned at court. To manifest their devotion to the consort of Louis XIV, the ambassadors had presented the Queen with a little black page called Nabo.

A few months later, in 1664, Maria Teresa had given birth to a hale and lively little girl with black skin. When this prodigy took place, the Chirurgeon Royal swore to the King that the newborn child's colour was a passing inconvenience due to congestion at birth. Days passed, however, and the child's skin showed no sign of lightening. The Chirurgeon Royal then said that perhaps that court blackamoor's over-insistent glances might have interfered with the Queen's pregnancy. "A glance?" replied the King. "It must have been most penetrating."

"A few days later, with the greatest discretion, Louis XIV had the page Nabo put to death."

"And Maria Teresa?"

"She said nothing. She was not seen either to weep or to smile. Indeed, she was not seen at all. Yet, from the Queen no one had ever succeeded in obtaining anything except words of kindness and pardon. She had always made a point of telling the King of every little thing, in proof of her own fidelity, despite the fact that he dared to appoint his own mistresses as her maids of honour. It was as though Maria Teresa had not known how to appear anything but colourless, opaque, almost devoid of any will of her own. She was too good, too good."

Devizé's phrase came to mind: it was indeed an error to judge Maria Teresa by appearances alone.

"Do you think that she dissimulated?" I asked.

"She was a Habsburg. She was a Spaniard. Two exceedingly proud breeds, and bitter enemies of her husband. How do you think that Maria Teresa felt, exiled on French soil? Her father loved her dearly and had agreed to lose her only in order to conclude the Peace of the Pyrenees. I was present at the Isle of Pheasants, my boy, when France and Spain concluded the treaty and decided the nuptials between Louis and Maria Teresa. When King Philip of Spain had to bid his daughter farewell, and knew that he would never again see her, he embraced her and wept disconsolately. It was almost embarrassing to see a King comport himself thus. At the banquet which followed the agreement, one of the most sumptuous that I have ever seen, he barely touched his food. And in the evening, before retiring, he was heard to groan between his tears, saying, 'I am a dead man,' and other silly phrases."

Melani's words left me speechless: I had never thought that powerful sovereigns, the masters of Europe's fate, might suffer so bitterly for the loss of a loved one's company.

"And Maria Teresa?"

"At first, she behaved as though nothing had happened, as was her wont. She had immediately let it be understood that her betrothed was pleasing to her; she smiled, conversed amiably and showed herself pleased to be leaving. But that night, everyone heard when in her chamber she cried in torment: '*Ay, mi padre, mi padre!*'"

"Then it is clear: she was a dissimulator."

"Exactly. She dissimulated hatred and love and simulated piety and fidelity. And so we ought not to be too surprised that no one should have known of the gracious exchanges of musical scores between Maria Teresa, Corbetta and Devizé. Perhaps it all took place under the King's nose!"

"And do you think that Queen Maria Teresa used the guitarists to hide messages in their music?"

"That is not impossible. I recall having read something of the sort many years ago, in a Dutch gazette. It was cheap scribblers' stuff, published in Amsterdam but written in French in order to spread poisonous rumours about the Most Christian King. It told of a young valet at the court of Versailles, by the name of Belloc, if I recall correctly, who wrote scraps of poetry for recital during ballets. In those verses were inserted in cipher the reproaches and sufferings of the Queen for the King's infidelities, and these were said to have been commissioned by Maria Teresa herself."

"Signor Atto," I then asked, "who is Mademoiselle?"

"Where have you heard that name?"

"I read it at the top of Devizé's score. There were written the words '*à Mademoiselle*'."

Although the diffuse light of the lantern was faint, I saw Abbot Melani grow pale. And suddenly in his eyes I read the fear which for the past couple of days had begun silently to consume him.

I then told him everything else about my meeting with Devizé: how I had accidentally stained the score with oil and how, when endeavouring to clean it, I had read the dedication "*à Mademoiselle*". I recounted the few things which Devizé had told me about Mademoiselle: namely, that she was a cousin of the King; and how the latter had, because of her past as a rebel, condemned her to remain a spinster.

"Who is Mademoiselle, Signor Atto?" I repeated.

"What matters is not who she is but whom she married."

"Married? But was she not to remain unmarried, as a punishment?"

Atto explained to me that matters were rather more complicated than Devizé's version. Mademoiselle, who was in reality called Anne Marie Louise, Duchess of Montpensier, was the richest woman in France. Riches, however, were not enough for her: she was utterly set upon marrying a king, and Louis XIV amused himself by forbidding her the joys of matrimony. In the end, Mademoiselle changed her mind: she said she no longer wished to become a queen and to end up like Maria Teresa, subjected to the whims of a cruel monarch in some distant land. At the age of forty-four, she then fell in love with an obscure provincial gentleman: a poor younger brother from Gascony, with neither skills nor fortune who, a few years earlier, had had the good luck to be liked by the King, becoming the companion of his amusements and even acceding to the title of Count of Lauzun.

Lauzun was a cheap seducer, said Atto scornfully, who had courted Mademoiselle for her money; but in the end, the Most Christian King consented to the marriage. Lauzun, however, being a monster of presumption, wanted festivities worthy of a royal wedding; "like the union of two crowns," he would boast to his friends. Thus, while the wedding was held up by too many preparations, the King had time to relent and again forbid the marriage. The betrothed couple begged, entreated, threatened; all to no avail. So they married secretly. The King found this out, and that was the ruin of Lauzun, who ended up in prison, in a fortress far from Paris.

"A fortress," I repeated, beginning to understand.

"At Pinerol," added the abbot.

"Along with..."

"Exactly, along with Fouquet."

Until that moment, explained Melani, Fouquet had been the only prisoner in the enormous fortress. However, he already knew Lauzun, who had accompanied the King to Nantes on the occasion of his arrest. When Lauzun was brought to Pinerol, the Superintendent had been languishing in a cell for over nine years.

"And how long did Lauzun remain there?"

"Ten years."

"But that is so long!"

"It could have been worse for him. The King had not set the duration of his sentence and could have held him at his pleasure."

"How come, then, that after ten years he was freed?"

That was a mystery, said Atto Melani. The only certain fact was that Lauzun was liberated a few months after the disappearance of Fouquet.

"Signor Atto, I no longer understand a thing," said I, unable to control the trembling which had seized my limbs. We were now almost back at the inn, filthy and overcome by cold.

"Poor lad," said Atto Melani pityingly. "In a few nights, I have compelled you to learn half the history of France and of Europe. But it will all be useful! If you were already a gazetteer, you would have enough to keep you writing for the next three years."

"But, in the midst of all these mysteries, even you no longer understand anything concerning our situation," I dared retort, disconsolate and panting with fatigue. "The more we struggle to understand, the more complicated matters become. This much I know: your sole interest is in understanding why the most Christian King had your friend Fouquet condemned twenty years ago. As for my little pearls, they are lost forever."

"These days, everyone is curious about the mysteries of the past," said Abbot Melani, calling me severely to order. "This is because the present mysteries are too frightening. I and you shall, however, resolve both. That, I promise you."

These words were, I thought, all too facile. I endeavoured to summarise for the abbot all that we had learned in six days of shared claustration at the Donzello. A few weeks earlier, Superintendent

Fouquet had come to our hostelry, in the company of two gentlemen. The first, Pompeo Dulcibeni, was familiar with the system of tunnels under the inn and used them to visit his fellow-countryman, the physician Tiracorda, who was at the present time caring for the Pope. Dulcibeni had, moreover, had a daughter by a Turkish slave, who had been stolen from him by a certain Huygens, backed by a man called Feroni, when Dulcibeni was in the service of the Odescalchi, in other words, the family of the Pope.

Fouquet's second companion, Robert Devizé, was a guitarist whose relations with Maria Teresa, Queen of France, were not clear. He was a pupil of Francesco Corbetta, an intriguing personage who had written and, before dying, donated to Maria Teresa the *rondeau* which we so often heard Devizé playing. The music sheet of this *rondeau*, however, bore a dedication to Mademoiselle, the cousin of the Most Christian King and wife of the Count of Lauzun. The latter had, for ten years, been the companion of Fouquet at Pinerol, before the Superintendent's death...

"You should say 'before his escape'," Atto corrected me, "seeing that he died at the Donzello."

"Correct. And then..."

"And then we have a Jesuit, a runaway Venetian, a harlot, a Neapolitan astrologer, a drunkard of a host, an English refugee and a physician from Siena: like all his colleagues, a murderer of defenceless Christians."

"And the two *corpisantari*," I added.

"Ah yes, the two monsters. And, last of all, we ourselves who are racking our brains while someone in the hostelry has the plague, bloodstained pages from the Bible are to be found in the galleries beneath the city, as well as phials full of blood and rats puking blood... too much blood, now that I come to think of it."

"What does it all mean, Signor Atto?"

"A fine question. How many times must I repeat to you? Think of the crows and the eagle. And behave like an eagle."

By that time, we were already climbing the stairs that led to the secret chamber in the Donzello; and soon after that, we separated, after giving each other an appointment for the morrow.

Day the Seventh

17TH SEPTEMBER, 1683

✠

Even in those days overburdened with emotion, there would sometimes arise and keep turning in my mind an edifying maxim which the
old lady who had so lovingly educated and instructed me was wont to
chant, as one does with children: never leave a book half-read.

It was with that wise precept in mind that I decided, upon rising,
to complete my reading of Stilone Priàso's astrological almanack. My
scrupulous teacher was not mistaken: better not to open a book than
to read it only in part, thus committing to memory a mere fragment,
together with an erroneous judgement. Perhaps, I reflected, the remaining pages might enable me to gain a more balanced view of the
obscure powers which I had hitherto attributed to that mysterious
booklet.

Upon awakening, moreover, I felt less faint than on the preceding
mornings; I had slept soundly and sufficiently, even after the carousel
of stalking and spying and narrow escapes which had led us to follow
Dulcibeni the whole way along gallery C until we came to the underground river; and, above all, after the surprising revelations concerning Devizé (and his mysterious *rondeau*) which the abbot and I had
discovered during our return to the inn.

My mind still refused to dwell upon that intricate story. Yet, now
I found an opportunity to finish reading the gazette which the *corpisantari* had taken from Stilone Priàso, and which I still kept under
the mattress of my little bed.

This small volume seemed to have predicted accurately the
events of the past few months. Now, I wanted to know what the
future held in store for us.

So I read the predictions for the third week of September, which
would soon be upon us.

> *The Vaticinations which are to be conjectured from the Starres will, during this
> Week, be given principally by Mercury, which will receive two Luminaries in*

its Domiciles and, being in the Third House, in Coniunction with the Sunne, promises Voyages undertaken by Princes, the Sending of voluminous Dispatches and divers Royall Embassies.

Jupiter and Venus conjoined seek to bring together in the Igneous Trine an Assembly of the Virtuous to treat of a League, or a Peace of great Importance.

My attention was drawn at once to "Voyages undertaken by Princes, the Sending of voluminous Dispatches" and "Royall Embassies" and no doubt remained in my mind: these must be the dispatches announcing the outcome of the battle for Vienna, which must by then have been decided.

Soon, indeed, a multitude of mounted messengers, perhaps despatched by the very sovereigns and princes who had taken part in the fray, would spread across Europe, bearing the verdict in three days to Warsaw, in five, to Venice, in eight or nine to Rome and Paris, and later still to London and Madrid.

Once again, the author of the almanack had found his mark: not only had he foreseen a great battle, but the frenetic spreading of the news on the morrow of the final clash.

And was not the "Assembly of the Virtuous to treat of a League, or a Peace of great Importance" of which the Almanack spoke, the peace treaty which would surely be sealed between victors and vanquished?

I read on, coming to the fourth and last week of September:

Ill Tidings for the Sick *may be received during this fourth Weeke of September, since the Sun rules the Sixth House and has given over the care of the Infirm to Saturn; hence, there shall reign Quartan Fevers, Fluxes, Dropsy, Swellings, Sciatica, Gout and Pain caused by the Stone. Jupiter, however, rules the Eighth House and will soon bring Health to many Patients.*

There would, then, be other threats to health: fevers, disturbances in the circulation of the humours, excessive water on the stomach, pains in the bones, legs and bowels.

These were all grave threats; yet, according to the almanack, they were not insuperable. The worst was indeed still to come:

The first Tidings of this Weeke may be somewhat violent, for they will be sent by Mars, the Ruler of the Ascendant, who, being in the Eighth House, may cause us to hear of the Deathe of Men by Poyson, Steele or Fire. Saturn in the Sixth House, which rules over the Twelfth House, promises Deathe to certain enclosed Noblemen.

Upon reading those last words, I became breathless. I threw the gazette far from me and, with clasped hands, implored heaven's aid. Perhaps nothing that I had read in the course of my life so marked my soul as those few, cryptic lines.

"Violent" events were, then, brewing; such as "the Death of Men by Poyson, Steele or Fire". Death was destined for "enclosed Noblemen": some of the guests at the Donzello were certainly noble and, for sure, all were "enclosed" because of the quarantine!

If ever I had needed another proof that the almanack (the work of the Devil!) foretold events, here I had it: it spoke of *us*, cloistered in the Donzello by the pestilence, and of the death of certain gentlemen among us.

Violent death, and by poison: and had not Superintendent Fouquet perhaps been poisoned?

I knew that a good Christian must not yield to despair, even when his plight is most tragic. I would, however, be lying if I were to pretend that I faced these unheard-of revelations with manly dignity. Never had I felt myself so abandoned, despite my foundling's condition, in thrall to stars which, for who knows how many centuries, perhaps since their course began, had determined my destiny.

Overcome by terror and desperation, I grasped the old rosary which I had received as a gift from the pious woman who had raised me, kissed it passionately and pocketed it. I recited three paternosters and realised that, in my fear of the stars, I had entertained doubts about divine providence, which every Christian should acknowledge as his sole guide. I felt a burning need to purge my soul and to receive the comfort of the Faith: the time had come for Confession before God; and, thank heaven, there was in the hostelry someone who could help me.

"Well, come in my son, you are right to cleanse your soul at a time as difficult as this."

As soon as he had heard the reason for my visit, Robleda welcomed me to his little chamber with great benevolence. The secret of Confession melted my heart and loosed my tongue and I honoured the sacrament with ardour and commitment.

Once he had given me absolution, he asked me the origin of so many sinful doubts.

Without mentioning the almanack, I reminded Robleda that a while before, he had spoken to me of the predictions concerning the

Angelic Pope and this conversation had caused me to meditate long on the topic of fate and predestination. During the course of these cogitations, the thought had come to me that some held all sublunary things to be determined by the influence of the stars, so that such events could be adequately foretold. I knew that the Church rejected such views, which indeed belonged among the doctrines to be condemned. Yet, the physician Cristofano had assured me that astrology could do much for medical practice, and was therefore a good and useful thing. That was why, torn between such conflicting views, I had thought to ask Robleda to enlighten and counsel me.

"Bravo, my boy, we must always turn to Mother Church when confronting the many and various uncertainties of existence. I can understand that, here in this hostelry, with such comings and goings of travellers, you should have heard speak of the illusions which soothsayers, astrologers and necromancers of all sorts spread among simple souls. You must not listen to such chatter. There exist two forms of astrology, one false and one true. The first sets out, on the basis of men's date of birth, to foretell the events in their lives and their future behaviour. This is a false and heretical doctrine, which, as you know, has long been forbidden. There is, however, a good and true astrology, the aim of which is to investigate the power of the stars through the investigation of nature, for the purpose, not of prediction, but the accumulation of knowledge. And if one thing is absolutely certain, it is that the stars do influence things here on earth."

In the first place, declared Robleda, glad of the opportunity to hold forth and to show off his science, we have the ebb and flow of the tides, known to all and caused by the mysterious influence of the moon. Likewise, mention should be made of the metals in the deep bowels of the earth, reached neither by the light nor the heat of the sun, and which must therefore be produced thanks to the influence of the stars. Many other experiences, too, (which he could have listed *ad abundantiam*) would be difficult to explain without admitting the intervention of celestial influences. Even that modest little plant, penny-royal (or *Mentha pulegium*), according to Cicero in *De Divinatione*, flowers only at the winter solstice—on the shortest day of the year. Other demonstrations of the power of heavenly bodies over bodies terrestrial could be drawn from meteorology: the rising and setting of the seven stars situated at the head of the constellation of Taurus, which the Greeks called the Hyades, are usually accompanied by abundant rainfall. And

what can be said of the animal kingdom? It is well known that, with
the waxing and waning of the moon, oysters, crabs and other similar
creatures lose vital energy and vigour. What Cristofano had said was,
moreover, true: Hippocrates and other highly skilful physicians knew
that dramatic shifts took place in the progression of illnesses at the
solstices and equinoxes. All of this was, said the Jesuit, in accordance with the teaching of the angelic doctor, Saint Thomas, and
with that of Aristotle, in the *Meteora*, and was confirmed by many
other philosophers, including Domingo Soto, Iavello, Dominique
Bagnes, and I could have learned far more, had I read *The True and
False Astrology*, a wise and truthful volume by his brother Jesuit
Giovanni Battista Grassetti; which had gone to press only a few months
previously.

"But if, as you say, good astrology is not in conflict with the Christian religion," I objected, "then there must exist a Christian astrology."

"And it does indeed exist," replied Robleda, now indulging himself in the display of his own knowledge, "and it is a pity that I do not
have with me the *Enriched Christian Zodiac or the Twelve Signs of Divine
Predestination*, a work of the purest doctrine and the product of the
ingenuity of my brother Jeremiah Drexel, published in this holy city
some forty years ago."

In that volume, explained Robleda, the twelve signs of the astrological tradition were at last replaced by as many symbols of the
One True Religion: a burning candle, a skull, a golden ciborium of
the Eucharist, a bare, unveiled altar, a rosebush, a fig tree, a tobacco
plant, a cypress, two lances conjoined with a crown of olive leaves, a
scourge, with fasces, an anchor and a shield.

"And would these be the signs of the Christian zodiac?" I inquired,
full of wonderment.

"More than that: each of these is the symbol of the eternal values
of the Faith. The burning candle represents the inner light of the
immortal soul, as it is written *Lucerna pedibus meis verbum tuum et lumen
semitis meis*, the cranium symbolises meditation upon death, the golden
ciborium represents the frequency of Confession and Communion,
the altar... Look, you have dropped something."

In drawing the rosary from my pocket, some of the leaves found
by Ugonio and Ciacconio, which I kept in the same pocket, had fallen
to the ground.

"Oh, it is nothing," I lied. "It is… a curious spice which they gave me at the market on the Piazza Navona a few weeks ago."

"Give it to me," quoth Robleda, almost tearing one of the leaves from my hand. He turned it over several times in his hand, visibly astonished.

"How curious," said he, at length. "I wonder how it came to be here."

"Why?"

"It is a plant that does not grow in Europe. It comes from far overseas, from Peru in the Western Indies."

"And what is it called?"

"*Mamacoca.*"

Padre Robleda then told me the surprising story of *mamacoca*, an unusual little plant which was to have much importance in the events of the days that followed.

In the beginning, he informed me, when the Western Indies were conquered and the local savages (followers of false religions and cultivators of blasphemy) duly subjugated, no sooner had the Jesuit missionaries undertaken the holy work of evangelisation than they passed at once to the study of the innumerable varieties of plants of the New World. It was an endless universe: while the ancient and authoritative *Materia Medica* of Dioscurides mentioned some three hundred plants in all, the physician Francisco Hernández had in the seventeen volumes of his *Historia Natural de las Indias* counted over three thousand plant species.

In the midst of all these marvellous discoveries, grave dangers were however concealed. It was in fact impossible for the colonists to distinguish between plants and drugs, between infusions and poisons, and, in the native population, between physicians and necromancers. The villages abounded in wizards who swore that, through the power of herbs and roots, they could raise the Demon or foretell the future.

"Like the astrologers!" I exclaimed, hoping to discover some connection with the events which had taken place at the Donzello.

"No, no, astrology has nothing to do with this," replied Robleda, disappointing my hopes. "I am speaking of far graver matters."

According to the magicians, it seems, every single plant could be used in two ways: to cure an illness or to see the Devil. And in the Indies, there seemed to abound plants suited to the second purpose.

Donanacal (thus, Padre Robleda seemed to me to pronounce the exotic name), which the Indians called the "wonder mushroom" was held to be able to bring about communication with Satan. The same suspicion hung over *oliuchi* seeds and another mushroom known as *peyote*. A plant called *paté* was used by the magicians to listen to the fallacious oracles of the Inferno.

The Inquisition therefore decided to burn all the fields cultivated with forbidden plants, along with, from time to time, a few magicians. But the fields were too extensive and the magicians too numerous.

"Fears arose for the integrity of Christian doctrine!" whispered Robleda, his voice burdened with concern, waving the leaf of *mamacoca* under my nose as though to put me on guard against the Evil One.

Because of these accursed plants, the tale resumed, even converted and baptised savages blasphemed against the holy name of the doctors of the Church. Some of these held that Saint Bartholomew had travelled to America for the sole purpose of discovering plants possessed of miraculous powers, and that Saint Thomas had also preached in Brazil, where he had found trees, the leaves of which were mortal poison, but that he had toasted these on fire and had transformed them into a wonder-working medicine. The natives converted to our faith then used a number of potent drugs during prayer: something obviously prohibited by doctrine. In sum, new heresies spread, which were both unusual and most pernicious.

"There were even those who taught new gospels," said Robleda in a trembling voice, returning the little leaf to me with an expression of disgust, as though it were pestiferous. "In these blasphemous gospels," he continued, crossing himself, "it was said that Christ, as soon as he attained manhood, had been compelled to flee because the devils had attacked him in order to steal his soul. Mary, when she returned home and did not find her son, mounted a donkey and set out in search of him. Soon, however, she lost her way and entered a forest where, out of hunger and desperation, she felt herself growing ever more faint. Jesus saw her in that state and came to her aid: he blessed a *mamacoca* bush which grew nearby. The donkey was drawn to that bush and would not leave it; thus, Mary understood that it had been blessed for her. She chewed a few leaves and, as if by a miracle, felt neither hunger nor weariness. She continued on her way until she came to a village where some women offered her food. Mary replied that she was not hungry and showed the blessed branch of *mamacoca*. She handed a leaf to the women, saying: 'Sow this, it will put forth roots and a bush will grow.' The women did as Mary had said and four days later a bush sprang up, laden with fruit. From the fruit came the seeds for the cultivation of *mamacoca*, of which women have been devotees ever since."

"But that is monstrous!" I commented. "Thus to blaspheme against the Madonna and Our Lord Jesus Christ, saying that they fed on witches' plants..."

"You have spoken well, it is indeed monstrous," said Robleda wiping the perspiration from his cheeks and his brow, "nor was that an end to it."

The prohibited specialities were so numerous that the colonists (and even the Jesuits, said Robleda resignedly) were completely unable to maintain any control over events. Who could safely distinguish *oliuchi* from *donanacal*, *peyote* from *cocoba*, *paté* from *cola*, opium from *maté*, or *guarana* from *mamacoca*?

"Was *mamacoca* used for prayer, too?"

"No, no," he replied with an air of slight embarrassment, "it was used for another purpose."

The leaves of that seemingly innocent bush, said the Jesuit, had the stupefying power to annul weariness, remove all hunger and make those who took it euphoric and vigorous. *Mamacoca* also, as the Jesuits themselves had discovered, calmed pain, gave new strength to broken bones, warmed the limbs and healed old wounds which were beginning to become infested with worms. Last, (and perhaps, according to Padre Robleda, most important), thanks to *mamacoca*, workers, farm hands and slaves were able to work for hours on end without tiring.

Among the conquistadores, there were those who thought that this plague should be exploited rather than extirpated. *Mamacoca* enabled the Indians to stand up to the most exhausting conditions; and the Jesuit missionaries in the Indies, observed Padre Robleda, were in constant need of labourers.

Consumption of the plant was therefore made lawful. Native workers were paid in leaves of the plant, which for them were worth more than money, silver, even gold. The clergy had permission to raise tithes on the crop and the revenues of many priests and bishops were paid thanks to the sale of *mamacoca*.

"But was this not an instrument of Satan?" I objected in astonishment.

"Ah, well…" stammered Padre Robleda, "the situation was very complex, and a choice had to be made. By granting the natives greater freedom to use *mamacoca*, more missions could be built, the better to bring them civilisation, in other words, to win over more souls to the cause of Christ."

I turned over the little leaf in the palm of my hand. I tore it and brought it to my nose, sniffing at it. It seemed to be a thoroughly ordinary plant.

"And how could this have come to Rome?" I asked.

"Perhaps some Spanish ship brought a cargo of it to Portugal. From there, it will have made its way to Genoa, or Flanders. What more can I say? I recognised the plant because a brother showed me some, and I have since seen it mentioned in letters from missionaries in the Indies. Perhaps the person who gave it to you knows more."

I was on the point of leaving when one last question came to mind.

"Just one more question, Padre. How does one consume *mamacoca*?"

"For heaven's sake, my boy, I trust that you do not intend to use it?"

"No, Padre, I am simply curious."

"Generally speaking, the savages chew it, after spreading saliva and some ashes on the leaves; but I do not exclude that there may be other ways of taking it."

⁊᭬᳓

I descended the stairs to prepare luncheon, not without first making a passing visit to the apartment of Abbot Melani to tell him what I had learned from Padre Robleda.

"Interesting, how very interesting," commented Atto, with an expression of deep absorption. "At present, however, I have no idea where this all leads. We shall have to reflect on the matter."

In the kitchen, I found Cristofano, as usual, shuttling back and forth between the cellars and the stoves. He attended to the preparation of the most diverse and, to tell the truth, singular remedies for the pestilence which held Bedfordi in its thrall. In those days, I had seen a growing ferment in the Sienese physician's activities with spices; and now, he seemed to be trying almost everything. I had even seen him finish off my master's reserves of game, on the grounds that it would go bad and that concealing its taste with spices, as Pellegrino did, was lethal to health. Yet, during the night, he had seized partridges, stock doves, woodcock, quails and hazel-hens, for the sole purpose of stuffing them with Damascene and Amarena plums, whereupon he placed the birds in a white canvas bag and put it under a press, thus extracting from the delicate meat a beverage with which he hoped to restore the poor Englishman to health. Hitherto, all his attempts to find an efficacious *remedium* appeared to have come to nothing. Yet, young Bedfordi still lived.

Cristofano said that he found the other guests to be in rather good health, with the exception of Domenico Stilone Priàso and Pompeo Dulcibeni: the Neapolitan had awoken with the first signs of a cold sore on his lips, while the elderly Marchigiano was suffering from an attack of the piles, doubtless caused by the dinner based on cows' teats. For both these cases, he explained, the remedy was the same: we would therefore prepare a caustic.

"It mortifies putrid and corrosive ulcers such as, for example, itching herpes and other rashes and eruptions," he pronounced, and then ordered me: "*Recipe*: the strongest vinegar."

He then mixed the vinegar with crystalline arsenic, sal-ammoniac and sublimated quicksilver. He ground the lot and put it to boil in a beaker.

"Good. Now, we need to wait until half of the vinegar has evaporated. Then I shall go up to Stilone Priàso and dry his blisters with the caustic. You, meanwhile, prepare luncheon: I have already selected a few turkeys, suited to the needs of our guests. Boil them with parsnips until they are light brown in colour and serve them up with a broth of grated bread."

I set to work. As soon as the caustic was ready, Cristofano gave me my last instructions before climbing the stairs to visit Stilone Priàso. "I shall have need of you with Dulcibeni. Meanwhile, I shall help you to serve the meal, so that you will soon be free, given the propensity of the guests at this hostelry to chatter with you for rather too long," he concluded meaningfully.

After luncheon, we went to feed Bedfordi. Thereafter, we were not a little busy with my master. Pellegrino seemed not to appreciate the effluvia of the cleansing meal personally prepared for him by the physician, which did in truth have the appearance of a curious, greyish porridge. My master at least seemed more lively. The slow but progressive improvements of the last few days did not disappoint my hopes that he might soon recover completely. He sniffed at the porridge, then looked all around him, closed his right hand into a fist and then raised it, rhythmically pointing his thumb at his mouth. This was the unmistakeable gesture with which Pellegrino was accustomed to mime his desire for a good drink of wine.

I was on the point of inviting him to be more reasonable and patient for at least a few more days, but Cristofano stopped me with his hand.

"Are you not aware of his greater presence of mind? Spirits call for spirits: we can certainly allow him half a glass of red wine."

"But he made free with the wine until the day when he fell sick."

"Precisely. The point is that wine should be consumed in moderation: it is nutritious, it aids the digestion, it produces blood, it comforts and calms, brings joy, clarity of mind and vivacity. So go down to the cellar and fetch a little red wine, my boy," said he, with a trace of impatience in his tone, "For a little beaker will do Pellegrino the world of good."

While I was descending the stairs, the doctor called after me "Please make sure that it is chilled! In Messina, when they began to use snow to chill wine and food, all pestiferous fevers caused by constipation of the first veins ceased forthwith. Since then, a thousand fewer have died each year!"

I reassured Cristofano: in addition to bread and leathern bottles full of water, we were kept regularly supplied with pressed snow.

I returned from the cellars with a little carafe of good red wine and a glass. Hardly had I filled it than the doctor explained that my master's failing had been an immoderate consumption of wine, and that could turn a man raving mad, stupid, lustful, garrulous and even murderous. Temperate drinkers included Augustus and Caesar; while winebibbers included Claudius, Tiberius, Nero and Alexander, who, out of drunkenness, would sleep two days in a row.

Thereupon, he grasped the glass and downed half of it in a single gulp. "It is not too bad; both robust and smooth," said he, raising the glass with the few remaining drops in it and observing its fine ruby colour. "And, as I was saying, the right dose of wine changes the vices of nature into their opposites, so that the impious man becomes pious, the miser, liberal, the proud, humble, the lazy, energetic, the timid, bold: mental taciturnity and sloth are transformed into astuteness and eloquence."

He emptied the glass, refilled it and then emptied it in one rapid gulp.

"But beware of drinking after fulfilling one's bodily functions or after the sexual act," he warned me, while wiping his lips with the back of one hand and pouring himself a third dose with the other. "It is best to drink after consuming bitter almonds and cabbage or, following one's meal, peaches, quince jelly, pomegranates and other astringents."

He then administered the few remaining sips to poor Pellegrino.

Thereupon, we repaired to Dulcibeni's chamber, where the latter seemed somewhat irked to see me at Cristofano's side. I soon understood why: the physician had asked him to uncover his private parts. The old man glanced at me and complained. I understood that I had violated his privacy, and turned around. Cristofano assured him that he would not need to expose himself to my sight and that he should not be ashamed before a physician. He then requested that he kneel on all fours upon the bed, leaning on his elbows, so that his sores would be well exposed. Dulcibeni consented unwillingly, not without first helping himself to the contents of his snuff box. Cristofano made me squat before Dulcibeni, so as to be able to grasp him firmly by the shoulders. The doctor would soon be beginning to anoint the haemorrhoids with his caustic, and a false movement could cause the liquid to flow onto his cullions or his tail, which would be cruelly injured thereby. When the physician warned him, Dulcibeni suppressed a shiver and took a pinch of his indispensable snuff.

Cristofano set to work. Initially, as expected, Dulcibeni struggled with the burning pain and emitted brief, restrained moans. In order to distract him, the doctor tried to engage him in conversation, asking from what city he came, how he had come to the Donzello from Naples and so on, all questions which I had prudently avoided putting to him. Dulcibeni (as Abbot Melani had foreseen) always replied in monosyllables, letting one conversational opening after another die away without supplying a single element of information that might be of use to me. The doctor then turned to the dominant topic of those days, namely the siege of Vienna, and asked him what they were saying about that in Naples.

"I would not know," he replied laconically, as I had expected.

"But there has been talk of this for months, all over Europe. Who do you expect to win, the Christians or the Infidels?"

"Both, and neither," said he with evident distaste.

I wondered whether, on this occasion too, Dulcibeni might launch into another soliloquy on the topic which now seemed so to irritate him, once the physician and I had left the apartment.

"What do you mean?" insisted Cristofano, while his manipulations drew a hoarse cry from Dulcibeni. "In a war, for as long as no treaty is concluded, there is always a victor and a loser."

The patient reared up and it was only by grasping him by the collar that I could hold him down. I could not understand whether it was the pain that so irritated him: the fact is that, this time, Dulcibeni preferred an interlocutor of flesh and blood to his reflection in the mirror.

"But what do you know of it? There is so much talk of Christians and of Ottomans, of Catholics and Protestants, of the faithful and the Infidels, as though the faithful and the Infidels really existed. Whereas, in reality, all alike scatter the seeds of hatred among the members of the Church: here, the Roman Catholics, there the Gallicans, and so on and so forth. But greed and the thirst for power profess no faith in anything but themselves."

"But I beg of you!" interrupted Cristofano. "To say that Christians and Turks are one and the same thing! What if Padre Robleda should hear you?"

Dulcibeni, however, was not listening to him. While he angrily sniffed the contents of his precious box (part of which, however, fell on the floor) his voice was sometimes coloured by rage, as though in protest at the painful burning of the sores which Cristofano was inflicting upon him. While holding him firm, I endeavoured not to look too directly at him, which was no easy thing to do, given the position which I was constrained to adopt.

At a certain juncture, the austere patient began to inveigh against the Bourbons and the Habsburgs, but also against the Stuarts and the House of Orange, as I had already heard him do in his bitter and solitary invective against their incestuous marriages. When the physician, good Tuscan that he was, uttered a few words in defence of the Bourbons (who were related to the Grand Duke of Tuscany, his prince), he checked him, raging with particular rancour against France.

"To what a pass have the antique feudal nobility come, they who were the mark and pride of that nation! The nobles who crowd Versailles today, what do you suppose they are now, but the King's bastards? Condé, Conti, Beaufort, the Duke of Maine, the Duke of Vendôme, the Duke of Toulouse... Princes of the Blood, they call them. But what blood? That of the whores who happened to pass through the Sun King's bed or that of his grandfather Henry of Navarre."

The latter, continued Dulcibeni, had marched on Chartres for the sole purpose of laying his hands upon Gabrielle d'Estrées who, before granting her favours, demanded that her father be made governor of the city and her brother, bishop. D'Estrées succeeded in selling herself to the King for her weight in gold, despite the fact that she was a veteran of the beds of Henry III, (from whom old d'Estrées had extracted six thousand écus), the banker Zamet, the Duke of Guise, the Duke of Longueville and the Duke of Bellegarde. And all that despite the ambiguous fame of her grandmother, the mistress of Francis I, Pope Clement VI and Charles de Valois.

"Should one be surprised," asked Dulcibeni, "if the great feudal lords of France wanted to purge the kingdom of such abominations, or if they stabbed Henry of Navarre? But it was already too late! The blind power of sovereigns has ever since despoiled and robbed them without mercy."

"It seems to me that you are exaggerating," retorted Cristofano, raising his eyes from his delicate work and anxiously observing his overheated patient.

In my eyes, too, Dulcibeni seemed to be exaggerating. Of course, he was exhausted by the painful burns inflicted by the caustic. Yet, the doctor's calm and almost distracted objections really did not merit those reactions of boiling wrath. The almost febrile trembling of his members suggested that, in reality, Dulcibeni was prey to a singular state of nervous overexcitement. He was calmed only by repeated pinches of snuff. I again promised myself that I would report all this as soon as possible to Abbot Melani.

"If I am to believe you," Cristofano then added, "one would conclude that there is nothing good at Versailles or indeed at any other court."

"Versailles, you speak to me of Versailles; where the noble blood of the fathers is daily defiled! What has become of the cavaliers of old? There they are, all herded together by the Most Christian King and his usurer Colbert in a single palace, squandering their inheritance on balls and hunting parties, instead of defending the fiefs of their glorious ancestors."

"But thus Louis XIV put an end to plotting," protested Cristofano. "The King his grandfather died by an assassin's dagger, his father died of poison and he himself as a child was threatened by the nobles in the Fronde revolt!"

"It is true. Thus, however, he has taken possession of their riches. And he has not understood that the nobility, who once were spread throughout France, may well have threatened the Sovereign but were also his best protection."

"What do you mean?"

"Every sovereign can control his kingdom only if he has a vassal in each province. The Most Christian King has done the opposite: he has united the aristocracy in a single body. And a body has only one neck. When the day comes that the people want to cut through it, a single blow will suffice."

"Come, come! That can surely never happen," said Cristofano forcefully. "The people of Paris will never behead the nobles. And the King..."

Dulcibeni ranted on without listening to the doctor: "History," he almost screamed, causing me to give a start, "will have no pity for those crowned jackals, sated with human blood and infanticide; evil oppressors of a people of slaves, whom they have sent to the slaughter every time that their homicidal fury has been unleashed by whatever their low, incestuous passion lusted after."

Every single syllable he pronounced with inflamed rage, his lips livid and contracted, and his nose all covered in powder from his many inhalations.

Cristofano gave up attempting to answer him: we seemed to be witnessing the outburst of a deranged mind. Besides, the physician had almost completed his painful duty and silently arranged pieces of fine gauze between the buttocks of the Marchigiano who, with a great sigh, let himself collapse exhausted on his side. And thus he remained, *sans culotte*, until we had left the room.

ॐॐ

No sooner had I informed him of Dulcibeni's lengthy harangue than Atto had no more doubts: "Padre Robleda was right: if he is not a Jansenist, no one is."

"And why are you so sure?"

"For two reasons: first, the Jansenists detest the Jesuits; and in that respect I think that Dulcibeni's discourse against the Society of Jesus could hardly have been plainer: the Jesuits are spies, traitors, papal favourites, and so on: the usual propaganda against the Order of Saint Ignatius."

"Do you mean that it is untrue?"

"On the contrary, it is all perfectly true, but only the Jansenists have the courage to say so publicly. Our Dulcibeni is indeed afraid of nothing: he is all the more unafraid in that the only Jesuit in the vicinity is that coward Robleda."

"And the Jansenists?"

"The Jansenists say that the Church of the origins was purer, like the torrents near a spring. They hold that several truths of the gospel are no longer as evident as they once were. To return to the Church of the origins, one must submit to the severest of trials, penances, humiliations and renunciations; and while bearing all this, one must place oneself in the merciful hands of God, forever renouncing the world and sacrificing oneself to divine love."

"Padre Robleda told me that the Jansenists like to remain in solitude…"

"Correct. They tend towards asceticism, severe and chastened customs: you will have noticed how Dulcibeni boils with indignation whenever Cloridia approaches…" sniggered the abbot. "It goes without saying that the Jansenists utterly detest the Jesuits, who permit themselves every freedom of conscience and action. I know that in Naples there is an important circle of followers of Jansenius."

"So that is why Dulcibeni settled there."

"Perhaps. It is a pity that since the very beginning, for a number of theological reasons which I shall not now attempt to explain to you, the Jansenists have been accused of heresy."

"Yes, I know. Dulcibeni could be a heretic."

"Forget that. It is not what matters. Let us move on to the second motive for reflection."

"Namely?"

"All that hatred for princes and sovereigns. It is… how could I put it? It is all too Jansenist a sentiment. The obsession with kings who commit incest, marry harlots, beget bastard children; and the nobles who betray their elevated destiny and grow soft. These are themes which lead to rebellion, to disorder and turbulence."

"And so?"

"Nothing. It seems curious to me; where do those words come from? And above all, where can they lead? We know much about him, but at the same time, we know too little."

"Perhaps such ideas have something to do with the business about three to dine, the brothers and the farm."

"Do you mean the strange expressions which we heard in Tiracorda's house? Perhaps. We shall see tonight."

Night the Seventh
BETWEEN *the* 17TH & 18TH SEPTEMBER, 1683

✠

From Doctor Tiracorda's cabinet, tremulous candlelight filtered, while Dulcibeni sat down and laid on the table a bottle full of a green-ish liquid. The doctor banged down on the board the goblets which had on the last occasion remained empty, because of the breaking of the bottle.

Atto and I crouched in the shadows of the next room, as we had done the night before. Our incursion into the house of Tiracorda had proved more difficult than expected: for a long while, one of the housemaids tidied up the kitchen, so that we were unable to leave the stables. Once the maid had ascended to the first floor, we tarried no little time in order to be quite certain that no one was moving from room to room any longer. While we were still waiting, Dulcibeni at last knocked at the door; the master of the house welcomed him and led him up to the study on the first floor, where we were now eavesdropping upon the pair.

We had missed the beginning of the conversation, and the two were once again testing one another with incomprehensible phrases. Tiracorda sipped placidly at the greenish beverage.

"Then I shall repeat," said the doctor. "A white field, a black seed, five sowers and two directing them. It is ab-so-lute-ly clear."

"It is no use, no use…" said Dulcibeni, defensively.

At that moment, by my side Atto Melani gave a slight start and I saw that he was silently cursing.

"Then, I shall tell you," said Tiracorda. "Writing."

"Writing?"

"But of course! The white field is the paper, the seed is the ink, the five sowers are the fingers of the hand and the two who direct the work are the eyes. Not bad, eh? Ha ha ha ha ha! Haaaaaa ha ha ha ha!"

The old *Archiater* once again gave himself up to ribald laughter.

"Remarkable," was Dulcibeni's sole comment.

At that moment, I too understood: enigmas. Tiracorda and Dulcibeni were amusing themselves with riddles. Even the mysterious phrases which we had overheard last night were certainly part of that same innocent entertainment. I looked at Atto and his countenance mirrored my own disappointment: once more we had been racking our brains for nothing. Dulcibeni, however, seemed to appreciate this pastime far less than his companion, and tried to change the subject as he had done during our previous visit.

"Bravo, Giovanni, bravo," said he, again filling the glasses. "But tell me now, how was he today?"

"Oh, nothing new. And did you sleep well?"

"For as long as I was able to," said Dulcibeni gravely.

"I understand, I understand," said Tiracorda, draining his glass and promptly refilling it. "You are so troubled," continued the physician. "But there are still a couple of things which you have not told me. Excuse me for dwelling on the past, but why did you not ask the Odescalchi for help with your daughter?"

"I did, I did," replied Dulcibeni. "I have already told you. But they said that they could do nothing for me. And then…"

"Ah yes, then came that nasty incident, the beating, the fall…" Tiracorda recalled.

"It was no fall, Giovanni. They struck me on the neck and then they threw me down from the second floor. It was a miracle that I escaped with my life," said Dulcibeni, somewhat impatiently, once again filling his friend's glass.

"Yes, yes, please pardon me, I should have remembered that from your collar; it is just that I am rather weary…" Tiracorda's voice was growing drowsy.

"Do not excuse yourself, Giovanni, but listen. Now it is your turn. I have three good ones."

Dulcibeni took out a book and began to read in a warm, resonant voice:

> To tell you from A unto Zed, I intend,
> What to name I would always presume;
> And if I should claim to have Names for it all,
> Why, then I'm but Ragges and Spume.
> The one thing that counts is to 'wait the Boys' Call;
> 'Tis for them that my Stuff I consume.
> And you, Masters, who tell 'em of me to inquire,
> Know well that I am the good Son of a Friar.

The reading continued with two, three, four more bizarre little rhymes, with brief pauses in between.

"What say you, Giovanni?" asked Dulcibeni at length, after reading the series of riddles.

The only reply was a rhythmic bronchial murmur. Tiracorda was asleep.

At that juncture, something unforeseen occurred. Instead of rousing his friend, who had obviously drunk several glasses too many, Dulcibeni returned the book to his pocket and tiptoed to the secret closet behind Tiracorda's back, from which we had seen the latter take two little glasses the night before. Dulcibeni opened the door to the cupboard and began to busy himself with a number of vases and containers of spices. He then pulled out a ceramic vase on which were painted the waters of a pond, a few aquatic plants and strange little animals which I was unable to identify. There were little holes in the sides of the vase, as though to allow air to enter. Dulcibeni raised the vase to the candlelight and, removing its lid, looked into it. He then replaced the vase in the cupboard and began to rummage about in there.

"Giovanni!"

A woman's voice, strident and most disagreeable, came from the staircase and seemed to be approaching. Paradisa, the terrible wife of Tiracorda was beyond any doubt arriving. For a few instants, Dulcibeni stood as though petrified. Tiracorda, who seemed to be fast asleep, gave a start. Dulcibeni probably succeeded in closing the secret cupboard before the doctor awoke and surprised him searching among his things. Atto and I could not, however, observe the scene: yet again, we were caught between two fires. We looked all around, in desperation.

"Giovanniiii!" repeated Paradisa, drawing ever nearer. In Tiracorda's study, too, the alarm must be at its height: we heard a discreet but frenetic shifting of chairs, tables, doors, bottles and glasses; the doctor was hiding the evidence of his alcoholic misdeed.

"Giovanni!" declaimed Paradisa at last with a voice the colour of a clouded sky, as she entered the antechamber. At that precise moment, Abbot Melani and I were face to the ground among the legs of a row of chairs against the wall.

"Oh sinners, oh wretches, oh lost souls," Paradisa began to chant, solemn as a priestess, as she drew near to the door of Tiracorda's study.

"But, my dear wife, here is our friend Pompeo..."

"Silence, child of Satan!" screamed Paradisa. "My nose does not deceive me."

As we could hear from our uncomfortable position, the woman began to turn the study upside down, moving chairs and tables, opening and noisily slamming doors, cupboards and drawers, and knocking statuettes and ornaments one against the other in her search for proof of misconduct. Tiracorda and Dulcibeni strove in vain to calm her, assuring her that never, but never had it so much as entered their minds to drink anything but water.

"Your mouth, let me smell your mouth!" screeched Paradisa. Her husband's refusal provoked yet more screams and a great to-do.

It was at that moment that we resolved to slip out from under the chairs where we were hiding and to flee in silence but with all possible speed.

Șș

"Women, women, curses. And we are even worse than they..."

Two or three minutes had passed and we were already underground, commenting upon the events which had just transpired. Atto was furious.

"I shall tell you what Tiracorda and Dulcibeni's mysteries were all about. The first one, that which you heard last night, do you remember it? One had to guess: what was there in common between 'Enter dumb into here' and 'Number to dine: three'. Solution: it is an anagram."

"An anagram?"

"Of course. The same letters in a sentence so disposed as to form another one. The second was a game to test one's presence of mind: a father has seven daughters; if each daughter has a brother, how many children has that father?

"Seven, multiplied by two: fourteen."

"Not even in your dreams! She has eight: as Tiracorda said, the brother of the one is the brother of the others. These are all silly things: that which Dulcibeni read this evening, which begins, 'To tell you from A unto Zed, I intend...' is utterly simple. The answer is: the dictionary."

"And the others?" I asked, stupefied by Atto's prompt wit.

"What does it matter?" he fumed. "I am not a seer. What we need to know is why Dulcibeni was trying to get Tiracorda drunk and then rummaging in his secret cupboard. And that we would have known, had it not been for the arrival of that madwoman Paradisa."

At that moment, I did indeed recall that little was known of Signora Paradisa in the Via dell'Orso. In the light of what we had seen and heard in Tiracorda's house, it was perhaps no accident that the woman almost never left the house.

"And now, what shall we do?" I asked, observing the rapid pace at which Atto was preceding me on the way back to the hostelry.

"We shall do the one thing that remains possible if we are to elucidate matters: we shall take a look in Pompeo Dulcibeni's chamber."

The one risk of such an operation was, of course, the sudden return of Dulcibeni. We, however, trusted to our own celerity, and to the relative slowness of the elderly Marchigiano, who would also need some time to disengage himself from Tiracorda's house.

"Pardon me, Signor Atto," I asked, after a few minutes' hard march, "but what do you expect to find in the apartment of Pompeo Dulcibeni?"

"What stupid questions you sometimes ask. Here we are facing one of the most tremendous mysteries in the history of France, and you ask what we shall find! And how should I know? Surely, something more about the imbroglio in which we are now caught up: Dulcibeni, friend of Tiracorda; Tiracorda, physician to the Pope; the Pope, enemy of Louis XIV; Devizé, pupil of Corbetta; Corbetta, friend of Maria Teresa and Mademoiselle; Louis XIV, enemy of Fouquet; Fouquet, travelling with Devizé; Fouquet, friend of the abbot who stands before you… what more do you want?

Atto needed to unburden himself, and to do so he must needs talk.

"And besides," he continued, "Dulcibeni's apartment was also that of the Superintendent, or have you forgotten?"

He left me no time to reply, but added: "Poor Nicolas, his destiny was to be searched, even after his death."

"What do you mean?"

"Louis XIV had the Superintendent's cell searched continuously and in every possible manner throughout the twenty years of his imprisonment at Pinerol."

"Whatever was he looking for?" I asked with a jolt of surprise.

Melani stopped and, singing with all his heart, intoned a sad air by Master Rossi:

Infelice pensier,
chi ne conforta?
Ohimé!
Chi ne consiglia?…*

Sighing, he adjusted his justaucorps, wiped his forehead and straightened his red stockings.

"Would that I knew what the King was looking for!" he answered disconsolately. "But I must needs explain: there are still a number of things which you should know," he added, after recovering his calm.

It was thus that, in order to make up for my ignorance, Atto Melani recounted to me the last chapter of the story of Nicolas Fouquet.

When the trial was over and he had been condemned to imprisonment for the rest of his days, Fouquet left Paris forever, bound for the fortress of Pinerol, his carriage making its way through the crowd which tearfully acclaimed him. He was accompanied by the musketeer d'Artagnan. Pinerol was situated in Piedmontese territory, on the border of the kingdom. Many wondered why so distant a place should have been chosen, and one which was, moreover, perilously close to the states of the Duke of Savoy. More than flight, however, the King feared Fouquet's many friends, and Pinerol represented the only way of removing him forever from their assistance.

As his gaoler, a musketeer was appointed from the escort which had accompanied Fouquet from one prison to another throughout the trial: Benigne d'Auvergne, Lord of Saint-Mars, personally recommended to the King by d'Artagnan. Saint-Mars was assigned eighty soldiers to guard one prisoner: Fouquet. He would report directly to the Minister for War, Le Tellier, Marquis de Louvois.

Fouquet's imprisonment was most rigorous: every communication with the outside world was forbidden him, whether oral or written: there were to be no visits of any kind or for whatever reason. He was not even permitted to take a breath of air within the confines of the fortress. He could read, but only such works as the King permitted, and one book at a time. Above all, he must not write: once returned, each book read by the prisoner was to be leafed through thoroughly by the faithful Saint-Mars, in case Fouquet might have annotated something or underlined some word. His Majesty charged himself with seeing to clothing, which was sent to Pinerol with each change of season.

* Unhappy thought, / Who can give comfort for't? / Alas! / Who can give counsel?

In that remote citadel, the climate was hard. Fouquet was not allowed to walk. Constrained to absolute immobility, the Superintendent's health declined rapidly. Despite this, he was denied the care of his personal physician, Pecquet. Fouquet did, however, obtain herbs with which to care unaided for his health. He was also allowed the company of two of his valets, who had agreed out of loyalty to share their master's fate.

Louis XIV knew how fascinating Fouquet's mind was. He could not refuse him the comforts of the Faith, but he recommended that his confessors should be changed frequently, lest he should win them over and use them to communicate with the outside world.

In June 1665, lightning struck the fortress and caused the explosion of a powder store. There were many deaths. Fouquet and his valets jumped out of a window. The chances of surviving that leap into the void were minimal; yet all three emerged unharmed. When the news reached Paris, poems circulated which commented upon the occurrence and called it a miracle: God wished to spare the Superintendent and to show the King a sign of His will. Many took up the cry: "Free Fouquet!" The King, however, did not yield; on the contrary, he persecuted whoever clamoured too loudly.

It was necessary to rebuild the fortress. In the meanwhile, Fouquet spent a year in the house of the Commissary for War of Pinerol, and then in another prison.

In the course of the work, Saint-Mars discovered among the ashes of Fouquet's furniture of what the Superintendent's intellect was capable. Louvois and the King were at once sent the little treasures of ingenuity found in the Squirrel's cell: notes written by Fouquet using a few capon's bones as a pen and as ink a little red wine mixed with lamp black. The prisoner had even managed to create an invisible ink and to find a hiding place for his writings in the back of a chair.

"But what was he trying to write?" I asked, shocked and moved by these pitiful stratagems.

"That has never been discovered," replied Atto. "All that was intercepted was sent to the King in great secret."

From that moment onwards, the King ordered that he should be searched thoroughly every day. Only reading then remained to him. He was allowed a Bible, a history of France, a few Italian books, a dictionary of French rhymes and the works of Saint Bonaventure (while those of Saint Jerome and Saint Augustine were not permitted him).

He began to teach Latin and the rudiments of pharmacy to one of his valets.

But Fouquet was the Squirrel in all things: his astuteness and industry could not be bridled. Goaded on by Louvois, who knew the Superintendent well and could not believe that he would allow himself to be so easily defeated, Saint-Mars made a careful inspection of his underclothing. He was found to be wearing little ribbons of lace trimmings covered in minute writing, and many inscriptions were also found on the back of the lining of his doublet. The King at once ordered that Fouquet was to be issued solely with black clothing and undergarments. Towels and napkins were numbered so as to avoid the possibility that he might take possession of them.

Saint-Mars laid the blame on the two valets who gave him no peace with their requests and who always strove to favour their master, to whom they were devoted body and soul.

The years passed, but the King's almost obsessional fear that Fouquet might somehow get away from him in no way lessened. Nor was he mistaken: towards the end of 1669 an attempt to help him escape was found out. It is not known who organised it, perhaps the family, but it was rumoured that Madame de Sévigné and Mademoiselle de Scudéry were not unconnected with it. The person who paid the price for this was an old servant, a moving example of fidelity. He was called La Forêt, and he had accompanied the Superintendent at the time of his arrest in Nantes. After the arrest, he had marched for hours and hours to escape the musketeers who had placed a cordon around the city. Thence, he reached the nearest postal stage, whence he rode with all speed to Paris in order to give the grim news of the arrest to Fouquet's pious mother. La Forêt had even gone so far as to wait by the roadside for the carriage bearing his master to Pinerol, so as to be able to salute him for the last time. Even d'Artagnan had been moved, for he had the convoy stopped and allowed the two to exchange a few words.

La Forêt was, then, the only person not to have lost all hope. He arrived at Pinerol in disguise and even succeeded in finding a number of informers within the fortress and communicating with his adored master by gestures, through a window. In the end, his attempt was discovered and the poor man was hanged immediately. Life became hard for Fouquet. His windows were barred. No longer could he see the sky.

His health declined. In 1670, Louvois travelled to Pinerol in person, sent by the King. After six years of refusals and prohibitions, Louis finally consulted the Superintendent's old physician, Pecquet.

"How strange. Did not the King wish to see Fouquet dead?"

"The one thing that is certain is that, from that moment on, Louis seemed to be concerned about the health of the poor Squirrel. Those of the Superintendent's friends who had not fallen into disgrace, like Pomponne (who had just been appointed Secretary of State), Turenne, Chéqui, Bellefonds and Charost, returned to the attack and sent petitions to the Most Christian King. The turning point, however, came later."

In 1671, the number of special prisoners at Pinerol grew to two. Another illustrious captive arrived at the fortress: the Comte de Lauzun.

"Because he had married Mademoiselle, the King's cousin," I interjected, remembering Abbot Melani's previous account.

"Bravo, I see that you have a good memory. And now the tale becomes really interesting."

After subjecting Fouquet to years of isolation, the decision to accord him a prison companion seems inexplicable. Even stranger is the fact that, in the immense fortress, he should have been given the cell next to Fouquet's.

Of Lauzun, all manner of things may be said, but not that he was an ordinary personage. At the outset, he was the youngest scion of a Gascon family, with neither fortune nor skill, a braggart and full of himself, who had, however, the good fortune to be liked by the King when the latter was very young and to become his boon companion. Although only a cheap seducer, he had succeeded in charming Mademoiselle, the very wealthy and very ugly 44-year-old cousin of the King. He was a difficult prisoner, and lost no time in making that quite clear. His attitude was tempestuous, bombastic, insolent; no sooner was he left in his cell than he set fire to it, also damaging a beam in Fouquet's cell. He then gave himself up to painful simulations of sickness or folly, with the clear aim of attempting to escape. Saint-Mars, whose experience as a gaoler was limited to guarding the Superintendent, was unable to tame Lauzun and, faced with such fury, came to call Fouquet "the little lamb".

Very early on (but this was discovered far later) Lauzun succeeded in communicating with Fouquet through a hole in the wall.

"But how is it possible that no one should have realised," I protested incredulously, "what with all the surveillance which Fouquet had to put up with every day?"

"I have asked myself the same question many times," agreed Abbot Melani.

Another year passed. In October 1675 His Majesty authorised Fouquet and his wife to correspond. The couple's letters were, however, first to be read by the King who arrogated himself the right to alter or destroy them. But there was more: without any logical reason, some twelve months later, the King had Fouquet sent a number of books on recent political developments. A little while later, Louvois sent Saint-Mars a letter for the Superintendent, adding that if the prisoner should request writing paper in order to reply, it was to be given to him. And that is what happened: the Superintendent wrote and sent two reports to Louvois.

"What did they contain?"

"No one has succeeded in finding out, although rumours immediately started in Paris that they had been copied throughout the city. Immediately afterwards, however, it became known that Louvois had sent them back to Fouquet, saying that they were of no interest to the King."

This was an inexplicable gesture, commented Melani: first, because if a memorandum is useless, it is simply thrown away; and secondly, because it is practically impossible that Fouquet should not have given the King some good counsel.

"Perhaps they wanted to humiliate him yet again," I speculated.

"Or perhaps the King wanted something from Fouquet which he would not give him."

The concessions, however, continued. In 1674, Louis authorised husband and wife to write to each other twice a year, even though the letters first passed through his hands. The Superintendent's health again worsened and the King became worried: he did not permit him to leave his cell, but had him visited by a physician sent from Paris.

From November 1677, he was at last permitted to take a little air; in whose company? Why, that of Lauzun, of course; and the two were even allowed to converse! With the proviso that Saint-Mars should listen to their every word and faithfully report all that was said.

The King's gracious concessions became more and more numerous. Now, Fouquet even received copies of the *Mercure Galant* and other gazettes. It seemed almost as though Louis wished to keep Fouquet informed of everything important that was happening in France and in Europe. Louvois recommended Saint-Mars to place the accent, in his dealings with the prisoner, on the military victories of the Most Christian King.

In December 1678 Louvois informed Saint-Mars of his intention to hold a free epistolary correspondence with Fouquet: the letters were to be rigorously sealed and secret, so that Saint-Mars' only duty was to see to their delivery.

Scarcely a month later, the astonished gaoler received an aide-mémoire penned by the King in person on the conditions to apply to Fouquet and Lauzun. The two could meet and converse as often as they pleased and could walk not only within the inner fortress but throughout the whole citadel. They could read whatever they wished, and the officers of the garrison were obliged to keep them company if they so desired. They could also request and receive any table games.

A few months passed and another opening came: Fouquet could correspond as much as he pleased with all his family.

"In Paris we were so excited," said Atto Melani, "for we were now almost sure that sooner or later the Superintendent would be freed."

A few months later, in May 1679, another long-awaited announcement was made: the King would soon allow all Fouquet's family to visit him. Fouquet's friends exulted. The months passed, one year passed. With bated breath they awaited the Squirrel's liberation which, however, never came. They began to fear some stumbling-block; perhaps Colbert was up to his usual tricks.

In the end, no pardon came. Instead, like a bolt of lightning reducing hearts to ashes, came news of the sudden death of Nicolas Fouquet in his cell at Pinerol, in his son's arms. It was 23rd March, 1680.

"And what about Lauzun?" I asked, as we climbed the vertical well that led back to the inn.

"Yes, Lauzun. He remained in prison a few months longer. Then he was freed."

"I do not understand; it is as though Lauzun had been imprisoned to stay close to Fouquet."

"That is a good guess. Yet, I wonder, what for?"

"Well, nothing comes to mind, except... to make him talk. To get Fouquet to say something which the King wished to know, something which..."

"That will do. Now you know why we are about to search Pompeo Dulcibeni's chamber."

The search was far less difficult than expected. I kept an eye on the corridor, while Atto entered the Marchigiano's chamber carrying only a candle. I heard him rummage for a long time, with intervals of silence. After a few minutes, I too entered, stirred both by the fear of being discovered and by curiosity.

Atto had already combed through a good many of Pompeo Dulcibeni's personal effects: clothing, books (amongst them the three volumes from Tiracorda's library), a few scraps of food, a passport to travel from the Kingdom of Naples to the Papal States and a number of gazettes. One of these was entitled: *Relation of what took place between the Caesarean Armies and the Ottomans on 10th July, 1683.*

"It concerns the siege of Vienna," murmured Abbot Melani.

The other gazettes too, of which there were over a dozen, also dealt with the same subject. We ended by examining the whole room hurriedly; no other object of any significance came to our attention. I was already inviting Abbot Melani to abandon the search when I saw him stop in the middle of the chamber, thoughtfully scratching his chin.

Suddenly, he rushed to the wardrobe and, finding the corner in which the dirty linen was piled, literally plunged into it, groping and pulling with his hands at the underclothing waiting to be laundered. At length, he grasped a pair of muslin drawers. He began to finger them in several places, until his hands concentrated on the piping through which passed the cord that holds up the drawers.

"Here we are. The chore was malodorous, but it was well worth the trouble," said Abbot Melani with satisfaction, extracting from Dulcibeni's drawers a small flattened coil. This consisted of several folded and compressed sheets of paper. The abbot unfolded them and placed them under the candle in order to read them.

I should be lying to the reader of these pages were I to hide the fact that the image of what took place in the minutes that followed remains engraved in my memory, as vivid as it is chaotic.

We began to read aloud avidly, almost in unison, the letter formed by those few leaves of paper. It was a long discourse in Latin, written in a senile, uncertain hand.

"*Optimo amico Nicolao Fouquet... mumiarum domino... tributum extremum... secretum pestis... secretum morbi... ut lues debelletur...* It is incredible, truly incredible," Abbot Melani murmured to himself.

Some of those words sounded strangely familiar to me. At once, however, he invited me to keep an eye on the corridor, in order not to be surprised by Dulcibeni's return. So I posted myself outside the door, keeping an eye on the stairs. While Abbot Melani completed his reading, I heard him muttering undisguised expressions of surprise and incredulity.

There then occurred what I was by now inured to fearing. Stopping his nose and his mouth, with his eyes narrowed and swollen, Abbot Melani rushed out from the chamber and placed the letter in my hands. He squirmed, again and again desperately repressing a dangerous sneeze.

I went straight to the last part of the letter, which he, in all probability, had been as yet unable to read. I, however, understood little of the content, owing to my excitement and to the bizarre contortions whereby Atto Melani was striving to mount his resistance to the beneficial release. My eyes moved directly to the end, where I understood why the words *mumiarum domino* had not sounded new to me when, almost incredulously, I deciphered the signature: *Athanasius Kircher I.H.S.*

Now at the limit of his resistance, Atto pointed at Dulcibeni's drawers, into which I hastily returned the letter. Obviously, we could not remove it. Dulcibeni would certainly discover that, with unforeseeable consequences. A few moments after we had left Dulcibeni's chamber and locked the door, Atto Melani exploded in a noisy, liberating, triumphal sneeze. Cristofano's door opened.

I took to the stairs and rushed down to the cellars. I heard the doctor reproving Abbot Melani. "What are you doing outside your chamber?"

The abbot needed all of his wits about him to arrange a clumsy excuse: he was on his way to call on Cristofano because, said he, of a sudden sneezing attack which was suffocating him.

"Good, then why are your shoes all muddy?" asked Cristofano angrily.

"Oh well... er... yes, indeed, they did get rather dirty on the journey from Paris and I have not yet had them cleaned here, what with all that has happened," stammered Atto. "But please, let us not talk here, we shall wake up Bedfordi,"—for the Englishman was indeed sleeping nearby.

The physician muttered something and I heard the door close. A few minutes later, I heard the two emerge once again.

"I do not like this business; now we shall see who else is playing the night wanderer," hissed Cristofano, knocking at a door. From within came Devizé's voice, half-smothered by sleep.

"No, it is nothing, excuse me, just a little check," explained the doctor.

My sweat ran cold. He was about to knock on Dulcibeni's door. Cristofano knocked.

The door opened: "Yes?"

Pompeo Dulcibeni had returned.

☙❧

After leaving a while for the waters to calm, I returned to await Atto Melani in my chamber. What we most feared had, alas, come to pass. Not only had Cristofano found Atto wandering about the inn, but Dulcibeni too had witnessed that nocturnal confusion. Clearly, he had returned to his apartment just when Atto was in Cristofano's chamber. At that moment, I myself was on the stairs, some way below. Thus, I did not hear Dulcibeni's return. The old gentleman must have descended the stairs between the little room and the first floor on tiptoe, despite the fact that he was moving in the dark. What had taken place then was bizarre, although not impossible.

What did seem almost incredible was the fact that Dulcibeni should have succeeded in making a timely return after all those comings and goings in the underground galleries, then in Tiracorda's house, and again in the tunnels; hauling himself up through the trapdoor with his own strength, walking in the dark, climbing steep stairs, and all in complete solitude. Dulcibeni was strongly built and far from short-winded. Too far, I thought, for a man of his age.

I did not have to wait long until Abbot Melani came to my door. He was not a little gloomy because of the stupid and ridiculous way in which we had been caught by Cristofano, arousing the suspicions of Dulcibeni himself.

"And what if Dulcibeni runs away?"

"I do not think he will do that. He would fear that Cristofano might raise the alarm and that, in dread of the Bargello's men, you and I might reveal the underground passage and the trapdoor leading directly to the house of his friend Tiracorda; which might irremediably compromise his mysterious plans. I am rather of the opinion that, whatever Dulcibeni may have in mind to do, after what has taken place tonight, he will quicken his pace. We must be on guard."

"Yet, finding that letter in his drawers, we did make a great discovery," I added, recovering my good humour. "By the way, what led you to find the hiding place so quickly?"

"I see that you cannot bear to think matters through. Who accompanied Dulcibeni when he came to the hostelry?"

"Devizé; and Fouquet."

"Good. And where did Fouquet hide his writings when he was imprisoned at Pinerol?"

"I thought about all that Abbot Melani had narrated to me an hour previously. "In chairs, in the lining of clothes, and in his undergarments!"

"Exactly."

"But then, Dulcibeni knows everything about Fouquet."

The abbot nodded his assent.

"So, Dulcibeni lied on the morning of our sequestration, when he told the Bargello's men that he had met the old Frenchman only recently," said I in amazement.

"Precisely. To have attained such a degree of intimacy, in reality, Dulcibeni and the Superintendent must have met a long time previously. Do not forget that Fouquet emerged from twenty years' imprisonment in a very poor state of health: I do not believe he can have moved around very much before settling in Naples. Nothing could be simpler than that he should have sought anonymous refuge in a circle of Jansenists, who are among the most bitter enemies of Louis XIV, and who are well established in that city."

"And there," I concluded, "he must have made the acquaintance of Dulcibeni, to whom he will have revealed his identity."

"Just so. That would mean that their friendship dates back three years, and not two months, as Dulcibeni would wish us to believe. And now, with God's help, we shall see this matter through to the end."

At this point, I felt bound to confess to Abbot Melani that I was not at all sure that I had fully understood the meaning of the letter which we had furtively read in Dulcibeni's chamber.

"Poor boy, you always need someone to tell you what to think. But it does not matter. That will happen, too, when you become a gazetteer."

As he had told me a few days earlier, Atto had met Kircher four years earlier, when he was already a dotard. The letter which we had just read seemed indeed to result from the great man's mental decline: it was addressed to "Monsieur le Surintendant des Finances Nicolas Fouquet", as though nothing had ever happened to the poor Squirrel.

"He had lost all sense of time," said Atto, "like those old men who think that they have become children again and ask for their mothers."

The content of the letter was, however, unequivocal. Kircher felt himself close to departure from this earth and was turning to his old friend Fouquet to thank him one last time. Fouquet, the Jesuit reminded him, had been the only potentate to whom he had confided his theory. The Superintendent had indeed cast himself down at Kircher's feet when the latter had illustrated for him in detail the great discovery of his life: the *secretum pestis*.

"Perhaps I understand!" I hastened to conclude, "It is the treatise in which Kircher writes of the pestilence. Dulcibeni spoke of it at the very beginning of our quarantine: Kircher wrote that the pestilence depended, not upon miasmas of unhealthy humours, but upon tiny beings, *vermiculi animati* or something of the sort. Perhaps that is the secret of the pestilence: invisible *vermiculi*."

"You could not be more mistaken," retorted Atto. "The theory of the *vermiculi* was never a secret: Kircher published it some thirty years ago in the *Scrutinium phisico-medicum contagiosae luis quae pestis dicitur*. In the letter in Dulcibeni's possession, there is far more: Kircher announces that he knows how to *praevenire, regere* et *debellare*."

"In other words, to prevent, regulate and defeat the pestilence."

"Bravo. And that is the *secretum pestis*. However, in order not to forget what I did manage to read, before coming to see you, I went into my chamber and there noted down all the most important phrases."

He showed me a few fragmentary words and phrases in Latin, rapidly scribbled onto a sheet of paper:

secretum morbi
morbus crescit sicut mortales
augescit patrimonium

senescit ex abrupto
per vices pestis petit et regreditur
ad infinitum renovatur
secretum vitae arcanae obices celant

"According to Kircher," Atto explained, "the plague is born, grows old and dies just like men. It feeds, however, at their expense: when it is young and strong, it endeavours to extend its estate as much as possible, like a cruel ruler exploiting his subjects, and through the infection brings about the massacre of an infinity of victims. Then, suddenly, it weakens and decays, like a poor old man at the end of his strength; and in the end, it dies. The visitation is cyclical: it attacks people and then rests; years later, it again attacks; and so on *ad infinitum*."

"Then it is a kind of... well, a thing that is forever turning around."

"Precisely: a circular chain."

"But then the plague can never be defeated, as Kircher promised."

"That is not so. The cycle can be modified, by recourse to the *secretum pestis*."

"And how does that work?"

"I have read that it is divided into two parts: the *secretum morbi*, to cause the plague; and the *secretum vitae*, to cure it."

"That means: a pestiferous malefice, and the antidote thereto."

"Precisely so."

"But then, how does it work?"

"I do not know. Indeed, Kircher did not really explain it. He insisted greatly, as far as I could understand from what I was able to read, on a single point. There is in the final stages of the pestilence something unexpected, mysterious, foreign to medical doctrine: after reaching its maximum strength, the disease *senescit ab abrupto*, or suddenly begins to come to an end."

"I do not understand, it is all strange," I commented. "Why did Kircher not publish his findings?"

"Perhaps he feared that someone might make improper use of them. It would take little to steal so precious a thing, once the manuscript was handed over to the printers. Now, can you imagine the disaster for the whole world if such secrets were to fall into the wrong hands?"

"He must, then, have greatly esteemed Fouquet to confide such a thing to him alone."

"I can tell you that one needed speak only once with the Squirrel to be won over by him. Kircher added, however, that the *secretum vitae* is hidden by *arcanae obices.*

"*Arcanae obices?* That means 'mysterious obstacles'. But what does it refer to?

"I have not the least idea. Perhaps it is part of the jargon of the alchemists, the spagyrists or the necromancers. Kircher knew religions, rituals, superstitions and devilries from all the world over. Or perhaps *arcanae obices* is a coded expression which Fouquet could decipher after reading the letter."

"But Fouquet could not receive the letter," I objected, "while he was in prison at Pinerol."

"That is a correct observation. Yet someone must have delivered it to him, since we found it among Dulcibeni's effects. So the decision to allow him to have it was taken by whoever controlled all his correspondence..."

I fell silent, not daring to draw the appropriate conclusions.

"... that is, His Majesty the King of France," said Atto, swallowing, as though he were frightened by his own words.

"But then," I hesitated, "the *secretum pestis...*"

"Was what the King wanted from Fouquet."

That, I thought, was all that we needed. Scarcely had Atto named him and it was as though the Most Christian King, First-Born and Most Dearly Beloved Son of the Church, had somehow entered the hostelry in a freezing, angry gust, and was about to sweep away all that remained of poor Fouquet within the walls of the Donzello.

"*Arcanae obices, arcanae obices,*" Melani chanted to himself, with his fingers drumming on his knees.

"Signor Atto," I interrupted him, "do you believe that, in the end, Fouquet revealed the *secretum pestis* to the King?"

"*Arcanae...* What did you say? I do not know, I really do not know."

"Perhaps Fouquet left prison because he had confessed," I proposed.

"Indeed, had he escaped, the news would have spread at once. I believe that matters must have gone otherwise: when Fouquet was arrested, there were found on him letters from a mysterious prelate which spoke of the secret of the pestilence. Those letters must have been kept by Colbert. If, when I entered the *Coluber's* study, more time had been given me, I should probably have discovered those too."

"And then?"

"And then began the trial of Fouquet. And now we know why the King and Colbert used every means to prevent Fouquet from being condemned to no more than exile: they wanted him in prison so that they could extort from him the *secretum pestis.* Moreover, not having understood who the mysterious ecclesiastic might be, they could turn only to Fouquet. Now, if they had understood that it was Kircher..."

"Of what use would the secret of the pestilence have been to them?"

It was all too clear, said Atto, growing fervent: control of the pestilence would have enabled Louis XIV to settle accounts once and for all with his enemies. The dream of using the plague for military purposes was, he said, centuries old. Already Thucydides told how the Athenians, when their city was decimated by the disease, suspected their enemies of the Peloponnesian League of having provoked the visitation by poisoning their wells. In more recent times, the Turks had tried (with scant success) to use the contagion to overcome besieged cities by catapulting infected bodies over the ramparts.

Fouquet held the secret weapon which the Most Christian King would have been more than delighted to use to bring to heel Spain and the Empire and to crush William of Orange and Holland.

His imprisonment had, then, been so rigorous only in order to convince Fouquet to talk, and to be quite sure that he would not pass the secret to one of his many friends. That was why he was forbidden to write. But Fouquet did not yield.

"Why ever should he have done so?" Abbot Melani asked himself rhetorically. "Keeping the secret to himself was his sole guarantee of remaining alive!"

Perhaps the Superintendent had for years simply denied that he really knew how to disseminate the pestilence; or perhaps he had put up a series of half-truths in order to gain time and to obtain less cruel conditions of imprisonment.

"But then, why was he freed?" I asked.

"The letter from Kircher, by now utterly delirious, had reached Paris and Fouquet could therefore no longer deny all knowledge, thus endangering his own life and that of his family. Perhaps in the end Fouquet did give in and promise the King the *Secretum pestis* in exchange for his own freedom. After that, however, he did not respect his agreement. That is why, then... Colbert's spies set their sights on him."

"Might not the contrary have been the case?" I asked.

"What do you mean to say?"

"Perhaps it was the King who did not respect the agreement."

"Enough of that. I will not permit you to opine that His Majesty..."

Atto never finished his sentence, caught up in a sudden vortex of who knows what thoughts. I understood that his pride could not bear to hear my hypothesis: that the King might have promised the Superintendent his freedom, while intending to eliminate him immediately afterwards. That had not happened solely because, as I began fervidly to imagine, Fouquet had somehow foreseen the move and succeeded in boldly avoiding the ambush. But perhaps my fantasy was getting the better of me. I studied the abbot's face: his eyes staring straight in front of him, he was following the same reasoning as me, of that I was sure.

"One thing, however, is certain," said he suddenly.

"And what might that be?"

"In Fouquet's flight and in the *secretum pestis*, other persons are involved: many others. Lauzun, first and foremost, who was surely sent to Pinerol in order to loosen Fouquet's tongue, perhaps against the promise that he would soon return to Mademoiselle, his wealthy little wife. Then, there is Devizé, who accompanied Fouquet here to the Donzello. Perhaps Corbetta, Devizé's master, is also part of the picture, for, like his pupil, he was utterly devoted to poor Queen Maria Teresa, as well as being an expert in cryptography. Do not forget that the *secretum vitae* has been somehow concealed in *arcanae obices*. Bear in mind also that Devizé has been lying from the start: do you remember his lies about the theatres in Venice? Last, but not least, we have Dulcibeni, Fouquet's confidant, in whose undergarments lay hidden the letter which speaks of the *secretum pestis*. He is but a merchant, yet when he speaks of the pestilence, one would think he was Paracelsus."

He stopped to draw breath. His mouth was dry.

"Do you think that Dulcibeni knows the *secretum pestis*?"

"That is possible. Now, however, it is late, and we should be terminating our discussion."

"All this story strikes me as absurd," said I, trying to calm him. "Do you not fear making too many suppositions?"

"I have already told you. If you would understand matters of state, you must take a different view of facts from that which you employ in the ordinary way. What counts is not what you think, but how. No one knows everything, not even the King. And, when you do not know, you must learn to suppose, and to suppose truths which may at first sight appear to be utterly absurd: you will then discover without fail that it is all dramatically true."

Ashen-faced, he went out, scanning the corridor to the left and the right, as though someone might be lying in ambush for him; yet Atto's fear, which had at last become fully manifest, was no longer such a mystery to me. No longer did I envy him his secret mission, his relations in many courts, his skills as a man of action and intrigue.

He had come to Rome in order to serve the King of France and to investigate a mystery. Now he knew that, if he would resolve that mystery, he must investigate the King himself.

Day the Eighth
18ᵀᴴ SEPTEMBER, 1683

✠

I awoke the next day gnawed by a certain febrile anxiety. Despite the long-drawn-out reflections in which Atto and I had engaged the night before and the little sleep which I had, yet again, allowed myself, I was perfectly vigilant and ready for action. What I might be able to do was in reality not very clear to me: too many mysteries haunted the inn and their sheer number prevented me from resolving any of them. Threatening or unattainable presences (Louis XIV, Colbert, Queen Maria Teresa, Kircher himself) had made their way into the hostelry and into our lives. The scourge of the pestilence had not yet left off from tormenting and terrifying us; some of our guests had, moreover, for days now assumed guises and comportments which were at once indecipherable and enigmatic. As though all that were not enough, the astrological almanack purloined from Stilone Priàso promised disastrous and death-dealing events for the days to come.

As I descended the stairs on my way to the kitchen, I heard the voice of Atto Melani resounding, quietly yet agonisingly:

> *Infelice pensier,*
> *chi ne conforta?*
> *Ohimé!*
> *Chi ne consiglia?...* *

Atto, too, must have felt confused and discouraged—and that, far more than me! I hastened on my way, deliberately refusing to dwell upon such disheartening thoughts. As usual, I diligently assisted Cristofano in the kitchen and in serving meals. I had prepared snails boiled and lightly fried in oil, with ground garlic, mint, parsley, spices and a slice of lemon; and these were greatly appreciated.

---

* Unhappy thought, / Who can give comfort for't? / Alas! / Who can give counsel?

I worked with a will, almost as though I were sustained by an excess of vital heat. This beneficial disposition of body and soul was crowned by an event as joyous as it was unexpected.

"Cloridia has asked for you," announced Cristofano after luncheon. "You are to go directly to her chamber."

The reason for that call (and this, Cristofano knew) was completely frivolous. I found Cloridia with her bodice half-unlaced and her head bent over the tub, washing her hair. The chamber was inundated with the effluvia of sweet essences. Stunned, I heard her ask me to pour onto her head the vinegar contained in a phial which lay upon her dressing table: later, I learned that she used it to make her tresses more lustrous.

While I went about this, I recalled the doubts which I had entertained about Cloridia's parting words at our previous encounter. Speaking to me of the extraordinary numerological coincidences between her date of birth and that of Rome, she had mentioned a wrong suffered in connection with her return to this city. She had then explained to me that she had found her way to the Donzello by following a certain *virga ardentis* (or ardent rod) which was also called "trembling" or "protruding". This, also because of the equivocal gesture with which she had accompanied her explanation, I had taken to be an indecent allusion. I had then promised myself that I would find out what she really meant. And now, the same Cloridia had suddenly called me and provided me with the opportunity to put my question.

"Pass me the towel. No, not that one, the smaller coarse linen towel," she commanded me, while twisting her hair.

I obeyed. She wrapped her hair in the cloth, after drying her shoulders.

"Would you comb my hair now?" she asked in honeyed tones. "It is so curly that it is almost impossible for me to disentangle it alone without pulling it."

I was happy to undertake so agreeable a service. She sat with her back to me, still half-free from the laces of her bodice, and explained to me that I should begin at the tips and then work back to the roots of her hair. This seemed to me to be the right time to ask her to recount to me what had brought her to the Donzello, and I reminded her of what she had told me last time that we met. Cloridia agreed.

"Then, what is the ardent or trembling rod, Monna Cloridia? I asked.

"Thy rod and thy staff do comfort me," she recited. "Psalm 22."

I breathed a sigh of relief.

"Are you not acquainted with this? It is simply a forked hazel branch, about a foot and a half long and a finger's breadth thick, cut not more than one year before. It is also known as the rod of Pallas, the Caduceus of Mercury, Circe's wand, Aaron's rod and Jacob's staff. Then there are other names: the divine, the lucent, protruding, transcendent, cadent or superior rod: all names given it by the Italians who work in the quicksilver mines of Trent and the Tyrol. It is akin to the Augur's Rod of the Romans, who used it in the place of the sceptre; to the rod which Moses used to smite the rock and bring forth water; to the rod of Asahuerus, King of the Medes and Persians, from whom Esther, once she had kissed its tip, obtained all that she asked."

And she plunged into an explanation of rare and lucid doctrine; for, as I well recalled, Cloridia was no mere strumpet, she was a courtesan: and no woman lived who could couple such sublime erudition with the amatory arts.

"The rod has been used for over two hundred years to discover metals, and for a century, to find water. But everyone knows that. Since time immemorial, however, it has been used to capture criminals and assassins in great numbers in the most distant countries: in the lands of Edom, Sarmatia, Getulia, Gothland, Rhaetia, Raphia, Hibernia, Sleasia, Lower Cirenaica, Marmaris, Mantiana, Confluentia, Prufuik, Alexandria Major, Argenton, Frisia, Gaeta, Cuspia, Livonia, Casperia, Serica, Brixia, Trabezond, Syria, Cilicia, Mutina, Arabia Felix, Malines in Brabant, Liburnia, Slavonia, Oxiana, Pamphilia, Garamantia and finally Lydia, which was formerly known as Maeonia, where flow the rivers Hermes and Pactolus, famed in poesy and song. In Gedrosia, an assassin was even followed for more than forty-five leagues over land and over thirty leagues by sea and arrested at last. With the rod, they had found out the bed in which he had slept, the table where he had eaten, his cooking pots and crockery."

Thus I learned from Cloridia that the mysterious rod works thanks to the porousness of bodies which constantly give off impalpable particles through a process of continual emanation. Somewhere between visible bodies and inconceivable and unintelligible beings there exists a median category of volatile agents, which are rather subtle and active, and are called corpuscles, or particles of matter, atoms or subtle matter.

These corpuscles are most mysterious but exceedingly useful. They may be an emanation of the very substance from which they originate, or else they may be a third substance, which the brain, (the receptacle thereof), distributes through the nerves and muscles to produce the various movements. In other cases, however, such corpuscles are present in the air near to the irradiating matter which uses the air as a vehicle whereby to conduct its own imprint to the absorbent matter.

"That is, for example, how bell and clapper function, imprinting an impulse on the nearby air, which in turn presses against other air, and so on, until it strikes our ear, which registers the sensation of the sound," explained Cloridia.

Now, it was such corpuscles which produced sympathy and antipathy, and even love.

"Indeed, the search for a thief or an assassin will be based upon antipathy. In the market at Amsterdam, I saw a herd of pigs grunt angrily at a butcher the moment that he approached them, all striving to hurl themselves at him, as far as the tethers tied around their necks would allow. This was because those swine had perceived the corpuscles of other pigs which had just been slaughtered by the butcher: corpuscles which impregnated the man's clothing, agitating the air all around him and disturbing the herd of living swine."

For this same reason, I learned (not without surprise) that the blood of a man assassinated, or even only wounded, (or that of a woman who has been violated), flows from the wound in the direction of the malefactor. The spirits and corpuscles which emanate from the blood of the victim envelop the evil-doer and are most strongly agitated because of the horror aroused by so cruel and sanguinary a man, and this makes it easy for the rod to follow suchlike and to find them out.

Yet, even if the act took place indirectly and at a distance, for example, on commission, or in the case of acts and decisions which have been the cause of death or violence for one or many, the rod is able to trace them, always with the proviso that it should start from the place where the crime was committed. The spirit of the guilty is indeed agitated by the mortal alarms to which the horror of so great a crime gives rise, and by the eternal fear of the ultimate torment which, as Holy Scripture says, ever watches at the gates of the wicked.

"'*Fugit impius nemine persequente*'": the impious flee, even when no one follows them," cited Cloridia with unexpected erudition, raising her head and letting her pupils shoot forth darts.

Likewise, it was through antipathy that, if a wolf's tail were to be hung on the wall of a cowshed, the cattle would be unable to eat; that the vine flees the cabbage; that hemlock keeps its distance from rue, and, although hemlock is a mortal poison, it will not be harmful if, immediately after it has been taken, one imbibes the juice of rue. Again, there is irreconcilable antipathy between the scorpion and the crocodile, the elephant and the swine, the lion and the cock, the crow and the owl, the wolf and the sheep, as well as the toad and the weasel.

"But, as I have already said, the corpuscles also produce sympathy and love," continued Cloridia, who then recited:

> *Vi son nodi segreti, vi son simpatie,*
> *il cui dolce accordo fa nelle anime armonie,*
> *sì che s'amano e l'una e l'altra, e si lasciano avviluppar*
> *da questi non so che, che non si posson esplicar.* *

"Well, my dear, what we are unable to explain is in fact the corpuscles. According to Giobatta Porta, there is, for instance, great sympathy between the male and the female palm, between the vine and the olive, between the fig and the myrtle. And it is out of sympathy that a maddened bull will grow calm when tied to a fig tree; or an elephant, upon seeing a ram. And know," said she, her voice growing softer, "that according to Cardano the lizard feels sympathy for man, and likes to look upon him and to seek his saliva, which he drinks avidly."

Meanwhile, she had stretched her arms behind her and, grasping the hand that combed her, had drawn me to her side.

"In the same way," she said, as though nothing had taken place, "the affection or secret attraction which we feel imperiously for certain persons from the first time that we encounter them is caused by an emission of spirits or corpuscles from that person which gently make their imprint on the eyes and the nerves, until they reach the brain and make for a sensation of agreeableness."

Trembling, I worked on her temples with the comb.

"And do you know something?" she added winningly. "This attraction has the magnificent power of rendering the object of our desires most perfect and most worthy in our eyes."

* There are secret ties, there are sympathies, / Whose sweet accord makes harmonies in Souls, / So then they love, and let themselves infolded be / In that I-know-not-what to which they have no key.

No one could ever have seen *me* as being most perfect, no, certainly not: this I repeated to myself as I struggled to master my violent emotion; yet meanwhile, I could not so much as articulate a single word.

Cloridia leaned her head against my chest and sighed.

"Now you must unravel the hair at the nape of my neck, without however hurting me: there the hair is most entwined but also most fragile and sensitive."

Having said which, she made me sit facing her, on her high bed, and placed her head in my lap, with her face downwards, showing me her neck. Still bewildered and confused, I felt the warmth of her breath upon my groin. I began again to comb her curls. I felt my head completely empty.

"I have not yet explained to you how to use the rod successfully," she began again, slowly, while I felt her find the most comfortable position.

"Remember, first and foremost, that nature has one single mechanism in all its operations and this alone can explain the movement of the rod. One must first of all dip the tip of the rod in some material, if possible humid and warm (like blood or other humours), which has to do with whatever is sought after. This is because touch can sometimes discover what the eyes cannot. Then one takes the rod between two fingers, holding it at the level of the belly. One can also balance it on the back of one's hand, but in my opinion that does not work. One should then proceed in the direction where one thinks what one seeks is to be found. One must walk back and forth, up and down, several times, until the rod rises: and thus, one can be sure that the direction one has taken is the right one. The inclination of the rod is, in fact, the same thing as the inclination of the needle of a compass: it responds to a magnetic attraction. The important thing, with the rod, is never to agitate it brusquely, for that may break the volume of vapours and exhalations coming from the place one seeks and which, by impregnating the rod, cause it to rise in the right direction. Every now and then, it is good to take in one's hands the two horns which are at the base of the rod, but without squeezing too much, and in such a way that the back of the hands faces the ground and taking care that the tip of the rod is always well raised and pointing towards the goal. You should also know that the rod will not move in just anyone's hands. This calls for a special gift and much art. For example, it will not move in the hands of someone whose perspiration is gross, rough and abundant, since such corpuscles will break the column of vapours, exhalations and smokes. It does, however, sometimes happen that the rod may not move even in the hands of someone who has previously used it successfully. (Not that I have ever experienced that, thank heavens.) What may occur is that something alters the constitution of the person handling the rod, causing their blood to ferment violently. Something in the air or food may produce acrid or acid salts. Overwork, staying up late at night or studies may cause perspiration which is excessively acrid and rough and passes from the hands to the interstices of the rod, thus hindering the column of vapours, so that these will not move. This is because the rod acts as a catalyser of the invisible corpuscles, like a microscope. You should see what a spectacle there is when the rod at last attains..."

Cloridia had broken off. Cristofano knocked.

"I thought I heard a cry. Is all well with you?" asked the physician, all out of breath from running up the stairs.

"Nothing to worry about. Our poor little prentice has just hurt himself while he was helping me, but it is a mere trifle. Good day to you, Signor Cristofano, and thank you," answered Cloridia with subtle hilarity.

I had cried out. And now I lay, faint with pleasure and shame, sprawled across Cloridia's bed.

I do not know how long afterwards or in what manner I took my leave. I remember only Cloridia's smile and the tender pat on the head which she bestowed on me before closing the door.

Overwhelmed by the most conflicting sentiments, I slipped down to my chamber like lightning and changed my breeches: I could not run the risk that Cristofano might see me so obscenely soiled. It was a fine warm afternoon and, almost without realising it, I fell asleep half-dressed on my couch.

☙❧

I awoke after an hour or so. I called on Abbot Melani to see whether he needed anything: in reality, recalling his heartbroken singing that morning, I felt sorry for him and did not wish him to feel alone. Instead, I found him in a good mood:

A petto ch'adora
è solo un bel guardo.
È solo un bel guardo!...[5]

* To an adoring bosom, / 'tis but a luscious glance. / 'Tis but a luscious glance...

He warbled joyously by way of a salutation. I looked at him without understanding.

"It seems I heard you in the distance, er, suffering this morning. You scared Cristofano, you know. He was in the doorway with me when we heard, up there in Cloridia's tower..."

"Oh, but you must not think, Signor Atto," I parried, blushing, "that Monna Cloridia..."

"But yes, of course," said the abbot, suddenly looking serious, "the fair Cloridia did nothing. 'To an adoring bosom', a bewitching glance suffices, as my master, Seigneur Luigi, so aptly put it."

I departed, consumed by the blackest shame, detesting Melani with all my heart.

In the kitchen, I found Cristofano pale and overcome by anxiety.

"The Englishman is in a bad way, a very bad way," he whispered upon seeing me.

"But all the cures which you have dispensed..."

"Nothing. A mystery. My prodigious *remedia*: all useless. Understood? And Bedfordi is dying. And we shall never get out from here. Done for. All of us, done for." He spoke in fits and starts and his voice sounded unnatural.

On his face I saw with anxiety a pair of tremendous bags under the eyes and a vacant, bewildered expression. His speech was fragmented and he seemed to have lost the use of verbs.

The Englishman's health had indeed never improved, nor had the patient ever regained consciousness. I looked around me; the kitchen was completely upside down. Vases, flasks, lit ovens, alembics and cups of all sorts invaded every surface: tables, chairs, corners, shelves, passages, even the floor. In the fireplace two cauldrons were boiling, and a fair number of cooking pots. I saw with horror chopped up on the fire our best provisions of lard, meat, fish and dried fruit from the pantry, all horribly mixed with unknown, stinking alchemical preparations. On the great table, on the plate rack, on the dresser, and on the pantry shelves lay an endless range of little pots full of oils and piles of powders of many colours. Next to each little pot or heap of powder was a label: Zedoary, Galangal, Long Peppers, Round Peppers, Juniper Berries, Rind of Lemons and of Oranges, Sage, Basil, Marjoram, Laurel Berries, Penny-royal, Gentian, Calamint, Leaves of Elder, Red Roses and White Roses, Spikenard, Cubeb, Rosemary, Mint, Cinnamon, *Calamatus Odoratus*, *Chamidrys Stocis*, *Meleghetta Maris*, Maize,

Thuris Albi, Hepatic Aloes, Wormwood Seeds, Wood of Aloes, Carda-
mom, Laurel Oil, Galbanum, Gum of Ivy, Incense, Cloves, Comfrey,
Nutmeg, White Burning Bush (*Dictamnus Albus*), Benzoin, New Yellow
Wax, Finest Turpentine and Cinders from the fire.

I turned to the physician to request an explanation, but then I
held back: pale and seemingly lost to the world, Cristofano wandered
confusedly from one side of the room to the other attending to a
thousand operations without completing any.

"You must help me. We shall risk all. Bedfordi's accursed tokens
have not opened. The disgusting things have not even matured. And
so we... we shall slice them clean off!"

"Oh no!" I exclaimed, for I knew well that to cut off tokens before
they have matured can be lethal for he sufferer from the pestilence.

"If the worst comes to the worst, he'll die anyway," he cut me
short with unusual harshness. "And here is the plan: first, he must
puke. But enough of the imperial musk. Something stronger will be
needed, for instance, my diaromatic: for distempers both intrinsic
and extrinsic. Two drachms on an empty stomach and out with the
vomit. It salves the body. It unburdens the head; and it provokes
sputum, a sign that it kills all maladies. *Recipe!*" Cristofano screamed
suddenly, causing me to jump. "Fine sugar, ground pearls, musk,
saffron, wood of aloes, cinnamon and the philosopher's stone: one
mixes all and reduces it to tablets, which are incorruptible. These are
miraculous against the pestilence. They refine the gross, corrupted
humours which generate the tokens. They comfort the stomach; and
they cheer the heart."

Bedfordi was in for trouble, I thought. Yet, on the other hand,
what choice had we? Every hope of salvation was vested in Cristofano, and in the Lord God.

The doctor, exhausted by so much agitation, issued repeated commands without giving me the time to execute them, and repeated
mechanically the recipes which he must have read in the medical
texts.

"Point the second: *elixir vitae* in order to restore the patient. That
enjoyed great success here in Rome in the visitation of '56. It pos-
sesses so many virtues: it cures many sorts of grave and malignant
infirmities. It is by nature most penetrative. Its virtue is desiccating
and it comforts all the places offended by any malady. It preserves
all things corruptible, salving catarrh, coughs and tightness of the

chest, and other similar complaints. It cures and heals all crude sorts of putrid ulcers and resolves all aches and pains caused by frigidity *et cetera.*"

For a moment, he seemed to vacillate, with his gaze lost in the void. I made to succour him, but suddenly he reprised: "Point the third: pills against the pestilence of Mastro Alessandro Cospio da Bolsena, Imola, 1527: great success. Armenian bolus, *terra sigillata*, camphor, tormentil, aloes hepatick: four drachms of each; the whole spread with juice of cabbages. And, a scruple of saffron. Point the fourth: medicine for buccal administration of Mastro Roberto Coccalino da Formagine; a great physician in the kingdom of Lombardy, 1500. *Recipe!*" he again screamed in strangled tones.

Thus, he commanded me to prepare a decoction of black hellebore, sienna, colocynth and rhubarb.

"The buccal medicine of Mastro Coccalino, we shall administer to him up his arse. Thus, it will encounter Mastro Cospio's pills half-way, and together they will get the better of that disgusting plague. And we shall win, yes, we shall win!"

We then ascended to the chamber where Bedfordi lay more dead than alive; and there I collaborated, not without horror, in putting into practice all that Cristofano had excogitated.

At the end of the cruel operation, the chamber resembled a knacker's yard: vomit, blood and excrement, all mixed in puddles, in itself the most disgusting and foul-smelling of spectacles. We proceeded to excise the tokens, spreading on the wounds vinegary syrup with *oleum philosophorum*, which, according to the doctor, would relieve the pain.

"And last, we bandage the wounds with wax plaster *gratiadei*," concluded Cristofano, panting rhythmically.

And I indeed prayed that we should be aided *gratia Dei*, by the grace of God, which we so dearly needed. The young Englishman had in no way reacted to the therapy. Indifferent to everything, he had not even been moved to groan with pain. We stared at him, awaiting some sign, whether good or bad.

With clenched fists, Cristofano gestured that I should hasten with him to the kitchen. All bathed in sweat and muttering to himself, he began roughly to pound a great quantity of aromas. He mixed them all and put them to boil in the finest aqua vitae in a retort, over a wind furnace which gave a very slow fire.

"Now, we shall have water, oil and phlegm. And all separated the one from the other!" he announced emphatically.

Very soon the vessel began to fill with a milky distillate, which then turned smoky and light yellow. Cristofano then changed receptacles, pouring this white water into a well-plugged iron vase.

"First, water of balsam!" he exclaimed, shaking the vase with exaggerated and grotesque joy.

He increased the fire under the retort, in which there had remained a boiling liquid which turned into an oil as black as ink.

"Mother of balsam!" announced Cristofano, pouring the fluid into a flask.

He then augmented the fire to the maximum, until all the substance came out from the retort. "Liquor of balsam: miraculous!" he rejoiced savagely, handing it to me in a bottle, together with the two other remedies.

"Shall I bring it to Bedfordi?"

"No!" he screamed, outrageously, pointing his index finger upwards as one might with a dog or a small child, and inspecting me from head to toe.

His eyes were narrowed and bloodshot: "No, my boy, this is not for Bedfordi. It is for us. All of us. Three excellent aquae vitae. The finest!"

In my hand, he placed the twisted flask, still hot, and with rustic frenzy poured himself a glass of the first liquor.

"But what are these for?" I asked, intimidated.

His sole response was to refill his glass and again pour it down his throat.

"For buggering fear, ah, ah!" swallowing a cup of the third aqua vitae and filling it for the fourth time.

He then forced me to make a mad toast with the empty retort which I held in my hand.

"Thus, when they bear us all off to die in the pest-house, we shall not even realise it, ah, ah, ah!"

Having said which, he threw the glass over his shoulder and emitted a couple of vigorous belches. He endeavoured to walk, but his legs became entangled. He fell to the ground, horribly white in the face, and at last lost his senses.

Seized by terror, I was about to call for help, when I restrained myself. If panic were to spread, the situation in the hostelry would descend into chaos; and we should then run the risk of being discovered by the watchman on guard. So I ran to enlist the help of Abbot Melani. With great care (and great effort) we succeeded in carrying the doctor up to his own chamber on the first floor almost without making any noise. I told the abbot of the young Englishman's agony and of the state of confusion into which Cristofano had fallen before collapsing.

The doctor meanwhile lay pale and inert on his bed, panting noisily.

"Is it the death rattle, Signor Atto?" I asked with a knot in my throat.

Abbot Melani leaned over and studied the patient's countenance.

"No: he is snoring," he replied amusedly. "Besides, I have always suspected that Bacchus had a hand in physicians' nasty mixtures. What's more, he has been working too hard. Let him sleep, but we shall keep an eye on him. One can never be too prudent."

We sat beside the bed. Speaking under his breath, Melani again asked after Bedfordi. He seemed very worried. The horrendous prospect of the pest-house was becoming ever more tangible. We reviewed, and rejected, the possibility of escaping through the underground galleries. Sooner or later, we would be recaptured.

Disconsolate, I tried to think about something else. So it was that I remembered that Bedfordi's chamber had still to be cleaned of the sick man's filth. I signalled to Atto that he could find me in the Englishman's chamber, next door, and went there to fulfil my unpleasant task. When I returned, I found Atto blissfully dozing in his chair. He slept with folded arms and his legs stretched out onto the chair which I had left vacant. I leaned over Cristofano. He was sleeping heavily and his face seemed already to have recovered a little colour.

Somewhat reassured, I had just squatted on a corner of the bed when I heard a sound of muttering. It was Atto. Uncomfortably installed on two chairs, his sleep was agitated. His hanging head oscillated rhythmically. With his fists folded against his chest he tugged at the lace of his cuffs, while his insistent moaning reminded one of an angry little boy facing a parent's reproof.

I listened intently: with his breathing troubled and uncertain, almost as though he were on the point of sobbing, Atto was speaking in French.

"*Les barricades, les barricades…*" he moaned softly in his sleep.

I recalled that Atto, when he was barely twenty, had fled Paris during the tumults of the Fronde with the royal family and his master, Le Seigneur Luigi Rossi. Now he babbled of barricades: perhaps in his sleep he was reliving the rebellion of those days.

I wondered whether I should not awaken him and free him from those ugly memories. Carefully, I got out of bed and brought my face close to his. I studied it. This was the first time that I was able to scrutinise Atto from so near, without coming under his vigilant and censorious eye. I was moved by the abbot's countenance, puffed up and stained by sleep: the cheeks, smooth and just beginning to sag, were redolent of the eunuch's solitude and melancholy. An ancient sea of suffering in the midst of which the proud and wayward dimple strove still, like one shipwrecked, to keep afloat, demanding the reverence and respect due to a diplomatic representative of His Most Christian Majesty. I felt my heart tighten, but was suddenly torn from my reverie.

"*Barricades… mystérieuses, mystérieuses. Barricades. Mystérieuses. Les barricades…*" Abbot Melani suddenly murmured in his sleep.

He was raving. Inexplicably, however, those words troubled me. Whatever could those barricades be in the mind of Abbot Melani? *Barricades mystérieuses.* Mysterious. What did those two words remind me of? It was as though the concept was not new to me…

Just then, Atto gave signs of waking. He no longer seemed in the least weighed down by suffering, as he had only moments before. On the contrary, upon seeing me, his face broadened at once into a smile and he chanted:

> *Chi giace nel sonno*
> *non speri mai Fama.*
> *Chi dorme codardo*
> *è degno che mora…*[*]

"Thus Le Seigneur Luigi, my master, would have upbraided me," he jested, stretching and scratching himself here and there. "Have I missed anything? How is our physician?" he then asked, seeing me so pensive.

"There is nothing new, Signor Atto."

---

[*] He who lies sleeping / lays no claim to Fame / He who cravenly sleeps / is worthy of death.

"I feel that I owe you an apology, my boy," said he, a moment later.

"What for, Signor Atto?"

"Well, perhaps I should not have teased you as I did, when we were in my chamber this afternoon; concerning Cloridia, I mean."

I replied that no apologies were necessary; in reality, I was as surprised as I was pleased by Abbot Melani's admission. With a more amiable disposition, I then recounted all that Cloridia had explained to me, dwelling especially upon the magical and surprising science of numbers, in which the destiny of each one of us is concealed. I then proceeded to tell him of the investigative powers of the ardent rod.

"I understand. The ardent rod is (how should I put it?) an unusual and fascinating subject," commented Atto, "in which Cloridia is surely well versed."

"Oh, you see, she was washing her hair and called for me to help comb it out," said I, ignoring Atto's subtle irony.

> *O biondi tesori*
> *inanellati,*
> *chiome divine, cori,*
> *labirinti dorati...*

He exclaimed to me, singing *sotto voce*. I blushed, at first in anger and shame, but then was at once overcome by the beauty of that aria, now utterly devoid of any accent of scorn.

> *... tra i vostri splendori*
> *m'è dolce smarrire*
> *la vita e morire...**

I let the melody transport me to thoughts of love: I lulled myself in the image of Cloridia's blonde and curly tresses, and I remembered her sweet voice. In my heart, I began to wonder whatever had brought Cloridia to the Donzello. It had been the ardent rod, that much she had told me. She had then added that the rod is moved by "antipathy" and by "sympathy". Which, then, had it been for her? Had she come to the inn following the trail of someone who had done her a grave wrong and upon whom she may perhaps have wished to take revenge? Or (oh, delicious thought!) had Cloridia come, guided

---

* O blonde treasures / Rings curled upon rings, / Divine tresses, choirs, / Golden labyrinths! ... Amidst your splendours / It is sweet to me to lose / My life, and die...

by that magnetism which leads us to find love and to which, it seems, the rod is rather sensitive? I began to daydream that perhaps it was so...

Su tutto allacciate,
legate, legate
gioir e tormento!...[*]

Atto's song, in tribute to the golden tresses of my courtesan of the honey-coloured skin, was in counterpoint to my thoughts.

Moreover, I continued in my musings upon love, those moments of... relaxation: had not Cloridia graciously bestowed them upon me, without ever a mention of money, (unlike that painful previous episode when I had consulted her concerning dreams)?

While I was thus engrossed, and Atto was so caught up in the vortex of song as no longer to hold back the flood of his voice, Cristofano opened his eyes.

He looked at the abbot with narrowed eyes, without however interrupting him. After a moment of silence, he even thanked him for having helped him. I heaved a sigh of relief. From his expression and his colouring, the doctor seemed to have recovered. His diction, again fluent and normal, soon reassured me as to the state of his health. This had been a mere passing crisis.

"Your voice is still splendid, Signor Abbot Melani," commented the physician, as he rose and adjusted his clothing. "Although it was somewhat imprudent on your part to allow the other guests on this floor to hear you. Let us hope that Dulcibeni and Devizé do not wonder what you were doing singing in my chamber."

After once again thanking Abbot Melani for his attentive assistance, Cristofano moved in my company towards the room next door, in order to visit poor Bedfordi, whilst Atto returned to his own chamber on the second floor.

Bedfordi lay immobile as ever. The doctor shook his head: "I fear that it is time to inform the other guests of this unfortunate young man's plight. If he should die, we must avoid panic breaking out in the hostelry."

We agreed that we should first warn Padre Robleda, so that he could administer Extreme Unction. I avoided mentioning to Cristofano that once, when requested by me, Robleda had refused to administer the

---

[*] All put up and tied, / Tied, tying together / Joy and torment!...

holy oil to the young Englishman, treating him as a Protestant, who was thus excommunicated.

Thus we knocked at the Jesuit's door. I foresaw all too well the reaction of the cowardly Robleda to our bad news: anxiety, stammering and, above all, noisy scorn for Cristofano's attitude. To my surprise, none of that came to pass.

"How come that you should not have tried to cure Bedfordi through the use of magnetism?" Robleda asked the physician, as soon as he had finished explaining the sad situation to him.

Cristofano remained speechless. Robleda then reminded him that, according to Father Kircher, the whole of creation was dominated by magnetism, so much so that the learned Jesuit had devoted a book to explaining the entire doctrine, clarifying once and for all that the world is nothing more than a great magnetic concatenation at the centre of which is God, the first and the one original magnet, towards Whom every object and every living being tends irremediably. Is not love (both human and divine) an expression of magnetic attraction? Indeed, is not every kind of fascination? The planets and the stars are, as all know, subject to reciprocal magnetism; but the celestial bodies are also inhabited by magnetic force.

"Well, yes," intervened Cristofano, "I do know the example of the compass."

"... which, of course, aids navigators and travellers to orient themselves; but there is far more to it."

What should we say of the magnetism exercised upon the waters by the sun and the moon, so evident from the tides? And, in plants, the universal *vis attractiva* is clearly to be found: the vegetal magnetic force triumphs in the *barometz*, said Robleda, as no doubt the doctor well knew.

"Mmm, yes indeed..." said Cristofano, hesitantly.

"What is that?" I asked.

"Well, my boy," said the Jesuit, adopting a paternal tone, "this is the celebrated plant from the lands of Tartary, which senses magnetically the presence of nearby sheep and then produces miraculous flowers in the form of sheep."

Analogous is the behaviour of the heliotropes, which magnetically follow the path of the sun (like the sunflower, from which Father Kircher had fashioned an extraordinary heliotropic clock) and that of the selenotropic plants, whose blossoms follow the moon instead.

Animals, too, are magnetic: while leaving aside the all too well-known examples of the torpedo and of the fisher frog, which attract and paralyse their prey, animal magnetism is clearly observable in the *anguis stupidus*, the enormous American serpent which lives immobile below ground and attracts prey to itself, mostly deer, which it calmly proceeds to envelop in its coils and to swallow, slowly dissolving in its mouth their flesh and even their hard horns. And, is not the faculty magnetic whereby the anthropomorphic fish, also known as sirens, attract unfortunate mariners into the waters?

"I understand," retorted Cristofano, slightly confused, "but our task is to cure Bedfordi, not to devour or to capture him."

"And do you perhaps believe that medicinal remedies do not act through their magnetic virtue?" asked Robleda, with skilful rhetoric.

"I have never heard of anyone being cured in that way," I observed dubiously.

"Well, it is quite naturally the therapy to be employed where all others have failed," said Robleda in defence of his contention. "What matters is not to lose sight of the laws of magnetism. First, one cures the sickness using every herb, stone, metal, fruit or seed which bears a similarity in colour, form, quality, figure *et cetera* with the diseased part. One observes the correspondences with the stars: heliotropic plants for solar types, lunar plants for lunatics, and so on and so forth. Then the *principium similitudinis*: kidney stones, for example, are cured with stones from the bladders of swine or other creatures which enjoy stony environs, such as crustaceans and oysters. The same is true of plants: the chondrilla, for example, the roots of which are covered in nodes and protuberances, are splendid for curing haemorrhoids. Finally, even poisons can act as antidotes; and in the same way, honey is excellent for healing bee stings, spiders' legs are used in poultices against spiders' bites..."

"Now, I understand," lied Cristofano. "Yet I fail to see with what magnetic therapy we should cure Bedfordi."

"But that is simple: with music."

Padre Robleda had not the slightest doubt: as Kircher had most clearly explained, the art of sounds entered too into the law of universal Magnetism. The ancients knew that the different musical modes were able through magnetism to stimulate the soul: the Doric mode inspired temperance and moderation, the Lydian, which was suitable for funerals, moved one to tears and lamentation; the Mixolydian mode aroused commiseration, piety and the like; the Aeolian and the Ionic induced sleep and torpor. If, then, one rubs the edge of a glass with a damp fingertip, it will emit a sound which will be propagated magnetically to all similar beakers placed in the immediate vicinity, thus provoking choral resonance. But the *magnetismus musicae* also has exceedingly powerful therapeutic capacities, which manifest most markedly in the cure of tarantism.

"Tarantism?" I asked, while Cristofano at last nodded his accord.

"In the city of Taranto, in the Kingdom of Naples," explained the physician, "a species of unusually noxious spider is often to be found, which are therefore known as tarantulas."

Their bite, Cristofano explained, produces effects which are, to say the least, terrifying: the victim first bursts into uncontrollable fits of laughter, ceaselessly rolling and twisting on the ground. He then jumps to his feet and raises his right arm high, as though unsheathing a sword, like a gladiator preparing solemnly for combat, and exhibits himself in a series of ridiculous gesticulations, before yet again casting himself down to the ground in another fit of hilarity. He then pretends again, with great pomp, to be a general or *condottiere*, whereupon he is seized with an irrepressible thirst for water and coolness, so that if he is given a vase full of water, he will plunge his whole head into it, shaking it frenetically as sparrows do when washing in a fountain. He then runs to a tree and climbs up it, remaining suspended therefrom, sometimes for many days. At last, he lets himself fall to the ground, exhausted and, kneeling bent double, he falls a-groaning and a-sighing and strikes the bare ground with his fists like an epileptic or a lunatic, invoking punishments and misadventures upon his own head.

"But that is terrible," I commented, horrified. "All that, just from the bite of a tarantula?"

"Of course," confirmed Robleda, "and that is without mentioning other extraordinary magnetic effects: the bite of the red tarantula causes the victim to become red in the face, green tarantulas make one turn green, and striped ones likewise cause the victim to come out in stripes, while aquatic ones induce a desire for water, those which dwell in hot places induce choler, and so on and so forth."

"And how is it cured?" I asked, growing curious.

"Perfecting the primitive knowledge of certain peasants from Taranto," said Robleda, rummaging in his drawers and then proudly showing us a leaf of paper, "Padre Kircher prepared an antidote."

He showed us a crumpled half-sheet of paper, covered in notes and pentagrams. We observed him with perplexity and no little suspicion.

"And with what does one play?"

"Well, the Tarantini perform it with tambourines, lyres, zithers, dulcimers and flutes; and, obviously, with guitars, like that of Devizé."

"In short," the physician retorted perplexedly, "you are saying that Devizé could cure Bedfordi with this music."

"Oh no, this is good only for the bite of the tarantula. We shall have to use something else."

"Another music?" I asked.

"We shall have to use trial and error. We shall leave the choice to Devizé. But remember, my sons: in desperate cases, the only true succour comes from the Lord; and," added Padre Robleda, "no one has ever discovered an antidote for the pestilence."

"You are right, Padre," I heard Cristofano say, while obscurely I remembered the *arcanae obices*. "And I wish to place my entire confidence in the theories of your colleague Kircher."

The physician, as he freely admitted, no longer knew to which saint to address himself; yet, still hoping that his cures might, sooner or later, have a beneficial effect upon Bedfordi, he would not deprive his moribund patient of one last desperate attempt. He therefore informed me that we would, for the time being, delay informing the other guests of the Englishman's desperate condition.

Later, when I was already serving dinner, Cristofano told me that he had set an appointment with Devizé for the morrow. The French musician, whose chamber was next to that of Bedfordi, would only have to play his guitar in the Englishman's doorway.

"So, do we take leave of one another until morning, Signor Cristofano?"

"No, I have fixed the appointment with Devizé immediately before luncheon. That is the ideal time: the sun is high and the energy of the musical vibrations can spread to the maximum. Good night, my boy."

Night the Eighth

BETWEEN *the* 18ᵀᴴ *&* 19ᵀᴴ SEPTEMBER, 1683

✠

"Closed! It is closed, damn it!"

That was to be expected, I thought, while Atto Melani pushed uselessly against the trapdoor that led to Tiracorda's stables. Already, when we were marching through the galleries, escorted by the subdued muttering of Ugonio and Ciacconio, this latest nocturnal expedition to the house of Tiracorda seemed to me destined to fail. Dulcibeni had discovered that we were keeping an eye on him. Perhaps he did not imagine that we had already spied upon him in Tiracorda's study, but he would never have wished to run the risk of being observed while conducting strange trafficking with (or against) his old friend. And indeed, after entering his fellow-countryman's home, he had made sure that the trapdoor was locked.

"Excuse me, Signor Abbot," said I while Atto wiped his hands nervously, "but perhaps it is better like this. If tonight Dulcibeni notices nothing strange while he is playing at riddles with Tiracorda, perhaps tomorrow we shall find our way free."

"Not a bit of it," replied Atto crossly, "he knows now that he is under observation. If he intends to accomplish something strange, he will do it as early as possible: even tonight; or tomorrow, at the latest."

"And so?"

"And so, we must find a way of entering Tiracorda's house, even if I really do not know how. We would need…"

"Gfrrrlubh," interrupted Ciacconio, stepping forward.

Ugonio looked at him frowning, as though in reproof.

"At last, a volunteer," commented Abbot Melani, satisfied.

A few minutes later, we were divided into two unequal groups. Atto, Ugonio and I marched along gallery C, in the direction of the underground river. Ciacconio, on the other hand, had climbed to the surface up the well which led from the same conduit to the Piazza della Rotonda, near the Pantheon. He had not been willing to explain to us how he intended to effect his entry into the house of Tiracorda. We had patiently explained to him, down to the smallest details, how the physician's house was laid out, but only at the very end did the *corpisantaro* candidly declare that the information would be absolutely of no use to him. We had even provided him with a sketch of the house, including the disposition of the windows; but, hardly had we separated than we heard resounding in the gallery a frenetic, goat-like sound of mastication. The life of our sketch, on which Ciacconio was horribly banqueting, had been all too brief.

"Do you think he will succeed?" I asked Abbot Melani.

"I have not the least idea. We explained to them *ad nauseam* every single corner of the house, but it is as though he already knew what to do. I cannot bear them, those two."

In the meantime, we were rapidly advancing towards the small underground river where, two nights previously, we had seen Dulcibeni mysteriously disappear. We passed close to the old and nauseating carcasses of the rats, and very soon we heard the sound of the subterranean watercourse. This time we were better equipped: at Atto's request, the *corpisantari* had brought with them a long and robust rope, a few iron nails, a hammer and a few long staves. These would be useful for the perilous and somewhat unwise operation which Atto intended at all costs to perform: to ford the river.

We stood for who knows how long, pensively observing the watercourse, which seemed more black, fetid and threatening than ever. I shivered, imagining a ruinous fall into that disgusting and hostile current. Even Ugonio seemed worried. I sought to bolster up my courage by addressing a silent prayer to the Lord.

Suddenly, however, I saw Atto move away from me and direct his gaze towards a point where the right-hand wall of the gallery formed an angle with the channel through which the river ran. For a few moments, Atto remained immobile opposite the corner between the two conduits. Then he stretched out a hand along the wall of the fluvial gallery.

"What are you doing?" I called out in alarm, seeing him lean dangerously towards the river.

"Keep quiet," he whispered, groping ever more eagerly at the wall, as though he were seeking something.

I was about to run to his assistance, fearing that he might lose his balance. It was precisely then that I saw him at last retreat from this dangerous exposure, grasping something in his left hand. It was a little painter of the kind which fishermen use to moor their boats on the Tiber. Atto began to pull on the cord, gradually coiling it. When at last there seemed to be resistance at the far end, Atto invited Ugonio and myself to look at the little river. Just in front of us, faintly illuminated by the light of the lantern, there floated a flat-bottomed boat.

ॐ

"I think that by now even you will have understood," said Abbot Melani soon afterwards, as we navigated in silence, driven by the current.

"No, I really do not," I admitted. "How did you manage to discover the boat?"

"It is simple. Dulcibeni had two possibilities: to cross the river or to go down it by boat. In order to take the river, however, he needed to have a boat moored at the point where the two galleries intersect. When we arrived, there was no trace of any boat; but, if there had been one, it would surely have been subject to the pull of the current."

"So, if it was secured by a rope," I guessed, "it would be pulled downstream by the current into the gallery to our right, where it flows down towards the Tiber."

"Exactly. The mooring had therefore to be secured to a point situated to the right in relation to gallery C, in other words, in the direction of the current. Had it been otherwise, we should have seen the hawser stretched from left to right, towards the boat. That was why I looked for the cord on the right. It was secured to an iron hook, which had been placed there who knows how long ago."

While I meditated upon this new proof of Abbot Melani's sagacity, Ugonio increased our pace by pulling gently on the two oars with which the boat was equipped. The bare landscape illuminated by our lantern was dull and monotonous. On the vaulted stone roof of the gallery, we heard the echo of the waves lapping against our fragile bark.

"But you were not sure that Dulcibeni had used a boat," I suddenly objected. "You said: 'Now, if there had been one...'"

"Sometimes, in order to know the truth, it is necessary to presuppose it."

"What do you mean?"

"It frequently happens like this in affairs of state: in the presence of inexplicable or illogical facts, one must figure out what must have been the indispensable condition which determined them, however incredible it may be."

"I do not understand."

"The most absurd truths, my boy, which are also the blackest ones, never leave any traces. Remember that."

"Does that mean that they will never be discovered?"

"Not necessarily. There are two possibilities: the first is that there may be someone who knows or who has understood, but who has no proof."

"And what then?" I asked, understanding very little of the abbot's words.

"He then constructs the proof which he does not have, so that the truth comes to the surface," replied Atto candidly.

"Do you mean that one can encounter false proofs of real facts?" I asked, open-mouthed.

"Bravo. But do not be surprised. You must not fall into the common error of believing, once it has been discovered that a document or a proof was counterfeited, that its content, too, is false. The contrary is likely to be true. Remember that when you become a gazetteer: often the most horrendous and unacceptable truths are contained in false documents."

"And what if even those are not available?"

"At that point, and this is the second assumption, it remains only to make suppositions, as I told you at the outset, and then to verify whether one's reasoning holds."

"If so, one must reason thus in order to understand the *secretum pestis*."

"Not yet," replied Melani. "First, one must understand the role of each of the actors, and above all the comedy which they are interpreting. And I believe that I have found it."

I looked at him in silence, with an expression which betrayed my impatience.

"It is a conspiracy against His Most Christian Majesty," exclaimed Atto solemnly.

"And who would be behind such a plot?"

"Why, that is clear: his wife, the Queen."

Seeing my incredulity, Atto was obliged to refresh my memory. Louis XIV had imprisoned Fouquet in order to extort from him the secret of the plague. Around Fouquet, however, moved personages who, like the Superintendent, had been humiliated or ruined by the Sovereign. First among these was Lauzun, imprisoned at Pinerol together with Fouquet and used as a spy; then, there was Mademoiselle, His Majesty's wealthy cousin, whom the King had forbidden to marry Lauzun. Moreover, Devizé, who had accompanied Fouquet to the Donzello, was faithful to Queen Maria Teresa, who had suffered all manner of infidelities, vexations and overbearing behaviour on the part of Louis XIV.

"But all this is no sufficient basis for holding that all of them plotted against the Most Christian King," said I, interrupting him to voice my doubts.

"That is true, but I ask you to consider: the King wants the secret of the pestilence. Fouquet refuses to give it to him, probably affirming that he knows nothing of it. When the letter full of Kircher's ravings which we have found on Dulcibeni comes into Colbert's possession, Fouquet can no longer deny all knowledge, on pain of his own life and that of his family. In the end, he reaches an agreement with the King and leaves Pinerol in exchange for the *secretum pestis*. Thus far, are we in agreement?"

"Yes. Agreed."

"Well, at this point, the King has triumphed. Do you suppose that, after twenty years of rigorous imprisonment and reduced to indigence, Fouquet will be content?"

"No."

"Would it have been human for him to gain some small satisfaction at the King's expense, before disappearing?"

"Why, yes."

"Exactly. Now, imagine: your immensely powerful enemy extorts from you the secret of the pestilence. He wants it at all costs, because he yearns to become even more powerful. However, he does not realise that you are also in possession of the secret of the antidote, the *secretum vitae*. If you cannot use that yourself, what will you do?"

"I could give it to someone... to a foe of my own enemy."

"Very good. And Fouquet had any number of such persons at his disposal, all ready to take their revenge on the Sun King: beginning with Lauzun."

"But why, in your opinion, did Louis XIV not realise that Fouquet also possessed the antidote to the pestilence?"

"This is my theory. As you will recall, in Kircher's letter, I also read *secretum vitae arcanae obices celant* or, in other words, the secret of life is concealed in mysterious obstacles, while the secret of the transmission of the pestilence is not. Well, I maintain that Fouquet was unable to deny that he knew the *secretum morbi* but succeeded in keeping to himself the secret of the antidote, adducing as a pretext—thanks to that phrase—that Kircher had hidden it from him too. This must have been quite easy for the Superintendent, seeing that the King's main interest was, if I know him well, how to spread the plague, not how to combat it."

"That does all seem rather complicated."

"But, it works. Now, consider this: with the secret of the pestilence in his hands, for whom might Louis XIV have been able to cause a few headaches?"

"Well, above all for the Empire," said I, thinking of what Brenozzi had told me.

"Very good. And perhaps for Spain too, with whom France has been at war for centuries. Is that not correct?"

"That is possible," I admitted, without understanding what Atto was getting at.

"But the Empire is in the hands of the Habsburgs, and Spain too. To what royal house does Queen Maria Teresa belong?"

"To the Habsburgs!"

"There we are: if we are to impose some order on the facts, we must therefore assume that Maria Teresa received, and used, the *secretum vitae* against Louis XIV. Fouquet may have given the *secretum vitae* to Lauzun, who will have passed it on to his beloved Mademoiselle, and she to the Queen."

"A queen, acting in the shadows against the King her husband," I reflected aloud, "why, that is unheard of."

"There too, you are mistaken," said Atto, "for there is a precedent."

In 1637, said the abbot, a year before the birth of Louis XIV, the secret services of the French Crown intercepted a letter from the Spanish ambassador in Brussels. The letter was addressed to Queen Anne of Austria, sister of King Philip IV of Spain and consort of King Louis XIII, in other words, the mother of the Sun King. From the missive, it was clear that Anne of Austria was in secret correspondence with her former country; and that, at a time when France and Spain were in open conflict. The King and Cardinal Richelieu ordered thorough but discreet inquiries. Thus, it was discovered that the Queen visited a certain convent in Paris rather too frequently: officially, to pray; but in reality, to exchange letters with Madrid and with the Spanish ambassadors in England and Flanders.

Anne denied that she had been engaged in espionage. She was then summoned for a private interview with Richelieu: the Queen risked imprisonment, the Cardinal warned icily, but a simple confession would save her. Louis XIII would pardon her only in exchange for a complete account of the news which she had learned in her secret correspondence with the Spaniards. The letters of Anne of Austria did not, indeed, relate solely to the usual complaints about the life of the court of Paris (where Anne was rather unhappy, as Maria Teresa was also to be). The Queen of France was exchanging precious political information with the Spaniards, perhaps in the belief that this could bring about an early end to the war. It was, however, against the interests of her kingdom. Anne confessed in full.

"In 1659, during the negotiations which led up to the Peace of the Pyrenees on the Isle of Pheasants," continued Atto, "Anne at last met her brother, King Philip IV of Spain, again. They had not seen each other for forty-five years. They had separated painfully when she, as a young princess barely sixteen years of age, had left for France forever. Anne tenderly embraced and kissed her brother. Philip, however, drew away from his sister's lips, looking her in the eyes. She said: 'Will you pardon me for having been such a good Frenchwoman?' 'You have my esteem,' said he. Ever since Anne had ceased to spy on his account, her brother had ceased to love her."

"But she was Queen of France, she could not..."

"I know, I know," said Atto sharply. "I told you that old story only to help you understand what the Habsburgs are like. Even when they marry a foreign king, they remain Habsburgs."

"The blackwater is walloping!"

We had been interrupted by Ugonio, who was showing signs of nervousness. After a relatively calm stretch, the little river had become more impetuous. The *corpisantaro* was using his oars with more vigour, trying in fact to slow us down. Rowing against the current, he had just decapitated one oar against the hard bed of the watercourse.

An awkward moment then arose: a little further on, the river divided into two branches, one twice as wide as the other. The noise and the speed of the waters were distinctly greater.

"Right or left?" I asked the *corpisantaro*.

"Decreasing the scrupules so as not to increase one's scrupules, and to obtain more benefice than malefice, I ignorify comprehension and navigate fittingly," said Ugonio, while Atto protested.

"Stay on the wider stream, do not branch off," said the abbot. "The other branch may lead nowhere."

Ugonio instead made a few decisive movements with his oar and steered us into the lesser channel, where our speed at once diminished.

"Why did you not obey me?" complained Atto, growing angry.

"The canaletto is conductive, but the grand canalisation is misodorous; while by decreasing the scrupules so as not to increase one's scrupules, and by fulfilling one's obligations, the Christian's jubilations are increased."

Rubbing his eyes as though he were suffering from a violent headache, Atto abandoned any attempt to understand Ugonio's mysterious explanation.

Very soon, Abbot Melani's suppressed rage was unleashed. After a few minutes of placid navigation, the vault of the new gallery began to become lower and lower.

"It is a secondary sewer, a curse upon you and your sparrow's brain," said Atto, turning to Ugonio.

"Yet it misodours not, howsoever well the other ramification may flow," replied Ugonio, without in any way losing his composure.

"But what does he mean?" I asked, worried about the roof, which was coming ever nearer to our heads.

"It misodours not, for all that it is overstrait."

We gave up all hope of interpreting Ugonio's verbal hieroglyphics, also because the gallery had in the meantime become so low that we had to crouch uncomfortably at the bottom of the boat. It was now almost impossible for Ugonio to row and Atto himself had to help the boat forward by pushing from the stern with one of the poles. The stink of the black waters, which was already in itself almost unbearable, had now become even more painful because of the posture which we were compelled to adopt and the suffocating space into which we were being forced. With a pang of regret, my thoughts went out to

Cloridia, to the intemperance of Master Pellegrino, to sunny days and to my bed.

Suddenly, we heard plashing around us, just next to our craft. Living beings of an unknown nature seemed to be moving excitedly in the waters around us.

"Rats," announced Ugonio. "They fugitate."

"How ghastly," commented Abbot Melani.

The vault was now even lower. Ugonio was forced to draw the oars aboard. Only Atto, in the stern, kept pushing our bark onward with rhythmic shoves from his pole against the bottom of the channel. The waters we were traversing were almost completely stagnant, yet deprived of their accustomed silence: for, all around us, in bizarre counterpoint to the rhythmic beat of Abbot Melani's pole, we were followed by the sinister gurglings of the rats.

"If I did not know that I was alive, I would say that, roughly speaking, we must be on the Styx," said Atto, panting from so much effort. "Always provided that I am not mistaken as to the first point," he added.

We now lay face upwards, pressed one against the other on the bottom of the craft, when we heard the acoustics of the gallery change and become gentler, as though the channel were about to widen. It was then that there appeared before our astonished eyes, on the roof of the gallery, a circle of crepitating fire, into which yellow and reddish tongues of flame seemed to want to draw us.

Disposed in a halo within the circle were three Magi, immobile and fatal. Enveloped in crimson tunics and long conical cowls, they observed us icily. Within the cowls, from pairs of round holes, flashing eyes observed us, evil and all-knowing. One of the three held a skull in his hand.

Overcome by the surprise, all three of us started in unison. The bark deviated slightly from its natural course and went askew, with its prow and poop scraping against the opposite sides of the channel; thus, it became stranded immediately under the circle of fire.

One of the three Magi (or were they perhaps sentinels of the Inferno?) leaned over, observing us with malevolent curiosity. He brandished a torch, which he waved several times, seeking the better to illuminate our countenances; his fellows consulted with one another in hushed tones.

"Perhaps I was indeed mistaken about that first point," I heard Atto stammer.

The second Magus, who held in his hand a great white candle, leaned forward in his turn. It was then that Ugonio exploded in a scream of infantile terror, struggling madly and involuntarily kicking me in the stomach and hitting Abbot Melani hard on the nose. Hitherto frozen by fear, we reacted with unpardonable discomposure, striking out in all directions. In the meanwhile, the bark had freed itself; so that, before we realised what was happening, our terrified trampling got the better of us and I heard one splash, then two, to either side of me.

The world folded in upon itself and all grew suddenly cold and dark while beings leapt forth from diabolical whirlpools and crawled over my face, sprinkling it with disgusting filth. I screamed in turn, but my voice was broken and fell like Icarus.

I shall never know for how long (for seconds? for hours?) that nightmare in the subterranean canal lasted. I only know that it was Ugonio who saved me, when with bestial vigour he pulled me from the waters, dumping me on hard planks so rudely that he almost broke my back.

Overwhelmed by terror, I had lost my memory. I must have dragged myself along the sewer, sometimes tiptoeing along the bottom, which I was just able to do, sometimes floating, and been saved in the end by Ugonio. Now I lay in the bottom of the boat, which had been righted and emptied of water.

My back was quite painful; I was panting from cold and fear, and still in thrall to its diabolical effects. Thus I believed that my eyes were deceiving me when, upon sitting up, I looked around me.

"Both of you may thank Abbot Melani," I heard Atto saying. "If, when I fell into the water, I had let go of the lantern, we should by now be food for the rats."

The faint light continued heroically to light up the way, offering our eyes the most unexpected of sights. Although struggling to penetrate the darkness, I could clearly discern that we were in the middle of a vast subterranean lake. Above our heads, as we were able to tell from the echo, an immense and majestic cavern opened up. All around us there spread black and threatening waters. But our bodies were safe. We had landed on an island.

ॐॐ

"To obtain more benefice than malefice, and to be more padre than parricide, I abominate the artefactor of this revolting, merdiloquent and shiteful spectacule. He is a disghastly felonable!"

"You are right. Whoever has done this is a monster," said Atto, for the first time completely in agreement with Ugonio.

It was not difficult to explore the islet upon which destiny (or rather, our carelessness and lack of the fear of God) had so kindly deposited us. The little strip of ground could be covered on foot in a few instants and I would not have said that it was any bigger than the modest little church of Santa Maria in Posterula.

It was, however, the middle of the island which caught the attention of Atto and Ugonio: it was there that several objects of varying sizes were gathered, and which I had difficulty in distinguishing clearly.

I felt my clothing: I was soaking wet and shivering with cold. I shook myself, striving to revive my inner heat, and in my turn disembarked, diffidently testing the cindery soil of the isle with my outstretched foot. I joined Atto and Ugonio who were searching here and there with expressions at once thoughtful and disgusted.

"I must say, my boy, that your talent for fainting is growing ever more refined," said Atto in welcome. "You are pale. I see that our recent encounter has terrified you."

"But who were they? Good heavens, they looked like…"

"No, they were not the guardians of the Inferno. It was only the *Societas Orationis et Mortis.*"

"The pious confraternity who bury abandoned corpses?"

"The very people. Do you not recall how they came to the inn to collect the body of poor Fouquet? Unfortunately, I too had forgotten that when they meet in procession, they wear tunics and cowls and bear torches, skulls and so on. Rather picturesque, really…"

"Ugonio too was terrified," I observed.

"I asked him why and he did not want to answer me. I am under the impression that the *Societas Orationis et Mortis* is one of the rare things that the *corpisantari* fear. The Company was proceeding along an underground gallery in which there is an opening above the sewer at exactly the same moment, alas, as we arrived on the scene. They heard us passing and leaned over to look, and panic played an unpleasant trick on us. Do you know what happened after that?"

"I… recall nothing," I admitted.

Atto briefly explained to me what had taken place: he and Ugonio had fallen into the water and the bark had suddenly lost its balance and capsized. I had remained imprisoned underneath the boat, with my body under the water and my head above it, which was why my screams had been stifled, as though under a bell. Terrified by the cataclysm, the rats which infested the waters had jumped onto me, running over my face and fouling me with their excrement.

I touched my face. It was true. I wiped myself with a sleeve, with my stomach turning in disgust.

"We were fortunate," continued Atto, while he guided me around the island, "for, between one scream and another, Ugonio and I managed to free ourselves of those disgusting beasts."

"Rats, not beasties," Ugonio promptly corrected him, while he gazed at a sort of cage which stood at our feet.

"Rats, mice, what you will! In short," Abbot Melani finished explaining to me, "we succeeded in bringing you and the bark out of that accursed sewer and finding our way into this underground lake. Fortunately, the three hooded ones did not attempt to follow us, and here we now are. Courage! You are not the only one to be cold. Just look at me: I too am soaked to the skin and covered in mud. Who could ever have imagined that I should ruin so many magnificent clothes in your wretched hostelry... But, come on now."

He showed me the bizarre workshop which occupied the centre of the isle.

Two large blocks of white stone lay on the ground and served as pedestals for two tables of dark, rotting wood. Upon one, I discovered a great array of instruments, pincers, pointed little knives and long butchers' knives, scissors and various blades without handles; bringing our lantern closer, I noted that they were all caked with congealed blood, of all shades from carmine to black. The table stank horribly of rotting carcasses. Among the knives were a couple of large, half-consumed candles. Abbot Melani lit them.

I moved to the other table, upon which lay other more mysterious objects: a ceramic vase, complete with its lid, decorated all over and with a number of holes in its side, which seemed strangely familiar to me; a little phial of transparent glass, the appearance of which also did not seem new to me; next to it, a voluminous orange-coloured earthenware basin about an arm's length in diameter, in the middle of which stood a strange metal harness. It was a sort of tiny gallows.

Upon a broad tripod stood a vertical stem which ended in two curved arms which, using a screw, could be hooped and tightened at will so as to garrotte any unfortunate homunculus attached thereto. The dish was half-full of water, so that the little scaffold (which was no higher than a jug) was completely immersed, apart from the garrotting hoops at the apex.

On the ground, however, stood the most singular item of the whole mysterious elaboratory: an iron cage, as tall as a small child, and with rather close, narrow bars; as though it were designed to imprison minuscule, lively and volatile creatures like butterflies or canaries.

I noticed a movement within the cage and looked more closely. A tiny grey creature was, in its turn, looking at me, fearful and furtive in its nest: a little wooden box filled with straw.

Atto brought the lantern closer so that I could see what he and Ugonio had already discovered. Now the sole hostage of the isle, visibly scared by our presence, I descried with surprise was a poor little mouse.

Around the cage, piled one against the other, stood other sinister devices, which we examined with cautious disgust: urns filled with yellowish powder, drippings, secretions, bilious humours, phlegm and mire; little jars filled with animal (or human?) fat, all mixed with ashes, dead skin and other revolting elements; retorts, alembics, glass jars, a bucket full of bones, surely of animals (which Ugonio nevertheless examined meticulously), a lump of putrescent meat, the rotting peel of fruit, nutshells; a ceramic vase filled with locks of hair, another glass one containing a mass of little serpents preserved in spirits; a little fishing net, a brazier with its bellows, old firewood, half-rotten leaves of paper, coals and pebbles; finally, a pair of large, filthy gloves, a pile of greasy rags and other sordid and vile objects.

"It is a necromancer's den," said I, thoroughly disconcerted.

"Worse still," retorted Atto, while we still roamed around that mad and barbarous bazaar. "It is the den of Dulcibeni, who lodges at your inn."

"And whatever would he be doing here?" I exclaimed in horror.

"It is difficult to say. What is certain is that he is doing something to rats which does not find favour with Ugonio."

The *corpisantaro* was still pensively observing the butcher's table, completely undisturbed by the mortiferous stench which emanated from it.

"He imprisons, he strangulates, he bistourifies. Thereafter, however, it surpasses all apprehension," said he at length.

"Many thanks, thus far I too had come," said Atto. "First, he captures rats with his fishing net, then he puts them into cages. Then he uses them for some strange sorcery and he strangles them using that strange little gallows. Then he quarters them, and in the end I have no idea what else he may do," said Atto with an acid smile. "All, no doubt, in accordance with the pious prescriptions of the Jansenists of Port-Royal. The one in the cage must be the sole survivor."

"Signor Atto," said I, nauseated by this triumph of obscenity, "does it not seem to you that there is something here which we have already seen?"

I pointed to the phial on the table, next to the miniature gallows.

By way of a reply, Atto extracted from his pocket an object whose existence I had practically forgotten. Unwrapping them from a handkerchief, he exhibited the fragments of the glass phial full of blood which we had found in gallery D. Then he compared them with the phial that was still intact.

"They are twins!" I remarked with surprise.

The broken phial was indeed identical, both in its form and in its greenish glass, to that which we had just found on the island.

"But we have already seen the decorated vase with a lid," I insisted. "It was, unless I am mistaken..."

"... in Tiracorda's secret room," added Atto, coming to my help.

"There we have it!"

"No, no. You are thinking of the vase in which Dulcibeni was rummaging when his friend had gone to sleep. This one, however, is far bigger and the designs painted on it are far more intricate. The motif of the decoration and the holes in the sides are, I will allow, almost identical. Perhaps they are the work of the same artisan."

The vase found on the islet also had lateral air-holes on it and was likewise decorated with pond plants and little swimming beings, probably tadpoles which played about between the leaves. I opened the lid, raised the vase to the lantern and immersed one finger: inside, there was greyish water, in which floated fragments of light white gauze; at the bottom, a little sand.

"Signor Atto, Cristofano told me that it is dangerous to handle rats during a time of pestilence."

"I know. I thought of that, too, the other night, when we encountered those two moribund rats which were spitting blood. Clearly, our Dulcibeni feels no such fear."

"The insula is not goodly, not justly, not sanitary," warned Ugonio in grave tones.

"I know, you brute, we shall be leaving it very soon. Instead of lamenting, you could at least tell me where we are, seeing as it is thanks to you that we came here."

"It is true," said I to Ugonio. "If, at the fork in the river, you had chosen to take the other branch, we should never have discovered Dulcibeni's island."

"It is no opera of delight, inaswhereandwhat concerns the occupation exercisioned with great artifice upon the altar of the insula."

Abbot Melani raised his eyes to heaven as though in extremities of distress. He fell silent for a moment, and suddenly cried out: "Then will somebody tell me where and what the deuce this damned insula is!" and his cry caused the whole vast cavern to reverberate.

The echoes died away. Without opening his mouth, Ugonio invited me to follow him. He pointed at the back of the huge stone block which served as the base for one of the tables, and nodded his head with a grunt of satisfaction, as though in reply to Abbot Melani's challenge.

Atto joined us. On the stone, a high-relief was visible, in which the figures of men and animals could be distinguished. Melani drew even closer and began impatiently to explore the carved surface with his fingertips, as though to confirm what he had just seen with his eyes.

"Extraordinary. It is a Mithraeum," he murmured. "Look, look here. A textbook example! There is everything here, the sacrifice of the bull, the scorpion..."

Where we stood, there had once, long ago, been an underground temple in which the ancient Romans adored the god Mithras. He was a god originating in the Orient who had in Rome come to rival in popularity Apollo, who, like him, represented the sun. That this was indeed an ancient shrine of Mithras was not in doubt: the image carved on one of the stones showed the god killing a bull, whose testicles were held in the claws of a scorpion, a typical depiction of Mithras. What was more, underground sites (always supposing that this place had been under the ground) were favoured by the worshippers of Mithras.

"We have found only the two large stones on which Dulcibeni places the tables he uses for his practices," concluded Abbot Melani. "Perhaps the remainder of the temple is at the bottom of the lake."

"And how could that be?"

"With all these underground rivers, every now and then the terrain down here settles. You have seen it yourself. Underground, there are not only conduits, tunnels and galleries, but grottoes, caverns, great hollows, whole Roman palaces integrated into buildings of more recent centuries. The waters of the rivers and the sewers carve the ground out blindly and every now and then a grotto crumbles, another one fills with water, and so on. That is the nature of the subterranean city."

I thought instinctively of the fissure which had opened in the wall of the staircase of the inn, a few days earlier, after we had heard a reverberation under the ground.

Ugonio was again showing signs of impatience. We decided to return the boat to the water and attempt to go back. Atto could not wait to see Ciacconio and to know the success or otherwise of his incursion into the house of Tiracorda. We again launched our humble vessel (which had fortunately suffered no significant damage) and prepared to return up the same narrow channel which had brought us to the subterranean Mithraeum.

Ugonio seemed in the worst of humour. Suddenly, just when we were about to embark, he jumped down from the boat and, raising a shower of gravel with his rapid little trot, returned to the island.

"Ugonio!" I called after him, astonished.

"Be quiet, he'll only be a moment," said Atto Melani, who must have foreseen what the *corpisantaro* was about to do.

A few moments later, indeed, Ugonio returned and jumped agilely into the bark. He seemed relieved.

I was about to ask him what the deuce had called him back, when suddenly I understood.

"Insula iniquitable," muttered Ugonio, speaking to himself.

He had freed the last rodent from its cage.

❧

Our return through the suffocating channel that flowed into the lake was somewhat less dramatic but just as wearying as the outward journey. The going was made all the slower and more painful by our fatigue and the fact that we were moving upstream, however weak the current may have been. No one spoke and in the poop Atto and Ugonio pushed with poles while I held the lantern and provided a counterweight in the prow.

After a while, I wanted to break the heavy silence, relieved only by the viscous slopping of water in the canal.

"Signor Atto, concerning this matter of the movements provoked by underground rivers, something bizarre befell me."

I told him that the astrological gazette which we had taken from Stilone Priàso had forecast for the month of September natural phenomena such as earthquakes and the like. A few days earlier, at exactly the time predicted, there had been heard in the bowels of the earth a sort of abysmal, menacing rumble and a fissure had appeared in the wall of the staircase. Was that only a fortuitous occurrence? Or did the author of the almanack know that in September phenomena of that nature were likely to take place?

"I can only tell you that I do not believe in such nonsense," said Abbot Melani with a scornful little laugh, "otherwise, I would have run to consult an astrologer to tell me the present, the past and the future. I do not believe that the fact of having been born on the 31st of March can..."

"Aries," muttered Ugonio.

Atto and I looked at one another.

"Ah yes, I was forgetting that you are... that you understand these things," said Atto, struggling to contain his laughter.

But the *corpisantaro* would not be intimidated. According to the great astrologer Arcandam, Ugonio imperturbably pronounced, the native of Aries, warm and dry in nature, will be dominated by wrath. He will be red-headed or fair and will almost always bear marks on his shoulders or on his left foot; he will have abundant hair, a thick beard, brightly coloured eyes, white teeth, well-formed jaws, a fine nose and large eyelids.

He will be observant and curious about the words and deeds of others and concerning every secret. His will be a studious, elevated, variable and vigorous spirit. He will have many friends. He will flee evil. He will be little inclined to illnesses, apart from the grave vexations caused him by headaches. He will be eloquent, solitary in his way of life, prodigal in necessary things: he will meditate upon fraudulent enterprises and will often employ threats. He will have good fortune in all kinds of wars as in negotiating all things.

In his early youth, he will be very contentious and choleric. He will suffer from inner irascibility which he will barely manifest. He will be a liar, and false; using soft words to cover dissimulation and lies, saying one thing and doing another, making marvellous promises but not keeping them. He will spend a part of his life in a position of authority. He will be avaricious and will therefore take care to acquire and to sell. He will be envious and therefore quick to anger, but even more, he will be envied by others, wherefore he will have many enemies and treacherous adversaries. As for misfortune, he may be beset by various calamities, so much so that he will not enjoy a single commodity without discommodiousness and peril for his property. He will possess a mutable inheritance, or he will soon lose what he had acquired and soon acquire what he had lost. But much wealth will be bestowed upon him.

He will make many voyages and will quit his country and his parents. From the age of twenty-three onwards, he will move on to better things and he will handle money. He will become rich at the age of forty and will attain a position of great dignity. He will succeed perfectly in whatever he undertakes; his good offices will be appreciated. He will not marry the woman who was first intended for him, but another whom he will love and from whom he will have noble sons. He will converse with ecclesiastics. In general, if he is born during the hours of daylight, he will be fortunate and held in great esteem by princes and lords. He will live to the age of eighty-seven years and three months.

Instead of mocking Ugonio, Atto and I listened to him in religious silence up to the end. Abbot Melani even left off using his boat-pole, while the *corpisantaro* humbly maintained his rhythm.

"Well, let us see," reflected Atto. "Wealthy, that is true. Skilful in negotiations, that is true. Fair-haired, at least until it went white, that is true. A great traveller, an observer of others' words and deeds: for sure. Fine eyes, white teeth, well-formed jaw, fine nose: yes, indeed. Eloquent, studious, elevated, variable and vigorous spirit: God forgive my immodesty, but that is not incorrect; on the contrary. What else? Ah yes, the esteem of princes, the company of prelates, and headaches. I do not know where our Ugonio fished up so much information from the sign of Aries, but it certainly is not all unfounded."

I avoided asking Atto Melani whether he also recognised himself in avarice, irascibility, fraudulence, envy and recourse to lies and threats, as mentioned in the astrological portrait. And nor did I ask

Ugonio why, among the many defects of those born under the sign of Aries, vanity had been omitted. I also took care not to mention the prophecy concerning marriage and children, which were obviously precluded in the case of the abbot.

"You truly know many things about astrology," I complimented the *corpisantaro* instead, recalling also his eloquent excursus into medical astrology a few nights previously.

"Perused, auscultated, verbalised."

"Remember, young man," interjected Abbot Melani, "that in this holy city, every house, every wall, every single stone is imbued with magic, with superstition, with obscure hermetic knowledge. Our two monsters must have read a few manuals of astrological consultations—one can find them everywhere, so long as the matter is not spoken of out loud. Scandal is but an entertainment for bumpkins: remember the story of Abbot Morandi."

It was at that moment that the sound of running water distracted us from our conversation: we had returned to the confluence with the main channel.

"Now we shall have to set to work with the oars," said Atto, while our boat gave itself up to the far faster and more forceful waters of the underground river.

A moment passed, then we all looked at one another speechlessly. "The oars," said I. "I think that we abandoned them when the trio of the *Societas Orationis et Mortis* made their appearance."

I saw Atto glare resentfully at Ugonio, as though awaiting an explanation.

"Aries also distractable," said Ugonio in his defence, trying to shift the blame for the loss of the oars to the abbot.

The little bark, now a helpless prey to the current, began to accelerate remorselessly. All attempts to use the poles to slow down our progress proved useless.

For a brief passage, we proceeded down the river; soon, however, a confluent poured in from the left, provoking a wave which compelled us to hold on tight to our poor piece of wood in order not to be thrown out. The roaring of the waters had grown ever louder and more overwhelming; the walls of the channel offered no hold. No one dared open his mouth.

Ugonio tried to use the cord which he had brought with him to hook onto any outcrop in the walls, but the bricks and stones that made these up were completely smooth.

Suddenly, I remembered that, on our outward journey, the *corpisantaro* had, however enigmatically, explained the reason why, when we came to the fork that led to the lake, he had not wished to proceed along the main channel.

"Did you not say that this river 'misodours'?" I asked him.

He nodded. "It misodours with the foulestest of fetidness."

Suddenly, we found ourselves in the midst of a sort of aquatic crossroads: from the left and from the right, two equal and contrary confluents hurled themselves with even greater force into our river.

That was the beginning of the end. The little bark, reeling drunkenly from that convolution of confluents, began to turn on itself, at first slowly and then vertiginously. We clung now, not only to the boat but to one another. The rotation soon made us lose our sense of direction, so that for a moment I had the absurd sensation of moving upstream, towards salvation.

Meanwhile a deafening roar drew ever nearer. The only reference point was our lamp which, with the greatest of difficulty, Atto continued to hold up, as though the fate of the world depended on it; around that point of light, everything spun madly. We seemed almost to be flying, I thought, transported by fear and vertigo.

That thought came true. Under the boat, the waters vanished, as though a magnetic force had raised us up and was about to deposit us mercifully upon the sands of salvation. For a brief and insane moment, I remembered the words of Padre Robleda about Kircher's Universal Magnetism, which comes from God and holds all things together.

But suddenly a blind, colossal force crashed against the bottom of the bark, throwing us from it at the same instant, and all became dark. I found myself in the water, drawn through icy, malignant eddies, lapped by filthy, disgusting foam, screaming with terror and despair.

We had gone over a waterfall, plummeting into an even more fetid and disgusting river. Not only had the impact with the water capsized the boat, but our lamp was lost. Only from time to time could I touch bottom with my feet, perhaps because here and there lay some large outcrop. Had that not been the case, I should surely have drowned. The stench was unbearable and my lungs were filled only by my panting from weariness and fear.

"Are you alive?" yelled Atto in the dark, while the roar of the cascade hammered at our ears.

A large blunt object struck me in the chest, leaving me breathless.

"Hold on, hold on to the boat, it is here between us," said Atto.

Miraculously, I managed to grasp the edge of the bark, while the current continued to drag us along.

"Ugonio," screamed Atto again, with all the breath that remained to him, "Ugonio, where are you?"

We were only two now. Certain at this moment that we were going to our death, we let ourselves be led by that poor wreck, floating in the midst of stinking fluids and other indescribable faecal waste.

"It misodoureth... now I understand."

"Understand what?"

"This is not just any channel. It is the Cloaca Maxima, the biggest sewer in Rome, built by the ancient Romans."

Our speed increased again, and, going by the sound, we knew that we were in a broad conduit the vault of which was rather low, perhaps hardly enough for the capsized hull of our little bark to pass. Now the roar of the waters had diminished, as we drew away from the waterfall.

Suddenly, however, the boat came to a stop. The vault was too low and had caused our poor craft to run aground in a comical, capsized position. Somehow, I managed to hold onto the edge. I raised an arm and felt with horror how close and oppressive was the roof of the vault. The air was dense and fetid: breathing had become almost impossible.

"What shall we do?" I panted, struggling desperately to keep my lips above the surface of the waters.

"There is no way back. Let us go with the current."

"But I cannot swim."

"I neither. But the water is dense, one has but to keep afloat. Lie on your back and try to keep your head erect," said he, spitting to cleanse his lips. "Move your arms a little from time to time, but do not struggle or you will sink."

"And then what?"

"We shall emerge somewhere."

"And what if, before that, the vault closes in completely?"

He did not reply.

Almost at the limit of our strength, we let ourselves be borne by the waves (if that disgusting mire could be so called) until my prophecy came true. The current again speeded up, as though we were on a slope; the air was so rarefied that I alternated long periods of holding my breath with sudden, agitated intakes; the foul gases thus inhaled provoked pains in my head and violent dizziness. It felt as though a remote and powerful whirlpool was about to swallow us.

Suddenly, the top of my head struck the roof of the gallery. The current ran even faster. This was the end.

I was about to vomit. Yet somehow I held back, as though at last about to obtain liberation and, with it, peace. Strangled, yet very close, I heard Atto's voice one last time.

"Alas, so it really is true," he murmured to himself.

Day the Ninth

19ᵀᴴ September, 1683

✠

"Look, look here. This one is young."

Hands and eyes of merciful angels were caring for me. I had come to the end of a long voyage. I, however, was no more: my body must have been elsewhere, while I enjoyed the beneficent warmth which heaven radiates upon all good souls. I waited to be shown the way.

A few timeless instants passed, then the hands of one of the angels gently prodded me. Light, indistinct murmurs were gradually awakening me. I could at last catch a droplet of that sweet celestial colloquy: "Search the other one better."

A few fleeting but perhaps eternal moments later, I understood that the winged celestial messengers had temporarily left me. Perhaps, for the time being, I no longer needed their charitable assistance. I then opened myself to the divine light which benign heaven extended over and around me and other poor wandering souls.

Contrary to all expectations, I still had eyes to see, ears to hear and flesh with which to feel the warm and holy dawn which utterly pervaded me. So I raised my eyelids and before me appeared the divine symbol of Our Lord, used centuries ago by the first Christians: a magnificent silver fish, which observed me benevolently.

At last, I looked up towards the light, but I had at once to raise my hand and cover my eyes.

It was day and I was under the sun, lying on a beach.

I soon understood that I was alive, although not in the best of condition. I sought in vain the two angels (or whatever they were) who had busied themselves about me. My head ached terribly and my eyes could not bear the light of day. Suddenly, I realised that I barely able to rise to my feet. My knees shook and the mud on which I walked threatened to make me to slip perilously.

Narrowing my eyes, I nevertheless looked around myself. I was no doubt on the banks of the Tiber. It was dawn and a few fishing boats sailed placidly on the waters of the river. On the far bank stood the ruins of the ancient Ponte Rotto—the Broken Bridge. To my right, lay the indolent profile of the Isola Tiberina, anointed by the two branches of the river which have for aeons caressed its banks. To my left, the quiet hill of Santa Sabina stood out against the quiet dawn sky. Now I knew where I was: a little further to the right was the outfall of the Cloaca Maxima, which had vomited Atto and me into the river. Fortunately, the current had not taken us downstream. I had a confused memory of having dragged myself from the water and cast myself down dejectedly upon the bare ground. It was a miracle to be alive; if all this had happened in winter, I thought, I should certainly have rendered my soul to the Lord.

Instead, I was comforted by the September sun, once more rising into a limpid sky; but hardly had my mind grown clearer than I realised that I was all filthy and numbed with cold, and an uncontrollable fit of shivering began to shake me from head to foot.

"Leave me, villain, leave me! Help!"

The voice came from behind me. I turned and found my way obstructed by a clump of tall bushes. I crossed it rapidly and found Abbot Melani lying on the ground, he too all covered in mud, and by now no longer in a state to cry out; he was vomiting violently. Two men, or rather, two dubious-looking individuals were leaning over him, but hardly did I approach than they took to their legs, disappearing behind a slight rise which dominated the beach. From the barks which were sailing in the vicinity, no fisherman seemed to have witnessed the scene.

Shaken by tremendous convulsions, Atto was throwing up the water which he had swallowed during our disastrous shipwreck. I held his head, hoping that the liquid expelled would not suffocate him. After a while, he was again able to speak and breathe normally.

"The two bastards…"

"Do not overstrain yourself, Signor Atto."

"… thieves. I shall catch them."

I had not then, indeed, I never had the courage to confess to Atto that in those two thieves I had recognised the two blessed angels of my awakening. Instead of caring for us, they had carefully inspected us with a view to robbery. The silvery fish which I had found by my side was no sacred epiphany, only some fishmonger's refuse.

"Anyway, they found nothing," Atto continued between one expectoration and another. "The little I had on me, I lost in the Cloaca Maxima."

"How do you feel?"

"How do you expect me to feel, in this condition and at my age?" said he, opening his filthy doublet and shirt. "If it were up to me, I would remain here in the sun until I feel a little warmer; but that, we cannot do."

I gave a start. Soon Cristofano would be beginning his matutinal rounds.

Followed by the curious glances of a group of fishermen who were preparing to disembark nearby, we moved away.

We took a little road parallel to the river bank, leaving Monte Savello to our right. Filthy and desperate as we were, the few passers-by looked upon us in dismay. I had lost my shoes and walked with a limp, coughing uncontrollably; Atto looked thirty years older and the clothing which he wore seemed to have been robbed from a tomb. He kept quietly cursing all the rheumatic and muscular pains provoked by those tremendous nocturnal labours and the soaking he had received. We were about to walk towards the Portico d'Ottavia, when he turned brusquely.

"I have too many acquaintances here. Let us change our route."

We then passed through the Piazza Montanara and crossed the Piazza Campitelli. More and more people were appearing on the streets.

In the labyrinth of narrow, tortuous, damp and gloomy alleyways, almost all of them unpaved, I savoured again the habitual alternation of dust and mire, the evil smells, the clangour and the cries. Swine large and small rooted in heaps of rubbish near steaming cauldrons of pasta and broad pans of fish already frying at that early hour, in flagrant disregard of all the notices and edicts of public health.

I heard Atto murmur something with disgust and vexation, while the sudden thunder of a cart's wheels covered his words.

Once it was quiet again, Abbot Melani continued: "How is it possible that, like pigs, we should have to seek peace in manure, serenity in rubbish, repose in this shambles of neglected streets? What is the point of living in a city like Rome if we must move like beasts and not like men? I beg you, Holy Father, deliver us from excrement!"

I looked at him questioningly.

"I am quoting Lorenzo Pizzati da Pontremoli," said he. "He may have been a parasite at the court of Pope Rospigliosi; but how right he was! It was he who penned this candid supplication to Clement IX some twenty years ago."

"But then, Rome has always been like this!" I exclaimed in surprise, always having imagined a very different and most fabulous environment for the city of the past.

"As I have already told you, I was in Rome at the time; well, in those days, the streets were repaired, albeit badly, almost every day. And if you consider all the sewers and pipes, too, the roads were always blocked by public works. To protect oneself from the mire of rainwater and refuse, one had to wear high boots, even in August. Pizzati was right: Rome has become a Babel in which people live in a continual clamour. It has ceased to be a city. It is a pigsty," exclaimed the abbot, stressing the last word.

"And did Pope Rospigliosi do nothing to improve matters?"

"On the contrary, my boy! But, if only you knew how pig-headed these Romans are. He tried, for example, to plan a public system for the collection of ordure; he commanded the citizens to clean the street before their doorways. All in vain!"

All of a sudden, the abbot pulled me violently to one side and we flattened ourselves against a wall. Only by a hair's-breadth did I thus escape the precipitous onrush of an enormous and luxurious carriage. The abbot's mood grew even darker.

"Carlo Borromeo was wont to say that in Rome, to have success, two things are necessary: to love God and to possess a carriage," Melani commented bitterly. "Do you know that in this city, there are more than a thousand of them?"

"Then it is perhaps they who account for the distant rumble which I hear even when no one is passing through the streets," said I, disconcerted. "But where do all those carriages go?"

"Oh, nowhere. It's simply the case that noblemen, ambassadors, physicians, famous advocates and Roman cardinals move about exclusively in carriages; even for the briefest of journeys. And that is not all: they are alone in their carriages, and sometimes, alone yet accompanied by several other carriages."

"Are their families so numerous?"

"No, of course not," said Atto, laughing. However, cardinals and ambassadors on official visits may proceed accompanied by up to three hundred carriages; with all the choked traffic and daily clouds of dust which that entails."

"Now, I can understand the brawl over a carriage station," said I, echoing him, "which I recently witnessed on the piazza in Posterula; the footmen of two carriages belonging to noblemen were going at each other hammer and tongs."

At that point, Atto turned off again.

"Even here, I could be recognised. There is a young canon... Let us cut across towards the Piazza San Pantaleo."

Exhausted as I was, I protested against all these complicated itineraries.

"Be quiet and do not attract attention to yourself," said Atto, unexpectedly tending to his faded white hair.

"It is a good thing that, in all this bestial confusion, no one is paying the slightest attention to us," he whispered, adding in an almost inaudible voice, "I hate being in this state."

It was wise, and Atto knew it, to traverse the great crowd at the market on the Piazza Navona, rather than be seen as isolated vagabonds in the middle of the Piazza Madama or the Strada di Parione.

"We must reach Tiracorda's house as early as possible," said Atto, "but without being seen by the Bargello's watchmen who are mounting guard in front of the inn."

"And, after that?"

"We shall try to enter the stables and take the underground galleries."

"But that will be extremely difficult; anyone might recognise us."

"I know. Have you any better ideas?"

We therefore prepared to plunge into the crowd at the market on the Piazza Navona. How immense was our disappointment when we found ourselves facing a half-empty square, animated only by sparse groups, in the centre of which, from the height of a box or a seat, bearded and sweaty orators waved their arms, haranguing and declaiming. No market, no vendors, no stalls piled up with fruit and vegetables, no crowd.

"The deuce, it is Sunday!" said Atto and I, almost in unison.

On Sunday, there was no market: that was why there were so few people in the streets. The quarantine and our too frequent adventures had made us lose count of the days.

As on all feast days, the priests were the lords of the piazza, preachers and pious men who, with edifying sermons attracted, some by the subtleties of their logic, some by the stentorian flow of their eloquence, small gaggles of students, scholars, loafers, mendicants, and even cutpurses, always ready to profit from the distraction of the other spectators. The gay quotidian chaos of the market had given way to a grave, leaden atmosphere; and, as though yielding to that atmosphere, clouds suddenly covered the sun.

We crossed the piazza stunned by disappointment, feeling even more naked and defenceless than we in fact were. We moved away from the centre of the square to the right-hand side, where we tiptoed along the walls, hoping to attract no attention. I was startled when a little boy, coming out from a nearby hut, pointed us out to the adult who was accompanying him. The latter stared briefly at us and then, fortunately, ceased to attend to our furtive and miserable presence.

"They will notice us, damn it. Let us try to merge into the crowd," said Atto, pointing out to me a nearby group of people.

So we mixed with a small but compact assembly, gathered around an invisible central point. We were just a few paces from the Cavalier Bernini's great Fountain of the Four Rivers in the middle of the piazza; the four titanic anthropomorphic statues of the aquatic deities, almost admonitory in their marmoreal potency, seemed to be participating in the pious atmosphere of the piazza. From within the fountain, a stone lion scrutinised me, ferocious but impotent. Above the monument, however, there stood an obelisk all covered in hieroglyphics and capped with a little golden pyramid, almost naturally pointing towards the Most High. Was this not precisely the obelisk which had been deciphered by Kircher, as someone had told me a few days earlier? But I was distracted by the crowd, which moved further forward, the better to listen to the sermon which I could hear coming from a few paces beyond.

In the forest of heads, backs and shoulders I could descry the preacher for only a few brief instants. His hat revealed him to be a Jesuit brother; he was a rotund purple-faced little man wearing a tricorn too big for his head and entertaining with torrential eloquence the small, tight group of spectators who had gathered around him.

"... And what is the life of devotion?" I heard him declaim. "I tell you that it is to speak little, to weep much, to be mocked first by this man, then by that, to tolerate poverty in one's life, suffering in one's body, insults to one's honour, injuries to one's interests. And, can such a life not be most unhappy? I tell you, yes it can!"

The crowd was stirred by a hubbub of incredulity and scepticism.

"I know," continued the preacher vehemently. "Persons who live the life of the spirit are accustomed to these evils and would even wish spontaneously to suffer from them. And if they do not find them upon their way, they go out hunting for them!"

Another murmur of disquiet traversed the crowd.

"Think of Simon of Cyrene, who feigned madness in order to be mocked at by the people. Think of Bernard of Clairvaux, who suffered from poor health and always took refuge in the iciest and most cruel of hermitages! And do you therefore account them to have been no more than miserable wretches? No, no, listen with me to what the great prelate Salviano said."

Abbot Melani caught my attention by pulling at my sleeve. "The way seems clear, let us go."

We moved towards the way out from the square nearest to the Donzello, hoping that those last footsteps would not hold any bad surprises for us.

"The great prelate Salviano may say what he will, but I cannot wait to get changed," complained Atto, nearing the limits of his patience and endurance.

Without having the courage to turn round, I had the disagreeable impression that someone was following us.

We were on the point of emerging safely from our perilous crossing when the unforeseeable occurred. Atto was proceeding ahead of me, skirting the wall of a palazzo, when from a little doorway I saw a pair of robust and decisive hands dart forth, seize him and drag him indoors by force. This terrible vision, together with my overwhelming weariness, almost caused me to lose my senses. I was petrified, unable to decide whether to run away or to call for help, in both of which cases I ran the risk of being identified and arrested.

Extricating me from the horns of this dilemma, there came from behind me a familiar voice, whose sound was so improbable as to appear celestial: "Get you ultraquickly into the coneyhole!"

Great though Abbot Melani's scorn for the *corpisantari* may have been, I believe that on this occasion he had no little difficulty in

hiding his gratitude for their intervention. Not only had Ugonio miraculously survived the Cloaca Maxima, but after rejoining Ciacconio, he
had tracked us down again and—although the method employed may
have been somewhat rough—had brought us to safety. It was, however,
Ciacconio who had dragged Atto through the little door on the Piazza
Navona, whither Ugonio now urged me to enter in my turn.

Once beyond the threshold, and without giving us the time to ask
any questions, the *corpisantari* made us pass through another little
door and climb down an exceedingly steep flight of stairs which in
turn led to a narrow and even more dismal windowless corridor. Ciacconio produced a lantern which, absurdly, he seemed to have been
concealing, already lit, in the folds of his grimy overcoat. Our saviour
seemed to be as soaked as we, and yet he trotted along as boldly and
rapidly as ever.

"Where are you taking us?" asked Atto, for once surprised and no
longer master of the situation.

"The Piazzame Navonio is perditious," said Ugonio, "and, to be
more padre than parricide, the subpantheon is more salubricious."

I remembered that, during one of our explorations of gallery C,
the *corpisantari* had shown us the way to an exit which led to the
courtyard of a palace behind the Pantheon, not far from the Piazza
della Rotonda. For a good quarter of an hour, they led us from cellar
to cellar, through an uninterrupted sequence of obscure doorways,
steps, abandoned store-rooms, spiral staircases and galleries. Every
now and then, Ugonio would bring out his ring laden with keys, open
a door, let us through, then lock the door behind us with four or
five turns of the key. Atto and I, already exhausted, were pushed and
dragged along by the two *corpisantari* like two mortal vessels whose
souls were ready to abandon them at any moment.

We arrived at last before a sort of great wooden portal which
opened creaking onto a courtyard. The daylight again hurt our pupils.
From the courtyard, we emerged into a little alleyway and from there
into another half-abandoned courtyard, to which we gained access
through a door without any lock.

"Ultraquickly into the coneyhole!" exhorted Ugonio, showing me
a wooden trap in the ground. We raised the lid, revealing a dark and
suffocating well. Across the top was laid an iron bar, from which hung
a rope; and this we swarmed down. We already knew where it led: to
the network of tunnels connected to the Donzello.

As the trapdoor closed over our heads, I saw the cowled heads of Ugonio and Ciacconio disappear into the light of day. I would have liked to ask Ugonio how he had managed to survive the wreck of our boat in the Cloaca Maxima and how the deuce he had got out from there, but I had no time. While I lowered myself, grasping the rope, for a fleeting instant it seemed to me that Ugonio's eyes met my own. Inexplicably, it seemed to me that he knew what I was thinking. I was happy that he was safe.

കൊ

Hardly had I returned to my chamber than I changed in a rush and hid my dirty, mud-stained clothing. At once, I betook myself to Cristofano's apartment, ready to justify my absence by an improbable visit to the cellars. Too exhausted to worry, I was ready to face questions and objections for which I was utterly unable to find a reply.

Cristofano, however, was sleeping. Perhaps still exhausted by the crisis of the day before, he had gone to bed without even closing his door. He lay clumsily sprawled across the bed, half-dressed.

I took care not to awaken him. The sun was low on the horizon; I still had time for something before the appointment we had fixed with Devizé in Bedfordi's chamber: to sleep.

Contrary to my expectations, this sleep did not restore me. My rest was troubled by tormented and convulsed dreams, in which I relived those terrible moments when I was under the capsized bark; then those disquieting discoveries on the islet of the Mithraeum, and lastly, the nightmare of the Cloaca Maxima, in which I believed that I had met with death. That was why, when Cristofano's fists pounded on my door, I arose almost wearier than before.

The physician did not seem to be in good form either. Two heavy bluish bags under the eyes marked his weary countenance; his gaze was watery and distant, and his posture, which I usually found so solid and erect, was slightly bent. He neither greeted me nor asked me anything, thank heavens, about the previous night.

On the contrary, I found myself reminding him that we would soon have to make the usual arrangements for our guests' breakfast. First, however, we must turn our minds to the emergency. It was time to put Robleda's theories to the test: Bedfordi's infection would, this time, be treated by the notes of Devizé's guitar. I went to inform the Jesuit that we were about to follow his advice. We called Devizé and

we then went to the adjoining chamber, where the poor Englishman
lay.

The young musician had brought his little stool with him so that
he could play in the corridor without entering the sickroom and thus
risking his own health. The door would remain open, so that the guitar's (we hoped) beneficent sound could penetrate within. Cristofano, however, posted himself right by Bedfordi's bed, in order to
observe the patient's reactions, if any.

I stood discreetly in the corridor, a few yards from the musician.
Devizé sat on his little stool, sought the most comfortable position
and began to tune his instrument. He soon broke off and warmed his
hands with an allemande. This, he followed with a courante, after
which he turned to a severe sarabande. He stopped again to tune and
asked Cristofano for news of the patient.

"Nothing new."

The concert continued with a gavotte and a gigue.

"Nothing new—nothing, nothing, nothing. He does not seem
even to hear," said the doctor, both discouraged and impatient.

It was then that Devizé at last played what I had long awaited,
the one piece which, among all the dances I had heard him perform,
seemed capable of capturing the attention and the heart of all the
guests at the inn: the superb *rondeau* which his master Francesco Corbetta had written for Maria Teresa, Queen of France.

As I suspected, I was not alone in awaiting those fatally fascinating notes. Devizé executed the *rondeau* once, then again, and then a
third time, as though to let it be understood that, to him, too, those
notes were—for unknown reasons—most sweet and delectable. We
all remained in silence, rapt in like manner. We had listened to this
music so many times, yet we could never hear it enough.

But while we were listening to the *rondeau* for the fourth time, my
pleasure in the sounds gave way to something utterly unexpected.
Lulled by the cyclical repetition of the *ritornello*, I suddenly thought:
what was it that Devizé had said about it on the first day? The alternate strophes of the *rondeau* "contain ever new harmonic assays,
which all conclude in an unexpected fashion, almost as though alien
to good musical doctrine. And after reaching its apogee, the *rondeau*
brusquely enters its finale."

And what had Abbot Melani read in the letter from Kircher? That
the plague, too, is cyclical and "there is in the final stages something

unexpected, mysterious, foreign to medical doctrine: after reaching the height of its strength, the disease *senescit ab abrupto*, or suddenly begins to come to an end."

The words used by Devizé to describe the *rondeau* were almost identical to those used by Kircher when speaking of the plague.

I waited until the music ended and at last put the question which I should have asked long—too long—before: "Signor Devizé, has this *rondeau* a name?"

"Yes, 'Les Barricades Mystérieuses'," he pronounced slowly.

I remained silent.

"In Italian, one says... *barricate misteriose*, mysterious barricades," he added, as though to fill the silence.

I froze, utterly speechless.

Mysterious barricades, *les barricades mystérieuses:* were those not the same obscure words which Atto Melani had muttered in his sleep the afternoon before?

I had no time to answer my own question. Already, my mind was galloping out of control towards other mysterious barricades, the *arcanae obices* of Kircher's letter...

My thoughts were swept away. Cast into a sea of suspicion and illusion by the exasperating buzz which those two Latin words had left in my mind, I was seized by vertigo. I rose suddenly to my feet and rushed straight to my chamber, under the astonished gaze of Cristofano and Devizé, who was just beginning to play the same piece once more.

I slammed the door behind me, crushed by the weight of that discovery and by all the consequences which, like the most ruinous of avalanches, it carried with it.

The terrible mystery of Kircher's *arcanae obices*, the mysterious obstacles which concealed the *secretum vitae*, had at last taken form before my very eyes.

I needed a pause for reflection, in total solitude, in my own room; not so much in order to clarify my ideas as to understand with whom I could share them.

Atto and I were on the trail of those *arcanae obices* or "mysterious barricades" which had the supreme capacity to overcome the pestilence, as mentioned by Kircher in the ravings of his last letter to Superintendent Fouquet; then, I had heard the abbot, in his sleep, name the still unidentified *barricades mystérieuses* in the language of his chosen country. And now, when I asked Devizé the name of the *rondeau* which he was playing in order to heal the plague-ridden Bedfordi, I learned that its very title was "Les Barricades Mystérieuses". Someone knew far more than he was prepared to admit.

҈

"But you really have no idea about anything!" exclaimed Abbot Melani.

I had just awoken him from a deep sleep in order to obtain explanations and suddenly the fire of the news had rendered incandescent both his words and his gestures. He asked me to repeat my account word for word: about Devizé who was playing the *rondeau* for Bedfordi's health and who had freely confessed to me that the music was entitled "Les Barricades Mystérieuses".

"Pardon me, but you must leave me a few minutes in which to reflect," said he, almost overcome by what I had told him.

"Yet you know that I desire your explanations, and that..."

"Yes, of course, of course, but now please let me think."

So, I had to leave him and again to knock at his door a few minutes later. From his eyes, which had regained their vigilance and pugnacity, I would have thought that he had never slept.

"Just at this moment when we are near to the truth, you have chosen to become my enemy," he began, in almost heartbroken tones.

"Not your enemy," I hastened to correct him, "but you must understand that..."

"Enough," he interrupted me. "Just try to reason for one moment."

"If you will permit me, Signor Atto, this time I am able to reason perfectly well. And I say to myself: how is it possible that you should know the title of that *rondeau*, and that it should also be the translation of *arcanae obices*?"

I felt proud to have that most sagacious of beings with his back to the wall. I stared at him suspiciously and accusingly.

"Have you finished?"

"Yes."

"Very well," said he at length, "now let me speak. In my sleep, you heard me murmur '*barricades mystérieuses*', if I have understood you correctly."

"Exactly."

"Well, as you know, that is more or less a translation of *arcanae obices*."

"Indeed. And I want to know once and for all how you knew…"

"Be quiet, be quiet, that is not the point."

"But you…"

"Trust me just this one last time. What I am about to tell you will make you change your mind."

"Signor Atto, I cannot follow these mysteries any longer, and besides…"

"You need follow nothing. We are there already. The secret of the *arcanae obices* lies here between us, and perhaps it is more yours than mine."

"What do you mean?"

"That you have seen it, or better, heard it more often than I."

"Pardon me?"

"The *secretum vitae* which protects against the plague is in that music."

This time, it was I who needed time to get used to the shocking news. In the marvellous *rondeau* which had so fascinated me, lay the centre of the mystery of Kircher and Fouquet, of the Sun King and Maria Teresa.

Atto gave me time to blush, a helpless prey to surprise, and to stammer defencelessly: "But I thought… it is not possible."

"That is what I too said to myself initially, but if you think about the matter, you will understand. Just follow my reasoning: have I not told you that Corbetta, Devizé's master, was expert at encrypting messages into his music?"

"Yes, that is true."

"Good. And Devizé himself told you that the *rondeau* 'Les Barricades Mystérieuses' was composed by Corbetta and that, before he died, he presented it to Queen Maria Teresa."

"That, too, is true."

"Well, the dedication of the *rondeau*, which you saw with your own eyes, is *'à Mademoiselle'*: the wife of Lauzun. Lauzun was in prison with Fouquet; and Fouquet had received the secret of the plague from Kircher. Now Fouquet, when he was still Superintendent, must have commissioned Corbetta to encrypt in music the *secretum vitae* (or *arcanae obices* or mysterious barricades, if you prefer) which brings salvation from the pestilence."

"But you told me that Kircher too knew how to encrypt messages in music."

"Certainly. Indeed, I do not exclude the possibility that Kircher may have passed on to Fouquet the *secretum vitae* already encrypted in a musical score. It is, however, probable that such music was still at a rather rough, preparatory stage. Do you remember what Devizé told you? Corbetta created the *rondeau*, rearranging it on the basis of an earlier melody. I am sure he was referring to Kircher. Not only that: Devizé himself, playing it again and again on his guitar, may have so perfected its performance that it became quite impossible to suspect that so sublime a harmony might conceal a message in ciphers. Incredible, is it not? I myself find it difficult to believe."

"And it is in the form of a *rondeau* that the Superintendent must jealously have conserved the *secretum vitae*."

"Yes, that music somehow survived all the misadventures which befell my friend Nicolas."

"Until in Pinerol..."

"... he confided it to Lauzun. But do you know what I think about this? That it was Lauzun himself who wrote the dedication '*à Mademoiselle*'. He will have given it to his wife to pass on to Queen Maria Teresa."

"Yet Devizé told me that the score was a gift from Corbetta to the Queen."

"A tall story, and one of no importance. A way of complicating a simple tale for you: the truth is that, after Corbetta, and before Maria Teresa came into possession of that *rondeau*, it passed through the hands of Fouquet, Lauzun and Mademoiselle."

"One thing does not make sense to me, Signor Atto: did you not suspect that Lauzun was imprisoned at Pinerol near to the Superintendent in order to extract the secret from him?"

"Perhaps Lauzun served two masters. Instead of spying on and betraying Fouquet, he may have preferred to talk openly to him—also because the Squirrel was most perspicacious. Thus, Lauzun will have helped him to win his own freedom from the King in exchange for the *secretum morbi*. But, and this would do him honour, he will have avoided revealing to His Most Christian Majesty the fact that Fouquet also possessed the *secretum vitae*, in other words, the *rondeau*. On the contrary, he and Mademoiselle will have availed themselves of the opportunity to revenge themselves on the King and to place the precious antidote to the plague in the hands of His Majesty's enemies: beginning, and it pains me greatly to say this, with his wife Maria Teresa, may the Lord keep her in His Glory."

I remained deep in thought, going over in my mind all the notions which Atto had set before me.

"There is truly something strange in that music," I observed, drawing all the threads of my memory together. "It is as though it... came and went, always the same, yet always different. I cannot explain this well, but it brings to mind what Kircher wrote about the pestilence: the distemper moves away, then returns; and in the end, it dies just when it has reached its paroxysm. It is as though... that music spoke of this."

"Indeed? So much the better. That there is in this music something mysterious and indefinable, I too, had thought, ever since I first heard it."

In the heat of our discussion, I had completely forgotten the reason for my calling upon Abbot Melani: to obtain an explanation of those words which he had pronounced in his sleep. Yet again, however, Atto would not let me speak.

"Listen to me. Two unresolved problems remain: first of all, to whom could the antidote of the *secretum vitae* against the *secretum morbi*, and thus against His Most Christian Majesty, be useful? Secondly: whatever is Dulcibeni plotting? How is it that he was travelling with Devizé and Fouquet before my poor friend,"—and here, Atto's voice again broke under the weight of emotion—"came to die at your hostelry?"

I was about to remind him that he had also to discover to whom or to what Fouquet's strange death was attributable, and what had become of my little pearls, when the abbot, paternally cupping my chin in the palm of his hand, continued: "Now I ask you, if I had known at what door to knock in order to find the *arcanae obices* mentioned by Kircher, would I have wasted all this time just for the pleasure of your company?"

"Well, perhaps not."

"*Certainly* not: I would have set my sights directly upon Devizé and the secret of his *rondeau*. Perhaps I would have succeeded without too much difficulty: it is possible that Devizé himself does not know what is embedded in the *rondeau* of the 'Barricades Mystérieuses'. And we could forget about Corbetta, Lauzun, Mademoiselle and all that horribly complicated tale."

At that precise moment, our eyes met.

"No, my boy. I must admit it, you are most precious to me, but I do not intend to deceive you in order to obtain your services. Now, however, Abbot Melani must ask you to make one last sacrifice. Will you still obey me?"

I was spared a reply by the echo of a scream: I had no difficulty in identifying the voice of Cristofano.

I left Abbot Melani and ran directly to Bedfordi's chamber.

"Triumph! Wonder! Victory!" the doctor kept repeating, his face purple with emotion, his hand on his heart and his back against the wall to prevent himself from falling.

The young Englishman, Eduardus Bedfordi, was sitting on the edge of his bed, coughing noisily.

"Could I have a drink of water?" he asked in a hoarse voice, as though he had awoken from a long sleep.

※

A quarter of an hour later, all the lodgers were gathered around the stunned Devizé, before Bedfordi's door. Jubilant and breathless at the happy surprise, the inhabitants of the Donzello had all flowed like a little torrent into the corridor on the first floor, and now they were bombarding one another with exclamations of amazement and questions to which they did not even expect an answer. They dared not yet approach Cristofano and the newly revived Englishman: the doctor had meanwhile regained his self-control and was meticulously examining his patient. His response was not long in coming: "He is well. He is very well, by Jove! I'd say that he has never been better!" exclaimed Cristofano, allowing himself to give way to an outburst of liberating laughter, which spread to all the others.

Unlike Signor Pellegrino, my master, Bedfordi had immediately recovered his normal consciousness. He asked what had happened and why he was bandaged everywhere and suffering such pain in all his members: the excision of the tokens and the incisions for bleeding him had played havoc with his young body.

He remembered nothing; and to every question that was put to him, by Brenozzi in the first place, he would react with bewilderment, opening his eyes wide and wearily shaking his head.

Looking more closely, I saw that not all were in the same humour. The rejoicing of Padre Robleda, Brenozzi, Stilone Priàso and my

Cloridia (who regaled me with a lovely smile) were in contrast to the absorbed silence of Devizé and Dulcibeni's waxen pallor. I observed Abbot Melani, lost in thought, ask something of Cristofano. He then withdrew and returned up the stairs.

It was only then that, in the general turmoil, Bedfordi at last understood that he had had the plague and had for days on end been given up for lost.

"But then, the vision..." he exclaimed.

"What vision?" came a chorus of questions.

"Well... I think that I have been in hell."

Thus he related that, of his illness, he remembered only having suddenly experienced a long, long fall downwards, and the fire. After who knows how long, no less a personage than Lucifer stopped before him. The Devil, with green skin, moustaches and a goatee on his chin (just like those of Cristofano, he pointed out) had planted one of his red hot talons, from which leapt tongues of fire, in his throat, and had tried to tear out his soul. Not succeeding in this, Lucifer had brandished his pitchfork and transfixed him with it again and again, almost draining him of all his blood. Then the foul beast had clutched his poor, exhausted body and thrown him into boiling pitch; and here Bedfordi swore that this had all seemed horribly real to him and that he would never have believed that one could suffer such pain. And in that pitch, the young man had remained for who knows how long, contorted by suffering, and he had begged God for forgiveness for all his sins and his little faith and had implored the Most High to rescue him from that infernal Hades. Then, darkness.

We all listened in religious silence; but now the guests' voices were competing for who should shout "Miracle!" the loudest. Padre Robleda, who throughout the narration had been continuously making the sign of the cross, stepped forward prudently from the group and, deeply affected, signed the air in blessing; whereupon some knelt and crossed themselves in turn.

Only the physician's countenance had darkened. He knew well, as did I, whence Bedfordi's vision came: it was none other than the delirious memory of the cruel therapies to which Cristofano had subjected him as he lay prostrate in the clutches of the pestilence. The diabolical claw which tried to tear out his soul was in reality the imperial musk with which Cristofano had induced vomiting; the cruel pitchfork of Lucifer, we recognised without difficulty as the harness which the physician had employed when bleeding his patient; lastly, the boiling pitch was none other than the cauldron over which we had placed Bedfordi for his steam bath.

Bedfordi was hungry, but, at the same time, he said he was suffering from a strong sensation of burning in the stomach. Cristofano then commanded me to warm him a little of the good broth of stock-dove which had already been prepared. This would both nourish him and pacify his bowels. At this juncture, however, the Englishman fell asleep.

We resolved then to let him rest and all descended together to the chambers on the ground floor. Oddly enough, no one was troubled by the fact that he had left his own apartment; nor did Cristofano remember to scold them all and make them return to their own chambers. The plague seemed to have gone; so, by tacit accord, our seclusion was at an end; and no one so much as mentioned it.

The guests of the Donzello seemed also to be suffering the pangs of great hunger; wherefore, I descended to the cellars, determined to cook something tasty and rich with which to celebrate. While with my head down almost to the ground among the boxes of snow I searched among kids' heads and feet, sweetbreads, legs of mutton and chicken, a multitude of thoughts passed through my mind. Bedfordi was cured. How was that possible? Devizé had played for him, as recommended by Padre Robleda: was the Jesuit's theory about the magnetism of music then true? It was indeed true that the Englishman seemed to have awoken only after "Les Barricades Mystérieuses"... But was that *rondeau* not supposed to be a mere cipher concealing the *secretum vitae*? That had at least been Abbot Melani's assumption. Now, however, the melody itself had perhaps proved to be the agent of the cure... No, I really could make no sense of the whole matter. I must speak of this with Abbot Melani as soon as possible.

Returning up the stairs, I heard the voice of Cristofano. In the dining hall, I saw that Atto had joined the group.

"What is one to say?" asked the physician, addressing the little assembly. "It may have been the magnetism of the music, as Father Robleda avers, or my remedies, I do not know. The truth is that no one knows why the pestilence disappears so suddenly. The most wondrous thing is that Bedfordi had shown no sign of improvement. On the contrary, he was near death, and I should soon have been compelled to inform you that all hope was lost."

Robleda nodded emphatically at that juncture, thus showing that he was already implicated in those desperate moments.

"I can tell you," continued Cristofano, "that this is not the first such case. There are those who explain such mysterious recoveries by contending that nothing of the pestilence remains in the furniture or in the houses or in material things, but can disappear overnight. I recollect that when I was in Rome during the Visitation of 1656, no remedy having been found, it was decided to initiate a great fast and many processions during which the people went barefoot, in sackcloth and ashes, begging forgiveness for their sins, their faces wet with tears, all mournful and dolorous. God then sent the Archangel Michael, who was seen by all the people of Rome on the 8th of May above the Castello with a bloody sword in his hand: from that moment on, the pestilence ceased and of the infection, nothing remained, not even in clothing or in beds, which are usually among the most dangerous vehicles of contagion. Nor is that all. The historians of antiquity also tell of such strange instances. In the year 567, it is told that there was a visitation of a most terrible and cruel pestilence throughout the world, and only a quarter of humanity survived. Yet the plague suddenly ceased and infection remained in no object."

"In the Plague of 1468," Brenozzi added in support of the physician's assertions, "more than thirty-six thousand died in Venice, and in Brescia, over twenty thousand; and many houses remained uninhabited. But these two visitations came to a sudden end and the infection was left in no thing. The same occurred during the visitations that followed: in 1485, the pestilence returned to Venice in the most horrendous form and killed many nobles, including even the Doge Giovanni Mocenigo; in 1527, it spread throughout the whole world and, finally, in 1556, it reappeared in Venice and all its dominions, although, thanks to the good governance of the senators, it did little damage. Nevertheless, at a certain point during every one of these visitations, the pestilence suddenly died out and not a trace of it remained. How, how can that be explained?" he concluded grandiloquently, growing red in the face.

"Well, I would until now have preferred to say nothing in order not to bring bad luck upon us," Stilone Priàso added solemnly, "but, according to the astrologers, because of the malign influence of the Dog Star during the last two weeks of August and the first three of September, all those contaminated by the pestilence should die within two or three days, or even within twenty-four hours. Indeed, in London, during the plague of 1665, that was the worst period, and it is said that in a single night, between one o'clock and three in the morning, more than thirty thousand persons perished. During the same period, nothing of the sort happened to us."

A shiver of fear and relief traversed the little assembly, while Robleda rose to poke around in the kitchen. As soon as the kids' heads, the gigot and the chicken began to give off their first sweet aromas, I served soup with asparagus and citrus fruit, in order to settle the stomach.

"I remember that, when I was in Rome in '56," said Cristofano, resuming his narration, "the pestilence was in full spate. I was then a young physician and my colleague, who had come to visit me, told me that the fury of the distemper was about to abate. Yet, it was precisely in that week that the bulletins reported more deaths than throughout the whole year, and I pointed this out to my fellow-practitioner. He gave me the most surprising of replies. 'Judging by the number of persons who are sick at this moment,' said he, 'if the distemper were still as fatal as it was two weeks or so ago, we should have had three times as many dead. Then, it killed within two to three days, but now it lasts eight to ten days. Two weeks ago, moreover, one sick person in five survived, while now we count at least three cures. You may be certain that next week's bulletin will show a far lower mortality, and that there will be ever more recoveries. The distemper has lost its virulence, and, although the number of those infected is enormous, however long the infection itself may last, the number of deaths will be ever less elevated.'"

"And was it so?" asked Devizé, visibly perturbed.

"Precisely so. Two weeks later, the bulletin showed half as many deaths. To tell the truth, many still died, but the number of those who recovered was far greater."

In the weeks that followed, it was to become even clearer, explained Cristofano, that his colleague had been right: within a month, deaths had almost ceased to be reported, although the sick still numbered tens of thousands.

"The distemper had lost its malignancy," repeated the doctor "and not gradually, but at the very height of its fury, when we were most desperate; just as has happened today in the case of the young Englishman."

"Only the hand of God could so swiftly interrupt the course of the distemper," commented the Jesuit with great emotion.

Cristofano gravely nodded in agreement: "Medicine was powerless in the face of the infection; death harvested thousands at every street corner; and, had matters continued thus for two or three more weeks, not a soul would have been left alive in Rome."

Once it had lost its death-dealing potency, the physician continued, the distemper killed only a small proportion of those infected. The physicians themselves were astounded by this. They saw that their patients were getting better; they sweated abundantly and their tokens soon matured, their pustules were no longer inflamed, fevers were not so extreme and they no longer suffered from terrible pain in the head. Even those physicians whose faith was less fervent were obliged to admit that the sudden decline of the pestilence was of supernatural origin.

"The streets filled with persons who had just been cured, with their necks and heads still bandaged; or limping from the scars left by the tokens in the groin. And all were exulting that they had escaped so great a peril."

It was then that Padre Robleda stood up and, drawing a crucifix from his black tunic, brandished it before his listeners, proclaiming: "How marvellous a change, O Lord! Until yesterday, we were buried alive, but Thou hast restored us to the land of the living!"

We knelt and, ardent in our gratitude, intoned our praise to the Most High, guided by the Jesuit. Whereupon, when luncheon was served, all sat down to eat with a great appetite.

I, however, could not free my mind from the thought of those words of Cristofano: the plague possessed it own obscure natural cycle, in accordance with which, after spreading, it suddenly dissipated, losing its virulence until, at last, it disappeared altogether. Mysteriously it departed, as it had come. *Morbus crescit sicut mortales, senescit ex abrupto...*: the distemper grows like mortals, and suddenly grows old. Were not those the same words as Abbot Melani had read in the strange letter from Padre Kircher which he had discovered in Dulcibeni's drawers?

After hastily consuming my meal at the big kitchen table, I found Atto in the dining hall. We understood one another at a glance. I would be calling on him as soon as possible.

So, I went to bring his luncheon to Pellegrino, who could be considered as cured, were it not for his continual giddiness. The doctor joined me there, advising me that he in person would bring his broth to the young Englishman.

"Signor Cristofano, could we not perhaps ask Devizé to play in my master's chamber, too, so that he might again become as sharp-witted as he once was?" I took the opportunity of asking him.

"I do not believe it would be of any use, my boy. Unfortunately, matters have not gone as I had hoped: Pellegrino will not fully recover that soon. I am certain that this was not a case of the spotted fever, nor indeed of the pestilence, as even you will have realised."

"Then what is wrong with him?" I murmured, troubled by the innkeeper's fixed, bewildered stare.

"Blood in the head, because of his fall down the stairs: a clot of blood which will only very gradually be reabsorbed. I think that we shall all leave here safe and sound before that happens. But, do not worry, your master has a wife, has he not?"

So saying, he departed. While feeding Pellegrino, I thought with a pang in my heart of his sad fate, when his severe spouse returned to find him in that vague condition.

∂∽∾

"Do you recall what we read?" asked Atto no sooner than I had entered his chamber. "According to Kircher, the pestilence is born, grows, becomes old and dies just like men. When it is about to die, it augments and reaches its greatest strength before expiring."

"Exactly as Cristofano said just now."

"Yes. And do you know what that means?"

"Perhaps that Bedfordi recovered on his own, or not thanks to the *rondeau*?" said I, hazarding a guess.

"You disappoint me, my boy. Do you really not understand? The plague in this hostelry was barely at its beginnings: it should have accomplished a massacre before losing its virulence. Instead, matters went otherwise. Not one of us others fell ill. And do you know what I think? Since Devizé, compelled to keep to his chamber, began to play the *rondeau* ever more frequently, those notes, spreading throughout the inn, have preserved us from the infection."

"Do you honestly believe that it is thanks to that music that no one else among us fell victim to the pestilence?" I asked sceptically.

"It is surprising, I know. But think now: in all history, it has never sufficed, when faced with the spread of the plague, simply to withdraw

alone to one's chamber. As for Cristofano's remedies to preserve us
from the infection, forget it!" said the abbot with a laugh. "Besides,
the facts speak for themselves: the doctor was in contact with Bedfordi every single day, after which, he visited all the others. Yet neither he nor any of us ever fell ill. How do you explain that?"

Indeed, I thought, if I was immune to the infection, one could not
say as much of Cristofano.

"Not only that," Atto continued, "once Bedfordi himself was directly exposed to the notes of the *rondeau*, just when he was about to
give up the ghost, he awoke and the distemper literally vanished."

"It is as though… Padre Kircher had discovered a secret which, in
those already suffering from the plague, speeds up the natural cycle
of the disease, inducing its extinction without having wrought any
harm. Yet this is also a secret capable of preserving the healthy from
the infection."

"Bravo, you have got it. The secretum vitae concealed in the *rondeau* functions precisely thus."

Bedfordi, concluded Atto, making himself at ease on his bed, was
all but resuscitated when Devizé played for him. The idea had come
from Padre Robleda, persuaded of the health-giving magnetism of
music. Initially, however, the French musician had played for a long
time without anything happening.

"You will have noticed that, after Bedfordi's recovery, I stopped
to speak to the doctor; well, he made it clear to me that only after
Devizé had begun to play the *rondeau* and had repeated it ad infinitum, did the Englishman show signs of life. I wondered: whatever is
hidden in those blessed 'Barricades Mystérieuses'?"

"I too had wondered about that, Signor Atto: the melody must
have mysterious powers."

"Exactly. As though in it Kircher had concealed a thaumaturgical
secret, yet the content was one with the casket; so much so as to ra-
diate its potent and health-giving effects to anyone who so much as
listened to the *rondeau*. Now do you understand?"

I assented, with rather less than true conviction.

"But could we not find out more about this?" I tried to ask. "We
could try to decrypt the *rondeau*. You understand music. I could attempt to borrow Devizé's scores from him and from there we could
work by trial and error; or perhaps we might even obtain something
from Devizé himself."

The abbot stopped me with a gesture.

"Do not imagine that he knows any more than we do," he retorted, smiling. "Besides, what does that all matter to us now? The power of music: there is the real secret. During these days and nights we have done nothing but rationalise: we wanted to understand everything and at all costs. Rather presumptuously, we meant to square the circle. And I was the first to behave thus:

> Qual è 'l geomètra che tutto s'affige
> per misurar lo cerchio, e non ritrova,
> pensando, quel principio ond'elli indige,
> tal era io a quella vista nova.*

as the poet says."

"The words of Seigneur Luigi, your master?"

"These words, no. They were penned a few centuries ago by my divine countryman, who is now out of fashion. What I mean to tell you is simply that while we racked our brains, we neglected to use our hearts."

"Did we then misinterpret everything, Signor Atto?"

"No. All that we discovered, all our insights and our deductions, were perfectly correct; but incomplete."

"Meaning?"

"Of course, in that *rondeau* there is encrypted I know not what formula of Kircher's against the pestilence. That, however, is not all that Kircher had to say. The *secretum vitae*, the secret of life, is something more. And that cannot be expressed: you will find it neither in words nor in numbers, but in music. That, then, is Kircher's message."

Atto, still half-reclining, had leaned his head against the wall and was looking dreamily over, and far beyond, my head.

I was disappointed: Abbot Melani's explanation did not calm my curiosity.

"But is there no way of deciphering the melody of the *Barricades Mystérieuses*? Thus we would at last be able to read the secret formula which protects against the pestilence," I insisted.

"Forget it. We could spend centuries here, studying those pages without finding a single syllable. There remains to us only what we

---

* As the geometer who tries all ways he can / To square the circle, yet cannot, / By thinking, find out the principle involved, / So was I, when faced with that new sight.—Dante *Paradiso*. (Translator's note.)

have seen and heard today: simply upon hearing it, that *rondeau* protects against the plague. That should suffice for us. In what manner it brings this about, it is not, however, given to us to understand: "'High fantasy here lost its power'," intoned the abbot, again quoting the poet, his countryman, and concluding: "That madman Athanasius Kircher was a great man of science and of the Faith, and with his *rondeau*, he gave us a great lesson in humility. Never forget that, my boy."

કે૦ન્જ

Resting on my couch, I awaited sleep, wearied by the hurricane of revelations and surprises. I was a prey to endless cogitations and stirrings of the soul. Only at the close of my conversation with Atto had I understood the double and inextricable magic of that *rondeau*: it was no accident if the "Barricades Mystérieuses" bore that name; and there was indeed no sense in deciphering them. Like Kircher, Abbot Melani had taught me a noble lesson: the profession of humility by a man in whom neither pride nor mistrust were in any way lacking. I mused vaguely for a long time yet upon the mystery of the "Barricades", while striving in vain to hum its touching melody.

I had also been touched by the paternal tone in which Atto had called me "my boy". I was lulled by that thought, so much so that only when I was on the point of falling asleep did I recollect that, for all his fine words and reassurances, he had not yet explained to me how come he had, the day before, pronounced the words "*barricades mystérieuses*", in his sleep.

I spent I know not how many hours resting in my little chamber. On my awakening, a sovereign silence reigned over the Donzello. The hostelry, once the uproar had died down, seemed to have fallen into lethargy: I pricked up my ears, yet I could hear neither Devizé's playing nor Brenozzi's importunate ramblings. Nor had Cristofano come to look for me.

It was still early to prepare supper, yet I resolved to descend to the kitchen: as I had already done at luncheon, only even more so, I desired adequately to celebrate the good news of Bedfordi's recovery and the return to the Donzello of the hope of freedom. I would prepare tasty little redwings, or thrushes, fresh as could be. On the stairs, I met Cristofano, whom I asked for news of the Englishman.

"He is well, very well," said he, contentedly. "He is only in pain... er... because of the cutting of the tokens," he added, with a hint of embarrassment.

"I had in mind to cook redwings for dinner. Do you think that would also be suitable for Bedfordi?"

The doctor smacked his lips: "More than suitable: the flesh of thrushes is excellent in savour, both substantial and nutritious, easily digested and good also for convalescents and for all those whose constitution is debilitated. They are now at their best. In winter, however, they arrive from the mountains of Spoleto and Terni, and are very fat, for they have during that season fed on myrtle and juniper berries. When they have eaten myrtle berries, they are, moreover, excellent for curing dysentery. But if you really do intend to cook them," said he with a touch of hungry impatience, "you would do well to make haste: the preparation takes time."

Once on the ground floor, I found that the other guests had descended and were all present, some engaged in conversation, some playing cards, others wandering freely. No one seemed willing to return to those chambers in which they had all feared they might die of the pestilence.

My Cloridia came to me with festive mien: "We are alive again!" she exclaimed happily. "Only Pompeo Dulcibeni is missing, it seems to me," and she looked at me questioningly.

At once, I felt dejected: here, once again, Cloridia was showing her interest in the elderly gentleman from the Marches.

"In truth, Abbot Melani is absent, too," said I, turning my back on her ostentatiously and rushing down to the cellars in order to choose all that I would be needing.

The dinner that followed was the most delicious since that of the cows' teats and—pardon my immodesty—was deservedly received with great and general applause. As I had already seen my master do, I prepared the redwings with the freest and most honest invention. Some, I prepared rolled in breadcrumbs and lightly fried in minced bacon with slices of ham, then covered with broccoli tips cooked in good fat and flavoured with lemon; others, I roasted, after lighting a good blaze, interspersed with sausages and slices of oranges and lemons; or I boiled them with salted stuffing, covered with small fennel or lettuce leaves bound with egg, serving them in nets as roulades or bunched with herbs, and a sauce of spiced *mostacciolo* cake.

Then, when cooking them, I made many *allo spiedo* (on skewers), *in crosta* (in pastry), or interlarded with slices of bacon and bay leaves, anointed with good oil and sprinkled with breadcrumbs. Nor did I fail to cook the redwings as Pellegrino best knew how to: stuffed with bacon and ham slices, sprinkled with cloves and served in a royal sauce; and finally, served in roulades, netted or in marrow leaves. Some other, rather bigger, birds I parboiled, then halved and fried. The whole dish I served with fried green vegetables, simply lacquered with sugar and lemon juice, without cinnamon.

By the time I completed my cooking, I was surrounded by the guests' joyous faces, as they hastened to serve themselves and to share the various dishes. Cloridia, to my surprise, served me my own portion; I had arranged for her a generous serving which I had not omitted to garnish deliciously with parsley and a slice of lemon. My blush was of the deepest crimson, but she did not give me time to breathe a word and with a smile joined the others at table.

In the meanwhile, Abbot Melani, too, had come downstairs. Dulcibeni, however, was not to be seen. I went to knock on his door and ask him whether he wished to dine. Even had I wished to obtain from him some indication of his future intentions, I would have had no means of doing so. He said from behind the door that he was not at all hungry, nor did he desire to talk with anyone. Rather than raise his suspicions, I did not insist. As I was leaving, I heard a by now familiar sound within, a sort of rapid, whistling sniff.

Dulcibeni was again at his snuff box.

Night the Ninth

BETWEEN *the* 19ᵀᴴ & 20ᵀᴴ SEPTEMBER, 1683

✠

"Urgentitious, perditious and sacrilegious," assured Ugonio, in a voice shaking unaccustomedly with excitement.

"Sacrilegious, what do you mean by that?" asked Abbot Melani.

"Gfrrrlubh," explained Ciacconio, devoutly crossing himself.

"Whene'er he verbalises a sacral mutter, or one that howorwhensoever implacates a holyecclesiasticon, or holysaintliness, or one eminentitious—for by fulfilling one's obligations the Christian's jubilations are increased—Ciacconio duefully denominates him with condescending, lucent and remanent respectuosity."

Atto and I looked at one another in perplexity. The *corpisantari* seemed unusually agitated and were trying to explain something to us concerning a personage of the Curia, or something of the sort, for whom they appeared to feel no little reverential fear.

Anxious to know the outcome of Ciacconio's incursion into the house of Tiracorda, Atto and I had found them in the Archives, busy as ever with their disgusting pile of bones and filth. According the dignity of language to Ciacconio's grunts, Ugonio had at once put us on guard: in the house of Dulcibeni's physician friend, something dangerous was about to take place, which it was urgent to circumvent and which concerned a high-ranking personage, perhaps a prelate, whose identity was, however, as yet unclear.

"First of all, tell me: how did you gain entry to Tiracorda's house?"

"Gfrrrlubh," replied Ciacconio with a sly smile.

"He entrified via the chimblypipe," explained Ugonio.

"Up the chimney? So that is why he was not even interested to know anything about the windows. But he will have made himself filthy… Excuse me, forget that I said that," said Atto, remembering that filth was the natural element of the two *corpisantari*.

Ciacconio had managed to climb without too much difficulty into the chimney of the kitchen on the ground floor. Thence, following

430

the sound of voices, he had succeeded in tracing Tiracorda and Dulcibeni to the study, where they were intent on conversing on matters incomprehensible to him.

"They parleyfied argumancies theoristical, and enigmifications, perhaps even thingamies necromaniacal."

"Gfrrrlubh," confirmed Ciacconio, nodding in confirmation, visibly disquieted.

"No, no, have no fear," interrupted Atto with a smile, "those were no more than riddles."

Ciacconio had overheard the enigmas with which Tiracorda enjoyed distracting himself with Dulcibeni and had taken them for obscure cabalistic rituals.

"In parleyfying, the doctorer intimidated that, perduring the nocturn, he would," added Ugonio, "ascend unto Monte Cavallo, there to therapise the sacrosanctified personage."

"I see. Tonight he will go to Monte Cavallo, in other words, to the papal palace, in order to treat that person, that exceedingly important prelate," Atto interpreted, looking at me with a significant expression.

"And then?"

"Then they ingurgitated alcohols magnomcumgaudio, and into the arms of Murphyus the doctorer fell."

Dulcibeni had again brought with him the little liqueur to which the doctor was so partial and with it had put him to sleep.

Here began the most important part of Ciacconio's narration. Hardly had Tiracorda entered the world of dreams than Dulcibeni took from a cupboard a vase decorated with strange designs, on the sides of which were various holes to let in the air. From his pocket, he had then extracted a little phial from which he had poured into Tiracorda's vase a few drops of liquid. Atto and I looked at one another in alarm.

"While effectifying this outpouring, he demurmured: "'For her...'""

"'For her'... How interesting. And then?"

"Then thereupon did the furiosa represent herself."

"The fury?" we both asked in unison.

The good wife Paradisa had burst into the study, where she had surprised her spouse in thrall to the fumes of Bacchus, and Dulcibeni in possession of the abhorred alcoholic potion.

"She greatly disgorgified herself, in manner most wrathful and cholerific," explained Ugonio.

From what we understood, Paradisa had begun to shower her husband with insults and repeatedly to hurl at him the beakers which had served for their toasts, together with the physician's instruments and whatever came to hand. In order to escape from all those projectiles, Tiracorda had been compelled to take refuge under the table while Dulcibeni had hastily returned to its place the decorated vase into which he had poured those drops of mysterious liquid.

"Exorbitrageous female: most inappropriate for the doctorer, who therapises in order to achieve more benefice than malefice," pronounced Ugonio, shaking his head, while Ciacconio nodded in concerned agreement.

It was, however, at that very moment that Ciacconio's mission suffered a setback. While Paradisa was venting her hatred for wine and grappa upon the defenceless Tiracorda, and Dulcibeni remained quietly in a corner, waiting for the storm to pass, Ciacconio seized the opportunity to satisfy his baser instincts. Already, before the woman's arrival, he had espied upon a shelf an object to his taste.

"Gfrrrlubh," he gurgled complacently, producing from his overcoat and showing us, polished and shining, a magnificent skull, complete with the lower jaw, which Tiracorda had probably used when teaching his students.

While Paradisa's raging grew incandescent, Ciacconio had crept into the study on all fours, making his way around the table under which Tiracorda had hidden, and had managed to purloin the skull without being seen. As chance would have it, a large candlestick which Paradisa had hurled at Tiracorda rebounded and struck Ciacconio. Offended and in pain, the *corpisantaro* leapt onto the table and met fire with fire, uttering as a war-cry the one and only sound of which his mouth was capable.

Upon the unexpected sight of that repulsive and deformed being, who was, moreover, threatening her with her own candlestick, Paradisa screeched at the very top of her voice. Dulcibeni remained where he stood, as though petrified, and Tiracorda flattened himself even more under the table.

Hearing Paradisa's cries, the servant girls came rushing down from the floor above, just in time to encounter Ciacconio who was hurrying towards the stairs down to the kitchen. The *corpisantaro*, finding himself faced with three fresh young damsels, could not resist the temptation to lay his clutches upon the one nearest to him.

The poor girl, lasciviously groped by the monster just where her flesh was softest and plumpest, instantly lost her senses; the second maid exploded into hysterical screams, whilst the third ran back to the second floor as fast as her legs could carry her.

"It is not cognisable whether she also pissified upon herself," added Ugonio, cackling rather vulgarly together with his companion.

Crowing savagely at the unhoped-for entertainment, Ciacconio succeeded in regaining the kitchen and the chimney whereby he had made his entry. This, he had rapidly (and in what manner remains inexplicable) ascended until he returned to the roof of Tiracorda's house, thus at last regaining his liberty.

"Incredible!" commented Atto Melani. "These two have more lives than a salamander."

"Gfrrrlubh," specified Ciacconio.

"What did he say?"

"That in the vessel there were not salamanthers but leechies."

"What? Perhaps you mean..." stammered Abbot Melani.

"Leeches," I broke in, "that is what was in the vase which Dulcibeni found so interesting..."

Abruptly, I stopped: a sudden intuition had jolted my thoughts.

"I have it, I have it!" I cried at length, while I saw Atto hanging on my every word. "Dulcibeni, oh my God!..."

"Go on, tell me," begged Melani, grasping me by the shoulders and shaking me like a sapling, while the two *corpisantari* looked on as curiously as two owls.

"... wants the Pope dead," I gasped.

We all four sat down, almost crushed by the unbearable weight of that revelation.

"The question is," said Atto, "what is the liquid which Dulcibeni secretly poured into the vase of leeches?"

"Something which he must have prepared on his island," I promptly replied, "in the elaboratory where he slices up rats."

"Precisely. He quarters them, then he drains their blood. They are sick rats, however," added Atto, "for we encountered a number of dead ones and others which were moribund, do you remember?"

"Of course I remember: they were bleeding freely from their snouts! Cristofano told me that this is just what happens to rats which are sick with the pestilence," I retorted excitedly.

"So they were rats with the plague," agreed Atto. "Using their blood, Dulcibeni prepared an infected humour. He then went to Tiracorda and put him to sleep with liquor. In this way, he was able to pour the pestiferous humour into the vase of leeches, which have thus become a vehicle for the distemper. With those leeches, Tiracorda will tonight bleed Innocent XI," concluded Atto in a voice made hoarse by emotion, "and he will infect him with the plague. Perhaps we are already too late."

"We have circled around this mystery for days, Signor Atto. We even heard Tiracorda say that the Pope was being treated with leeches!" I interjected, blushing.

"Good heavens, you are right," replied Melani, growing gloomy after a moment's reflection. "That was the first time that we heard him talk with Tiracorda. How could I have failed to understand?"

We continued to reason, to remember and to conjecture, completing and rapidly reinforcing our reconstruction.

"Dulcibeni has read many medical tomes," continued the abbot. "One can hear that whenever he touches on the subject. So he knows perfectly well that during visitations of the plague, rats fall ill; and so from them, or rather, from their blood, he can obtain all that he needs. Moreover, he accompanied Fouquet, who knew the secrets of the pestilence, on his travels. Lastly, he is well acquainted with Kircher's theory: the plague is transmitted, not by miasmas, odours or stenches, but *per animalcula*: through minuscule beings which can transmigrate from one being to another: from rats to the Pope."

"It is true!" I recalled. "At the beginning of our quarantine, we all discussed theories of the plague together, and Dulcibeni explained the theories of Kircher down to their minutest details. He knew them so well that it seemed he had never thought of anything else; for him this seemed to be almost…"

"… a ruling passion. The idea of contaminating the Pope must have come to him some time ago; probably, when he was speaking of the secrets of the plague with Fouquet, during the three years which the Superintendent spent in Naples."

"But then, Fouquet must have trusted Dulcibeni implicitly."

"Certainly. So much so that we found Kircher's letter in his undergarments. Otherwise, why should Dulcibeni have helped a blind old man so generously?" commented the abbot sarcastically.

"But where will Dulcibeni have procured the *animalcula* that transmit the plague?" I asked.

"There are always outbreaks here and there, although they do not always develop into major visitations. I seem to recall, for instance, that there were outbreaks on the borders of the Empire, around Bolzano. No doubt, Dulcibeni will have obtained the blood of infected rats there, with which he began his experiments. Then, when the time was ripe, he came to the Donzello, just next to Tiracorda's house, and continued to infect rats in the underground city, so as to have a ready supply of freshly infected blood."

"In other words, he kept the plague alive, passing it from one rat to another."

"Precisely. Perhaps, however, something caused him to lose control of his activities. In the underground galleries, everything was to be found: infected rats, phials of blood, lodgers at the inn coming and going... too much movement. In the end, some invisible germ, some *animalculum*, reached Bedfordi and our young Englishman was infected with the distemper. Better thus: it could have struck down you or me."

"And Pellegrino's illness, and the death of Fouquet?"

"The plague has nothing to do with all that. Your master's illness has turned out to be simply the result of a fall, or little else. Fouquet, however, according to Cristofano (and in my view, too), was poisoned. And I would not be surprised if he was killed by Dulcibeni himself."

"Oh heavens, the assassination of Fouquet, too?" I exclaimed in horror. "But, to me, Dulcibeni did not seem too unpleasant a character... After all, he has suffered greatly from the loss of his daughter, poor man; his way of life could hardly have been more modest; and he was able to gain the confidence of old Fouquet, assisting and protecting him..."

"Dulcibeni intends to kill the Pope," Atto cut me short, "you were the first to understand that. Why, then, should he not have poisoned his friend?"

"Yes, but..."

"Sooner or later, we all make the mistake of trusting the wrong person," said he, silencing me with a grimace. "And besides, you have already heard how the Superintendent always trusted his friends too much," he added, shivering a little at his own words. "If, however, you have a taste for doubts, I have a far greater one: when he is bled tonight, the Pope will be infected by Tiracorda's leeches and will die of the pestilence. Why? Only because the Odescalchi did not help Dulcibeni to find his daughter?"

"So, what are you saying?"

"Are you not struck by how flimsy a motive this is for taking the life of a Pontiff?"

"Well, yes, indeed…"

"It amounts to so little, so very little," repeated Atto, "and I have the impression that Dulcibeni must have some other motive for so bold an undertaking. Just now, however, I cannot go beyond that."

While we two were thus reflecting, Ugonio and Ciacconio were also deep in discussion. In the end, Ugonio stood up, as though impatient to be on his way.

"Concerning the matter of mortal risks, how did you manage to save yourself from the wreck of our bark on the Cloaca Maxima?" he asked the *corpisantaro*.

"Sacramentum of salvage, this was done by Baronio."

"Baronio? And who would that be?"

Ugonio looked at us with solemn mien, as though he were about to make a grave announcement: "When and wheresoever, he intervenerates to salvage a personable acquaintance in emergentitious necessity," said he, while his companion invited us with a series of pulls and pushes to rise and follow him.

Thus, guided by the *corpisantari*, we again set out in the direction of conduit C.

After a few minutes' march, Ugonio and Ciacconio suddenly stopped. We had entered the first part of the gallery, and I seemed to hear a discreet rustling sound grow closer and closer. I became aware, too, of a strong, disagreeable, bestial stench.

Suddenly, Ugonio and Ciacconio bowed down, as though to worship an invisible deity. From the thick darkness of the gallery, I could just descry a number of greyish outlines, jumping up and down.

"Gfrrrlubh," proffered Ciacconio, deferentially.

"Baronio, of all the *corpisantari*, Excellentissimus, Caporal and Conducentor," announced Ugonio solemnly.

☙❧

That the people of darkness who formed the *corpisantari* might be fairly numerous was doubtless foreseeable; but that it should be guided by a recognised chief to whom the stinking mass of seekers after relics accorded prestige, authority and quasi-thaumaturgical powers—that, we really had not expected.

And yet here was the novelty which now faced us. The mysterious Baronio had come to meet us, almost as though he had sensed our approach, surrounded by a dense group of followers. They were a motley crowd—if one can use the word motley for shades only of grey and of brown—composed of individuals not too dissimilar to Ugonio and Ciacconio: attired at best in miserable and dusty cloaks, their hands and faces concealed by cowls and over-long sleeves, the acolytes of Ugonio, Ciacconio and Baronio formed the most frightful rabble conceivable to the mind of man. The penetrating stench which I had smelled before the meeting was no more and no less than the clarion call that heralded their coming.

Baronio stepped forward. He could be distinguished by the fact that he was slightly taller than those who accompanied him.

Hardly had we met, however, than there occurred something unforeseeable: the head of the *corpisantari* made a rapid withdrawal and two of his stunted adepts instantly stepped in to form a shield before him. Hedgehog-like, the entire assembly of *corpisantari* formed into a phalanx, emitting a rumble of mistrustful mutterings.

"Gfrrrlubh," then spoke forth Ciacconio, and suddenly the group appeared to lower their guard.

"You scarified Baronio: he misbegot you for a daemunculus subterraneus," said Ugonio, "but I did reinsure him, and can conswear, that you are a goodlious comrade-in-harms."

The head of the *corpisantari* had taken me for one of those little demons which—according to their bizarre beliefs—inhabit the subterranean darkness and whom the searchers after relics have never seen but of whose existence they are horribly certain. Ugonio explained to me that such beings, who were said to inhabit the vast regions under the ground, had been amply described by Nicephorus, Caspar Schott, Fortunius Licetus, Johannes Eusebius Nierembergius and by Kircher himself, who broadly discussed the nature and customs of the *daemunculi subterranei*, as well as of the Cyclops, the giants, pygmies, monopods, tritons, sirens, satyrs, cynocephali and acephali (or dog-headed and headless beings).

Now, however, there was nothing to be feared. Ugonio and Ciacconio stood guarantors for me and for Atto. The other *corpisantari* were therefore presented to us, answering (although my memory may betray me) to such appellations as Gallonio, Stellonio, Marronio, Salonio, Plafonio, Scacconio, Grufonio, Polonio, Svetonio and Antonio.

"Such an honour," said Atto, restraining his ironic disgust only with the greatest of difficulty.

Ugonio explained that it was Baronio who had guided the group which came to his assistance when our little bark had capsized, leaving us at the mercy of the Cloaca Maxima. Now, too, the head of the *corpisantari* had mysteriously perceived (by virtue, perhaps, of the same miraculous olfactory sensibility possessed by Ciacconio, or of other out-of-the-ordinary faculties) that Ugonio wished to meet him, and he had come to the encounter from the deep bowels of the earth; or perhaps, more simply, from the trapdoor which led into the underground tunnels from the Pantheon.

The *corpisantari* seemed to be united by bonds of brotherhood and Christian solidarity. Through the mediation of a cardinal with a passionate interest in relics, they had informally petitioned the Pope for the right to form an arch-confraternity; but the Pontiff had ("strangefully", commented Ugonio) failed as yet to respond to that request.

"They rob, they deceive, they smuggle, and then they behave like so many church mice," Atto whispered to me.

Ugonio then fell silent, leaving the floor to Baronio. At last the uninterrupted bustling of the *corpisantari*—perennially intent upon scratching, scraping away dead skin and scurf, coughing and spitting, and toothlessly chewing away at invisible and disgusting aliments—ceased.

Baronio puffed up his chest, pointed severely upwards and, pointing a clawed index heavenward, declaimed: "Gfrrrlubh!"

"Extraordinary," Atto Melani commented icily, "they all speak the same... language."

"It is no linguafrank, it is a vote," Ugonio intervened with some irritation, perhaps understanding that Atto was subtly deriding his leader.

Thus we learned that the limited lexical capacity of the *corpisantari* was a consequence, not of ignorance or stupidity but of a pious vow.

"Until the sacral object is disgoverned, we have voted not to verbalise," said Ugonio, who then explained that he alone was free of that pledge so as to be able to maintain contacts between the community of the *corpisantari* and the outside world.

"Ah yes, and what would this sacred object be which you so ardently seek?"

"Ampoule with the true Sanguine Domini Nostri," said Ugonio, while the rest of the troop made the sign of the cross as one man.

"Yours is indeed a noble and holy quest," said Atto, turning to Baronio with a smile.

"Pray that they should never be released from that vow," he then whispered to me so as not to be overheard, "or in Rome they will all end up talking like Ugonio."

"That is improbabilious," Ugonio replied unexpectedly, "whereinasmuch the undersignified is Germanic."

"Are you German?" asked Atto in astonishment.

"I proveniate from Vindobona," came the *corpisantaro*'s stiff reply.

"Ah, so you were born in Vienna," translated the abbot. "That would account for your speaking so..."

"... I commandeer the italic tongue, not as an immigrunter, but as if 'twere my own motherlingo," Ugonio hastened to add, "and am most gratificated to your worshipful decisionality for the complement of esteem wherewith you do adub me."

Once he had finished with complimenting himself for his awkward and ramshackle eloquence, Ugonio explained to his companions what was at stake: a dubious individual, lodging at our hostelry, had excogitated a plan to assassinate His Holiness Innocent XI using pestiferous leeches, and that at a time when in Vienna the fate of Christendom hung in the balance. The dastardly plot was to be enacted that very night.

The *corpisantari* received the news with expressions of profound indignation, approaching panic. A brief but excited debate took place, which Ugonio summarised for us. Plafonio proposed that they should withdraw in prayer and beg for the intercession of the Most High. Gallonio, on the other hand, favoured a diplomatic initiative: a delegation of *corpisantari* should visit Dulcibeni and request that he desist from his plan. Stellonio joined the discussion, expressing a very different opinion: they should enter the Donzello, capture Dulcibeni and execute him without further ado. Grufonio observed that such a scheme would provoke disagreeable counter-actions, such as the arrival of the Pontifical Guards. Marronio added that entry into premises shut up on grounds of suspected pestilence would thereafter incur undeniable risks. Svetonio pointed out that such an action would in any case be of no use for the purpose of foiling Dulcibeni's plot: if Tiracorda visited the Pope (and here Grufonio once more made the sign of the cross) all was lost. Tiracorda must therefore be stopped at all costs. The entire body of *corpisantari* then turned to Baronio, who harangued them efficaciously: "Gfrrrlubh!"

Baronio's rabble then began to jump up and down and to grunt in a furious, warlike manner; whereupon, as we watched, it dispersed and transformed itself, forming double ranks, like a band of soldiers, all marching into conduit C in the direction of Tiracorda's house.

Atto and I witnessed all this impotently, quite out of our depth; Ugonio, who had remained with us together with his usual companion, had to explain to us what was happening: the *corpisantari* had decided to intercept Tiracorda come what may. They would position themselves in the little roads around the old *Archiater*'s house, in order to ambush his carriage when it set out for the pontifical palace of Monte Cavallo.

"And we, Signor Atto, what shall we do to stop Tiracorda?" I asked, seized by agitation and the desire to fight with all my might against whoever threatened the life of the Vicar of Christ.

The abbot, however, was not listening to me. Instead, he simply replied to Ugonio's explanation with the words: "Ah, so that is how matters stand," proffered in a colourless voice.

He had lost all control over the situation and did not seem very pleased about that.

"Well then, what are we to do?"

"Tiracorda must be stopped, that is for sure," said Melani, striving to regain a decisive demeanour. "While Baronio and the others control the surface, we shall look after the underground galleries. Look here."

Under our eyes, he stretched out a newly revised version of the map of the underground city which he had drawn up previously but lost in the disaster of the Cloaca Maxima. The new map also showed conduit C, including the intersection with the little subterranean river leading to Dulcibeni's elaboratory and the Cloaca Maxima. The continuation of conduit D was also visible, up to the exit in Tiracorda's stables, just next to the Donzello.

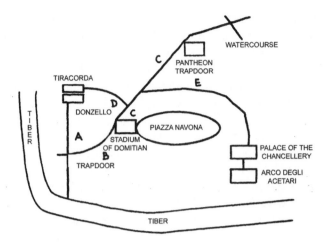

"In order to intercept Tiracorda, it will not suffice to control the streets around the Via dell'Orso," explained Atto. "We simply cannot ignore the possibility that the doctor may, in the interests of secrecy, prefer to pass through the underground galleries, taking conduits D, C, B and A, in that order, and emerging on the banks of the Tiber."

"But why?"

"He might, for example, travel some way by boat, moving upstream to the harbour of Ripetta. That would lengthen his itinerary but make it almost impossible to follow him. Or he might surface at some point unknown to us. It will be as well if we divide our tasks so as to be ready for all contingencies: Ugonio and Ciacconio will keep an eye on galleries A, B, C and D."

"Will that not be rather too much for the two of them on their own?"

"They are not two, but three: there is also Ciacconio's nose. You and I, my boy, shall explore the part of conduit B where we have never yet been; just to make quite sure that Tiracorda cannot get by that way."

"And Dulcibeni?" I asked. "Do you not fear that he too may be wandering underground?"

"No. He has done all that he could: to infect the leeches. Now it will suffice that Tiracorda should visit the Pope and apply those leeches."

Ugonio and Ciacconio departed at once, almost at a run, taking conduit C in the reverse direction. As we began our march, I found myself unable, however, to contain my overpowering curiosity: "Signor Atto, you are an agent of the King of France."

He looked askance at me. "Yes, and what are you getting at?"

"Well, it is just that... after all, this Pope is surely no friend of the Most Christian King, and yet you wish to save him, is that not so?"

He stopped. "Have you ever seen a man beheaded?"

"No."

"Well, you should know that when the head is rolling down from the scaffold, its tongue can still move. That is why no prince is ever content when one of his peers dies. He fears that rolling head and the dangerous things which that tongue might utter."

"Then, sovereigns never have anyone killed."

"Well, that is not exactly the case... they may do so, where the Crown itself is in jeopardy. But politics, and remember this, my boy, real politics consists of balances, not bloodshed."

I observed him surreptitiously; the uncertainty in his voice, the pallor of his face, his shifty eyes, all betrayed the return of Abbot Melani's fears: despite his fine words, I had clearly detected his fumbling. The *corpisantari* had left him no time for reflection: they had rapidly taken the initiative and were organising the rescue of Innocent XI; an heroic enterprise which Atto had not undertaken with such celerity and into which he had now been catapulted by surprise. There was now no turning back. He tried to mask his unease by hastening his steps, thus showing me only his stiff and nervous back.

Once we had reached the Archives, we searched in vain for some trace of Ugonio and Ciacconio. The two must be waiting there already, well hidden in some corner.

"It is we! Is all well?" asked Atto in a loud voice.

From behind some archway enveloped in darkness, Ciacconio's unmistakeable grunt replied in the affirmative.

We therefore resumed our exploration and, as we walked, again began to converse.

It had, we both agreed, been inexcusably short-sighted on our part not to have collated the very clear clues which had come to our attention during the previous few days. Fortunately, it was still possible to catch the mad horse of truth by the mane. Atto tried once more to sum up the elements of which we were aware: "Dulcibeni worked for the Odescalchi, as an accountant or something of the kind. He had a daughter called Maria, by a Turkish slave. The maiden was abducted by the former slave-trader Feroni and by his right-hand man Huygens, surely in order to satisfy one of the latter's caprices. Maria was probably taken very far away, to somewhere in the north. In order to trace her, Dulcibeni then turned to the Odescalchi, but they did not help him. This is why Dulcibeni detests them, and will naturally feel special hatred for the powerful Cardinal Benedetto Odescalchi, who has in the meantime become Pope. Moreover, after the abduction, something strange happens. Dulcibeni is assaulted and thrown from a window, probably with the intention of killing him. Are we agreed?"

"Agreed."

"And here the first obscure point arises: why would someone, acting perhaps on the orders of Feroni or the Odescalchi, have wished to be rid of him?"

"Perhaps to prevent him from recovering his daughter."

"Perhaps," said Atto with scant conviction. "But you have heard that all his searches were in vain. I am more inclined to believe that Dulcibeni had become a danger for someone."

"But Signor Atto, why was Dulcibeni's daughter a slave?"

"Did you not hear Tiracorda? Because her mother was a Turkish slave whom Dulcibeni was unwilling to marry. I am not well informed on the trade in negroes and Infidels, but—according to Dulcibeni—the bastard child was also considered to be a slave of the Odescalchi. I only wonder: why did Huygens and Feroni not simply buy her?"

"Perhaps the Odescalchi did not wish to sell her."

"Yet they did sell her mother. No, I think it was rather Dulcibeni who opposed his daughter's being ceded; that would explain why she was abducted, perhaps with the support of the Odescalchi themselves."

"Do you mean to say that such an abominable action might have had the backing of the family?" I asked, horrified.

"Surely. And perhaps that of Cardinal Benedetto Odescalchi himself, who has since become Pope. Do not forget that Feroni was exceedingly wealthy and quite powerful. That would suffice to explain why the Odescalchi should not have wished to help Dulcibeni to find his daughter."

"But what means had Dulcibeni to oppose the sale, if the girl was the property of the Odescalchi?"

"You rightly ask: what means had he? That, I think, is the point. Dulcibeni must have unsheathed an arm that posed a real threat to the Odescalchi and left them no choice but to arrange the abduction with Feroni and to try to have Dulcibeni silenced forever."

Feroni: I was about to tell the abbot that the name did not sound new to me. However, being unable to recall where I had heard it, I held my peace.

"An arm against the Odescalchi. A secret perhaps... who knows," murmured the abbot, with a lubricious gleam in his eyes.

An inadmissible secret in the past of the Pope: I understood that Atto Melani, secret agent of His Most Christian Majesty, would have given his life to know what that might have been.

"We must come to a conclusion, damn it!" he exclaimed at the end of his cogitations. "But first, let us recapitulate: Dulcibeni hatches the idea of assassinating no less a personage than the Pope. He can surely not hope to obtain an audience with the Pontiff and to stab him with a knife. How can one kill a man from a distance? One may attempt to poison him; but it is exceedingly difficult to introduce poison into the Pope's kitchens. Dulcibeni, however, works out a more refined solution. He remembers that he has an old friend who will serve his purpose: Giovanni Tiracorda, Physician in Chief to the Pope. Pope Odescalchi—and this Dulcibeni knows—has always suffered from delicate health. He is Tiracorda's patient, and Dulcibeni can take advantage of the situation. Just at this moment, moreover, tormented by the fear that the Christian armies might be defeated in Vienna, the condition of Pope Innocent XI has worsened. The Pope is treated by blood-letting, and this is effected by means of leeches which, of course, feed on blood. So, what does Dulcibeni do? Between one riddle and another, he gets Tiracorda drunk. This is not too difficult a task, because the physician's wife, Paradisa, is a bigot and half-crazed: she believes that alcohol leads to the damnation of the soul. So Tiracorda is compelled to drink in secret, and thus almost always to gulp down large quantities at speed. As soon as he is inebriated, his friend Dulcibeni infects the leeches intended for treating the Pope with the pestiferous humour which he has produced on his islet. The little creatures will sink their teeth into the Pontiff's holy flesh and he will be attacked by the infection."

"How horrible!"

"I would not say that. This is simply what a man thirsting for vengeance is capable of. Do you recall our first incursion into Tiracorda's house? Dulcibeni asked him: 'How are they?'", referring, as we now know, to the leeches which he planned to infect. Then, however, Tiracorda accidentally broke the bottle of liquor and Dulcibeni was compelled to postpone his operation. Last night, however, his plans progressed smoothly. While he was infecting the leeches, he pronounced the words, 'For her'": he was fulfilling his vendetta against the Odescalchi for the abduction of his daughter."

"But," I observed, "he needed a quiet place in which to prepare his plan and to carry out his operations."

"Bravo. And above all to cultivate the pestiferous humour, using arts unknown to us. After capturing rats, he caged them on his island and inoculated them with the infection. Then he extracted their blood and so treated it as to produce the infected humour. It was surely he who lost the leaf from the Bible in the galleries."

"So could he also have stolen my little pearls?"

"Who else? But, do not interrupt me," said Atto, cutting me short, and adding: "After the beginning of the quarantine and your master's being taken ill, Dulcibeni, in order to continue to have access to the underground galleries and, thus, to the isle of the Mithraeum, had to filch a key from Pellegrino's ring and to have a copy made by a locksmith. He wrapped a copy of the key in Komarek's page from the Bible; but, what with all that trafficking with rats, leeches and alembics, it was inevitable that he should have accidentally stained it with blood."

"On the island, we also found a vase for leeches almost identical to Tiracorda's," I observed, "and then, there were all those instruments..."

"He used the vase, I imagine, to keep a few leeches in and perhaps to make certain that they could feed on infected blood without themselves being killed by it. When, however, he understood that he was not the only one to take walks in the underground galleries, and that someone might be on his trail, he got rid of the little creatures which might have provided evidence of his criminal designs. The apparatus and instruments on the islet, however, were used not only for his experiments on rats, but also for preparing the pestiferous humour. That is why everything called to mind the cabinet of an alchemist: alembics, unguents, crucibles..."

"And that sort of gallows?"

"Who knows? Perhaps to keep the rats still while he bled them, or to cut them up and collect their blood."

And that was why, we repeated once more, we had found dying rats in the galleries: they had either escaped from or survived Dulcibeni's experiments, and we had encountered them before they died. Finally, the glass phial full of blood which we had found in gallery D had certainly been lost by Dulcibeni, who had perhaps attempted unsuccessfully to infect his friend Tiracorda's leeches directly with the rats' blood.

"But in the underground galleries, we also found leaves of *mamacoca*," I observed.

"That, I am unable to explain," admitted Abbot Melani. "Those had nothing to do with the pestilence or with Dulcibeni's plot. Another point: I cannot conceive how it was possible for Dulcibeni, day after day, and even at night, to run, to row, to climb and to escape our attempts to stalk him with the energy of a young boy. It seems almost as though someone must have helped him."

While we were engaged in such discussions, we came to the trapdoor at the intersection between conduits A and B. The left-hand branch of B was the last of the three passages which we had undertaken to explore a few days earlier, in order to complete our understanding of the galleries under the Donzello.

Contrary to our usual practice, therefore, we did not lower ourselves through the trapdoor leading from gallery B to A, as we would have done in order to return to the Donzello, but continued on our way. Thanks to the plan drawn up by Atto, it was clear to me that we were proceeding in the direction of the river, with the inn to our right and the Tiber to our left.

The gallery offered no surprises of any kind, until we came across a square stairwell not dissimilar to that all too familiar one which led down from the secret chamber in the Donzello to the galleries below.

"But if we take this, we shall emerge in the Via dell'Orso," said I, as we began to climb the stairs towards the surface.

"Not quite, perhaps a little more to the south, in the Via Tor di Nona."

The ascent led to a sort of vestibule with a floor of old bricks, again very like that which we had crossed so many times on our sorties from the hostelry.

On the ceiling of this vestibule, our eyes (and above all our probing hands) discovered a sort of heavy lid of iron or perhaps lead, which muffled all vibrations and resisted any attempts to open it. We needed to remove that last obstacle in order to discover to which point on the surface our path had led us. We put our backs to the heavy disc, and, with a great heave, pushing vigorously against the last step of the stone stairway, our combined efforts managed to shift it, with a loud clanging on the flagstones, just enough for us to squeeze out from under the ground. As we did so, we glimpsed and heard a violent struggle, which was taking place only a few yards from where we emerged.

We moved forward under the dim nocturnal light. In the semi-darkness, I could distinguish a carriage in the middle of the road, upon which two torches set on either side cast a sinister, oblique light. Suffocated cries came from the postillion, who was struggling to break free of the grip of several individuals. One of the attackers had taken the reins and stopped the horses, which were whinnying and snorting nervously. Just then, another individual slipped out of the carriage, holding a voluminous object in his arms (or so it seemed to me). There could be no question about it, the carriage was being robbed.

Although confused by my lengthy peregrinations under the ground, I instinctively recognised our surroundings as the Via Tor di Nona which, parallel to the Tiber, leads to the Via dell'Orso: Abbot Melani's estimate of where we would emerge had proved correct.

"Quick. Let us get closer," murmured Atto, pointing at the carriage.

The scene of violence which we were witnessing had almost paralysed me; I knew that, very nearby, at the end of the Sant'Angelo Bridge, a detachment of guards were usually stationed. The risk of being involved in so grave a crime did not dissuade me from following the abbot who, keeping prudently close to the wall, was approaching the scene of the robbery.

"Pompeo, help! Guards, help!" a voice whined from within the carriage.

The weak, stifled voice of the passenger belonged without the shadow of a doubt to Giovanni Tiracorda.

In a flash, I understood: the man in the driver's box, who uttered hoarse little cries as he vainly struggled against overwhelming forces, was certainly Pompeo Dulcibeni. Against our every expectation, Tiracorda had asked him to accompany him on his errand to serve the

Pope at the palace of Monte Cavallo. The physician, being too old and weak to drive his own carriage, had preferred to be accompanied by his friend, rather than by some anonymous coachman, on his delicate and secret mission. The *corpisantari*, however, had lain in wait nearby and had intercepted the carriage.

It was all over in a few moments. Hardly had the bag been extracted from within the coach than the four or five *corpisantari* who were immobilising Dulcibeni released their prey and took to their legs; they passed very close and disappeared behind us in the direction of the trap from which we had just emerged.

"The leeches, they must have taken the leeches," said I, excitedly.

"Shhh!" warned Atto, and I understood that he had no intention of participating in what was taking place. Some of the inhabitants of the surrounding houses, hearing the noise of the brawl, had meanwhile come to their windows. The guards might arrive at any moment.

From within the carriage came Tiracorda's feeble complaints, while Dulcibeni descended from his box, probably in order to succour his friend.

It was then that something incredible occurred. A fast-moving shadow, turning back from the trap into which the *corpisantari* had disappeared, approached in a zigzag and slipped back into the carriage. He still seemed to be carrying under his arm the voluminous object which we had seen him snatch from poor Tiracorda.

"No, you wretch, no—not the crucifix! There is a relic..."

The physician's imploring voice echoed piteously in the night as, after a brief struggle, the shadow emerged from the opposite side of the carriage. A fatal error: here, Pompeo Dulcibeni awaited him. We heard the cruel, sharp crack of the whip which he had recovered and which he now used to hobble the marauder's legs, causing him to fall to the ground. As he struggled uselessly to rise from the dust, by the light of one of the torches, I recognised the clumsy hunchbacked figure of Ciacconio.

We drew a little closer, thus risking being seen. With our view partly obscured by the still open door of the carriage, we heard the whip crack once again, and then a third time, accompanied by Ciacconio's inimitable grunt, this time carrying a clear note of protest.

"Filthy dogs," said Dulcibeni, as he placed something back in the carriage, closed the door and jumped back into the box, urging on the horses.

Once again, the sheer speed of the sequence of events prevented me from considering the motives of prudence and of the intellect, and even the righteous fear of God, which should have persuaded me to escape from the perilous influence of Abbot Melani and not to involve myself in rash, criminal and violent deeds.

That was why, still set on our bold plan to save the life of Our Lord Innocent XI, I did not dare draw back when Abbot Melani, dragging me from the shadows, guided me towards the carriage just as it was moving away.

"Now or never," said he when, after a brief chase, we leapt onto the footmen's platform behind the body of the carriage.

Hardly had we grasped the great handles behind the coach when there was another thud on the platform and rapacious hands gripped me, almost causing me to fall into the road. Almost overcome by this last shock, I turned and found myself facing the horribly deformed and toothless grin of Ciacconio, who held in his hands a crucifix to which was tied a pendant.

Thus weighted down by a third unasked-for passenger, the carriage meanwhile tilted sharply to one side.

"Filthy dogs, I shall kill you all," said Dulcibeni, while his whip cracked again and again.

The carriage turned left, along the Via del Panico, while on the far side the disorderly band of *corpisantari* watched impotently as our vehicle made off. Clearly they had all returned to the surface when Ciacconio failed to rejoin them. Three or four of them set out to follow us on foot, while we again veered to the right at the Piazza di Monte Giordano in the direction of the Santa Lucia sewer. Because of the ambush, Dulcibeni had been unable to take the road to Monte Cavallo and seemed now to be proceeding haphazardly.

"You've played another of your tricks, is that not so, you ugly beast!" cried Abbot Melani to Ciacconio as the carriage gathered speed.

"Gfrrrlubh," grunted Ciacconio in self-justification.

"Do you see what he has done?" replied Atto, turning to me. "As though winning were not enough, he had to turn back to rob the carriage of the crucifix with the relic, which Ugonio already tried to filch the first time we entered Tiracorda's stables. And thus, Dulcibeni has recovered the leeches."

Behind us, the *corpisantari* did not abandon their chase, even if they were already losing ground. Just then (we had again turned left)

we heard the tremulous, terrorised voice of Tiracorda, who was leaning out from the window: "Pompeo, Pompeo, they are following us,
and there is someone here behind..."

Dulcibeni did not reply. An unexpected and exceedingly violent
explosion deafened us, while a cloud of smoke momentarily deprived us of our sight and our ears were pierced by a cruel, lacerating
whistle.

"Down! He has a pistol," Atto exhorted us, crouching on the platform.

While I followed his example, the carriage again accelerated. Already sorely tried by the assault of the *corpisantari*, the horses' nerves
had been unable to withstand the sudden detonation.

Instead of taking shelter, Ciacconio opted as usual for the most
insane solution and climbed on top of the carriage, crawling towards
Dulcibeni and holding by some miracle onto that unsafe roof which
bounced in every direction. A few moments passed and the crack of
the whip compelled him at once to renounce his attack.

We were emerging at high speed from the Via del Pellegrino into
the Campo di Fiore, when I saw Ciacconio, still clinging precariously
to the carriage roof, remove the pendant with the relic and hurl the
holy cross at Dulcibeni with all his might. The carriage tilted slightly
to the right, which gave us the impression that the missile had found
its target. Ciacconio tried again to advance, perhaps attempting to
take advantage of the opportunity before Dulcibeni had time to reload his pistol.

"If Dulcibeni does not stop the horses, we shall end up against a
wall," I heard Atto say, his voice almost drowned out by the clatter of
the wheels on the cobblestones.

Again, we heard the whip crack; instead of slowing down, our
speed was increasing. I noticed that we were driving almost in a
straight line.

"Pompeo, oh my God, stop this carriage!" we heard Tiracorda
whine from within the carriage, his voice just audible despite the
metallic screech and clatter of wheel-rims and horseshoes.

By now, we had crossed Piazza Mattei and even Piazza Campitelli;
the wild charge of the coach through the night, leaving Monte Savello behind on our right, seemed utterly devoid of sense or any hope
of safety. While the flames of the two side torches gaily streaked the
darkness, the rare and furtive night wanderers, enveloped in their

cloaks and unknown to all save the moon, speechlessly witnessed our noisy onrush. We even crossed the night watch on their rounds, but they had neither the time nor the means to stop and interrogate us.

"Pompeo, I beg of you," Tiracorda yet again implored, "stop, stop at once."

"But why does he not stop, and why does he keep driving straight on?" I screamed to Atto.

As we crossed the Piazza della Consolazione, Dulcibeni's whip and Ciacconio's grunting could no longer be heard. We peeked cautiously over the roof and beheld Dulcibeni, standing in his box, exchanging with Ciacconio a wild, disorderly rain of blows and kicks. No one held the reins.

"My God," exclaimed Atto, "that is why we never turned."

It was then that we entered the long tetragonal esplanade of the Campo Vaccino—the Cows' Field—where one can see all that remains of the antique Roman Forum. To our left, the Arch of Septimius Severus, to our right, the ruins of the Temple of Jupiter Stator and the entrance of the Orti Farnesiani joined in the desperate frenzy harassing our eyes. Before us, drawing ever nearer, was the Arch of Titus.

Our ride became all the more hazardous, given the barbarously uneven terrain of the Campo Vaccino. Somehow, we avoided two Roman columns which lay on the ground. At last, we passed under the Arch of Titus and ran down the hill, ending the descent at a mad velocity. Nor did it seem that anything could stop us now, while Dulcibeni's angry voice screamed, "Filthy dog, go to hell!"

"Gfrrrlubh," Ciacconio insulted him in turn.

Something large, greyish and ragged then rolled down from the carriage, just as the team of horses, exhausted yet triumphant, entered the ample space over which, for sixteen centuries, the ruins of the Colosseum have loomed in magnificent indifference.

As we approached the imposing amphitheatre, we heard a dry crack under our feet. The rear axle had yielded to the excessive demands of the long ride, causing our vehicle to skid and tilt violently to the right. Before the carriage turned over, screaming in terror and shock, Atto and I let ourselves fall and roll on the ground, miraculously escaping being smashed by the spokes of the great wheels spinning wildly just next to us; the horses fell heavily, while the carriage with

its two passengers toppled, then slipped and slid sideways some way
further over a broken patch of earth, stones and weeds.

❧❧

After a few instants of comprehensible confusion, I rose to my feet. I
was in a sorry state, but uninjured. The carriage lay on its side, with
one wheel still spinning in the void, suggesting unenviable consequences for its passengers. The torches on either side were smoking,
having gone out.

We knew that the grey thing which had been thrown down not
long before must have been poor Ciacconio, hurled by Dulcibeni
from the moving vehicle. But our attention was at once captured by
something else. Atto pointed at one of the carriage doors, flung open
and pointing heroically heavenward. We understood each other instantly: without a moment's hesitation, we leapt inside the carriage,
where Tiracorda lay groaning, and in a swoon. Swifter than Atto, I
seized a heavy little chest from the hands of the Chief Physician,
within which clinking sounds betrayed the probable presence of a
vase. It seemed beyond a doubt to be the same object which we had
seen seized from Ciacconio: the container of the robust hermetic
vase used by physicians for transporting leeches.

"We have it!" I exulted. "Now let us flee!"

But even before I could complete my sentence, a powerful grip
tore me from within the carriage, dumping me on the hard flagstones, where I rolled painfully like a little bundle of rags. It was
Dulcibeni, who had perhaps recovered his wits at that very moment.
Now he was trying to tear the little chest from my grasp; but I,
clasping it in my arms with all the strength that remained in me,
had closed around my prize, shielding it with my arms, chest and
legs. Thus, every attempt by Dulcibeni ended up with him lifting
me and my precious load together, without succeeding in separating
us.

While Dulcibeni struggled thus, crushing me with his powerful
weight and inflicting upon me many painful bruises, Abbot Melani
attempted to turn away the fury of the ancient Jansenist. All in vain:
Dulcibeni seemed to possess the strength of a hundred men. We all
three rolled on the ground, in a furious, tumbling entanglement.

"Let me go, Melani," yelled Dulcibeni, "you do not know what
you are doing!"

"Do you really mean to assassinate the Pope, all because of your daughter? All because of a little half-caste bastard?"

"You cannot…" gasped Dulcibeni, while Atto succeeded for a moment in twisting his arm, thus stifling him.

"Did the daughter of a Turkish whore bring you to this?" continued Atto scornfully, while, coughing hoarsely from the effort, he was forced to let go of Dulcibeni's arm.

Pompeo hit him hard on the nose, which caused the abbot to groan no little, and left him rolling semi-conscious on the ground.

Turning back to me, Dulcibeni found me still clasping the little chest. Paralysed by fear, I dared not even move. He grasped me by the wrists and, almost tearing me apart, freed the container of the vase from my grasp. He then ran back to the carriage.

I followed him with my eyes in the moonlight. A little later, he emerged from the carriage, jumping nimbly to the ground. He held the chest under his left arm.

"Give me the other one. Yes, that is it, it is just behind," said he, speaking to someone within.

He then reached inside the carriage and drew out what appeared to be a pistol, unless my eyes betrayed me. Rather than reload his first arm, he had preferred to take a second pistol, ready for use. Meanwhile, Atto had risen and was rushing towards the carriage.

"Abbot Melani," said Dulcibeni, half scornful and half threatening, "since you enjoy stalking people so much, you may now complete your work."

He then turned and began to run in the direction of the Colosseum.

"Stop! Give me that bag!" called Atto.

"But Signor Atto, Dulcibeni…" I objected.

"… is armed. I am aware of that," replied Abbot Melani, crouching prudently near the ground. "But that is no reason to let him escape us."

I was struck by Atto's decisive tone and in a blinding insight, I understood what was agitating his heart and his thoughts and why, that evening, he had climbed without a moment's hesitation onto the back of Tiracorda's carriage, taking the mortal risk of following Dulcibeni.

Atto's natural predisposition to embroil himself in obscure intrigues and the potent pride which caused him to puff up his chest when he detected the presence of plotters, all those things which he felt and wanted and tended naturally to desire, remained unsatisfied. Dulcibeni's half-unveiled revelations had drawn Melani into their vortex. And now the abbot could not, would not withdraw. He wanted to know, come what may. Atto was not running in order to tear the leeches from Dulcibeni's hands: he wanted his secrets.

While those images and those thoughts rushed before my eyes at a speed a thousand times greater than that of Tiracorda's carriage, Dulcibeni fled towards the Colosseum.

෭~ჟ

Dulcibeni disappeared in the twinkling of an eye behind the dark portico of the Colosseum. Atto dragged me to the right, as though he intended to follow the same route as the man he was pursuing, but outside the colonnade.

"We must surprise him before he reloads his pistol," he whispered to me.

Dodging from side to side, we drew near to the arches of the Colosseum. We stopped first by one of the mighty load-bearing columns, draping ourselves like ivy around the stone blocks. Then we slipped into the colonnade: of Dulcibeni, there was no trace or sound.

We advanced a few paces, listening intently. It was only the second time in my life that I found myself among the ruins of the Colosseum, but I did know that the place was often infested, not only by owls and bats, but by all manner of bawds, thieves and wrongdoers who hid there in order to avoid justice and to perpetrate their execrable practices. The darkness made it almost impossible to see anything; now and again, one could distinguish only whatever was open to the sky and the pale light of the moon.

We proceeded cautiously along the great arcade, almost more at pains to avoid stumbling on some half-buried lump of stone than to track down our prey. The vault of the portico and the wall to our right echoed our every sound; the latter separated the arcade from the interior of the amphitheatre, and was pierced at regular intervals by vertical slits which allowed one to peer into the great arena. Apart from the padding of our feet and the swishing sounds of such gestures as we inevitably made, there was silence. That was why we jumped when, clearly and directly, a voice came out of the dark: "Poor Melani, slave to your king unto the bitter end."

Atto stopped: "Dulcibeni, where are you?"

There followed a moment's silence.

"I am ascending to heaven, I want to see God from closer quarters," whispered Dulcibeni from an unidentifiable place, which sounded at once distant and near at hand.

We looked fruitlessly around us.

"Stop and let us talk," said Atto. "If you do so, we shall not denounce you."

"So you wish to know, Abbot. Well, then I shall give you satisfaction. But first, you must find me."

Dulcibeni was moving away; but neither behind, nor before us under the portico, nor outside the Colosseum.

"He is already inside," concluded Atto.

Only far later, a long time after these events, did I discover that the wall which separates the interior of the amphitheatre from the arcade, while allowing one to see into the great arena, was regularly penetrated by criminals. One could obtain lawful access to the arena only through the big wooden gates situated at either end of the edifice, and these were obviously closed at night. Thus, to make a useful secret hiding place of the ruins, men and women engaged in nefarious activities would open up breaches in the surrounding wall, which the authorities rarely repaired as swiftly as they should.

Clearly, Dulcibeni had passed through one of these gaps. Abbot Melani at once set about exploring the nearby part of the wall, in search of the passage.

"Come on, come on, Melani," Dulcibeni's voice derided us all the while, growing ever more distant.

"Damn it, I cannot... ah, here we are!" exclaimed Atto.

It was not so much a hole as a simple widening of one of the slits in the surrounding wall, reaching up to the waist of a person of normal height. We helped each other through this gap. As I lowered myself into the arena, I felt myself shaken by a powerful tremor of fear. From outside, a hand had gripped my shoulder. I thought with alarm that this must be one of the criminals who infest the area at night, and was about to cry out when a familiar voice invited me to remain silent: "Gfrrrlubh."

Ciacconio had retraced us, and now he was about to join forces with us in the difficult task of capturing Dulcibeni. While the *corpisantaro* slipped through the opening, I breathed a sigh of relief and passed the news on to Atto.

The abbot had already moved ahead to scout the place out. We were in one of the many corridors which extend round the central space, whose sands were, centuries ago, stained by the blood of gladiators, lions and Christian martyrs, all sacrificed to the delirium of the pagan mob.

We proceeded in single file under high stone walls sloping down towards the centre of the Colosseum, which once framed the central arena and which must once—as could readily be conjectured—have supported the tiers on which the public sat. The nocturnal hour, the damp and the stink of the walls, arches and half-ruined bridges, and the crazed fluttering of bats, all rendered the atmosphere gloomy and menacing. The stench of mould and organic waste made it difficult even for Ciacconio, with his miraculous sense of smell, to determine which direction we should take in order to find Dulcibeni. Several times, I saw the *corpisantaro* point his huge nose upwards, panting and sniffing like an animal, but all in vain. Only the moonlight, which was reflected even on the white stone of the highest tiers of the edifice, afforded us some partial comfort and enabled us to proceed, although we had no lamp, without falling into one of the many chasms that opened up between one ruin and another.

After yet more useless reconnoitring, Atto lost patience and halted.

"Dulcibeni, where are you?" he cried.

The unquiet silence of the ruins was the only response.

"Shall we try dividing our forces?" I asked.

"On no account," replied Atto. "By the way, where have all your friends gone?" he asked Ciacconio.

"Gfrrrlubh," replied the latter, gesticulating and making it clear that the rest of the *corpisantaro* rabble would soon be arriving.

"Good. We shall need reinforcements to collar…"

"Slave of crowned heads, are you not coming to catch me?"

Dulcibeni had once more called us to action. This time, the voice came unequivocally from above our heads.

"Stupid Jansenist," commented Atto in a low voice, clearly irritated by the provocation, then he called out: "Come closer, Pompeo, I only want to talk with you."

In response, we heard resounding laughter.

"Very well, then I shall come up," Atto retorted.

That was in truth more easily said than done. The interior of the Colosseum, between the central arena and the façade, was a labyrinthine series of ruined walls, mutilated architraves and decapitated columns, in which the difficulty of orienting oneself was exacerbated by the lack of light.

Over centuries, the Colosseum had been, first, abandoned, then stripped of its marble and stone by many pontiffs for the (justified and sacrosanct) construction of many churches; as I have said, of the former terraces sloping down to the arena, there remained only the supporting walls. These radiated from the perimeter of the arena to the top of the curved outer wall. Parallel to these ran the narrow passages connecting the many concentric circular corridors which completely surrounded the stadium. The whole formed an inextricable maze through which we now moved.

We followed one of the circular corridors some way, endeavouring to draw nearer to the point from which Dulcibeni's voice had issued. The attempt proved useless. Atto looked questioningly at Ciacconio. The *corpisantaro* again explored the air with wide open nostrils, to no effect.

Dulcibeni must have realised our difficulties, because he almost immediately showed his presence again: "Abbot Melani, you are making me lose my patience."

Contrary to all our expectations, the voice was anything but far off; yet the echoes produced by the ruins made it impossible to detect from which direction the fugitive's mocking words came. Curiously, the moment that the sonorous reflections of his voice died out, I seemed to hear a brief and repeated whistling sound, which seemed familiar to me.

"Did you hear?" I asked Atto in a very small voice. "It seems that... I think that he is taking snuff."

"Strange," commented the abbot. "At a time like this..."

"I heard him doing that this evening, too, when he did not come down to dinner."

"In other words, when he was on the point of setting out to complete his plan," noted Abbot Melani.

"Precisely. I also saw him take snuff just before his soliloquy about crowned heads, when he went on about corrupt sovereigns and so forth. And I noticed that, after taking snuff, he seemed more awake and vigorous. It was as though he used it to think more clearly, or... to gain strength—yes, that is it."

"I think that I have just fathomed this," murmured Atto under his breath, but he suddenly broke off.

Ciacconio was pulling us by the sleeves, drawing us towards the centre of the arena. The *corpisantaro* had moved out of the labyrinth, the better to follow the scent of Dulcibeni. Hardly had he entered the open space when he gave a start. "Gfrrrlubh," said he, indicating a point on the immense and impervious perimeter walls of the Colosseum.

"Are you sure?" we asked in unison, vaguely put out by the danger and inaccessibility of the place.

Ciacconio nodded and we at once set out for our objective.

The great perimeter walls of the stadium were composed of three superimposed orders of arches. The point indicated by Ciacconio was an arch at the intermediate level, at a height above ground perhaps exceeding that of the entire Locanda del Donzello.

"How are we to get up there?" asked Abbot Melani.

"Get some help from your monsters," we heard Dulcibeni cry; this time Atto had spoken without lowering his voice sufficiently.

"You are quite right, that is a good idea!" he yelled back. "You were not mistaken," he then added, turning to Ciacconio, "the voice does come from up there."

Ciacconio was meanwhile beating a path in all haste across the labyrinth. He led us towards one of the two great wooden gates which were left open in daytime to give access to the interior of the amphitheatre. Just in front of the gate there rose a great, steep staircase which entered into the majestic body of the Colosseum.

"He must have come up this way," murmured Melani.

The stairs did indeed lead to the first storey of the building, in other words to the level of the second order of arches. Hardly had we ascended the last steps than we emerged into the open and found ourselves in an enormous corridor which ringed the entire amphitheatre. Here, rising no little above the level of the auditorium, the moonlight spread more surely and more generously. Spectacular was the view over the central space and the ruins of the tiers of seats; and, above us, the enormous walls that contained the entire mass of the circus, standing out majestically against the heavens. With our breath short after our rapid climb, for an instant we halted and almost forgot our objective, ravished by so grandiose a spectacle.

"You are almost there, spy of kings," the harsh, grating voice of Dulcibeni called us from the right.

From there, came a detonation that terrified us, and almost instantly we flattened ourselves on the ground. Dulcibeni had fired at us.

We were then startled by a loud clatter a few paces away. I approached on all fours and found Dulcibeni's pistol, half-broken by the hard impact.

"Two misses, what a pity! Take courage, Melani, now we are on an equal footing."

I handed the arm to Atto, who looked thoughtfully in Dulcibeni's direction. "There is something that escapes me," he commented, as we approached the place from which the voice and the pistol had come.

For me, too, something was amiss. Already, as we ascended the great staircase, I had been assailed by no few doubts. Why had Dulcibeni drawn us into that bizarre moonlight pursuit among the ruins of the Colosseum, thus losing precious time and risking being caught by the police *in flagrante delicto*?

Why should he have wanted so much to attract Abbot Melani all the way up here with the promise that he would reveal to him all that he wanted to know?

Meanwhile, as we clambered breathlessly over the last time-worn tiers of seats, we heard the echo of distant cries, sounding something like the warlike bustle of troops converging upon an agreed objective.

"I knew it," commented Abbot Melani, panting. "It was impossible that a few *caporioni* and members of the watch should not show up. Dulcibeni could not hope to pass unobserved after that episode with the runaway carriage."

With his mocking provocations, our prey had facilitated our search. Yet it at once became clear that it would be very difficult indeed for us to approach him. Dulcibeni had in fact hauled himself up on top of one of the walls supporting the terraces; from the corridor in which we stood, the wall climbed obliquely to a window in the perimeter wall, at almost the highest point of the Colosseum.

There he was, comfortably seated under the window with his back to the wall, still holding the chest with the leeches tightly in his arms. I was astounded by the extraordinary way in which he had succeeded in taking refuge up there; under the oblique wall on top of which he had ventured there yawned a horrible and most perilous gulf, and anyone who fell into it would meet with a ghastly death. Beyond the window, there was a chasm as deep as two entire palaces were high, yet Dulcibeni did not seem in the least perturbed by this. Three awesome and sublime worlds opened up around the fugitive: the great arena of the Colosseum, the tremendous abyss beyond the façade, and the starlit night which set the seal on the grandiose and fatal theatre of that night's events.

Under the Colosseum, in the meantime, we seemed to hear the voices and presence of strangers: the men of the watch must have arrived. We were separated from our prey by a space of empty air as wide as a middling city street.

"So here they are, the saviours of the usurer with the tiara, of the insatiable beast from Como," and he exploded into what seemed to me to be forced, unnatural laughter, the fruit of an insane blend of wrath and euphoria.

Atto glanced questioningly at me and Ciacconio.

"I have understood, you know," said Atto.

"Tell me, tell me, Melani, tell me what you have understood," exclaimed Dulcibeni.

"The tobacco is not tobacco…"

"Oh, how clever. Do you know what I have to say to that? You are quite right. So many things are not what they appear to be."

"You inhale those strange dried leaves, what are they called…?" insisted Atto.

"*Mamacoca*," I exclaimed.

"How perspicacious! I am lost in admiration," Dulcibeni replied caustically.

"That is why you are not tired at night," said the abbot. "But then in the daytime you become irascible and feel the need to have more and more of it, and so you continue to stuff your nostrils with it: and then you declaim complete speeches before your mirror, imagining that you still have your daughter with you. And when you launch into one of your insane diatribes about sovereigns and crowns, you become inflamed, and no one can stop you, because that herb sustains your body, but it… In short, it confuses the mind, which becomes possessed. Or am I mistaken?"

"I see that you have amused yourself teaching the art of spying [to yo]ur little prentice instead of leaving him to his natural destiny [as a so]urce of amusement for princes and of astonishment for fair[-goers and fi]dlers," replied Dulcibeni, with roars of laughter which he [aimed sc]ornfully at me.

It was, moreover, true that I had spied at the Jansenist's door and had then gone to recount all that I had heard to the abbot.

Dulcibeni then bounded nimbly along the oblique wall, oblivious of the chasm beneath his feet and (despite the burden of the little chest which he still carried) hauled himself onto the top of the great wall of the façade, the width of which exceeded three paces.

There our adversary now stood, majestically dominating us from above. A few yards away from him rose a great wooden cross, higher than a man, placed above the façade of the Colosseum to signify the consecration of the monument to the memory of the Christian martyrs.

Dulcibeni glanced downwards, outside the Colosseum. "Take courage, Melani. Reinforcements will soon be arriving. There is a group of guards down there."

"Then tell me, before they arrive," Atto rejoined, "why do you want the death of Innocent XI?"

"Rack your brains," said Dulcibeni, withdrawing from the edge of the great wall; at that precise moment, Atto was climbing in his turn onto the narrow cornice that led to the perimeter wall.

"What has he done to you, damn it?" Atto continued with a strangled voice. "Has he dishonoured the Christian faith, has he covered it in shame and ignominy? Is that what you think? Say it, Pompeo, admit that you are possessed, like all the Jansenists. You hate the world, Pompeo, because you cannot manage to hate yourself."

Dulcibeni did not reply. Meanwhile Atto, holding tightly onto the naked stone, was climbing painfully along the wall that led up to him.

"The experiments on the island," he continued, clumsily grappling on all fours with the top of the wall, "the visits to Tiracorda, the nights in the underground galleries... You did all that for a bastard, half-Infidel bitch, you poor madman. You should thank Huygens and that slobbering old Feroni if they did her the honour of ripping open her maidenhead before they threw her into the sea."

I was shocked by the cruel obscenities which Abbot Melani had unexpectedly unleashed. Then I understood. Atto was provoking Dulcibeni to make him explode. And he succeeded.

"Silence, castrato, shame of God, you who can only get your arse ripped open," screamed Dulcibeni from afar. "That you liked plunging your cock in the shit, that I knew; but that your head was full of it too..."

"Your daughter, Pompeo," Atto continued, taking advantage of the moment, "old Feroni wanted to buy her, is that not so?"

Dulcibeni let out a groan of surprise: "Go on, you are getting close," was, however, all that he replied.

"Let us see," said Atto, panting from the effort of his climb, yet drawing ever closer to Dulcibeni. "Huygens looked after Feroni's affairs; therefore, he often dealt with the Odescalchi, and so with you too. One day he discovered your little girl and took a fancy to her. That idiot Feroni, as usual, wanted to give her to him at all costs. He offered to buy her from the Odescalchi, perhaps even to sell her again when Huygens grew tired of her. Perhaps he obtained her from Innocent XI himself when he was still a cardinal."

"He obtained her from him and from his nephew Livio, damned souls," Dulcibeni corrected him.

"You could not legally oppose the sale," continued Atto, "because you had not deigned to marry her mother, a wretched Turkish slave, and so your daughter belonged not to you but to the Odescalchi. Then you found a remedy: to rake up a scandal against your masters, a stain on the honour of the Odescalchi. In short, you blackmailed them."

Dulcibeni again remained silent, and this time his silence seemed more than ever to be a confirmation.

"I am lacking only one date," Atto asked. "When was your daughter abducted?"

"In 1676," Dulcibeni replied icily. "She was only twelve years old."

"Just before the conclave, is that not so?" said Atto, taking another step forward.

"I believe you have understood."

"The election of the new Pope was being prepared, and Cardinal Benedetto Odescalchi, who had lost the previous conclave by a hair's-breadth, was determined to triumph this time. But with your threats, you held him in your power: if a certain item of news were to reach the ears of the other cardinals, there would have been an enormous scandal, and goodbye to the election. Am I on the right track?"

"You could not be more right," said Dulcibeni, without concealing his surprise.

"What was the scandal, Pompeo? What had the Odescalchi done?"

"First, finish your own little story," Dulcibeni invited him scornfully.

The night wind, which at that height makes itself felt more acutely, whipped relentlessly at us; I trembled, without knowing whether it was from cold or fear.

"With pleasure," said Atto. "By threatening them, you believed that you could prevent the sale of your daughter. Instead, you signed your own death warrant. Feroni, perhaps with the complicity of the Odescalchi themselves, abducted your daughter and thus closed your mouth for long enough for Benedetto to be elected Pope. After which, you tried to find the child. But you were not clever enough."

"I raked through Holland from end to end. God only knows that I could do no more!" roared Dulcibeni.

"You did not find your daughter and you were the victim of a strange incident; someone caused you to fall from a window, or something of the sort. Yet you escaped with your life."

"There was a hedge below, I was lucky," explained Dulcibeni. "Pray continue."

Atto hesitated before this latest exhortation from Dulcibeni. Even I wondered why he was doling out so much rope to us.

"You fled Rome, hunted down and terrorised," continued Melani. "The rest, I already knew: you converted to Jansenism and in Naples you met Fouquet. There is, however, something else which I do not understand. Why take revenge now, after so many years? Perhaps because... Oh my God, now I see."

I saw the abbot bring his hand to his forehead in a gesture of surprise. He had, meanwhile, in a bold balancing act, crossed another stretch of the wall, drawing even closer to Dulcibeni.

"Because there is a battle now for Vienna and if you kill the Pope, the Christian alliance will collapse, the Turks will win and will devastate Europe. Is it not so?" exclaimed Atto in a voice hoarse with astonishment and indignation.

"Europe has already been devastated: by her own kings," retorted Dulcibeni.

"Oh, you wretched madman," replied Atto. "You would like... you want..." and he sneezed three, four, five times with unaccustomed violence, at the risk of losing his grip on the wall and tumbling into the abyss.

"Damn it," he swore, thoroughly put out. "Once there was only one thing that made me sneeze: textiles from Holland. And now at last I know why I have been sneezing so much since I entered that accursed hostelry."

I too understood: it was the fault of Dulcibeni's old Dutch clothing. Yet, I suddenly recalled, Atto had sometimes sneezed upon my arrival. Perhaps I was just returning from the Jansenist's apartment. Or...

This was no time for such cogitations. I observed Dulcibeni move along the top of the amphitheatre's façade, first to the left, then to the right, continuing to keep an eye on Tiracorda's carriage.

"You are still hiding something, Pompeo," cried Atto, recovering from his bout of sneezing and regaining his balance as he straddled the wall. "With what did you manage to blackmail the Odescalchi? What is the secret with which you held Cardinal Benedetto in your power?"

"There is no more to be said," Dulcibeni cut him short, again looking in the direction of the Chief Physician's carriage.

"Ah no, that is all too convenient! Besides, your daughter's story does not hold water: it is simply not enough to explain an attempt on the life of a Pope. Come, come: first, you were not even willing to wed her mother, and now you would do all this to avenge her? No, that makes no sense. Besides, this Pope is a friend of you Jansenists. Speak, Pompeo."

"It is no business of yours."

"You cannot..."

"I have no more to say to a spy of the Most Christian King."

"Yes, but with your leeches, you wanted to do the Most Christian King a great favour: to free him of the Pope and Vienna at a blow."

"Do you really believe that Louis XIV will defeat the Turks too?" replied Dulcibeni invidiously. "Poor deluded creature! No, the Ottoman tide will cut off the head of the King of France, too. No regard for traitors: that is the victor's rule."

"So is this then your plan for palingenesis, your hope for a return to the pure Christian faith, you true Jansenist?" retorted Atto. "Yes, of course, let us sweep away the Church of Rome and the Christian sovereigns, let the altars go up in flames! Thus we shall return to the times of the martyrs: our throats cut by the Turks, but firmer and stronger in the Faith! And you believe that? Which of us is the more deluded? Dulcibeni?"

Meanwhile, I had moved away from Atto and Dulcibeni, reaching a sort of little terrace, near the stairs which we had climbed to the first storey; from that viewpoint, I could observe what was taking place outside the Colosseum, and I understood why Dulcibeni was looking down with so much interest.

A group of the Bargello's men were busying themselves around the carriage, and in the distance the voice of Tiracorda could be heard. Some of them were observing us; soon, I imagined and feared, they would come up and capture us.

Suddenly, however, I had cause to shiver, not on account of the freshness of the late night wind: a howl arose, nay, a savage chorus which came from all sides of the open space before the Colosseum, and a diffuse crackling sound which seemed to be caused by the throwing of many stones and projectiles.

The horde of *corpisantari* (who had evidently planned their incursion with care) poured screaming into the forecourt of the Colosseum, armed with clubs and sticks and charging at full speed, without even giving the Bargello's men time to understand what was happening. Our view was somewhat improved by the light which the guards' torches spread here and there on the scene.

The ambuscade was sudden, barbarous, pitiless. A group of attackers emerged from the Arch of Constantine, a second descended from the wall around the orchards overlooking the ruins of the Curia Hostilia, another rushed out from the ruins of the Temple of Isis and Serapis. The warlike cry of the assailing mob rose high and wild, utterly disconcerting their victims, who numbered only five or six.

A pair of guards who were more cut off from the group, almost paralysed with surprise, were the first to suffer the blows, scratches, kicks and bites of the three *corpisantari* arriving from the Arch of Constantine. The clash came in a chaotic scrimmage of legs, arms, heads bestially grasped, a rudimentary brawl devoid of any military orderliness. The blows dealt out were, however, certainly not mortal, seeing that the victims, although badly thrashed, soon beat an indecorous retreat towards the street that leads to San Giovanni. Two other guards (those, in fact, who in all probability were on the point of entering the Colosseum in order to arrest us), terrorised by the filthy *corpisantaro* band, made off without so much as a blow, running as fast as their legs would carry them in the direction of San Pietro in Vincoli, followed by a bunch of verminous attackers, among whose cries I seemed to discern the unmistakeable eloquence of Ugonio.

Matters, however, went differently for the two guards near to Tiracorda's carriage: one of the pair defended himself ably with his sabre, succeeding in keeping a trio of *corpisantari* effectively in check. Meanwhile, his companion, the only one on horseback, hauled up to the saddle a third, plump and clumsy personage who (unless my eyes deceived me) had a bag hanging from his neck. It was Tiracorda, whom the guard had doubtless recognised as the victim of the criminal events of the night, and had decided to bear to safety. Hardly had the horse carrying the two ridden off towards the sanctuary of Monte Cavallo than the guard who remained on foot resigned himself to flight, disappearing into the darkness. The Colosseum returned to the realm of silence.

My attention switched back to Atto and Dulcibeni, who had also been distracted by the real battle which had taken place before our eyes.

"It is all over, Melani," said the latter. "You have won, with your subterranean monsters, with your mania for spying and intrigue, with that insane curiosity which makes you crawl like a bedbug under the clothing of princes. Now, I shall open this bag and give you its contents, which the little prentice here would perhaps like to lay his hands on even more than you."

"Yes, it is all over," repeated Atto with a weary sigh.

He had almost reached the end of the wall and was a few yards now from Dulcibeni's feet. Soon, he would be able to climb onto the outer wall of the Colosseum and stand face to face with his antagonist.

I was not, however, of the same opinion as the abbot: it was by no means all over. We had stalked, followed, investigated, reasoned for nights and nights. All in order to find the answer to one question above all others: who had poisoned Nicolas Fouquet, and how? I was astounded that among the thousand questions which Atto had put to Dulcibeni, that was the one question for which he had found no time. But, if he did not ask it, I was still there.

"Why kill the Superintendent too, Signor Pompeo?" I dared then to ask.

Dulcibeni raised his eyes to heaven and burst into lugubrious laughter.

"Ask that question of your dear Abbot, my boy!" he exclaimed. "Ask him how come his dear friend Fouquet felt ill after his foot bath. Get him to tell you also why Abbot Melani became so agitated and why he tormented the poor man with his questions and would not even let him die in peace. And then... ask him what was so potent in the water of Fouquet's foot bath, ask him which poisons kill so perfidiously."

I looked instinctively at Atto, who said nothing, as though caught off balance.

"But you..." he tried feebly to interrupt.

"I put one of my little mice to swim in that water," Dulcibeni continued, "and after a few moments, I saw him perish in the most horrible way imaginable. A powerful poison, Abbot Melani, and a treacherous one: well dissolved in a foot bath, it penetrates through the skin and under the toenails without leaving a trace, and ascends through the body to the bowels, inexorably destroying them. A true work of art, such as only the French master perfumers can create, is that not so?"

I recalled then that, on my second visit to Fouquet's body, Cristofano had found on the floor, next to the basin containing the foot bath, a few pools of water; this, despite the fact that I myself had dried the floor carefully that very morning. In taking his sample, Dulcibeni must have spilled a little. I shivered when I remembered that I had touched a few drops of that fatal liquid: too little, fortunately, to suffer even so much as a slight malaise.

Then, turning to Atto, Dulcibeni added: "Did the Most Christian King perhaps entrust a very special task to you, Signor Abbot Atto Melani? Something terrible, but which you could not refuse? A proof of supreme fidelity to the King?"

"Enough of that, I cannot permit such talk!" warned Atto, at last hauling himself up onto the great wall surrounding the Colosseum.

"What vile lies against Fouquet did the Most Christian King feed to you when he commanded you to eliminate him?" insisted Dulcibeni. "You obeyed, squalid slave that you are. But then, when he was dying in your arms, the Superintendent murmured something to you which you did not expect. I can imagine it, yes: some reference to obscure secrets, a few babbled phrases which perhaps no one could ever have understood. But it was enough for you to realise that you were a pawn in a game the existence of which you did not so much as suspect."

"You are raving, Dulcibeni, I do not…" Atto tried once again to interrupt him.

"Ah! You are under no obligation to say anything: those words will remain forever a secret between you and Fouquet, that is not what matters," cried Dulcibeni, facing the wind which was growing ever more impetuous. "But at that moment, you understood that the King had lied to and exploited you. And you began to fear for yourself. Then you got it into your head to investigate all the guests at the inn: you were trying desperately to discover the real reason why you had been sent to kill your friend."

"You are mad, Dulcibeni, you are mad and you are trying to accuse me in order to cover up your own guilt, you are…"

"And you, boy," Dulcibeni interrupted him, turning again towards me, "ask your abbot, too: why were Fouquet's last words "*'Ahi, dunqu'è pur vero'*"? Is that not strangely reminiscent of an aria famous in the Superintendent's golden days? Abbot Melani, you cannot have failed to recognise it: tell me, how many times did you sing it in his presence? And he meant to remind you of those words, as he died with the pain of your betrayal. Like Julius Caesar, when he saw that among the ruffians who were stabbing him was his beloved Brutus."

Atto had ceased to respond. He had climbed onto the great wall, and now he and Dulcibeni confronted one another. But the abbot's silence had another cause: Dulcibeni was about to open the box of leeches.

"I promised you, and I always keep my promises," said Dulcibeni. "The contents are all yours."

Then he approached the edge of the wall and turned the little chest upside down, opening it onto the void.

But from the chest (even I could see this from a distance) came nothing. It was empty.

Dulcibeni laughed.

"Poor imbecile," said he to Melani, "did you really believe that I would waste all this time for the sole pleasure of being insulted by you?"

Instinctively, my eyes and Atto's sought each other, sharing the same thought: Dulcibeni had drawn us up there for the sole purpose of creating a diversion. He had left the leeches in the carriage before fleeing into the Colosseum.

"Now they are on their way with their master, bound for the veins of the Pope," he added mockingly, "and no one can stop them."

Atto sat down, overcome; Dulcibeni dropped the chest into the void, outside the Colosseum. A few seconds later, we heard a sad, muffled thump.

Dulcibeni took advantage of the respite to take his snuff box out once more and treat himself to a great sniff of *mamacoca*; then he threw the little box into the void too, turning his arm in a gesture at once triumphal and derisive.

It was that last throw, however, that cost him his balance. We saw him sway a little, then try to regain an erect position, at last bending to the right, where the great wooden cross stood.

It all happened in a matter of moments. He brought his hand to his head, as though assailed by a sharp, cruel pain, or a sudden loss of control, and collided with the cross, the presence of which—I thought—he had not in any way foreseen.

The collision with the wooden symbol deprived him of his already precarious equilibrium. I saw his body fall into the Colosseum, in instants dropping the height of many men placed one above the other. Fortunately—and this saved his life—the first impact was with a slightly sloping brick shelf. Then Dulcibeni's body landed on a great stone slab, which received it mercifully, as a riverbed receives the wrecks of ships overcome by the force of the tempest.

Only with the help of the other *corpisantari* were we able to raise the inert body of Dulcibeni. He was alive, and a few minutes later, he even regained consciousness.

"My legs... I can no longer feel them," were his first words.

Under the guidance of Baronio, the *corpisantari* found a hand-cart nearby, perhaps left there by some fruit vendor. It was old and rickety, but, thanks to the united forces of the *corpisantari*, we managed to use it to transport Dulcibeni's poor injured body. Of course, Atto and I could have abandoned the wounded man among the ruins of the Colosseum, but we at once agreed that so to do would be pointlessly cruel and dangerous; he would sooner or later be found and, what was more, would be missing from the roll-call at the inn, thus inevitably provoking an inquiry on the part of Cristofano, and then, by the authorities.

I felt relieved by our shared decision to save Dulcibeni: the melancholy and tragic history of his daughter had not left me indifferent.

The march back to the Donzello was interminable and funereal. We followed the most tortuous of routes and the strangest short-cuts in order to avoid once again being surprised by the Bargello's men. The *corpisantari*, taciturn and peevish, were disheartened by their failure to prevent Tiracorda from escaping with the leeches and mortified both by the bitterness of defeat and the fear that, by the morrow, the Pope might be mortally infected. On the other hand, Dulcibeni's desperate condition inspired no one with the idea of denouncing him; the savage assault which the *corpisantari* had just inflicted upon the Bargello's men counselled prudence and silence. It would be in all our best interests that there should remain in the minds of the guardians of order only memories of this night, but no traces.

In order not to form too large and visible a group, most of the *corpisantari* left us, not without a hurriedly grunted farewell. Seven of us remained: Ugonio, Ciacconio, Polonio, Grufonio, Atto, Dulcibeni (loaded onto the hand-cart) and myself.

We proceeded in a group, taking turns to push the cart. We were near to the Gesù church, in the vicinity of the Pantheon, where we were to regain the underground galleries in order to return to the Donzello. I noticed that Ciacconio was not keeping up with us and had fallen behind. I observed him: he was walking with difficulty and dragging his feet. I drew this to the attention of those at the front of the group and we waited for Ciacconio to catch up with us.

"All the haste leaves him windified," commented Ugonio.

It did not seem to me that Ciacconio was merely exhausted. Hardly had he rejoined us than he leaned against the cart, then sat down on the ground, with his back to the wall, and remained motionless. His breathing was short and light.

"Ciacconio, what is wrong with you?"

"Gfrrrlubh," he replied, pointing to the left-hand side of his belly.

"Are you tired, or unwell?"

"Gfrrrlubh," he replied, repeating the same gesture, and seeming to have nothing to add to that.

Instinctively (and despite the fact that any bodily contact with the *corpisantari* was to be regarded as far from desirable) I touched Ciacconio's clothing at the place which he had indicated. It seemed damp.

I shifted the folds of material a little and became aware of a disagreeable but familiar odour. Everyone had meanwhile gathered round, and it was Abbot Melani who drew even closer. He touched Ciacconio's clothing and brought his hand to his nose.

"Blood. Good heavens, let us open his clothing!" he said, nervously undoing the cord which kept Ciacconio's old overcoat closed. He had a wound just halfway up his belly, from which blood was seeping continuously and had already stained a great patch of material. The wound was most grave, the haemorrhage copious, and I was astounded that Ciacconio should still have had the strength to walk until now.

"My God, he needs help, he cannot come with us," I said, shocked through and through by our discovery.

There was a long moment's silence. It was all too easy to understand what thoughts were traversing the mind of the group. The ball which had struck Ciacconio had come from Dulcibeni's pistol. Without intending it, he had mortally wounded the unfortunate *corpisantaro*.

"Gfrrrlubh," said Ciacconio, then, pointing out with one hand the road which we were following and gesturing that we should continue on our way. Ugonio knelt down and drew near to him. There followed a rapid and unintelligible parley between the two, during which Ugonio twice raised his voice as though to convince his companion of his own opinion. Ciacconio, however, repeated the same murmur again and again, each time more feebly and breathlessly.

It was then that Atto understood what was about to happen: "My God, no, we cannot leave him here. Call your friends," he said, turning to Ugonio. "Let them come and fetch him. We must do something, call someone, a chirurgeon..."

"Gfrrrlubh," said Ciacconio in a slight, resigned whisper, which fell among us as the most definitive human reasoning of which one could conceive.

Ugonio, for his part, laid his hand gently on his companion's shoulder, then stood up as though the conversation were at an end. Polonio and Grufonio then approached the wounded man and exchanged confused and mysterious arguments with him in an uninterrupted murmur. At length, they all knelt down together and began to pray.

"Oh no," I wept, "it cannot, it must not be."

Even Atto, who had hitherto manifested so little sympathy for the *corpisantari* and their bizarre qualities, could not contain his emotion. I saw him draw aside and hide his face and I noticed that his shoulders were shaken by convulsive movements. In silent, liberating sobs, the abbot was at last releasing his pain: for Ciacconio, for Fouquet, for Vienna, for himself; a traitor perhaps, but one betrayed, and alone. And, while I bethought myself of Dulcibeni's last mysterious words about the death of Fouquet, I felt dark shadows gather between Atto and myself.

In the end, we all went down on bended knee to pray, while Ciacconio's breathing became ever shorter and more suffocated; until Grufonio left briefly, to warn (or so I surmised) the rest of the *corpisantari* who, within a few minutes, arrived. Soon they would remove the poor body and accord it a decent burial.

It was then, before my eyes, that the last heartrending seconds of Ciacconio's life ran out. While his companions gathered around him, Ugonio compassionately supported the head of the dying man; with a gesture, he invited us all to keep silent and interrupt our prayers. The quiet of the night fell over the scene and we could heart the last words of the *corpisantaro:* "Gfrrrlubh."

I looked questioningly at Ugonio who, between sobs, translated: "*Lachrymae in pluvia.*"

Then the poor man ceased breathing.

There was no need for further explanations. In those words, Ciacconio had carved his own fleeting adventure on earth: we are as teardrops in the rain; hardly shed, and already lost in the great flow of mortality.

After Ciacconio's remains had been borne away by his friends, we went again on our way with our hearts weighed down by bitter, indescribable pain. I walked with bowed head, as though propelled by a force outside of me. My suffering was such that during the remainder of our march, I had not even the courage to look at poor Ugonio, fearing that I would be unable to hold back my tears. All the adventures which we had faced together with the two *corpisantari* returned to mind: our explorations of the subterranean maze, the beating of Stilone Priàso, the incursions into Tiracorda's house... I imagined then how many other vicissitudes he must have shared with Ciacconio, and, confronting his state of mind with my own, I understood how desperately he would miss his friend.

Such was our mourning that it overshadowed all my memories of the rest of the journey: the return underground, the exhausting march through the tunnels, the conveyance into the hostelry, then into his chamber, of Dulcibeni. In order to hoist him up, we had to cobble together a sort of stretcher, removing a few planks from the cart which we had used on the surface. The injured man, now feverish and semi-conscious, aware only of having suffered grave and perhaps irreversible wounds, was thus transported, tied up like a sausage in its skin, and raised from one trapdoor to another, from one stair to the next, and only at the cost of inhuman efforts by twelve arms: four *corpisantari*, Atto and I.

It was already dawn when the *corpisantari* took their leave of us, disappearing into the little closet. Obviously, I feared that Cristofano might hear the passing of our cortège, however quiet, above all when we hauled Dulcibeni up into the little room and then down the stairs of the hostelry to the first floor. When, however, we passed in front of his chamber, we heard only the peaceful, regular vibration of his snores.

I had also to bid Ugonio farewell. While Atto stood aside, the *corpisantaro* grasped my shoulders firmly with his clawed hands; he knew that it was hardly probable that we should ever meet again. I would no longer descend into his subterranean world, nor would he ever emerge under the dome of heaven, save under cover of night, when poor, honest folk (like myself) lie abed, sleeping away the exhausting labours of the day. Thus we left one another, with heavy hearts; nor indeed, did I ever see him again.

࿐

I needed urgently to retire to bed and to avail myself of the little time that remained to Atto and me in which to recuperate our strength. Yet, too shaken by events, I already knew that I would never be able to find sleep. I therefore decided to take advantage of the situation to note down in my diary the events which had just taken place.

The temporary leave-taking from Atto was a matter of a moment, and of a look which each of us read in the eyes of the other: several hours ago by now, Dulcibeni's pestiferous leeches would already have attacked the soft, tired flesh of Innocent XI.

Everything depended upon the course which the illness took: whether it was slow or, as in so many cases, fulminating.

Perhaps the new day would already bring with it the news of his death; and with it, perhaps, the outcome of the battle for Vienna.

EVENTS BETWEEN
the 20TH & 25TH SEPTEMBER, 1683
✠

The notes which I consigned to my little book that night were the last to be written. The events that followed left me no time (nor did they inspire any desire) to continue writing. Fortunately, those last days of our sequestration at the Donzello have remained very clear in my memory, at least in their essentials.

On the next day, Dulcibeni was found in his bed wretchedly soaked in his own urine, incapable of rising or even so much as moving his legs. All our attempts to make him walk, or even to control his lower limbs, proved useless. He could not feel his feet anymore; one could even pierce his flesh without him experiencing any physical sensation. Cristofano warned of the gravity of the situation; he had, he said, met with many cases of the kind. Among the most similar was the case of a boy working in a marble quarry who fell from badly made scaffolding, striking the ground violently with his back; on the next day, he awoke in his bed in the same condition as Dulcibeni, and, alas, thereafter he was never to recover the use of his legs, remaining handicapped for life.

However, all hope was not lost, Cristofano insisted, digressing into a whole series of reassurances which seemed to me as vague as they were verbose. The patient, who remained feverish, did not seem to be aware of his grave condition.

Of course, the serious accident of which Dulcibeni was the victim provoked a string of questions from Cristofano, who was certainly not so foolish as not to understand that the Marchigiano—and those who had brought him back—had been able to leave and return to the inn.

The bruises, cuts and scratches which Atto and I had sustained in our fall from Tiracorda's carriage also called for an explanation. While Cristofano dispensed his cures—medicating the wounds with his specially prepared balsam and celestial water and anointing the bruises with *oleum philosophorum* and electuary of magisterial marsh mallow—we were constrained to admit that, yes, Dulcibeni had left the hostelry, seeking a way of fleeing the quarantine and, from the secret closet, had ventured forth into the network of tunnels under the inn. We two had, however, been watching him for some time, having guessed his intentions, and had followed him and brought him back. On returning, he had lost his balance and had fallen into the little well that led back to the inn, and this had caused the grave injury which now condemned him to his bed.

Dulcibeni was, moreover, in no position to deny the story: the day after the fall, his fever was exceedingly high, depriving him almost completely of his powers of both reasoning and speech. Only gradually did he regain his wits, and then he would groan interminably, complaining of atrocious, unending pains in the back.

Perhaps that painful spectacle also inclined Cristofano to indulgence; our tale was clearly full of gaps and improbabilities, nor would it have stood up to a serious interrogation, especially if conducted by two of the Bargello's men. Having regard, probably, to the extraordinary recovery of Bedfordi and to the likelihood of an early end to the quarantine, the doctor weighed up the risks and advantages and was kind enough to pretend that he believed our version, without informing the sentinel (who was still on guard before the doorway of the inn) of what had happened. At the end of our reclusion, he said, he would endeavour to ensure that Dulcibeni received all possible cures. These happy resolutions were probably inspired, too, by the festive atmosphere which was just then beginning to spread across the city, and of which I shall now speak.

߷

Already, rumours had begun to circulate concerning the outcome of the battle of Vienna. The first to be heard were on the 20th, but only on the night of Tuesday 21st (and the details of this I obviously obtained later) did Cardinal Pio receive a note from Venice with news of the flight of the Turkish army from Vienna. Two days later, again at night, other letters arrived from the Empire announcing the Christian victory. Gradually, the details had become more precise: the city of Vienna, so long besieged, had at last been relieved.

On the 23rd day of September, the official announcement of the victory reached Rome, borne in the dispatches of Cardinal Bonvisi:

eleven days earlier, on 12th September, the Christian troops had routed the hosts of God's enemies.

The details were to arrive with the gazettes of the succeeding weeks, but in my memory the tales of that glorious triumph all blend into one moment: that of the exciting and exalting moment when we learned of the victory.

When the stars came out on the night of the 11th and 12th September, the serried ranks of the Ottoman host were heard making their prayers, with piercing cries; this was also evident from the lamps and fires, lit in great symmetry, together with the double lights of the superb pavilions of the Infidel encampment.

Our men, too, had prayed long and hard: the Christian forces were far inferior to those of the Infidels. At the first light of dawn on 12th September, the Capuchin friar, Marco d'Aviano, a great arouser and inspirer of the Christian army, celebrated mass with the Christian commanders in a little Camaldolese convent on a height called the Kahlenberg, which dominates Vienna from the right bank of the Danube. Immediately afterwards, our troops formed ranks, ready for victory or death.

On the left wing were Charles of Lorraine with the Margrave Hermann and the young Ludwig Wilhelm; Count von Leslie and Count Caprara; Prince Lubomirski, with his fearsome Polish armoured cavalry; then Mercy and Tafe, the future heroes of Hungary. Together with dozens of other princes, the still unknown Eugene of Savoy prepared for his baptism by fire; like Charles of Lorraine, he had left Paris to flee the Sun King, and was subsequently to cover himself in glory, reconquering eastern Europe for the Christian cause. The Prince Elector of Saxony, too, prepared his troops, assisted by Field Marshal Goltz and the Prince Elector of Bavaria, with the five Wittelsbachs. In the centre of the Christian lines, next to the Bavarians, stood the Franconian and Swabian troops; besides them, the princes and rulers of Thuringia, from the glorious houses of Welf and of Holstein; then came other great names like the Margrave of Bayreuth, Field Marshals and Generals Rodolfo Baratta, Dünewald, Stirum, Baron von Degenfeld, Kàroly Pàlffy and many other heroic defenders of the cause of Christ. Finally, the right wing was held by the valorous Poles, King Jan Sobieski and his two lieutenants.

When they beheld that powerful deployment of friendly forces, the hard-pressed defenders of Vienna immediately gave way to jubilation, launching dozens of salvoes of rockets.

The army was sighted from Kara Mustapha's camp too; but when the Turks decided to react, it was too late: the attackers were already charging down the slopes of the Kahlenberg at breakneck speed. The Grand Vizir and his men then emerged precipitously from their tents and their trenches, in their turn, deploying in battle order. In the centre stood Kara Mustapha and the great mass of the Spahis; by his side, the impious Infidel preacher Wani Effendi with their sacred standard; and before him, the Agha with his regiments of sanguinary janissaries. On the right wing, near the Danube, the cruel Voivodes of Moldavia and Walachia, Vizir Kara Mehmet of Diyarbakir and Ibrahim Pasha, from Buda; on the left wing, the Khan of the Tartars and a great number of pashas.

The gentle green heights outside the walls of Vienna, with their many vineyards, were the theatre of the battle. The first, memorable, clash took place in the narrows of the Nussberg, between the Christian left wing and the janissaries. After prolonged battling back and forth, the imperial troops and the Saxons succeeded at midday in breaking through and chasing the Turks back to Grinzing and Heiligenstadt. Meanwhile, the troops of Charles of Lorraine reached Döbling and approached the Turkish encampment, while Count Caprara's Austrian cavalry and Lubomirsky's armoured horsemen made the Moldavians bite the dust after bitter fighting, chasing their remnants back along the Danube. Meanwhile, from the heights of the Kahlenberg, King Jan Sobieski hurled down the Polish cavalry, after the German and Polish infantry had cleared the way for them, chasing the janissaries from house to house, from vine to vine, from haystack to haystack, and, with cruel obstinacy, driving them from Neustift, from Pötzleinsdorf and from Dornbach.

The Christians' hearts trembled when Kara Mustapha tried to take advantage of the enemy's moves and to drive wedges into the gaps created by their powerful advance. These attempts were, however, short-lived: Charles of Lorraine sent his Austrians in to attack, making them converge on the right. In Dornbach, they cut off the retreat of the Turks, who were trying to withdraw towards Döbling. Meanwhile, the Polish cavalry smashed through all resistance, driving the enemy back as far as Hernals.

At the centre, in the front line, while the glorious Sarmatian military ensign fluttered above, the King of Poland rode with the falcon's wing raised on the tip of his lance, splendid and indomitable, alongside Prince Jakob, barely sixteen and already a hero, flanked by his knights with their armour marvellously ornamented by their multicoloured surcoats, by plumes and by precious stones. To the cry of "Jesumaria!" the lances of the hussars and of King Jan's heavy cavalry swept away the Spahis and charged towards the tent of Kara Mustapha.

The latter, observing the clash between his own men and the Polish cavalry from his command post, instinctively looked up to the green standard in the shade of which he stood. That sacred standard was precisely what the Christians were aiming at. He then yielded to fear, and decided to withdraw, dragging with him in his inglorious retreat, first the Pashas, then the whole body of his troops. The centre of the Turkish host then gave way, too; the rest of the army panicked, and defeat turned to disaster.

The besieged Viennese at last took courage and dared to sally forth through the Scottish Gate, while the Turks fled, abandoning to the enemy their immense encampment, overflowing with incalculable treasures; not, however, without first cutting the throats of hundreds of prisoners and dragging with them as slaves six thousand men, eleven thousand women, fourteen thousand young girls and fifty thousand children.

The military victory was so complete and triumphant that no one thought of stopping the fleeing Infidels. For fear of a return of the Turks, the Christian soldiers, on the contrary, remained on guard through the night.

The first to enter the tent of Kara Mustapha was King Jan Sobieski, who took as booty the horsetail and the steed left behind by the defeated commander, as well as the many oriental treasures and marvels abandoned by the dissolute miscreant satrap.

On the next day, the dead were counted: the Turks had lost ten thousand men on the field of battle, three hundred cannon, fifteen thousand tents and mountains of arms. The Christians mourned two thousand dead, including, alas, General de Souches and Prince Potocki; but there was no time for sadness: all Vienna yearned to welcome the victors, who entered in triumph the city which they had saved from the Infidel hordes. King Jan Sobieski wrote humbly to the Pope, attributing the victory to a miracle: *venimus, vidimus, Deus vicit.**

❧☙

It was, as I said, only later that we were to learn all this in detail. Yet, around the Donzello, jubilation was growing: on 24th September,

---

* We came, we saw, God conquered. (Translator's note.)

a notice was posted in all the churches of Rome ordering that the
Ave Maria should be sounded that very evening by all bells to thank
the Lord for the defeat of the Turks; gay lights were placed in all
windows and with universal and excessive exultation the bells rang
out, while rockets, Catherine wheels and little mortars went off all
around. Thus, from our windows, one could hear not only the people giving vent to their joy but above all the loud explosions of the
fireworks, whose flashes illuminated the roofs of embassies, the Cas-
tel Sant'Angelo, the Piazza Navona and the Campo di Fiore. Having
flung open the shutters and glued ourselves to the bars of the hostelry's windows, we witnessed in the street the burning in effigy of
vizirs and pashas, amidst the uncontainable joy of the populace. We
beheld entire families, groups of boys, clusters of young men and old,
marching back and forth bearing torches, as though crazed, lighting
up the sweet September night and accompanying, with their laughter, the silvery counterpoint of the bells.

Even those who dwelled close to our hostelry and who had hitherto taken care not to approach our windows for fear of contagion, now
shared with us their joy, their gibes, their cries of gladness. It seemed
that they felt the approach of our liberation, almost as though the triumph of Christian arms in Vienna portended the release of our poor
inn from the menace of the plague.

Although still sequestered, we too were overcome by immense
joy; it was I myself who brought the news to each of the guests. We all
celebrated together in the chambers on the ground floor, embracing
each other and drinking toasts with the greatest and most cheerful
exultation. I, above all, was in seventh heaven; Dulcibeni's plan to
strike at the heart of Christian Europe had come too late, even if I
was still anxious about the health of the Pope.

Besides all these genuine manifestations of joy, in the news which
was circulating among the populace and which reached us from the
street, there were two circumstances which I found somewhat unexpected and worthy of reflection.

First, from one of the watchmen (who were continuing to keep an
eye on the inn, in the absence of further orders) we came to know
that the Christian victory had been aided by an inexplicable series of
errors on the part of the Turks.

The armies of Kara Mustapha had, in fact, by means of the novel
technique of mines and trenches, reduced the city walls of Vienna

and, in the opinion of the victors themselves, could unquestionably have carried out a concentrated and victorious assault long before the arrival of King Jan Sobieski's reinforcements. Yet, instead of rapidly unleashing the decisive attack, Kara Mustapha had, quite inexplicably, made no move, wasting several precious days. Nor had the Turks taken the trouble to occupy the heights of the Kahlenberg, which would have given them a decisive tactical advantage. Not only that: they had neglected to confront the Christian reinforcements before they crossed the Danube, thus allowing them to draw irremediably close to the beleaguered city.

Why all this had happened, no one could tell. It was as though the Turks had been waiting for something... Something which made them feel sure of victory. But, what could that be?

Secondly, another strange circumstance: the outbreak of the plague, which had been ravaging the city for months, suddenly died out, for no apparent reason.

To the victors, this series of miracles was seen as a sign from divine providence, the same benign providence which had to the last sustained the desperate forces of the besieged and Jan Sobieski's liberating troops.

The culmination of the festivities in Rome took place on the 25th day; of that, I shall recount more later, since my concern here is to tell of other important facts which came to my acquaintance during those days of sequestration.

The strange manner in which the plague in Vienna had suddenly been extinguished gave me no little cause for reflection. After terrorising the besieged even more than the Ottoman foe could, the pestilence had rapidly and mysteriously petered out. This factor had been decisive: had the infection persisted and spread among the population of Vienna, the Turks would certainly have prevailed without the slightest difficulty.

It was impossible not to consider that news in the light of what Atto and I had so laboriously uncovered or deduced, all of which I strove to sum up in my mind. Louis XIV hoped for a Turkish victory in Vienna, the better to carve up Europe with the Infidels. In order to achieve his dreams of dominion, the Sun King counted upon using the infectious principle of the *secretum pestis*, in other words the *secretum morbi*, which he had at last succeeded in extracting from Fouquet.

At the same time, however, the consort of the Most Christian King, Maria Teresa, was striving to achieve a diametrically opposed design. Proudly attached to the destiny of the House of Habsburg which occupied the imperial throne and of which she herself was a scion, the Queen of France strove secretly to impede her husband's plans. Indeed, according to the theory advanced by Atto, Fouquet had succeeded in delivering to Maria Teresa, through Lauzun and Mademoiselle (both of whom detested the Sovereign no less than Maria Teresa herself), the only antidote capable of countering the secret weapon of the plague: the *secretum vitae*, that is, the *rondeau* with which Devizé had beguiled us during those days at the Donzello, and which seemed even to have cured Bedfordi.

Nor was it by chance that the antidote should have been in the hands of Devizé; the *rondeau*, although probably composed by Kircher in its original, crude form, had been perfected and consigned to paper by the guitarist Francesco Corbetta, a past master of the art of enciphering secret messages in musical notes.

Even thus simplified, the picture was as hard on the intellect as on the memory. Yet, if the method which Atto Melani had taught me held water (to act on suppositions, where one has not the benefit of knowledge), then everything fell into place. One must use one's powers of reasoning persistently in order to uncover what was needed to explain patent absurdities.

I therefore asked myself: if Louis XIV had wished to deliver the *coup de grâce* to the dreaded Habsburgs, who flanked him on either side in Austria and in Spain, and above all to the hated Emperor Leopold, where would he have unleashed the plague? Why, in Vienna; the answer astounded me with its simplicity.

Was that not the decisive battle for the fate of Christianity? And was I not aware, ever since I had overheard the conversation between Brenozzi and Stilone Priàso, that the Most Christian King was secretly playing on the side of the Turks in order to catch the Empire in the teeth of an infernal trap set between East and West?

Nor was that all. Was it not true that there had for months been an outbreak of the plague in Vienna, which had spread apprehension amongst all the heroic, beleaguered warriors? And was it not also true that the infection had died out, or had been mysteriously tamed by some arcane invisible agent, thus saving the city and all Western Europe?

Although deeply immersed in such meditations, I myself found it difficult to accept the logical conclusions to which they gave rise: the plague in Vienna had been unleashed by agents of Louis XIV, or by anonymous cut-throats in their employ, thus putting into effect the occult science of the *secretum morbi*. That was why the Turks had not moved for days and days, despite the fact that Vienna was in their grasp: they were awaiting the dreaded effects of the infection sent by their secret ally, the French sovereign.

The infamous sabotage had, however, encountered no less powerful adverse forces: the emissaries of Maria Teresa had arrived in Vienna in time to dispel the threat, activating the *secretum vitae* and thus overcoming the infection. How this was done, I would never know. What is, however, certain is that the vain hesitations of the Turkish army were to cost Kara Mustapha his head.

This summary, so overcrowded with events, risked seeming too fanciful, indeed almost fantastical. Did not all the interweaving of the affairs of Kircher and Fouquet, Maria Teresa and Louis XIV, Lauzun and Mademoiselle, Corbetta and Devizé also smack of folly? Yet, I had spent entire nights in Atto Melani's company reconstructing, piece by piece, in a sort of divine madness, all that senseless intrigue, which had become more real for me than the life which continued outside the walls of the Donzello.

My imagination was peopled by the shadowy agents of the Sun King, intent upon spreading the pestilence throughout poor Vienna when the city was already *in extremis*; on the other side, the defenders, the shadow-players of Maria Teresa. All of them were investigating secret formulae concealed in the pentagrams of Kircher and Corbetta, agitating retorts and alembics and other obscure instruments (like those seen on Dulcibeni's island) and reciting incomprehensible hermetic phrases in some abandoned cloister. Thereafter, some would have poisoned—and others cleansed—waters, orchards, streets. In the invisible struggle between the *secretum morbi* and the *secretum vitae* the vital principle had in the end triumphed: the same one which had enthralled my heart and my mind as I listened to the *rondeau* played on Devizé's guitar.

From the latter, of course, I would not be able to draw so much as a syllable. Yet his role was almost completely clear, and so were the images which it conjured up in my mind: Devizé receives from the Queen the original copy of the "Barricades Mystérieuses"; he is then

ordered to go to Italy—to Naples—there to seek out an aged traveller with a double identity... In Naples, he finds Fouquet, already
in Dulcibeni's company. Perhaps he shows the old Superintendent
the *rondeau* which, years before, he had placed in the trusted hands
of Lauzun for delivery to the Queen. But Fouquet is blind; he will
have taken those sheets of paper in his bony hands, caressed and
recognised them. Devizé will then have played the *rondeau*, and the
old man's last uncertainties will have vanished amidst tears of emotion: the Queen has succeeded; the *secretum vitae* is in good hands,
Europe will not succumb to the madness of a single sovereign. And
she, before taking her leave of this earth, has, by the hand of Devizé,
obtained this last reassurance.

Devizé and Dulcibeni, by common accord, decide to bring their
protégé to Rome where, in the shadow of the Pope, the threatening
emissaries of the Sun King are hampered in their movements. Of
course, Dulcibeni has other designs... And, still in Rome, while playing his "Barricades Mystérieuses" for us, Devizé knows that Maria
Teresa has sent to Vienna the enigmatic quintessence of those notes,
to bar the way to the plague which threatens to result in a Turkish
triumph.

Now, of all this, Devizé would never breathe a word. His devotion
to Maria Teresa, if genuine, would surely not have been exhausted
with the Sovereign's death. Moreover, the consequences of being
identified as a plotter against the Sun King would certainly be lethal.
Here again, I applied the rule which Atto Melani had taught me,
thus relieving Devizé of so perilous a task. I, a humble apprentice
to whom no one accorded the least importance, would speak in his
place, only a few, well-turned phrases. Not by his speech would I
judge him, but by his silence.

A favourable opportunity was soon to arise. He had called me late
in the afternoon, requesting a further light meal. I brought him a
modest basket with a little salami and a few slices of bread, which he
devoured voraciously. No sooner had he set to than I took my leave
and made for the door.

"By the way," said I carelessly, "I hear, Sir, that Vienna is indebted
to Queen Maria Teresa for having been spared by the plague."

Devizé grew pale.

"Mmm," he mumbled in alarm, with his mouth full, rising to look
for a sip of water.

"Oh, has it gone down the wrong way? Do have something to drink," said I, handing him a little jug which I had brought with me but had not placed near to him.

As he drank, he screwed up his eyes in puzzlement.

"Do you want to know who told me that? Well, you will be aware that, since his unfortunate accident, Signor Pompeo Dulcibeni has suffered greatly from fevers, and during one such crisis he spoke at great length when I happened to be present."

This was a great lie, but Devizé swallowed it as eagerly as the water which he had just gulped down.

"And what... what else did he say?" he stammered, wiping his mouth and chin with his sleeve and endeavouring to remain calm.

"Oh, so many things which I have not perhaps even understood. The fever, you know... If I am not mistaken, he did mention a certain Fooky, or something of the sort and, I think, a certain Lozen," said I, deliberately distorting the names. "He spoke of a fortress, of the plague, of a secret of the pestilence or something like that, then, of an antidote, of Queen Maria Teresa, of the Turks, and even of a plot. In other words, he was delirious, you know how that happens. At the time, Doctor Cristofano was worried, but now poor Signor Dulcibeni is no longer in danger and has only to worry about his back and his legs, which..."

"Cristofano? Did he hear too?"

"Yes, but you know how it is when a physician is at work: he hears yet he does not hear. I also spoke of this to Abbot Melani, and he..."

"You did what?" roared Devizé.

"I told him that Dulcibeni was sick and feverish and that he was raving."

"And did you tell him... everything?" he asked, overcome by terror.

"How am I to remember, Signor Devizé?" I replied, politely piqued. "I only know that Signor Pompeo Dulcibeni was so far gone as no longer to be much with us, and Abbot Melani shared my concern on that account. And now, Sir, if you will excuse me," said I, slipping through the door and taking my leave.

Besides checking upon Devizé's knowledge, I had allowed myself to take a little revenge on him. The panic which had seized the guitarist could not have been more eloquent; not only did he know what I and Atto knew but—as expected—he had been one of those most deeply involved. That was why I chuckled at the dreadful suspicion which I had sown in his mind: that Dulcibeni's delirious outburst (which had, of course, never happened) might, through me, have reached the ears, not only of Cristofano but of Abbot Melani. And, that if Atto so desired, he could denounce Devizé as a traitor to the King of France.

My spirit was still oppressed by all the scornful treatment which the guitarist had always heaped upon me. Thanks to a few well-chosen lies, tonight I would at last enjoy the rich sleep of a gentleman, while his lot would be the troubled sleep of the outcast.

I must confess there was still one person with whom I would and should have liked to share that extreme intellectual solace, but those times had passed. I could no longer ignore the fact that, since his confrontation with Dulcibeni on the wall of the Colosseum, all was changed between Atto Melani and myself.

Certainly, he had unmasked Dulcibeni's criminal and blasphemous plot. Yet, at the moment of truth, I had seen him vacillate—and not on his legs, like his adversary. He had climbed the Colosseum as an accuser, he came down accused.

I had been stunned by his indecision in responding to Dulcibeni's allusions to the death of Fouquet. I had known him to hesitate before, but always only for fear of obscure, impending dangers. When he faced Dulcibeni, however, it was as though his stammerings arose, not from fear of the unknown, but from what he knew perfectly well and must keep hidden. Thus, Dulcibeni's accusations (the poison poured into the foot-bath, the order to kill received from the King of France), although unsupported by any evidence, sounded more final than any sentence.

Then, there was that strange, suspicious coincidence: as Dulcibeni had recalled, Fouquet's last words were "*Ahi, dunque è pur vero*"— "Alas, so it is really true"—a verse from an aria by Maestro Luigi Rossi which I had one day heard Atto sing in the most heartbroken tones. "Alas, so it is really true... that you have changed your mind." Thus the verse ended, like an unambiguous act of accusation.

Again, I had heard those same words murmured when, almost drowning in the Cloaca Maxima, we in our turn came close to leaving this world. Why, even then, in the face of death, had that verse come to his lips?

With the eyes of fantasy, I imagined that I had traitorously taken the life of a dear friend, and tried to immerse myself in the guilt that would surely consume me after such an act. If I had heard my friend's last words, would they not perhaps resound forever in my ears, until they found an open echo in my mouth?

And when Dulcibeni had accused him, reproaching him with that heartbreaking, lamenting verse, I had heard Melani's voice break under the weight of guilt, whatever the cause of that guilt might be.

No longer was he the Atto Melani I had known; neither the same fascinating mentor, nor the same trusted leader. He was again Atto Melani, the castrato, whom I had come to know when I overheard the talk of Devizé, Cristofano and Stilone Priàso: Abbot of Beaubec by the prerogative of the King of France, intriguer, liar, traitor, spy of exceptional skill; and perhaps an assassin, too.

I remembered then that the abbot had never given me a satisfactory explanation as to why, in his sleep, he had murmured the words "*barricades mystérieuses*": and I at last understood that he must have heard them repeated, without understanding their meaning, when he was shaking the dying Fouquet by the shoulders and—as Cristofano had reported—crying out questions which were destined to remain forever unanswered.

In the end, I felt great pity for the abbot, deceived, as Dulcibeni had said, by his own King. By now I knew that Atto had omitted something from his account of his search through Colbert's study: he had shown to Louis XIV the letters which revealed Fouquet's presence in Rome.

I was utterly at a loss to comprehend: how, how could he have had the nerve thus to betray his former benefactor? Perhaps Atto had wished once more to demonstrate his unfailing devotion to his Most Christian Majesty. It would be an important gesture: offering the King on a silver platter the man whose friendship had, some twenty years previously, condemned him to exile far from France. Yet, this had been a fatal error, and the King had repaid the faithful castrato with yet another betrayal. He had dispatched him to Rome precisely to assassinate Fouquet, without revealing to him the true reasons for that terrible command, or the abyss of death and hatred within his own heart. Who knows what absurd tale the King concocted, or what shameful lies he employed to besmirch once more the trampled honour of the old Superintendent.

During those last days which I spent in the Donzello, I was beset by the shameful image of Abbot Melani selling the life of his poor old friend to the Sovereign, and then knowing not how to avoid carrying out that cruel despot's atrocious commands.

How had he had the gall to act out for me the part of the broken-hearted friend? He must have needed to draw upon all his art as a theatrical castrato, so spoke my raging thoughts. Or perhaps those tears were real; but they were tears only of remorse.

I do not know whether Atto wept when, constrained by his Sovereign's commands, he was preparing his hasty departure for Rome in order to put an end to Fouquet's life, or whether he executed his orders like an obedient servant.

He must have been unnerved by the last weary words of the blind old Superintendent when he was dying by his hand; by those laboured phrases which babbled of mysterious barricades and obscure secrets, but perhaps even more by those opaque and honest eyes. He must then have understood that he was the victim of his King's lies.

Once the irremediable had taken place, he could but try to understand. That was why he had undertaken all those investigations, with my unwitting collaboration.

Soon, my thinking could take me no further. Nor could I escape from the throes of my disgust for Abbot Melani. I ceased to speak to him. With my reflections, the old trust between us had dissolved, and along with it, the familiarity which had so swiftly grown between us during those few days of life together at the Donzello.

Yet, no one more than he had been a master and an inspiration to me. I therefore strove to maintain, at least outwardly, the obliging solicitude to which I had accustomed him. From my eyes and voice, however, the light and warmth which only friendship can confer, had departed.

I observed the same transformation in him; now we were strangers to one another, and he knew it. Now that Dulcibeni was bedridden and all his plans had been foiled, Abbot Melani had no longer any foe to overcome, any ambush to set, any enigma to solve; and now that the imperatives of action had all fallen away, he no longer sought to justify himself in my eyes or to offer me explanations of his behaviour, as he had hitherto done in response to my repeated remonstrances. In the last few days, he had withdrawn into an embarrassed silence, one which only guilt could have erected around him.

Only once, one morning, while I was in the kitchen, preparing luncheon, did he take my arm and squeeze my hands in his. "Come

to Paris with me. My house is spacious, I shall arrange for you to receive the best instruction. You shall be my son," said he in grave and
heartfelt tones.

I felt something in my hand; I opened it, and there were my three
marguerites, the little Venetian pearls given to me by Brenozzi. I
should have realised: he had stolen them from under my nose, that
first time we visited the little closet, in order to induce me to take
part in his investigations.

And now he was returning them to me, thus putting an end to his
last deception. Was this perhaps an attempt at reconciliation?

I thought one moment, then decided: "You wish me to become
your son?!" I exclaimed, with a cruel laugh for the castrato who could
never have any.

And, opening my fist, I let the pearls fall to the floor.

That vain little act of revenge placed a tombstone on our relations; with those three little pearls, there rolled away our pacts, our
trust, our affection and all that had brought us so close in the past
few days. It was all over.

❧❦

All was not, however, resolved. Something was still missing from the
picture which we had built up: what could be the real reason behind
the atrocious hatred which Dulcibeni bore the Odescalchi and, in
particular, Pope Innocent XI? A motive did indeed exist: the abduction and disappearance of Dulcibeni's daughter. Yet, as Atto had correctly noted, this did not seem to be the only motive.

It was when I was racking my brains over this question, a couple of
days after the night of the Colosseum, that I received, blinding and
unexpected, one of those rare insights which, like lightning bolts,
illuminate one's life. (At the time of writing, I speak from experience.)

Once again, I turned over in my memory what I had learned from
the reconstruction which Abbot Melani had presented to Dulcibeni.
The latter's twelve-year-old daughter, a slave of the Odescalchi, had
been abducted and carried off to Holland by Huygens and Francesco
Feroni, a slave merchant.

Where was Dulcibeni's daughter now? A slave in Holland, since
Feroni's right-hand man had been besotted with her; or sold in some
other land. I had, however, heard that some of the most beautiful

slave girls did, sooner or later, succeed in gaining their freedom: by means of prostitution, obviously, which I knew to be a flourishing trade in those lands reclaimed from the sea.

What would she have looked like? If she were still alive, she would now be about nineteen years old. From her mother, whose skin was dark, she would certainly have inherited a similar complexion. It was difficult to imagine her face, without having known her mother's. She would surely have been ill-treated, imprisoned, beaten. Her body, I thought, must bear the signs of this.

"How did you know?" was Cloridia's only question.

"From your wrists—the scars on your wrists. And also, your talk of Holland, the Italian merchants whom you so abominate, the name of Feroni, the coffee which reminds you of your mother, your way of always asking after Dulcibeni, your age and the colour of your skin, your search with the divining rod, which brought you here. And then there was the Arcana of Justice, do you remember?: the reparation of past wrongs, of which you spoke to me. Lastly, the sneezes of Abbot Melani, who is sensitive to Dutch materials. And you and your father are the only persons to wear those in this hostelry."

Naturally, Cloridia was not satisfied with these explanations, and, in order to justify my intuition, I had to recount to her a great part of my adventures during the preceding days. Initially, she did not, of course, believe many of my revelations, despite the fact that I had omitted many events which I myself would have found fantastic or improbable.

Obviously, it was rather difficult to prove to her that her father had plotted an attempt on the life of the Pope, and of this she became convinced only a long time afterwards.

In the end, however, after lengthy and patient explanations, she believed in my good faith and in most of the facts with which I had acquainted her. The narration, interspersed with her many questions, took almost a whole night, during the course of which we naturally paused at times to rest and, during those pauses, it was I who requested and she who instructed.

"And did he never suspect it?" I asked her at the end.

"Never, I am sure of that."

"Will you tell him?"

"At first, I wanted to do so," she replied after a brief silence. "I had sought him so long... But now I have changed my mind. In the first place, he would not believe me; and then, the news would not even make him happy. And then, you know, there is my mother: I cannot forget that."

"Then we two shall be the only ones to know," I observed.

"It will be better that way."

"That no one else should know?"

"No, better that you too should know," said she, caressing my head.

అఁఀ

At this juncture, one last item of news was impatiently awaited, and not only by myself. The universal jubilation for the victory at Vienna filled the city with joyous festivities. Dulcibeni's efforts to destroy the True Religion in Europe had come too late. But, what of the Pope? Had Tiracorda's leeches already taken effect? Perhaps the author of the victory over the Turks was at that very moment tossing and turning feverishly under his blankets, stricken by the plague. We certainly would not have been able to know this then; certainly not from the prison of our chambers. Soon, however, we were to be overtaken by events which at long last freed us from our imprisonment.

I have already had cause to mention that, in the days before the beginning of the quarantine, strong reverberations had been heard, coming from the ground under the inn, and immediately afterwards Master Pellegrino had discovered a fissure in the wall of the staircase on the first floor. The phenomenon had, of course, given rise to no little concern; but that had, however, been overshadowed by the death of Fouquet, the imposition of the quarantine and many successive events. However, Stilone Priàso's astrological almanack had, as I had been able to read with my own eyes, predicted for those days "earthquakes and subterranean fires". If this had been a mere coincidence, it seemed designed to perturb even the calmest of spirits.

The memory of those subterranean rumblings still instilled a certain disquiet in my soul, made all the greater by the crack in the staircase which—I could not decide whether this was the work of my imagination—seemed every day to grow longer and deeper.

It was perhaps because of that state of anxiety that, on the night of the 24th and 25th September, I awoke in the small hours. I opened my eyes, finding my dark, damp chamber even narrower and more suffocating than usual. What had disturbed me? I had no need to relieve my bladder, nor had I been awoken by some loud noise. No: it was a sinister, diffuse creaking, coming from I knew not where. It was like the groan of pebbles grinding against each other, as though they were being slowly crushed by a gigantic millstone.

Thought and action were one: I flung open my door and rushed into the corridor, then down to the lower floors, yelling at the top of my voice. The inn was about to collapse.

Cristofano, with praiseworthy presence of mind, at once warned the night watchman, so that he should let us escape to the safety of the street. The evacuation of the Donzello, observed with a mixture of curiosity and unease by some neighbours who had at once rushed to their windows, was neither easy nor devoid of perils. The creaking came from the stairs, where the fissure had, in the space of a few hours, grown into a chasm. As usual, it required the courage of a few (Atto Melani, Cristofano and myself) to bear the helpless Dulcibeni to safety. The convalescent Bedfordi managed on his own. Thus, too, my master, although confused, found the usual presence of mind to utter imprecations against his misfortune. Once we were all outside, it seemed almost as though the peril had ceased. It would not, however, have been wise to return, and that was emphasised by the noise of a great fall of rubble within. Cristofano consulted closely with the watchman.

This led to the decision that we should turn to the nearby monastery of Celestine fathers who would surely take pity on our sad condition and be willing to offer us succour and shelter.

And so they were; awoken in the middle of the night, the fathers welcomed us without great enthusiasm (perhaps also because of the suspicion of pestilence during the preceding days) but with pious generosity, assigning us to little cells, in which each of us could find the most dignified and comfortable refuge.

The great news of the following day, Saturday 25th September, arrived as soon as we awoke. The city was still immersed in the festive climate of the Viennese victory celebrations, and hardly had I poked my nose out from my little cell than I saw how this carelessly relaxed attitude had affected even the Celestine fathers. None of them was keeping any special watch over us, and the only supervisory visit that I received was that of Cristofano, who had slept in the same cell as Dulcibeni, in order to be able to assist him with any nocturnal difficulties. He confirmed with a trace of surprise that we seemed not to be subject to restrictions of any kind and that whoever wished to do so could walk out from any of the monastery's many doors. In the coming days, he thought that some would inevitably make their way out. He did not, however, know that the first such escapade would take place within only a few hours.

It was an indiscreet conversation between two Celestine fathers outside my door that brought to my attention the event which was to take place that very evening: in the Basilica of Saint John Lateran, the victory at Vienna was to be celebrated with a great *Te Deum*; and this solemn rite of thanksgiving was to be conducted by His Beatitude Pope Innocent XI in person.

I spent almost the entire day in my cell, apart from a couple of visits to Dulcibeni and Cristofano, and one to Pellegrino. My poor master was now beset by sufferings of both body and mind: it had been explained to him that the inn was in danger and that in the early hours of the morning, the stairs had completely collapsed, together with the landings and walls giving onto the inner courtyard. I myself gave a start upon hearing that news: it meant that in all probability the secret closet through which one could gain access to the galleries beneath had been lost. I would have liked to share that news with Abbot Melani, but it was too late.

When the afternoon light was already eroded by the soft embrace of twilight, it was not difficult for me to slip out from my cell and from the monastery, through an unguarded side door. For a modest sum (which I took from the few savings I had salvaged during our flight from the Donzello), I gained the complicity of a young servant of those friars, so as to be certain of finding the same door open on my return.

I was not fleeing; I had only one aim, and once I had satisfied that I would again retire to the monastery of the Celestines. It took no little time to reach the basilica of Saint John, where a huge crowd of people was gathering. From the monastery, I went first to the Pantheon, then to the Piazza San Marco and thence to the Colosseum. Within a few minutes, after proceeding down the street that leads straight from the amphitheatre to the basilica, I found myself at last in the Piazza of Saint John Lateran, surrounded by an anxious, febrile multitude which was growing by the minute. I therefore approached the entrance of the basilica, where I saw that I had arrived only just in time: flanked by two wings of the jubilant crowd, His Holiness emerged at just that moment.

As I tiptoed to see him better, I received a blow on the ear from the elbow of an old man who was trying to barge past me.

"Hey, take care, boy," he said rudely to me, as though it was he who had been struck.

Despite the many necks and heads towering above me, by slipping with difficulty through the crush, I managed at last to catch sight of His Beatitude, just before he mounted his carriage, retreating from the plaudits and attention of the multitude. I saw him, just when he saluted the faithful and, with a smiling, amiable gesture, blessed us once, twice, three times. Taking advantage of my youthful agility, I had managed to come within a few feet of the Holy Father; thus I could scrutinise his countenance from nearby and discern the colour in his cheeks, the light in his eyes and even his complexion.

I am not a physician, nor am I a seer. It was perhaps only my hunger to know the truth that stimulated my faculties of observation to an almost supernatural degree, beyond the confines of common experience, thus enabling me to see that there was not a trace of sickness in him. He had the face of one who has suffered greatly, that is true; but his suffering was of the soul, long wracked by anxiety for the fate of Vienna. Just next to me, I heard two aged prelates whisper that, upon receiving the joyous news of the victory, Innocent XI had been seen weeping like a child, kneeling on the ground and wetting the tiles of his chamber with his compassionate tears.

But sick, no, that he was not; this was clear from his luminous expression, his rosy complexion, and lastly from the brief but vigorous movement with which he mounted the step to his carriage before disappearing into it. Not far off, I suddenly descried the placid face of Tiracorda. He was surrounded by a group of young men (perhaps his students, I thought). Before the strong hand of a pontifical guard pushed me back, I had time to overhear Tiracorda: "But no, you are too kind. It is through no merit of mine... It was the hand of the Lord: after the happy victory, I no longer needed to do anything."

Now I was certain. Once he had learned of the victory at Vienna, the Pontiff had felt better and leeching had become pointless. The Pope was safe and sound. Dulcibeni had failed.

I remarked that I was not alone in knowing this. A little way off in the crowd, I recognised, without myself being seen, the agitated and suspicious visage of Abbot Melani.

❧❧

I returned to the monastery on my own, lost in the crush of people swarming homeward in disorder, without catching sight of Abbot Melani or making any attempt to retrace him. All around me, exuberant comments abounded: on the ceremony, the health of the Pope, and his glorious work for Christendom. Quite by chance, I found myself in the midst of a group of Capuchin friars, who wended their way cheerfully, waving torches and thus perpetuating the rejoicings of the *Te Deum*. From their conversation I gleaned a number of curious details (the truth of which I was to ascertain during the months that followed) of what had taken place during the siege of Vienna. The fathers spoke of reports received from Marco d'Aviano, the Capuchin friar who had so valiantly dedicated himself to the League against the Turks. At the end of the siege—I heard them tell this with their tongues loosened by emotion—the Polish king had disobeyed the orders of Emperor Leopold and had made his solemn entry into Vienna, acclaimed as victor by all the Viennese. The Emperor, as he himself had confessed to Marco d'Aviano, envied him not for his triumph, but for the love his subjects bore him; all Vienna had seen Leopold abandon the capital to its fate, escaping like a thief, and now they were enthusiastically cheering a foreign king who had just risked his life, that of his people, and even that of his firstborn son, to save it from the Turks. Obviously, the Habsburg monarch would now exact payment from Sobieski for what he had done. When they did at last meet, the Emperor was peevish and icy. "I am petrified," Sobieski confessed to his people.

"But then the Lord has so arranged matters that all will be for the best," concluded one of the Capuchins, conciliatingly.

"Yes, indeed, if God so wills it," echoed one of his brothers. "In the end, all is for the best."

Those wise words still echoed in my head when, on the next day, I was informed by Cristofano that within a few days we would all be freed from the restrictions of the quarantine. Taking advantage of the festive spirit, the doctor had succeeded in persuading the authorities that there was no longer the slightest danger of any infection. The only person still in need of assistance was Pompeo Dulcibeni, whose condition was explained to the guards by an accidental fall down the stairs of the Donzello. As for Dulcibeni himself, he was, alas, a candidate for perpetual immobility. Cristofano would be able to help him for a few more days; then he too would be returning to the Grand Duchy of Tuscany.

Who would take care, I thought to myself with a bitter smile, of the man who had attempted to assassinate the Pope?

Events of the Year 1688

✠

Five years had passed since the terrible adventure at the Donzello. The inn had not re-opened. Pellegrino had been taken away by his wife, to stay with relatives, I presume.

Cloridia, Pompeo Dulcibeni and I dwelled in a modest farmhouse outside the city walls, beyond the San Pancrazio gate, where I am even now consigning these words to paper. The days and the seasons were, then as now, measured only by the harvesting of our little field and the care of the few farmyard animals purchased with Dulcibeni's savings. I was already familiar with every hardship of the fields; I had learned to grub in the soil with my bare hands, to question the wind and the sky, to barter my own fruit for that of others' toil, to bargain and to detect cheating. I had learned to leaf through the pages of books in the evening with a peasant's swollen, dirty hands.

Cloridia and I lived as man and wife. No one could ever have blamed us for that: in our remote area, we never so much as saw a priest, even for the Easter blessing.

Since he had at length become resigned to the loss of his legs, Pompeo had grown even more taciturn and irritable. He no longer resorted to inhaling ground *mamacoca* leaves, the drug from Peru which he had obtained in Holland. Thanks to this, he had also ceased to be seized by those states of gloomy exaltation which had enabled him to sustain his wild excursions into the galleries under the Donzello.

He still could not understand why we had taken him in and provided him with shelter and assistance. At first, he suspected that we were motivated by the not inconsiderable savings with which he could endow us. He never learned about Cloridia. Nor did she ever wish to reveal to him that she was his daughter. In her heart, she had never pardoned him for permitting the sale of her mother.

When enough time had passed to protect her from the anguish of memories, Cloridia at last recounted to me the vicissitudes which she had suffered after being torn from her father. Huygens had persuaded the child that he had bought her from Dulcibeni. He had kept her hidden and then, when he tired of her, he had sold her to other wealthy Italian merchants before returning to Feroni in Tuscany.

For long years, she had travelled in the retinue of these merchants, and then of others, and yet others, more than once being bought and resold. From that to the ancient and shameful art, the step had been short; but with the money she had secretly and with great efforts set aside, she had bought back her freedom. Opulent and liberal, Amsterdam was the ideal city for that vile trafficking in bodies. At last, however, she was overcome by the urge to retrace her father and to ask him to explain why he had abandoned her, and this, aided by the science of numbers and the ardent rod, had brought her to the door of the Donzello.

Despite all that she had suffered and the sad memories which often robbed her of sleep, Cloridia assisted Dulcibeni with constancy and devotion. He, for his part, ceased to treat her with disdain. He never asked her any questions about her past, thus sparing her the embarrassment of having to lie.

Pompeo soon asked me to go and recover the trunks full of books which he had left in Naples. He presented them to me, announcing that, with time, I would come more and more to appreciate their value. Thanks to those books, and the discussions which arose from reading them, little by little, Dulcibeni's tongue loosened. In time, he switched from observations to memories, and from these to teachings. He taught, however, on the basis not only of doctrine but of experience; one who has traded for years throughout Europe, and in the service of a powerful house like that of the Odescalchi, will have much to tell. There remained between us, however, hanging in the air, that unrevealed mystery: why had Dulcibeni made an attempt on the life of the Pope?

One day, he confided, he would unveil the secret. I knew, however, that given his proud, stubborn nature, to ask him for it would, have been utterly useless. I must wait.

❧

In the autumn of 1688, the gazettes bore news of the gravest and most painful occurrences. The heretical prince William of Orange had, with his fleet, crossed the English Channel and disembarked at a place called Torbay. His army advanced and met with almost no resistance. Within a matter of days, he had usurped the English throne, deposing the Catholic King James II of the House of Stuart, guilty of having only two months previously sired from his second wife the long-desired male heir to the throne, who would have robbed the Prince of Orange of all hope of ever becoming King of England. With William's incursion, England fell into the hands of the Protestant heretics and was thus forever lost to Rome.

When I informed Dulcibeni of the dramatic news, Pompeo made no comment of any kind. He was seated in the garden, stroking a kitten which lay in his lap. He seemed tranquil. Yet, suddenly I saw him bite his lip and chase the little creature away, with trembling fist, banging hard on the nearby table.

"What has come over you, Pompeo?" I asked, jumping to my feet and fearing that he might be unwell.

"He has done it, the wretch! He has done it at last!" he panted, staring at the horizon beyond my head in cold fury.

⇛⇚

It had all started almost thirty years ago. It was then, Dulcibeni recounted, that the Odescalchi family had besmirched itself with the most infamous of crimes: aiding heretics.

It was about 1660. At that time, William of Orange was still a child. The House of Orange was, as ever, short of money. To give an idea of what that meant, William's mother and grandmother had pawned all the family jewels.

For Holland, there were portents of tremendous wars in the European theatre; and indeed, these were not long in breaking out: first, against England, then France. Fighting these wars cost money: huge sums of money.

After a series of highly secret overtures, of which not even Dulcibeni knew the details, the House of Orange turned to the Odescalchi. They were the most solvent moneylenders in Italy, nor did they draw back from the transaction.

Thus, the wars of heretical Holland were financed by the Catholic family of Cardinal Odescalchi, the future Pope Innocent XI.

The whole loan operation was, of course, conducted shrewdly and with all possible discretion. Cardinal Benedetto Odescalchi lived in Rome; his brother, who was the principal of the family business, resided in Como. The money for the Orange family was, however, sent to Venice through two trusted men of straw, so that it would in no way be possible to retrace it to the family of Innocent XI. The loans were, moreover, not addressed directly to members of the House of Orange, but to secret intermediaries: Admiral Jean Neufville, the financier Jan Deutz, the merchants Bartolotti, and to Jan Baptista Hochepied, Amsterdam councillor.

From the latter, this money was then redirected to the House of Orange, in order to finance the wars against Louis XIV.

"And what about you?" I interrupted.

"I went back and forth to Holland on behalf of the Odescalchi; I made sure that the letters of exchange arrived at their destination and were duly encashed, and that the relevant receipt was obtained. Moreover, I made sure that all took place far from prying eyes."

"In other words, the money of Pope Innocent XI was used to finance the heretics' landing in England!" I concluded, utterly shocked.

"More or less. The Odescalchi, however, only lent money to the Dutch until some fifteen years ago, while William has only now landed in England."

"So, what happened then?"

Something bizarre had then taken place, explained Dulcibeni. In 1673, Carlo Odescalchi, the brother of the future Pope, had died. Thus, Cardinal Odescalchi was no longer able to follow the family business from Rome and decided to suspend the loan to the Dutch. The game had become too dangerous and the pious Cardinal could no longer risk discovery. His image must remain immaculate. He was far-sighted: within three years, the conclave took place which was to make him Pope.

"But he had lent money to the heretics!" I exclaimed, scandalised.

"Listen to the rest of it."

With time, the debt of the House of Orange to the Odescalchi had increased beyond all measure, to over five hundred and fifty thousand scudi. Now that Benedetto had been elected Pope, how was all that money to be recouped? In the event of insolvency, the initial agreement stipulated that the Odescalchi would be able to lay claim to William's private property. Now, however, Benedetto Odescalchi, having become Pontiff, was in the public eye: he could not impound the property of a heretic prince, for that would also reveal the loans to that prince. And that would lead to a dreadful scandal. It is true that in the meantime Benedetto had made an apparent donation of all his goods to his nephew Livio, but in reality it was well known that it was still he who continued obstinately to control everything.

Besides, there was another problem. William was still short of money, since his Dutch creditors (in other words, the wealthy families of Amsterdam) had tightened their purse-strings. Thus, Innocent XI was in danger of never seeing his money again.

That was why, said Dulcibeni, Innocent XI had always been so hostile to Louis XIV: the Most Christian King of France was the only one who could bar the way to William's mounting the throne of England. Only Louis XIV came between Innocent XI and his money.

The Odescalchi had in the meantime succeeded in keeping all this secret. In 1676, however, a little before the conclave, the Huygens incident took place: the right-hand man of the slave merchant Francesco Feroni (who also had dealings with the Odescalchi) became infatuated with Pompeo Dulcibeni's daughter by a Turkish slave and—with the support of Feroni—wanted to take possession of her. Dulcibeni could not oppose this legally, since he had not married the child's mother. So he let the Odescalchi understand that, if Huygens and Feroni did not renounce their claims, indiscretions might circulate which would be somewhat dangerous for Cardinal Benedetto: a matter of loans with interest, granted to Dutch heretics... And Cardinal Odescalchi could then bid the conclave adieu...

The rest, I already knew: the maiden was abducted and Dulcibeni defenestrated, escaping death only by a miracle. Pompeo had to go into hiding, while Benedetto Odescalchi was elected Pope.

"Until now, the Pontiff will not have been able to lay his hands upon the money loaned to William of Orange. I am quite sure of that; I know how these matters are managed. Nevertheless, that will all now be settled," Dulcibeni concluded.

"Why is that?"

"It is quite clear: now William will become King of England and he will somehow manage to repay his debts to the Pope."

I fell silent. I was confused and felt lost.

"So that was what lay behind your plans: the visits to Tiracorda, the experiments on the island... Abbot Melani was right: you were not motivated solely by your daughter's abduction. It was as though you were acting to punish the Pope—I do not know how to put this—for betraying..."

"For betraying religion, precisely that. For lucre, he bartered the honour of the Church and of Christendom. Now, never forget that disease of the body is nothing compared to that of the soul. That is the true pestilence."

"Yet, you wanted the ruin of all Christendom: that was why you chose to infect the Pope during the siege of Vienna."

"The siege of Vienna… There is something else that you should know; and it concerns not only the gold of the Odescalchi but the Emperor too."

"The Emperor?" I exclaimed.

"The ploy was straightforward, and this time, too, it was conducted in great secrecy. In order to finance the war against the Turks, the House of Habsburg had been subsidised from the coffers of the Apostolic Chamber. At the same time, however, the Emperor contracted a private loan with the Odescalchi. In surety, the Pope's family received the quicksilver extracted from the imperial mines."

"And what did the Odescalchi do with that quicksilver?"

"That is simple. They resold it to the Dutch heretics; to be quite precise, to the Protestant banker Jan Deutz."

"But then Vienna owes its salvation to the heretics!"

"In a sense, that is true. Nevertheless, the city was saved above all by the money of the Odescalchi. And you may be certain that they will obtain a return of the favour which they did the Emperor; and here, I am not speaking only of money."

"What do you mean?"

"In time, the Emperor will surely grant the Pope, or his nephew and sole heir, Livio, some great political favour. Wait a few years, and you will see."

September 1699

✠

I am now closing this memoir. As I write, eleven years have passed since William of Orange's landing in England. The heretical sovereign still reigns there, and his reign is a successful one: the honour of religion and of the English Catholics was sold by Innocent XI for mere lucre.

Pope Innocent will not, however, be repeating that miserable business. He expired ten years ago, after a long and painful agony. The autopsy showed that his bowels had rotted and his kidneys were full of stones. Someone has already proposed that he should be held up as an exemplar and beatified.

Pompeo Dulcibeni has left us, too. He died this year, as a good Christian, after much prayer and sincerely repenting his sins, which were not few. It happened one day in April; we had perhaps eaten rather more than we should and he (who was always too red in the face and had, in his last years, tended to partake too much of the bottle) asked me to help him to bed, so that he might take a little rest. He never rose again.

What I am today, I believe that I owe in great part to him: he had, so to speak, become my new mentor, God only knows how different from Abbot Melani. Thanks to his long and sorrow-laden sojourn on this earth, Pompeo was able to reveal much to me of his life and sufferings, while always seeking to transmit all that he told me with the comforts of the Faith and in the fear of God. I have read all the volumes which he gave me: books of history, theology, poetry and even medicine, along with some containing the rudiments of the science of commerce and business ventures, in which Dulcibeni was so deeply versed and which, these days, one can no longer permit oneself to ignore. This makes me think that I may perhaps have penned these memoirs of former times with today's thoughts in my mind, often attributing to the poor, destitute prentice of the Donzello words and cogitations with which God has graced me only of late.

I have, moreover, found that my greatest discoveries came, not from the tomes of political or moral doctrine, but from those of medicine. I have burned much midnight oil to convince myself that I was, in reality, never immune to the plague, as Cristofano had assured me at the beginning of our quarantine; my unfortunate condition in no way protected me from infection. The doctor had lied, perhaps in order to avail himself of my services, and had invented everything: from the fable of the sodomising African homunculus to the classifications of Caspar Schott, Fortunius Licetus and Johannes Eusebius Nierembergius, in none of whose works did I find any mention of my supposed immunity. Cristofano knew perfectly well that stature bears no relation to the pestilence. Against infection, it avails me nothing to be what I am, a poor dwarf: "a source of amusement for princes and of astonishment for fairground idlers", as Dulcibeni once put it so scornfully.

I shall, nevertheless, always be grateful to Cristofano: thanks to his venial lie, my pygmy breast was blown up with pride. That was never to recur. My cruelly diminutive stature resulted only in my being abandoned at an early age and the derision of the entire human race; and that, despite the fact that—as Cristofano once stressed—I was to be counted among the more fortunate of my kind, the *mediocres* in stature, and not the *minores* or, worst of all, the *minimi*.

When I look back to the adventure of the Donzello, the mocking laughter of the Bargello's men still rings in my ears, as they shoved me violently into the hostelry at the start of the quarantine: and then, there was Dulcibeni, who amused himself by ascribing to me the Latin tag of *pumilio*, or "little dwarf". I can still see, as though he were there, the obscene vice of Brenozzi, pinching the celery between his thighs, just at the height of my nose; and the *corpisantari* when they mistook me for one of the *daemunculi subterranei*, the minuscule demons which people their nightmares. And I can see myself, almost as though I had been created for that underworld, as I moved agilely before Atto through the narrow tunnels under the hostelry.

In those days at the Donzello, my unhappy condition weighed upon me not less than throughout the rest of my life. I have, however, preferred to leave that in the shadows in my evocation of the great theatre of those events; who would ever accord the slightest credence to the words of one whom only a few wrinkles differentiate from a small boy?

❧⁓❧

Dulcibeni's revelations have, in the time that has intervened, been confirmed by the facts. The nephew of Innocent XI, Livio Odescalchi, who was the Pope's sole heir, has for a derisory price purchased from the Emperor the Hungarian fief of Sirmio (acting, so it is whispered in Rome, against the advice of the officials of the Imperial Household). To add to the lustre of that most profitable transaction, the Emperor even made him a Prince of the Holy Roman Empire. Yet, every excessive gift always, it is said, hides the repayment of a favour. So it was true: the Emperor too was indebted to the Odescalchi. Now he has repaid that money with interest.

Livio Odescalchi himself seems to feel no shame for his odious and bare-faced trafficking. Upon the death of Innocent XI, it is said that his fortune amounted to more than a million and a half scudi, as well as the fief of Ceri. He at once laid his hands on the dukedom of Bracciano, the marquisate of Roncofreddo, the county of Montiano and the lordship of Palo, as well as on the Villa Montalto at Frascati. He was even on the point of buying the fief of Albano, but the Apostolic Chamber itself managed *in extremis* to snatch the transaction from him. Finally, after the death of King Jan Sobieski, the victor of Vienna, Livio attempted to succeed him on the throne of Poland with an offer of eight million florins.

There is no point in waxing indignant: money—that infamous scourge, without land and without pity—has never ceased to corrupt Europe and will ever more trample underfoot the honour of the Faith and of crowns.

☙❧

I am no longer the innocent boy of those days at the Donzello. The things I then saw and heard, and which I shall never be able to reveal to anyone, have marked my life forever. The Faith has not abandoned me; yet, inevitably, the sentiments of devotion and fidelity which every good Christian should foster for his Church have been forever corrupted.

The act of confiding my memories to these pages has, if nothing else, helped me to overcome the moments of greatest discomfort in my life. The rest has been provided for by prayer, the companionship of Cloridia and the reading with which I have nourished my spirit over the years.

Three months ago, Cloridia and I were at last joined in matrimony: we seized upon the opportunity when a mendicant friar arrived in our wretched locality.

A few days ago, I sold a few bunches of grapes to a cantor from the Sistine Chapel. I asked him if he ever happened to sing arias by Luigi Rossi.

"Rossi?" he replied, furrowing his eyebrows. "Ah yes, I think I have heard that name, but it must be old stuff, from the days of the Barberini. No," he added, laughing, "nowadays no one remembers him: today in Rome, all glory goes to the great Corelli, did you not know that?"

Only now do I realise how I have let the years flow past beyond the threshold of my little house. No, I do not know that Corelli; but I do know that I shall never forget the name of the Le Seigneur Luigi or the sublime accents of his arias, which were already out of fashion when Abbot Melani evoked them for himself and for me.

From time to time, sometimes even in my dreams, I recollect the voice and sharp little eyes of Atto Melani, whom I imagine bent by age in his house in Paris, that spacious house in which he had once invited me to go and live.

Fortunately, the weariness of my labours banishes nostalgia: our farm has grown and there is always more work. Among other things, we sell fresh vegetables and good fruit to the nearby villa of the Spada family, where they often call upon me for some other services.

Whenever my work allows, however, I turn to my memories of Atto's words and repeat to myself that phrase of his about solitary eagles and flocks of crows, inwardly seeking to reproduce the tone, the intonations and the intentions, although I know them to be both audacious and ill-advised.

Oft have I returned in vain to the Via dell'Orso, to ask the new occupants of the house where the Donzello stood (now there are only apartments for rent) whether any letters have arrived for me from Paris, or whether anyone has ever asked after the one-time prentice. Every time, as I feared, my hopes have been dashed.

Time has helped me to understand. Only today have I understood that in reality Abbot Melani never intended to betray Fouquet. It is true that Atto gave the Sun King the letters which he had stolen from Colbert, from which the Superintendent was found to be hiding in Rome. However, before then, the King had already begun to show clemency for Fouquet; he had alleviated the conditions of his imprisonment and by now there was even hope that he might be freed. Everyone believed that his liberation was being delayed by Colbert as usual: so why should it not have been a good idea to bring the *Coluber*'s letters to the King? Melani could certainly not foresee that the King's mind would, as soon as he laid eyes on the letters stolen by Atto from Colbert's study, move as swiftly as lightning to a deadly conclusion: Fouquet was in Rome with the *secretum pestis*, and perhaps he would give it to the Pope, who was sustaining the defenders of Vienna...

Louis XIV could not permit his plans to fail at precisely that moment, when his pact with the Turks was on the point of yielding fruit. He will have coldly dismissed Atto. He will have accorded himself time for reflection. He will have recalled him a little later and told him who knows what deceitful tale. Whatever that may have been, I am sure of the conclusion of that meeting: Atto was sent to accomplish an extreme and tragic act of fidelity to the Crown.

Today, all this no longer seems horrible to me. I look back almost with tenderness at the stratagem of robbing those little pearls off me in order to involve me in his investigations. And I wish I could turn back to that last day when I saw Atto Melani: Signor Abbot, please stop, I should like to tell you...

The chance was lost and now that is impossible. We were separated, then and forever, by my boyish candour, my disappointed enthusiasm and my impatience. Now, I know that it was wrong to sacrifice friendship on the altar of purity, confidence on that of reason, sentiment on that of sincerity.

One cannot befriend a spy without bidding farewell to the truth.

෯෨෯

All the prophecies came true. On the first days of the quarantine, I dreamed that Atto gave me a ring and that Devizé played the trumpet. Well, in my Cloridia's book on the interpretation of dreams, I have read that the ring is a symbol of the good conjoined with difficulty, while the trumpet signifies occult knowledge, such as the secret of the pestilence.

In my dream, I had seen Pellegrino rise from the grave: a presage of travails and harm, which did indeed befall us all. In those dream fantasies I saw salt scattered, symbolising assassination (the death of Fouquet); and then, a guitar, indicative of melancholy and labour without reputation (I and Cloridia, unknown and neglected on our little plot). Only one symbol had been favourable, and Cloridia knew that well: the cat, which signals lust.

Stilone Priàso's astrological almanack had also predicted all that befell us: not only the collapse of the inn, but also the imprisonment of a group of gentlemen (the quarantine at the Donzello), a city besieged (Vienna), malignant fevers and venomous distempers (which struck more than one guest), the death of a sovereign (Maria Teresa), and the journeys of ambassadors (bringing news of the victory in Vienna). Only one vaticination had not come true; or rather, it had been overtaken by an even greater force: the "Barricades Mystérieuses" had prevented the death of "certain enclosed noblemen", as foreseen by the almanack.

All this has helped me to come to a decision, or rather, to free myself of an old and unhealthy desire.

No longer do I wish to become a gazetteer. Nor is this only because of the doubt (incompatible with the Faith) that our destinies may be governed by the caprices of the stars. It was something else that extinguished that old ardour in me.

In the gazettes which, since the adventure of the Donzello, I have had occasion to read in great numbers, I have found nothing of what Atto taught me. I am not speaking of facts: I already knew that the real secrets of sovereigns and states are never to be found in the broadsheets which are sold in our city squares. What is most lacking from the gazetteers' accounts is the courage to think matters through to their conclusion, a thirst for knowledge, and bold and honest testing of the intellect. It is not that newspapers are quite useless: they are simply not made for searchers after the truth.

I could certainly, even with the poor abilities at my disposal, have changed that state of affairs; but whoever dared divulge the mysteries of Fouquet and Kircher, Maria Teresa and Louis XIV, William of Orange and Innocent XI, would at once be arrested, bound in chains and thrown forever into the prison for the insane.

What Atto said is true: knowing the truth is of no use to those who write gazettes. On the contrary, it is the greatest of obstacles.

Silence is the only known salvation.

What no one can restore to me and which I most sorely miss are not, however, words, but sounds. Of the "Barricades Mystérieuses" (alas, I could keep no copy) there remains to me only a faint and patchy memory, some sixteen years old.

I have made of it a sort of solitary divertissement, a joyous contest with my own memory. How was it, how did that passage sound, that chord, that bold modulation?

When the dog days of summer dry the head and the knees, I sit down under the oak that shades our modest cottage, in Pompeo Dulcibeni's favourite seat. Then I close my eyes and gently hum Devizé's *rondeau*: once, twice, and then again, in the sure knowledge that my every attempt will be more faded, more uncertain, more distant from the truth.

A few months ago, I sent a letter to Atto. Not having his address in Paris, I sent it to Versailles, in the hope that someone would forward it to him. I am sure that everyone at court knows the famous castrato abbot, counsellor to the Most Christian King.

I confided to him my deep pain at having taken my leave without first expressing to him my gratitude and devotion. I offered him my services, begging him to do me the favour of accepting them and calling myself his most faithful servant. Last of all, I mentioned to him that I had written these memoirs, based upon my diary of those days, of which Atto will not even have suspected the existence.

Yet he has not so far replied to me. Thus, an atrocious suspicion has in recent times begun to disturb my mind.

What will Atto have reported to the Most Christian King on his return to Paris? Will he have succeeded in concealing all those royal secrets which he had discovered? Or will he have lowered his guard, browbeaten by so many questions, thus enabling the King to perceive that he was privy to too many infamies?

Thus, I sometimes imagine a nocturnal ambush in some obscure alleyway, a stifled cry, the footsteps of fleeing ruffians and Atto's body lying in blood and mire...

I shall not give up. Struggling with my fantasies, I continue to hope. And as I await the post from Paris, I sometimes quietly sing a verse or two of his old master, Le Seigneur Luigi:

> *Speranza, al tuo pallore*
> *so che non speri più.*
> *E pur non lasci tu*
> *di lusingarmi il core...*

> Hope, from your pallor
> I know you hope no more.
> And yet you do not cease
> From flattering my heart...

Addendum

✠

Dear Alessio,

You will at last have completed your reading of my two old friends' opus. It will now be up to you to take the final step that will place it in the hands of the Holy Father. While consigning these lines to paper, I pray that the Holy Spirit may inspire your reading and the decision to which it gives rise.

Almost forty years have passed since I received by post the typescript narrating the tale of the Donzello and its dwarf apprentice. Obviously, my first thought was that here was a work in which fantasy was predominant. True, the two authors had (or so they said) drawn upon a historical document: the unpublished memoir of an apprentice, dating back to 1699. I knew moreover, as a priest and a scholar, that the text was correct in regard to Abbot Morandi and Tommaso Campanella, the Jansenists and the Jesuits, the ancient *Societas Orationis et Mortis*, as well as the no longer existent monastery of the Celestines, and even the bizarre beliefs circulating in the seventeenth century concerning Confession and Extreme Unction. Finally, the many examples of lexical licence and a certain cavalier handling of Latin quotations all point indisputably to the language in use in the seventeenth century.

Indeed, the characters often indulge in all the linguistic and terminological excesses of the writers of baroque treatises, including their heavy pomposity.

Apart, however, from those few points, what was in fact freely invented? Doubt was unavoidable; and not only because of the audacious and at times bewilderingly sensational character of the plot, but the very representation of the two protagonists, who—as I have already mentioned—resemble all too closely the traditional duo of investigators comprising Sherlock Holmes and his assistant and narrator, Watson; not to mention Agatha Christie's Poirot and Hastings, all of whom likewise show a preference for investigating in enclosed spaces (trains, ships, islands): just like the Locanda del Donzello...

Do we not also find in the seventeenth-century memoirs of *La-zarillo de Tormes* an analogous teacher-and-pupil couple, an old man and a young one? And what are we to say then of Dante and his *"maes-tro e duca"* Virgil, who guides and instructs him in infernal galleries all too like the subterranean tunnels beneath the Donzello?

I therefore assumed that I had before me a *Bildungsroman*, to employ the terminology of literary experts, among whom I certainly cannot be numbered: in other words, a novel which instructs; in this instance, written in the form of a memoir. Is it not perhaps true that the ingenuous apprentice becomes an adult in the course of the nights spent underground following Abbot Melani and his teachings?

Be that as it may, I soon realized that such considerations did not answer the question: who was the author of this text? My two friends, or the apprentice himself? Or both? And, if so, in what proportions?

For as long as the presumed models that I found remained distant in time, I was completely unable to reach any conclusion. What point was there in obstinately referring back to the fact that in the work of Aretino or, better, in Boccaccio's *Decameron*, the narrative is divided up into days, and, above all—just as in the Donzello—the characters are held in captivity because of the plague and, in order to while the time away, tell each other the most varied tales? Might that not be the model present in the mind of our unknown apprentice?

"Books always speak of other books and every story tells a tale which has already been told": so I concluded, to quote someone whose name I forget. I therefore desisted from such wild-goose chases.

There were, however, a number of blatant borrowings which cast far deeper doubts upon the authenticity of the entire text: for example, one of the tirades in which Pompeo Dulcibeni rails against crowned heads, accusing them of opportunism and incest, was lifted in part, without a by-your-leave, from a famous speech by Robespierre, to which the authors themselves jokingly referred by leaving Dulcibeni on his bed *"sans culotte"*.

Finally, the text contains no few excesses, such as the eccentric figures of Ugonio and Ciacconio: modelled on the archetype of the tomb-robbers or *tombaroli*, those predators of antiquities who still infest our land to this day; like the other *corpisantari* Baronio and Gallonio, they take their names from famous seventeenth-century scholars and explorers of the catacombs. Not to mention the courtesan Cloridia who, when listening to and interpreting the apprentice-boy's dreams, has him lie down on her bed and sits behind his head, obviously in anachronistic imitation of the psychoanalyst's typical posture.

Even the malevolent representation of the personage of Pope Innocent XI seemed to me no more than a clumsy attempt to upset historical reality. As a good citizen of Como, I was of course well acquainted with the figure and the work of this Pope and fellow-citizen. Likewise, I was aware of the malign comments and calumnies which—even during his lifetime—were spread concerning him, for obvious purposes of political propaganda, and which Padre Robleda so foolishly divulged to the young apprentice. Such insinuations had, however, been amply disproved by the most serious historians. To take one example, Papasogli had penned an excellent though weighty monograph of over three hundred pages on the Blessed Innocent XI. Published nearly a century ago, in the 1950s, this work had done much to cleanse his memory of all deceit. Even before that, Pastor, that giant among Church historians, had cleared away many suspicions.

Nor was this the only improbability: there was also the story of Superintendent Fouquet.

In the apprentice's tale, Fouquet dies in the Locanda del Donzello, poisoned by Atto Melani on 11th September, 1683; yet, even in school text-books we read that the Superintendent died in the fortress of Pinerol in 1680, and not in Rome in 1683! A number of fanciful historians and novelists have, it is true, put forward the hypothesis that Fouquet did not die in prison, and the question is too old and too worn for me to need repeat it here. Voltaire, who was able to speak with the Superintendent's still surviving relatives, held that we shall never know with certainty when or where he died. Yet it really did seem to me excessive to affirm, as I had read in the opus sent to me by my two old friends, that Fouquet died in Rome, in a hostelry, assassinated on the orders of Louis XIV.

Here, I had found something that simply could not hold water, a mere manipulation of history. I was at that point close to consigning the typescript to the waste-paper basket. Had I not found the proof that it was a forgery? I was soon, however, to discover that matters were not quite so simple.

Everything began to become more and more unclear when I decided to study the figure of Fouquet in depth. For centuries, the Superintendent has been held up by history books as the veritable prototype of the venial and corrupt minister. Colbert, on the contrary, passes for a model statesman. According to Atto Melani, however, the honest Fouquet was an innocent victim of the envy and hostility of the mediocre Colbert. At first, I ascribed that surprising reversal to pure fantasy, all the more so in that I found in the text echoes of an old novel about Fouquet by Paul Morand. I was, however, soon to revise my beliefs. I found in a library an authoritative essay penned by the French historian, Daniel Dessert, who, a century ago—documents in hand— spoke out to restore Fouquet's merited glory and to unmask the baseness and conspiracies of Colbert. In his admirable essay, Dessert set out point by point (and proved unequivocally) all that Atto told the young man in defence of the Superintendent.

Unfortunately, as so often happens to those who call hoary old myths into question, the precious work of Dessert was consigned to oblivion by the consortium of historians, whom Dessert had made so bold as to accuse of laziness and ignorance. It is, nevertheless, significant that no historian has ever had the courage to disprove his weighty and impassioned study.

Thus, the dramatic case of Fouquet, as evoked with such feeling by Abbot Melani, was anything but a mere narrative invention. Not only that: continuing my library research, I also verified the acquaintance between Kircher and Fouquet which, although not clearly documented, is quite probable, given the fact that the Jesuit (Anatole France mentions this in his opuscule on Fouquet, and it is partially borne out in Kircher's writings) really was interested in the Superintendent's mummies.

Even the thoroughly mysterious tale of Fouquet's sequestration at Pinerol, as I have scrupulously verified, is authentic in every detail. The Sun King really did seem to be holding the Superintendent in prison for fear of what he knew; yet it has never been discovered what that might have been. The ambiguous Comte de Lauzun is also faithfully represented, he who for ten years was imprisoned at Pinerol, where he succeeded in communicating secretly (and quite inexplicably) with Fouquet and was released immediately after the Superintendent's demise.

The book did, then, contain a number of solid and well-documented references to historical reality.

"Now, what if it were all true?" I found myself thinking, as I turned the pages of this disturbing typescript.

࿐

At that juncture, I was unable to restrain myself from undertaking a number of other library searches, in the hope of uncovering some gross error which might demonstrate the falseness of my two friends' writings, and which might enable me to be free of the question. I must confess, I was afraid.

Alas, my suppressed fears were borne out. With unimaginable rapidity, bursting out from dictionaries, encyclopaedias and contemporary manuals, there emerged before my eyes—exactly as I had read in the typescript—descriptions of Rome, quarantine measures, all the theories concerning the plague, both in London and in Rome, Cristofano's remedies and the apprentice's menus; and similarly with Louis XIV, Maria Teresa, the Venetian mirror-makers, even down to Tiracorda's riddles and the plan of the underground galleries in the Holy City.

My head was in a whirl of thoughts about the divining rod, the interpretation of dreams, numerological and astrological doctrines, the saga of *mamacoca* (i.e. coca); and lastly, the battle for Vienna, including the secrets of French siege technique which the Turks had so mysteriously acquired, as well as the mystery of the strategic errors which led to the Infidels' ruinous defeat.

In the Casanatense Library in Rome, still incredulous before an original page from the Bible printed by Komarek, I gave myself up for lost: all that I had read proved stupefyingly authentic, down to the most insignificant details.

Albeit unwillingly, I found myself bound to continue. Instead of errors, I had found proven facts and circumstances. I was beginning to feel myself the victim of an astute trap, an evil system of wheels within wheels, a spider's web in which, the further one penetrates, the more one is ensnared.

I therefore decided to look into the theories of Kircher: I already knew quite a few things about his life and writings, but I had never heard either of the *secretum pestis* or indeed of the supposed *secretum vitae* capable of dispelling the plague, let alone of a *rondeau* in which its secret was encrypted. It is true that I had, like Padre Robleda, read Kircher's *Magnes, sive de arte magnetica*, in which the German Jesuit claims that music has therapeutic powers and even recommends the use of a melody composed by himself as an antidote for the bite of the tarantula. I also knew that in modern times Kircher had been labelled a charlatan: in his treatise on the plague, for example, he

claimed that he had seen the bacilli of the disease under the microscope. Yet, the historians object, in Kircher's time, there did not exist
sufficiently powerful magnifying lenses. So, was it all invented?

If that were the case, I would need to assemble all the necessary
proofs. In the first place, I clarified my ideas about the disease known
as the plague: this is the bubonic plague, caused by the bacillus *Yers-
inia pestis* which is transmitted by fleas to rats, and by the latter to
man. It has nothing to do with the various animal plagues, or with
the so-called pulmonary plague which from time to time strikes in
the Third World.

. The surprise came when I read that bubonic plague has not existed for centuries, nor does anyone know why.

I even found myself smiling when I read that in Europe (and even
earlier in Italy) the plague practically disappeared at the turn of the
seventeenth and eighteenth centuries, almost contemporaneously
with the events at the Donzello. I was expecting that.

Many theories exist about its mysterious disappearance, yet none
is definitive. Some see in this a consequence of more advanced measures of sanitation adopted by mankind; others, however, think that
we must thank the arrival in Europe of *Rattus norvegicus* (the brown
rat) which supplanted *Rattus rattus* (the black rat), which is host to
Xenopsilla cheopis, the flea that acts as carrier of the plague bacillus.
Others attribute the merit to new brick and tile buildings, replacing
those built of timber and straw, or to the removal of domestic grana-
ries, which drove rats from housing. Yet others insist upon the role
played by pseudo-tuberculosis, a benign illness which has the effect
of giving immunity to bubonic plague.

From academic discussions, however, only one thing emerges
with certainty: between the seventeenth and eighteenth centuries,
Europe was mysteriously freed of its most ancient scourge, just as
Kircher had promised to bring this about by applying his secrets.

The coincidences grew even thicker when I thought of the enigma
of the "Barricades Mystérieuses", the *rondeau* which seems to be the
casket enclosing the *secretum vitae*, just as Kircher's tarantella contains
the antidote to the bite of the tarantula. But it was at this juncture
that, may the Lord pardon me, I had the secret satisfaction of at last
discovering a fatal historical error.   .

I needed only to leaf through any old musical dictionary to learn
that the "Barricades Mystérieuses" was not the work of the scarcely

known guitarist and composer Francesco Corbetta, as stated in the text of my two friends, but was written by François Couperin, the celebrated French composer and harpsichordist, who was born in 1668 and died in 1733. The *rondeau* is taken from the first book of his *Pièces de Clavecin*; it was, thus, written for the harpsichord, and not the guitar. Most importantly, it was first published only in 1713: thirty years after the events which are supposed to have taken place in the Locanda del Donzello. The anachronism committed by the two young writers was serious enough to deprive their work of any claim to authenticity, let alone verisimilitude.

Once I had discovered that grave and unexpected inconsistency, it seemed useless to confute the rest of that ingenious narrative. How could a text containing so serious an error possibly threaten the glorious memory of the Blessed Innocent XI?

For some time, in moments of ease at the day's end, I would skim lazily through the typescript, and my thoughts would go out more to the two writers of those pages than to the contents of the story. This disturbing tale, full of poisonous gossip concerning the Pope my countryman, seemed to me an open provocation, even a bad joke. In my soul, there prevailed that distaste and natural mistrust which, I must confess, I have always felt for journalists.

The years passed. By now, I had almost forgotten my two old friends, and with them the typescript which lay buried in an old chest. In an excess of prudence, I had, however, kept it well hidden from the prying eyes of strangers, who might have read it without being armed with the requisite counter-poisons.

I could not yet know how wise that precaution would prove to be.

❧

Three years ago, when I was informed that His Holiness wished to reopen the process of canonisation of Pope Innocent XI, I could not so much as remember where that pile of faded yellow papers might be. Yet it was soon to knock again at my door.

It happened in Como, one damp November evening. Following the pressing insistence of some friends, I was present at a concert organised by an excellent musical association in my diocese. Towards the end of the first half, the nephew of an old companion from my student days played the piano. It had been a hard day and I had, until then, participated rather distractedly in the evening's proceedings. Suddenly, however, an insinuating and ineffable motif attracted me as no music ever had. It was a dance, baroque in style, but with dreaming accents and harmonies which undulated back and forth from Scarlatti to Debussy, from Franck back to Rameau. I have always been a lover of good music and am the proud possessor of a not inconsiderable record collection. If, however, I had been asked from which century those timeless notes came, I would not have known how to answer.

Only at the end of the piece did I open the programme, which I had forgotten on my knees, and read the title of the music: "Les Barricades Mystérieuses".

Once again, the apprentice-boy's account had not lied. That music had an incomparable power to enchant, to confound, unaccountably to fascinate the heart and the mind. After listening, the memory could not shake itself loose. I was not surprised that the young man should have been so perturbed by it, or that, years later, he still continued to turn that motif over in his memory. The mystery of the *secretum vitae* was wrapped within another mystery.

This was not in itself enough to enable me to say that all the rest was true, but it was too much for me to resist the temptation to continue to the bitter end.

The morning after, I acquired a costly complete recording of Couperin's many *Pièces de Clavecin*. After listening to it most attentively for days and days, the conclusion seemed evident: no music of Couperin's resembled the "Barricades Mystérieuses". I consulted dictionaries, I read monographs. The few critics who mentioned it all agreed that Couperin had composed nothing else like it. The dances from Couperin's *suites* almost all have a descriptive title: "Les Sentiments", "La Lugubre", "L'Âme-en-peine", "La Voluptueuse", and so on. There are also titles like "La Raphaèle", "L'Angélique", "La Milordine" or "La Castellane": each alluded to some lady who was well-known at court and whom contemporaries would amuse themselves recognizing in the music. Only for the "Barricades Mystérieuses" did no explanation exist. A musicologist defined the piece as "truly mysterious".

It was as though it were someone else's work. But then, whose could it be? Full of bold dissonances, of languishing, distilled harmonies, the "Barricades" are too far removed from the sober style of Couperin. In an ingenious interplay of echoes, both anticipated and delayed, the four voices of the polyphony merge in the delicate clockwork of an arpeggio. This is the *style brisé*, which the harpsichordists had copied from the lute players. And the lute is the closest relative of the guitar...

I began to admit the hypothesis that "Les Barricades Mystérieuses" might really have been written by Corbetta, as the apprentice-boy had said. But why then had Couperin published it under his own name? And how had it come into his hands?

According to the manuscript, the author of the *rondeau* was the obscure Italian musician Francesco Corbetta. It all seemed to be a pure invention: the idea had never entered any musicologist's mind. There was, however, an interesting precedent: even when Corbetta was still living, controversies broke out as to the authorship of some of his pieces. Corbetta himself accused one of his pupils of stealing some of his music and publishing it under his own name.

I was able to verify without the slightest difficulty that Corbetta really had been Devizé's master and friend: it was therefore all the more likely that some scores must have passed from the one to the other. In those days, there was little printed music and musicians personally copied whatever was of interest to them.

When Corbetta died in 1681, Robert Devizé (or de Visée, according to modern orthography) already enjoyed great fame as a virtuoso and teacher of the guitar, the lute, the theorbo and the large guitar. Louis XIV in person required him to play for him almost every evening. Devizé frequented the foremost court salons. There he played in duo with other celebrated musicians, including, as it happens, the harpsichordist François Couperin.

So, Devizé and Couperin did know one another and they played together; in all probability, they will have exchanged compliments, opinions, advice, perhaps even confidences. We know that Devizé amused himself playing Couperin's music on the guitar (some of his transcriptions have come down to us). It is not improbable that Couperin will in turn have tried his friend's *suites* for guitar on the harpsichord. And it is inevitable that notebooks and scores should have passed from hand to hand. Perhaps, one evening, while Devizé was distracted by the coquettishness of some court ladies, Couperin may have taken that fine *rondeau* with the strange title from his friend's papers, thinking that he would return it the next time that they met.

Under the charm of that celestial music, and of the mystery that was taking form under my eyes, in a short time I again devoured the whole tale, minutely noting in a little exercise book all events and circumstances that would need verification. I knew that only thus could I clear my heart forever of the shadowy suspicion: was that strange story only a clever invention which, manipulating the truth, spread falsehood?

The fruit of the three years' work which followed is all in the pages which you are about to read. I would advise you that, in the event of your wishing to consult them, I have kept Photostat copies of all the documents and books cited.

One enigma above all caused me great anxiety, since it risked transforming the canonisation of the Blessed Innocent XI into a catastrophe. That was Dulcibeni's great secret, the origin of all his troubles and the real motive behind all his plotting: was Innocent XI really in cahoots with William of Orange?

Unfortunately, the apprentice mentions the question only in the final pages of his memoir, when Dulcibeni's enigma is dissolved. Nor had my two friends chosen to enrich the story with other relevant information, acting on their own initiative. Why on earth, I wondered with extreme disappointment, had two curious journalists like themselves failed to do so? Perhaps, I hopefully surmised, they had not succeeded in finding anything against the great Odescalchi.

My duty nevertheless required me to investigate and authoritatively to dispel all shadows and calumnies from the image of the Blessed Innocent. I therefore reread the revelations which the apprentice learned in the end from Pompeo Dulcibeni.

According to the Jansenist, William's debt to the Pope was secured by the Prince of Orange's personal possessions. Where, then, were his possessions? I realised that I had no idea where William's personal fief was situated. Perhaps in Holland? I looked at an atlas, and when I at last located Orange, I could hardly contain my surprise.

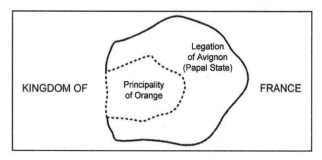

The Principality of Orange was situated in the south of France, surrounded by the Legation of Avignon. The latter was in fact a state of the Church; since the Middle Ages, Avignon had been part of the Papal States. And, in its turn, the Legation of Avignon was surrounded by France! A bizarre situation: the Principality of Orange was surrounded by its Catholic enemy, encircled in turn by another enemy: Louis XIV, the great adversary of Innocent XI.

So the search must be conducted in Avignon; or rather, among the documentation pertaining to Avignon. I therefore obtained a special pass to the Secret Archives of the Vatican and spent several weeks there. I already knew where I must search: in the diplomatic and administrative correspondence between Avignon and Rome. I sorted through piles of correspondence, hoping to find some mention of Orange, William, or loans of money. For days and days, I found nothing. I was about to give up when, in a package of letters completely devoid of any interest, I found three loose quarto notebooks. These dated back to the last months of 1689, a few months after the death of Innocent XI. The new Pope, Alexander VIII Ottoboni, had only just ascended to the papal throne. Alas, the three quarto notebooks seemed comprehensible only to initiates:

```
22 76 18 11 97 46 98 64 48 36
71 37 81 18 73 67 14 38 69
2610 48 46 31 22 14 76
39 0 71 48 76 98 13 48 76
39 37 71 44 22 41 67 14
0 22 34 13 83 78 89 5
77 44 0 64 0 39 93 14 11
48 97 84 34 48 11 76 0
2499 0 55 0 71 11 37 18 16
34 73 93 39 0 29 22 76 18
22 97 97 37 98 38 2575
5 36 14 34 0 76 13 84 18
79 69 2347 94 18 22 19
19 14 78 2316 97 48 94
36 34 37 14 18 71 71 73
18 22 97 46 39 37 46
88 48 71 19 34 37 76 16 37
19 0 98 46 18 13 13 48 39
93 0 34 94 20 97 14 77 76
37 14 38 69 2610 555
48 2336 0 55 64 0 16
```

37 71 73 39 0 16 44 48 16
39 14 19 14 18 81 0 34 31
22 18 16 73 34 48 79 71...

And so on, for twelve pages, with a total of twenty-four columns like that reproduced here. It was a letter in cipher, and at first I despaired of understanding anything.

Fortunately, however, the ciphers used in the letter were those habitually employed at the time by the Vatican Secretariat of State. I therefore compared the letter with other deciphered letters and succeeded at length in decoding a brief preliminary passage:

UNSUDDITOFEDELISSIMODELLASANTASEDEEDIBVONTALENTOGENTIL-
HVOMOAVIGNONESE,MIHAFATTOPERVENIREUNALETTERA,ALUISCRITTA-
DAVNSVDDITODELPRINCIPEDEORANGES...

It took me days of work to obtain a correct and legible version of the text. I was, moreover, compelled to keep a number of indecipherable terms in figures, but these were fortunately not necessary for understanding the text. It was a letter from Monsignor Cenci, Papal Vice-Legate of Avignon, who was writing to Rome in order to describe a strange negotiation:

A most faithful Subject of the Holy See and one of goodly Talents, a Gentleman of Avignon, has passed to me a Missive, sent to him by a Subject of the Prince of Orange, which tells of the great Desire of the Subjects of that Principality to come under the Dominion of the Holy See...

If he speaks to me of that Matter, I shall listen to and report all that he tells me, nor shall I accept or reject 2657. It seems there can be no Doubt but that this is being done with the Agreement of the House of Orange...

My Ministry has obliged me to communicate what I know concerning this exceedingly important Negotiation. The enclosed Folio contains a Copy of the aforementioned Letter, which was written to Signor Salvador, Auditor of the Rota of Avignon, by Monsieur de Beaucastel, Gentleman, of Courteson...

Here was what had happened: Monsieur de Beaucastel, a gentleman of the small town of Courthézon and a subject of the Prince of Orange, had first contacted a priest at Avignon, the Auditor of the Rota Paolo de Salvador, and then Vice-Legate Cenci. Beaucastel was the bearer of a proposal which was, to say the least, surprising: the Principality of Orange desired to offer itself to the papacy. I was astonished: how could the subjects of William of Orange, who were, for the most part Protestants, wish to give themselves to the papacy? And how could they be so sure that William would consent thereto?

Rummaging further in the correspondence between Rome and Avignon, I found the other letters exchanged between Cenci and the Vatican Secretariat of State, and even the initial missive from Beaucastel to Salvador. At the risk of seeming over-meticulous, I note that these documents, hitherto unknown to historians, are to be found in the Secret Archives of the Vatican, *Fondo segreteria di Stato—legazione di Avignone*: folder 369 (Monsieur de Beaucastel to Paolo de Salvador, 4th October, 1689), folder 350 (two letters from Monsignor Cenci to the Vatican Secretariat of State, undated, and one from Cardinal Ottoboni to Cenci, dated 6th December, 1689) and in folder 59 (Monsignor Cenci to Cardinal Ottoboni, 12th December, 1689).

The few letters in cipher were all accompanied by their decoded version. I noted with surprise, however, that the only one which I had translated—the first and most important of all—was not thus accompanied. It was as though someone, in view of the extreme gravity of the contents, had arranged for the disappearance of the deciphered version... Moreover, the letter was not in its proper place, far from the packet of letters which contained the other missives.

Despite the difficulties, I succeeded at long last in reconstructing an extraordinary story, which no historian had yet brought to light.

The motive for the citizens of Orange wishing to come under the papal flag was as simple as it was troubling. William of Orange had accumulated a mountain of debt to Innocent XI; and the subjects of Orange, who had already had to disburse a great deal of money to the papacy, thought that they could best resolve their problems by directly offering their own annexation to the state of the Church: "Here in the Kingdom," writes Monsignor Cenci, "it is quite widely believed that the Prince of Orange still owes the previous pontificate large sums, in payment whereof he believes he can offer possession of a State from which he can gain little capital."

Precisely for that reason, however, not all the subjects of Orange were in agreement: "In the Past, we have already given too much Money to the Church!" protested Monsieur de Saint-Clément, former Treasurer of the Principality.

In Rome, however, Beaucastel's proposal was coldly turned down. The Secretary of State, Cardinal Rubini, and the nephew of the new

Pope, Cardinal Ottoboni, ordered Cenci to reject the embarrassing offer. It could not be otherwise: the new Pope knew absolutely nothing about such debts. It was, moreover, out of the question that the glorious Pope Innocent XI might have lent money to a heretic prince...

I was deeply shocked. The letters found in the Secret Archives of the Vatican confirmed what Dulcibeni had revealed to the young apprentice: William of Orange had been in debt to Innocent XI. Not only that: if the Prince of Orange did not pay up, that would result in the seizure of his personal property. Indeed, the debt had become so high that William's possessions and his subjects considered spontaneously donating themselves!

☙❧

I could not, however, remain content with this. I had to find confirmation of the declarations of the subjects of Orange. I therefore needed to clarify my ideas about William: where did he obtain the money to finance his warlike undertakings? And who had financed the invasion of England?

All the histories of the Glorious Revolution, as the coup d'état whereby the Prince of Orange grabbed the throne of England is now called, sing from the same hymnal: William is good, William is strong, William is so idealistic and disinterested that he does not even want to become King!

If we are to believe the historians, the valiant William seems to have lived on air: but who on earth had given him, since his youth, the wherewithal to fight and to defeat the armies of Louis XIV? Someone must have found him the money to pay for the munitions, the mercenaries (who in those days accounted for the greater part of all armies), the cannons and a few generals worthy of the name.

All the European monarchs then bogged down in wars were beset by the same problems of finding money with which to finance them. The Prince of Orange, however, had an advantage: if there was one city in which money circulated in the seventeenth century—a great deal of money—it was Amsterdam, where, not by chance, the banks of Jewish moneylenders flourished. The capital of the United Provinces was the richest financial market in Europe, just as Cloridia, and later the other guests, told the apprentice of the Donzello.

I consulted a few good books on economic history and discovered that, in the days of William of Orange, a good many of the businessmen in Amsterdam were Italian. The city was full of names like Tensini, Verrazzano, Balbi, Quingetti, and then there were the Burlamacchi and the Calandrini who were already present in Antwerp (almost all of whom were mentioned in the apprentice's tale, first by Cloridia, then by Cristofano). They were Genoese, Florentine, Venetian, all merchants and bankers, some also agents of Italian Principalities and Republics. The most enterprising had succeeded in penetrating the closed circle of the Amsterdam aristocracy. Others were well placed in the lucrative but perilous slave trade: such was the case of Francesco Feroni.

The most interesting case, however, was that of the Bartolotti, from Bologna: originally humble brewers, then merchants, and, in the end, the most prosperous of financiers. They had intermarried with a Dutch family until all trace of their original Italian blood was lost. In fact, the Protestant Bartolotti had in the space of a few decades become wealthy enough to be able to finance the House of Orange, lending money in quantity, first to William's grandfather, then to the Prince himself. The loans were sometimes secured against mortgages on lands in Holland and Germany.

Money against land: according to Dulcibeni, the Odescalchi had entered into an identical pact with the House of Orange. An interesting coincidence.

For the time being, I had learned enough about the Italian merchants and financiers of the House of Orange. It was time to pass on to the Odescalchi, and to get their papers to talk.

I spent months and months, I no longer recall how many, in the archives of Palazzo Odescalchi and the Rome State Archives, with only the help of one young assistant, both of us tormented by the cold and the dust, all day long with our heads bent over papers. We combed through all the papers of Innocent XI, in search of anything that could lead us to William of Orange: letters, contracts, rescripts, reports, memoranda, diaries, ledgers. All to no avail.

Much time had passed since the start of my research, and I had the feeling that I had run into the sands. I began to toy with the idea of giving up: until the thought came to me that Dulcibeni had spoken of Venice, saying that all the money for Holland had been sent from there. And in Venice, there was a branch of the Odescalchi concern: it was there that I must seek the way through to my goal.

From the will of Carlo Odescalchi, Benedetto's elder brother, I
learned that the property of the family had always remained *commune
et indivisa* between the two: in other words, what belonged to the one
belonged to the other. That was why the Pope seemed so poor on paper. Only by examining his brother's accounts was I able to discover
how much he really possessed.

Carlo Odescalchi was in fact the fulcrum of the family's economic
activity: he administered the family's considerable possessions in
Lombardy; he also directed from Milan the branch in Venice, which
was managed by two procurators. I therefore sought the two books
containing the Inventory of Property referred to in Carlo's will. These
could have resolved the problem. If a list of debtors were annexed to
them, William of Orange would have appeared among them. Strangely enough, however, there was no trace of any such inventory.

I then took a look at Carlo's private ledgers, and at last found what
I sought. In the heavy vellum-bound volumes kept by the brother of
the Blessed Innocent XI until his death, and today held by the State
Archives of Rome, there emerged trading and transactions on a colossal scale: millions and millions of scudi. A small proportion of the
operations concerned commercial transactions: revenue from excise
duties and rents. Then came what interested me: hundreds of financial operations, largely carried out from Venice by two procurators,
Cernezzi and Rezzonico, who received commissions for these transactions. The blood in my temples throbbed violently when I saw that
most of these operations were directed towards Holland. I wondered
how the matter had never yet come to light; an archivist explained
to me that these two ledgers had for centuries lain forgotten in the
cellars of Palazzo Odescalchi and had only recently been sold to the
State Archives of Rome. No one had yet looked into them.

It was not difficult to get to the bottom of the matter. Between
1660 and 1671, Carlo Odescalchi had ordered payments in various
currencies from Venice to Holland totalling 153,000 scudi: a sum almost equal to the entire, gigantic annual outgoings of the ecclesiastical state (173,000 scudi) at the time when Benedetto was elected
pope.

Within the space of nine years, between 1660 and 1669, the
Odescalchi sent a good 22,000 scudi to the financier Jan Deutz,
founder and proprietor of one of the principal Dutch banks. The
Deutz family were literally a piece of Holland, not only for the vast

wealth which they had accumulated, but the government posts which they occupied at all levels, and their links of kinship and marriage with the most prominent members of the country's ruling class. Jan Deutz's brother-in-law had been the Grand Pensioner Jan de Witt, preceptor and mentor of the young William III. Jan Deutz the Younger, the banker's son and partner, was a member of the Amsterdam city council from 1692 until 1719; Deutz's daughters and granddaughters married burgomasters, generals, merchants and bankers.

That was only the beginning: between June and December 1669, a further 6000 scudi were sent by the Odescalchi to a company of which Guillelmo Bartolotti, one of William of Orange's financiers, was a partner. That was the decisive proof: the Odescalchi sent money to the Bartolotti, and they lent it to William. Thus, the money passed from the coffers of the Odescalchi to those of the House of Orange.

The more I knocked, the more doors opened up to me. Between November 1660 and October 1665, the Venetian procurators of the Odescalchi sent another 22,000 scudi to a certain Jean Neufville. Now, Neufville was certainly no minor figure in William's entourage; his daughter Barbara married Hiob de Wildt, who served first as Secretary of the Admiralty at Amsterdam and later as Admiral-General, appointed by William himself. The de Wildts had, moreover, always had ties with the House of Orange; Hiob's grandfather, Gillis de Wildt, had been appointed to the Haarlem city council by Prince Maurice of Orange. Hiob de Wildt, however, gathered the finance necessary for the invasion of England in 1688 and, after William ascended to the English throne in 1688, acted as his personal representative in Holland.

Finally, in October 1665, a small sum was also sent by the Odescalchi's procurators to the company of Daniel and Jan Baptista Hochepied, the first of whom was a member of the Council of Amsterdam as well as Chairman of the East India Company: the commercial and financial powerhouse of Protestant Holland.

So it was true. Dulcibeni had invented nothing: the Dutch secretly financed by the Odescalchi were precisely those whom the Jansenist had finally revealed to the young apprentice. This tied in with one important detail: in order to leave no traces, the money was sent to friends of the House of Orange by the two Venetian proxies of the Odescalchi, Cernezzi and Rezzonico. Sometimes Carlo Odescalchi

noted in his ledgers that such and such an operation was to be made
in the name of Cernezzi and Rezzonico, but the money was his; and
thus, his brother's too.

Finally, I also found loans to the slaver Francesco Feroni: 24,000
scudi in ten years, from 1661 to 1671: who knows how much those
loans may have earned? That would explain the Odescalchi's willing-
ness to accept Feroni's claims on Dulcibeni's daughter.

Not only that: the Odescalchi had also lent money to the Genoese
Grillo and Lomellini, holders of the Spanish royal charter for the traffic in slaves, and in their turn friends and financiers of Feroni. Since
these documents, too, have never been studied by historians, I shall
indicate where they are to be found (Archivio di Stato di Roma, *Fondo
Odescalchi*, XXIII, A (1), p. 216. Cf. also XXXII E (3), (8)).

I checked how many scudi were sent by the Odescalchi to Holland and have drawn up a graph of these operations:

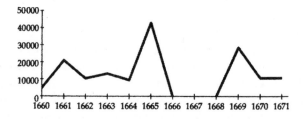

The money was certainly used to finance wars. That is confirmed
by the dates: in 1665, for instance, when payments reached their
maximum of 43,964 scudi, Holland went to war with England.

My work would have been considerably easier if I had been able to
compare Carlo Odescalchi's ledgers with his commercial correspondence. Strangely, however, the letters from 1650 until 1680, which
must give the names of debtors in Holland, are nowhere to be found:
they are neither in the Rome State Archives nor in the Archives of
Palazzo Odescalchi, the only two places holding the family's documents where these may be consulted.

Nor is it the first time that there have been strange disappearances in this affair. Louis XIV had a high-ranking spy in his pay
in Rome: Cardinal Cybo, a close collaborator of Innocent XI. Cybo
passed the French a most precious piece of information: the Vatican
Secretary of State Lorenzo Casoni was in secret contact with the
Prince of Orange.

Whether true or false, at the end of the eighteenth century, unknown hands spirited away the volumes of Casoni's correspondence preserved in the Vatican.

❧❧

Even the saddest and most embarrassing details of my two old friends' typescript have turned out to be true. It was not possible, I had at first thought, that Innocent XI and his family should have disposed of Cloridia as their own chattel, going so far as to cede her to Feroni, like common slave merchants.

After consulting a number of well-documented papers on the subject, however, I was compelled to revise my ideas. Like many patrician families, the Odescalchi family kept slaves as a matter of course. Livio Odescalchi, the Pontiff's nephew, for example, was the master of fifteen-year-old Ali, a native of Smyrna. And the Blessed Innocent XI possessed Selim, a nine-year-old Moorish boy. Nor was that all.

In 1887, the Archivist Emeritus Giuseppe Bertolotti published in an obscure specialist periodical, the *Rivista di Disciplina Carceraria* (*Review of Prison Discipline*), a detailed study on slavery in the Papal State. From this emerged a surprising picture of the Blessed Innocent, which is certainly not to be found in any of his biographies.

All the popes, down to and beyond the baroque age, made use of slaves acquired or captured in war, either on the pontifical galleys or for private purposes. But the contracts signed by Innocent XI in regard to slaves were by far the most cruel, observed Bertolotti, who was disgusted by the "slaver's contracts in human flesh" personally subscribed to by the Pontiff.

After years of inhuman labour, the galley slaves, by now incapable of working any longer, begged to be freed. To ransom them, Pope Innocent claimed the poor savings which, year after year, these wretched slaves had somehow scraped together. Thus, Salem Ali from Alexandria, suffering from a disease of the eyes and declared unfit for work by the doctors, had to pay 200 scudi into the papal coffers in order to be freed from the chains of the papal galleys. Ali Mustafa, from Constantinople, acquired from the Maltese galleys for 50 scudi and suffering from "incapacity owing to pains and sciatica" had to pay 300 scudi into the Vatican treasury. Mamut Abdi from Toccado, sixty years old, of which twenty-two had been spent in slavery, had to part with 100 scudi. Mamut Amurat, from the Black Sea, Sixty-five years old and in poor health, could afford only 80 scudi.

Those without money were made to wait until death resolved the problem. Meanwhile, they were thrown into prison, where the doctors found themselves having to cope with poor bodies destroyed by overwork and hardships, horrible ulcers and unhealed wounds decades old.

Upset by this discovery, I looked for the documents used by Bertolotti, who described them as "easily consulted". Here again, I drew a blank: these too had disappeared.

The documents should have been in the Rome State Archives, *Acta Diversorum* of the Chamberlain and Treasurer of the Apostolic Chamber for the year 1678. The Chamberlain's volumes cover all the years until 1677, then start again in 1679; the volume for 1678 is the only one missing.

As for the Treasurer, a single miscellaneous volume covers operations between 1676 and 1683. Here, too, there is no trace of those for 1678.

࿇

Belua insatiabilis, insatiable beast: was that not what the prophecy of Malachy called Innocent XI?

After months spent coughing amidst the dust of seventeenth-century manuscripts, I took up a printed work, the *Epistolario Innocenziano*: one hundred and thirty-six letters written by Benedetto Odescalchi over a period of twenty years to his nephew Antonio Maria Erba, a Milanese senator. The patient curator of this volume, Pietro Gini of Como, cannot have realised, in his enthusiastic devotion, what kind of material he was feeding to the printers.

These are, it is true, private letters. But it is precisely from his family correspondence that the man's overbearing character and his attitude to money emerge. Cadastral acts, lands, inheritances, mortgaged loans, claims for damages, sums to be demanded, confiscations from debtors. Every sentence, every line, every note is poisoned by an obsessive fixation with money. Apart from a few other family disputes and inquiries after the health of spouses, the letters of Innocent XI contain nothing else.

There abounds, however, advice on how to keep close watch over money, and how to obtain repayment from debtors. It is always better not to have anything to do with the courts of law, the Pope reflects in a letter dated 1680, but if one wants to see one's money back, then one should be the first to sue: there will always be time to come to an arrangement.

Even his close circle seemed somewhat perplexed by the Pope's consuming passion. A manuscript note by his nephew Livio, from about 1676, states that "some minister" must be found "to correspond about the family's business affairs, for if the Pope continues to want to do everything with his own head and in his own hand, his health will not be able to stand the strain."

The obsession with money consumed even his flesh.

༈

Dear Alessio, now I know. Under my eyes, day after day, the memoirs of the apprentice of the Donzello have become reality. The secrets which, in the end, Pompeo Dulcibeni revealed to the young man, and which motivated his attempt on the life of Innocent XI, are all true.

The Blessed Innocent was an accomplice of Protestant heretics, thus gravely damaging Catholic interests: he allowed England to be invaded by William of Orange for the sole purpose of obtaining repayment of a monetary debt.

Pope Innocent was also a financier of the slave trade, nor did he renounce the personal possession of slaves; and he treated those who were old and dying with sanguinary cruelty.

He was a niggardly and avaricious man, incapable of raising himself above material concerns, obsessed by the thought of lucre.

The figure and the work of Innocent XI were thus unjustly celebrated and elevated, using false, devious and partial arguments. Evidence was concealed: the inventory of the will of Carlo Odescalchi, the letters and commercial receipts of the Odescalchi archives from 1650 until 1680, the correspondence of Secretary of State Casoni, the contracts concerning the redemption of slaves cited by Bertolotti, together with other papers of which I shall have to report the, at best, inexplicable disappearance in my final documents.

Thus the lie triumphed in the end. The financier of heretics was pronounced the Saviour of Christendom. The greedy merchant became a wise administrator; the stubborn politician, a capable statesman. Revenge was dressed up as pride, the miser was called frugal, the ignorant man became simple and plain-living, evil stole the clothing of goodness; and goodness, abandoned by all, became earth, dust, smoke, shadow, nothing.

Now, perhaps, I understand the dedication chosen by my two friends: "To the defeated". Fouquet was defeated: to Colbert, glory; to him, ignominy. Defeated, too, was Pompeo Dulcibeni, who could not obtain justice: his leeches failed. Defeated, likewise, was Atto Melani: he was constrained by the Sun King to kill his friend Fouquet. And, despite a thousand vicissitudes, he failed to extract from Dulcibeni his closely guarded secret. Defeated was the apprentice-boy who, faced with the vision of evil, lost his faith and his innocence: from aspirant gazetteer, he descended to taking refuge in the hard and simple life of a son of the soil. Defeated, too, was his very memory which, although composed with so much care and labour, lay forgotten for centuries.

All the agitation of these personages was in vain. Against the malign forces of injustice which dominate the history of the world, they were powerless. Their strivings were, perhaps, useful only to themselves, to discover and to understand what—for a long, long time—none would be privileged to know. Those strivings served perhaps above all to augment their sufferings.

If this should be a novel, it is the novel of labour lost.

ঔৎঔ

I hope that you will, dear Alessio, pardon me for the outburst to which I abandoned myself in these last lines. For my part, I have done what I could. It will be for historians one day to complete the labour of selection from the archives, the scrupulous verification of sources, of circumstances, of details.

First, however, it will be for His Holiness, and for Him alone, to judge whether the opus of my two friends should be published or kept secret. The implications of its dissemination would be manifold, nor would they concern only the Church of Rome. How, indeed, will the British Orangemen be able stubbornly and arrogantly to parade through the streets of Derry and Belfast when, on the 12th of July each year they celebrate the anniversary of the Battle of the Boyne, the victory in which William of Orange finally crushed the Catholic forces? What meaning will be left to their celebration of Protestant extremism when they know that they owe that victory to a pope?

The ancient vaticinations do not lie; the Holy Father will now take the right, the inspired, decision. According to the prophecy of Saint Malachy, as evoked by Padre Robleda, our well-beloved (and rather long-lived) Pontiff will be the last, and the holiest Pope: *De Gloria Olivae*, as he is called in the prophecy.

I am aware that the list of popes attributed to Malachy has long been recognised as a forgery dating from the sixteenth century, and not the Middle Ages. Yet no scholar has succeeded in explaining how it correctly foresaw the names of modern popes right down to the present day.

That list tells us that time has now run out: *Fides intrepida* (Pius XI), *Pastor angelicus* (Pius XII), *Pastor et nauta* (John XXIII), *Flos florum* (Paul VI), *De Medietate Lunae* (John Paul I), *De labore Solis* (John Paul II) and last of all *De Gloria Olivae*: all the 111 Pontiffs. The Holy Father is, then, perhaps he who will prepare the return of Peter to this earth, when each shall be judged and every wrong set right.

Cloridia told the apprentice that she had come to Rome following the way of numbers and the oracle of the Tarot: the Arcana of Judgement called for "the reparation of past wrongs" and the "equitable judgement of posterity". If the prophecy of Malachy is true, then, that time has come.

All too often, history has been insulted, betrayed, distorted. If, now, we do not intervene, if we do not proclaim the truth out loud, if the writings of my two friends are not published, it is possible that evidence will continue to disappear: that the letters of Monsieur de Beaucastel and Monsignor Cenci will be lost, placed by mistake in the wrong folder, or that the ledgers of Carlo Odescalchi will vanish inexplicably, as have so many documents.

I know, dear Alessio, that you are concerned to respect the schedules which your office lays down. For that very reason, I trust that you will transmit these papers to His Holiness with all diligence, so that he may weigh up whether to order a late, yet still timely, *imprimatur.*

Notes

✠

The Donzello

The Locanda del Donzello all'Orso ("The Squire with the Bear") really did exist. I was able to find its precise location thanks to the *Status Animarum* (the census carried out each year at Easter by the parishes of Rome) of the former parish of Santa Maria in Posterula, the little church which was once near the inn. In the nineteenth century, the church and the *piazzetta* in which it stood were demolished to make way for the construction of the new embankments of the Tiber. Yet the yearly censuses have been preserved and may be consulted in the historical archives of the Vicariate of Rome.

The former inn was situated exactly where the apprentice said: in a sixteenth-century house at the beginning of Via dell'Orso, where numbers 87 and 88 now stand. The main entrance is a fine studded *portone*; nearby, one can see the broad doorway with an oblong arch which in 1683 led to the dining room of the inn, and which today is the entrance to an antique shop. The building was acquired a few decades ago and renovated by a family which still lives there and lets out a number of apartments for rent.

By means of a series of searches through the cadastral records, I was able to verify that the building has undergone a number of changes between 1683 and the present day; without, however, radically altering its original appearance. The ground-floor and first-floor windows, for example, no longer have grilles; the attic has become the third floor, above which there is now a terrace. The order of windows facing onto the alleyway at the corner of the Via dell'Orso has been completely bricked up but is still visible. The little tower which was supposed to house the courtesan Cloridia has been extended and now forms an extra storey. Of the other storeys there remain only the structural walls, all partition walls having been changed several times over the centuries. Not even the little closet which hid the secret stairway giving access to the underground galleries has survived; in the place where that stairway was, a series of apartments have been added on in more recent times.

In other words, the inn is still there, as though time had stopped. With a little imagination, one could hear the voice of Pellegrino or the mutterings of Padre Robleda behind those ancient windows.

Time has mercifully spared other documents, which have proved decisive for my research. In the Orsini section of the Capitoline historical archives,

I found a precious register of the guests at the Donzello up until the end of the year 1682. The volume, in a rough parchment binding, was entitled, in a shaky hand: *Book in which are noted all of those who came to lodge at the Cammera Locanda of Sig.ra Luigia de Grandis Bonetti, at the Bear.* A manuscript note within confirms that the inn was known as the Donzello.

From the register of guests, surprising coincidences emerge. According to the apprentice, the proprietor of the Donzello, Signora Luigia, died a violent death caused by an attack by two gypsies.

Well, the register of the inn breaks off suddenly on 20th October, 1682. It seems that, around that date, the innkeeper Luigia Bonetti met with a serious accident; we hear nothing of her until the date of her death on 29th November of the same year (I was able to verify this in the register of deaths of the parish of Santa Maria in Posterula).

But that is not all. I could not believe my eyes when, in the register of guests at the Donzello, I found a number of familiar names: Eduardus Bedfordi, twenty-eight years of age, Englishman; Angelo Brenozzi, twenty-three years of age, Venetian; and lastly, Domenico Stilone Priàso, thirty years of age, Neapolitan; all had lodged at the inn between 1680 and 1681. The three young men were, in other words, people of flesh and blood, and had really stayed at the Donzello at the time when it was kept by Signora Luigia, before the arrival of the apprentice.

I therefore searched also for traces of the apprentice himself, who unfortunately never reveals his name in his memoir, and for information concerning his master, Pellegrino de Grandis.

The boy said he was taken into service by Pellegrino in the spring of 1683, while Pellegrino had, on his arrival from Bologna with his wife and two daughters, taken up temporary lodgings near the Donzello, "waiting for the few passing guests to vacate the premises".

So, all that is borne out. In the *Status Animarum* I discovered that the *palazzetto* of the Donzello housed several families of tenants that spring: a few pages further on, I first found mention of a certain Pellegrino de Grandis, from Bologna, a cook by trade, along with his wife Bona Candiotti and two daughters. They were accompanied by a twenty-year-old apprentice called Francesco. Was he, perhaps, the young dwarf at the inn?

In the following year, new lodgers were again to be found at the Donzello: a sign that the damage described by the apprentice at the end of his account had been repaired, but Pellegrino did not continue his activity as innkeeper. Nor are there any further traces of him or his young helper.

Personages and documents

The physician from *Le Marche*—the Marches—Giovanni Tiracorda, was born in the village of Alteta in the province of Fermo and was one of the most noted *Archiaters* (or physicians to the Pope) of his time, caring for Innocent XI on several occasions. As I have been able to ascertain (again through the *Status Animarum* of the church of Santa Maria in Posterula), he really did live in the Via dell'Orso, near to the inn, with his wife Paradisa and three servant girls. His plump and jovial figure, just as the boy described him, corresponds exactly to a caricature by Pier Leone Ghezzi preserved in the Vatican Library. The books, the furniture, the ornaments and the plan of the interior of Tiracorda's house, as described by the apprentice, all correspond down to the last detail to the inventory of goods attached to the physician's last Will and Testament, which may be consulted in the State Archives of Rome.

Even the capricious character of the doctor's wife Paradisa seems to correspond to the truth. In the Archives of the Pio Sodalizio dei Piceni (Pious Association of Citizens of Ascoli Piceno) in Rome, there are to be found the few documents of Tiracorda's which escaped the ravages of the Napoleonic troops stationed in the Holy City. Amongst the remaining papers, I consulted a series of legal cases brought against Paradisa after her husband's death. From a number of expert opinions, it emerged that the lady was no longer in possession of her mental faculties.

I have found no few mentions of the surname Dulcibeni in the city of Fermo, in the Marches, during the course of the two visits which I made there; unfortunately, I did not find anyone who in the seventeenth century answered to the name Pompeo. I did, however, find confirmation of the existence in Naples of an important circle of Jansenists: probably that to which Dulcibeni belonged.

In the Medici Archives in Florence, I was able to verify almost in its entirety the story of Feroni and Huygens; upon his return to Tuscany from Holland, Francesco Feroni wished to contract an aristocratic marriage for his daughter Caterina. The girl was, however, completely besotted with her father's right-hand man, Antonius Huygens, from Cologne; so much so that she had fallen ill of "continuall Fever, which has since become a tertian Fever". Despite that, Huygens continued to work for Feroni, even managing the subsidiary of his business in Livorno. Here, too, the apprentice's memoir spoke the truth.

Concerning the Sienese physician Cristofano, I have traced only information concerning his father, who bore the same name, the well-known Superintendent for Health Cristofano Ceffini, who was indeed active during the plague epidemic at Prato in 1630. He also left a *Libro di Sanità*—a book of health—listing the rules which health officials were to observe in the event of a plague outbreak.

Luigi Rossi, the master of Atto Melani, lived in Rome and Paris, where he was young Atto's friend and mentor. All the verses which Abbot Melani sings are taken from his songs. Le Seigneur Luigi (as he is referred to in original scores scattered throughout the libraries of Europe) never took the trouble during his lifetime to have his operas printed; yet these were highly success-ful, and the monarchs of the time competed to have them performed. Thus, Luigi Rossi, while being regarded in the seventeenth century as the greatest of all European composers, had already fallen into oblivion by the dawn of the new century.

I have succeeded in finding only two recordings of his love songs, but I was lucky. I actually found the two passages sung by Atto and was thus able to listen to them, enchanted by their wonderful melodies.

The astrological almanack of Stilone Priàso, which so troubled the ap-prentice of the Donzello, was published in December 1682 and may be con-sulted at the Biblioteca Casanatense, in Rome. It was, I confess, with some disquiet that I discovered that the author really had predicted that the bat-tle of Vienna would take place in September 1683. That is a mystery and, I think, destined to remain so.

At the Biblioteca Casanatense, thanks to the professionalism and ex-treme courtesy of the librarians, I was also able to trace the astrological manual from which was drawn the horoscope of Aries that Ugonio recited to Atto and the boy during their underground peregrinations. This little trea-tise was published in Lyons in the year 1625, just a year before the birth of Abbot Melani: *Livre d'Arcandam Docteur et Astrologue traictant des prédictions d'Astrologie*. Well, in the case of Atto, Arcandam's vaticinations seem to have been remarkably accurate, including even his life span: eighty-seven years, as foretold by the astrologer.

Atto Melani

All the circumstances of the life of Atto Melani contained in the appren-tice's account are authentic. Castrato singer, diplomat and spy, Atto served, first the Medici, then Mazarin, and finally the *Roi Soleil*, but also Fouquet and an indefinite number of cardinals and noble families. His career as a castrato was long and glorious, and his singing was celebrated—as he himself boasted to the apprentice-boy—by Jean de la Fontaine and Francesco Redi. Besides being mentioned in all the principal musical dictionaries, the name of Atto Melani appears in the correspondence of Mazarin and in the mem-oirs of several French writers.

Atto Melani was also accurately described by the apprentice-boy, both in regard to his appearance and his character; to appreciate this, one has but to stop and look at the funerary monument erected in his memory in the church of San Domenico in Pistoia. Looking up, one meets the abbot's sharp eyes and can recognise the mocking fold of his lips and the impertinent dimple on his chin. The Marquis de Grammont describes the young Atto Melani in his memoirs as "amusing, and far from stupid". And one has only to read one of Atto's many letters, scattered like *disjecta membra* throughout all the libraries of Italy, to marvel at his gay and ironic, gossipy and exceedingly acute style.

In his correspondence, one finds many of the teachings which Atto imparted to the young apprentice, beginning with his learned (and eminently debatable) reasoning as to why it was absolutely licit for a Christian King to ally himself with the Turks.

Even the guide to the architectural marvels of Rome, which Abbot Melani was writing in his room at the Donzello, between one adventure and another, seems to have been anything but an invention. Atto's guide is in fact extraordinarily similar to an anonymous manuscript which was first published by a small Roman publishing house in 1996, under the title *Lo Specchio di Roma Barocca* (*The Mirror of Baroque Rome*). The anonymous writer of the manuscript was a cultivated, well-to-do abbot, well informed about all things political and with good connections at the papal court, a misogynist and a Francophile. That sounds like a portrait of Abbot Melani.

Not only that: the author of the guide must have sojourned in Rome between 1678 and 1681, just like Atto, who in fact met Kircher in 1679.

Like Atto Melani's guide, *Specchio di Roma Barocca* remained incomplete. The author abandoned the work in the midst of a description of the church of San Atanasio dei Greci. Incredibly, Atto interrupted his work at the same point, struck down by the memory of his meeting with Kircher. Is that only a coincidence?

Atto, moreover, really did know Jean Buvat, the scribe who—as we read in the apprentice's account—looked after his correspondence in Paris, imitating his handwriting perfectly. Buvat was a copyist at the Bibliothèque Royale, highly skilled in deciphering parchments and an excellent calligrapher. He worked for Atto too, and the latter recommended him—unsuccessfully—to the prefect of the Library for an increase in pay (cf. *Mémoire-Journal de Jean Buvat* in: *Révue des Bibliothèques*, October/December 1900 pp. 235–236).

History was, however, kinder to Buvat than to Atto; while Abbot Melani was consigned to oblivion, Buvat had a notable part in *Le Chevalier d'Harmentel* by Alexandre Dumas, Père.

Atto and Fouquet

I found a brief biography of Atto (Archivio di Stato di Firenze, *Fondo Tordi* n. 350) p. 62) written a few years after his death by his nephew Luigi, from whom we learn that he really was a friend of Fouquet, as we read in the apprentice's memoir. Indeed, according to Atto's nephew, the Superintendent corresponded copiously with Abbot Melani. Of that correspondence, to tell the truth, no trace has ever been found.

What, then, were Atto's real relations with the Superintendent?

When Fouquet was arrested, Atto was in Rome. As was mentioned in the apprentice's memoir, he had fled from the wrath of the Duc de la Meilleraye, Mazarin's powerful heir, who had seen the castrato poke his nose into his house too often and had asked the King to exile him. In Paris, however, it was rumoured that he was involved in the Fouquet scandal.

From Rome, in the autumn of 1661, Atto wrote to Hugues de Lionne, Minister of Louis XIV. It is a heartfelt letter (traced by me in the archives of the Ministry of Foreign Affairs in Paris, *Correspondance politique*, Rome (142), pp. 227 et seq.; the original being in French), in which the tormented syntax and the spelling mistakes reveal the depth of his anxiety:

Rome, on the last day of October, 1661

You tell me that there is no Remedie for my Sicknesse and that the King is still irritated with me.

To write this to me is to notify me that I am under Sentence of Death, and you have been inhuman, knowing my Innocence as you do, not in some Way to have gilded the Pill, for you are not unaware of how much I adore the King, or of the Passion which I have always had to serve him as he should be served.

Had God wished that I should not have loved him so and that I should have been more attached to Monsieur Fouquet: at least I would be justly punished for a Crime which I had committed, and I should not lament for myself. Now, however, I am the most wretched young Man in the World, nor shall I ever be able to console myself, for I do not consider the King as a great Prince, but as a Person for whom I experienced the transports of a Love as great as a Human Person can know. I aspired only duteously to serve him and well to merit his goode Graces, without in any way thinking of the least Rewarde, and I can tell you that I would not have remayned so long in France, even during the Lifetime of the Lord Cardinall [Mazarin], were it not for the Love which I bore the King.

My Soul is not strong enough to bear so great a Misfortune.

I dare not compleyn, not knowing to whom to impute such a Disgrace, and even if it seems to me that the King does me a great Injustice, yet I cannot so muche as murmur, since he was right to be surprised that I had an exchange of Correspondence with Monsieur le Surintendant.

He had due Cause to believe me to be a perfidious and wicked Person, seeing that I sent to Monsieur Fouquet the Drafts of Letters which I addressed to His Majesty. He is right to condemn my Conduct and the Terms of which I employ [*sic*] when writing to Monsieur Fouquet.

If, my poor Monsieur de Lionne, the King has treated me justly, declaring that he is displeased with me, because the Hande that has betrayed all his Letters deserves to be cut off, yet my Heart is innocent, and my Soul has committed no Errour: they have ever been faithfull to the King, and if the King would be just, he must condemn the one, and absolve the others; for the extreme Love which my Heart has borne the King has led my Hande to err. It has erred because I have felt to Excesse the Desire to return close to him; and because, in my Tyme of Need, abandoned by all, I believed the Surintendant to be the beste and most faithfull Minister of the King, who manifested his Goodnesse to him more than to any Other.

These are the four Motives which led me thus to write to Monsieur Fouquet, and there is not a single Worde in my Letteres that I cannot justify, and if the King would condescend to have the Goodnesse to grant me that Grace, which has never been refused to any Criminel, please have all my Letters examined, and may I be put to the Question, may I go to Prisoun, even before replying, so as to be punished, or to be pardoned, if such are my Desarts.

Nothing will be found in the Letteres which I have written to Monsieur Fouquet, except that I wrote to him at the Tyme when I fell in Disgrace, which prooves that I did not know him before that.

Those Accounts will not be found to shewe that he made any Summe of Monnaye over to me, or that I was one of those who received a Pension from him.

By Means of some of his Letteres, I can well prove the Truth of all that he wrote me, and that he, knowing the Reasoun which led me to write to him, told me (whether truthfully or in Flatterie) that he would emploie his goode Offices with the King and that he wished to take Care of my Interests.

And here is a Copie of the last Lettere, the only one which I have received since my arrival in Rome. Should you desire the Originall, you have but to tell me...

Atto confessed then that, when he wrote to the King, he passed the draft of his letters to the Superintendent! These were letters from an agent of France, and they were addressed to the Sovereign himself: a mortal sin.

Atto, however, denied that he had done this for money: he had contacted Fouquet only after falling in disgrace, in other words when the ire of the Duc de la Meilleraye exploded and he needed a place to hide (just as Devizé recounted in the apprentice's memoir).

In proof of what he claimed, Atto sent a copy of the letter which Fouquet had written to him. It is a moving document: the Superintendent wrote to the castrato on 27th August, 1661, only a few days before his arrest. This is one of the last letters that he wrote as a free man.

Fontainebleau, 27th August, 1661

I have received your letter of the first of this month, together with that from Cardinal N.

I would have written to you earlier, if I had not had a fever which kept me in bed for two weeks and which left me only yesterday.

I am preparing to leave the day after tomorrow to accompany the King to Britanny, and I shall endeavour so to arrange matters that the Italians do not intercept our letters again; I shall speak of this to Monsieur de Neveaux as soon as I arrive in Nantes.

Do not worry about your interests, since I am taking special care of them, and although in the past few days my indisposition has prevented me from conversing with the King as usual, I have not failed to bear witness to him of your zeal in his service, and he is well pleased about that.

This letter will be delivered to you by Monsieur l'Abbé de Crécy, whom you can trust. I have read with pleasure what you communicate to me on behalf of Cardinal N., and I beg you to tell him that there is nothing that I would not do to serve him. I also beg you to be so kind as to present my compliments to Madame N.; I always honour her perfectly and am completely at her service.

The confusion in which I now find myself on the eve of so important a journey prevents me from replying in greater detail to all the content of your letter. Send me a memorandum of what is owed to you of your pension and you may be sure that I shall fail in nothing to demonstrate to you the esteem in which I hold you and how much I desire to serve you.

If Fouquet really wrote thus to Atto (the original, if it existed, has been lost) it was not a brilliant idea to try to disculpate himself by showing these lines to the King. What took place between the castrato and the Superintendent was too ambiguous, the climate surrounding them too charged with suspicions: intercepted letters, confidential mail, a Cardinal N. (perhaps Rospigliosi, Atto's friend?) and a mysterious Madame N. (perhaps Maria Mancini, Mazarin's niece, the King's former mistress who may also have been in Rome at that time?)

But above all, the ballet which Atto and Fouquet danced around the King drew suspicion. The first passed his own correspondence with Louis XIV secretly to the second, who in his turn recommended his friend to the Sovereign. And then, there was that pension with which Fouquet promised to help Atto...

Despite the scandal in which he found himself involved, Fouquet did not betray his friend. During his trial, when he was asked about their relations, Fouquet replied evasively, thus succeeding in saving Atto from prison; I have found full confirmation of this in the minutes of the trial, exactly as Devizé told the guests of the Donzello.

Atto Melani's last years

In his last years, the castrato Melani must have been weighed down by solitude. That perhaps explains why he spent the last part of his life at his house in Paris, with two nephews, Leopoldo and Domenico. So it may well be true that, as the apprentice of the Donzello says in his manuscript, he had offered to take him with him.

On his deathbed, Atto ordered that all his papers were to be packed and taken to the house of a trusted friend. He knew that during his agony, his house would be full of curious bystanders and profiteers, hungry to find out his secrets. And perhaps he was thinking back to the time, as he told the apprentice-boy, of his own trespassing in the study of the less far-sighted Colbert.

The initial dedication

Rita and Francesco told me that they had found the apprentice's memoirs among Atto's papers. Now, how had they ended up there? To understand that, we must read attentively the mysterious initial dedication, the anonymous letter, without sender or addressee, which precedes the apprentice's tale:

> Sir,
>
> in conveying to you these Memoirs which I have at last recover'd, I dare hope that Your Excellency will recognise in my Efforts to comply with your Wishes that Excess of Passion and of Love which has ever been the cause of my Felicity, whenever I have had Occasion to bear Witness thereof to Your Excellency.

In the last pages of his account, the apprentice, consumed by remorse, writes to Atto, again offering him his friendship. However, he lets slip the fact that he had kept a diary, and had subsequently compiled a detailed memoir of what had taken place at the inn.

The apprentice says that Atto never replied, and he even fears for the latter's life. We, however, know that the sly abbot made good his escape and lived for many years afterwards. He must, therefore, have received that letter. I can even imagine the first instant of pleasure registering on his face when he read those lines, followed by fear; and then, by resolve: he charged some faithful miscreant to go to Rome and filch the apprentice's memoir before it fell into the wrong hands. Those pages revealed too many secrets and accused him of the most horrendous crimes.

The anonymous dedication will, then, have been written to Atto by his ruffian, once the latter had fulfilled his task. That explains why Rita and Francesco said to me that they had found the apprentice's memoir among Melani's papers.

Did Atto and the apprentice ever meet again? Perhaps, one day, Abbot Melani, seized by nostalgia, may have suddenly ordered his *valet de chambre* to fill his travelling trunks, as he must set out urgently for the court of Rome...

INNOCENT XI *&* WILLIAM OF ORANGE:
DOCUMENTS

✠

History in need of rewriting

The liberation of Vienna in 1683, the religious disputes between France and the Holy See, the conquest of England by William of Orange in 1688 and the end of English Catholicism, the political isolation of Louis XIV in the face of the other powers, the entire European political picture in the second half of the seventeenth century and during the decades that followed: a whole chapter of European history will need rewriting in light of the documents which reveal the secret manoeuvrings of Pope Innocent XI and the Odescalchi family. But to do that will mean raising a curtain of silence, hypocrisy and lies.

The historian Charles Gérin (*Révue des questions historiques*, XX, 1876, p. 428) points out that, when in 1689 Louis XIV and James II asked Innocent XI to stem the financial aid being sent to the Habsburgs (who were continuing to push back the Turks) and to send money urgently for the Catholic troops of the Stuart king, fighting in Ireland against the heretical forces of William of Orange, the Pope responded with phrases whose full significance can only be appreciated today. He explains that in Vienna he is fighting "a perpetual crusade" in which he, like his predecessors, has taken "a personal part". He is furnishing the allies with "his own galleys, his own soldiers and his own money" and defending, not only the integrity of Christian Europe, but "his particular interests as a temporal Sovereign and an Italian Prince". After the landing of the Prince of Orange, Innocent XI betrayed himself with a revealing phrase, reported by Leopold von Ranke (*Englische Geschichte, vornehmlich im Siebzehnten Jahrhundert*, Vol. III, Leipzig, 1870. p. 201.): *Salus ex inimicis nostris*, salvation comes from our enemies.

The loans of Innocent XI to William of Orange

Unfortunately, Atto Melani was right when he told of the trial of Fouquet: history is written by the victors. And, to this day, official historiography has always been the victor. About Innocent XI, no one has been able (or willing) to write the truth.

The first to speak of the loans of Innocent XI to William of Orange were a few anonymous pamphlets which the French put into circulation following the Protestant prince's landing in England (cf. J. Orcibal, *Louis XIV contre Innocent XI*, Paris 1949, pp. 63–64 and 91–92). According to the memoirs of Madame de Maintenon, moreover, the Pope is said to have sent William sums to the tune of 200,000 ducats for the landing in England; but these memoirs are of dubious authenticity. These were all rumours promulgated by the French for the evident purpose of defaming the Pontiff. Hearsay was spread by essayists and pamphleteers, who provided no proof of their assertions.

Rather more insidious for the memory of Innocent XI was Pierre Bayle's entry in his famous *Dictionnaire historique et critique*. Bayle issues a reminder that Innocent was born into a family of bankers and reports a satirical comment which was appended beneath the statue of Pasquino in Rome on the day when Cardinal Odescalchi was elevated to the pontificate: *Invenerunt hominem in telonio sedentem.* In other words: they have chosen a Pope seated at the usurer's table.

This was no piece of gossip disseminated for purposes of propaganda. Bayle, a great pre-Enlightenment intellectual, could not be accused of vulgar pro-French partisan motives. He was, moreover, quite close to the facts about which he was writing (his dictionary was published in 1697).

No historian, however, attempted to clarify the facts, to follow the tracks left by the clandestine pamphlets and Bayle. The truth about the Odescalchi was thus kept to a handful of pamphlets and the dusty dictionary of a Dutch philosopher who repudiated his own writings (Bayle converted from Calvinism to Catholicism and back, and ended up by rejecting all credos).

Hagiography, meanwhile, triumphed without firing a shot, and Innocent XI passed into history. The facts seemed incontrovertible: in 1683, Vienna was liberated thanks to the man who had mobilised the Catholic princes and sent subsidies from the Apostolic Chamber to Austria and Poland. Innocent XI was a heroic and ascetic pope who had put an end to nepotism, restored order to the Church's finances, forbidden women to appear in public in short sleeves, put an end to the insanity of the Carnivals and closed the theatres of Rome, those places of perdition.

After his death, a deluge of letters arrived from all over Europe; every reigning house asked for him to be beatified. The process of beatification began as early as 1714, thanks to the solicitude of the Pope's nephew Livio. Witnesses still living were heard, documents acquired, and biographical events reconstructed, going back to the Pope's infancy.

Almost at once, however, a number of obstacles arose, which slowed down the progress of the investigation. Perhaps mention was made of the old French pamphlets and of Bayle's Dictionary: malicious scribblings, hearsay, unproven and perhaps impossible to prove, and yet, even in the case of a chaste, virtuous and heroic life like that of Benedetto Odescalchi, such things must needs be taken into consideration. Opposition on the part of France is also suspected, where the elevation of an old and bitter enemy was not viewed kindly. The process of beatification, already weighed down by innumerable and highly creditable procedural documents, ground to a halt: from a rushing torrent, it had turned into a muddy and sluggish trickle, disappearing into the sands.

Decades passed. There was no more talk of Innocent XI until 1771, when the British historian John Dalrymple published his *Memoirs of Great Britain and Ireland*. And perhaps one can catch here glimpses of what had slowed down the investigation. In order to understand Dalrymple's thesis, one must, however, take a step back in time and widen one's view to cover the European political panorama on the eve of William of Orange's landing in England.

In the last months of 1688, a new and exceedingly grave outbreak of political tension had occurred in Germany. For months, the nomination of the new Archbishop of Cologne had been awaited. France wanted at all costs that this office should go to Cardinal Fürstenburg. If the manoeuvre had succeeded, Louis XIV would have won a precious bridgehead towards central Europe, gaining military and strategic predominance; and that, the other princes could not tolerate. Innocent XI himself had refused his—legally indispensable—consent to Fürstenburg's nomination. During these same weeks, all Europe was watching anxiously the military manoeuvres of William of Orange's troops. What was William preparing? Was he on the point of intervening against the French to resolve by force of arms the question of the Archdiocese of Cologne, thus sparking off a tremendous conflict throughout Europe? Or was he—as some suspected—on the point of invading England?

Here, then, is Dalrymple's thesis: William of Orange succeeded in persuading the Pope that he intended to use his troops against the French. Innocent XI who, as usual, could not wait to obstruct the plans of Louis XIV, fell into the trap and lent William the money necessary to maintain his army. The Prince of Orange crossed the Channel instead and won England over for ever to the Protestant religion.

Thus, heresy was said to have triumphed thanks to Church finances. Even if he had been deceived, the Pope had nevertheless armed a Protestant prince against a Catholic one.

This hypothesis had already been circulated in anonymous pamphlets at the time of Innocent XI and Louis XIV. On this occasion, however, Dalrymple produced decisive proofs: two long and detailed letters from Cardinal d'Estrées, Ambassador Extraordinary of Louis XIV to Rome, addressed to the French Sovereign and to Louvois, the Sun King's Minister for War.

According to the two missives, the closest collaborators of Innocent XI were already informed well in advance of William of Orange's real intentions: the conquest of England. At the end of 1687—a year before the invasion of England by the Protestant prince—the Vatican Secretary of State Lorenzo Casoni was alleged already to be in contact with a Dutch burgomaster, sent secretly by William of Orange. Among Casoni's servants, there was, however, a traitor; thanks to the latter, Casoni's missives to the Emperor Leopold I were intercepted. From these letters, it was learned that the Pope had placed large sums of money at the disposal of the Prince of Orange and of the Emperor Leopold I, so that they could fight the French in the conflict which was on the point of breaking out over the question of the Archbishop of Cologne. From Casoni's letters to the Emperor, William's real intentions also emerged clearly: not to provoke a conflict in central Europe against the French, but the invasion of England, of which the ministers of Innocent XI would thus have been perfectly aware.

D'Estrées' letter struck a mortal blow against the process of beatification. Even if Innocent XI had been in the dark about William's real plans, namely the annihilation of Catholicism in England, it emerged absolutely clearly that he had financed him for warlike purposes and, moreover, against the Most Christian King.

A whole series of historians took up the letters produced by Dalrymple, thus demolishing the reputation of Benedetto Odescalchi. Besides this, doubts had also arisen on strictly doctrinal matters, and these further complicated the progress of the beatification, which seemed thus to have been irremediably compromised.

A period of time proportionate to the gravity of these circumstances had to pass before someone found the courage and lucidity necessary to reopen the question. Only in 1876 did a masterly article by the historian Charles Gérin cause history to take a 180-degree turn. In the *Révue des questions historiques*, Gérin demonstrates rigorously and with a wealth of arguments that the letters from d'Estrées published by Dalrymple were gross forgeries, once again attributable in all probability to French propaganda. Inexactitudes, errors, improbabilities, and above all a series of blatant anachronisms voided them of all credibility.

As though that were not enough, Gérin demonstrated that the originals of the letters, which, according to Dalrymple, were supposed to be in the archives of the Ministry of Foreign Affairs in Paris, were nowhere to be found. Dalrymple himself, Gérin observed, had candidly confessed that he had never seen the originals and had relied on a copy sent to him by an acquaintance. The repercussions of Gérin's article, although limited to historians' circles, were considerable. Dozens of authors (including the celebrated Leopold von Ranke, doyen of the historians of the papacy) had drawn blithely upon Dalrymple's *Memoirs* without taking the trouble to verify his sources.

The conclusion was unavoidable. With blind symmetry, once the letters had been proved false, all the facts to which they referred became false and all that went in the opposite direction was taken to be true. Where accusations are based upon false documentation, the accused immediately becomes innocent.

The by now time-worn question of the relations between Innocent XI and William of Orange, which seemed to have been resolved forever by Gérin, was unexpectedly resurrected by the German historian Gustav Roloff at the beginning of the First World War. In an article published in 1914 in the *Preussischer Jahrbücher*, Roloff brought to light new documents concerning Innocent and the Prince of Orange. From a report by a Brandenburg diplomat, Johann von Görtz, it was discovered that in July 1688, a few months before William's landing on the English coast, Louis XIV had secretly requested Emperor Leopold I of Austria (Catholic, but a traditional ally of the Dutch) not to intervene if France invaded Holland. Leopold, however, already knew that the Prince of Orange intended to invade England, and he therefore found himself faced with a dramatic dilemma: whether to support Catholic France (detested, however, throughout Europe), or heretical Holland.

According to Görtz's report, the Emperor's doubts were dispelled by Innocent XI. The Pope is alleged to have communicated to Leopold that he should absolutely not endorse Louis XIV's actions and designs, since the latter "derived, not from a just passion for the Catholic Religion, but from the intention to throw all Europe into the sea, and consequently, England too".

Leopold, after ridding himself of the burden of religious doubt, did not hesitate to enter into further pacts of support for and alliance with William, thus favouring the invasion of England by a Dutch heretic. The advice from Innocent XI which made for this resolve followed soon after William's coup, the imminence of which he should have known from his representative in London, the Nuncio D'Adda. Of course, Roloff adds, no letter from Innocent XI has been found, in which he communicated his opinion to Leopold; but it may readily be assumed that the latter will have taken the form of a rapid and discreet oral communication through the Papal Nuncio in Vienna.

Roloff himself was not, however, at all satisfied with his own explanation. Something else must have been involved, said the German historian. "If Innocent had been a Renaissance Pope, his behaviour could easily have been explained by political opposition to France. However, that motivation was no longer adequate in the period following the great wars of religion." The Pope's actions were, indeed *must* have been determined by some other factor, of which the oppressive presence could still only be sensed.

The matter was not resolved. In 1926, another German historian, Eberhard von Danckelmann, went onto the counter-attack with the declared intention of winning the decisive battle against all talk of an alliance of interests between the Protestant William III of Orange and the Pope. In an article which appeared in the periodical *Quellen und Forschungen aus italienischen Archiven und Bibliotheken*, Danckelmann directly attacks Roloff's thesis. Not only was Innocent XI not informed of the Prince of Orange's expedition, says Danckelmann, citing a number of letters from the Vatican's diplomatic representatives, but he followed with anguish the unfolding of the situation in England.

Then we came to the heart of the matter. Revealing his hand almost nonchalantly, Danckelmann adds that it had in the past been rumoured that the

Prince of Orange owed the Pope large sums of money; debts in consequence of which William is alleged to have considered renouncing his Principality of Orange in favour of Innocent. These sums, Danckelmann points out, are alleged to have been lent specifically for the purpose of the English expedition.

In five lines, Danckelmann drops his bombshell. It is true that Saint-Simon in his *Mémoires* adopted the same poisonous hypothesis (which Voltaire was to dismiss as improbable). No serious and well-documented modern historian, however, had ever taken seriously the scandalous idea that the Blessed Innocent XI might have lent money to the Prince of Orange to overthrow the Catholic religion in England.

Roloff himself had done no more than conclude that the Pope knew in advance of the Prince of Orange's intention to invade England, and had done nothing to prevent him. But he made no claim that William had been financed by Innocent XI. Danckelmann had, however, decided to give a name—even while confuting it—to that unknown factor which, according to Roloff's intuition, must have guided the Pope's manoeuvrings and caused him secretly to support William: money.

The hypothesis that Innocent financed William's undertaking, Danckelmann argues, naturally depends upon one premise: that the Pope knew of the Prince of Orange's imminent landing in England, as Roloff claimed to have proved. Once he had taken the English throne, William would have found it easy to honour his debts to the Pope, to whom he would sooner or later have repaid them all, with interest, as to any other moneylender.

Instead, Danckelmann swears, the Pope did not know. He was owed nothing by William, nor did he expect the forthcoming invasion of England. This is proved, according to Danckelmann, by the letters exchanged shortly before William's landing, between the Secretary of State, Cardinal Alderano Cybo, the Nuncio to Vienna, Cardinal Francesco Bonvisi, and the Nuncio to London, Ferdinando D'Adda. According to these missives, the Pope was most alarmed by the Prince of Orange's military manoeuvres, nor was there any hint of a secret understanding between William and the Holy See. The Pope, therefore, did not know.

Even if it were to be admitted that Innocent had channelled money to William, Danckelmann continued, the money would certainly have had to pass through the Papal Nunciature in London. But payments from Rome to the London Nunciature, scrupulously checked by the German scholar, showed no trace of financing for William. The documents examined, Danckelmann complacently concludes, "completely clarify the question". Roloff's thesis is demolished and, with it, any claim that dares affirm that the Pope lent money to the House of Orange: Q.E.D.

Danckelmann's rashness is quite astonishing. With a little research, however, a number of interesting facts come to light: the Barons von

Danckelmann had been closely linked with the House of Orange since the time of William III. They had been raised to the nobility by the Prince Elector Frederick of Brandenburg, the uncle of William III. They came, moreover, from the county of Lingen, which was part of the estates of the House of Orange. Danckelmann, however, omits to inform his readers of these personal connections (cf. *Kürschners deutscher Gelehrter Kalender*, Berlin 1926, II, p. 374; C.J.M. Denina, *La Prusse litteraire sous Frédéric II*, Berlin 1791, I, *ad vocem*; A. Rössler, *Biografisches Wörterbuch zur deutschen Geschichte*, Munich 1973–1975, *ad vocem*).

In 1956, the beatification of Pope Innocent XI at long last took place, aided and abetted—in the view of some—by the Cold War: the Turks had become a metaphor for the Soviet empire, while the Pope of the day cast himself as carrying the flame of his heroic predecessor three centuries previously. Pope Innocent XI had saved the West from the Turkish tide; Pope Pius XII would protect it from the horrors of communism.

For too long, the truth was made to wait out in the cold. Once the official version had crystallised, historians went to unprecedented lengths to stick only to what had already been said. Perhaps perturbed by too many questions both too old and too new, they cast only an indifferent glance over the mystery that forever links William III of Orange, the Prince who re-established the Anglican religion in England, and the greatest Pope of the seventeenth century.

Meanwhile, papers, essays and theses abounded on depilation in the Middle Ages, the daily life of deaf mutes under the *Ancien Régime* and the world-view of millers in Lower Galicia. No one, however, took the trouble to tackle that great historical question mark and, sharing the dust of the archives in which they lay, honestly to peruse the papers of the Odescalchi and Beaucastel.

The mercenary Pope

The fact remains: no one has ever attempted to tell the truth about Innocent XI. In the Biblioteca Nazionale Vittorio Emanuele in Rome, there is a curious opuscule written in 1742 and entitled *De supposititiis militaribus stipendis Benedicti Odescalchi*, by Count Giuseppe Della Torre Rezzonico. Rezzonico's purpose is to dispel a widespread rumour following the death of Innocent XI, namely that the Blessed had, in the years of his youth, fought as a mercenary in Holland under the Spanish flag, suffering, among other things, a serious wound to his right arm. Rezzonico claims that Benedetto Odescalchi had been a soldier as a very young man, but only in the communal militia of Como, not as a mercenary.

It is perhaps unfortunate that the author was a relative of that Rezzonico who, from Venice, acted as a proxy for the Odescalchi; it is also a pity that the Rezzonico family should have had ties of kinship with the family of Innocent XI. It would doubtless have been preferable if a historian more detached from the events of which he speaks had set out to disprove the military past of the Blessed. However, a number of facts make one regret the absence of a closer examination. According to Pierre Bayle, the young Benedetto Odescalchi was wounded in the right arm when fighting as a mercenary in Spain. Curiously, as confirmed by official medical sources, the Pope suffered from great pain in that very member until his death.

Quite apart from the merits or demerits of the above, it is surprising that this obscure aspect of the life of Pope Innocent should have been neglected for decades. From within Rezzonico's volume, there fell out a card from the library, showing the name of the last person to consult it: the card was signed "Baron v. Danckelmann, 16 April 1925". Since then, no one had turned those pages.

True and false

Atto Melani says wisely, when instructing the young apprentice: what false papers proclaim is not always false. Even the forged letters of d'Estrées published by Dalrymple fall into that bizarre class of document. It is no accident that another letter, this time authentic, published by Gérin, from the Cardinal d'Estrées to Louis XIV dated 16th November, 1688, confirms the contacts between Count Casoni and William of Orange:

> Cardinal Cybo [...] has learned that, through the good offices of a cleric who came last year from Holland bearing letters from certain missionaries in that country, who had been given to hope that the States-General would accord freedom of conscience to the Catholics, he [Casoni] had come to a kind of understanding with a man depending upon the Prince of Orange and who held out hope for that freedom: that the said man upheld the missionary in the conviction that the Prince of Orange had great respect for the Pope and would do many things for him; that in recent times these relations had grown firmer and that the Prince of Orange had certainly given it to be understood that he had only good intentions.

The circumstance referred to by d'Estrées is credible, if only because the source of the information, Cardinal Cybo, was a spy in the pay of Louis XIV (Orcibal, *op. cit.*, p. 73, note 337). On 9th December, the French sovereign sent this irate reply to d'Estrées:

> If he wanted to restore good relations with me, the Pope would remove Casoni for good, together with the criminal correspondence which he has carried on with the Prince of Orange.

The memoirs of Madame de Maintenon, which speak of loans by Innocent XI to William of Orange, are apocryphal, yet may they too not tell the truth?

The revolution of 1688

All this is not limited to a mere academic discussion. In order to appreciate the scope of the Glorious Revolution, and therefore of Innocent XI's action, we shall again give the floor to Roloff:

> The revolution in which William of Orange overthrew the Catholic James in 1688 marked the transition from one period to another no less than the other great European revolution, the French one of 1789. For England, the accession of the Prince of Orange meant not only the definitive establishment of the evangelical faith, but also the stabilisation of the rule of Parliament and the opening of the way which was to lead to the reign of the House of Hanover, which has continued to this day. The victory of Parliament over James II made possible the creation of both the parties which have divided government between themselves throughout English history [i.e. Tories and Whigs]. Power passed durably into the hands of the aristocracy of birth and of money, who represented mercantile interests in general.

Moreover (and this is what should have mattered most to the Pope), after the Orange victory, the laws which excluded Catholics from public life became notably harsher; during the reign of James II, 300,000 Englishmen had professed themselves to be Catholic. In 1780, the number had decreased to only 70,000.

William's debts

The money in the Prince of Orange's pocket: these accounts should have been checked at the outset. In the biographies of William of Orange, however, this one fundamental chapter always remains somewhat nebulous: who financed the armies which he commanded in defence of Holland? No answer has been given to this question, but only because the question has never been put firmly enough. Yet, some scholar might have been expected to show a little curiosity.

According to the Anglican Bishop Gilbert Burnet, William's contemporary and friend, the Prince of Orange "came into the world under great disadvantages [...] His private affairs were also in a very bad condition: two great jointures went out of his estate, to his mother, and grandmother, besides a vast debt that his father had contracted to assist the King [of England]." (cf. *Bishop Burnet's History of His Own Time*, London 1857, p. 212.)

Burnet had played an active part in preparing the revolution of 1688. He had been one of the few people to be informed of the planned landing in England and he was by William's side at the most delicate moments of the coup, including the final march on London from the coast. It would not, therefore, be surprising if he should have concealed other facts, which would have been more embarrassing for the Crown and the Anglican faith.

The German historian Wolfgang Windelband cites a letter from William to his friend Waldeck, written shortly before he ascended to the English throne: "If you knew the existence I am leading, you would certainly feel pity for me. The only consolation that remains to me is that God knows it is not ambition that drives me" (cit. in Windelband, Wolfgang "Wilhem von Oranien und das europäische Staatensystem", in *Von Staatlichem Werden und Wesen. Festschrift Erich Marks zum 60. Geburtstag*, Aalen 1981).

Are these, asks Windelband in astonishment, the words of one who has just fulfilled the dream of a lifetime? And I would add: are these not the words of someone who has pressing and unavowable money problems?

His English subjects did not regard the new King as a champion of frugality. As von Ranke points out (*Englische Geschichte*, cit.), in 1689 William asked Parliament for a permanent personal income, like that enjoyed by the Stuart kings who had preceded him: "It is necessary for our security to have money at our disposal." Parliament was mistrustful: the King was granted only an annual income, with the express proviso that it should be voted for "no longer" than one year at a time. William seemed profoundly upset and regarded the refusal as a personal insult; but he had no means of opposing it. It was precisely at that period—note the coincidence—that the secret negotiations between Beaucastel, Cenci and the Vatican Secretariat of State took place.

If one observes carefully, the whole history of the House of Orange is full of revealing episodes, in which the Protestant princes' relationship with money seems to have been painful, to say the least. According to the English historian Mary Caroline Trevelyan, "William II's ambitions* would have troubled them [the States-General] very little if, in his capacity as Captain-General of the Republic, he had not tried to maintain a larger army than they were prepared to pay for." In order to find the money necessary for defence, William II even stooped to violence, imprisoning no fewer than five of the leading deputies of the States of Holland in 1650 and marching on Amsterdam (Renier G.J., *William of Orange*, London 1932, pp. 16–17).

In 1657, again according to Mary Trevelyan, the mother of William III had pawned her jewels in order to meet the desires of her brothers. In January 1661 she died in England. In May of the following year, William's grandmother, Princess Amalia of Solms, had an inquiry opened with a view to reclaiming the jewels. Her secretary, Rivet, wrote to Huygens, William's secretary, that, "our

* William II was the father of William III. (Translator's note.)

little master is constantly talking about them" (Trevelyan, M.C., *William III and the Defence of Holland 1672–1674*, London 1930, p. 22).

The princes of Orange needed considerable financial resources in order to finance their warlike undertakings. In the months leading up to the landing in England, even the papal agents in Holland were aware of William's pressing needs: in mid-October, they reported (and Danckelmann noted the occurrence) that, because of strong winds, ten to twelve vessels from William's fleet had not returned from manoeuvres on the high seas, and the Prince of Orange was in great distress because the delay in preparations was costing him 50,000 *livres* a day.

Need, when acute, can cause a prince to stoop to unworthy actions, including fraud and treason. According to the historian of numismatics, Nicolò Papadopoli (*Imitazione dello zecchino veneziano fatta da Guglielmo Enrico d'Orange (1650–1702)*, in *Rivista italiana di numismatica e scienze affini*, XXIII [Vol. III], 1910), in the seventeenth century the mint of the Principality of Orange shamelessly forged Venetian coin (zecchini), easily escaping all sanctions. When, in 1646, the fraud was discovered, the *Serenissima Repubblica* of Venice was engaged in the war of Candia against the Turks and was, in fact, taking arms and troops from Holland; so the Venetians were compelled to suffer the insult in silence. It is probable that the princes of Orange also forged the *ungar* (or Hungarian ducat), which was the normal currency in Holland.

The financiers of the landing in England

William of Orange was, then, poor; or rather, perennially in debt and in search of money for his wars. One needs, therefore, to know who his financiers were, beginning with those with whom dealings were overt.

The political and military activities of William of Orange, including the invasion of England, were sustained by three principal sources of finance: the Jewish bankers, the Admiralty of the city of Amsterdam, and a number of patrician families.

The Jewish bankers occupied a prominent place in the financial life of Amsterdam and all of Holland. Among them, the Baron Lopes Suasso stood out; besides acting as diplomatic intermediary between Madrid, Brussels and Amsterdam, he generously financed William. According to contemporaries, he advanced him 2 million Dutch florins without any guarantee, referring to the loan with the famous phrase: "If you are fortunate, you will return it to me; if you are unfortunate, I am willing to lose it." Other financial help for William came from the *Provediteurs-General* (as he himself called them) Antonio Alvarez Machado and Jacob Pereira, two Sephardi Jewish bankers (cf. Swetschinski, D. and Schoenduve, N., *De familie Lopes Suasso, financiers van Willem III*, Zwolle 1988).

No less important for William was the support of the Admiralty of Amsterdam, which, according to the historian Jonathan Israel, supplied about sixty per cent of the warships and crews that disembarked in England. According to contemporary estimates, these numbered about 1800 men who, when the landing was imminent, worked watches day and night.

Finally, William obtained contributions from several Dutch families, although this was beset with a thousand difficulties. Obsessed by the dangers of arming a prince, Israel observed, the patricians of Amsterdam arranged matters in such a way that the funds which they advanced were not officially destined for the English expedition, as though that was entirely William's business and not that of Amsterdam and all the United Provinces. William therefore had in the end to stand with a burning fuse in his hand: the responsibility was his and the debts were his. To achieve this window-dressing, the money was advanced under a fictitious heading, so that nothing should appear in the public accounts. Part of the finance was, for instance, secretly drawn from the 4 million florins which the United Provinces had collected in July before the expedition to improve their system of fortifications. All this is explained by the fact that in the end William's personal property stood surety with his creditors, in other words, the Principality of Orange. On the other hand, William was to become King of England, which was supposed to enable him to resolve all his problems of indebtedness (Israel, J., "The Amsterdam Stock Exchange and the English Revolution of 1688" in *Tijdschrift voor Geschiedenis* 103 (1990), pp. 412–440).

The Bartolotti

Next, come the hidden financiers: the Odescalchi. The Pope's family may perhaps not have directly financed William's landing in England, but it is certain that they had for a long time channelled money to the House of Orange via highly tortuous and secret routes. The most interesting of the channels in question was that of the Bartolotti, the family of which Cloridia speaks to the apprentice in their first conversation. This family came from Bologna, but soon their blood was completely mixed with that of the van den Heuvel family, which continued to bear the Italian name solely for hereditary reasons.

Well integrated into the Dutch aristocracy, some of the Bartolotti-van den Heuvel family obtained high office: they became commanders of the Amsterdam infantry, regents of the city or Calvinist pastors. Ties with the ruling class were at last crowned by the marriage of the daughter of Costanza Bartolotti with Constantin Huygens, Secretary to William III of Orange (Elias, J.E., *De vroedschap van Amsterdam*, Amsterdam 1963, I, 388-389).

It was, however, possible to ascend the social ladder only by accomplishing a corresponding ascent in regard to wealth; and, in the space of a few decades, the Bartolotti had become among the most powerful bankers, in a position to serve the great, including the House of Orange. Guillelmo Bartolotti, for instance, was among the organizers of a loan of 2 million florins at 4 per cent to Frederick Henry of Orange, William's grandfather. And it was with Guillelmo that William's grandmother, Amalia of Solms, had pawned her family jewels.

The son of Guillelmo Bartolotti, who took his father's name, lent money with interest and did business with a partner called Frederik Rihel (both figure among the debtors in the ledgers of Carlo Odescalchi, Archivio di Stato di Roma, *Fondo Odescalchi*, Libri mastri, XXIII A2 p. 152). From his father, Guillelmo Bartolotti the younger inherited not only money and real estate but also letters of credit. And, when his mother, too, died in December 1665, Guillelmo Bartolotti the younger became a creditor of William III of Orange, who was then just fifteen years old. The Prince of Orange in fact owed the Bartolotti 200,000 florins, to be reimbursed on the basis of two bonds. The first, of 150,000 florins was guaranteed by a mortgage "on the domain of the city of Veere and its polders". The remaining sum was guaranteed by a mortgage on "certain estates in Germany", where the Orange family did in fact have some possessions (Elias, *op. cit.*, I, p. 390).

As we have seen, in two of the three above-board channels used by the Prince of Orange and identified by historians (i.e. the Admiralty in Amsterdam, noble Dutch families and Jewish bankers) the money of the Odescalchi was circulating. Loans from the family of Innocent XI had ended up in the hands of the Admiralty (in the person of Jean Neufville, who was made an admiral by William of Orange himself) and of numerous families of the Dutch economic and financial aristocracy: the Deutz, Hochepied and the Bartolotti, all of whom are mentioned in Carlo Odescalchi's ledgers.

Two channels out of three, then, were supplied by the family of the Blessed Innocent. In their support of the House of Orange, the Odescalchi had only one rival: the Jewish bankers. It may be a coincidence, but among the many strict measures introduced by Innocent XI during his pontificate, one specifically affected the world of finance. The Blessed Innocent banned Jews, on pain of severe penalties, from exercising banking activities, the very field in which the Odescalchi family excelled. This grave measure, which marked the end of a long period of tolerance by the popes, brought about the economic downfall of Rome's Jewish community who, until the nineteenth century, were forced to stand impotently by while their debts piled up and their takings collapsed. At the same time, Pope Innocent gave strong backing to the charitable institution known as Monte di Pietà, which—while in itself a worthy and socially beneficial initiative—took even more resources and customers away from the Jewish bankers.

This ban on the lending of money with interest was introduced by Innocent XI in 1682. In the same year, the Jewish banker Antonio Lopes Suasso had granted William of Orange a loan of 200,000 guilders. A coincidence?

The secret of the ledgers

Deciphering Carlo Odescalchi's ledgers proved a time-consuming task. The keeping of account books was made compulsory by the Venetian authorities in the sixteenth century in order to guarantee and protect commerce. No sooner had the measure been introduced, however, than it was cleverly circumvented by merchants, who transformed their books into dense and incomprehensible lists of figures and names, drawn up by trusted accountants under the direct supervision of their principal and only decipherable by the latter. Carlo Odescalchi did even more: he compiled his ledgers personally in an almost illegible hand. Family account books, like those of Carlo Odescalchi, were the receptacles of even more recondite secrets and of the most delicate private matters. They were kept under lock and key in inaccessible hiding places and often destroyed before they could fall into the hands of strangers (cf. for example: Alfieri, V., *La partita doppia applicata alle scritture delle antiche aziende mercantili veneziane*, Turin 1881).

The double entry system, a technique applied—however crudely—by Italian merchants, does not appear to have been employed in the accounts of the Odescalchi. Transactions are mixed without any strict chronology or charging-in account. Investments are shown, but the results of single operations remain unknown and, above all, the final overall result.

It would all have been far simpler had it been possible to consult the company's journals which describe the transactions, the amounts of which are entered in the ledgers; but the journals have unfortunately not been kept. The inventory of Carlo Odescalchi's estate could also have helped retrace any loans made to William of Orange, but there is no trace of the inventory either.

Carlo the diligent

The Biblioteca Ambrosiana in Milan (fondo Trotti n. 30 and 43) holds the diary, never located hitherto, which Carlo Odescalchi kept meticulously from 1662 until his death. Unfortunately, it tells us nothing about the family business; it contains methodical notes concerning health of the author, the meetings of the day, the weather. On 30th December, 1673, an anonymous hand described the dying man's last moments: the administering of Extreme Unction, the spiritual assistance provided by two fathers of the Society of Jesus, death faced with the fortitude "of a true *Cavagliere*". There follows a brief eulogy of his qualities: prudence, humility, justice. But, above all, "he was most diligent in noting all his business with his own hand, which was useful in ensuring that nothing should be lost after his death, and all inventories could be made of movable and fixed property, credits and external interests."

In praise of the deceased, the anonymous commentator spends more words on the precision with which he kept and recorded accounts and business documentation than on his moral virtues. The *"Cavaghere"* Carlo Odescalchi must have been a master archivist. How is it, then, that neither the inventory of his legacy nor the journals of his ledgers can be found?

Repayment of the loan

Was the Odescalchi's loan to William of Orange ever repaid? To answer that question, one must look into another no less extraordinary affair.

Innocent XI passed away in August 1689. A few months later, his death was followed by that in Rome of Christina of Sweden, the sovereign who, some thirty years previously, had converted from Protestantism to the Catholic religion and had moved to Rome, under the protection of the papacy.

Before dying, Christina made Cardinal Decio Azzolino her heir. The Cardinal who had, for long years, been her counsellor and intimate friend, was himself to die only a few months later, and the estate of Queen Christina passed into the hands of a relative, Pompeo Azzolino.

Pompeo, an obscure provincial gentleman (the Azzolino family came from Fermo, in the Marche, like Tiracorda and Dulcibeni) found himself the possessor of the gigantic legacy of Christina of Sweden: over two hundred works of art by Raphael, Titian, Tintoretto, Rubens, Caravaggio, Michelangelo, Domenichino, Van Dyck, Andrea del Sarto, Bernini, Guido Reni, the Carracci, Giulio Romano, Parmigianino, Giorgione, Velázquez and Palma the Elder; tapestries inlaid with gold and silver thread designed by Raphael; hundreds of drawings by famous artists, an entire gallery of sculptures, busts, heads, vases and marble columns; more than six thousand medals and medallions; arms, musical instruments, valuable furniture; jewels stored in Holland, financial claims on the Swedish and French crowns, as well as claims on certain properties in Sweden; and lastly, Christina's extraordinary library, with thousands of printed books and manuscripts which contemporaries regarded as priceless.

When he inherited Christina's treasure, Pompeo refrained from jumping for joy. Christina's estate was also heavily burdened with debts, and, unless he could sell it as soon as possible, he risked ending up strangled by creditors. Very few have the means to acquire a patrimony of such dimensions; this meant perhaps entering into negotiations with some prince, provided he was not too indebted. But Pompeo was a *parvenu*; he did not know even where to begin, and Rome was full of adventurers ready to pull the wool over the eyes of this timid gentleman who had just arrived from the provinces.

Pompeo endeavoured to simplify matters, selling the estate undivided, but the operation proved difficult and risky. The creditors began to become nervous. Pompeo then decided hurriedly to dismantle the estate and to sell single collections and individual items. The tapestries and other precious furnishings (including a mirror designed by Bernini) soon went to the Ottoboni, the powerful family of the new Pontiff, Alexander VIII; the books enriched the Vatican Library.

Nevertheless, the complications only increased. Apart from debts, Christina's estate entailed a number of insidious legal disputes. Sweden laid claim to Christina's jewels held in Holland, as a banker's security, and had them seized by the Amsterdam magistrates.

A diplomatic incident with Sweden was the last thing that Pompeo wanted. He was advised to petition the person best placed to mediate with the Swedes and to influence matters in Holland: Prince William of Orange, who had now become King of England.

In March 1691, Pompeo Azzolino therefore addressed a petition to William, begging for his protection and help in the matter of the jewels. The response was, to say the least, unexpected: no sooner had he learned that the estate of Christina was for sale than he proposed to purchase all that remained of it, immediately requesting an inventory of the collections.

This was a bolt out of the blue. Until a few days previously, Pompeo had still been selling off paintings one by one and he could hardly believe that he could now sell the lot in one go. What was even more surprising was that William, who had always had to go begging for the money to finance his military undertakings, should feel the need to spend a fortune on pictures and statues. Even the Sun King had declined the opportunity to acquire Christina's collections when his ambassador in Rome, Cardinal d'Estrées, had advised him of the possibility of purchasing those treasures.

Then came the second dramatic surprise. Another buyer made an offer: Livio Odescalchi, the nephew of Innocent XI.

For 123,000 scudi, Livio snatched the lot from under William's nose and bought almost all that remained of the estate. Incredibly, not only did William not take the thing badly, but remained on the best of terms with Pompeo Azzolino. In a flash, the whole complicated business of the inheritance had been resolved.

This epilogue was as surprising as it was improbable. A Protestant king who is perennially short of money proposes to buy an exceedingly costly art collection. A nephew of the Pope (who had, incidentally, lent that king a huge sum of money) clinches the deal by a hair's-breadth, yet all the monarch does is to compliment the buyer (Montanari, T., "La dispersione delle collezioni di Cristina di Svezia. Gli Azzolino, gli Ottoboni e gli Odescalchi" in *Storia dell'Arte*, No. 90 (1997), pp. 251–299).

A few figures: the Odescalchi had lent William about 153,000 scudi and Livio bought Christina's collection for the not far inferior price of 123,000 scudi.

What refined minds were at work! By the end of 1688, William had at last become King of England, which placed him in a position to reimburse his debt to the Odescalchi. In the following year, however, Innocent XI had died. How could he repay? Probably, at that moment, only part of the debt had been reimbursed. The opportunity created by the legacy of Christina of Sweden was, then, not to be missed. Livio made the purchase, but William paid, through some discreet intermediary.

After so many wars, the secret pact between the House of Odescalchi and that of Orange had, then, ended with the greatest of discretion. It is not hard to imagine the scene. While admiring a Tintoretto or a Caravaggio in the golden light of a Roman afternoon, a trusted representative of William will have passed an envelope containing a letter of exchange to an emissary of Livio Odescalchi; the while, singing the praises of the late and great Christina of Sweden.

Livio and the Paravicini

It was, then, perhaps thanks to the estate of Christina of Sweden that William of Orange was able to repay his debt to the Odescalchi. But the family of Innocent XI had lent at least 153,000 scudi, on which interest must be calculated. Pompeo Azzolino, when he sold Christina's estate to Livio Odescalchi, received only 123,000 scudi. What became of the difference?

Carlo Odescalchi, the brother of Innocent XI, had died in 1673. In 1680, the Odescalchi's business in Venice was liquidated, while that in Genoa had already closed down years before. What trusted expert and go-between then remained to Innocent XI through whom to recover the first tranche of the loan?

He certainly could not entrust this to his nephew Livio, not only because he was too exposed to the eyes of the world. Livio was the prototype of the rich and spoiled young man: sulky, rebellious, introverted, capricious, unstable, perhaps even prone to tears. He loved money, but only when others had earned it. His uncle, Benedetto, kept him far from affairs of state; he wanted him to continue the family line. But, almost as though he were getting his own back, Livio never married. Nor did he ever take the trouble to leave Rome and visit the Hungarian estates of Sirmio which he had acquired from the Emperor. Pope Innocent XI had closed all the theatres? After his uncle's death, Livio took his revenge by purchasing a box at the Tor di Nona theatre. From his uncle, he perhaps inherited a certain tendency to avarice and cunning: when the Austrian Ambassador asked him to change a few imperial ducats into Roman currency, Livio tried clumsily to cheat him, offering forty baiocchi to a ducat, when the official exchange rate was forty-five. As a result, the ambassador, following the fashion of the time for facile anti-Semitism, spread the word that the nephew of Innocent XI did business "like a Jew" (Landau, M., *Wien, Rom, Neapel—Zur Geschichte des Kampfes zwischen Papsttum und Kaisertum*, Leipzig 1884, p. 111, note 1).

Livio also committed a serious gaffe in relation to the Emperor, to whom he promised to send a loan and a military contingent: 7000 soldiers to support the imperial troops as soon as they arrived in the Abruzzi. In exchange, he demanded the title of Prince of the Empire. As we know, the title was granted him, and Livio did indeed lend the Emperor a modest sum of money; but of the 7000 troops, no trace was ever seen.

A victim of hypochondriac fixations, the nephew of the Blessed Innocent kept careful note in his diary of his medical consultations as well as collecting reports on autopsies. In minuscule, illegible handwriting, he recorded obsessively the most insignificant potential signs of illness. Attracted to the occult, he passed his nights in alchemical experiments and wearisome searching for remedies, for which he was prepared to pay handsomely, even to complete strangers (*Fondo Odescalchi* XXVII B6 Archivio di Palazzo Odescalchi, III B6. Nos. 58 and 80). And when his morbid personality suffered too much from his uncle's impositions, he would find relief noting down malevolent observations and gossip, almost as though he were pursuing some infantile vendetta (*Fondo Odescalchi,* Diario di Livio Odescalchi).

Never could such a man have borne the weight of oppressive secrets, of compromising meetings, of decisions on which there could be no going back. The task of obtaining repayment of William's debt called for an expert go-between, swift-acting and with the requisite sang-froid.

Innocent XI had recourse to such a man in Rome, one well able to care for his interests faithfully and discreetly. This was the banker Francesco Paravicini, who came of a family close to the Odescalchi. He had the competence and the down-to-earth qualities of a true businessman and followed the most varied economic affairs of the future Pope: from rent collection to the acquisition of guaranteed loans, from the encashment of sums sent to Rome by relatives to debt collection. Already, way back in 1640, it was Paravicini who, acting on the instructions of Carlo Odescalchi, had purchased two Chancellery Prelates' secretariats and one presidency (cost: 12,000 scudi) on behalf of Benedetto, thus inaugurating with money, as was then the normal practice, his entry into the ecclesiastical hierarchy.

The Paravicini family must, then, have enjoyed the complete confidence of the Odescalchi. As soon as Cardinal Benedetto became Pope, he appointed two other Paravicini, Giovanni Antonio and Filippo, to posts as secret treasurers as well as paymasters-general of the Apostolic Chamber; responsible, in other words, for all manner of donations ordered by the Holy See or by the Pope himself. At the same time, however, the new Pontiff abolished the offices of paymaster at the pontifical legations of Forlí, Ferrara, Ravenna, Bologna and Avignon; the latter benefice was, for no clear reason, awarded to the Paravicini (Archivio di Stato di Roma, *Camerale I—Chirografi.* 169, 237, 239, 10th October 1676 and 12th June 1667, and *Carteggio del Tesoriere generale della Reverenda camera apostolica,* years 1673–1716. Cf. also Nardi, C, *I Registri del pagatorato delle soldatesche e dei Tesorieri della legazione di Avignone e del contado venaissino nell'Archivio di Stato di Roma*, Rome 1995).

Why go to the trouble of entrusting an office in distant Avignon, where the paymaster-general had only to deal with the routine expenditure of the Apostolic Palace and the soldiers' pay, to the Paravicini, who resided in Rome? (Curiously, the moment that Innocent XI died and the French occupation of Provence came to an end, the office of paymaster at Avignon was restored to Pietro Del Bianco, whose family had held it for generations.)

The depth of the Pope's confidence in Giovanni Antonio and Filippo Paravicini is also borne out by a number of revealing details. When it became necessary to provide the apostolic nuncios at Vienna and Warsaw with the funds necessary for the war against the Turks, the money of the Holy See was made to travel via the markets of Ulm, Innsbruck and (yet again) Amsterdam through trusted intermediaries of the Pope: besides the well-known Rezzonico, the two Paravicini. Would the latter not, then, have been the ideal mediators to encash the money reimbursed by the Prince of Orange? (*Fondo Odescalchi*, XXII A13 p. 440.)

The phrases of Monsieur de Saint-Clément and Monsieur de Beaucastel reported by Monsignor Cenci lead one to suspect that, in order to pay off the debts contracted with the Pope's family, a sort of "Odescalchi tax" had been imposed on the citizens of Orange. Once the money became available, the safest and most economical solution would, then, have been to hand it over at a place only a few kilometres distant from Orange: in Avignon itself, perhaps, for which the trusted Paravicini were responsible. William's treasurer would have delivered periodically to an intermediary of the Pope a simple letter of exchange, in some obscure corner of the Provencal countryside; no more straw men or international bank accounts and triangulations.

Other untraceable papers

In order to find documentary proof of this hypothesis, it was necessary to search through the acts of the Avignon repository kept in the Rome State Archives. From these papers, it will be learned that, no sooner had the Paravicini taken up their duties as paymasters than they entered at once into credit. Instead of making payments, they received several thousand scudi, deriving from cash compensations. This is an interesting clue. Unfortunately, there is a serious, inexplicable lacuna in the Avignon registers: five years are missing, between 1682 and 1687, almost half of the pontificate of Innocent XI.

In order to dispel doubts, it would have been useful to consult the correspondence of the hierarchical superior of the Paravicini, the treasurer-general of the Apostolic Chamber. This too is, however, missing; for all the years between 1673, the year of Carlo Odescalchi's death, and 1716.

Conclusions

In the aftermath of the Second World War, a few years before the beatification of Innocent XI, the Secret Archives of the Vatican acquired the Zarlatti papers, an archival bequest containing documents relative to the Odescalchi and the Rezzonico families. This bequest was established from the eighteenth century onwards; it would have been interesting to know whether at that time there still existed traces of the old relationships between Benedetto Odescalchi, his brother Carlo and their procurator in Venice. That, however, will never be known. Those responsible for the Vatican Secret Archives themselves noted the "strange dispersions" and "obvious extrapolations" suffered by the bequest as soon as it was deposited in the Vatican: folders separated from the original bequest, left unsigned (i.e. unidentifiable). (Cf. Pagano, S. "Archivi di famiglie romane e non romane nell'Archivio segreto vaticano" in *Roma moderna e contemporanea* I, September/December 1993, pp. 194; 229–231. Strange disappearances of documents are also reported in Salvadori, V. (ed.), *I carteggi delle biblioteche lombarde: Censimento descrittivo*. Vol. II, Milan 1986, p. 191.

Perhaps someone wished to take all possible precautions...

Pieces of Music Performed in *Imprimatur*

✠

For more information about the music in Imprimatur, *and to listen to samples, go to* http://polygon.birlinn.co.uk/. *Page references are provided below:*

1.   The mysterious *rondeau* (pp. 29–31)
     Performed on the piano

2.   "Disperate speranze" (p. 35)
     Luigi Rossi

3.   "Ai sospiri, al dolore" (p. 64)
     Luigi Rossi

4. & 5.   Story of Fouquet (pp. 64 *et seq.*)
     Luigi Rossi, passacaglia and courante

6.   "Chaconne des Harlequins" (p. 69)
     Jean-Baptiste Lully

7   "Piango, prego e sospiro" (p. 97)
     Luigi Rossi

8.   The mysterious *rondeau* (p. 98)
     Performed on the harpsichord

9.   "A chi vive ogn'or contento" (p. 104)
     Luigi Rossi

10.   "In questo duro esilio" (p. 112)
     Luigi Rossi

11.   "Chaconne des Harlequins" (p. 135)
     Robert Devizé after Jean-Baptiste Lully

12.   "Fan battaglia i miei pensieri" (p. 173)
     Luigi Rossi

13.   "Speranza, al tuo pallore" (p. 190)
     Luigi Rossi

14.   *Amanti, sentite,* which contains:
     "Son faci le Stelle", (p. 207); "A petto ch'adora", (p. 368); "Chi giace nel sonno", (p. 374)
     Luigi Rossi

15.   The mysterious *rondeau* (p. 226)
     Performed on the harp

16.   "Ma, quale pena infinita!" (p. 235)
       Luigi Rossi

17.   *Gigue in E major* (p. 243)
       Robert Devizé

18.   Chaconne (p. 243)
       Robert Devizé

19.   "Ahi, dunqu'è pur vero" (p. 252)
       Luigi Rossi

20.   "Lascia speranza, ohimé" (p. 253)
       Luigi Rossi

21.   The mysterious *rondeau* (pp. 293–94)
       Performed on the theorbo

22.   Sarabanda & "Noi siam tre donzellette" (p. 301)
       Luigi Rossi

23.   "Fantaisie caprice de chaconne" (pp. 316–17)
       Francesco Corbetta

24.   "Infelice pensier" (pp. 346, 362)
       Luigi Rossi

25.   "O biondi tesori" (pp. 375–76)
       Luigi Rossi

26.   The mysterious *rondeau* (pp. 379–80)
       Performed on the guitar

27.   Tarantella (pp. 412–14 *et seq.*)
       Athanasius Kircher

28.   The mysterious *rondeau* (pp. 412–14 *et seq.*)
       Performed on the piano